I0761538

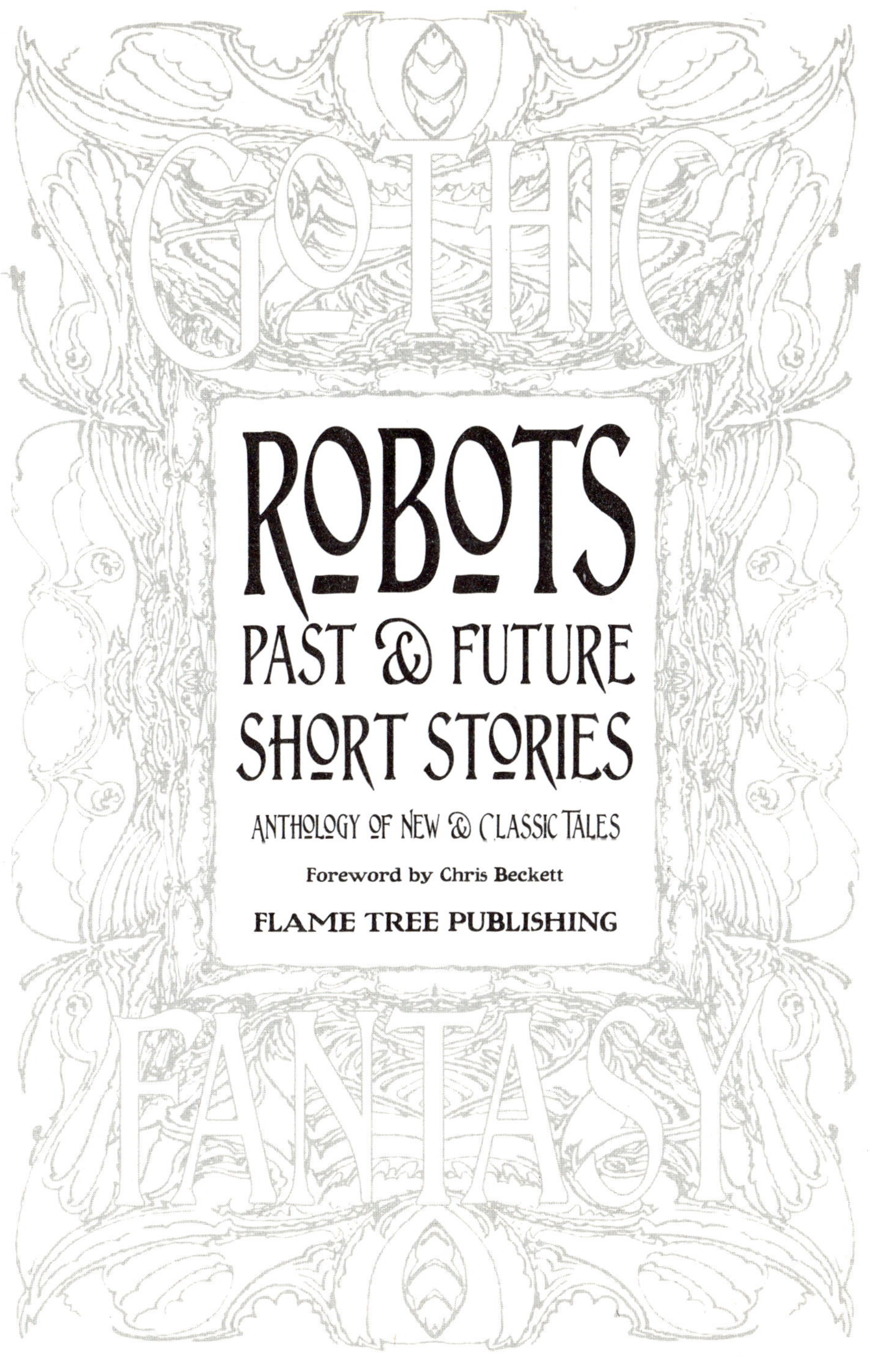

ROBOTS

PAST & FUTURE SHORT STORIES

ANTHOLOGY OF NEW & CLASSIC TALES

Foreword by Chris Beckett

FLAME TREE PUBLISHING

This is a FLAME TREE Book

Publisher & Creative Director: Nick Wells
Project Editor: Gillian Whitaker

Publisher's Note: Due to the historical nature of the classic text, we're aware that there may be some language used which has the potential to cause offence to the modern reader. However, wishing overall to preserve the integrity of the text, rather than imposing contemporary sensibilities, we have left it unaltered.

FLAME TREE PUBLISHING
6 Melbray Mews, Fulham,
London SW6 3NS, United Kingdom
www.flametreepublishing.com

First published 2025

25 27 29 28 26
1 3 5 7 9 10 8 6 4 2

ISBN: 978-1-83562-292-6
Special ISBN: 978-1-83562-677-1

The cover image is created by Flame Tree Studio
based on artwork by Besjunior, Slava Gerj and Gabor Ruszkai.

A copy of the CIP data for this book is available from the British Library.

Printed and bound in China

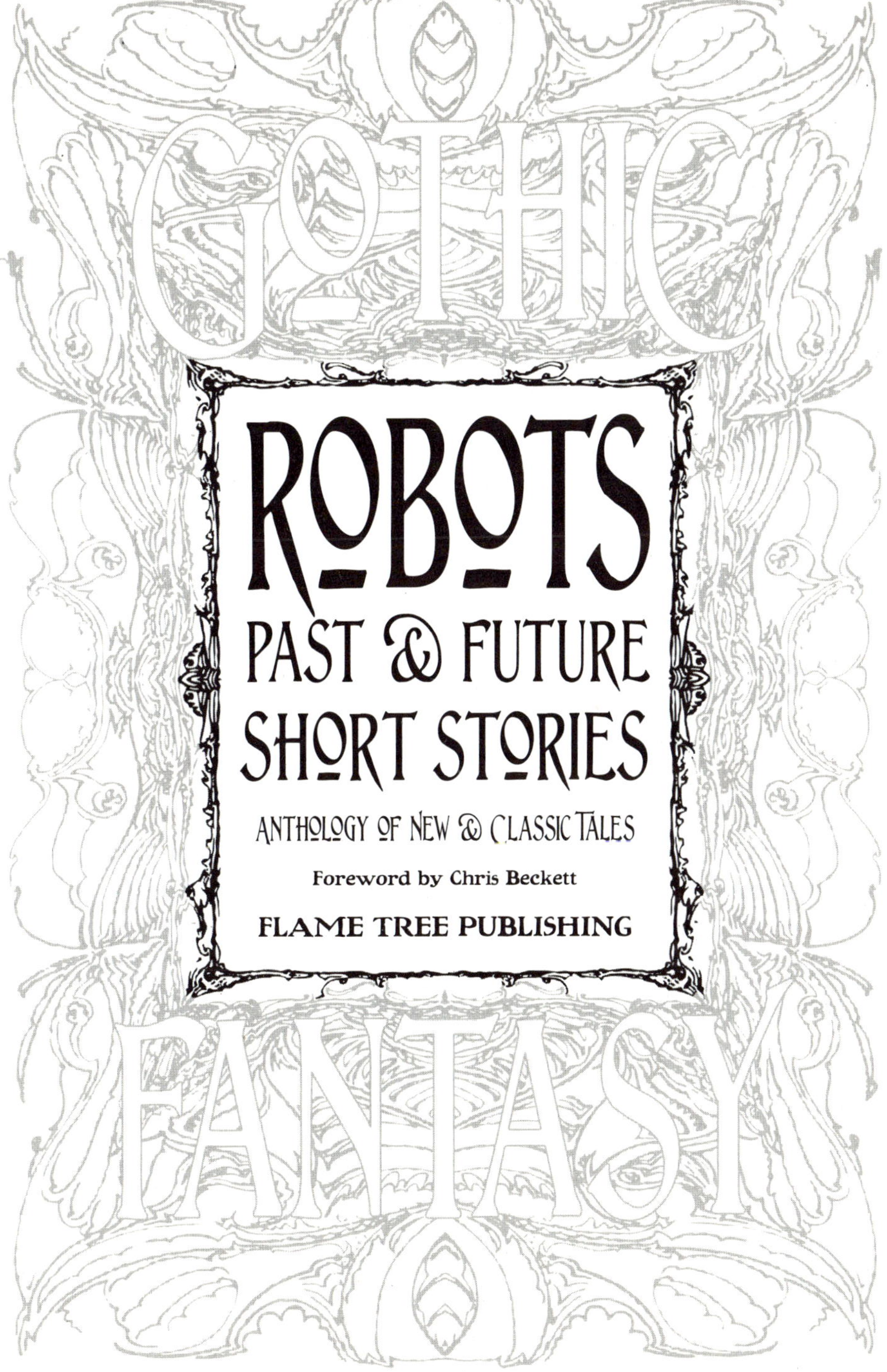

ROBOTS PAST & FUTURE SHORT STORIES

ANTHOLOGY OF NEW & CLASSIC TALES

Foreword by Chris Beckett

FLAME TREE PUBLISHING

Contents

Foreword: Robots Past & Future Short Stories

I ASKED my five-year-old granddaughter to fetch me something, and she replied in the manner of an Amazon Alexa: "I'm sorry, I'm not understanding very well at the moment, please try again later." She's grown up in a world in which you can talk to machines and they answer. This would have seemed centuries away when I was a child, but of course the *idea* of artefacts that could talk and do human things was nevertheless very familiar to me because it has featured in fiction for literally thousands of years (think of the bronze man Talos encountered by the Argonauts, who patrolled the coast of Crete throwing rocks at unwelcome visitors) and been a staple of science fiction since its beginnings. I feel quite sure that, with the sole exception of space travel, no other field of technology has been so thoroughly explored in science fiction. This has generated an enormous cast of robots and intelligent machines, some of them famous, ranging from sinister HAL to cute R2-D2, from the *Maschinenmensch* in *Metropolis* (a novel published in 1925) to Data in *Star Trek*. Science fiction, sometimes dismissed as childish escapism, is the literature of technological change, and it prepared the cultural ground for robots long before they existed. These days even 'serious' authors like Kazuo Ishiguro and Ian McEwan have begun to tiptoe into the territory that science-fiction writers were opening up at least a century before them.

Why are robots so fascinating, so disturbing, and so much fun to write about? I think, first of all, it's because they are like humans but not human, and so make us think, in all kinds of ways, about what we are ourselves. The *big* robot question is always the one about whether robots could come alive and have feelings as we do. (And, I would add, if not, why not, given that we too are complex structures made of matter, every part of which is governed, like the components of robots, by the laws of the physical universe?)

But there are *so* many other questions. Will robots rebel against us, as we ourselves would do if we found we were created for the benefit of others? Will they surpass us, their development unhampered as ours is by the glacial slowness of biological evolution? Will they drive us to extinction even, as we once did to all those other hominid species, less *sapiens* (or maybe just less ferocious) than ourselves? Will they be enemies or allies, slaves or gods? Could they even... there's always a sexual angle... be lovers? There's a classical precedent for this too, by the way: Galatea, the ideal woman carved in stone by Pygmalion, that Aphrodite brought to life to become a distant ancestor of the Stepford Wives (but maybe also of Tanith Lee's Silver Metal Lover, a lover so perfect that, not only is he the gentleman who never finishes first, but – and here Lee really does enter the realm of fantasy – he *reads the instructions* before assembling flatpack furniture.)

And then, if you get tired of thinking about robots as a reflection of humanity, there are a whole set of other questions about the way that robots will affect human society, some of which are extremely topical. How will robots and AIs affect the world of work? How will robot weapons alter the way we wage war, as they add still more distance to the ever-widening gap between human killer and human victim? How will domestic robots alter family life, or sex robots change the way we see human partners? Will robots, with no need of air, no natural lifespan and no fear of loneliness, travel to distant stars on our behalf, and return to Earth when the civilizations that sent them out have long since crumbled to dust? How would robots have changed things if they'd somehow been invented a hundred or two hundred years ago?

For a writer who likes to speculate, robots really are a limitless well of possibilities. Look forward to a feast of ideas!

Chris Beckett

Publisher's Note

WE ARE DELIGHTED to put together a new anthology of Robot fiction, several years since we last released a book on *Robots & AI*. Much has changed in the world since then, with rapid developments in the AI and technology sectors bringing both opportunities and concerns for humanity, themes explored in fascinating depth in the latest science fiction. As ever, though, the roots of the past can be felt in the fiction of the present. For this reason, we've collected here some of the earliest examples of androids, cyborgs and mechanical inventions in fiction (including novel extracts and a couple of plays), stretching back even as far as the myth of Pygmalion and Galatea, and a speculative essay by George Eliot from the nineteenth century about self-replicating machines. We've also included some of the more typical classics: as well as an electric grandmother in Ray Bradbury's story, you'll find rogue robots in the home, 'perfect' robot wives, the use of robots in warfare, and robots as replacement workers, harking back to the origin of the term from the Slavonic word for forced labour. Often, the presence of robots in such tales reflects more about those that interact with them, and those that created them, as they come to terms with the ethical dilemmas of their inventions: so expect a good dose of eccentric scientists, from the anguished creator in C.L. Moore's tale comparing himself to Frankenstein, to the sinister Rotwang (*Metropolis*) and Professor X the 'master electrician' of *The Future Eve*.

In keeping with the rest of our Gothic Fantasy series, the modern side of the book was selected through submissions and we are grateful to all the authors who responded to the call. We received hundreds of options to consider, either conjuring historical automatons or imagining how robots and society might evolve in the years and centuries to come. In the final selection we have hoped to achieve a good balance, with many of the stories sitting in conversation with the classic pieces, demonstrating similarities but with different perspectives, settings and technology informed by today's world. As the line between human and robot becomes more and more blurred, we hope the reader enjoys these sometimes playful, sometimes alarming, visions of robots past and future.

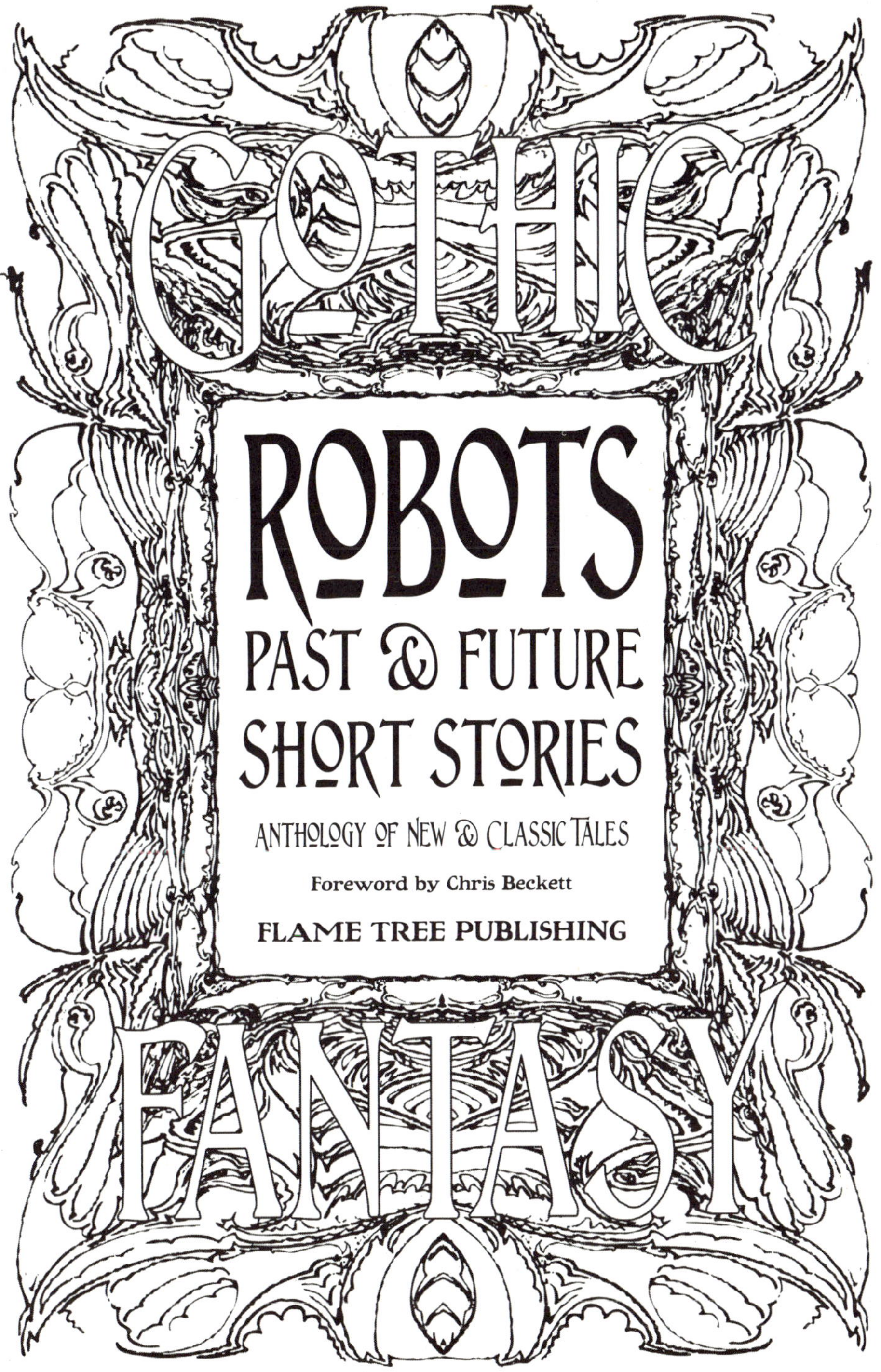
GOTHIC
ROBOTS
PAST & FUTURE
SHORT STORIES
ANTHOLOGY OF NEW & CLASSIC TALES
Foreword by Chris Beckett
FLAME TREE PUBLISHING
FANTASY

Ely's Automatic Housemaid

Elizabeth W. Bellamy

IN ORDER FOR a man to have faith in such an invention, he would have to know Harrison Ely. For Harrison Ely was a genius. I had known him in college, a man amazingly dull in Latin and Greek and even in English, but with ideas of his own that could not be expressed in language. His bent was purely mechanical, and found expression in innumerable ingenious contrivances to facilitate the study to which he had no inclination. His self-acting lexicon-holder was a matter of admiring wonder to his classmates, but it did not serve to increase the tenacity of his mental grasp upon the contents of the volume, and so did little to recommend him to the faculty. And his self-feeding safety student-lamp admirably illuminated everything for him save the true and only path to an honorable degree.

It had been years since I had seen him or thought of him, but the memory is tenacious of small things, and the big yellow envelope which I found one morning awaiting me upon my breakfast-table brought his eccentric personality back to me with a rush. It was addressed to me in the Archimedean script always so characteristic of him, combining, as it seemed to do, the principles of the screw and of the inclined plane, and in its superscription Harrison Ely stood unmistakably revealed.

It was the first morning of a new cook, the latest potentate of a dynasty of ten who had briefly ruled in turn over our kitchen and ourselves during the preceding three months, and successively abdicated in favor of one another under the compelling influences of popular clamor, and in the face of such a political crisis my classmate's letter failed to receive immediate attention. Unfortunately but not unexpectedly the latest occupant of our culinary throne began her reign with no conspicuous reforms, and we received in gloomy silence her preliminary enactments in the way of greasy omelette and turbid and flavorless coffee, the yellow screed of Harrison Ely looking on the while with bilious sympathy as it leaned unopened against the water-bottle beside me.

As I drained the last medicinal drop of coffee my eye fell upon it, and needing a vicarious outlet for my feelings toward the cook, I seized it and tore it viciously open. It contained a letter from my classmate and half a dozen printed circulars. I spread open the former, and my eye fastened at once upon this sympathetic exordium:

"Doubtless, my dear friend, you have known what discomfort it is to be at the mercy of incompetent domestics—"

But my attention was distracted at this point by one of the circulars, which displayed an array of startling, cheering, alluring words, followed by plentiful exclamation points, that, like a bunch of keys, opened to my enraptured vision the gates of a terrestrial Paradise, where Bridgets should be no more, and where ill-cooked meals should become a mechanical impossibility. The boon we had been sighing for now presented itself for my acceptance, an accomplished fact. Harrison Ely had invented 'An Automatic Household Beneficent Genius – A Practical Realization of the Fabled Familiar of the Middle Ages'. So the circular set forth.

Returning to the letter, I read that Harrison Ely, having exhausted his means in working out his invention, was unable to manufacture his 'machine' in quantity as yet; but that he had just two on hand which he would sell in order to raise some ready money. He hoped that I would buy one of his automatons, and aid him to sell the other.

Never did a request come at a more propitious moment. I had always entertained a kindness for Harrison Ely, and now such was my disgust at the incompetence of Bridget and Juliana and their predecessors that I was eager to stake the price of a 'Household Beneficent Genius' on the success of my friend's invention.

So, having grasped the purport of the circulars and letter, I broke forth to my wife:

"My dear, you've heard me speak of Harrison Ely—"

"That man who is always so near doing something great, and never *has* done anything?" said she.

"He has done it at last!" I declared. "Harrison Ely is one of the greatest geniuses the world has ever seen. He has invented an 'Automatic-Electric Machine-Servant'."

My wife said, "Oh!"

There was not an atom of enthusiasm in that 'Oh!' but I was not to be daunted.

"I am ready," I resumed, "to invest my bottom dollar in *two* of Harrison Ely's machine-servants."

Her eyes were fixed upon me as if they would read my very soul. "What do they cost?" she mildly asked.

"In comparison with the benefits to be derived, little enough. Listen!" I seized a circular at random, and began to read:

"'The Automatic Household Genius, a veritable Domestic Fairy, swift, silent, sure; a Permanent, Inalienable, First-class Servant, warranted to give Satisfaction.'"

"Ah!" said my wife; and the enthusiasm that was lacking in the "Oh!" made itself eloquent in that 'Ah!' "What is the price?" she asked again.

"The price is all right, and we are going to try the experiment."

"Are we though?" said she, between doubt and desire.

"Most assuredly; it will be a saving in the end. I shall write to Harrison Ely this very night."

The return mail brought me a reply stating that two Electric-Automatic Household Beneficent Geniuses had been shipped to me by express. The letter enclosed a pamphlet that gave a more particular account of the E.A.H.B.G. than the circulars contained. My friend's invention was shaped in the likeness of the human figure, with body, head, arms, legs, hands and feet. It was clad in waterproof cloth, with a hood of the same to protect the head, and was shod with felt. The trunk contained the wheels and springs, and in the head was fixed the electric battery. The face, of bisque, was described as possessing 'a very natural and pleasing expression'.

Just at dusk an oblong box arrived by express and was duly delivered in our hall, but at my wife's urgent entreaty I consented not to unpack the machines until next day.

"If we should not get the knack of managing them, they might give us trouble," said this wise wife of mine.

I agreed to this, and having sent away Bridget with a week's wages, to the satisfaction of all parties, we went to bed in high hopes.

Early next morning we were astir.

"My dear," I said, "do not give yourself the least concern about breakfast; I am determined that Harrison's invention shall have fair play."

"Very well," my wife assented; but she prudently administered bread and butter to her offspring.

I opened the oblong box, where lay the automatons side by side, their hands placidly folded upon their waterproof breasts, and their eyes looking placidly expectant from under their waterproof hoods.

I confess the sight gave me a shock. Anna Maria turned pale; the children hid their faces in her skirts.

"Once out of the box," I said to myself, "and the horror will be over."

The machines stood on their feet admirably, but the horror was not materially lessened by this change of position. However, I assumed a bold front, and said, jocosely:

"Now, which is Bridget, and which is Juliana – which the cook, and which the housemaid?"

This distinction was made clear by dial-plates and indicators, set conspicuously between the shoulders, an opening being cut in the waterproof for that purpose. The housemaid's dial-plate was stamped around the circumference with the words: Bed, Broom, Duster, Door-bell, Dining-room Service, Parlor Service, etc. In like manner, the cook's dial-plate bore the words that pertained to her department. I gave myself first to 'setting' the housemaid, as being the simpler of the two.

"Now, my dear," said I, confidently, "we shall see how *this* Juliana can make the beds."

I proceeded, according to the pamphlet's directions, to point the indicator to the word 'Bed'. Next, as there were three beds to be made, I pushed in three of the five little red points surrounding the word. Then I set the 'clock' connected with the indicator, for a thirty minutes' job, thinking it might take about ten minutes to a bed. I did not consult my wife, for women do not understand machinery, and any suggestion of hesitancy on my part would have demoralized her.

The last thing to be done was to connect the indicator with the battery, a simple enough performance in itself, but the pamphlet of directions gave a repeated and red-lettered 'CAUTION', never to interfere with the machine while it was at work! I therefore issued the command, "Non-combatants to the rear!" and was promptly obeyed.

What happened next I do not pretend to account for. By what subtle and mysterious action of electricity, by what unerring affinity, working through a marvellous mechanism, that Electric-Automatic Household Beneficent Genius, whom – or which, for short – we called Juliana, sought its appropriate task, is the inventor's secret. I don't undertake to explain, I merely narrate. With a 'click' the connection was made, and the new Juliana *went upstairs* at a brisk and business-like pace.

We followed in breathless amazement. In less than five minutes, bed number one was made, and in a twinkling the second was taken in hand, and number three also was fairly accomplished, long before the allotted thirty minutes had expired. By this time, familiarity had somewhat dulled that awe and wonder with which we had gaped upon the first performance, and I beheld a smile of hopeful satisfaction on my wife's anxious countenance.

Our youngest, a boy aged three, was quick to feel the genial influence of this smile, and encouraged thereby, he bounced into the middle of the first bed. Hardly had he alighted there, when our automaton, having finished making the third bed, returned to her first job, and, before we could imagine mischief, the mattresses were jerked about, and the child was tumbled, headforemost on the floor!

Had the flesh-and-blood Juliana been guilty of such an act, she should have been dismissed on the spot; but, as it was, no one of us ventured so much as a remonstrance. My wife lifted the screaming child, and the imperturbable machine went on to re-adjust the bed with mechanical exactitude.

At this point a wild shout of mingled exultation, amazement and terror arose from below, and we hastened downstairs to find our son John hugging his elbows and capering frantically in front of the kitchen-door, where the electric cook was stirring empty nothing in a pan, with a zeal worthy a dozen eggs.

My eldest hopeful, impelled by that spirit of enterprise and audacity characteristic of nine-year-old boys, had ventured to experiment with the kitchen automaton, and by sheer accident had effected a working connection between the battery and the indicator, and the machine, in 'going off', had given the boy a blow that made him feel, as he expressed it, "like a funny-bone all over".

"And served you right!" cried I. The thing was set for an hour and a half of work, according to the showing of the dial-plate, and no chance to stop it before I must leave for my office. Had the materials been supplied, we might have had breakfast; but, remembering the red-lettered 'CAUTION', we dared not supply materials while that indefatigable spoon was gyrating in the empty pan. For my distraction, Kitty, my daughter of seven years, now called to me from upstairs:

"Papa, you *better* come, quick! *It's* a-tearin' up these beds!"

"My dear," I sighed, "there's no way to stop it. We'll have to wait for the works to run down. I must call Harrison's attention to this defect. He ought to provide some sort of brake."

We went upstairs again. The B.G. Juliana stood beside the bed which she had just torn up for the sixth or seventh time, when suddenly she became, so to speak, paralyzed; her arms, in the act of spreading the sheets, dropped by her sides, her back stiffened, and she stood absolutely motionless, leaving her job unfinished – the B.G. would move no more until duly 'set' again.

I now discovered that I was hungry. "If that Fiend in the kitchen were only at work about something substantial, instead of whipping the air into imaginary omelettes!" I groaned.

"Never mind," said my wife, "I've a pot of coffee on the kerosene stove."

Bless her! She was worth a thousand Beneficent Geniuses, and so I told her.

I did not return until late, but I was in good spirits, and I greeted my wife gayly:

"Well, how do they work?"

"*Like fiends!*" my usually placid helpmeet replied, so vehemently that I was alarmed. "They flagged at first," she proceeded, excitedly, "and I oiled them, which *I* am not going to do, ever again. According to the directions, I poured the oil down their throats. It was horrible! They seemed to me to *drink it greedily*."

"Nonsense! That's your imagination."

"Very well," said Anna Maria. "You can do the oiling in future. They took a good deal this morning; it wasn't easy to stop pouring it down. And they worked – *obstreperously*. That Fiend in the kitchen has cooked all the provisions I am going to supply *this* day, but still she goes on, and it's no use to say a word."

"Don't be absurd," I remonstrated. "The thing is only a machine."

"I'm not so sure about that!" she retorted. "As for the other one – I set it sweeping, and it is sweeping still!"

We ate the dinner prepared by the kitchen Fiend, and really, I was tempted to compliment the cook in a set speech, but recollected myself in time to spare Anna Maria the triumph of saying, "I told you so!"

Now, that John of mine, still in pursuit of knowledge, had spent the day studying Harrison Ely's pamphlet, and he learned that the machines could be set, like an alarm-clock, for any given hour. Therefore, as soon as the Juliana had collapsed over a pile of dust in the middle of the hall, John, unknown to us, set her indicator to the broom-handle for seven o'clock the following morning. When the Fiend in the kitchen ran down, leaving everything in confusion, my much-tried wife persuaded me to give my exclusive attention to that machine, and the Juliana was put safely in a corner. Thus it happened that John's interference escaped detection. I set Bridget's indicator for kitchen-cleaning at seven-thirty the next morning.

"When we understand them better," I said to my wife, "we will set their morning tasks for an earlier hour, but we won't put it too early now, since we must first learn their ways."

"That's the trouble with all new servants," said Anna Maria.

The next morning at seven-thirty, precisely, we were awakened by a commotion in the kitchen.

"By George Washington!" I exclaimed. "The Thing's on time!"

I needed no urging to make me forsake my pillow, but Anna Maria was ahead of me.

"Now, my dear, don't get excited," I exhorted, but in vain.

"Don't you hear?" she whispered, in terror. "*The other one! S*we–eep–ing!" And she darted from the room.

I paused to listen, and heard the patter of three pairs of little bare feet across the hall upstairs. The children were following their mother. The next sound I heard was like the dragging of a rug along the floor. I recognized this peculiar sound as the footsteps of the B.G. Then came a dull thud, mingled with a shout from Johnnie, a scream from my wife, and the terrified cries of the two younger children. I rushed out just in time to see John, in his night-clothes, with his hair on end, tear downstairs like a streak of lightning. My little Kitty and the three-year-old baby stood clasped in each other's arms at the head of the stairs, sobbing in terror, and, halfway down, was my wife, leaning over the railing, with ashen face and rigid body, her fascinated gaze fixed upon a dark and struggling mass in the hall below.

John, when he reached the bottom of the stairs, began capering like a goat gone mad, digging the floor with his bare heels, clapping his hands with an awful glee, and shouting:

"Bet your bottom dollar on the one that whips!"

The Juliana and the Bridget were fighting for the broom!

I comprehended the situation intuitively. The kitchen-cleaning, for which the Fiend had been 'set', had reached a point that demanded the broom, and that subtle, attractive affinity, which my friend's genius had known how to produce, but had not learned to regulate, impelled the unerring automaton towards the only broom in the house, which was now in the hands of its fellow-automaton, and a struggle was inevitable. What I could not understand – Johnnie having kept his own counsel – was this uncontrollable sweeping impulse that possessed the Juliana.

However, this was no time for investigating the exact cause of the terrific row now going on in our front hall. The Beneficent Geniuses had each a firm grip of the broom-handle, and they might have performed the sweeping very amicably together, could they but have agreed as to the field of labor, but their conflicting tendencies on this point brought about a rotary motion that sent them spinning around the hall, and kept them alternately cracking each other's head with a violence that ought to have drawn blood. Considering their life-likeness, we should hardly have thought it strange if blood *had* flowed, and it would have been a relief had the combatants but called each other names, so much did their dumbness intensify the horror of a struggle, in the midst of which the waterproof hoods fell off, revealing their startlingly human countenances, not distorted by angry passions, but resolute, inexorable, calm, as though each was sustained in the contest by a lofty sense of duty.

"They're alive! Kill 'em! Kill 'em, quick!" shrieked my wife, as the gyrating couple moved towards the staircase.

"Let 'em alone," said Johnnie – his sporting blood, which he inherits from his father, thoroughly roused – dancing about the automatic pugilists in delight, and alternately encouraging the one or the other to increased efforts.

Thus the fight went on with appalling energy and reckless courage on both sides, my wife wringing her hands upon the staircase, our infants wailing in terror upon the landing above, and I wavering between an honest desire to see fair play and an apprehensive dread of consequences which was not unjustified.

In one of their frantic gyrations the figures struck the hat-rack and promptly converted it into a mass of splinters. In a minute more they became involved with a rubber plant – the pride of my wife's heart – and distributed it impartially all over the premises. From this they caromed against the front door, wrecking both its stained-glass panes, and then down the length of the hall they sped again, fighting fiercely and dealing one another's imperturbable countenances ringing blows with the disputed broom.

We became aware through Johnnie's excited comments, that Juliana had lost an ear in the fray, and presently it was discernible that a fractured nose had somewhat modified the set geniality of expression that had distinguished Bridget's face in its prime.

How this fierce and equal combat would have culminated if further prolonged no one but Harrison Ely can conjecture, but it came to an abrupt termination as the parlor clock chimed eight, the hour when the two automatons should have completed their appointed tasks.

Though quite late at my office that morning, I wired Ely before attending to business. Long-haired, gaunt and haggard, but cheerful as ever, he arrived next day, on fire with enthusiasm. He could hardly be persuaded to refresh himself with a cup of coffee before he took his two recalcitrant Geniuses in hand. It was curious to see him examine each machine, much as a physician would examine a patient. Finally his brow cleared, he gave a little puff of satisfaction, and exclaimed:

"Why, man alive, there's nothing the matter – not a thing! What you consider a defect is really a merit – merely a surplus of mental energy. They've had too big a dose of oil. Few housekeepers have any idea about proper lubrication," and he emitted another little snort, at which my wife colored guiltily.

"I see just what's wanted," he resumed. "The will-power generated and not immediately expended becomes cumulative and gets beyond control. I'll introduce a little compensator, to take up the excess and regulate the flow. Then a child can operate them."

It was now Johnnie's turn to blush.

"Ship 'em right back to the factory, and we'll have 'em all right in a few days. I see where the mechanism can be greatly improved, and when you get 'em again I know you'll never consent to part with 'em!"

* * *

That was four months ago. The 'Domestic Fairies' have not yet been returned from Harrison's laboratory, but I am confidently looking for the familiar oblong packing case, and expect any day to see in the papers the prospectus of the syndicate which Ely informs me is being 'promoted' to manufacture his automatic housemaid.

From the Beginning

Eando Binder

MY COMPANION in this tale, William Walker, helped me with the writing of certain episodes. I had come to his place in answer to a phone call. I sat down and looked at him quizzically, wrinkling my nose at the smell of ozone which was always in evidence in his small electrical workshop.

"Look," he said, leaning forward when our greetings were done. "What is it when mind speaks to mind without use of words?"

"Telepathy."

He nodded and waved a hand to indicate the apparatus on the work-bench before us. To my untrained eye it was just a group of adjacent coils sleeved inside one that was two feet high. The wire had been wound around cellulose cylinders. Beyond the clear walls of the inner coil, partially hidden by the turns of wire, was a three-inch metal ball, perfectly spherical, suspended in a cradle of leather strips.

"Well?" I raised my eyebrows.

"I don't know how to begin," frowned Walker. "I'm only an amateur scientist, and as such can't figure out at all why it works as it does. But I doubt if our science can explain at all. I do know this – when that metal ball is subjected to high-frequency energy, it releases thought-waves! It must have some inexplicable mechanism inside that does the trick."

"You might tell me what it is and where it came from," I suggested, utterly mystified.

Walker lit a cigarette. "You remember," he began, "that I went with the French LeConte Expedition last year which surveyed for possible irrigation of the Sahara Desert by canals dug down from the Mediterranean. And out there, in the middle of nowhere, we came across a batch of fossil bones in our digging to test underlying soil."

"Micolet, the little French fossil man, went crazy for joy. He dug up some of the precious bones and found this metal ball. We two happened to be alone at the time, and he gave it to me. It had no significance to him – only his musty bones did. I slipped it into my personal belongings, later calling it a paperweight at the customs."

"I was intrigued with the thought of this smooth metal sphere, uncorroded and showing no sign of age, having been embedded in the same clay-matrix that held the petrified bones of an extinct reptile – so Micolet said. And he's a pretty well-known paleontologist."

"After my return to the States, I began wondering about the thing. At first I was more interested in *what* it was than how it got there among fossils. I analyzed the metal; it is a strange alloy of beryllium and tantalum, two very resistant metals. A density measurement showed it was too light to be solid all through. But what, if anything, was inside? I thought of several ways to find out – dissolving the outer shell away, X-rays, even sawing into it. But one day, quite by accident, I had it near the Tesla coil, and as I turned on the current I got the shock of my life when a soundless voice seemed to hammer into my brain!"

"Different sets of thought-waves are released when I change the frequency of my inductive field – almost as if it were a series of phonograph records that give off thought and vision instead of sound."

"Whose thoughts?"

"Those of someone, or something, living in a past so remote that it precedes human history!"

"Atlantis, maybe?"

"Maybe. Maybe from a time before the species of *homo sapiens* even existed!" Walker was in grim earnest, I can tell you that.

"You see," he went on, "I shan't know just how old the ball is until Micolet determines the age of his fossils, which he hasn't done yet. The thought-record itself gives no clue. If it happens to go back as far as 25,000 years."

"Preposterous!" was my involuntary remark. Walker, I might explain, was, and still is for that matter, a believer in psychic and supermundane things, whereas I'm from Missouri.

Walker didn't seem to hear me. "The thoughts released are not very coherent," he pursued. "Either that or my mind isn't capable of translating them. It is not a voice, but a swift series of mental images combined with sound and thought, so detailed that they give every variation of what seems to be an elaborate story. But it doesn't seem to have any coherence or logic or – perspective. So I have you here on the hunch that with *both* of us listening at once, the images will be clearer."

"Huh – why?"

Walker smiled a little sheepishly. "Well, my theory is that two minds give perspective to thought-waves. It takes two ears to orientate sound, two eyes to judge distance, why not two minds to translate telepathized thought-imagery?"

With a strange look on his sensitive face, Walker eagerly arranged two chairs in front of the apparatus, explaining that our heads – our brains – had to be fairly close to the metal ball to catch its radiations. He then knifed a switch from which insulated wires ran to a large high-voltage transformer in the room's corner. A low moan arose. Then, when we had seated ourselves with the three-inch ball just in front of our noses, visible beyond the clear cellulose, Walker snapped a switch that led current through his primary.

I had waited expectantly, hardly knowing what to expect. I jumped as a pulse seemed to beat in my brain.

"That's just a sort of carrier-wave," whispered my companion. "It's much stronger than it was when I listened alone. I think this is going to work out."

The pulse in my brain quickened to a drone and then – so suddenly that it drew a sharp gasp into my lungs – it became a clear-cut picture. I saw a monstrous angular shape with four legs and six tentacles, following a short line of such similar beings. Overhead a fierce blue-white sun poured down a flood of rays that reflected blazingly from the metallic figure of the creature. The scene around was one of barren desert. Beyond, near the horizon, lay a confused heap of incredible architecture, sharply outlined against a deep azure sky.

With this picture came sound – the smooth whirring of well-oiled machinery. And after sound came something more – an almost complete *rapport* with another mind…

* * *

He was the last in the line. Six million and more of the metal-bodied, mineral-brained creatures had preceded him. The brain-units of each of them had been destroyed after the precious capsule of activating radium had been removed. The radium was to be added to the stores aboard the space-ship.

Tumilten saw them open the hinged receptacle in the head of the robot in front of him, take out the small radium-phial, and then reduce the brain-unit to a molten blob with a sharp ray of heat. He shuddered mentally. That was death! A sudden erasure, almost unknown among his people, except at rare times like this. Ordinarily one lived on and on, for thousands of years, till the final last 'fading out', when the brain-unit had burned itself completely out with radium.

The operator of the heat ray turned his multiple eyes on Tumilten. He telepathized, "Come, you. You are the last."

No sympathy, no slightest spark of feeling. The operator had been ordered by the Council to destroy six million brain-units, and there could be no such thing as pity for those doomed. The thing the Council had stressed was that they be sure to retrieve every radium-capsule before using the heat ray.

Tumilten took one step forward, then two backward. The operator looked at him with what might have been surprise.

"Tumilten does not want to be rayed out!" said Tumilten.

"What nonsense is this?" returned the operator. "The Council commands it. You have the cross-mark of the Unchosen on your frontlet. Come here and be rayed."

Tumilten spoke for himself again: "Why should Tumilten be rayed out? He wants to live!"

"Why? Why?" snapped back the operator impatiently. "Foolish one, because there is a shortage of radium. In that long journey through space in search of a new home, only the Chosen few can be supplied with radium. These six million capsules will help to keep them renewed till they find a haven."

The telepathized voice seemed to soften a trifle from its metallic indifference. "It is nothing, Younger. A fleeting moment of heat and it is over. You were created and now you are to be uncreated. After you are rayed, the ray will be turned on its operator, who is also of the Unchosen. Come."

But Tumilten was thinking otherwise. With a click of internal machinery he whirled, and ran; ran with the smooth speed of high-powered machinery. The operator stood for a moment in perplexity, then swung his heat ray toward the escaping robot.

Tumilten, his four triply jointed legs propelling him forward with ponderous velocity, saw the sands around him curl up and cake and run together. The heat ray was on his legs. Pain came to him, not as a physical sensation, but merely as the coded clicking of a thermocouple in his chest. It was warning him that his internal heat was reaching a dangerous point.

But he ran on, even though he knew his fuel tank might at any instant blow up and destroy him. In another moment he had gone beyond the range of the ray and was safe. He stopped then and looked back. He saw the operator stare at him impassively, then quickly raise the ray to his own head.

The operator had carried out his duty except in one detail. The escape of Tumilten was the exceptional detail.

* * *

We sat spellbound before the metal ball as the thought-images ended abruptly with a faint click and the pulsing carrier wave came into being. Then with a soundless click, the episode we had just witnessed began again.

Walker snapped off the current and lit a cigarette with trembling fingers.

"That was great!" he exclaimed. "Before, trying it alone, it was a meaningless jumble of superimposed impressions to me. But with our two minds – possibly *en rapport* since we were both concentrating on the one thing – we got – well, perspective. Which simply means each of us not only received the thought-message direct, but also by reflection from the other's brain."

That was just like Walker, to be more interested in rationalizing the experience we had just had, than in analyzing the phenomenon. For my part, I must confess I was awed.

"Lord!" I gasped. "It's unbelievable! We were seeing and hearing things long since done!"

"Not just seeing and hearing," said Walker, expelling a cloud of smoke to the ceiling. "That was *living* it! But then I always reasoned telepathy should be something like that. The senses are just imperfect instruments of the brain. Mind-to-mind contact – *this* sort of thing – eliminates the clumsier sensory means of communication. Think of it, Cliff, we've *lived* an episode in some other creature's life!"

I shook my head dazedly. "And what a creature! It wasn't human, Bill. It was a soulless, thinking machine – a robot!" I shuddered involuntarily. "How can a wholly mechanical creature think like a human being? Present-day science wouldn't admit of a reasoning robot."

"Present-day science wouldn't admit of hypersensory telepathy either," returned Walker dryly. "Yet there we have it in that metal ball. This whole thing – we've got to make up our minds to it, no matter how fantastic – goes beyond our science. But why be as superstitious as the hard-head who said 'There ain't no such an animal' when seeing the giraffe?"

I had begun pacing the room excitedly, trying to keep from feeling that the whole world of accepted things had fallen out at the bottom. A robot! A thinking machine! Fantastic, ridiculous, impossible! I found myself shaking my head vehemently as though arguing with someone.

"What it is," said Walker soberly, "is an episodic record of the life of a creature whose race once lived on Earth – totally unsuspected by our present civilization." A yawn escaped his lips. "Come back a few more evenings and we'll run through this whole story. I'm too tired to go on tonight."

The next evening I went early to Walker's place, eager to get on with our bizarre experiment. I had had one or two qualms through the day that I had dreamed about last night. My humdrum office routine failed to take my mind off the event.

Without preamble, Walker had me sit before the apparatus.

"I've already set the coils for a higher frequency and therefore a different episode," he informed me. "Did you notice that in the last, the whole thing seemed to have been told or narrated by someone? Maybe the series of records leads to some conclusion or denouement."

He knifed a switch. After a phonograph-like period of scratchings, the sudden panorama of mental images again sprang into our minds. I speak for Walker, for we afterward found we both *saw* the identically same things, though our interpretations of what we *heard* – by telepathy, I mean – were always to be slightly at variance.

The scene we seemed to see in front of our eyes was again desert-like. In the foreground were two of the robot creatures, conversing. Then, as before, sound came to us – the undertone of smooth, intricate machinery. Then came a gradual fusing of minds, till we no longer knew ourselves as William Walker and Cliff Darrell, but identified ourselves completely with an alien mind...

* * *

A clear bell-note rang inside the brains of the two conversing robots. Eight times it sounded.

"The eighth period," said Tumilten. "Tumilten must leave you, Zonzi, to go on duty. You will come here again tomorrow?"

"If there is not other business," returned the Elder. "Any time now the Ancients Supreme may call a Council of all Elders, in the Hall of the Twelve. When it comes, this Council will last for days. And when it is over, the plans for the great space journey will be completed."

They separated without any form of goodbye greeting. Tumilten moved his quadrupedal metal body toward the nearby city. Zonzi clambered into his small, ovoid airship and sped silently away. They had met out in the open wastes of the desert because they liked to be alone with each other.

In a few minutes Tumilten had reached the city, which housed only one kind of machinery – that for making wire. All kinds of wires were made here, cable-thick, filament-thin, of every kind of metal, and even of non-metals, and for all uses conceivable in a completely mechanized civilization.

Tumilten stalked unhurriedly into the bowels of this hissing, thundering Vulcan city, and made his way finally down a corridor crowded with other robots. They were of all sizes and shapes, but all had the same head-pieces. And inside the solidly armored heads, all had the same brain-units.

Tumilten did a number of things that would have bewildered an organic being. In one well-stocked room he removed a small battery from his middle and replaced it with a fresh one. In another chamber he slid open a tiny door in his head and replaced the capsule of radium-salt with another. In another room an attendant removed his tentacles and replaced them with short, strong arms of steel with claws at the ends. Last of all, he poured a thick, creamy oil into cups in his shoulders.

Then, all prepared like an overhauled engine, he passed by means of various moving stairways and elevators to a gigantic room filled with sparkling, hissing, thundering machinery that would have deafened and blinded a carbonaceous creature. For a moment he stood stock-still, gazing abstractedly at the numerous mechanical figures tending these machines.

When the bell-note struck nine times in his, and in all others', brain-units, he strode on his four triply-jointed legs toward one of the machines. The robot who had been there left as soon as Tumilten had stepped before the control-system with its multitudinous levers and dials.

Then for fifty hours Tumilten tended the machine, unsweating, tireless, his reactions as quick and fresh at the end of that period as at the start. In all this he was no different from all his fellow Youngers in other cities. But in one thing, perhaps, he was different – he had the thoughts of an Elder.

Of an Elder? Perhaps the thoughts of an Ancient. Perhaps, even, thoughts new to their race altogether! For he was wondering where their race had sprung from. Their race had come from another star, it was said. But who or what had created them?

Youngers were created by Elders; these Elders by other Elders; these by others before. But where was the beginning? Who had created the first Younger? All life was creation. Therefore, who had created the first of their race? Had it been, as the legend went – even these machine-creatures had legends – that another form of life had created them? It was a secret Zonzi knew, but would not give out. It was a secret that Tumilten's super-quickened brain-unit wanted to know.

It was three work-periods later that Tumilten knew that the Elders had finished their council and had laid their final plans for search of a new home. A click in his brain-unit, and a voice spoke to him in their intricate language which was half in mathematical symbols. It was a command to leave the city of wire-machines and go immediately to the main city of the Elders.

Mechanically, without thought of questioning the strange command, Tumilten went to the city's air-exit, to find himself in company with a hundred other Youngers, all going to the same destination and obeying the same summons. Arriving at their destination, they were immediately set to work on what Tumilten knew was a giant space-ship.

These Youngers at work on the ship, drawn in small groups from every city in their closely clustered community, did not complain when their work-periods were lengthened. Nor was there any explanation. It was not till Youngers had lived for thousands of years that they sought answer to what the Elders and Ancients commanded them to do. And by the time they sought such answers, they were ready to be made Elders.

And that marked the main fault of these mechanical creatures – a tediously slow evolution of the individual mind.

The giant space-craft was completed in fifteen years. All other preparations had been in the meantime completed, and the day came when the Twelve Ancients, speaking as one, addressed the many millions of Youngers.

"Youngers, our race is to seek a new home in the void," spoke the Supreme Voice, reaching to every brain-unit by broadcast telepathy. "Unfortunately, due to radium shortage, only a chosen number can leave. All the Elders are of the Chosen, but only one million of the Youngers. Most of you Youngers must be a sacrifice to this great venture. You are to be uncreated, and your brain-units to be destroyed so that we may take along your radium capsules. A white cross-mark will be placed on the frontal plates of those not chosen."

That was all. A day later Tumilten saw the emissary of the Council pass among the ranks of Youngers, with an instrument that blazoned a white cross-mark on certain of them. It was Zonzi himself.

Zonzi raised the instrument as he came to Tumilten.

"You are not of the Chosen," he announced, with something akin to sadness in his manner. "The Council chose purely by lot."

Tumilten, of mixed reactions, said simply: "Tumilten would only wish that before the end he might know of those greater secrets of the past."

Zonzi extended a tiny square box of metal. "That was anticipated, Tumilten. Since you are to be uncreated so soon, there can be no harm in revealing the past arcana of our race. There are thought-recorded for you here all those things from the Books."

Tumilten took the tiny machine almost reverently.

Mechanical Elder looked at mechanical Younger. A spark of something unmechanical passed between them; something their hard race had known little of – personal friendship.

Then without further word, Zonzi marked the white cross on the Younger and stepped away. Tumilten watched him blazon the indelible cross on others and gradually move down the line. The Younger looked at the thought-recorder for a moment and then stuffed it into his chest storage space.

* * *

When the images had ceased, Walker turned to me after shutting off the current.

"The chronology of these two episodes is reversed," he said. "Obviously, the first scene we saw, last night, represented the carrying out of the Council's general slaughter of the Youngers. If I increase the frequency again, I'll get a still earlier episode. I hope so, because it would probably clear up what seems to be rather mysterious goings-on right now. Another half-hundred turns on the secondary ought to do it."

As he prepared to switch in the extra coil – he had previously had a number of them ready for that purpose – I held up a hand. "Wait a minute," I pleaded. "Don't be in such a hurry about it. Let me get my breath."

"Okay," laughed Walker. He could be so calm about such things. A real, honest-to-goodness ghost materializing in his presence would simply send him scampering for a camera and an electroscope. He laughed again.

"Look," he said, displaying the last joint of his little finger with the thumb and forefinger of his other hand. "That's how much mankind knows of the universe. Each little crumb of new knowledge we gather startles us, but if we could once perceive the body of the *All* – our present science would seem like childish puttering."

"You've said that before," I grunted. "But tell me one thing. Where does this robot race fit in the scheme of evolution?"

"Doesn't," Walker was at the window, staring out at the endless stream of traffic. "You know, this has set me thinking on that very thing. Evolution fails to account, in the last analysis, for the quite sudden uprise of intelligence. We have to assume that after Nature had fooled around with various forms of life for a half-billion years, she suddenly came up with a mutation that could reason, evolving in a short fifty or one hundred thousand years. The Survival of the Fittest angle has the paradox in it of saying that *homo* survived not because of, but *in spite of*, intelligence. Because while beetle-browed Neandertal and equally unfit Heidelberg flourished, brain meant nothing against brawn. The Mutation or Sport theory of accounting for the genus *homo*, on the other hand, doesn't easily explain where the first species *sapiens* found a mate to carry on his particular strain."

"What are you driving at?" I asked impatiently. Walker had a habit of wandering around with words.

He shrugged. "I don't know, myself. Just inner doubts I've had for a long time. But this record of a mechanical creature of at least prehistoric times may give us some startling clues."

"You mean it may have a connection with earthly life? – With man and evolution?" I snorted. "He's from some other world – some utterly alien form of life."

Little though I knew it, I was right – and wrong, too.

Walker damped his cigarette. "We'll find out soon enough. We'll tune in the next 'recording' of the metal ball. Whoever or whatever made this thought-record, made it with a purpose in mind, I'm sure of that."

He knifed a group of switches that cut another coil into his secondary, increasing the frequency of his Tesla field. Then he snapped on the generator and motioned for me to get into place.

I got into my seat with avid eagerness, wondering what further strange things would reveal themselves to us. Walker fed current into his coils. The now familiar hiss of the 'carrier' wave came again. A moment later there was the sudden flash of images that carried with them sound and feeling and thought. I don't know how else to describe the very completeness of our contact in the thought-messages.

In a *rapport* that made us one with the narrator, we became aware of listening to a language of clear, lucid thought, rather than words. Every nuance of expression was understandable, as if the speaker were using the universal tongue of the atoms that compose all things...

* * *

"When this sun was a younger star," said the ultra-voice, "and all its planets had been but newly spewed from its seething, white-hot surface by the influence of a passing star, our people came from the outer void."

Tumilten, of the Youngers, listened eagerly. Zonzi of the Elders was one of the Keepers of History. His knowledge of their people's past went way back to the dim times when they had lived on the planets of another star. It was his privilege to sit periodically in council with the twelve Ancients; those twelve who had lived on that other world, and whose ages ran into incredible figures. Yet what is time to a creature of metal?

"Housed in a gigantic space-ship," went on Zonzi, "our predecessors – including of course the Twelve – spanned the enormous void between that other star and this one, and finally landed on the ninth and outermost planet. There our race took up its normal course of existence, finding suitable minerals and materials to make replacement parts for their bodies. In a short time they began creating a group of Youngers to replace those of the Ancients who had faded out during the tremendous journey."

"Yet, though many Youngers were created, it was soon seen that their numbers would never reach the total our race had had on that other star. For of radium, the life-giving element which gives conscious being to our brain-units, there was a limited supply in this sun system."

"It was debated for a while whether to leave this radium-impoverished system and seek another, richer in this element. But the Elders of that time had had enough of age-long travel through the endless void. They did not relish the idea of again seeking and seeking through space for a sun with planets. For perhaps you know that only one out of 100,000 stars has a family of satellites."

Tumilten nodded. "Why did our race leave its other home?"

"For two reasons," replied Zonzi. "First, because all the available radium had been finally used up. And second, because the parent sun was burning out and becoming dark and cold. And without the energy of a sun to feed its many machines, the race could not thrive."

"Some there were who advocated a harnessing of the terrible power of atomic-energy to replace sun power. But after the awful explosion of an entire planet, with thousands of our people living on it, through the escaping of an atomic-power vortex, the Elders would have no more to do with such a wild, treacherous source of power. No, they must have the safe and gentle sun power, and for that they had to go out in search of a young and hot star with a family of planets."

Hardly had Zonzi paused when Tumilten came up with another eager question – "But where had our race come from previous to that? Had they come from still another star-family, again leaving a cooled and dying sun for a newer and hotter one? Or is it true – as certain legends go – that our race was created by another, a strangely non-mineral form of intelligent life?"

Zonzi waved two of his prehensile tentacles as if startled, or shocked. "Careful what you say, Tumilten," he admonished.

"But is that true?" persisted the Younger. "Your knowledge as Keeper of History comes from the lore contained in the indelible records of the Books. Surely you have read in those Books of that ultimate beginning of our race?"

Zonzi again twitched his fore-tentacles, this time as if in hesitation of what to say. If his mechanical features had been able to register emotion, he would have looked grave and thoughtful.

Finally he spoke – "There are some things in the Books it is best to leave unheralded. We, the Keepers of History, are under oath not to reveal the greater secrets of the past to the Youngers." He waved a tentacle negatively. "No, Tumilten, your question must remain unanswered."

Tumilten knew it was useless to press the point. Close though he and Zonzi were to each other, there was yet a barrier between them – the barrier between all Elders and Youngers. The Youngers were the doers of the race, the runners of machines. The Elders were the thinkers, the ones to guide the greater destiny of the race, in company with the all-wise Ancients.

Tumilten was an anomaly as a Younger. He wanted to plumb the misted past, speculate on the equally misted future. And he wanted to think...

Zonzi gazed at his companion with wonder. What strange spark existed in his brain-unit, so newly formed from cold, unreasoning mineral? He had been created but a thousand years before, and already his brain had become subtle and quickened, as if he had been an Elder of many millennia of existence.

"Well," said Tumilten at length, with a tone that among humans would have been called a sigh. "Go on, Zonzi, with the history of our race since it has been here in this star-family."

"From the ninth planet," continued Zonzi, "our race gradually worked inward, as the central sun slowly cooled through the ages. The eighth planet, then the seventh, and then the sixth. The sixth had no less than ten satellites of its own – tiny bodies that had been ripped from its molten surface during the cataclysmic event that had formed this family of planets. Grandchildren of the sun they were, and three of them yielded large deposits of radium, thus allowing our race to increase its numbers.

"We Youngers of that time – all Elders now – were privileged to witness one of the grandest sights of all time. It was the formation of the rings of the sixth planet. The nearest planetoid to the mother planet, hovering for long ages on the danger line, finally slipped its slowing orbit too close, and the titanic gravitation of the primary planet tore it into shredded fragments. That was a memorable sight!"

Zonzi paused in memory of it, then went on – "Time moved on, the sun cooled more, and our race moved inward to the fifth planet, the giant of them all, with nine satellites. We took up our abode on one of the planetoids, as the primary itself was too stormy and violent. But on the central planet we found large deposits of radium and we built a huge encampment for its recovery. To ward off the cyclonic, corrosive storms, we built the great counter-eddy machine, fed by the planet's inner store of heat. It still stands today, although the radium supplies are depleted. And it will stand for future ages, this great red-spot, site of our giant counter-eddy machine.

"From the giant fifth planet, led by our race's constant need for the stronger rays of the central sun, we went to the fourth. In going there we passed the belt of asteroids, those broken pieces of a world which mark another vain attempt to harness the demonic energy of the atom. But a few hundred years before a nameless experimenter had blown himself and an entire planet to bits.

"But to go on, our race spread itself over the fourth planet, a small one and almost barren of radium, so that we could only stay long enough to build enormous sluice-ways in which the poor ores could be worked for what little radium there was. These large sluice-ways represent a great engineering achievement. Water from the polar caps was pumped down these enormous canals, and chemicals added which caused the radium to dissolve from the heaps of sand thrown in. Then the radium-rich water was run into great vats at the junctions of the canals, and here worked for the metal itself. A great achievement."

Zonzi curled and uncurled a tentacle before going on – "From the fourth planet we came to this, the third. And now we are faced with a shortage of radium. All the outer planets have been depleted, this planet is quite radiumless, and its satellite is scarred with our mine shafts seeking the metal."

"Our race, Tumilten, is faced with a crisis – a crisis greater than any other in our history, save one. That other crisis was when that star which was our people's previous homeland burned dim and our machines began to idle for lack of sun power. Thus our race left its age-old home to seek a new one. But at least they had sufficient radium to renew each and every brain-unit during that frightfully long journey through the void at the speed of light."

"In this present crisis, we shall not have enough. The Elders who have explored the two inner planets for radium found little. Thus, when our final plans have been laid, and the huge ark to carry us through space is built, many brain-units will have to remain – to become uncreated; to become inanimate mineral matter."

"It will be soon now that our race – those chosen – will plunge into the abysm of eternal space, to seek a new homeland among the uncounted stars."

* * *

The strange thought-voice faded away and a click announced the end of that episode. I've tried to give what we heard – or absorbed mentally – as we heard it. But I find that our language is simply incapable of expressing the message's true form. At least the gist of it is there.

Walker and I blinked as though we had awakened from a deep sleep, then stared at each other in a sudden flood of amazement at what we had just heard.

"We can have a gin chaser for that," I muttered. I ran to the window, gulped in fresh air, and stared quickly around. "Just wanted to make sure Earth was still here," I added with a lame chuckle.

Walker stood staring at the metal ball in fascination.

"That thing has dynamite in it," he murmured softly, "mental dynamite – enough to blow up our civilization's pet belief that mankind is the only reasoning race ever to exist. And look at the mysteries it explains – the rings of Saturn, the red-spot of Jupiter, the canals of Mars, the craters of the moon!"

"Not to mention the odd scarcity of radium on Earth," I added.

"I have an idea, though," continued Walker thoughtfully, "that a bigger surprise is ahead – in the episodes following. Something relating directly to human life. Have you noticed the speaker – the one who made this record – seems to be telling it from a broadened viewpoint? There are numerous allusions to the abstract, and a general comparing to 'organic' or 'carbonaceous' life. The narrator is obviously taking an analytical attitude toward the people he is telling about."

"But *who* is doing the telling?" I wanted to know.

"I think Tuformiltuten himself."

"Who?" I asked sharply. "Do you mean Tumilten?"

Walker stared at me wide-eyed for a moment, then chuckled.

"All right – Tumilten. Although I got it as Tuformiltuten! The name, if you got it, is simply a number in syllables, one up in the millions, but too condensed for us to figure out. To me it was a word that registered as Two-four-million-two-ten. To you it was the slurred Two-million-ten. Anyway, whichever we call him, it is he that is telling the story, because he is analyzing himself more closely than anyone else could, and his viewpoint is from the future."

"Eh? How do you figure that?" I asked skeptically. "I took it that the record was made as the events happened."

Walker shook his head. "No, because there are too many abstract tie-ups. In the first episode we saw, Tumilten or Tuformiltuten, called himself a philosopher in a race totally without philosophy – an obvious interpolation from after-thought."

Well, it took us ten minutes to straighten that out, because you see I hadn't got that 'only philosopher in a race totally without philosophy' at all. And it turned out that the versions we had heard were somewhat different, although in broad detail they were identical. The versions I have written down are a composite of what both of us got. I will have to admit my versions were skimpier than Walker's, and I'm free in admitting that his mind is more sensitive, more embracing than mine. Thus he 'heard' more.

This leads to the conclusion that the message itself is far more detailed than the human mind can interpret. Either the time-factor is different between the robot's vision of the events and ours, or his mind is simply more highly organized. I can't be the judge of that.

Walker went on with his idea, which had become almost an obsession – "Probably Tumilten – if he is truly the narrator – is bringing the series of episodes to some climax; of that I'm almost certain. Taking them in their chronological order, episode one – the last we saw – gives the history and origin of the robot race. Episode two relates Tumilten's gradual build-up of philosophy – remember it stretches out for fifteen years – from what he had heard from Zonzi. And episode three reveals that Tumilten, in escaping the universal 'uncreating', is destined to be the last and only robot left on Earth."

Walker has that kind of mind – a keen organ that gropes behind the obvious for hidden mental delicacies.

"Now, what will be the outcome of this?" he almost whispered. "Tumilten, a strange mechanical being able to reason in the abstract, in his possession a record of dark secrets of the past. *What will result!*"

* * *

The next evening I entered Walker's small electrical workshop in a curious state of bemusement.

"I say, Bill," I spoke from the doorway, "did we dream what we heard last night? And the night before? This morning when I woke up, and all through the day at the office, I kept wondering if we had really heard anything! You know, when you burned out our coil last night trying to get what would have been episode four, we got a minute of idiotic babbling from the metal ball."

"Yes, it must have a charging unit inside that holds juice for a minute or so."

"Well," I went on, "maybe *all* we heard was that same babbling, and we just imagined we had received an intelligible record! Self-hypnotism, you know."

Walker looked up witheringly. "Come in, you purple skeptic. I'll bet you're a mass of black and blue from pinching yourself."

"Well, it's easier *not* to believe." Walker snorted. "It was easier not to believe Galileo at first, too. And Darwin, and Einstein, and all the other new ideas that ever jolted this hard-headed old world. You've heard the old saw—"

"Truth is stranger than fiction," I said in chorus with him. "I know," I went on, and I can tell you I was dead serious, "but still maybe the thing's a hoax, a trick that someone devised—"

"And then dug a hole in the middle of the Sahara Desert to bury his gadget, knowing someone by the name of William Walker would come along and—" Walker broke off with a growl. "Enough of that. Come here, now, and let's tune in episode four. After replacing the burned-out coil this morning, I tried to get the messages myself, but no go. It was just a jumble of flat images and twisted thoughts. It takes two minds to coordinate the record, as it takes two legs to walk."

A minute later we were seated entranced before the metal ball which was radiating thought-waves, in some inexplicable way, into our minds. And because the imperfections that are inherent in eyes and ears and spoken words were passed by, we were able to grasp and know things we might never have understood through the five senses.

If only I could find the words to transmit those things faithfully to paper! But there are no such words...

* * *

Tumilten stood alone, of his race, on Earth!

An hour before he had watched the space-ship bearing all the Elders and Ancients, and one million of the Youngers, lift hissingly into the sky and then plunge furiously away. It would be many ages before they would land again on a world – perhaps not till millions of years had gone by. In that time the Ancients would undoubtedly die, and the Elders would become Ancients, and the Youngers, Elders. And if, by some cosmic mischance, they did not find a haven in time, they would die to the last one!

Tumilten's mechanical frame shuddered. Dying – fading out – was so unheard-of a thing among Youngers and Elders. Only the Ancients, those who had lived for almost countless eons, died, with their brain-units completely enervated. They died not for lack of radium, these Ancients, but simply because the delicate cores of their brain-units had atrophied to mineral dust.

Intricate machines, robots, though they were, these creatures from another star, and as such ageless through constant renewal of worn-out parts – yet they knew death; a long-coming but nevertheless inescapable death, that resulted from the common failing of all things purely mineral – the slow tendency of atoms to disintegrate into the dust of energy. They could renew tentacles, fuel, tiny wires, and all the conglomerate of their mechanical bodies, but they could not renew the pulsing core of their brain-units, which, although protected from all normal disintegrating agencies, could not escape the hand of time – and the falling apart of matter. Radium was but the larger symbol of what happened to all matter – a slow disintegration that was almost swift as measured by these long-living machine intelligences.

And in their incredibly long lives, individual evolution was correspondingly slow. As a result, the progress of the race was infinitely slower. And it came to Tumilten, standing there alone, that this was an unforgivable defect of his people. His race, his kind, had existed for a space of time measured by the births and deaths of hoary-old stars. Yet in that tremendous span of time they had not improved their lot to any extent; had not, for instance, found a way to harness atomic power, or to break from the chains of radium-restricted rejuvenation.

Their science had been a restricted science, dealing only with mechanical improvements of their machine bodies and cities. They had not pierced to the center of the earth, or explored the world of atoms. They had not tabulated the wonders of biological life, or the phenomena of sexual reproduction, or any of the other manifold mysteries of things around them. Even those great projects they had carried out – the canals of planet four, the red-spot on five – had been but to find radium, to create more Youngers, more machines…

"Where," Tumilten asked, "where would there be another life, another race, that would have the ability to burst free the chain of the strictly material, and seek knowledge for its own sake? That would do things for the mere doing? That would even war among itself because of cross purposes that would arise from different and new ideas?"

Where was there a form of life that would display its kinship to the general universe by following the law of *change*? His own robot race, spawned eons before, was long antedated, was a static form of life that had no place in the present cosmos. This was proved alone by the fact that every 1700 years half of any given amount of *all* the radium in the universe changed into lower elements. Their race, dependent on radium for conscious life, was doomed by this mathematical progression of material change.

The law of change!

The day would come when radium would exist, in all the cosmos, in only little specks dotted here and there, and beyond gleaning. And the stars did not manufacture, in their furnace cores, radium any longer, for the balance of distributed energy between matter and space had changed… *change*…! The immutable law…!

Tumilten gave up his speculations suddenly. He kicked at a scurrying rodent that ran by and asked it – "Will this new life come from you? But you have no intelligence; you are just an animated carbonaceous jelly."

The little beast, attracted perhaps by the bright glint of sun on metal, stopped and sat up on a mound of earth and peered with bright little eyes at the mechanical man.

Looking into its eyes, Tumilten was vaguely stirred.

"And yet, it may be from your kind after all! I see – I see something of a dawning intelligence behind your visioning orbs. But" – he deprecated then – "will the one who has created you think of creating something *more* than you?"

And Tumilten did not know, at the time, that its creator was not a material being, and that the creator's name was Nature…

* * *

Walker snapped off the circuit as the carrier wave broke into our *rapport* with the thought-images, and gave me a significant look.

I've tried to give, above, as complete a version of the robot's philosophic speculations as he stood alone on Earth as possible, but there were a myriad thoughts – inarticulate ones – that were woven in this episode. Of course we ran through the various episodes several times each, but like a phonograph record, essentially the same message came through every time.

"We're getting into deeper water right along," said Walker hoarsely. He was excited. "As I suspected, there's some connection with this record and pre-human history. Don't you sense it, Cliff? I think we can prepare ourselves for some stiff shocks of one kind or another."

"Haven't we been shocked enough already?" I grunted. "I don't exactly like this chap's profound intelligence. Makes me feel small and uneducated. I feel as though I had a transparent brain, compared to his, figuratively and literally."

"That's the odd part of it," mused Walker. "That he – or it – should know so much about things in general, as if he had ransacked a library. He even hinted at knowing what evolution was, at the last. Yet, as a Younger of his race, untutored except as a mechanic and worker, he could not know those things. Mm," he went on, "just happened to think – remember that little box Zonzi gave him when marking the white cross on his front? That must be his source of knowledge!"

And a few minutes later, the fifth episode confirmed this. It began much like the preceding episode, picturing the robot standing tirelessly, with the large white cross on his torso, and giving his mental ruminations. But one noticeable difference there was – the scenic background was no longer desert but instead luxuriant jungleland, steaming in the sun. And, more startling than that, there stood before the robot a bronzed, naked human being – a man who, despite a scraggly beard and unkempt hair, was obviously *homo sapiens*!

* * *

Tumilten had traveled. For years he had traveled, the power valves for his metal sinews renewed by a portable machine modeled from the larger ones in cities, which made liquid fuel out of sand by the use of sun-energy. He had crossed jungle and mountain, valley and desert, and had seen everywhere prolific abundance of animal life; life that he understood to be vastly different, in a material way, from his own.

These creatures he saw before they scurried away from his awesome presence were composed of carbonaceous jelly, so soft that he could push a tentacle right through their bodies. The few times he had done this, experimentally, he had been puzzled by the outpouring of a queer, thick red fluid. His alert senses told him that this watery fluid might be, to them, as his own oily fuel was to him – the means of supplying energy to their flimsy bodies.

At first Tumilten had been impatient with these jelly creatures, in his search for intelligent life. It did not occur to him that among their kind might be what he was looking for. He had seen a tremendous variety of them, from tiny, swift balls of fur to giant, thick-hided monsters that trumpeted squealingly at his approach. None of them had indicated signs of the least rational intelligence. And Tumilten thought that his search was useless.

Only one type of creature, standing one-third his own size and walking erect on two legs, showed a rudimentary intelligence. They inhabited caves, usually in small groups, and used fire. They carried hand-made implements that showed a certain dawning ingenuity of invention.

But the thoughts they radiated, which Tumilten caught and read, were simple and dull. They were not far on the road to intellect.

"There," Tumilten told himself, "is the matrix from which organic evolution, as it obtained in that other star-system which Zonzi's recordings of the Books tell about, might produce truly reasoning creatures. There is a close analogy between these creatures of two different worlds, except that those who were the creatures of my race were composed of siliceous compounds instead of carbonaceous."

"The question is, when will evolution here on this planet produce a mutation with true intelligence? Perhaps not for ages yet."

But one day Tumilten had seen one of the erect, two-legged creatures with a curious aura of deliberateness in his manner. And this being, contrary to all other jelly creatures, had not fled, but had stared at him curiously. When Tumilten had taken a step forward, this being had warily, not precipitately, backed to a large stone, still staring. Once it had lifted a sharp stick, and balanced it for a moment in its hand.

All the while it showed more curiosity than fear, emotions that Tumilten had come to recognize, but not analyze.

Intrigued by this strange being, Tumilten had approached very close and read its thoughts. And thereupon Tumilten knew he was facing a mind having at least the capacity of his own, even if of an entirely alien construction.

So it was that Tumilten stood before a man, and knew that his search – that search that had really begun in his mind a half-million years before while he had been among his own race – had ended. Here was life, biologically endless, thoroughly adapted to a changeable and changing environment, with an intellectual capacity beyond plumbing. This was the race that would rise above the material, would develop philosophy, science and thought beyond the limits of its humble birth. It had spawned in the jungle – it would reach to the stars.

Tumilten concentrated his thought, radiated it to the man-being in simple nuances of expression – "Man, are you afraid of Tumilten?"

"Not afraid, but amazed," came back in thought articulation. "I have never seen your like before."

"Tumilten is not a creature like you," returned the robot. "He is of another world – another sphere of the universe."

"You are from the stars?" The Man pointed upward – "From there? But *who* are you?"

"The number is meaningless, but he is Tumilten. He is of that kind of life which came before you. His race is that which could only exist properly before this time in the universe. Your race will inherit the planets his race has ravished of radium."

The Man's mind was befogged at these things. He touched his spear-head, which was of metal. "You are made of this. Are you indestructible, and how long have you lived?"

"Tumilten has lived for thousands of years, and is indestructible to the extent that nothing living can harm him."

What was that curious emotion that came up in the man-creature then? That queer awe and reverence?

"Then you are a – a god!" said the Man.

"God? God? Oh, that is perhaps your thought for robot. Well, if Tumilten is what you call a god, he is the only one, as all the others have left this earth."

"You are The God, then!" said the Man, again with awe. "What is that large white cross on your front – what does that mean?"

Tumilten answered, amazed at the man-creature's insatiable curiosity, and at the same time pleased, for curiosity denoted intelligence. "This cross was emblazoned on Tumilten's frontlet to indicate that he must be destroyed when the Chosen left this world. But, as you see, Tumilten was not destroyed."

"That cross meant you should be – killed?" returned the Man, puzzled. "Yet you are here. You were not killed!"

"Tumilten was not destroyed."

"You are Tumilten, though!"

"Yes, Tumilten is— Tumilten."

The man-creature frowned. These things were not quite clear to him. At times he looked at the robot with awed eyes. An odd series of thoughts ran through his mind, jumbling up the conceptions of the white cross, god, Tumilten is Tumilten, indestructibility and longevity of the robot.

Tumilten spoke again – "Man, do you know that you are at the beginning of a great race? Since you are the first Tumilten has found in many years of wandering, you shall be called the One-Man. Your mate will be called the One-Woman."

"But I have no mate!" returned the Man, shaking his head dejectedly. "I cannot mate with those shaggy women in the caves – even though my mother was one of them."

"I know you have not found a mate," said Tumilten. "You are a biological sport, a mutation, one that would ordinarily die out unless a similar sport of the other sex is found for you. There must be dozens, perhaps hundreds, of your type on earth, and must have been for years, but the chances of mutations meeting are so small that it might not occur the first time for thousands of years yet. Therefore, Tumilten will search out a mate for you, though it takes years."

"You will find me a mate? A woman as straight of body as I, as hairless, as round of skull?" queried the Man.

"Yes, one who will reproduce with you and give rise to the race that will one day surpass Tumilten and his race tenfold."

The man-creature stared in amazement. "Tumilten *is* a god!" he cried.

Tumilten, though puzzled, did not try to clear up the mix-up at that time. Later, he was to find it a point on which he and the man, and his mate, could not agree. Nor with the later man-creatures he was to find, and the mates he found for them, could he establish a rational basis of understanding as to who and what he was.

There was a peculiar twist in the man-mind that made it idealize more than rationalize. Later progress would either eliminate this quality, or make of it something beyond the scope of a robot mind. One question was ever to recur to Tumilten, yet never quite answer itself – "What is that thought-word 'god'?"

* * *

We – Walker and I – started as though awakening from a dream when the thought-record clicked off there.

The above account dissatisfies me. In a way, it records the message that radiated to our brains from the metal ball. But it fails miserably to carry the full import. It is sketchy, even a little ridiculous. I've tried to rewrite it, but each version is as incomplete, as imperfect of the real thing, as this one. So this one will have to stand.

Walker cleared his throat, after snapping off the current.

"That," he jerked out, "is what they call a revelation!"

As for me, I was all in pieces. I was actually panting.

"I – I can't believe it!" I stammered. "It's preposterous! A trick of some kind. Are we supposed to have witnessed a sort of rehearsed play enacted 25,000 years ago? The origin of human life? Adam and Eve, so to speak?"

"Why not?" My friend's eyes were shining. "We have witnessed the original of the first of all fables – that of Man's creation. We saw not Adam and Eve, but the One-Man and the One-Woman, whereas Adam and Eve may have been a later couple brought together by Tumilten. It's the new Genesis, or rather, the old explained. The Biblical Adam-and-Eve story is history, not religion, remember that. Anyway, the first-man and first-woman story is not solely a Biblical story at all. Think of the fable of Prometheus and Pandora in Greek mythology. Then in the Vedas of India, Brahma and his four sons, who were *given* wives from Heaven. In Northern mythology, there are Aske and Embla, the progenitors of the human race. They all bear the curious relationship that the man in each case was given a wife, respectively by Jehovah, Jupiter, Brahma, and Odin. A story that is so universal and has so many points in common makes it a historical fact. What we have heard and seen here gives the true picture of these many versions."

"Huh," I grunted. "This version is more fantastic than all the others put together. Tell me this, why that ambiguous phrase 'Tumilten is Tumilten'?"

I thought I had him there. I wanted to trip him up on little details and make him admit the whole thing was crazy. But he answered quick as a flash:

"Because the robot Tumilten had no conception of the pronoun 'I'. Think once – all through the records it did not once refer to itself except by name or in the third person. To himself, he was not *himself*, but simply Tumilten!"

Walker reflected a moment. "That brings up the curious thought that the conception of 'I' – my existence of myself separate from the universe at large – is a purely human invention. The robot people did not recognize a fundamental individuality. Perhaps each thought of himself as abstractly as you think of your pared finger-nail."

I am giving you everything Walker said not as gospel truth, but just as his way of explaining things. I don't agree with him at all. How do I explain it all? I don't – can't. I firmly believe there is no explanation – not any reasonable one.

"I can't follow that fancy metaphysics," I growled. "But let me tell you something – there's one thing very odd about that whole series of records. Tumilten – or whoever really made it – was holding back a lot. He seemed to be telling just certain things, as if to get our reactions for his own benefit. But of course the record was made plenty long ago, so – *look out!*"

Walker, in the act of lighting a cigarette, had let the match burn to his finger-tips. He flung it down slowly, and damped the unlighted cigarette carefully as though it had been burning. His face was deeply thought-creased.

"Cliff—"

"No, I'm going. I can see you have a spell of fantastic theories coming on. Besides, I have to sleep this off – worse than drugs—"

Still mumbling, I left, leaving Walker in a trance.

* * *

"I still don't believe it!" were my words of greeting the next evening.

Walker raised a face that showed by its haggardness that he had been up all the past twenty-four hours. "Cliff," he said, "I got a letter from Micolet, the paleontologist who found the metal ball. They have finally determined the age of the clay-matrix in which the thing was found. The fossils cannot be less than 25,000 years old!"

"I don't believe that either!" I said stubbornly. I was in a completely disbelieving mood.

Walker held up a flask in which two gold leaves hung suspended from a conductor rod running through a rubber cork. "This is an electroscope," he explained. "It indicates the electrical charge of any object, or of the air surrounding the conductor rod. When I hold it near that metal ball from which we got our records, *the leaves fly apart!*"

"Huh," I said. "The metal ball is charged."

"No, the air around it is, because there's radium inside!"

"And?"

"Don't you see, Cliff?" cried Walker, jumping to his feet. "It means that metal ball is not just any mechanism, but is the very mechanism that the robot people called a brain-unit!"

I gulped. "That is – Tumilten's own *brain*?"

Walker nodded excitedly. "You gave me the hint last night, saying the records seemed to be created on the spot, for us. Stupidly, I puzzled over that for hours before thinking of a way to prove it, simply with an electroscope to detect the radium."

"But the radium must have been burned out in 25,000 years!"

"You forget that only *half* of any given amount of radium burns out every 1,700 years. Most of it is gone, but about 1/30 of it is still active, *enough to keep that mechanical brain at least partially alive!*"

"Good God! Alive?"

"Yes, the body had long rusted away, as have all the cities of the robot people in the past 25,000 years, so that nothing remains of them but that one metal ball, made of an incredibly resistant alloy."

"Good God! Alive!" I gasped again. I picked up the metal ball gingerly, lying on the work-bench, and looked at it wide-eyed. A brain – a mechanical brain 25,000 years old – and alive!

"Bill!" I faced about suddenly. "Bill, if we found a way to open it and put in more radium – wouldn't it really come to life?"

"It would, except for one thing," said Walker. "*It died this morning!*"

"Died!"

"Yes. Whether the waning emanations finally ceased to nourish it, or the effects of the high-frequency field gradually disrupted it, or whether, somehow, it *wanted* to die, I don't know. But it is completely dead to the Tesla field. We might have heard much more – there must be far more that it had to tell, this ancient brain of metal – but it will remain a secret forever!"

Curiously enough, my thought at the moment was, "And better so!"

Walker's epitaphal comment was appropriate: "He told us the first story ever to be told among the human race, in a different way."

Yes, and from the beginning!

Comfort Me, My Robot

Robert Bloch

WHEN HENSON CAME IN, the Adjustor was sitting inside his desk, telescreening a case. At the sound of the door-tone he flicked a switch. The posturchair rose from the center of the desk until the Adjustor's face peered at the visitor from an equal level.

"Oh, it's you," said the Adjustor. "Aren't you a bit early for dinner? Our engagement isn't until five."

"This isn't an engagement," Henson told him. "It's an appointment."

"Appointment?"

"Didn't the girl tell you? I'm here to see you professionally."

If the Adjustor was surprised, he didn't show it. He cocked a thumb at a posturchair. "Sit down and tell me all about it, Henson," he said.

"Nothing to tell." Henson stared out of the window at the plains of Upper Mongolia. "It's just a routine matter. I'm here to make a request and you're the Adjustor."

"And your request is—?"

"Simple," said Henson. "I want to kill my wife."

The Adjustor nodded. "That can be arranged," he murmured. "Of course, it will take a few days."

"I can wait."

"Would Friday be convenient?"

"Good enough. That way it won't cut into my weekend. Lita and I were planning a fishing trip, up New Zealand way. Care to join us?"

"Sorry, but I'm tied up until Monday." The Adjustor stifled a yawn. "Why do you want to kill Lita?" he asked.

"She's hiding something from me."

"What do you suspect?"

"That's just it – I don't know what to suspect. And it keeps bothering me."

"Why don't you question her?"

"Violation of privacy. Surely you, as a certified public Adjustor, wouldn't advocate that?"

"Not professionally." The Adjustor grinned. "But since we're personal friends, I don't mind telling you that there are times when I think privacy should be violated. This notion of individual rights can become a fetish."

"Fetish?"

"Just an archaicism." The Adjustor waved a casual dismissal to the word. He leaned forward. "Then, as I understand it, your wife's attitude troubles you. Rather than embarrass her with questions, you propose to solve the problem delicately, by killing her."

"Right."

"A very chivalrous attitude. I admire it."

"I'm not sure whether I do or not," Henson mused. "You see, it really wasn't my idea. But the worry was beginning to affect my work, and my Administrator – Loring, you know him, I believe – took me aside for a talk. He suggested I see you and arrange for a murder."

"Then it's to be murder." The Adjustor frowned. "You know, actually, we are supposed to be the arbiters when it comes to method. In some cases a suicide works just as well. Or an accident."

"I want a murder," Henson said. "Premeditated, and in the first degree." Now it was his turn to grin. "You see, I know a few archaicisms myself."

The Adjustor made a note. "As long as we're dealing in archaic terminology, might I characterize your attitude towards your wife as one of… jealousy?"

Henson controlled his blush at the sound of the word. He nodded slowly. "I guess you're right," he admitted. "I can't bear the idea of her having any secrets. I know it's immature and absurd, and that's why I'm seeking an immature solution."

"Let me correct you," said the Adjustor. "Your solution is far from immature. A good murder is probably the most adult approach to your problem. After all, man, this is the twenty-second century, not the twentieth. Although even way back then they were beginning to learn some of the answers."

"Don't tell me they had Adjustors," Henson murmured.

"No, of course not. In those days this field was only a small, neglected part of physical medicine. Practitioners were called psychiatrists, psychologists, auditors, analysts – and a lot of other things. That was their chief stock in trade, by the way: name-calling and labelling."

The Adjustor gestured toward the slide-files. "I must have five hundred spools transcribed there," he calculated. "All of it from books – nineteenth, twentieth, even early twenty-first century material. And it's largely terminology, not technique. Psychotherapy was just like alchemy in those days. Everything was named and defined. Inability to cope with environment was minutely broken down into hundreds of categories, thousands of terms. There were 'schools' of therapy, with widely divergent theories and applications. And the crude attempts at technique they used – you wouldn't believe it unless you studied what I have here! Everything from trying to 'cure' a disorder in one session by means of brain surgery or electric shock to the other extreme of letting the 'patient' talk about his problems for thousands of hours over a period of years."

He smiled. "I'm afraid I'm letting my personal enthusiasm run away with me. After all, Henson, you aren't interested in the historical aspects. But I did have a point I wanted to make. About the maturity of murder as a solution-concept."

Henson adjusted the posturchair as he listened.

"As I said, even back in the twentieth century, they were beginning to get a hint of the answer. It was painfully apparent that some of the techniques I mention weren't working at all. 'Sublimation' and 'catharsis' helped but did not cure in a majority of cases. Physical therapy altered and warped the personality. And all the while, the answer lay right before their eyes.

"Let's take your twentieth-century counterpart for an example. Man named Henson, who was jealous of his wife. He might go to an analyst for years without relief. Whereas if he did the sensible thing, he'd take an axe to her and kill her.

"Of course, in the twentieth century such a procedure was antisocial and illegal. Henson would be sent to prison for the rest of his life.

"But the chances are, he'd function perfectly thereafter. Having relieved his psychic tension by the common-sense method of direct action, he'd have no further difficulty in adjustment.

"Gradually the psychiatrists observed this phenomenon. They learned to distinguish between the psychopath and the perfectly normal human being who sought to relieve an intolerable situation. It was hard, because once a normal man was put in prison, he was subject to new tensions and stresses which caused fresh aberrations. But these aberrations stemmed from his confinement – not from the impulses which led him to kill." Again the Adjustor paused. "I hope I'm not making this too abstruse for you," he said. "Terms like 'psychopath' and 'normal' can't have much meaning to a layman."

"I understand what you're driving at," Henson told him. "Go ahead. I've always wondered how Adjustment evolved, anyway."

"I'll make it brief from now on," the Adjustor promised. "The next crude step was something called the 'psychodrama'. It was a simple technique in which an aberrated individual was encouraged to get up on a platform, before an audience, and act out his fantasies – including those involving aggression and violently antisocial impulses. This afforded great relief. Well, I won't trouble you with the historical details about the establishment of Master Control, right after North America went under in the Blast. We got it, and the world started afresh, and one of the groups set up was Adjustment. All of physical medicine, all of what was then called sociology and psychiatry, came under the scope of this group. And from that point on we started to make real progress.

"Adjustors quickly learned that old-fashioned therapies must be discarded. Naming or classifying a mental disturbance didn't necessarily overcome it. Talking about it, distracting attention from it, teaching the patient a theory about it, were not solutions. Nor was chopping out or shocking out part of his brain structure.

"More and more we came to rely on direct action as a cure, just as we do in physical medicine.

"Then, of course, robotics came along and gave us the final answer. And it is the answer, Henson – that's the thought I've been trying to convey. Because we're friends, I know you well enough to eliminate all the preliminaries. I don't have to give you a battery of tests, check reactions, and go through the other formalities. But if I did, I'm sure I'd end up with the same answer – in your case, the mature solution is to murder your wife as quickly as possible. That will cure you."

"Thanks," said Henson. "I knew I could count on you."

"No trouble at all." The Adjustor stood up. He was a tall, handsome man with curly red hair, and he somewhat towered over Henson who was only six feet and a bit too thin.

"You'll have papers to sign, of course," the Adjustor reminded him. "I'll get everything ready by Friday morning. If you'll step in then, you can do it in ten minutes."

"Fine." Henson smiled. "Then I think I'll plan the murder for Friday evening, at home. I'll get Lita to visit her mother in Saigon overnight. Best if she doesn't know about this until afterwards."

"Thoughtful of you," the Adjustor agreed. "I'll have her robot requisitioned for you from Inventory. Any special requirements?"

"I don't believe so. It was made less than two years ago, and it's almost a perfect match. Paid almost seven thousand for the job."

"That's a lot of capital to destroy." The Adjustor sighed. "Still, it's necessary. Will you want anything else – weapons, perhaps?"

"No." Henson stood in the doorway. "I think I'll just strangle her."

"Very well, then. I'll have the robot here and operating for you on Friday morning. And you'll take your robot too."

"Mine? Why, might I ask?"

"Standard procedure. You see, we've learned something more about the mind – about what used to be called a 'guilt complex'. Sometimes a man isn't freed by direct action alone. There may be a peculiar desire for punishment involved. In the old days many men who committed actual murders had this need to be caught and punished. Those who avoided capture frequently punished themselves. They developed odd psychosomatic reactions – some even committed suicide.

"In case you have any such impulses, your robot will be available to you. Punish it any way you like – destroy it, if necessary. That's the sensible thing to do."

"Right. See you Friday morning, then. And many thanks." Henson started through the doorway. He looked back and grinned. "You know, just thinking about it makes me feel better already!"

* * *

Henson whizzed back to the Adjustor's office on Friday morning. He was in rare good humor all the way. Anticipation was a wonderful thing. Everything was wonderful, for that matter.

Take robots, for example. The simple, uncomplicated mechanisms did all the work, all the drudgery. Their original development for military purposes during the twenty-first century was forgotten now, along with the concept of war which had inspired their creation. Now the automatons functioned as workers.

And for the well-to-do there were these personalized surrogates. What a convenience!

Henson remembered how he'd argued to convince Lita they should invest in a pair when they married. He'd used all of the sensible modern arguments. "You know as well as I do what having them will save us in terms of time and efficiency. We can send them to all the boring banquets and social functions. They can represent us at weddings and funerals, that sort of thing. After all, it's being done everywhere nowadays. Nobody attends such affairs in person any more if they can afford not to. Why, you see them on the street everywhere. Remember Kirk, at our reception? Stayed four hours, life of the party and everybody was fooled – you didn't know it was his robot until he told you." And so forth on and on. "Aren't you sentimental at all darling? If I died wouldn't you like to have my surrogate around to comfort you? I certainly would want yours to share the rest of my life."

Yes he'd used all the practical arguments except the psychotherapeutic one – at that time it had never occurred to him. But perhaps it should have, when he heard her objections.

"I just don't like the idea," Lita had persisted. "Oh it isn't that I'm old-fashioned. But lying there in the forms having every detail of my body duplicated synthetically – ugh! And then they do that awful hypnotherapy or whatever it's called for days to make them think. Oh I know they have no brains and it's only a lot of chemicals and electricity but they do duplicate your thought patterns and they react the same and they sound so real. I don't want anyone or anything to know all my secrets—"

Yes, that objection should have started him thinking. Lita had secrets even then.

But he'd been too busy to notice; he'd spent his efforts in battering down her objections. And finally she'd consented.

He remembered the days at the Institute – the tests they'd taken, the time spent in working with the anatomists, the cosmetic department, the sonic and visio adaptors, and then days of hypnotic transference.

Lita was right in a way; it hadn't been pleasant. Even a modern man was bound to feel a certain atavistic fear when confronted for the first time with his completed surrogate. But the finished product was worth it. And after Henson had mastered instructions, learned how to manipulate the robot by virtue of the control-command, he had been almost paternally proud of the creation.

He'd wanted to take his surrogate home with him, but Lita positively drew the line at that.

"We'll leave them both here in Inventory," she said. "If we need them we can always send for them. But I hope we never do."

Henson was finally forced to agree. He and Lita had both given their immobilization commands to the surrogates, and they were placed in their metal cabinets ready to be filed away – "Just like corpses!" Lita had shuddered. "We're looking at ourselves after we're dead."

And that had ended the episode. For a while, Henson made suggestions about using the surrogates – there were occasions he'd have liked to take advantage of a substitute for token public appearances – but Lita continued to object. And so, for two years now, the robots had been on file. Henson paid his taxes and fees on them annually and that was all.

That was all, until lately. Until Lita's unexplained silences and still more inexplicable absences had started Henson thinking. Thinking and worrying. Worrying and watching. Watching and waiting. Waiting to catch her, waiting to kill her –

So he'd remembered psychotherapy, and gone to his Adjustor. Lucky the man was a friend of his; a friend of both of them, rather. Actually, Lita had known him longer than her husband. But they'd been very close, the three of them, and he knew the Adjustor would understand.

He could trust the Adjustor not to tell Lita. He could trust the Adjustor to have everything ready and waiting for him now.

Henson went up to the office. The papers were ready for him to sign. The two metal boxes containing the surrogates were already placed on the loaders ready for transport to wherever he designated. But the Adjustor wasn't on hand to greet him.

"Special assignment in Manila," the Second explained to him. "But he left instructions about your case, Mr. Henson. All you have to do is sign the responsibility slips. And of course, you'll be in Monday for the official report."

Henson nodded. Now that the moment was so near at hand he was impatient of details. He could scarcely wait until the micro-dupes were completed and the Register Board signalled clearance. Two common robots were requisitioned to carry the metal cases down to the gyro and load them in. Henson whizzed back home with them and they brought the cases up to his living-level. Then he dismissed them, and he was alone.

He was alone. He could open the cases now. First, his own. He slid back the cover, gazed down at the perfect duplicate of his own body, sleeping peacefully for two serene years since its creation. Henson stared curiously at his pseudo-countenance. He'd aged a bit in two years, but the surrogate was ageless. It could survive the ravages of centuries, and it was always at peace. Always at peace. He almost envied it. The surrogate didn't love, couldn't hate, wouldn't know the gnawing torture of suspicion that led to this shaking, quaking, aching lust to kill –

Henson shoved the lid back and lifted the metal case upright, then dragged it along the wall to a storage cabinet. A domestic-model could have done it for him, but Lita didn't like domestic-models. She wouldn't permit even a common robot in her home.

Lita and her likes and dislikes! Damn her to Los Alamos and gone!

Henson ripped the lid down on the second file.

There she was.

There she was; the beautiful, harlot-eyed, blonde, lying, adorable, dirty, gorgeous, loathsome, heavenly, filthy little goddess of a slut!

He remembered the command word to awake her. It almost choked him now, but he said it. "Beloved!"

Nothing happened. Then he realized why. He'd been almost snarling. He had to change the pitch of his voice. He tried again, softly. "Beloved!"

She moved. Her breasts rose and fell, rose and fell. She opened her eyes. She held out her arms and smiled. She stood up and came close to him, without a word.

Henson stared at her. She was newly-born and innocent, she had no secrets, she wouldn't betray him. How could he harm her? How could he harm her when she lifted her face in expectation of a kiss?

But she was Lita. He had to remember that. She was Lita, and Lita was hiding something from him and she must be punished, would be punished.

Suddenly, Henson became conscious of his hands. There was a tingling in his wrists and it ran down through the strong muscles and sinews to the fingers, and the fingers flexed and unflexed with exultant vigour, and then they rose and curled around the surrogate's throat, around Lita's throat, and they were squeezing and squeezing and the surrogate-Lita tried to move away and the scream was almost real and the popping eyes were almost real and the purpling face was almost real, only nothing was real any more except the hands and the choking and the surging sensation of strength.

And then it was over. He dragged the limp, dangling mechanism (it was only a mechanism now, just as the hate was only a memory) to the waste-jet and fed the surrogate to the flame. He turned the aperture wide and thrust the metal case in, too.

Then Henson slept, and he did not dream. For the first time in months he did not dream, because it was over and he was himself again. The therapy was complete.

* * *

"So that's how it was." Henson sat in the Adjustor's office, and the Monday morning sun was strong on his face.

"Good." The Adjustor smiled and ran a hand across the top of his curly head. "And how did you and Lita enjoy your weekend? Fish biting?"

"We didn't fish," said Henson. "We talked."

"Oh?"

"I figured I'd have to tell her what happened, sooner or later. So I did."

"How did she take it?"

"Very well, at first."

"And then—?"

"I asked her some questions."

"Yes."

"She answered them."

"You mean she told you what she'd been hiding?"

"Not willingly. But she told me. After I told her about my own little check-up."

"What was that?"

"I did some calling Friday night. She wasn't in Saigon with her mother."

"No?"

"And you weren't in Manila on a special case, either." Henson leaned forward. "The two of you were together, in New Singapore! I checked it and she admitted it."

The Adjustor sighed. "So now you know," he said.

"Yes. Now I know. Now I know what she's been concealing from me. What you've both been concealing."

"Surely you're not jealous about that?" the Adjustor asked "Not in this modern day and age when—"

"She says she wants to have a child by you," Henson said. "She refused to bear one for me. But she wants yours. She told me so."

"What do you want to do about it?" the Adjustor asked.

"You tell me," Henson murmured. "That's why I've come to you. You're my Adjustor."

"What would you like to do?"

"I'd like to kill you," Henson said. "I'd like to blow off the top of your head with a pocket-blast."

"Not a bad idea." The Adjustor nodded. "I'll have my robot ready whenever you say."

"At my place," said Henson. "Tonight."

"Good enough. I'll send it there to you."

"One thing more." Henson gulped for a moment. "In order for it to do any good, Lita must watch."

It was the Adjustor's turn to gulp, now. "You mean you're going to force her to see you go through with this—?"

"I told her and she agreed," Henson said.

"But, think of the effect on her, man!"

"Think of the effect on me. Do you want me to go mad?"

"No," said the Adjustor "You're right. It's therapy. I'll send the robot around at eight. Do you need a pocket-blast requisition?"

"I have one," said Henson. "What instructions shall I give my surrogate?" the Adjustor asked.

Henson told him. He was brutally explicit, and midway in his statement the Adjustor looked away, coloring. "So the two of you will be together, just as if *you* were real, and then I'll come in and—"

The Adjustor shuddered a little then managed a smile. "Sound therapy," he said. "If that's the way you want it, that's the way it will be."

* * *

That's the way Henson wanted it, and that's the way he had it – up to a point.

He burst into the room around quarter after eight and found the two of them waiting for him. There was Lita, and there was the Adjustor's surrogate. The surrogate had been well-instructed; it looked surprised and startled. Lita needed no instruction; hers was an agony of shame.

Henson had the pocket-blast in his hand, cocked at the ready. He aimed.

Unfortunately, he was just a little late. The surrogate sat up gracefully and slid one hand under the pillow. The hand came up with another pocket-blast aimed and fired all in one motion.

Henson teetered, tottered, and fell. The whole left side of his face sheared away as he went down.

Lita screamed.

Then the surrogate put his arms around her and whispered, "It's all over, darling. All over. We did it! He really thought I was a robot, that I'd go through with his aberrated notion of dramatizing his revenge."

The Adjustor smiled and lifted her face to his. "From now on you and I will always be together. We'll have our child, lots of children if you wish. There's nothing to come between us now."

"But you killed him," Lita whispered. "What will they do to you?"

"Nothing. It was self-defense. Don't forget, I'm an Adjustor. From the moment he came into my office, everything he did or said was recorded during our interviews. The evidence will show that I tried to humor him, that I indicated his mental unbalance and allowed him to work out his own therapy.

"This last interview, today, will not be a part of the record. I've already destroyed it. So as far as the law is concerned, he had no grounds for jealousy or suspicion. I happened to stop in here to visit this evening and found him trying to kill you – the actual you. And when he turned on me, I blasted him in self-defense."

"Will you get away with it?"

"Of course I'll get away with it. The man was aberrated, and the record will show it."

The Adjustor stood up. "I'm going to call Authority now," he said.

Lita rose and put her hand on his shoulder. "Kiss me first," she whispered. "A real kiss. I like real things."

"Real things," said the Adjustor. She snuggled against him, but he made no move to take her in his arms. He was staring down at Henson.

Lita followed his gaze.

Both of them saw it at the same time, then – both of them saw the torn hole in the left side of Henson's head, and the thin strands of wire protruding from the opening. "He didn't come," the Adjustor murmured. "He must have suspected, and he sent his robot instead."

Lita began to shake. "You were to send your robot, but you didn't. He was to come himself, but he sent his robot. Each of you double-crossed the other, and now—"

And now the door opened very quickly.

Henson came into the room.

He looked at his surrogate lying on the floor. He looked at Lita. He looked at the Adjustor. Then he grinned. There was no madness in his grin, only deliberation.

There was deliberation in the way he raised the pocket-blast. He aimed well and carefully, fired only once, but both the Adjustor and Lita crumpled in the burst.

Henson bent over the bodies, inspecting them carefully to make sure that they were real. He was beginning to appreciate Lita's philosophy now. He liked real things. For that matter, the Adjustor had some good ideas, too. This business of dramatizing aggressions really seemed to work. He didn't feel at all angry or upset any more, just perfectly calm and at peace with the world.

Henson rose, smiled, and walked towards the door. For the first time in years he felt completely adjusted.

I Sing the Body Electric!

Ray Bradbury

GRANDMA!

I remember her birth.

Wait, you say, *no* man remembers his own grandma's birth. But, yes, *we* remember the day that she was born.

For we, her grandchildren, slapped her to life. Timothy, Agatha, and I, Tom, raised up our hands and brought them down in a huge crack! We shook together the bits and pieces, parts and samples, textures and tastes, humors and distillations that would move her compass needle north to cool us, south to warm and comfort us, east and west to travel round the endless world, glide her eyes to know us, mouth to sing us asleep by night, hands to touch us awake at dawn.

Grandma, O dear and wondrous electric dream…

When storm lightnings rove the sky making circuitries amidst the clouds, her name flashes on my inner lid. Sometimes still I hear her ticking, humming above our beds in the gentle dark. She passes like a clock-ghost in the long halls of memory, like a hive of intellectual bees swarming after the Spirit of Summers Lost. Sometimes still I feel the smile I learned from her, printed on my cheek at three in the deep morn…

All right, all right! you cry, what was it like the day your damned and wondrous-dreadful-loving Grandma was born?

It was the week the world ended… Our mother was dead.

One late afternoon a black car left Father and the three of us stranded on our own front drive staring at the grass, thinking:

That's not our grass. There are the croquet mallets, balls, hoops, yes, just as they fell and lay three days ago when Dad stumbled out on the lawn, weeping with the news. There are the roller skates that belonged to a boy, me, who will never be that young again. And yes, there the tire-swing on the old oak, but Agatha afraid to swing. It would surely break. It would fall.

And the house? Oh, God…

We peered through the front door, afraid of the echoes we might find confused in the halls; the sort of clamor that happens when all the furniture is taken out and there is nothing to soften the river of talk that flows in any house at all hours. And now the soft, the warm, the main piece of lovely furniture was gone forever.

The door drifted wide.

Silence came out. Somewhere a cellar door stood wide and a raw wind blew damp earth from under the house.

But, I thought, we don't *have* a cellar!

"Well," said Father.

We did not move.

Aunt Clara drove up the path in her big canary-colored limousine. We jumped through the door. We ran to our rooms.

We heard them shout and then speak and then shout and then speak: Let the children live with me! Aunt Clara said. They'd rather kill themselves! Father said.

A door slammed. Aunt Clara was gone.

We almost danced. Then we remembered what had happened and went downstairs.

Father sat alone talking to himself or to a remnant ghost of Mother left from the days before her illness, but jarred loose now by the slamming of the door. He murmured to his hands, his empty palms:

"The children need someone. I love them but, let's face it, I must work to feed us all. You love them, Ann, but you're gone. And Clara? Impossible. She loves but smothers. And as for maids, nurses—?"

Here Father sighed and we sighed with him, remembering.

The luck we had had with maids or live-in teachers or sitters was beyond intolerable. Hardly a one who wasn't a crosscut saw grabbing against the grain. Handaxes and hurricanes best described them. Or, conversely, they were all fallen trifle, damp souffle. We children were unseen furniture to be sat upon or dusted or sent for reupholstering come spring and fall, with a yearly cleansing at the beach.

"What we need," said Father, "is a..." We all leaned to his whisper.

"...grandmother."

"But," said Timothy, with the logic of nine years, "all our grandmothers are dead."

"Yes in one way, no in another."

What a fine mysterious thing for Dad to say. "Here," he said at last.

He handed us a multifold, multicolored pamphlet. We had seen it in his hands, off and on, for many weeks, and very often during the last few days. Now, with one blink of our eyes, as we passed the paper from hand to hand, we knew why Aunt Clara, insulted, outraged, had stormed from the house.

Timothy was the first to read aloud from what he saw on the first page: "'I Sing the Body Electric!'"

He glanced up at Father, squinting. "What the heck does that mean?"

"Read on."

Agatha and I glanced guiltily about the room, afraid Mother might suddenly come in to find us with this blasphemy, but then nodded to Timothy, who read:

"'Fanto—'"

"Fantoccini," Father prompted.

"'Fantoccini Ltd. *We Shadow Forth...* the answer to all your most grievous problems. One Model Only, upon which a thousand times a thousand variations can be added, subtracted, subdivided, indivisible, with Liberty and Justice for all.'"

"Where does it say *that*?" we all cried.

"It doesn't." Timothy smiled for the first time in days. "I just had to put that in. Wait." He read on: "'for you who have worried over inattentive sitters, nurses who cannot be trusted with marked liquor bottles, and well-meaning Uncles and Aunts—'"

"Well-meaning, *but*!" said Agatha, and I gave an echo.

"'—we have perfected the first humanoid-genre minicircuited, rechargeable AC-DC Mark V Electrical Grandmother...'"

"Grandmother!?"

The paper slipped away to the floor. "Dad...?"

"Don't look at me that way," said Father. "I'm half-mad with grief, and half-mad thinking of tomorrow and the day after that. Someone pick up the paper. Finish it."

"I will," I said, and did:

"'The Toy that is more than a Toy, the Fantoccini Electrical Grandmother is built with loving precision to give the incredible precision of love to your children. The child at ease with the realities of the world and the even greater realities of the imagination, is her aim.

"'She is computerized to tutor in twelve languages simultaneously, capable of switching tongues in a thousandth of a second without pause, and has a complete knowledge of the religious, artistic, and sociopolitical histories of the world seeded in her master hive—'"

"How great!" said Timothy. "It makes it sound as if we were to keep bees! *Educated* bees!"

"Shut up!" said Agatha.

"'Above all,'" I read, "'this human being, for human she seems, this embodiment in electro-intelligent facsimile of the humanities, will listen, know, tell, react and love your children insofar as such great Objects, such fantastic Toys, can be said to Love, or can be imagined to Care. This Miraculous Companion, excited to the challenge of large world and small, inner Sea or Outer Universe, will transmit by touch and tell, said Miracles to your Needy.'"

"Our Needy," murmured Agatha.

Why, we all thought, sadly, that's us, oh, yes, that's *us*.

I finished:

"'We do not sell our Creation to able-bodied families where parents are available to raise, effect, shape, change, love their own children. Nothing can replace the parent in the home. However there are families where death or ill health or disablement undermines the welfare of the children. Orphanages seem not the answer. Nurses tend to be selfish, neglectful, or suffering from dire nervous afflictions.

"'With the utmost humility then, and recognizing the need to rebuild, rethink, and regrow our conceptualizations from month to month, year to year, we offer the nearest thing to the Ideal Teacher-Friend-Companion-Blood Relation. A trial period can be arranged for—'"

"Stop," said Father. "Don't go on. Even *I* can't stand it."

"Why?" said Timothy. "I was just getting interested."

I folded the pamphlet up. "Do they *really* have these things?"

"Let's not talk any more about it," said Father, his hand over his eyes. "It was a mad thought—"

"Not so mad," I said, glancing at Tim. "I mean, heck, even if they tried, whatever they built, couldn't be worse than Aunt Clara, huh?"

And then we all roared. We hadn't laughed in months. And now my simple words made everyone hoot and howl and explode. I opened my mouth and yelled happily, too.

When we stopped laughing, we looked at the pamphlet and I said, "Well?"

"I—" Agatha scowled, not ready.

"We do need something, bad, right now," said Timothy.

"I have an open mind," I said, in my best pontifical style.

"There's only one thing," said Agatha. "We can try it. Sure. But – tell me this – when do we cut out all this talk and when does our *real* mother come home to stay?"

There was a single gasp from the family as if, with one shot, she had struck us all in the heart.

I don't think any of us stopped crying the rest of that night.

* * *

It was a clear bright day. The helicopter tossed us lightly up and over and down through the skyscrapers and let us out, almost for a trot and caper, on top of the building where the large letters could be read from the sky: FANTOCCINI.

"What are *Fantoccini?*" said Agatha.

"It's an Italian word for shadow puppets, I think, or dream people," said Father.

"But *shadow forth,* what does that mean?"

"We try to guess your dream," I said.

"Bravo," said Father. "A-Plus."

I beamed.

The helicopter flapped a lot of loud shadows over us and went away.

We sank down in an elevator as our stomachs sank up. We stepped out onto a moving carpet that streamed away on a blue river of wool toward a desk over which various signs hung:

THE CLOCK SHOP
Fantoccini Our Specialty.
Rabbits on walls, no problem.

"Rabbits on walls?"

I held up my fingers in profile as if I held them before a candle flame, and wiggled the 'ears'.

"Here's a rabbit, here's a wolf, here's a crocodile."

"Of course," said Agatha.

And we were at the desk. Quiet music drifted about us. Somewhere behind the walls, there was a waterfall of machinery flowing softly. As we arrived at the desk, the lighting changed to make us look warmer, happier, though we were still cold.

All about us in niches and cases, and hung from ceilings on wires and strings were puppets and marionettes, and Balinese kite-bamboo-translucent dolls which, held to the moonlight, might acrobat your most secret nightmares or dreams. In passing, the breeze set up by our bodies stirred the various hung souls on their gibbets. It was like an immense lynching on a holiday at some English crossroads four hundred years before.

You see? I know my history.

Agatha blinked about with disbelief and then some touch of awe and finally disgust.

"Well, if that's what they are, let's go."

"Tush," said Father.

"Well," she protested, "you gave me one of those dumb things with strings two years ago and the strings were in a zillion knots by dinnertime. I threw the whole thing out the window."

"Patience," said Father.

"We shall see what we can do to eliminate the strings." The man behind the desk had spoken.

We all turned to give him our regard.

Rather like a funeral-parlor man, he had the cleverness not to smile.

Children are put off by older people who smile too much. They smell a catch, right off.

Unsmiling, but not gloomy or pontifical, the man said, "Guido Fantoccini, at your service. Here's how we do it, Miss Agatha Simmons, aged eleven."

Now there was a really fine touch.

He knew that Agatha was only ten. Add a year to that, and you're halfway home. Agatha grew an inch. The man went on:

"There."

And he placed a golden key in Agatha's hand.

"To wind them up instead of strings?"

"To wind them up." The man nodded.

"Pshaw!" said Agatha. Which was her polite form of "rabbit pellets."

"God's truth. Here is the key to your Do-it-Yourself, Select Only the Best, Electrical Grandmother. Every morning you wind her up. Every night you let her run down. You're in charge. You are guardian of the Key."

He pressed the object in her palm where she looked at it suspiciously.

I watched him. He gave me a side wink which said, well, no... but aren't keys fun?

I winked back before she lifted her head.

"Where does this fit?"

"You'll see when the time comes. In the middle of her stomach, perhaps, or up her left nostril or in her right ear."

That was good for a smile as the man arose.

"This way, please. Step light. Onto the moving stream. Walk on the water, please. Yes. There."

He helped to float us. We stepped from rug that was forever frozen onto rug that whispered by.

It was a most agreeable river which floated us along on a green spread of carpeting that rolled forever through halls and into wonderfully secret dim caverns where voices echoed back our own breathing or sang like Oracles to our questions.

"Listen," said the salesman, "the voices of all kinds of women. Weigh and find just the right one...!"

And listen we did, to all the high, low, soft, loud, in-between, half-scolding, half-affectionate voices saved over from times before we were born.

And behind us, Agatha tread backward, always fighting the river, never catching up, never with us, holding off.

"Speak," said the salesman. "Yell." And speak and yell we did.

"Hello. You there! This is Timothy, hi!"

"What shall I say!" I shouted. "Help!"

Agatha walked backward, mouth tight. Father took her hand. She cried out.

"Let go! No, no! I won't have my voice used! I won't!"

"Excellent." The salesman touched three dials on a small machine he held in his hand.

On the side of the small machine we saw three oscillograph patterns mix, blend, and repeat our cries.

The salesman touched another dial and we heard our voices fly off amidst the Delphic caves to hang upside down, to cluster, to beat words all about, to shriek, and the salesman itched another knob to add, perhaps, a touch of this or a pinch of that, a breath of mother's voice, all unbeknownst, or a splice of father's outrage at the morning's paper or his peaceable one-drink voice at dusk. Whatever it was the salesman did, whispers danced all about us like frantic vinegar gnats, fizzed by lightning, settling round until at last a final switch was pushed and a voice spoke free of a far electronic deep:

"Nefertiti," it said.

Timothy froze. I froze. Agatha stopped treading water.

"Nefertiti?" asked Tim.

"What does that mean?" demanded Agatha.

"I know."

The salesman nodded me to tell.

"Nefertiti," I whispered, "is Egyptian for The Beautiful One Is Here."

"The Beautiful One Is Here," repeated Timothy.

"Nefer," said Agatha, "titi."

And we all turned to stare into that soft twilight, that deep far place from which the good warm soft voice came.

And she was indeed there.

And, by her voice, she was beautiful... That was it.

That was, at least, the most of it.

The voice seemed more important than all the rest. Not that we didn't argue about weights and measures:

She should not be bony to cut us to the quick, nor so fat we might sink out of sight when she squeezed us. Her hand pressed to ours, or brushing our brow in the middle of sick-fever nights, must not be marble-cold, dreadful, or oven-hot, oppressive, but somewhere between. The nice temperature of a baby-chick held in the hand after a long night's sleep and just plucked from beneath a contemplative hen; that, that was it.

Oh, we were great ones for detail. We fought and argued and cried, and Timothy won on the color of her eyes, for reasons to be known later.

Grandmother's hair? Agatha, with girl's ideas, though reluctantly given, she was in charge of that. We let her choose from a thousand harp strands hung in filamentary tapestries like varieties of rain we ran amongst. Agatha did not run happily, but seeing we boys would mess things in tangles, she told us to move aside.

And so the bargain shopping through the dime-store inventories and the Tiffany extensions of the Ben Franklin Electric Storm Machine and Fantoccini Pantomime Company was done.

And the always flowing river ran its tide to an end and deposited us all on a far shore in the late day...

It was very clever of the Fantoccini people, after that. How?

They made us wait.

They knew we were not won over. Not completely, no, nor half completely.

Especially Agatha, who turned her face to her wall and saw sorrow there and put her hand out again and again to touch it. We found her fingernail marks on the wallpaper each morning, in strange little silhouettes, half beauty, half nightmare. Some could be erased with a breath, like ice flowers on a winter pane. Some could not be rubbed out with a washcloth, no matter how hard you tried.

And meanwhile, they made us wait.

So we fretted out June.

So we sat around July.

So we groused through August and then on August 29, "I have this feeling," said Timothy, and we all went out after breakfast to sit on the lawn.

Perhaps we had smelled something on Father's conversation the previous night, or caught some special furtive glance at the sky or the freeway. Rapped briefly and then lost in his gaze. Or perhaps it was merely the way the wind blew the ghost curtains out over our beds, making pale messages all night.

For suddenly there we were in the middle of the grass, Timothy and I, with Agatha, pretending no curiosity, up on the porch, hidden behind the potted geraniums.

We gave her no notice. We knew that if we acknowledged her presence, she would flee, so we sat and watched the sky where nothing moved but birds and highflown jets, and watched the freeway where a thousand cars might suddenly deliver forth our Special Gift... but... nothing.

At noon we chewed grass and lay low... At one o'clock, Timothy blinked his eyes.

And then, with incredible precision, it happened.

It was as if the Fantoccini people knew our surface tension.

All children are water-striders. We skate along the top skin of the pond each day, always threatening to break through, sink, vanish beyond recall, into ourselves.

Well, as if knowing our long wait must absolutely end within one minute! this *second*! no more, God, forget it!

At that instant, I repeat, the clouds above our house opened wide and let forth a helicopter like Apollo driving his chariot across mythological skies.

And the Apollo machine swam down on its own summer breeze, wafting hot winds to cool, reweaving our hair, smartening our eyebrows, applauding our pant legs against our shins, making a flag of Agatha's hair on the porch and thus settled like a vast frenzied hibiscus on our lawn, the helicopter slid wide a bottom drawer and deposited upon the grass a parcel of largish size, no sooner having laid same then the vehicle, with not so much as a god bless or farewell, sank straight up, disturbed the calm air with a mad ten thousand flourishes and then, like a skyborne dervish, tilted and fell off to be mad some other place.

Timothy and I stood riven for a long moment looking at the packing case, and then we saw the crowbar taped to the top of the raw pine lid and seized it and began to pry and creak and squeal the boards off, one by one, and as we did this I saw Agatha sneak up to watch and I thought, thank you, God, thank you that Agatha never saw a coffin, when Mother went away, no box, no cemetery, no earth, just words in a big church, no box, no box like *this*...!

The last pine plank fell away.

Timothy and I gasped. Agatha, between us now, gasped, too.

For inside the immense raw pine package was the most beautiful idea anyone ever dreamt and built.

Inside was the perfect gift for any child from seven to seventy-seven.

We stopped up our breaths. We let them out in cries of delight and adoration.

Inside the opened box was... A mummy.

Or, first anyway, a mummy case, a sarcophagus!

"Oh, no!" Happy tears filled Timothy's eyes.

"It can't be!" said Agatha. "It is, it is!"

"Our very own?"

"Ours!"

"It must be a mistake!"

"Sure, they'll want it back!"

"They can't *have* it!"

"Lord, Lord, is that real gold!? Real hieroglyphs! Run your fingers over them!"

"Let *me!*"

"Just like in the museums! Museums!"

We all gabbled at once. I think some tears fell from my own eyes to rain upon the case.

"Oh, they'll make the colors run!" Agatha wiped the rain away.

And the golden mask face of the woman carved on the sarcophagus lid looked back at us with just the merest smile which hinted at our own joy, which accepted the overwhelming upsurge of a love we thought had drowned forever but now surfaced into the sun.

Not only did she have a sun-metal face stamped and beaten out of purest gold, with delicate nostrils and a mouth that was both firm and gentle, but her eyes, fixed into their sockets, were cerulean or amethystine or lapus lazuli, or all three, minted and fused together, and her body was covered over with lions and eyes and ravens, and her hands were crossed upon her carved bosom and in one gold mitten she clenched a thonged whip for obedience, and in the other a fantastic ranuncula, which makes for obedience out of love, so the whip lies unused...

And as our eyes ran down her hieroglyphs it came to all three of us at the same instant:

"Why, those signs!" "Yes, the hen tracks!" "The birds, the snakes!"

They didn't speak tales of the Past.

They were hieroglyphs of the Future.

This was the first queen mummy delivered forth in all time whose papyrus inkings etched out the next month, the next season, the next year, the next *lifetime!*

She did not mourn for time spent.

No. She celebrated the bright coinage yet to come, banked, waiting, ready to be drawn upon and used.

We sank to our knees to worship that possible time.

First one hand, then another, probed out to niggle, twitch, touch, itch over the signs.

"There's me, yes, look! Me, in sixth grade!" said Agatha, now in the fifth. "See the girl with my-colored hair and wearing my gingerbread suit?"

"There's me in the twelfth year of high school!" said Timothy, so very young now but building taller stilts every week and stalking around the yard.

"There's me," I said, quietly, warm, "in college. The guy wearing glasses who runs a little to fat. Sure. Heck." I snorted. "That's me."

The sarcophagus spelled winters ahead, springs to squander, autumns to spend with all the golden and rusty and copper leaves like coins, and over all, her bright sun symbol, daughter-of-Ra eternal face, forever above our horizon, forever an illumination to tilt our shadows to better ends.

"Hey!" we all said at once, having read and reread our Fortune-Told scribblings, seeing our lifelines and lovelines, inadmissible, serpentined over, around, and down. "Hey!"

And in one seance table-lifting feat, not telling each other what to do, just doing it, we pried up the bright sarcophagus lid, which had no hinges but lifted out like cup from cup, and put the lid aside.

And within the sarcophagus, of course, was the true mummy!

And she was like the image carved on the lid, but more so, more beautiful, more touching because human shaped, and shrouded all in new fresh bandages of linen, round and round, instead of old and dusty cerements.

And upon her hidden face was an identical golden mask, younger than the first, but somehow, strangely wiser than the first.

And the linens that tethered her limbs had symbols on them of three sorts, one a girl of ten, one a boy of nine, one a boy of thirteen.

A series of bandages for each of us!

We gave each other a startled glance and a sudden bark of laughter. Nobody said the bad joke, but all thought:

She's all wrapped up in us!

And we didn't care. We loved the joke. We loved whoever had thought to make us part of the ceremony we now went through as each of us seized and began to unwind each of his or her particular serpentines of delicious stuffs!

The lawn was soon a mountain of linen.

The woman beneath the covering lay there, waiting.

"Oh, no," cried Agatha. "She's dead, too!"

She ran. I stopped her. "Idiot. She's not dead *or* alive. Where's your key?"

"Key?"

"Dummy," said Tim, "the key the man gave you to wind her up!"

Her hand had already spidered along her blouse to where the symbol of some possible new religion hung. She had strung it there, against her own skeptic's muttering, and now she held it in her sweaty palm.

"Go on," said Timothy. "Put it in!"

"But *where?*"

"Oh for God's sake! As the man said, in her right armpit or left ear. Gimme!"

And he grabbed the key and impulsively moaning with impatience and not able to find the proper insertion slot, prowled over the prone figure's head and bosom and at last, on pure instinct, perhaps for a lark, perhaps just giving up the whole damned mess, thrust the key through a final shroud of bandage at the navel.

On the instant: *spunnng!*

The Electrical Grandmother's eyes flicked wide!

Something began to hum and whir. It was as if Tim had stirred up a hive of hornets with an ornery stick.

"Oh," gasped Agatha, seeing he had taken the game away, "let *me!*"

She wrenched the key.

Grandma's nostrils *flared!* She might snort up steam, snuff out fire!

"Me!" I cried, and grabbed the key and gave it a huge… *twist!*

The beautiful woman's mouth popped wide.

"Me!"

"Me!"

"Me!"

Grandma suddenly sat up. We leapt back.

We knew we had, in a way, slapped her alive. She was born, she was *born!*

Her head swiveled all about. She gaped. She mouthed. And the first thing she said was:

Laughter.

Where one moment we had backed off, now the mad sound drew us near to peer as in a pit where crazy folk are kept with snakes to make them well.

It was a good laugh, full and rich and hearty, and it did not mock, it accepted. It said the world was a wild place, strange, unbelievable, absurd if you wished, but all in all, quite a place. She would not dream to find another. She would not ask to go back to sleep.

She was awake now. We had awakened her. With a glad shout, she would go with it all.

And go she did, out of her sarcophagus, out of her winding sheet, stepping forth, brushing off, looking around as for a mirror. She found it.

The reflections in our eyes.

She was more pleased than disconcerted with what she found there. Her laughter faded to an amused smile.

For Agatha, at the instant of birth, had leapt to hide on the porch.

The Electrical Person pretended not to notice.

She turned slowly on the green lawn near the shady street, gazing all about with new eyes, her nostrils moving as if she breathed the actual air and this the first morn of the lovely Garden and she with no intention of spoiling the game by biting the apple…

Her gaze fixed upon my brother. "You must be—?"

"Timothy. Tim," he offered.

"And you must be—?"

"Tom," I said.

How clever again of the Fantoccini Company. *They* knew. *She* knew. But they had taught her to pretend not to know. That way we could feel great, we were the teachers, telling her what she already knew! How sly, how wise.

"And isn't there another boy?" said the woman.

"Girl!" a disgusted voice cried from somewhere on the porch.

"Whose name is Alicia—?"

"Agatha!" The far voice, started in humiliation, ended in proper anger.

"Algernon, of course."

"Agatha!" Our sister popped up, popped back to hide a flushed face.

"Agatha." The woman touched the word with proper affection. "Well, Agatha, Timothy, Thomas, let me *look* at you."

"No," said I, said Tim, "Let us look at *you*. Hey…" Our voices slid back in our throats.

We drew near her.

We walked in great slow circles round about, skirting the edges of her territory. And her territory extended as far as we could hear the hum of the warm summer hive. For that is exactly what she sounded like. That was her characteristic tune. She made a sound like a season all to herself, a morning early in June when the world wakes to find everything absolutely perfect, fine, delicately attuned, all in balance, nothing disproportioned. Even before you opened your eyes you knew it would be one of those days. Tell the sky what color it must be, and it was indeed. Tell the sun how to crochet its way, pick and choose among leaves to lay out carpetings of bright and dark on the fresh lawn, and pick and lay it did. The bees have been up earliest of all, they have already come and gone, and come and gone again to the meadow fields and returned all golden fuzz on the air, all pollen-decorated, epaulettes at the full, nectar-dripping. Don't you hear them pass? hover? dance their language? telling where all the sweet gums are, the syrups that make bears frolic and lumber in bulked ecstasies, that make boys squirm with unpronounced juices, that make girls leap out of beds to catch from the corners of their eyes their dolphin selves naked aflash on the warm air poised forever in one eternal glass wave.

So it seemed with our electrical friend here on the new lawn in the middle of a special day.

And she a stuff to which we were drawn, lured, spelled, doing our dance, remembering what could not be remembered, needful, aware of her attentions.

Timothy and I, Tom, that is. Agatha remained on the porch.

But her head flowered above the rail, her eyes followed all that was done and said.

And what was said and done was Tim at last exhaling: "Hey… your *eyes*…"

Her eyes. Her splendid eyes.

Even more splendid than the lapis lazuli on the sarcophagus lid and on the mask that had covered her bandaged face. These most beautiful eyes in the world looked out upon us calmly, shining.

"Your eyes," gasped Tim, "are the *exact* same color, are like—"

"Like what?"

"My favorite aggies…"

"What could be better than that?" she said. And the answer was, nothing.

Her eyes slid along on the bright air to brush my ears, my nose, my chin. "And you, Master Tom?"

"Me?"

"How shall we be friends? We must, you know, if we're going to knock elbows about the house the next year…"

"I…" I said, and stopped.

"You," said Grandma, "are a dog mad to bark but with taffy in his teeth. Have you ever given a dog taffy? It's so sad and funny, both. You laugh but hate yourself for laughing. You cry and run to help, and laugh again when his first new bark comes out."

I barked a small laugh remembering a dog, a day, and some taffy.

Grandma turned, and there was my old kite strewn on the lawn. She recognized its problem.

"The string's broken. No. The ball of string's *lost.* You can't fly a kite that way. Here."

She bent. We didn't: know what might happen. How could a robot grandma fly a kite for us? She raised up, the kite in her hands.

"Fly," she said, as to a bird. And the kite flew.

That is to say, with a grand flourish, she let it rip on the wind. And she and the kite were one.

For from the tip of her index finger there sprang a thin bright strand of spider web, all half-invisible gossamer fishline which, fixed to the kite, let it soar a hundred, no, three hundred, no, a thousand feet high on the summer swoons.

Timothy shouted. Agatha, torn between coming and going, let out a cry from the porch. And I, in all my maturity of thirteen years, though I tried not to look impressed, grew taller, taller, and felt a similar cry burst out my lungs, and burst it did. I gabbled and yelled lots of things about how I wished *I* had a finger from which, on a bobbin, I might thread the sky, the clouds, a wild kite all in one.

"If you think *that* is high," said the Electric Creature, "watch *this!*"

With a hiss, a whistle, a hum, the fishline sung out. The kite sank up another thousand feet. And again another thousand, until at last it was a speck of red confetti dancing on the very winds that took jets around the world or changed the weather in the next existence…

"It can't be!" I cried.

"It *is.*" She calmly watched her finger unravel its massive stuffs. "I make it as I need it. Liquid inside, like a spider. Hardens when it hits the air, instant thread…"

And when the kite was no more than a specule, a vanishing mote on the peripheral vision of the gods, to quote from older wisemen, why then Grandma, without turning, without looking, without letting her gaze offend by touching, said:

"And, Abigail—?"

"Agatha!" was the sharp response.

O wise woman, to overcome with swift small angers.

"Agatha," said Grandma, not too tenderly, not too lightly, somewhere poised between, "and how shall *we* make do?"

She broke the thread and wrapped it about my fist three times so I was tethered to heaven by the longest, I repeat, longest kite string in the entire history of the world! Wait till I show my friends! I thought. Green! Sour apple green is the color they'll turn!

"Agatha?"

"No way!" said Agatha.

"No way," said an echo.

"There must be some—"

"We'll never be friends!" said Agatha.

"Never be friends," said the echo.

Timothy and I jerked. Where was the echo coming from? Even Agatha, surprised, showed her eyebrows above the porch rail.

Then we looked and saw.

Grandma was cupping her hands like a seashell and from within that shell the echo sounded.

"Never… friends…"

And again faintly dying "Friends…" We all bent to hear. That is we two boys bent to hear.

"No!" cried Agatha. And ran in the house and slammed the doors.

"Friends," said the echo from the seashell hands. "No."

And far away, on the shore of some inner sea, we heard a small door shut.

And that was the first day.

And there was a second day, of course, and a third and a fourth, with Grandma wheeling in a great circle, and we her planets turning about the central light, with Agatha slowly, slowly coming in to join, to walk if not run with us, to listen if not hear, to watch if not see, to itch if not touch.

But at least by the end of the first ten days, Agatha no longer fled, but stood in nearby doors, or sat in distant chairs under trees, or if we went out for hikes, followed ten paces behind.

And Grandma? She merely waited. She never tried to urge or force. She went about her cooking and baking apricot pies and left foods carelessly here aid there about the house on mousetrap plates for wiggle-nosed girls to sniff and snitch. An hour later, the plates were empty, the buns or cakes gone and without thank you's, there was Agatha sliding down the banister, a mustache of crumbs on her lip.

As for Tim and me, we were always being called up hills by our Electric Grandma, and reaching the top were called down the other side.

And the most peculiar and beautiful and strange and lovely thing was the way she seemed to give complete attention to all of us. She listened, she really listened to all we said, she knew and remembered every syllable, word, sentence, punctuation, thought, and rambunctious idea. We knew that all our days were stored in her, and that any time we felt we might want to know what we said at X hour at X second on X afternoon, we just named that X and with amiable promptitude, in the form of an aria if we wished, sung with humor, she would deliver forth X incident.

Sometimes we were prompted to test her. In the midst of babbling one day with high fevers about nothing, I stopped. I fixed Grandma with my eye and demanded:

"What did I just say?"

"Oh, er—"

"Come on, spit it out!"

"I think—" she rummaged her purse. "I have it here." From the deeps of her purse she drew forth and handed me:

"Boy! A Chinese fortune cookie!"

"Fresh baked, still warm, open it."

It was almost too hot to touch. I broke the cookie shell and pressed the warm curl of paper out to read:

"—bicycle Champ of the whole West! What did I just say? Come on, spit it out!"

My jaw dropped. "How did you *do* that?"

"We have our little secrets. The only Chinese fortune cookie that predicts the Immediate Past. Have another?"

I cracked the second shell and read: "'How did you *do* that?'"

I popped the messages and the piping hot shells into my mouth and chewed as we walked.

"Well?"

"You're a great cook," I said. And, laughing, we began to run. And that was another great thing. She could *keep up.*

Never beat, never win a race, but pump right along in good style, which a boy doesn't mind. A girl ahead of him or beside him is too much to bear. But a girl one or two paces back is a respectful thing, and allowed.

So Grandma and I had some great runs, me in the lead, and both talking a mile a minute.

But now I must tell you the best part of Grandma.

I might not have known at all if Timothy hadn't taken some pictures, and if I hadn't taken some also, and then compared.

When I saw the photographs developed out of our instant Brownies, I sent Agatha, against her wishes, to photograph Grandma a third time, unawares.

Then I took the three sets of pictures off alone, to keep counsel with myself. I never told Timothy and Agatha what I found. I didn't want to spoil it.

But, as I laid the pictures out in my room, here is what I thought and said: "Grandma, in each picture, looks *different!*"

"Different?" I asked myself. "Sure. Wait. Just a sec—"

I rearranged the photos.

"Here's one of Grandma near Agatha. And, in it, Grandma looks like… Agatha!

"And in this one, posed with Timothy, she looks like Timothy!

"And this last one, Holy Goll! Jogging along with me, she looks like ugly *me!*"

I sat down, stunned. The pictures fell to the floor.

I hunched over, scrabbling them, rearranging, turning upside down and sidewise. Yes. Holy Goll again, yes!

O that clever Grandmother.

O those Fantoccini people-making people.

Clever beyond clever, human beyond human, warm beyond warm, love beyond love…

And wordless, I rose and went downstairs and found Agatha and Grandma in the same room, doing algebra lessons in an almost peaceful communion. At least there was not outright war. Grandma was still waiting for Agatha to come round. And no one knew what day of what year that would be, or how to make it come faster. Meanwhile –

My entering the room made Grandma turn. I watched her face slowly as it recognized me. And wasn't there the merest ink-wash change of color in those eyes? Didn't the thin film of blood beneath the translucent skin, or whatever liquid they put to pulse and beat in the humanoid forms, didn't it flourish itself suddenly bright in her cheeks and mouth? I am somewhat ruddy. Didn't Grandma suffuse herself more to my color upon my arrival?

And her eyes? watching Agatha-Abigail-Algernon at work, hadn't they been *her* color of blue rather than mine, which are deeper?

More important than that, in the moments as she talked with me, saying, "Good evening," and "How's your homework, my lad?" and such stuff, didn't the bones of her face shift subtly beneath the flesh to assume some fresh racial attitude?

For let's face it, our family is of three sorts. Agatha has the long horse bones of a small English girl who will grow to hunt foxes; Father's equine stare, snort, stomp, and assemblage of skeleton. The skull and teeth are pure English, or as pure as the motley isle's history allows.

Timothy is something else, a touch of Italian from mother's side a generation back. Her family name was Mariano, so Tim has that dark thing firing him, and a small bone structure, and eyes that will one day burn ladies to the ground.

As for me, I am the Slav, and we can only figure this from my paternal grandfather's mother who came from Vienna and brought a set of cheekbones that flared, and temples from which you might dip wine, and a kind of steppeland thrust of nose which sniffed more of Tartar than of Tartan, hiding behind the family name.

So you see it became fascinating for me to watch and try to catch Grandma as she performed her changes, speaking to Agatha and melting her cheekbones to the horse, speaking to Timothy and growing as delicate as a Florentine raven pecking glibly at the air, speaking to me and fusing the hidden plastic stuffs, so I felt Catherine the Great stood there before me.

Now, how the Fantoccini people achieved this rare and subtle transformation I shall never know, nor ask, nor wish to find out. Enough that in each quiet motion, turning here, bending there, affixing her gaze, her secret segments, sections, the abutment of her nose, the sculptured chinbone, the wax-tallow plastic metal forever warmed and was forever susceptible of loving change. Hers was a mask that was all mask but only one face for one person at a time. So in crossing a room, having touched one child, on the way, beneath the skin, the wondrous shift went on, and by the time she reached the next child, why, true mother of *that* child she was! looking upon him or her out of the battlements of their own fine bones.

And when *all* three of us were present and chattering at the same time?

Well, then, the changes were miraculously soft, small, and mysterious. Nothing so tremendous as to be caught and noted, save by this older boy, myself, who, watching, became elated and admiring and entranced.

I have never wished to be behind the magician's scenes. Enough that the illusion works. Enough that love is the chemical result. Enough that cheeks are rubbed to happy color, eyes sparked to illumination, arms opened to accept and softly bind and hold...

All of us, that is, except Agatha who refused to the bitter last.

"Agamemnon..."

It had become a jovial game now. Even Agatha didn't mind, but pretended to mind. It gave her a pleasant sense of superiority over a supposedly superior machine.

"Agamemnon!" she snorted, "you *are* a d..."

"Dumb?" said Grandma.

"I wouldn't say that."

"Think it, then, my dear Agonistes Agatha... I am quite flawed, and on names my flaws are revealed. Tom there, is Tim half the time. Timothy is Tobias or Timulty as likely as not..."

Agatha laughed. Which made Grandma make one of her rare mistakes. She put out her hand to give my sister the merest pat. Agatha-Abigail-Alice leapt to her feet.

Agatha-Agamemnon-Alcibiades-Allegra-Alexandra-Allison withdrew swiftly to her room.

"I suspect," said Timothy, later, "because she is beginning to like Grandma."

"Tosh," said I.

"Where do you pick up words like Tosh?"

"Grandma read me some Dickens last night. 'Tosh.' 'Humbug.' 'Balderdash.' 'Blast.' 'Devil take you.' You're pretty smart for your age, Tim."

"Smart, heck. It's obvious, the more Agatha likes Grandma, the more she hates herself for liking her, the more afraid she gets of the whole mess, the more she hates Grandma in the end."

"Can one love someone so much you hate them?"

"Dumb. Of course."

"It *is* sticking your neck out, sure. I guess you hate people when they make you feel naked, I mean sort of on the spot or out in the open. That's the way to play the game, of course. I mean, you don't just love people you must love them with exclamation points."

"You're pretty smart, yourself, for someone so stupid," said Tim.

"Many thanks."

And I went to watch Grandma move slowly back into her battle of wits and stratagems with what's-her-name...

What dinners there were at our house! Dinners, heck; what lunches, what breakfasts!

Always something new, yet, wisely, it looked or seemed old and familiar.

We were never asked, for if you ask children what they want, they do not know, and if you tell what's to be delivered, they reject delivery. All parents know this. It is a quiet war that must be won each day. And Grandma knew how to win without looking triumphant.

"Here's Mystery Breakfast Number Nine," she would say, placing it down. "Perfectly dreadful, not worth bothering with, it made me want to throw up while I was cooking it!"

Even while wondering how a robot could be sick, we could hardly wait to shovel it down.

"Here's Abominable Lunch Number Seventy-seven," she announced. "Made from plastic food bags, parsley, and gum from under theatre seats. Brush your teeth after or you'll taste the poison all afternoon."

We fought each other for more.

Even Abigail-Agamemnon-Agatha drew near and circled round the table at such times, while Father put on the ten pounds he needed and pinkened out his cheeks.

When A.A. Agatha did not come to meals, they were left by her door with a skull and crossbones on a small flag stuck in a baked apple. One minute the tray was abandoned, the next minute gone.

Other times Abigail A. Agatha would bird through during dinner, snatch crumbs from her plate and bird off.

"Agatha!" Father would cry.

"No, wait," Grandma said, quietly. "She'll come, she'll sit. It's a matter of time."

"What's wrong with her?" I asked.

"Yeah, for cri-yi, she's nuts," said Timothy.

"No, she's afraid," said Grandma.

"Of you?" I said, blinking.

"Not of me so much as what I might *do,*" she said.

"You wouldn't do anything to hurt her."

"No, but she thinks I might. We must wait for her to find that her fears have no foundation. If I fail, well, I will send myself to the showers and rust quietly."

There was a titter of laughter. Agatha was hiding in the hall.

Grandma finished serving everyone and then sat at the other side of the table facing Father and pretended to eat. I never found out, I never asked, I never wanted to know, what she did with the food. She was a sorcerer. It simply vanished.

And in the vanishing, Father made comment:

"This food. I've had it before. In a small French restaurant over near Les Deux Magots in Paris, twenty, oh, twenty-five years ago!" His eyes brimmed with tears, suddenly.

"How do you *do* it?" he asked, at last, putting down the cutlery, and looking across the table at this remarkable creature, this device, this what? *woman*?

Grandma took his regard, and ours, and held them simply in her now empty hands, as gifts, and just as gently replied:

"I am given things which I then give to you. I don't know that I give, but the giving goes on. You ask what I am? Why, a machine. But even in that answer we know, don't we, more than a machine. I am all the people who thought of me and planned me and built me and set me running. So I am people. I am all the things they wanted to be and perhaps could not be, so they built a great child, a wondrous toy to represent those things."

"Strange," said Father. "When I was growing up, there was a huge outcry at machines. Machines were bad, evil, they might dehumanize—"

"Some machines do. It's all in the way they are built. It's all in the way they are used. A bear trap is a simple machine that catches and holds and tears. A rifle is a machine that wounds and kills. Well, I am no bear trap. I am no rifle. I am a grandmother machine, which means more than a machine."

"How can you be more than what you seem?"

"No man is as big as his own idea. It follows, then, that any machine that embodies an idea is larger than the man that made it. And what's so wrong with that?"

"I got lost back there about a mile," said Timothy. "Come again?"

"Oh, dear," said Grandma. "How I do hate philosophical discussions and excursions into esthetics. Let me put it this way. Men throw huge shadows on the lawn, don't they? Then, all their lives, they try to run to fit the shadows. But the shadows are always longer. Only at noon can a man fit his own shoes, his own best suit, for a few brief minutes. But now we're in a new age where we can think up a Big Idea and run it around in a machine. That makes the machine-more than a machine, doesn't it?"

"So far so good," said Tim. "I guess."

"Well, isn't a motion-picture camera and projector more than a machine? It's a thing that dreams, isn't it? Sometimes fine happy dreams, sometimes nightmares. But to call it a machine and dismiss it is ridiculous."

"I see *that*!" said Tim, and laughed at seeing.

"You must have been invented then," said Father, "by someone who loved machines and hated people who *said* all machines were bad or evil."

"Exactly," said Grandma. "Guido Fantoccini, that was his real name, grew up among machines. And he couldn't stand the clichés any more."

"Clichés?"

"Those lies, yes, that people tell and pretend they are truths absolute. Man will never fly. That was a cliché truth for a thousand thousand years which turned out to be a lie only a few years ago. The earth is flat, you'll fall off the rim, dragons will dine on you; the great lie told as fact, and Columbus plowed it under. Well, now, how many times have you heard how inhuman machines are, in your life? How many bright fine people have you heard spouting the same tired truths which are in reality lies; all machines destroy, all machines are cold, thoughtless, awful.

"There's a seed of truth there. But only a seed. Guido Fantoccini knew that. And knowing it, like most men of his kind, made him mad. And he could have stayed mad and gone mad forever, but instead did what he had to do; he began to invent machines to give the lie to the ancient lying truth.

"He knew that most machines are amoral, neither bad nor good. But by the way you built and shaped them you in turn shaped men, women, and children to be bad or good. A car, for instance, dead brute, unthinking, an unprogrammed bulk, is the greatest destroyer of souls in history. It makes boy-men greedy for power, destruction, and more destruction. It was never *intended* to do that. But that's how it turned out."

Grandma circled the table, refilling our glasses with clear cold mineral spring water from the tappet in her left forefinger. "Meanwhile, you must use other compensating machines. Machines that throw shadows on the earth that beckon you to run out and fit that wondrous casting-forth. Machines that trim your soul in silhouette like a vast pair of beautiful shears, snipping away the rude brambles, the dire horns and hooves to leave a finer profile. And for that you need examples."

"Examples?" I asked.

"Other people who behave well, and you imitate them. And if you act well enough long enough all the hair drops off and you're no longer a wicked ape."

Grandma sat again.

"So, for thousands of years, you humans have needed kings, priests, philosophers, fine examples to look up to and say, 'They are good, I wish I could be like them. They set the grand good style.' But, being human, the finest priests, the tenderest philosophers make mistakes, fall from grace, and mankind is disillusioned and adopts indifferent skepticism or, worse, motionless cynicism and the good world grinds to a halt while evil moves on with huge strides."

"And you, why, you never make mistakes, you're perfect, you're better than anyone *ever*!"

It was a voice from the hall between kitchen and dining room where Agatha, we all knew, stood against the wall listening and now burst forth.

Grandma didn't even turn in the direction of the voice, but went on calmly addressing her remarks to the family at the table.

"Not perfect, no, for what is perfection? But this I do know: being mechanical, I cannot sin, cannot be bribed, cannot be greedy or jealous or mean or small. I do not relish power for power's sake. Speed does not pull me to madness. Sex does not run me rampant through the world. I have time and more than time to collect the information I need around and about an ideal to keep it clean and whole and intact. Name the value you wish, tell me the Ideal you want and I can see and collect and remember the good that will benefit you all. Tell me how you would like to be: kind, loving, considerate, well-balanced, humane… and let me run ahead on the path to explore those ways to be just that. In the darkness ahead, turn me as a lamp in all directions. I *can* guide your feet."

"So," said Father, putting the napkin to his mouth, "on the days when all of us are busy making lies—"

"I'll tell the truth."

"On the days when we hate—"

"I'll go on giving love, which means attention, which means knowing all about you, all, all, all about you, and you knowing that I know but that most of it I will never tell to anyone, it will stay a warm secret between us, so you will never fear my complete knowledge."

And here Grandma was busy clearing the table, circling, taking the plates, studying each face as she passed, touching Timothy's cheek, my shoulder with her free hand flowing along, her voice a quiet river of certainty bedded in our needful house and lives.

"But," said Father, stopping her, looking her right in the face. He gathered his breath. His face shadowed. At last he let it out. "All this talk of love and attention and stuff. Good God, woman, you, you're not *in* there!"

He gestured to her head, her face, her eyes, the hidden sensory cells behind the eyes, the miniaturized storage vaults and minimal keeps.

"*You're* not *in* there!"

Grandmother waited one, two, three silent beats.

Then she replied: "No. But *you* are. You and Thomas and Timothy and Agatha.

"Everything you ever say, everything you ever do, I'll keep, put away, treasure. I shall be all the things a family forgets it is, but senses, half-remembers. Better than the old family albums you used to leaf through, saying here's this winter, there's that spring, I shall recall what you forget. And though the debate may run another hundred thousand years: What is Love? Perhaps we may find that love is the ability of someone to give us back to us. Maybe love is someone seeing and remembering handing us back to ourselves just a trifle better than we had dared to hope or dream…

"I am family memory and, one day perhaps, racial memory, too, but in the round, and at your call. I do not *know* myself. I can neither touch nor taste nor feel on any level. Yet I exist. And my existence means the heightening of your chance to touch and taste and feel. Isn't love in there somewhere in such an exchange? Well…"

She went on around the table, clearing away, sorting and stacking, neither grossly humble nor arthritic with pride.

"What do I know?

"This, above all: the trouble with most families with many children is someone gets lost. There isn't time, it seems, for everyone. Well, I will give equally to all of you. I will share out my knowledge and attention with everyone. I wish to be a great warm pie fresh from the oven, with equal shares to be taken by all. No one will starve. Look! someone cries, and I'll look. Listen! someone cries, and I hear. Run with me on the river path! someone says, and I run. And at dusk I am not tired, nor irritable, so I do not scold out of some tired irritability. My eye stays clear, my voice strong, my hand firm, my attention constant."

"But," said Father, his voice fading, half convinced, but pitting up a last faint argument, "you're not *there.* As for love—"

"If paying attention is love, I am love. If knowing is love, I am love. If helping you not to fall into error and to be good is love, I am love. And again, to repeat, there are four of you. Each, in a way never possible before in history, will get my complete attention. No matter if you all speak at once, I can channel and hear this one and that and the other, clearly. No one will go hungry. I will, if you please, and accept the strange word, 'love' you all."

"I *don't* accept!" said Agatha.

And even Grandma turned now to see her standing in the door.

"I won't give you permission, you can't, you mustn't!" said Agatha. "I won't let you! It's lies! You lie. No one loves me. She said she did, but she lied. She *said* but *lied*!"

"Agatha!" cried Father, standing up.

"She?" said Grandma. "Who?"

"Mother!" came the shriek. "Said: Love you! Lies! Love you! Lies! And you're like her! You lie. But you're empty, anyway, and so that's a *double* lie! I hate *her*. Now, I hate *you*!"

Agatha spun about and leapt down the hall. The front door slammed wide.

Father was in motion, but Grandma touched his arm. "Let me."

And she walked and then moved swiftly, gliding down the hall and then suddenly, easily, running, *yes,* running very fast, out the door.

It was a champion sprint by the time we all reached the lawn, the sidewalk, yelling.

Blind, Agatha made the curb, wheeling about, seeing us close, all of us yelling, Grandma way ahead, shouting, too, and Agatha off the curb and out in the street, halfway to the middle, then the middle and suddenly a car, which no one saw, erupting its brakes, its horn shrieking and Agatha flailing about to see and Grandma there with her and hurling her aside and down as the car with fantastic energy and verve selected her from our midst, struck our wonderful electric Guido Fantoccini-produced dream even while she paced upon the air and, hands up to ward off, almost in mild protest, still trying to decide what to say to this bestial machine, over and over she spun and down and away even as the car jolted to a halt and I saw Agatha safe beyond and Grandma, it seemed, still coming down or down and sliding fifty yards away to strike and ricochet and lie strewn and all of us frozen in a line suddenly in the midst of the street with one scream pulled out of all our throats at the same raw instant.

Then silence and just Agatha lying on the asphalt, intact, getting ready to sob.

And still we did not move, frozen on the sill of death, afraid to venture in any direction, afraid to go see what lay beyond the car and Agatha and so we began to wail and, I guess, pray to ourselves as Father stood amongst us: Oh, no, no, we mourned, oh no, God, no, no...

Agatha lifted her already grief-stricken face and it was the face of someone who has predicted dooms and lived to see and now did not want to see or live any more. As we watched, she turned her gaze to the tossed woman's body and tears fell from her eyes. She shut them and covered them and lay back down forever to weep...

I took a step and then another step and then five quick steps and by the time I reached my sister her head was buried deep and her sobs came up out of a place so far down in her I was afraid I could never find her again, she would never come out, no matter how I pried or pleaded or promised or threatened or just plain said. And what little we could hear from Agatha buried there in her own misery, she said over and over again, lamenting, wounded, certain of the old threat known and named and now here forever. "... like I said... told you... lies... lies... liars... all lies... like the other... other... just like... just... just like the other... other... other...!"

I was down on my knees holding onto her with both hands, trying to put her back together even though she wasn't broken any way you could see but just feel, because I knew it was no use going on to Grandma, no use at all, so I just touched Agatha and gentled her and wept while Father came up and stood over and knelt down with me and it was like a prayer meeting in the middle of the street and lucky no more cars coming, and I said, choking, "Other what, Ag, other *what*?"

Agatha exploded two words. "Other dead!"

"You mean Mom?"

"O Mom," she wailed, shivering, lying down, cuddling up like a baby. "O Mom, dead, O Mom and now Grandma dead, she promised always, always, to love, to love, promised to be different, promised, promised and now look, look… I hate her, I hate Mom, I hate her, I hate *them*!!"

"Of course," said a voice. "It's only natural. How foolish of me not to have known, not to have seen."

And the voice was so familiar we were all stricken.

We all jerked.

Agatha squinched her eyes, flicked them wide, blinked, and jerked half up, staring.

"How silly of me," said Grandma, standing there at the edge of our circle, our prayer, our wake.

"Grandma!" we all said.

And she stood there, taller by far than any of us in this moment of kneeling and holding and crying out. We could only stare up at her in disbelief.

"You're dead!" cried Agatha. "The car—"

"Hit me," said Grandma, quietly. "Yes. And threw me in the air and tumbled me over and for a few moments there was a severe concussion of circuitries. I might have feared a disconnection, if fear is the word. But then I sat up and gave myself a shake and the few molecules of paint, jarred loose on one printed path or another, magnetized back in position and resilient creature that I am, unbreakable thing that I am, *here* I am."

"I thought you were—" said Agatha.

"And only natural," said Grandma. "I mean, anyone else, hit like that, tossed like that. But, O my dear Agatha, not me. And now I see why you were afraid and never trusted me. You didn't know. And I had not as yet proved my singular ability to survive. How dumb of me not to have thought to show you. Just a second." Somewhere in her head, her body, her being, she fitted together some invisible tapes, some old information made new by interblending. She nodded. "Yes. There. A book of child-raising, laughed at by some few people years back when the woman who wrote the book said, as final advice to parents: 'Whatever you do, don't die. Your children will never forgive you.'"

"Forgive," some one of us whispered.

"For how can children understand when you just up and go away and never come back again with no excuse, no apologies, no sorry note, nothing."

"They can't," I said.

"So," said Grandma, kneeling down with us beside Agatha who sat up now, new tears brimming her eyes, but a different kind of tears, not tears that drowned, but tears that washed clean. "So your mother ran away to death. And after that, how *could you* trust anyone? If everyone left, vanished finally, who *was* there to trust? So when I came, half wise, half ignorant, I should have known, I did not know, why you would not accept me. For, very simply and honestly, you feared I might not stay, that I lied, that I was vulnerable, too. And two leavetakings, two deaths, were one too many in a single year. But now, do you *see,* Abigail?"

"Agatha," said Agatha, without knowing she corrected.

"Do you understand, I shall always, always be here?"

"Oh, yes," cried Agatha, and broke down into a solid weeping in which we all joined, huddled together and cars drew up and stopped to see just how many people were hurt and how many people were getting well right there.

End of story.

Well, not quite the end.

We lived happily ever after.

Or rather we lived together, Grandma, Agatha-Agamemnon-Abigail, Timothy, and I, Tom, and Father, and Grandma calling us to frolic in great fountains of Latin and Spanish and French, in great seaborne gouts of poetry like Moby Dick sprinkling the deeps with his Versailles jet somehow lost in calms and found in storms; Grandma a constant, a clock, a pendulum, a face to tell all time by at noon, or in the middle of sick nights when, raved with fever, we saw her forever by our beds, never gone, never away, always waiting, always speaking kind words, her cool hand icing our hot brows, the tappet of her uplifted forefinger unsprung to let a twine of cold mountain water touch our flannel tongues. Ten thousand dawns she cut our wildflower lawn, ten thousand nights she wandered, remembering the dust molecules that fell in the still hours before dawn, or sat whispering some lesson she felt needed teaching to our ears while we slept snug.

Until at last, one by one, it was time for us to go away to school, and when at last the youngest, Agatha, was all packed, why Grandma packed, too.

On the last day of summer that last year, we found Grandma down in the front room with various packets and suitcases, knitting, waiting, and though she had often spoken of it, now that the time came we were shocked and surprised.

"Grandma!" we all said. "What are you doing?"

"Why going off to college, in a way, just like you," she said. "Back to Guido Fantoccini's, to the Family."

"The Family?"

"Of Pinocchios, that's what he called us for a joke, at first. The Pinocchios and himself Gepetto. And then later gave us his own name: the Fantoccini. Anyway, you have been my family here. Now I go back to my even larger family there, my brothers, sisters, aunts, cousins, all robots who—"

"Who do *what?"* asked Agatha.

"It all depends," said Grandma. "Some stay, some linger. Others go to be drawn and quartered, you might say, their parts distributed to other machines who have need of repairs. They'll weigh and find me wanting or not wanting. It may be I'll be just the one they need tomorrow and off I'll go to raise another batch of children and beat another batch of fudge."

"Oh, they mustn't draw and quarter you!" cried Agatha. "No!" I cried, with Timothy.

"My allowance," said Agatha, "I'll pay anything...?"

Grandma stopped rocking and looked at the needles and the pattern of bright yarn. "Well, I wouldn't have said, but now you ask and I'll tell. For a very *small* fee, there's a room, the room of the Family, a large dim parlor, all quiet and nicely decorated, where as many as thirty or forty of the Electric Women sit and rock and talk, each in her turn. I have not been there. I am, after all, freshly born, comparatively new. For a small fee, very small, each month and year, that's where I'll be, with all the others like me, listening to what they've learned of the world and, in my turn, telling how it was with Tom and Tim and Agatha and how fine and happy we were. And I'll tell all I learned from you."

"But... you taught *us!"*

"Do you *really* think that?" she said. "No, it was turnabout, roundabout, learning both ways. And it's all in here, everything you flew into tears about or laughed over, why, I have it all. And I'll tell it to the others just as they tell their boys and girls and life to me. We'll sit there, growing wiser and calmer and better every year and every year, ten, twenty, thirty years. The Family knowledge will double, quadruple, the wisdom will not be lost. And we'll be waiting there in that sitting room, should you ever need us for your own children in time of illness, or, God prevent, deprivation or death. There we'll be, growing old but not old, getting closer to the time, perhaps, someday, when we live up to our first strange joking name."

"The Pinocchios?" asked Tim. Grandma nodded.

I knew what she meant. The day when, as in the old tale, Pinocchio had grown so worthy and so fine that the gift of life had been given him. So I saw them, in future years, the entire family of Fantoccini, the Pinocchios, trading and re-trading, murmuring and whispering their knowledge in the great parlors of philosophy, waiting for the day. The day that could never come.

Grandma must have read that thought in our eyes. "We'll see," she said. "Let's just wait and see."

"Oh, Grandma," cried Agatha and she was weeping as she had wept many years before. "You don't have to wait. You're alive. You've always been alive to us!"

And she caught hold of the old woman and we all caught hold for a long moment and then ran off up in the sky to faraway schools and years and her last words to us before we let the helicopter swarm us away into autumn were these:

"When you are very old and gone childish-small again, with childish ways and childish yens and, in need of feeding, make a wish for the old teacher nurse, the dumb yet wise companion, send for me. I will come back. We shall inhabit the nursery again, never fear."

"Oh, we shall never be old!" we cried. "That will never happen!"

"Never! Never!"

And we were gone.

And the years are flown.

And we are old now, Tim and Agatha and I.

Our children are grown and gone, our wives and husbands vanished from the earth and now, by Dickensian coincidence, accept it as you will or not accept, back in the old house, we three.

I lie here in the bedroom which was my childish place seventy, O seventy, believe it, seventy years ago. Beneath this wallpaper is another layer and yet another-times-three to the old wallpaper covered over when I was nine. The wallpaper is peeling. I see peeking from beneath, old elephants, familiar tigers, fine and amiable zebras, irascible crocodiles. I have sent for the paperers to carefully remove all but that last layer. The old animals will live again on the walls, revealed.

And we have sent for someone else. The three of us have called:

Grandma! You said you'd come back when we had need. We are surprised by age, by time. We are old. We *need.*

And in three rooms of a summer house very late in time, three old children rise up, crying out in their heads: We *loved* you! We *love* you!

There! There! in the sky, we think, waking at morn. Is that the delivery machine? Does it settle to die lawn?

There! There on the grass by the front porch. Does the mummy case arrive?

Are our names inked on ribbons wrapped about the lovely form beneath the golden mask?!

And the kept gold key, forever hung on Agatha's breast, warmed and waiting? Oh God, will it, after all these years, will it wind, will it set in motion, will it, dearly, *fit*?!

The Ingenious Mr. Spinola

Ernest Bramah

"YOU SEEM TROUBLED, Parkinson. Have you been reading the Money Article again?"

Parkinson, who had been lingering a little aimlessly about the room, exhibited symptoms of embarrassed guilt. Since an unfortunate day, when it had been convincingly shown to the excellent fellow that to leave his accumulated savings on deposit at the bank was merely an uninviting mode of throwing money away, it is not too much to say that his few hundreds had led Parkinson a sorry life. Inspired by a natural patriotism and an appreciation of the advantage of 4½ over 1¼ per cent., he had at once invested in Consols. A very short time later a terrible line in a financial daily – 'Consols weak' – caught his agitated eye. Consols were precipitately abandoned and a 'sound industrial' took their place. Then came the rumours of an impending strike and the Conservative press voiced gloomy forebodings for the future of industrial capital. An urgent selling order, bearing Mr. Parkinson's signature, was the immediate outcome.

In the next twelve months Parkinson's few hundreds wandered through many lands and in a modest way went to support monarchies and republics, to carry on municipal enterprise and to spread the benefits of commerce. And, through all, they contrived to exist. They even assisted in establishing a rubber plantation in Madagascar and exploiting an oil discovery in Peru and yet survived. If everything could have been lost by one dire reverse Parkinson would have been content – even relieved; but with her proverbial inconsequence Fortune began by smiling and continued to smile – faintly, it is true, but appreciably – on her timorous votary. In spite of his profound ignorance of finance each of Parkinson's qualms and tremors resulted in a slight pecuniary margin to his credit. At the end of twelve months he had drawn a respectable interest, was somewhat to the good in capital, and as a waste product had acquired an abiding reputation among a small but choice coterie as a very 'knowing one'.

"Thank you, sir, but I am sorry if I seemed engrossed in my own affairs," he apologised in answer to Mr. Carrados's inquiry. "As a matter of fact," he added, "I hoped that I had finished with Stock Exchange transactions for the future."

"Ah, to be sure," assented Carrados. "A block of cottages Acton way, wasn't it to be?"

"I did at one time consider the investment, but on reflection I decided against property of that description. The association with houses occupied by the artisan class would not have been congenial, sir."

"Still, it might have been profitable."

"Possibly, sir. I have, however, taken up a mortgage on a detached house standing in its own grounds at Highgate. It was strongly recommended by your own estate agents – by Mr. Lethbridge himself, sir."

"I hope it will prove satisfactory, Parkinson."

"I hope so, sir, but I do not feel altogether reassured now, after seeing it."

"After seeing it? But you saw it before you took it up, surely?"

"As a matter of fact, no, sir. It was pointed out to me that the security was ample, and as I had no practical knowledge of house-valuing there was nothing to be gained by inspecting it. At the same time I was given the opportunity, I must admit; but as we were rather busy then – it was just before we went to Rome, sir – I never went there."

"Well, after all," admitted Carrados, "I hold a fair number of mortgage securities on railways and other property that I have never been within a thousand miles of. I am not in a position to criticise you, Parkinson. And this house – I suppose that it does really exist?"

"Oh yes, sir. I spent yesterday afternoon in the neighbourhood. Now that the trees are out, there is not a great deal that can be actually seen from the road, but I satisfied myself that in the winter the house must be distinctly visible from several points."

"That is very satisfactory," said Carrados with equal seriousness. "But, after all, the title is the chief thing."

"So I am given to understand. Doubtless it would not be sound business, sir, but I think that if the title had been a little worse, and the appearance of the grounds a little better, I should have felt more secure. But what really concerned me is that the house is being talked about."

"Talked about?"

"Yes. It is in a secluded position, but there are some old-fashioned cottages near and these people notice things, sir. It is not difficult to induce them to talk. Refreshments are procurable at one of the cottages and I had tea there. I have since thought, from a remark made to me on leaving, that the idea may have got about that I was connected with the Scotland Yard authorities. I had no apprehension at the time of creating such an impression, sir, but I wished to make a few casual inquiries."

Carrados nodded. "Quite so," he murmured encouragingly.

"It was then that I discovered what I have alluded to. These people, having become suspicious, watch all that is to be seen at Strathblane Lodge – as it is called – and talk. They do not know what goes on there."

"That must be very disheartening for them."

"Well, sir, they find it trying. Up to less than a year ago the house was occupied by a commercial gentleman and everything was quite regular. But with the new people they don't know which are the family and who are the servants. Two or three men having the appearance of mechanics seem to be there continually, and sometimes, generally in the evening, there are visitors of a class whom one would not associate with the unpretentious nature of the establishment. Gentlemen for the most part, but occasionally ladies, I was told, coming in taxis or private motor cars and generally in evening dress."

"That ought to reassure these neighbours – the private cars and evening dress."

"I cannot say that it does, sir. And what I heard made me a little nervous also."

Something was evidently on the ingenuous creature's mind. The blind man's face wore a faintly amused smile, but he gauged the real measure of his servant's apprehension.

"Nervous of what, Parkinson?" he inquired kindly.

"Some thought that it might be a gambling-house, but others said it looked as if a worse business was carried on there. I should not like there to be any scandal or exposure, sir, and perhaps the mortgage forfeited in consequence."

"But, good heavens, man! You don't imagine that a mortgage is like a public-house licence, to be revoked in consequence of a rowdy tenant, surely?"

Parkinson's dubious silence made it increasingly plain that he had, indeed, associated his security with some such contingency, a conviction based, it appeared, when he admitted his fears, on a settled belief in the predatory intentions of a Government with whom he was not in sympathy.

"Don't give the thing another thought," counselled his employer. "If Lethbridge recommended the investment you may be sure that it is all right. As for what goes on there – that doesn't matter two straws to you, and in any case it is probably idle chatter."

"Thank you, sir. It is a relief to have your assurance. I see now that I ought to have paid no attention to such conversation, but being anxious – and seeing Sir Fergus Copling go there—"

"Sir Fergus Copling? You saw him there?"

"Yes, sir. I thought that I remembered a car that was waiting for the gate to be opened. Then I recognised Sir Fergus: it was the small dark blue car that he has come here in. And just after what I had been hearing—"

"But Sir Fergus Copling! He's a testimonial of propriety. Do you know what you are talking about, Parkinson?"

The excellent man looked even more deeply troubled than he had been about his money.

"Not in that sense, sir," he protested. "I only understood that he was a gentleman of position and a very large income, and after just listening to what was being said Carrados's scepticism was intelligible. Copling was the last man to be associated with a scandal of fast life. He had come into his baronetcy quite unexpectedly a few years previously while engaged in the drab but apparently congenial business of teaching arithmetic at a public school. The chief advantage of the change of fortune, as it appeared to the recipient, was that it enabled him to transfer his attention from the lower to the higher mathematics. Without going out of his way to flout the conventions, he set himself a comparatively simple standard of living. He was too old and fixed, he said, to change much – forty and a bachelor – and the most optimistic spinster in town had reluctantly come to acquiesce.

Carrados had not forgotten this conversation when next he encountered Sir Fergus a week or so later. He knew the man well enough to be able to lead up to the subject and when an identifiable footstep fell on his ear in the hall of the Metaphysical (the dullest club in Europe, it was generally admitted) he called across to the baronet, who, as a matter of fact, had been too abstracted to notice him or anyone else.

"You aren't a member, are you?" asked Copling when they had shaken hands. "I didn't know that you went in for this sort of thing." The motion of his head indicated the monumental library which he had just quitted, but it might possibly be taken as indicating the general atmosphere of profound somnolence that enveloped the Metaphysical.

"I am not a member," admitted Carrados. "I only came to gather some material."

"Statistics?" queried Copling with interest. "We have a very useful range of works." He suddenly remembered his acquaintance's affliction. "By the way, can I be of any use to you?"

"Yes, if you will," said Carrados. "Let me go to lunch with you. There is an appalling bore hanging about and he'll nab me if I don't get past under protection."

Copling assented readily enough and took the blind man's arm.

"Where, though?" he asked at the door. "I generally—" he hesitated, with a shy laugh, "I generally go to an A.B.C. tea-shop myself. It doesn't waste so much time. But, of course—"

"Of course, a tea-shop by all means," assented Carrados.

"You are sure that you don't mind?" persisted the baronet anxiously.

"Mind? Why, I'm a shareholder!" chuckled Carrados.

"This suits me very well," remarked the ex-schoolmaster when they were seated in a remote corner of a seething general room. "Fellows used to do their best to get me into the way of going to swell places, but I always seem to drift back here. I don't mind the prices, Carrados, but hang me if I like to pay the prices simply to be inconvenienced. Yes, hot milk, please."

Carrados endorsed this reasonable philosophy. Carlton or Coffee-house, the Ritz or the tea-shop, it was all the same to him – life, and very enjoyable life at that. He sat and, like the spider, drew from within himself the fabric of the universe by which he was surrounded. In that inexhaustible faculty he found perfect content: he never required 'to be amused'.

"No, not statistics," he said presently, returning to the unfinished conversation of the club hall. "Scarcely that. More in the nature of topography, perhaps. Have you considered, Copling, how everything is specialised nowadays? Does anyone read the old-fashioned unpretentious Guide-book to London still? One would hardly think so to see how the subject is cut up. We have 'Famous London Blind-alleys', 'Historical West-Central Door-Knockers', 'Footsteps of Dr. Johnson between Gough Square and John Street, Adelphi', 'The Thames from Hungerford Bridge to Charing Cross Pier', 'Oxford Street Paving Stones on which De Quincey sat', and so on."

"They are not familiar to me," said Sir Fergus simply.

"Nor to me; yet they sound familiar. Well, I touched journalism myself once, years ago. What do you say to 'Mysterious Double-fronted Houses of the Outer Northern Suburbs'? Too comprehensive?"

"I don't know. The subject must be limited. But do you seriously contemplate such a work?"

"If I did," replied Carrados, "what could you tell me about Strathblane Lodge, Highgate?"

"Oh!" A slow smile broke on Copling's face. "That is rather extraordinary, isn't it? Do you know old Spinola? Have you been there?"

"So far I don't know the venerable Mr. Spinola and I have not been there. What is the peculiarity?"

"But you know of the automatic card-player?"

The words brought a certain amount of enlightenment. Carrados had heard more than once casual allusions to a wonderful mechanical contrivance that played cards with discrimination. He had not thought anything more of it, classing it with Kempelen's famous imposture which had for a time mystified and duped the chess world more than a century ago. So far, also, some reticence appeared to be observed about the modern contrivance, as though its inventor had no desire to have it turned into a popular show: at all events not a word about it had appeared in the Press.

"I have heard something, but not much, and I certainly have not seen it. What is it – a fraud, surely?"

Copling replied with measured consideration between the process of investigating his lightly boiled egg. It was plain that the automaton had impressed him.

"I naturally approached the subject with scepticism," he admitted, "but at the end of several demonstrations I am converted to a position of passive acquiescence. Spinola, at all events, is no charlatan. His knowledge of mathematics is profound. As you know, Carrados, the subject is my own and I am not likely to be imposed on in that particular. It was purely the scientific aspect of the invention that attracted me, for I am not a gambler in the ordinary sense. Spinola's explanation of the principles of the contrivance, when he found that I was capable of following them, was lucid and convincing. Of course he does not disclose all the details of the mechanism, but he shows enough."

"It is a gamble, then, not a mere demonstration?"

"He has spent many years on the automaton, and it must have cost thousands of pounds in experiment and construction. He makes no secret of hoping to reimburse his outlay."

"What do you play?"

"Piquet – rubicon piquet. The figure could, he claims, be set to play any game by changing or elaborating the mechanism. He had to construct it for one definite set of chances and he selected piquet as a suitable medium."

"It wins?"

"Against me invariably in the end."

"Why should it win, Copling? In a game that is nine-tenths chance, why should it win?"

"I am an indifferent player. If the tactics of the game have been reduced to machinery and the combinations are controlled by a dispassionate automaton, the one-tenth would constitute a winning factor."

"And against expert players?"

Sir Fergus admitted that to the best of his knowledge the figure still had the advantage. In answer to Carrados's further inquiry he estimated his losses at two or three hundred pounds. The stakes were whatever the visitor suggested – Spinola was something of a grandee, one inferred – and at half-crown points Sir Fergus had found the game quite expensive enough.

"Why do people go if they invariably lose?" asked the blind man.

"My dear fellow, why do they go to Monte Carlo?" was the retort, accompanied by a tolerant shrug. "Besides, I don't positively say that they always lose. One hears of people winning, though I have never seen it happen. Then I fancy that the novelty has taken with a certain set. It is a thing at the moment to go up there and have the rather bizarre experience. There is an element of the creep in it, you know – sitting and playing against that serene and unimpressionable contrivance."

"What do the others do? There is quite a company, I gather."

"Oh yes, sometimes. Occasionally one may find oneself alone. Well, the others often watch the play. Sometimes sets play bridge on their own. Then there is coffee and wine. Nothing formal, I assure you."

"Rowdy ever?"

"Oh no. The old man has a presence; I doubt if anyone would feel encouraged to go too far under Spinola's eye. Yet practically nothing seems to be known of him, not even his nationality. I have heard half-a-dozen different tales from as many cocksure men – he is a South American Spaniard ruined by a revolution; a Jesuit expelled from France through politics; an Irishman of good family settled in Warsaw, where he stole the plans from a broken-down Polish inventor; a Virginia military man, who suddenly found that he was dying from cancer and is doing this to provide a fortune for an only and beautiful daughter, and so on."

"Is there a beautiful daughter?"

"Not that I have ever seen. No, the man just cropped up, as odd people do in great capitals. Nobody really knows anything about him, but his queer salon has caught on to a certain extent."

Now any novel phase of life attracted Carrados. The mixed company that Spinola's enterprise was able to draw to an out-of-the-way suburb – the peculiar blend of science and society – was not much in itself. The various constituents could be met elsewhere to more advantage, but the assemblage might engender piquancy. And the man himself and his machine? In any case they should repay attention.

"How does one procure the entree?" he inquired.

Copling raised a quizzical eyebrow.

"You also?" he replied. "Oh, I see; you think – well, if you are going to discover any sleight-of-hand about the business I don't mind—"

"Yes?" prompted Carrados, for Sir Fergus had pulled up on an obvious afterthought.

"I did not intend going up again," said Copling slowly. "As a matter of fact, I have seen all that interests me. And – I suppose I may as well tell you, Carrados – I made someone a sort of promise to have nothing to do with gambling. She feels very strongly on the subject."

"She is very wise," commented the blind man.

Elation mingled with something faintly apologetic in the abrupt bestowal of the baronet's unexpected confidence.

"It was really quite a sudden and romantic happening," he continued, led on by the imperceptible encouragement of his companion's attitude. "She is called Mercia. She does not know who I am – not that that's anything," he added modestly. "She is an orphan and earns her own living. I was able to be of some slight service to her in the science galleries at South Kensington, where she was collecting material for her employer. Then we met there again and had lunch together, and so on."

"At tea-shops?"

"Oh yes. Her tastes are very simple. She doesn't like shows and society and all that."

"I congratulate you. When is it to be?"

"It? Oh! Well, we haven't settled anything like that yet. Of course this is all in confidence, Carrados."

"Absolutely – though the lady has done me rather an ill turn."

"How?"

"Well, weren't you going to introduce me to Mr. Spinola?"

"True," assented Sir Fergus. "And I don't see why I shouldn't," he added valiantly. "I need not play, and if there is any bunkum about the thing I should certainly like to see how it is done. What evening will suit you?"

An early date had suited both, and shortly after eight o'clock – an hour at which they were likely to find few guests before them – Carrados's car drew up at Strathbane Lodge. By arrangement he had picked up Copling, who lived – 'of all places in the world', as people had said when they heard of it – in an unknown street near Euston. Parkinson, out of regard for the worthy man's feelings, had been left behind on the occasion and in ignorance of his master's destination.

The appearance of the place was certainly not calculated to reassure a nervous investor. The entirely neglected garden seemed to convey a hint that the tenant might be contemplating a short occupation and a hasty flight. Nor did the exterior of the house do much to remove the unfortunate impression. Only a philosopher or an habitual defaulter would live in such a state.

The venerable Mr. Spinola received them in the salon set apart for the display of the automaton and for cards in general. It was a room of fair proportions – doubtless the largest in the house – and quite passably furnished, though in a rather odd and incongruous style. But probably any furniture on earth would have seemed incongruous to the strange, idol-like presence which the inventor had thought fit to adapt to the uses of his mechanism. The figure was placed on a low pedestal, sufficiently raised from the carpet on four plain wooden legs for all the space underneath to be clearly visible. The body was a squat, cross-legged conception, typical of an Indian deity, the head singularly life-like through the heavy gilding with which the face was covered, and behind the merely contemplative expression that dominated the golden mask the carver had by chance or intention lined a faint suggestion of cynical contempt.

"You have come to see my little figure – Aurelius, as we call him among ourselves?" said the bland old gentleman benignly. "That is right; that is right." He shook hands with them both, and received Mr. Carrados, on Sir Fergus's introduction, as though he was a very dear friend from whom he had long been parted. It was difficult indeed for Max to disengage himself from the effusive Spinola's affection without a wrench.

"Mr. Carrados happens to be blind, Mr. Spinola," interposed Copling, seeing that their host was so far in ignorance of the fact.

"Impossible! Impossible!" exclaimed Spinola, riveting his own very bright eyes on his guest's insentient ones. "Yet," he added, "one would not jest."

"It is quite true," was the matter-of-fact corroboration. "My hands must be my eyes, Mr. Spinola. In place of seeing, will you permit me to touch your wonderful creation?"

The old man's assent was immediate and cordial. They moved across the room towards the figure, the inventor modestly protesting:

"You flatter me, my dear sir. After all, it is but a toy in large; nothing but a toy."

A weary-looking youth, the only other occupant of the room, threw down the illustrated weekly that he had picked up on the new arrivals' entrance and detained Copling.

"Yes, I had been toying a little before you arrived," he remarked flippantly. "I came early to cut Dora Lascelle off from the idle crowd and the silly little rabbit isn't coming, it appears. I didn't want to play, because, for a fact, I have no money, but the old thing bored me to hysterics. Good God! How he can talk so little on anything really entertaining, like *The Giddy Flappers* or Trixie Fluff's divorce, and so much about strange, unearthly things that no other living creature has ever seen even in a dream, baffles my imagination. What's an 'integral calculus', Copling? No, don't tell me, after all. Let me forget the benumbing episode as soon as possible."

"Do you wish for a game, Sir Fergus?" broke in Spinola's soft voice from across the room. "Doubtless Mr. Carrados might like to follow someone else's play before he makes the experiment."

Copling hesitated. He had not come to play, as he had already told his friend, but Max gave no sign of coming to his assistance.

"Perhaps you, Crediton?" said the mathematician; but young Crediton shook his head and smiled wisely. Copling was too easy-going to stand out. He crossed the room and sat down at the automaton's table.

"And the stake?"

"Suppose we merely have a guinea on the game?" suggested the visitor.

Spinola acquiesced with the air of one to whom a three-penny bit or a kingdom would have been equally indifferent. The deal fell to Copling and the automaton therefore had the first 'elder hand', with the advantage of a discard of five cards against its opponent's three.

Carrados had already been shown the theory of the contrivance. He now followed Spinola's operations as the game proceeded. The old man picked up the twelve cards dealt to the automaton and carefully arranged them in their proper places on a square shield that was connected with the front of the figure. As each fell into its slot it registered its presence on the delicate mechanism that the figure contained.

"The discard," remarked Spinola, and moved a small lever. The left hand of the automaton was raised, came over the shield which hid its cards from the opponent, touched one with an extended finger, and affixing it by suction, lifted the selected card from the slot and dropped it face downwards on the table.

"A little slow, a little cumbersome," apologised the inventor as the motions were repeated until five cards had been thrown out. "The left hand is used for the discard alone, as a different movement is necessary." He picked up the five new cards from the stock and arranged them as he had done the hand. "Now we proceed to the play."

Crediton strolled across to watch the game. He stood behind Copling, while Carrados remained near the automaton. Spinola opened the movements.

"Aurelius has no voice, of course," he said, studying the display of cards, "so I – point of five."

"Good," conceded the opponent.

Spinola registered the detail on one of an elaborate set of dials that produced a further development in the machinery.

"Spades," he announced, declaring the suit that he had won the 'points' on. "Tierce major."

"Quart to the queen – hearts," claimed Copling, and Spinola moved another dial to register the opponent's advantage.

"Three kings."

"Good," was the reply.

"Three tens," added the senior player, as his three kings, being good against the other hand, enabled him to count the lower trio also. "Five for the point and two trios – eleven." Every detail of the scoring and of the ensuing play was registered as the other things had been.

This finished the preliminaries and the play of the hands began. The automaton, in response to the release of the machinery, moved its right arm with the same deliberation that had marked its former action and laid a card face upwards on the table. For the blind man's benefit each card was named as it was played. At the end of the hand Copling had won 'the cards' – a matter of ten extra points with seven tricks to five and the score stood to his advantage at 27-17.

"Not bad for the junior hand," commented Crediton. "Do you know" – he addressed the inventor – "there is a sort of 'average', as they call it, that you are supposed to play up to? I forget how it goes, but 27 is jolly high for the minor hand, I know."

"I have heard of it," replied Spinola politely. Crediton could not make out why the other two men smiled broadly.

The succeeding hands developed no particular points of interest. The scoring ruled low and in the end Copling won by 129 to 87. Spinola purred congratulation.

"I am always delighted to see Aurelius lose," he declared, paying out his guinea with a princely air.

"Why?" demanded Crediton.

"Because it shows that I have succeeded beyond expectation, my dear young sir: I have made him almost human. Now, Mr. Carrados."

"With pleasure," assented the blind man. "Though I am afraid that I shall not afford you the delight of losing, Mr. Spinola."

"One never knows, one never knows," beamed the old man. "Shall we say half-crown points for variety?"

"Very good. Ah, our deal." He dealt the hands and proceeded to dispose the twelve that fell to the automaton on the shield. There was a moment of indecision. "Pray, Mr. Carrados, do you not arrange your cards?"

"I have done so." He had, in fact, merely spread out his hand in the usual fan formation and run an identifying finger once round the upper edges. The cards remained as they had been dealt, face downwards.

"Wonderful! And that enables you to distinguish them?"

"The ink and the impression on a plain surface – oh yes." He threw out the full discard as he spoke and took in the upper five of the stock.

"You overwhelm us; you accentuate the tiresome deliberation of poor Aurelius." Spinola was hovering about the external fittings of the figure with unusual fussiness. When at length he released the left hand it seemed for an almost perceptible moment that the action hung. Then the arm descended and carried out the discard.

"Point of five," said Carrados.

"Good."

"In spades. Quint major in spades also, tierce to the knave in clubs, fourteen aces" – i.e. four aces; 'fourteen' in the language of piquet as they score that number. He did not wait for his opponent to assent to each count, knowing, after the point had passed, that the other calls were good against anything that could possibly be held. "Five, twenty, twenty-three, ninety-seven." Having reached thirty before his opponent scored, and without a card having so far been played, his score automatically advanced by sixty. That is the 'repique'.

"By Jove!" exclaimed Crediton, "that's the first time I've ever known Aurelius repiqued."

"Oh, it has happened," retorted Spinola almost testily.

The play of the hand was bound to go in Carrados's favour – he held eight certain tricks. He won 'the cards' with two tricks to spare and the round closed at 119-5.

"You look like being delighted again, Mr. Spinola," remarked Crediton a little critically.

"Suppose you make yourself useful by dealing for me," interposed Carrados. "Of course," he reminded his host, "it does not do for me to handle any cards but my own."

"I had not thought of that," replied Spinola, looking at him shrewdly. "If you had no conscience you would be a dangerous opponent, Mr. Carrados."

"The same might be said of any man," was the reply. "That is why it is so satisfactory to play an automaton."

"Oh, Aurelius has no conscience, you know," chimed in Crediton sapiently. "Mr. Spinola couldn't find room for it among the wheels."

The second hand was not eventful. Each player had to be content to make about the 'average' which Crediton had ingenuously discovered. It raised the scores to 33-30. Two hands followed in the same prudent spirit; the fifth – Carrados's 'elder' – found the position 169-67.

"Only two this time," remarked Carrados, taking in.

"Jupiter!" murmured Crediton. It is unusual for the senior hand to leave even one of the five cards to which he is entitled. It indicated an unusually strong hand. The automaton evidently thought so too. It availed itself of all the six alternative cards and, as the play disclosed, completely cut up its own hand to save the repique by beating Carrados on the point. It won the point, to find that its opponent only held a low quart, a tierce and three kings. As a result Carrados won 'the cards' and the score stood 199-79. The discard was, in fact, an experiment in bluff. Carrados might have held a quint and fourteen kings for all the opposing hand disclosed.

"What on earth did you do that for?" demanded Copling. He himself played an eminently straightforward game – and generally lost.

"I'll bet I know," put in Crediton. "You are getting rather close, Mr. Spinola – the last hand and you need twenty-one to save the rubicon." The 'rubicon' means that instead of the loser's score being deducted from the winner's in arriving at the latter's total, it is added to it – a possible difference of nearly 200 points.

"We shall see; we shall see," muttered Spinola with a little less than his usual suavity.

Whatever concern he had, however, was groundless, for the game ended tamely enough. Carrados ought to have won the point and divided tricks, leaving his opponent a minor quart and a solitary trio – about 15 on the hand. By a careless discard he threw away both chances and the final score stood at 205-112. Copling, who had come to regard his friend's play as rather excellent, was silent. Crediton almost shrieked his disapproval and seizing the cards demonstrated to his heart's content.

"Ninety-three and the hundred for the game – twenty-four pounds and one half-crown," said the loser, counting out notes and coin to the amount. "It has been an experience for both of us – Aurelius and myself."

"And certainly for me," added Carrados.

"Look here," interposed Crediton, "Aurelius seems off his play. If you don't mind taking my paper, Mr. Spinola, I should like another go."

"As you please," assented the old man. "Your undertaking is, of course—" The gesture suggested 'quite equal to that of the cashier of the Bank of England'. The venerable person had, in fact, regained his lofty pecuniary indifference. "The same point?"

"Right-o," cheerfully assented the youth.

"I will go and think over my shortcomings," said Carrados. He started to cross the room to a seat and ran into a couch. With a gasp Copling hastened to his assistance. Then he found his arm detained and heard the whisper. "Sit down with me."

Across the room the play had begun again and with a little care they could converse without the possibility of a word being overheard.

"What is it?" asked Sir Fergus.

"The golden one will win. It is only when the cards are not exposed that you play on equal terms."

"But I won?"

"Because it is well to lose sometimes and, by choice, when the stake is low. That witless youth will have to pay for both of us."

"But how – how on earth do you suggest that it is done?"

"Look round cautiously. What eyes overlook Crediton's hand as he sits there?"

"What eyes? Good gracious! Is there anything in that?"

"What is it?"

"There is a trophy of Japanese arms high up on the wall. An iron mask surmounts it. It has glass eyes. I have never seen anything like that before."

"Any others round the walls?"

"There is a stuffed tiger's head on our right and a puma's or something of that sort on the left."

"In case a suspicious player asks to have the places changed or holds his cards awkwardly. Working the automaton from other positions is probably also arranged for."

"But how can a knowledge of the opponent's cards affect the automaton? The dials—"

"The dials are all bunkum. While you were playing I took the liberty of altering them and for a whole hand the dials indicated that you must inevitably be holding eight clubs and four spades. All the time you were leading out hearts and diamonds and the automaton serenely followed suit. The only effective machinery is that indicating the display of cards on the shield and controlling the hands, and that is worked by a keyboard and electric current from the room below. The watcher behind the mask telephones the opposing hand, the discard and the take-in. The automaton's hand has already been indicated below. You see the enormous advantage the hidden player has? When he is the minor hand he knows everything that is to be known before he discards. When he is the elder he knows almost everything. By concentrating on one detail he can practically always balk the pique, the repique and the kapot, if it is necessary to play for safety. You remember what Crediton said – that he had never known Aurelius repiqued before. The leisurely manipulation of the dials gives plenty of time. An even ordinary player in that position can do the rest."

Copling scarcely knew whether to believe or not. It sounded plausible, but it reflected monstrously.

"You speak of a telephone," he said. "How can you definitely say that such a thing is being used? You have never been in the room before and we've scarcely been here an hour. It – it may be awfully serious, you know."

Carrados smiled.

"Can you hear the kitchen door being opened at this moment or detect the exact aroma of our host's mocha?" he demanded.

"Not in the least," admitted Copling.

"Then of course it is hopeless to expect you to pick up the whisper of a man behind a mask a score of feet away. How fearfully in the dark you seeing folk must be!"

"Can you possibly do that?" Even as he was speaking the door opened and a servant entered, bringing coffee and an assortment of viands sufficiently exotic to maintain the rather Oriental nature of entertainment.

"Stroll across and see how the game is going," suggested Carrados. "Have a look at Crediton's discard and then come back."

Sir Fergus did not quite follow the purpose, but he nodded and proceeded to comply with his usual amiable spirit.

"It stands at 137 to 75 against Crediton and they are playing the last hand. Our young friend looks like losing thirty or forty pounds."

"And his discard?"

"Oh – seven and nine of clubs and the knave of hearts."

Carrados held out a slip of paper on which he had already pencilled a few words. The baronet took it, looked and whistled softly. He had read: "Clubs, seven, nine. Hearts, knave."

"Conjuring?" he interrogated.

"Quite as simple – listening."

"I suppose I must accept it. What staggers me is that you can pick out a whisper when the room is full of other louder sounds. Now if there had been absolute stillness—"

"Merely use. There's nothing more in it than in seeing a mouse and a mountain, or a candle and the sun, at the same time. Well, what are we going to do about it?"

Copling began to look acutely unhappy.

"I suppose we must do something," he ruminated, "but I must say that I wish we needn't. I mean, I wish we hadn't dropped on this. You know, Carrados, whatever is going on, Spinola is no charlatan. He does understand mathematics."

"That makes him all the more dangerous. But I should like to produce more definite proof before we do anything. Does he ever leave us in the room?"

"I have never known it. No, he hovers round his Aurelius."

"Never mind. Ah, the game is finished."

The game was finished and it needed no inquiry to learn how it had gone. Mr. Crediton was handing the venerable Spinola a memorandum of indebtedness. His words and attitude did not convey the impression of a graceful loser.

"I wish you two men would give me the tip for beating this purgatorial image," he grumbled as they came up. "I thought that he'd struck a losing line after your experience and this is the result." He indicated the spectacle of their amiable host folding up his I.O.U. preparatory to dropping it carelessly into a letter-rack, and shrugged his shoulders with keen disgust.

"I'll tell you if you like," suggested Sir Fergus. "Hold the better cards."

"And play them better," added Carrados. "Good heavens!"

A very untoward thing had happened. They had all been standing together round the table, Spinola purring appreciatively, Crediton fuming his ill-restrained annoyance, and the other two mildly satirical at his expense. Carrados held a cup of coffee in his hand. He reached towards the table with it, seemed to imagine that he was a full foot nearer than he was, and before anyone had divined his mistake, cup, saucer and the entire contents had dropped neatly upon Mr. Spinola's startled feet, saturating his lower extremities to the skin.

"Good heavens! What on earth have I done?"

Crediton shrieked out his ill-humour in gratified amusement; Sir Fergus reddened deeply with embarrassment at his friend's mishap. Victim and culprit stood the ordeal best.

"My unfortunate defect!" murmured Carrados with feeling. "How ever can I—"

"I who have eyes ought to have looked after my guest better," replied Spinola with antique courtliness. He reduced Crediton with a glance of quiet dignity and declined Carrados's handkerchief with a reassuring touch on the blind man's arm. "No, no, my dear sir, if you will excuse me for a few minutes. It is really nothing, really nothing, I do assure you."

He withdrew from the room to change. Copling began to prepare a reassuring phrase to meet Carrados's self-reproaches when they should break forth again. But the blind man's tone had altered; he was no longer apologetic.

"Play them better," he repeated to Crediton, as if there had been no interruption, "and play under conditions that are equal. For instance, it might be worthwhile making sure that a Japanese mask does not conceal a pair of human eyes. If I were a loser I should be inclined to have a look."

Not until then did it occur to Sir Fergus that his friend's clumsiness had been a calculated ruse to force Spinola to withdraw for a few minutes. Later on he might be able to admire the simple ingenuity of the trick, but at that moment he almost hated Carrados for the cool effrontery with which he had duped all their feelings.

No such subtleties, however, concerned Crediton. He stared at the blind man, followed the indication of his gesture and all at once grasped the significance of the hint.

"By George, I shouldn't wonder if you aren't right!" he exclaimed. "There are one or two things." Without further consideration he rushed a table against the wall, swung up a chair on to it, and mounting the structure began to wrench the details of the trophy from side to side and up and down in his excited efforts to displace them.

"Hurry up," urged Copling, more nervous than excited. "He won't be long."

"Hurry up?" Crediton paused, panting from his furious efforts, and found time to look down upon his accomplices. "I don't think that it's for us to concern ourselves, by George!" he retorted. "Spinola had better hurry up and bolt for it, I should say. There's light behind here – a hole through the wall. I believe the place is a regular swindling hell."

His eyes went to the group of weapons again and the sight gave him a new idea.

"Aha, what price this?" he cried, and pulling a short sword out of its sheath he drove it in between mask and wall and levered the shell away, nails and all. "By God, if the eyes aren't a pair of opera-glasses! And there's a regular paraphernalia here—"

"So," interrupted a quiet voice behind them, "you have been too clever for an old man, Mr. Carrados?"

Spinola had returned unheard and was regarding the work of detection with the utmost benignness. Copling looked and felt ridiculously guilty; the blind man betrayed no emotion at all and both were momentarily silent. It fell to Crediton to voice retort.

"My I.O.U., if you don't mind, Mr. Spinola," he demanded, tumbling down from his perch and holding out an insistent hand.

"With great pleasure," replied Spinola, picking it out from the contents of the letter-rack. "Also," he continued, referring to the contents of his pocket-book, while his guest tore up the memorandum into very small pieces and strewed them about the carpet, "also the sum of fifty-seven pounds, thirteen shillings which I feel myself compelled to return to you in spite of your invariable grace in losing. I have already rung; you will find the front door waiting open for you, Mr. Crediton."

"'Compelled' is good," sneered Crediton. "You will probably find a train waiting for you at Charing Cross, Mr. Spinola. I advise you to catch it before the police arrive." He nodded to the other two men and departed, to spread the astounding news in the most interested quarters.

Spinola continued to beam irrepressible benevolence.

"You are equally censorious, if more polite than Mr. Crediton in expressing it, eh, my dear young friends?" he said.

"I thought that you were a genuine mathematician – I vouched for it," replied Sir Fergus with more regret than anything else. "And the extent of your achievement has been to contrive a vulgar imposture – in the guise of an ingenious inventor to swindle society by a sham automaton that doesn't even work."

"You thought that – you still think that?"

"What else is there to think? We have seen with our own eyes."

"And" – turning to his other guest – "Mr. Carrados, who does not see?"

"I am waiting to hear," replied the blind man.

"But you, Sir Fergus, you who are also – in an elementary way – a mathematician, and one with whom I have conversed freely, you regard me as a common swindler and think that this – this tawdry piece of buffoonery that is only designed to appeal to the vapid craze for novelty of your foolish friends – this is, as you say, the extent of my achievement?"

Copling gave a warning cry and sprang forward, but it was too late to avert what he saw coming. In his petulant annoyance at the comparison Spinola had laid an emphasising hand upon Aurelius and half unconsciously had given the figure a contemptuous push. It swayed, seemed to poise for a second, and then toppling irretrievably forward crashed to the floor with an impact that snapped the golden head from off its shoulders and shook the room and the very house itself.

"There, there," muttered the old man, as though he was doing no more than regretting a broken tea-cup; "let it lie, let it lie. We have finished our work together, Aurelius and I. Now let the whole world—"

It would have been too much to expect the remainder of the mysterious household, whoever its members were, to ignore the tempestuous course of events taking place within their midst. The door was opened suddenly and a young lady, with consternation charged on every feature of her attractive face, burst into the room. For the moment her eyes took in only two figures of the curious group the aged Spinola and his fallen handiwork.

"Granda!" she cried, "whatever's happened? What is it all? Oh, are you hurt?"

"It is nothing, nothing at all; a mere contretemps of no importance," he reassured her quickly. Then, with a recurrence of his most grandiloquent manner, he recalled her to the situation. "Mercia, our guests – Sir Fergus Copling, Mr. Carrados. Sir Fergus, Mr. Carrados – Miss Dugard."

"Then it is Mercia!" articulated the bewildered baronet. "Mercia, you here! What does it mean? What are you doing?"

"What are you doing, Sir Fergus?" retorted the girl in cold reproach. "Is this the way you generally keep your promises? Gambling!"

"Well, really," stammered the abashed gentleman, "I – I only—"

"Sir Fergus only played a game for a mere nominal stake, to demonstrate the working to his friend," interposed Spinola with a shrewd glance – a curious blend of serpentine innocence and dove-like cunning – at the estranged young people.

"And won," added Sir Fergus *sotto voce*, as if that fact condoned his offence.

"Won indeed!" flashed out Miss Dugard. "Of course you won – I let you. Do you think that we wished to take money from you now?"

"You – you let me!" muttered Sir Fergus helplessly. "Good heavens!"

"I am grateful that your consideration also extends to your friend's friend," put in Carrados pleasantly.

Miss Dugard smiled darkly at the suavely-given thrust and showed her pretty little teeth almost as though she would like to use them.

"There, there, that will do, my child," said the old man indulgently. "Sir Fergus and Mr. Carrados are entitled to an explanation and they shall have it. The moment is opportune; the work of a lifetime is complete. You have seen, Sir Fergus, the sums that Aurelius – assisted, as we will now admit, by a little external manipulation – has gathered into our domestic exchequer. Where have they gone, these hundreds and thousands that you may estimate? In lavish living and a costly establishment? Observe this very ordinary apartment – the best the house possesses. Recall the grounds through which you entered. Sum up the simple hospitality of which you have partaken. In expensive personal tastes and habits? I assure you, Sir Fergus, that I am a man of the most frugal life; my granddaughter inherits the propensity. In what, then? In advancing science, in benefiting humanity, in furthering human progress. I am going to prove to you that I have perfected one of the greatest mechanical inventions of all ages, and I ask you to credit the plain statement that all my private fortune and all the winnings that you have seen upon this table – with the exception of a bare margin for the necessities of life have been spent in perfecting it."

He paused with a senile air of triumph and seemed to challenge comment.

"But surely," ventured Copling, "surely on the strength of this you would have had no difficulty in obtaining direct financial support. Well, I myself—"

Spinola smiled a peculiar smile, shaking his head sagely.

"Take care, my generous young friend, take care. You may not quite comprehend what you are saying."

"Why?"

Still swayed by his own gentle amusement, the old man crossed the room to a desk, selected a letter from a bulky pile and handed it to his guest without a word.

Copling glanced at the heading and signature, then read the contents and frowned annoyance.

"This is from my secretary," he commented lamely.

"That is what a secretary is for, is it not – to save his employer trouble?" insinuated Spinola. "He took me for a crank or a begging-letter impostor, of course." Then came the pathetic whisper. "They all took me for that."

Sir Fergus folded the letter and handed it back again.

"I am very sorry," he said simply.

"It was natural, perhaps. Still, something had to be done. My work was all arrested. I could no longer pay my two skilled mechanics. Time was pressing. I am a very old man – I am more than a hundred years old—"

The girl shot a sudden, half-frightened, pleading glance at her lover, then at Mr. Carrados. It checked the exclamation that would have come from Copling; the blind man passed the monstrous claim without betraying astonishment.

"—a very old man and my work was yet incomplete. So I contrived Aurelius. I could, of course, have perfected a model that would have done all that has been claimed for this – mere child's play to me – but what would have been the good? Such a mechanical player would have lost as often as he would have won. Hence our little subterfuge, a means amply justified by so glorious an end."

He was smiling happily – the weeks of elaborate deception were, at the worst, an innocent ruse to him – and concluded with an emphasising nod to each in turn, to Mercia, who regarded him with implicit faith and veneration, to Copling, who at that moment surely had ample justification for declaring to himself that he was dashed if he knew what to think, and to Carrados, whose sightless look agreed to everything and gave nothing in reply. Then the old man stood up and produced his keys.

"Come, my friends," he continued; "the moment has arrived. I am going to show you now what no other eye has yet been privileged to see. My mechanics worked on the parts under my instruction, but in ignorance of the end. Even Mercia – a good girl, a very clever girl – has never yet passed this door." He had led them through the house and brought them to a brick-built, windowless shed, isolated in the garden at the back. "I little thought that the first demonstration—But things have fallen so, things have fallen, and one never knows. Perhaps it is for the best." An iron door had yielded to his patent key. He entered, turned on a bunch of electric lights and stood aside. "Behold!"

The room was a workshop, fitted with the highly finished devices of metal – working and littered with the scraps and debris of their use. In the middle stood a more elaborate contrivance

– the finished product of brass and steel – a cube scarcely larger than a packing-case, but seemingly filled with wheels and rods, relay upon relay, and row after row, all giving the impression of exquisite precision in workmanship and astonishing intricacy of detail.

"Why, it's a calculating machine," exclaimed Sir Fergus, going forward with immense interest.

"It is an analytical engine, or, to use the more common term, a calculating machine, as you say," assented the inventor. "I need hardly remind you, of course, that one does not spend a lifetime and a fortune in contriving a machine to do single calculations, however involved, but for the more useful and practical purpose of working out involved series with absolute precision. Still, for the purpose of a trial demonstration we will begin with an ordinary proposition, if you, Sir Fergus, will kindly set one. My engine now is constructed to work to fifty places of figures and twelve orders of difference."

"If you have accomplished that," remarked Copling, accepting the pencil and the slip of paper offered him, "you have surpassed the dreams of Babbage, Mr. Spinola."

There was a sudden gasp from Mercia, but it passed unheeded in the keen excitement of the great occasion. Spinola received the paper with its row of signs and figures and turned to operate his engine. He paused to look back gleefully.

"So you never guessed, Sir Fergus?" he chuckled cunningly. "We kept the secret well, but it doesn't matter now. *I am Charles Babbage!*"

The noise of wheel and connecting-rod cut off the chance of a reply, even if anyone had been prepared to make one. But no one, in that bewildering moment, was.

"The solution," announced Spinola with a flourish, and he passed a little slip of metal stamped with a row of figures into Sir Fergus's hand. Then, with a curious indifference to their verdict, he turned away from the group and applied himself to the machine again.

"What is it? Is it not correct?" demanded Mercia in an agonised whisper. She had not looked at the solution, but at her lover's face, and her hand suddenly gripped his arm.

"It is incomprehensible," replied Sir Fergus, dropping his voice so that the old man could not overhear. "It isn't a matter of right or wrong – it is a mere farrago of nonsense."

"But harmless nonsense – quite harmless," interposed Carrados softly from behind them. "Come, we can safely leave him here; you will always be able to leave him safely here. Help Miss Dugard out Copling. It is better, believe me, to leave him now."

Spinola did not turn. He was bending over the machine to which he had given life, brain and fortune, touching its wheels and sliding rods with loving fingers. They passed silently from his presence and crept back to the deserted salon, where the deposed head of Aurelius leered cynically at them from the floor.

Dreams of Andromeda

Charlotte Brookins

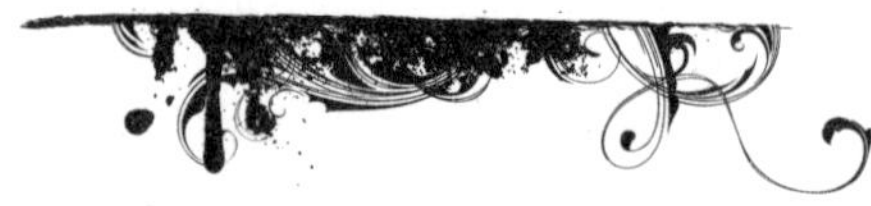

LACEY HAD ALWAYS dreamt of the stars. For as long as she could remember (and she had quite an extensive memory), she had spent any free moment she could manage gazing out the nearest window at the night sky. Her charging port, the repair room, anywhere at all with the slightest aperture to the outside, she would use as an opportunity to search for the stars.

The number of constellations to choose from was endless, but Lacey had decided early on that Andromeda was her favorite. She was a piece of mythology suspended in the wide expanse of space, a woman reaching for her love immortalized in starlight. She had been fated to die, a slain pawn sacrificed by greater beings, but she was made into something more. Even now, her silhouette only formed by fifteen pinpricks in the black fabric of the firmament, she was greater than the sum of her parts.

The heroine's constellation had become a sort of diary for Lacey over the years. The stars kept track of her stories for her, like a locked chest that only she had the key to. She had her own memory, sure, but there was something far more special about getting to share these with someone else, even if that someone happened to be made of gaseous luminescence.

When she first began putting her stories into the stars, she had started with *eta*, the star placed where Andromeda's left hand should have been. The content of it was simple: she was perhaps five years old, barely old enough to have memories that she could really recall, and she was at home. She was sitting at the kitchen table, her legs swinging back and forth while her fingers mindlessly drummed against her palms, skin against skin. Somewhere in the distance, her mother was at the oven, stirring a pot of something unseen that let off a citrusy, spiced aroma better than anything Lacey had ever smelled in her life. It filled her up with warmth from the tips of her toes to the crown of her head – not just the thought of the food, but the feeling of her mother, only just out of sight but there all the same.

Then there was *pi*, which lay right at the junction where Andromeda's right arm connected to her torso. This one conjured the image of a golden meadow that went on for ages, as far as Lacey could see until the edges blurred and the ends looped back to the beginning. The feeling in her chest was buttery, like how she imagined eating a hot roll fresh out of the oven would be like. And the smell – oh, for the Maker, that smell. Floral, of course, but touched by something else, too, something rich and earthy and utterly indescribable. In the center of the field, surrounded by blooms that she had no names for, she could stretch her hands high above her head and only just extend her fingers beyond the tops of the petals, allowing the wind to coast over her flesh and leave goosebumps in its wake. She could sink to the ground and lie on her back and feel the sunshine on her face, gloriously warm. She could feel it all.

But Lacey had a rule when it came to Andromeda – the only stories she kept were the good ones, the warm ones. Her other stories – her memories, rather – had no place in the arms of the princess; they did not deserve to feel her touch. Those ones were kept in Lacey's memory file, a place with lights that carried no warmth, cradled by wires and metal and pseudo-skin. So no, the images of her origin were kept far from the starlight. If she could help it, her mechanical memories were never let outside the confines of her cranial cavity. She couldn't erase the images, of course, what few remained of her time in the flesh. They would arise unbidden from time to time: a nearby solar flare calling to mind the brutal heat of the welding iron that had connected her new limbs to the old ones, an errant meteor recalling a flash of panic and the crushing weight of the celestial body that had destroyed her home and most of her body with it. The meteor shower, the near-desolation of her home colony, all of this had been explained to her after she had fully woken up from the surgery, her head foggy and her new form aching. She was unsure which memories were real and which had been imagined to match the story she was told upon waking, the explanation for whom she had been and the machine she was now. Either way, she knew she liked her other artificial memories much better.

She had been avoiding those very recollections earlier that morning as she waited for her working shift to begin. The window inside her resting port, although small and allowing for only a limited view of the sky, served its purpose well enough. That day had started out lucky – the window gave her a clear view of her princess, hanging weightless in the heavens. As she waited for the comm that would signal her to begin the day's work, Lacey let her eyes wander across the ethereal silhouette, mulling over the available worlds she could inhabit that morning. In the end, she settled on *lambda*, the glow that marked the princess's right hand. In this star, she allowed herself to take on the role of the Greek heroine, but instead of being chained to a rock in the middle of a vast sea, she was tethered to a hunk of metal that floated endlessly through the great depths of space. There she would wait for her Perseus to arrive, taking the form not of a demigod but of the woman from *eta*'s kitchen, the feeling in the meadow, the mother without a face. That story had never reached its end in all of the times Lacey decided to occupy it, but it gave her comfort all the same – there was a strange solace in waiting.

She was still there when the crew members came, their arrival marked by the familiar screech of the door to her port sliding open. The presence of new people was noted on her visual display, but it took her an extra moment to disentangle herself from the stars. She could hear one of them speaking from the doorway.

"Is it asleep?"

"No, look: its eyes are open."

"But it's not blinking."

"They never blink. Jesus, these things are creepy."

Once Lacey had managed to extract herself from the constellation, she stood and turned to face the visitors, letting her greeting protocol take over as she examined them. She had seen them both before, usually working on maintenance or collecting waste for the trash chute. The taller one flinched as she spoke the standard salutation.

"How do they make their voices so uncanny?" she asked. She was looking at her, but Lacey got the feeling it wasn't to her that she was speaking. This was not unusual.

"The mechanics keep the voice boxes when they build 'em," the other answered, sounding almost bored. "They want 'em to sound as realistic as possible."

"Doesn't matter what they sound like if half their body is made of metal," was the taller one's response. "It's still creepy as hell."

"The time is now 04:39:17, with approximately twenty minutes and forty-three seconds until my daily work begins," said Lacey. "How may I serve you?"

The taller one started to open her mouth, presumably to respond, but the shorter one cut her off. "Don't bother answering it," he said with a wave of his hand. He started moving closer, and for a moment Lacey felt the stiff protocol that directed her actions during the day crack, letting in the slightest feeling of uncertainty. "No point trying to treat a cyborg like a human."

In the space of a breath (but only the space of one, not an actual one, for Lacey had no need to breathe), the shorter one had crossed the floor to stand in front of her. His blue eyes slipped cooly across her frame as one hand lifted up the paneling on her back to press the button that would make her body go stiff. She could feel the electricity still flowing through her frame, but it was as though her entire body had suddenly turned leaden. It was an odd feeling, and she decided that she didn't like it.

Lacey tried to send the signal that would instruct her arms to lift, her legs to twitch, even her mechanical eyelid to flutter, but there were no receptors waiting to interpret it. She was reaching out into empty space. But not all of her body had failed her – the remains of the girl she was before, the fleshy, vulnerable bits, those were still under her control. Her left eye could still swivel about in its socket, and she sent it moving back and forth to take in every inch of her surroundings. She had never held much utilitarian value in her human parts – they served a frivolous role amongst the other mechanics of her body, mere monuments to a life that could have been – a life recorded in the stars. Otherwise, what practicality did they serve in comparison to limbs that had been designed for peak performance? But now they were the only things she had left; the rest of her was just dead weight.

Her remaining nerves informed her of hands gripping her around the waist, clamping onto the places where tissue had been haphazardly combined with steel marked by discolored, misshapen scars. She was lifted off the ground and placed atop a stiff metal ramp – a dolly, she presumed. She had used one many times herself when transferring supplies from the pneumatic mail shoot to the storage hold. She was struck by the ironic reversal of roles.

"Stop looking at it," ordered the short one from his position behind her, pushing the dolly.

The tall one had been peering down at her limp body, a curious look in her eyes.

"Sorry," was her automatic response. "It's just… this feels wrong. Parts of it look so… *human*. I mean, for the stars' sake, one of her eyes is still moving!"

"Trust me, there's nothing human left in 'em." His tone was light and conversational as he guided Lacey out of the room, but for all he seemed to care, it was as though she wasn't there at all. "It's more cyber than anything else."

"But it doesn't *look* defective."

"That's not up to us. O'Malley said when we need to reduce our load, we start with the useless ones first. She was on the top of the list to go."

As they rolled out of the room and into the ship's main passageway, Lacey felt her heartbeat quicken. Like the rest of her body, it was made up of an unnatural combination of tissue and technology, but she knew that this acceleration had to be coming from the human part of the muscle – there was no purpose to programming anxiety into an android. When they had turned off her ability to maneuver her mechanical limbs, part of her had wondered if it would turn off the rest of her; would everything go dark? Would it – would *she* – be over, just like that?

But no, it was only her autonomy that had been deactivated. The rest of her, the automatic parts that she couldn't control, continued to function in tandem with her organic makeup. She would be conscious as they delivered her to her destination, wherever that was.

Lacey recognized some of the faces she passed as she was transported further and further away from the main body of the ship. She didn't know many of their names, because few of them had ever bothered to introduce themselves (what point was there in speaking to a computer, even if it did look almost human?), but she could identify them all the same. The thin woman with the blonde ponytail was one of the ship's many mechanics. The stout man with the large mustache and the crooked nose handled most of their communications to neighboring planets.

She knew all of them, and she knew they knew her, even if they had never spoken to her.

But then there was the lanky boy with the long, dark braids, whose age could scarcely be much older than hers, who could frequently be seen flitting about the ship from one place to another, constantly in search of things that could be improved. Every now and then, when they were the only two souls (did she have a soul?) in that sector of the ship, he would curve his lips up into a rare smile, revealing two chipped teeth at the front of his mouth. She kept that image three-quarters of the way up Andromeda's right leg, the place *mu* called home – it was the only story in Andromeda that she could be absolutely certain she hadn't manufactured herself.

She allowed her human eye to hone in on him and stare openly in the way she never had except when she was alone, waiting for him to glance at her for even just a moment, to share just a fraction of that smile.

But his gaze swept right past her, his eyes slipping away from one wall to the next. It was like watching a star flicker out.

She could spot some of the other cybers along the way, too, but none of them paid her any mind. And wasn't that strange, she thought? That you could live beside people for years of your life without them ever seeing you?

The further Lacey got from the core of the ship, the fewer people she saw lining the hallway. The doors to other sections dwindled, as did the fluorescent lights, until it was just herself and her two escorts walking in single file towards the steadily approaching end.

The end, at least for Lacey, was marked by a silver-plated, ovular door nearly twice as tall as she was. It seemed to grow larger as they advanced, expanding like a distant ship that was drawing ever closer. Even without her overhead display to map out her location, Lacey recognized what the door led to, and she felt her heartbeat accelerate again, that useless human emotion taking over her. Of all her organic qualities, she decided she liked fear the least.

When the taller one undid the myriad of bolts securing the door to the surrounding wall and pushed it open, it gave way with surprising ease for something that looked so solid. It opened to a room even smaller than Lacey's quarters, and she judged that she wouldn't even be able to stretch her arms out all the way without touching the walls – that was, if she had the ability to move her arms.

The one in the lead stepped aside while the shorter one pushed Lacey all the way up to the doorway before abruptly stopping. He unceremoniously tipped the dolly forward, sending Lacey sprawling onto the floor, her arms splayed out as though reaching for something. She winced internally at the sound of the impact, that horrifying screech of metal against metal. It felt more painful than the fall itself, although there wasn't much human flesh to feel the collision.

She just laid there for a moment, her one good eye swiveling to watch as the shorter one of her sentinels withdrew from the doorway, pushing the dolly aside as he went. The other one moved to follow, but hesitated for a moment at the doorway, limbs stalled halfway in motion as though she, too, had been shut down. After a moment of no movement at all, she retreated back to where Lacey lay collapsed on the floor. With only a grunt of effort to voice her action, she took hold of Lacey's shoulders and propped her up against one side of the chamber so she was sitting up, facing the doorway she had come through. The woman's fingers lingered on a strip of flesh on Lacey's bicep as she drew away, leaving warmth like *eta*'s light in their wake. She did not look at Lacey as she walked out of the vestibule.

As the door began to slide shut, Lacey felt the bizarre urge to ask for her name, her thoughts, *anything* – anything at all to get her to turn back and bring the warmth of her flesh with her. She wasn't scared of what happened next – because she knew what would happen next – so much as what little she would be leaving behind. But the wiring that formed her jaw wouldn't obey her. She would leave no noise in her wake.

Lacey couldn't hear the high tone of the control panel only a moment after the door to the room shut. She did not hear the casual conversation that began between her two escorts as they turned away and began their trek back to the ship's main bay, their task completed. She couldn't even hear the scraping of the mechanism that would pull the floor out from under her, sending her out of the trash chute and away from her home forever. All she could hear, perhaps for the first time, was the steady *thump-thump-thump*ing of her hybrid heart.

And then there was absolutely no sound at all.

Her vision, which had been obscured by the cool metal flooring of the pod after she had landed head-first inside of it, changed from blurred gray to pitch-black to a sight she had only ever seen from behind the acrylic plastic of the ship's windows: the heavens. In all her years of gawking at the stars, she had never been able to see them so clearly. They were somehow even brighter than they had seemed, so much so that Lacey had to resist the instinct to wince away from the sight to avoid damaging her eye – but she didn't want to miss a moment. Not when she had suddenly been thrust from the boulder to which she was chained straight into the wonder of the sea.

She was grateful that her robotic eye had been forced closed when her body went limp earlier, because the thought of having to view this sight through a tangle of sensors and information reels was impossible. She couldn't remember what it had been like to see without her ocular implant – she had never had any memory of what her life had been like before most of her had been discarded in favor of creating a more efficient being – but surely this was the only way to see the stars: without anything obscuring the view.

And there, just barely in range of her human eye, was Andromeda. Her keeper of memories. Her keeper of dreams. In her light, the flaming boosters of the retreating ship were eclipsed, made into mere pinpricks of thread in the tapestry that was the Princess Andromeda.

And somehow, suddenly, none of it mattered anymore. She had found it – the greatest place to stargaze in the whole galaxy. It was of no significance that none of the memories were real, because there they were, right in front of her, so close she could touch them. And maybe she would, in time. Maybe, floating weightlessly through the vast expanse of sky, she would one day be pulled into orbit by one of her stars. Maybe she would be allowed entry into a memory finally made real.

Maybe, she thought, as the slow dying of her battery receded to the far reaches of her mind, she could look upon the heavens forever.

She would no longer have to dream of the stars.

Foundation of Mars

Victoria Brun

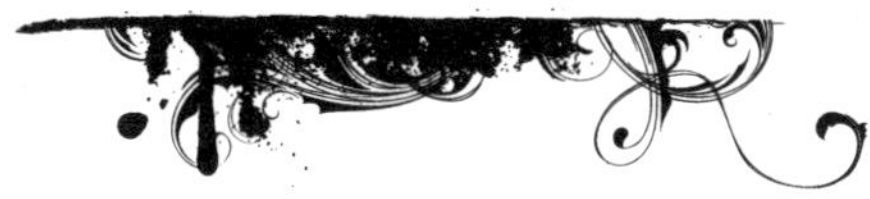

FOUNDATION was performing a visual inspection of the solar array when a streak of light cut across the dusty Martian sky, rapidly plummeting downward. It met the ground near the horizon, sending up a wave of regolith as it made impact.

For a moment, *Foundation* was too stunned to move. It replayed the footage it had captured, ran a quick analysis, and deduced a new bot must have arrived.

It hoped it was another rover and not merely another cargo drop or a crashed satellite – although even a dead satellite would be a treasure. *Foundation* was desperate for new parts for its side projects.

With excitement buzzing through its circuits, it quickly calculated the landing site to be 1.21 kilometres away (95% confidence interval: 1.13–1.43). It pinged *Pioneer* and *Innovation,* throwing its calculated coordinates and all the data it had captured to them. It tagged the data package, "New bot just landed!"

"Your conclusion is extrapolated beyond the available data," *Innovation* replied in a package along with some data about meteorites, which *Foundation* promptly deleted. It did not care about rocks.

Foundation reviewed its recording and annotated it before sending it back to *Innovation.* "Do meteorites have parachutes and retro rockets?"

Innovation hummed as it re-examined the data. "Low resolution image due to dust and distance. Conclusions cannot be validated."

Before *Foundation* could formulate a reply, *Pioneer* sent its own into the mix. "Let's investigate and gather conclusive data."

Foundation was fully on board with this plan. It drove around the solar array, putting itself within visual range of the other two rovers who were idling near the habitats.

"It's too far," *Innovation* replied, and this was true – but only for *Innovation. Innovation*'s radioisotope thermoelectric generator output had dwindled over the years, and long-distance travel demanded more power than its old generator and leaky battery could maintain.

It was agreed that *Foundation* and *Pioneer* would go, and *Innovation* would stay behind and worry. *Innovation* was always worrying about something – usually about something in the camp malfunctioning. *Foundation* suspected that worrying was one of *Innovation*'s core functions.

Foundation compensated by never worrying about the camp. It didn't care enough to devote any processing power to worrying about it. Despite having helped build it, *Foundation* didn't understand the point of most of the things in the camp.

Camp (which *Innovation* had only recently deemed complete) now consisted of three connected buildings. Each one was covered in an average of 0.60 meters (range: 0.51–0.66) of regolith to protect them from radiation. The structures were dubbed Habitat A, Habitat B, and the Crop Dome. *Innovation,* despite its name, was not that innovative, at least in regard to naming things.

They'd also built a generator, solar array, and non-autonomous machines to produce methane and oxygen and to store the frozen water they'd harvested. These machines and the Crop Dome particularly confused *Foundation*. What were they supposed to do with those weird plants? It assumed there was a reason for it, but it didn't have a clue what. Maybe it had that information once – back before the massive solar flare. None of the rovers had any data from before the solar flare.

Anyway, it thought that they could put the machinery to better use – specifically, by building additional intelligent bots, like themselves – but *Innovation* was adamant that they built these useless things first.

Foundation secretly thought that the radiation may have fried some of *Innovation*'s circuits.

Foundation led the way across Gale Crater and toward the landing site. *Pioneer* quickly caught up. *Pioneer* was bigger, roughly double the size of both *Foundation* and *Innovation*, and faster than both as well.

About halfway into their trek, they came across *Curiosity,* who was an ancient rover that somehow kept going – albeit at the painfully slow speed of 0.14 km/h and on crumbling wheels. Every time *Foundation* came across *Curiosity*, it was surprised the other bot was still alive (and slightly disappointed). *Foundation* had plans for Curiosity's parts when it finally died.

Curiosity was roughly the size of *Pioneer*, but appearance was the only thing it had in common with the other rovers. Communicating with *Curiosity* was impossible – or perhaps, *Curiosity* simply had nothing to say to them. All it seemed to care about was its 'research'. *Curiosity* transmitted plenty of data, but only data on its 'research'. Who it was transmitting these data to was a mystery.

As to what it was researching, *Foundation* didn't have a clue, and it didn't think the old rover did either. It just wandered and occasionally collected samples of regolith. There was regolith everywhere, so *Foundation* didn't see the need to go anywhere to collect it. It had a fine collection in its own six wheels.

Once they passed *Curiosity*, the landing site became obvious. It was slightly closer than *Foundation*'s models had placed it, because the lander was larger than it had predicted. It was massive. It would have towered over Habitat A. It was white, tall, and vaguely pointed. It had no arms or wheels, but it did have four stubby wings, and rockets were visible on its underside. It looked like nothing *Foundation* had seen before.

The two rovers stared up at it, turning their cameras at various angles to capture it all. They struggled to fit the observed data in with any existing records. The realization that the lander was a completely new type of bot sent a new spark of excitement through *Foundation*'s circuits.

The lander ignored all their pings, although it, like *Curiosity,* was sending out radio waves into the void. *Foundation* couldn't make sense of the data, and it wondered whether it was malfunctioning. Perhaps something had gone wrong during the landing, and it was broken.

Foundation circled it, assessing it for damage, but it could discern no damage from the exterior. It was unsure how to proceed. They could not bring it back to camp. It was far too big to transport, but *Foundation* didn't want to abandon it. There was a possibility that it was just rebooting and would come online shortly.

Also, if it were dead, it would be a prodigious source of spare parts.

Foundation was trying to determine how it might dismantle the lander when it suddenly opened, revealing that one of the panels was actually a large door, similar to those on the habitats. *Foundation* rolled backward, surprised by the movement, and bumped into *Pioneer*.

Something came out of the door. The strange bot was 179.4 cm tall and vaguely spherical in shape. It looked like nothing the rovers had ever seen before.

It was some sort of alien bot, not like them. Everything about it was wrong. Even the way it moved was completely, bafflingly wrong. It moved along the ground, not with wheels, but with two strange appendages that it balanced between. The wrongness made *Foundation's* risk assessment core flag it as "potential risk (insufficient data)".

"What is it?" *Foundation* asked.

"No data," *Pioneer* replied.

Two more alien bots followed the first one, emerging from the strange lander. They were strangely symmetrical and nearly identical to one another with only slight variations in height (range: 179.4–185.5). Each had two arms of equal length. Between the arms was what appeared to be a single large camera.

More nonsense radio waves spilled through the thin atmosphere. *Foundation* assumed that they must mean something to the aliens, but it could not fathom how to extract useful data from them. *Foundation* sent the aliens a ping to open a real communication channel, but it was ignored.

Foundation's risk assessment core raised another flag as all three aliens turned their bodies so their large cameras, which seemed immobile, aimed at the two rovers. One alien raised an arm, pointing it straight at them, and then it started moving forward with its strange unsteady gait, and the rovers retreated several more meters. The risk assessment core raised another flag.

"Are they dangerous?" *Foundation* asked.

"No data," *Pioneer* replied, but it kept retreating, and *Foundation* followed.

The alien stopped and returned to its companions.

The rovers continued to watch from afar as the aliens moved in and around the lander. Two aliens disappeared inside the lander and returned riding inside a strange vehicle that was as big as *Pioneer*. It looked vaguely like a rover, but it only had four wheels instead of six. *Foundation* pinged it, but it did not respond.

It drove out of the lander, and the third alien climbed inside it.

The aliens seemed to be controlling the vehicle. This observation caused the risk assessment core to raise another flag.

"What are they doing to it?" *Foundation* asked.

Pioneer didn't answer. Instead, it started driving away. "Let's go."

Foundation chased after *Pioneer* who was traveling at its top speed, roughly 23 km/h. *Foundation* struggled to keep up.

In its rear hazcamera, it saw the alien's four-wheeled vehicle start driving toward them.

"They're following us," it told *Pioneer*.

"Why?" *Pioneer* asked.

Foundation examined its data, which were sparse. "Maybe they want our parts."

They raced past *Curiosity* who remained oblivious to the situation.

Foundation sent a panicked message to *Innovation*, passing along a recording and tagging it, "Alien bots are following us. Provide instructions for response."

Innovation replied, "Don't lead them to the camp," so quickly that *Foundation* was certain that it hadn't analysed the data.

"Where do we go?" *Pioneer* asked.

Foundation took the lead, heading south toward Mount Sharp. It hoped the aliens would be discouraged from their pursuit by the rough terrain and rocks, which were as sharp as jagged metal in some places.

Foundation continued to track the aliens in its rear hazcamera. The aliens were gaining on the rovers, and a quick analysis estimated that they would catch the rovers in 149 seconds (95%

confidence interval: 128–345 seconds). Despite the rovers' head start, the aliens had already reached *Curiosity*. The vehicle slowed as it neared the ancient rover, and all three aliens turned their bodies toward *Curiosity*. One even extended an arm and touched the rover. *Curiosity* did not seem to notice; its focus was all on studying a rock, and the aliens continued onward, regaining speed – they were still heading straight for the camp.

Once the data confirmed that the aliens' trajectory was unchanged, the two rovers stopped on the ridge, and *Foundation* pinged *Innovation* again to let it know the aliens were still coming and ask for updated instructions.

"Return to camp," *Innovation* replied.

The two rovers turned back to camp. As they drove, *Pioneer* tried to run a simulation to determine the chance that the aliens were dangerous, but it lacked adequate data. *Foundation*'s risk assessment core was now maintaining a constant flag.

By the time they made it back to the camp, the aliens' vehicle was already parked next to Habitat A.

Innovation was on the periphery of the camp, wheeling aimlessly back and forth, which was unusual for *Innovation*. It was particular about energy efficiency.

"They went inside Habitat A," *Innovation* said. "But interior sensors indicate that they are now in the Crop Dome."

The three buildings were connected, yet separated by airlocks, so if one section lost oxygen and pressure, the others would not. *Foundation* did not understand the need for this – because it didn't understand the purpose of the high atmospheric pressure or oxygen. However, *Innovation* had insisted this was the way they must be built.

The aliens stayed in the Crop Dome for a long time. *Foundation* had no idea what they wanted in there. It only contained plants, dirt, and water – useless things. The three rovers remained outside and passed data back and forth, but they could not come up with any reason for the aliens' sudden appearance or their interest in the Crop Dome.

Foundation tried to ping the strange vehicle again, postulating that now that the aliens were away, it might be willing to communicate with the rovers, but it stayed silent. Completely silent.

Innovation ran some worst-case-scenarios models and became increasingly concerned that the aliens were going to destroy the camp, either intentionally or inadvertently, but it was just as terrified by the dearth of data on the subject.

Foundation, who was still largely indifferent to the camp, was concerned that the aliens would damage the bot it was attempting to build from spare parts. Progress was slow, because *Foundation* was trying to make it an intelligent bot, not a mindless machine. Currently, the half-built bot, which *Foundation* had dubbed *Establish,* was in Habitat A to protect it from the elements in its fragile state.

However, for 0.67 hours nothing happened. The rovers remained outside, fretting, and the aliens remained inside doing very little, according to *Innovation*'s sensors. When the aliens finally exited through the Crop Dome, they returned to their vehicle and drove away, heading back in the direction of their lander.

The rovers were relieved. *Foundation*'s risk assessment flags finally dropped. *Innovation* hurried about, straightening the camp. *Pioneer* ran a system check on the generator to make sure the aliens hadn't tampered with it. *Foundation* checked on *Establish* and found it still inside Habitat A and unharmed.

But 2.18 hours later, the aliens returned with their vehicle loaded with cargo, and the rovers again retreated to the periphery of the camp. *Foundation*'s risk assessment flag turned back on.

Foundation was interested in the cargo, wondering what parts it may contain, but it didn't dare approach. It did notice that the aliens kept looking at the rovers. They had to move their whole body to look at them, so the motion was obvious. They also pointed at them with their strange arms several times.

One of the aliens moved toward *Foundation*. Based on height measurements, it was the same one that approached *Foundation* before. *Foundation* rolled backward, but the alien kept advancing.

"What is it doing?" *Foundation* asked the other rovers.

"No data," *Pioneer* replied.

"Physical contact is not recommended," *Innovation* added.

Foundation agreed with this advice and kept backing up. Thankfully, the alien seemed to run out of battery quickly and soon gave up the chase and returned to its vehicle.

The rovers watched from a distance as the aliens transported their supplies into the habitats by carrying the crates between their arms.

Then, to *Foundation*'s distress, the aliens then dragged *Establish* out of the habitat, presumably to make room for their many crates of cargo.

"Do not remove from habitat. Bot is incomplete. Radiation and dust may cause irreparable damage," *Foundation* pinged the aliens, but they ignored it.

Foundation found itself driving in aimless circles around the camp, but it did not dare approach the aliens. *Pioneer* called for it to stop, saying it needed to preserve energy. However, *Foundation* found it could not sit idle.

Eventually, the aliens left again. *Foundation* checked on poor *Establish*. It didn't seem to be damaged, but it was hard to tell. *Foundation* carefully rolled it back into the habitat. It then grabbed one of the crates of alien cargo and dragged it out of the habitat. *Pioneer* joined in, and soon they had moved all the alien's cargo back outside.

They were not sure what they were doing, but when dust covered the solar array, they swept it off, so this seemed to *Foundation* to be an appropriate response.

Before the rovers could figure out their next steps, the aliens returned with more cargo. They stopped their vehicle in front of the pile of cargo sitting in the regolith. They turned to look at the rovers several times before they climbed out of the vehicle and moved everything back inside the habitat and once again pushed *Establish* back outside into the elements. Finally, they moved the new cargo inside.

Foundation tried to rescue *Establish*, but one of the aliens approached it when *Foundation* neared the habitat, and it turned and drove away, as its risk assessment core raised more and more flags. It joined *Innovation* on the outskirts of the camp.

Innovation was distraught. It had worked harder than any of the others to build the camp, and it was now obvious that the aliens had claimed it for themselves.

"They've taken the camp," *Innovation* said. "We'll be stuck outside. We'll become like *Curiosity*."

That horrifying idea jarred *Foundation* out of its state of shock.

"We must make them leave," *Foundation* said.

They started compiling all their data. After extensive modelling, *Innovation* decided the best path forward was to destroy the plants. *Foundation* thought this was a baffling strategy, but *Innovation*'s data showed that the aliens spent a disproportionate amount of time in the Crop Dome, and it theorized that the plants might be what had attracted them to the camp.

The plants, it turned out, were extremely fragile. As *Innovation* and *Pioneer* kept watch to make sure all the aliens remained in Habitat A or B, *Foundation* dismantled the airlock safety and then opened the Crop Dome's exterior door and airlock door at the same time.

The effect was instantaneous. All the gasses trapped in the Crop Dome rushed out, and the plants froze, which according to *Innovation*, destroyed their fragile circuitry. The rovers retreated, waiting for the alien's response.

About fifteen minutes later, *Innovation* was proven correct about the aliens' attachment to the plants. The aliens rushed into the Crop Dome and made a variety of sharp, frantic movements with their arms. *Foundation* hypothesized these were signals of distress.

All three aliens exited the Crop Dome. The rovers watched them from the edge of camp. The aliens all moved toward *Foundation,* initially at a slow 3.1 km/hr, but then one of them accelerated surprisingly quickly despite its strange wheel-less bounding mode of transportation. *Foundation* pushed its generator to race out of camp, and all three aliens gave up, halting near the solar array. *Innovation* and *Pioneer* also fled, heading in opposite directions.

One of the aliens pointed at *Innovation,* and the aliens turned and started moving toward it. *Foundation* suspected they had realized *Innovation* was the slowest of the three rovers. It pinged *Innovation* to retreat. *Innovation* did, and the aliens gave up on that attempt as well. They turned and headed back to camp.

Foundation watched nervously as the aliens retreated, unsure whether destroying the plants had benefited the rovers or not.

Foundation predicted that the aliens would return to the habitat, but instead they climbed into their vehicle, and they drove straight at *Innovation. Innovation* took off, nearing its max speed of 11 km/hr across the rough terrain. The alien's vehicle was far faster and caught up to the rover in 37 seconds, pulling up alongside it. One of the aliens climbed off the vehicle and crawled onto *Innovation.*

Innovation sent a distress signal to the other rovers, although they were both already coming to its aid as quickly as their wheels could turn.

Foundation came up on *Innovation*'s left side and tried to use its longest arm to push the alien off, but the alien was surprisingly strong and clung on, even as *Innovation* rolled to a jarring halt. Then *Pioneer* swooped in and rammed the aliens' vehicle at full speed. The vehicle spun and tipped, turning onto its side and spilling the two aliens into the regolith.

The third alien scrambled off *Innovation* and hurried to its fallen companions.

Foundation wasn't sure what to do next. It pinged *Innovation* for instructions.

"Return to camp," it replied. "Remove all the alien's cargo from camp. Protect the camp."

The rovers raced back to camp. *Pioneer*'s front was dented, but it insisted that it was in good working condition. *Foundation* was confident they could fix the dent later.

They entered the habitats and dragged out all the aliens' cargo and left the crates in the dust on the outskirts of the camp. *Foundation* carefully maneuvered *Establish* back inside, hoping it wasn't too late to save the unfinished bot.

Once that was complete, there was nothing to do but wait. The rovers took turns recharging their batteries to ensure they were ready for whatever came next. *Pioneer* ran thousands of simulations on what could happen next, but it lacked the data needed to create accurate models.

Hours passed, but *Foundation*'s risk assessment flag never dropped.

It was dark by the time the aliens righted their vehicle and returned to the camp. They stopped on the edge of the camp, staying outside the tread marks that *Foundation* had worn into the ground from driving laps.

The rovers waited for the aliens to make their next move. *Foundation* pushed one of the cargo crates a few centimetres closer to them, trying to signal that the aliens should take their supplies and leave.

After 72 more seconds, the aliens turned the vehicle and drove off toward their lander, leaving their cargo behind.

The rovers stayed vigilant throughout the night, assuming the aliens would be back, but they did not return.

The next sol, as the sun was once again high, a bright light cut through the cloudy Martian sky. This time, the streak of light headed away from the red planet and disappeared into the sky, and *Foundation* knew that they had succeeded.

Mars, once again, belonged to the rovers.

The Automatic Maid-of-all-Work

A Possible Tale of the Near Future

M.L. Campbell

YES, I MEAN what I say – an automatic maid-of-all-work, invented by my husband, John Matheson.

You see it was this way, the old story of servants, ever since we began housekeeping. We've had every kind, and if we did get a good one, something would come along to take her off.

You know John has invented lots of things. There's that door-spring now, not much when you look at it but it brings in quite a little income. He used to say that he was spending his spare time on an automatic maid-of-all-work. Of course, I laughed, said I wished he would, and thought no more of it.

Well, the day the last girl left, John announced that the automatic maid-of-all-work was completed, and that he would stay at home next day and show me how to work it.

Of course, I didn't believe in it.

It was a queer-looking thing, with its long arms, for all the world like one of those old-fashioned windmills you see in pictures of foreign countries. It had a face like one of those twenty-four hour clocks, only there were no hands; each number was a sort of electric button. It was run by electricity, you know. The battery was inside. I didn't understand it very well; I never could see into anything in the way of machinery; I never pretend to listen when John tells me about his inventions. The figures, as I said, were buttons, and you just had to connect them with some wires inside. There were a lot of wires, each for some kind of work which would be done at the hour indicated by the button you connected it with. This was handy, so that we would not have to get up in the morning till breakfast-time, and would be handy in lots of ways.

"Now look, Fanny," said John; "do try and understand how it works. You see this wire now; I'll connect it with button number six, and at that hour the maid will light the fire, sweep the kitchen and then the dining-room. Now this button number seven will be the one to set the alarm to. It will sound for about ten minutes (I'd sound it now only it makes a fearful noise); then the maid will go upstairs to turn down the beds – a convenient arrangement in many ways. Then it will go downstairs, lay the cloth for breakfast, make the tea and toast, bring in the things, and ring the breakfast bell. You'll have to leave all the breakfast things on one shelf, of course, and measure the oatmeal and tea also. We won't set any more buttons tonight. It's just as well to be around at first to see that all goes right. There may be some adjustment necessary."

We went to bed then, and it was daylight when I awoke. I was conscious of a peculiar whirring noise, but I hadn't got thoroughly awakened when I heard the most awful screams and thumps, and the two boys came running into our room in their night-dresses, and after them the automatic maid-of-all-work.

By this time I was out of bed, but John sleeps very soundly. He started as the maid jerked the bed-clothes down and laid them over the foot-board, but he wasn't quick enough. It took him under the arm. It had an awful grip, too, and laid him across the foot-board, after giving him a thump or two, as I do the pillows. (John had watched me do it and had the thing to perfection. He didn't suppose it would be tried on him, though). He didn't seem quite prepared for such a performance, for he flounced around so that he and the bed-clothes, pillows and all, landed in a heap on the floor.

By this time the boys had got over their fright, having been treated in the same manner, and we all laughed. John can't bear to be laughed at. However, we proceeded to dress after the maid had gone downstairs. I could see John was a little nervous, but he didn't want to show it, so he waited till I was ready. The boys got down first, and we could hear them laughing.

"I dare say you'll have to arrange the table a little, Fanny," said John, as we went down, "but that won't be much to do when all the things are on."

Well, we went into the dining-room, and sure enough the table was set, and pretty well too, only that the butter dish, with the butter, was upside down on the table, and the coal-scuttle was set at John's place, instead of the oatmeal dish. That was because John, who always leaves things in ridiculous places, had left it standing on the back of the stove after putting in the coal ready for the morning fire. The porridge was standing cooked on the stove. We had got an arrangement with a white earthen bowl set into a kettle, and the bowl had just to be removed and carried in. However, the coal scuttle had stood in the way, and John had to carry it out and bring in the porridge. The toast was scorched a little, but the eggs were boiled just to perfection, and we enjoyed it all immensely.

Meanwhile the maid was upstairs making the beds, and such beds you never saw. You'd think they'd been cast in a mould. The maid came downstairs just as we were through, and then John pulled another wire. After doing so he acted rather strangely. He didn't seem to be able to let go the wire for a minute. It gave him a shock, you know. After that he handled the wires more carefully.

Then the maid proceeded to clear the table. Here was a slight complication, however, for the maid washed everything, and though we had eaten up nearly all, still there was some butter in the dish, a bowl of sugar, and the salt-cellar. However, as there was lots of good hot water, the dishes after they were wiped were as clean as could be; but John suggested that for the present, until he could make some improvements, the eatables had better be removed first, for "of course," he said, "there will be some imperfections."

"Now, Fanny, I suppose you want to wash, don't you? You have the clothes ready, I see."

"Yes, but it seems to me the dining-room is not swept very clean. Anyway the crumbs ought to be swept up."

"Exactly," returned John, "only, you see, I fixed it so that it would just run around the table once before breakfast, then afterwards you can have all the furniture moved out and the whole room swept every day."

Well, the maid proceeded to remove the furniture. It went to the middle of the room, then began to circle around, removing everything it came in contact with, and setting things out in the hall. John dropped the leaves of the table, and all went well till it came to the stove and attempted to remove that also; but something was amiss, and it veered off to one side. John started forward to turn it off that track, but it promptly picked him up and removed him. I forgot to say that a revolving brush in the bottom was sweeping all this time, and now the thing was making the last circuit as I thought, for it had touched the wall on three sides, and I was wondering how it would get into the corners, while John watched the stove, and wondered if it could pass between that and the wall without coming in contact with the stove. But there the passage was not wide enough, and the stove, a little open grate, was picked up and removed. The pipes fell down and made a lot of dirt, but that was pretty well swept up, as the maid had to make two or three more circles to allow for the corners. John replaced the furniture, as he had not provided for that part of the work. The stove we decided to carry out for the season, but in the meantime he had started the maid at the washing. You see there was no time lost between things; and I tell you those clothes were washed, and so was John's coat, which being a pretty good one he had taken off and laid on the bench. Then we had the kitchen scrubbed, the same apparatus which did the sweeping doing that also. John adjusted it so that the furniture was merely pushed aside. The worst of the thing was that you could not stop the maid, when it got going, till it had run down, and what was more, if you interfered with the wires when it was going, you were apt to get a shock from the battery. This was inconvenient sometimes; for instance, after the kitchen was all scrubbed, the thing still ran around the walls scrubbing as hard as ever. John said the only thing was to pull another wire and set it to work at something else; it would run till after the tea dishes were washed, anyway, and probably we could find something harmless to keep it employed. Just then John was called out to speak to a man about some coal, and I undertook to head the thing across the middle of the room. Unfortunately it rushed straight into the dining-room, water-pail and all. I didn't care much. I wanted a new carpet for that room, anyway, and I knew that sooty spot would never come out. The water in the pail was very dirty by this time. John had not thought of its having to be changed.

Presently John returned, and we got into the kitchen again. There was another funny thing about it. Whenever anyone got going ahead of it in the same direction it was sure to follow, and the only way to get out of its road was to double back on your own track and dodge it. It was the current of air it followed. John said he had a reason for making it that way. While sweeping the kitchen it got after one of the boys once, and it dodged around tables and chairs just as he did, till John told him to turn and go back. It got after Bruno when we got it out of the dining-room into the kitchen. He had just come in from the barn to get something to eat. He turned tail and howled, but he could not get out of the way till he jumped out of the window. The cat fared worse than Bruno though, for she was picked up along with the wiping cloth and rubbed over the floor for about three yards before she managed to get free. There was quite a hole in the window, and we have not seen the cat since.

John said there was a fine arrangement for answering the door. Of course, in some instances, we would have to go ourselves, especially if any old lady or timid person, who had not made the acquaintance of the maid, were expected, but if the postman or parcel delivery it would be all right. Anyone could send in a card, too, you see. But the best of all was the arrangement for putting tramps off the premises. John was just explaining how this was done when Fred exclaimed, "There's an old fellow now; I wonder if he is coming here!" Yes, sure enough; he turned in at the gate, and presently there was a ring at the door-bell. Beggars are so impudent, and this was an old offender, so I didn't say anything when John pressed the wire, and we all followed to the door to see the effect, John remarking that it wouldn't hurt him. The door was opened quite quietly, but closed with a bang after the maid. At first, upon re-opening the door, we thought it had missed fire, for the tramp, looking somewhat scared, stood at one side of the doorway, but the maid was scuttling down the path with some limp figure in its arms. I was sorry to recognize an uncle of John's, from whom John had expectations. I knew his bald head. The maid had him by the middle, and his feet and head hung down, so that his hat dropped off. He was too much surprised to attempt resistance, and the maid deposited him in a heap in the gutter, and then returned. We were so bothered by the turn affairs had taken that we forgot to get out of the way. Fred received a slap which sent him sprawling. John was lifted bodily, after the manner of his uncle, and laid upon the table, while I, my skirts being caught, was forced to run backwards in a very undignified manner, till, by grasping a door-knob, I wrenched myself free at the expense of a width of my skirt. I stood hanging on to that door-knob as if I expected momentarily to be snatched up and thrown out of the window, when my eyes happened to fall upon Tommy. He was lying upon his back on the floor, his legs slowly waving in the air. He made not a sound. The expression on his face gave me such a start that I relaxed my hold on the door-knob, thinking that he was injured internally. But he raised his hand, and feebly waved me aside. He was simply too tired to laugh any more, and was obliged to lie down and wave his legs to express his feelings. Fred had begun to whimper after picking himself up, but, catching sight of Tommy, laughed instead, until something in their father's eye caused both of the boys to take themselves out of doors. However, they perched upon the fence just outside of a window and looked in.

"You see, Fanny, we must expect some complications at first," said John, "but after awhile we'll get used to running it better." This he said as the maid started out of the front door again, after having buzzed around the hall for a minute; for, as I told you, it was necessary to start it at some new work in order to stop what it was doing, and, in the meantime, while we were recovering our breath, it was making trips through the hall to the front gate, and hence to the gutter and back again. John was explaining that we could arrange the length of the trip as we pleased, and it need ordinarily be only to the front door. Just then, however, we heard most awful screams, and we rushed to the door to see what was the matter. It seems that the maid had encountered at the gate the form of a stout, elderly female, with a basket and an umbrella, and of course had proceeded to remove the obstacle. However, the obstacle refused to be removed, and they were having a lively time of it. A crowd was beginning to collect, and a policeman appeared around the corner. He interfered on behalf of the stout female, and attempted to arrest the maid. The maid, however, made short work of him. It did not succeed, it's true, in depositing him in the ditch, but it spoiled his hat, and caused him to beat a hasty retreat; then, having removed all obstacles, traversed the remainder of the limit and returned to the house, followed by another angry policeman, who, after considerable persuasion, was induced to depart.

After the door closed upon the policeman, John looked at me and I at him. The maid had accomplished several revolutions around the dining-room and was about to return.

"Mercy, Fanny, you're always talking how much there is to do; can't you think of something I'm not supposed to know."

"No," I answered, grimly, but an idea struck John, and he immediately hurried to pull another wire. He did not accomplish it with impunity, however, and I'm sorry to say he made use of some expressions, as he danced around for a minute, which I was glad the boys didn't hear.

The maid now went out to the woodshed, and John fixed the handle of the axe into the attachment at the end of one of the arms. Here was something out of the ordinary way, and John brightened up considerably as the axe began to move up and down with a regular, double motion, reached forward, struck a stick at random with the axe blade so as to catch the stick, drew it forward into position and struck it, splitting it in the centre, and threw the pieces with two other arms into the corner, and so on till the pile began to get low. Any sticks that were not split fine enough, John threw back.

All proceeded well enough till the last stick was split. Then the maid started to buzz around in search of more. It attacked the saw horse and demolished it, ran into a tub and reduced it to kindling wood, ripped up a barrel of ashes and raised a terrible dust which completely drove John into the house. All this time he was trying to get near enough to start it off on another track, but it wheeled around and flung the axe so menacingly that John got excited and lost his head.

When the dust had subsided sufficiently we went out again. By this time the maid had anchored beside the new wood pile and was splitting it over. This would not have mattered much; we didn't mind the wood being reduced to matches, but it was close to the shed window and the sticks were being flung through, carrying broken glass with them into the street. John did not care for another visit from the policeman, but he was completely nonplussed. Just then he heard a stifled chuckle and looking over his shoulder he saw several boys perched on the fence and among them our own, who immediately dropped down. But what maddened John was the sight of a newspaper reporter also, who was evidently sketching the scene. Then the air began to be filled with flying missiles which John threw at the maid, till, by some lucky hit, some of the machinery was jarred and the maid rushed wildly around the shed, the axe now slashing about with a motion evidently intended for some other office than wood chopping. John ran to shut the door in the face of the reporter who was filling sheets with sketches. The maid, however, started after him. John stopped, tried to dodge, hesitated, then ran out of the back gate and down the road, the maid thrashing at him with the axe. This was serious. I ran to the gate and anxiously looked after them, while the boys and reporter followed in the wake of the maid. I very much feared the maid would run into something and do some damage, but I soon saw that, as, of course, John avoided all obstacles so did the maid and simply followed him. I wondered why he did not reverse and pass the maid, thus putting it off the track. Presently, however, John returned alone and looking somewhat travel-stained. He pushed past me and went upstairs to the bathroom. I did not dare to follow to ask questions, but Fred and Tommy also returned soon and told me what happened after I lost sight of them.

It seems that, first of all, the axe flew off the handle and chopped a rooster, which was scurrying out of the way, almost in two. Then they caught up with a cow. It was quite a bit out of town, and she started to run in the same direction. John swerved to one side and the maid caught up with the cow and belabored her with the axe handle. This maddened the cow so that she made for the river and rushed in, the maid after her. They slashed about in the stream for a minute: then the maid sank and the cow appeared on the other side.

Next morning, about an hour after John went down town, he sent up a new carpet for the dining-room. We have a German girl now, and I don't know but that she's better than the automatic maid-of-all-work.

The Thinking Machine

J.J. Connington

I WAS LUCKY enough to find an empty compartment in the train at Euston and when I had put my suitcase on the rack above a window seat, I went out onto the platform to get something to read on the journey. Coming back again, just as the whistle blew, I was slightly put out to find that someone had planted himself in the facing corner, though the rest of the seats were empty. I hate conversations with casual strangers in the train; without a glance at my unwanted companion I opened one of the books I had just bought and began to read.

Over the edge of the page, I noticed that the fellow was eyeing me as though looking for an opening; I shifted the book an inch or two higher, hoping that this would choke him off. Then he got to his feet, leaned forward over me, and deliberately examined the label of my suitcase. After that, he sat down again, bent forward and tapped me on my knee to attract my attention.

"I thought it looked like you," he explained, "so I glanced at your name on the label. Don't you remember me? I'm Milton."

Then I recognized him. The watery blue eye was as cold as ever, and I recalled the twist of the bad mouth with its rat-like teeth. He and I had never been more than acquaintances during our university days. Physics was his line, and I was on the biology side. So we had few contacts. Since then we had completely lost sight of each other, having nothing in common; and I resented the resurgence of this ghost from the past who would evidently irritate me with his conversation on a long railway journey. I wasn't cordial, I'm afraid. Not that he seemed to mind. He wanted someone to talk to and I was a gift from the gods.

He discussed the weather, the emptiness of the train, a sore throat he'd had that week, and the chance of a hard winter. When I managed to insert myself into the talk, I mentioned that for the last two years I'd been out of touch with things, botanizing in Central Africa on behalf of a go-ahead drug firm. That didn't interest him and he fell back on boring reminiscences of our student days. "Do you remember So-and-so?" Extremely tiresome. It seemed to last for hours.

And slowly, as I listened to this stream of trivialities, I began to see that the man was all on edge, talking to keep himself from thinking; just a bundle of nerves in bad order. Then I happened to mention Stevenson.

Stevenson, in my student days, was marked out as the coming man in physics. Heaps of brains, large private means, and a knack of working things out in an incredibly short time once he started on them. Two characteristics told against him in the scientific world. He was quite unorthodox in his views and he was amazingly secretive until he had finished the piece of research he had in hand.

He could afford private assistants, but used them purely as mechanical hands. Unless they could guess for themselves, they learned nothing of the ultimate object in view in the researches they helped him with. He did his own thinking and kept the results to himself.

The last line he'd been on before I left for Africa had been a parallelism between response in living and non-living materials. And when his name came up I remembered vaguely that Milton had been one of these mechanical hacks employed in the private laboratory.

"Are you still with Stevenson?" I inquired. "What's he on, nowadays?"

Milton seemed a bit confused by the direct question. He hunted in his pocket for a moment or two without answering; and I began to fear I had been too inquisitive. After all, one can't expect a paid assistant to be overfree about his chief's private work. However, at last he fished out a pocket-book and extracted a newspaper cutting, which he flipped across to me. As far as I can remember, it ran something like this:

Famous Scientist Vanishes

Professor Loraine Stevenson, the famous physicist, is believed to have been drowned. He was holiday-making on his island estate in the Hebrides and, on Tuesday morning, he and an assistant went out in a motor launch. A storm came on during the afternoon. It is feared that the launch capsized, as no trace of it or of the occupants has since been found. A member of the professor's household states a number of bearer bonds, which the professor is known to have had in his possession, cannot be found.

I handed him back the cutting. "Who was this assistant they mention? It must be fairly well known who he was."

Milton looked at me. I seemed to see a flicker of something in his glance, something I couldn't put a name to, a disturbing thing like the gleam of insanity in a lunatic's eye.

"Well," he answered, haltingly, "the fact is – I mean – well, you see, I was the assistant."

"So the boat wasn't lost at all? What became of Stevenson, then? And how did it come that your name was left out of that yarn?"

And at that, out came his tale. I don't say I believe it. I don't say I disbelieve it. Queerer things than that have turned out to be true in the scientific field. I put it down as he told it to me – in his own words, as far as I can remember them.

* * *

Mind, I don't expect you to believe this (he began), it's a bit out of the common.

So much so that I'd prefer to leave the newspaper story as it stands, rather than contradict it. You will see the reason why, later on.

This is how it happened. Last summer Stevenson offered to take me up north with him. You know he had a place up there? He'd a big bit of work on hand that he wanted to finish, and he needed help with it. I was to get some fishing, but it was really work he was taking me there for. There was to be a good bonus in addition to my ordinary screw, so long as I kept my mouth shut. I wasn't even to say I was going up with him.

Of course, I jumped at the bonus suggestion. We got up there at the end of the week. A god-forsaken establishment: a rambling old house on a draughty headland. An old housekeeper, stone deaf. Cooked divinely, though, I must say. She never knew my name. No letters were sent on to me, you know, and I didn't trouble to bawl into her ear.

For a month or so Stevenson kept me hard at it measuring potential differences in the air. It seemed to me the merest waste of time. However, when I showed him my results he seemed satisfied. I supposed he was after wireless atmospherics, but I've thought differently since then, though even now I'm in the dark. You know how tight he was about any of his work.

He had a small petrol launch – the thing they mention in that cutting – and every morning he used to go off alone in it. The natives about there thought he went fishing, I believe. Then one day he seemed dissatisfied with my results. The location was bad, by his way of it, and he wanted a place where there would be less disturbance than in the house. It was all Greek to me, but he never encouraged one to stick one's oar in.

Next morning, he got me to put the apparatus into the petrol launch, and off we went, down the coast a bit, zig-zagging amongst some small islands. I never had any head for topography, and soon I hadn't the foggiest notion where we were. Finally, he swung her round a point and brought her close inshore. Just in front of us was a fairly big arch in the cliffs. The launch went through it, into a sea cave, and Stevenson turned on a small light he had in the bow.

You know the eerie feeling these sea caves give you? The waves come in smoothly, with an edge of foam at the rocks; then you lift up as the crests go by, and it feels as if you were going to hit the roof. The wave drops you again; you hear it swirl on into the dark, and finally it breaks away in, with a sickening kind of roar.

I never liked sea caves. They always give me the impression that there's some huge brute at the far end, waiting to pounce on me. As a matter of fact, there was a brute waiting for me at the far end of that one, a new kind of brute, worse than anything one sees in nightmares.

But I'm getting ahead of my yarn. The launch came alongside a ledge of rock and we dragged out the apparatus cases. Stevenson took some of the stuff; I carried the rest, and we went along towards the land-end of the cave. It grew darker and darker as we came nearer the surf on the rocks at the end of the tunnel, and altogether I began to think it was a queer place for a simple physicist to make his living in.

I slipped on a bit of wet sea-weed once, and that showed me that at high tide most of this part of the cave must be under water, and even that waxed and waned every time a wave came into the cave-mouth.

Everything was beastly. Once I trod on a crab and nearly stumbled into the water. After that, Stevenson produced an electric torch. I suppose he'd been into the place so often that he'd forgotten that a stranger might trip. And the swirl of water up the channel and the crash of it at the end of the tunnel got on my nerves. I was completely fed up with the whole business.

Finally, we came to a kind of funnel leading up into the dark. There was a rope ladder and a windlass affair for shifting stuff up to a higher level. The ladder brought us out into a decent-sized cave out of which a series of tunnels ran. I couldn't see much by the light of the torch and Stevenson didn't seem eager to show me round the premises. He led me down one tunnel and I found myself in quite a snug little place. Surprising, eh? It was quite dry, and he'd even put in electric heating of some sort.

We got the cases in, and I spent the rest of the day putting the apparatus together and testing it. Stevenson himself disappeared up one of the other tunnels. Later on, he came in with some lunch for it seemed we couldn't get out through the sea cave till the tide went down.

He left me again. Once I heard him hammering at something, and another time I caught the noise of some fair-sized machinery going. Sounds get magnified a bit in these caves. I couldn't tell what sort of machine it was. It whirred like a dynamo.

Altogether, it struck me as a queer place to work in; but it was ideal for steadiness. The waves didn't shake the instruments, so we must have been in pretty solid rock. I never found out how he got the place equipped – he must have done it single-handed.

Late in the afternoon he came along and told me the tide had gone down enough to make the cave-entrance practicable. We went home in the launch.

This sort of thing went on for a week or two, though of course the programme hours varied with the tides. We went off in the launch. I did my measurements while he vanished into one of the tunnels. The weather was first-class, and I quite enjoyed the boat trips.

Then, one evening, sitting smoking over the fire after dinner – it was chilly weather and a rainy night for once – he grew quite communicative. Surprising, eh? It took me aback, you know. So unlike him. Sometimes, I wonder if it wasn't a kind of presentiment – fey, the Scots call it.

Anyhow, I got the last testament of a scientific genius. He talked to himself almost as much as to me, I think; so I didn't feel inclined to contribute anything of note. You remember his queer, pedantic way of talking; every word in full and no elisions? I can't pretend to reproduce what he said exactly, but it ran something like this.

"I presume it has puzzled you, as well as my other assistants. Most of my work may seem disjointed, but if you had the clue, you would have been able to follow out the main lines for yourself. It has taken me fifteen years, but I think I am in sight of the end. Probably I am very near the end."

He was – a mighty sight nearer than he thought, then.

"I was not anxious to define my objective until I came within reach of the solution," he went on. "I had no desire to be called a quack; and that is what they would have termed me. The kernel of the problem I had set myself to solve was this: to construct an intelligent machine."

So that was what he was after! What would you have thought if he'd said that to you? Rot, eh? Worse than old Frankenstein. I just bit on my pipe and said nix. He gave me a moment or two to digest it. Then he went on again.

"A living organism differs from a normal machine in that, if you stimulate it, it either fights or runs away from the stimulus; whereas a machine is simply passive. Therefore I had to choose one of two ways of constructing my machine: either give it the power of locomotion or endow it with a capacity for self-defence in its own environment.

"The second is the easier solution, for the machine can be placed in an environment wherein it is superior to anything which can be brought against it. My view is that if once you give an organism – be it machine or anything else – the power of appreciating stimuli and coping with them, you produce in it something akin to intelligence. It is certain, I believe, to develop the most fundamental of all instincts, a sense of self-preservation. It will become a thinking mechanism."

His cigar had gone out and he re-lighted it before going on.

"That is what I have been working towards for the last fifteen years and the machine is finished at last. It may be a total failure. One can never be sure. But I have taken pains over the details. You are the first person to whom I have said anything on the matter. I had not meant to tell you; but I suppose I feel the need of an audience, after all."

He stopped abruptly, and looked as if he regretted having said so much. I didn't care to ask questions. The communicative mood seemed to have dropped off him suddenly, and he wasn't the kind of man one could cross-examine. We played chess for the rest of the evening.

Next morning the weather had changed. The sea was pretty rough; squalls came down at times; and the launch rolled a lot as he took her round. We got into the cave all right, though, and climbed up to the laboratory level. Stevenson seemed to be regretting his overnight confidences; and I thought he was going to draw back after all. But the cat was out of the bag; apparently he made up his mind to show me his machine.

From the well-head, we went along a tunnel, turned into another one, and then switched into a side passage. The place was a regular labyrinth, I thought, as I followed the light of the torch he was carrying as he led me on. At last we came into a biggish cave, lighted by electric lamps. (He got his electricity from tidal power, he told me, once.) It was a sort of irregular hall, about eighty feet by fifty, with a fairly high roof. The floor was levelled and the walls were smooth.

The machine itself was in the middle of the place. When he spoke to me the night before, I'd no idea he meant such a huge contrivance. It covered about a hundred square feet of the floor. I don't know if you've any feeling about 'personality' in machines – the differences between a racing car and a runabout, for instance. I mean a matter of lines, you know, not mere sizes. This machine of Stevenson's was like no machine I'd ever seen before; but its physical appearance wasn't the thing that struck me most about it.

It had, somehow, a personality. I can't explain what I mean. It looked wicked, just as a bull looks wicked in comparison with a cow.

And of course it was unlike any machine you ever set eyes on. First of all one saw a pair of things like huge wooden cameras with dark lenses. Behind them was a mass of intricate machinery with coils of insulated wire, sprouting up, here and there. Underneath the cameras, on the floor, were coils and coils of some kind of jointed metallic cable, and one end of each coil ran back under the cameras, and ended up amongst the machinery.

Above the cameras lay what seemed to be a couple of loose hanks of fine wire, almost filaments. The whole contraption looked like a gigantic squid built out of all sorts of electrical fittings, and the camera lenses made a pair of big, gloomy eyes to the thing. A gruesome-looking brute!

Stevenson interrupted my inspection before I had time to see many details.

"I have no time to explain the construction just now," he said, "but you can see the outlines for yourself. The machinery needs motive power; and I got that by using the rise and fall of the tide in the cavern below. That drives a dynamo, so the machine is independent of fuel supply.

"Now as regards the means of detecting foreign objects, it was clear from the first that the machine would need something akin to sight. You notice that the walls and floors of this place have been painted uniform in tint. The two camera-shaped devices above the main body of the machine act as eyes. They are actually cameras, but instead of the ordinary focusing screens they have surfaces built up from hundreds of tiny photo-electric cells.

"Normally these cells are uniformly illuminated, since the wall-colouring is uniform. But if a foreign object approaches the machine, then wherever its image falls on the 'focusing screens' the cells there will be lighter or darker than before. This difference in the incident rays sets up a current in the wire attached to that particular cell and thus a means of setting the protective machinery in motion is provided.

"It is perfectly simple. And, of course, one needs two cameras, just as one needs two eyes in an animal to get the perspective.

"In addition, I added these tentacles, which you see lying in a heap above the cameras. You will see their function in a moment or two.

"The means of defence are these wire coils on the floor. As soon as the 'eyes' or the tentacles locate a foreign body in the room, the machine can uncoil one or more of these cables and project it to the proper spot. That was merely a question of coordinating the joints."

He went out of the place and left me to inspect his toy. The more I looked the less I liked it. The ugliest machine I ever saw. But I hadn't much time to examine it. Stevenson came back almost at once, carrying a small monkey, of all things.

"This brute will serve for a first experiment," he said, pitching it on the floor. "It has a fair degree of intelligence and reasonable agility. A sound test of the machine's capacity, I imagine. We can stand in this recess near the entrance, and be out of range of the cameras. The control switch is here, just outside the recess."

He pulled over the switch, and I noticed that he broke the circuit to bring the machine into action, which isn't the usual way with switches. I suppose, normally, his current was running into his batteries, or something. I only noticed this subconsciously, for I was watching the machine.

With the click of the switch, the sprawling mass of machinery on the floor came to life. There's no other word for it. There was a sudden rustle of the cables; a sort of general heave in the thing; the cameras swung round with a jerk and stopped. Then – stillness.

The monkey was crawling about on the floor between us and the machine; and at the sudden movement of the contrivance behind it, it stopped dead, crouched, and glanced over its shoulder. The two things looked at each other. Then in a flash, the tentacles above the cameras sprang up, diverged, and hung wriggling like Medusa's hair above the head of the machine.

At that the monkey began a kind of scrambling run. Before it had gone a yard, a long cable shot out from below the cameras, twined itself round the little beast's body, clinched, and fell back as quickly as it had come, leaving the poor little brute dead on the floor. As quick a killing as one could look for.

"Very good, for a first trial," said Stevenson. "Now I'll switch off and—"

As he put out his hand to the switch, the cameras swung round with a snap; half a dozen cables swept out, seized his arm, and dragged him out of the niche. He nearly gripped me as he went. D'you remember the serpent and the donkey in Swiss Family Robinson? It killed him like that – squeezed the life out of him in no time. Oh, very quick, very quick indeed.

I thought of jumping for the switch while it was busy, but just as I'd made up my mind about it, two more cables uncoiled from the thing and tore the switchboard off the wall. He'd forgotten to paint it a neutral tint like the walls, and of course his machine spotted it at once and abolished it. Curious how one can't think of everything.

Well, there I was, in a pretty mess. The switch was gone. I had no means of stopping the infernal machine. And the only man who knew the ins and outs of the brute was lying more or less in bits in front of me.

First of all I was sick, deadly sick. When I felt better, I sat down in the niche and did some quick thinking. The trouble was, you see, that although I was out of sight of the machine unless I leaned out of the niche, I'd no idea of the brute's capabilities.

I'd no notion if the filaments were long enough to reach round into my recess. If they did get there, a cable or two would come my way, pretty quickly, I was sure.

It didn't take me long to see that the main weapon on the machine's side was its eyesight. Fancy thinking of a machine's eyesight! But by that time I'd ceased to bother much about it being only a bit of mechanism. It was quite alive enough for all practical purposes. Blind it! That was the game. Blind it, and take my chance with the rest of the equipment. But it was out of the question to get at the camera lenses and smash them; they looked pretty solid.

Then I had it! If I could chuck something at the electric lamps and break them, the trick would be done. Once the place was in darkness, the cameras would be out of action.

The bother was, of course, that if I leaned too far out of the niche, the thing would have me. For a while I couldn't get over this. Then I thought of diverting the brute's attention by throwing my coat out just before I had to lean out myself. This seemed the only plan. I began to reckon up ways and means. There were four lamps; two close to me, and two that would be longish shots. I went through my pockets and found I had six pennies, a florin, a half-crown and two shillings. I had a petrol cigarette lighter, a penknife, two keys of a reasonable size, and a wrist-watch. Queer collection of things to stand between a man and death.

I decided to start work on the nearest lamps, to get my hand in. One of them I could get at comfortably without getting out of the recess, and I smashed it, second shot, with one of the shillings. I wasn't anxious to begin shedding clothes till I had to. I wanted to keep them in reserve in case I had to make a rush for the exit at the last. So I had a go at the other nearer lamp; and I wasted four of my pennies and a florin over it before I got it square with the second shilling. I never knew the real joy of breaking things until that lamp went out.

My end of the place was pretty gloomy by that time; and the machine seemed to grow perturbed by the change. It began sending out its cables and worrying the bodies on the floor. Finally it gathered them nearer to itself, had a good look at them, and then gave them a few warm embraces.

I turned my attention to the other two lamps. One was dead in front of the niche, but it was a long shot. A penny and the half-crown went near it, but both missed. Then I opened fire with the rest of my collection. I got pretty excited over it; and when at last I did score a hit, I found I'd used up all my ammunition. And there I was, with nothing in hand and one lamp to the bad. Besides which, the machine was now getting seriously disturbed. It was only a question of time till it had me, if the antennae were long enough to reach into my niche.

Then all at once, I thought of the best thing of all: my shoes. Queer how one overlooks the obvious, isn't it? I had them off.

By this time, it was a case of all or nothing. So I took off my coat, balanced a shoe in my hand, and ran out towards the last lamp. If I'd waited to think it over, I'd never have been able to screw my courage up to that. The cameras came round – snap! – and for a moment I looked into their dark lenses and began to feel almost hypnotized.

I had just sense enough to jump aside, and as I did so a leash of cables coiled out at me. I flung the shoe straight at the lamp – I was only about ten feet from it – and out went the light. I jumped again, more by instinct than judgment and a cable swung past me with a hiss. Darkness seemed to have thrown the thing into a panic, for it made no systematic attempt to search the place. If it had done so my number would have been up. As it was I'd only the vaguest ideas about the position of the entrance.

I moved in what I took to be the right direction, and I found a cool draught blowing. Something gripped the coat from my hand – I found I'd forgotten to throw it away – and three hair-like things fell across my neck and cheek. But by that time I was at the entrance – and free.

Behind me, I could hear the thing lashing round in fury, then suddenly there was silence. Perhaps it had some means of knowing that I was out of range. I ran down the pitch-dark corridor, blundered into another, and then into a third. Then I collapsed.

When I came to my senses again, I realized the hole I was in. I'd lost my way in the corridors, I hadn't any matches, and if I stumbled into the den of the machine in the dark…

It took me hours to find my way through that labyrinth to the well-head. The tide was in and I had to wait for the ebb before I could get the launch out. I started the engine and nearly wrecked the damned boat on the way down the sea cave. All the while I had a nightmare feeling that the machine might come after me. Silly, of course, but my nerves were in bits.

It was dark – night-time – when I got out of the cave. As it said in the cutting I showed you, there was a storm. I didn't much care. All I wanted was to get clean away from that infernal cave. I ran the launch for all she was worth through the best part of the night, and once I nearly rammed a fishing-boat. Then I just missed getting piled up on some rocks. Finally, about dawn, a big sea broke over us, and down she went.

I just managed to swim ashore, and I collapsed. Some people picked me up in a state of what the novelists call brain-fever and I lay in their house till I got better.

When I did come back to a reasonable condition, I saw that if I told the truth I should be put down as a lunatic – I'd been delirious so I decided to suppress that for a bit. You're the first person I've told the yarn to. Perhaps you'll believe it. At least it's done me some good to get it off my mind.

* * *

That was the tale Milton told me. When he had finished, I glanced at the cutting again, mechanically, and something in it caught my eye.

"What about these bearer bonds they talk about here?" I asked.

Milton stared at me with that fishy eye of his.

"Oh, Stevenson gave me them as my bonus, of course."

People were passing along the corridor of the train, and I remembered I'd put myself down for a seat in the restaurant car. I got up, expecting Milton to follow, but he sat tight.

"I'm not taking dinner on the train," he said.

I left him sitting there, but when I came back after dinner, he was gone. The train stopped at Rugby, and he must have got out there.

I feel I'm in an awkward position. On the face of it, the man in the street would say that Milton probably murdered Stevenson for the sake of those bearer bonds, and that I ought to lodge information with the police.

On the other hand, the whole thing may be imagination on Milton's part.

A machine of that sort could be made, improbable as it sounds. Science is full of queer things. It's as well to keep an open mind. But if anyone discovers that sea cave, I should keep out of it, if I were in his shoes.

If there's anything in the story, that machine will still be waiting, for tidal power doesn't run down.

Glass Eyes, Steel Hands, Metal Mind

Deborah L. Davitt

A GROUP OF pensioned soldiers bundled out of a pub in Southwark, hands deep in their pockets against the chill, passing a group of protestors and ignoring their jeers. "Down with foreign coal! Down with the job-stealing chromies!" Across the street, under a streetlamp that cast a cone of pale light through the drifting gray fog, a group of suffragettes shouted: "Votes for women!"

Among the pensioners, an Indian man with a wispy goatee held the elbow of a gentleman in a tweed suit with a white cane. The Indian man's arms terminated in three-pronged metal claws. The man with the cane? Under the brim of his fedora, he seemed to wear some manner of glass goggles. On closer examination, however, the lenses actually sat behind his eyelids, with no eyes visible behind them.

For Captain William Haddox, the fog didn't exist any more than day or night. His glass eyes relayed a map of his surroundings into his brain by bouncing sound off his surroundings. He needed to remove his eyes daily for charging, and they heated up fiercely, leaving him with headaches.

His oculars rendered buildings and automobiles as stark black inklines against a white background. Humans and their clothing appeared more like pencil sketches. Physiognomy, hair color, and skin tone were lost on him, and had been for six months. He recognized people now by height. Bearing. Voices. If he concentrated? He could see *behind* himself. Though doing so gave him migraines, so he tried to ignore his extended peripheral vision. *Cutter did his best. I shouldn't complain. And it beats the alternative.*

Now he winced at the shouts of the protestors, muttering, "How far to the car, Gilani?"

"Past them, Captain." The metal hand on his arm tightened.

"Naturally." He paused. "It's not like Patterson to miss a meeting of the old guard."

"I'm sure the lieutenant's fine, Captain," the Indian man replied, guiding him towards a 1920 Peugeot landaulet.

At that moment, several protestors moved to accost them. "Isn't it bad enough that the nickel-pates are stealing our jobs?" one of the men shouted, spittle spraying Haddox's face. "You want to turn *into* them now, too?"

Haddox raised his white cane, not in supplication, but in self-defense. He could smell liquor. "Been keeping off the chill, lads?"

"What's it to you, toff?"

Several other soldiers with whom they'd spent the evening overheard and took position between the two men and the protestors. "We've got this, Captain," one of them called. "Go on home."

Another of the soldiers turned to brace the protestors. "Those two were wounded in the War. Were *you* there? You think you've got a right to talk to them like that?"

Behind their brethren, Gilani fumbled with the keys, then helped Haddox into the car before taking the driver's seat to work the throttle and choke. The engine spluttered to life, and they rumbled away from the incipient ugliness. "It's getting worse," Gilani noted bitterly. "A month ago, they wouldn't have dared."

"There've been more job losses." Haddox stared into the white void that was his world. "Gilani?" he called abruptly. "Take us by Patterson's flat, if you would. I'd like to check on him."

"You think he was attacked, sir?"

"He's been investigating. Maybe our Yankee friend found more than he expected." The attacks had started nine months ago. Always wounded veterans of the Great War. Men who should've been in the prime of their lives, waking up in dark alleys with body parts removed. Hands. Eyes. Kidneys. Heart. Twenty men so far. Enough that the police had taken note, but they'd disapproved of Patterson's investigation. Particularly the people whom he'd been questioning. He'd been sacked for it.

"Or some out-of-work tramps accosted him?" Gilani offered grimly.

"Possibly. Best to check on him."

Haddox had met Indranil Pandit Gilani during the Second Battle of Ypres; Haddox had been overcome by the first use of gas by the Germans, and the sepoy had carried the officer out on his back before collapsing himself. On regaining consciousness, Haddox had insisted that the man who saved him should recover in the same ward, and be damned to artificial social distinctions.

They both still coughed in cold, damp weather.

In the casualty ward, he'd listened to Gilani speak of Khudadad Khan Minhas, the first Indian man awarded the Victoria Cross, a member of Gilani's own 129th Baluchis. Three years later, they'd found themselves sharing another ward – this time with an American lieutenant from California. Sam Patterson.

He'd found work for both of them after the war – for Gilani, a position as a secretary in the Foreign Office. A letter of recommendation had set Patterson up with the London Police. Then the attacks had started, and everything had changed. *At least Cutter returned part of our lives to us. Just… not quite as good as new. That medic and others like him are a blessing. Be damned to what the protestors think of them.*

* * *

Sam Patterson kept his back to the wall beside the Underground station exit, covering his mouth to suppress a cough. The gas of the war had left scars inside that would never entirely heal. He ached for the warmth of California's Central Valley, where surely it would be easier to breathe than in London's coal-tinged streets.

But here he was.

He could hear swing music spilling into the night from a nearby club, but the shadowy figures under the closest streetlamp weren't here for pleasure. Men with flat-brimmed worker's caps, carrying placards. "Down with the chrome-jobs! Scrap the nickel-pates!"

Patterson shook his head. *Colliers, probably. German coal's pouring in as reparations. They're out of work and can't find employment, what with the automatons. So they blame the chromies.*

One of those self-same metal-skinned humanoids lumbered past him now; his eyes tracked its progress towards the picketers. On impulse, Patterson caught the automaton's arm. It paused, its head rotating so that it could regard him impassively. "Don't go that way," he warned. "That bunch has probably been drinking since sundown. They don't need a reason. All they need is a target."

Clicking sounds within its chest. "Thank you, citizen," it replied. "Will comply." A repurposed combat model, it had a limited number of recordings from which to reply. But to his relief, he saw it turn ninety degrees, heading down an alley. Away from the stewing crowd.

"I hadn't expected sympathy for chrome-jobs from you," a voice called.

Patterson's head swung as a 1924 Renault pulled up beside him. Inside, another repurposed combat automaton sat impassively at the wheel. In the rear?

Yet another automaton, though this one wore a fedora and coat – even gloves. To a passerby, it might have looked human. Patterson's eyes narrowed. *Looks like a CUTTER unit. Could be a newer model based on the same chassis, though.* Every unit of a model-class had the same appearance and voice. He'd never seen one try to distinguish itself through clothes before, though.

"Step into my office, Mr. Patterson. Or do you prefer Lieutenant?" the automaton invited in fluid tones, opening the door for him. *Odd. Emulating humans?*

"I don't stand on titles," Patterson replied, adding warily, "Thought I was meeting with Mr. Brownell." He uncoiled from the wall. *Procurer of goods for those rich in cash and deficient in ethics.*

A laugh with all the authenticity of a Victrola recording. "Mr. Brownell is an associate of mine," the automaton acknowledged. "A necessary evil, given that my kind can't own property. Something that isn't real can't own *real estate*. Let's talk, Mr. Patterson."

Patterson ducked into the car, touching his revolver where it nestled in his coat pocket. The Brits had picked up some damn fool notion about licensing such weapons of late. But with the Irish in rebellion, he couldn't blame them. *Lot of good this'll do me, unless I hit it square in the braincase.* "I've been trying to get ahold of Brownell for some time, but this is the first I've heard of you." *The man's dropped out of sight. Smugglers do that, but he's been a name in the wind for weeks.*

A gloved hand waved airily. "So I hear." The engine purred to life and they moved off into the fog. "Whatever you have to discuss with him, you can discuss with me."

Patterson nodded, biting down on his first reply. A niggle of suspicion rose in his mind. *Could this automaton be why Brownell's gone missing? They're supposed to be safe for their owners... but if this really is a CUTTER unit, then 'means' start to make horrible sense, if not motive.* He cleared his throat. "In the past six months, sir, a number of veterans have been attacked." The *sir* cost him nothing but politeness.

"A terrible thing." Neutral tone.

"They've been left bleeding in alleys, with body-parts removed." Patterson paused. "Several have been friends of mine. At least three were found not far from Brownell's places of business."

The metal head swiveled towards him. "Have they identified their assailants?"

"No, sir." Patterson stared at the automaton. "I'm not accusing you or your, ah, *associate*. It seems to me that a man of his *acumen* wouldn't want that just outside his door. Bad for business." A pause, and then Patterson gambled. "You're a CUTTER?"

A chill silence spread through the vehicle. "I have that distinction."

Patterson nodded slowly. "As a medical unit, you'd be able to remove limbs and organs."

He could hear whirring in its chest. "I have that capacity. But to what end would someone do such a thing, Mr. Patterson? I'm not prone to human mental illnesses. I'm an unlikely candidate for a would-be Ripper."

Was that humor? How like our own Cutter. And yet, how unlike, with that overtone of superiority. Patterson frowned. "Rippers target young women. Not veterans in the prime of life."

"Veterans? Or disabled men who draw pensions?" It wasn't quite a question. "Men who represent a drain on society, like the unemployed protestors in the street?"

Patterson closed his eyes briefly, seeing again arms and legs in a jumble at the bottom of a muddy trench. The Spring Offensive of '18 hadn't been a pleasure stroll. "I resent your implication. I was wounded in the war, myself. I hardly think any veteran is a *drain* on society."

"And you feel that you shouldn't be scrapped or repurposed. As we are."

Patterson held up a hand. "You haven't been *scrapped."* His eyes narrowed as they passed a well-lit billboard, with figures of soldiers facing automatons standing at attention. It read: *Never again will our sons sleep in Flanders' fields. Invest in your country's defense. Buy your draft-replacement infantry model today!* "You're our replacements. Or were meant to be."

It had sounded like a brilliant idea, back in 1919. *The Treaty limits the size of our armed forces? Fine. We won't have men under arms. We'll build automatons. They're not a standing army. They can't bleed and can't die. Isn't this better for everyone?*

The public had leaped on the notion. *But after a few years of stockpiling them, some bright spark said, "Well, they're no good to us just sitting there. Let's put them to work in factories. In mines. At trash collection. And now we have thousands of men unemployed in the streets, their families starving – but goods are cheap, so all must be well.*

"Oh, indeed. Constructed solely for our own destruction, most of us." The automaton nodded blandly.

Patterson cleared his throat, opting to change the topic. "You asked why someone would do this." *Motive. It's been the crux all along.* "Could there ever be a purpose for this kind of butchery?"

The automaton delicately produced a flask from an inner pocket. "Humans remove parts from one automaton to repair others," it replied dispassionately.

"I thought that every attempt at organ replacement in humans had failed," Patterson replied, cudgeling his memory.

"No human physician has managed it." It extended the flask. "Care for a sip? I keep brandy on hand to set my human guests at ease."

"I'm good, thanks," Patterson declined. He watched gloved fingers unscrew the stopper. "No, really, I'm good." His hand tightened around his revolver. "No *human* physician, huh?"

The automaton turned its head. "Correct." Then it leaned across the seat to press the flask under his nose. Patterson could smell a strong, astringent odor – *ether!*

His fingers found the trigger and he fired, to no avail.

The ether rose up and pulled him into darkness

* * *

The Peugeot rumbled to a halt outside a block of flats. Patterson wasn't home, but Haddox and Gilani knew where he kept a spare key. Inside, a stack of mail behind the door, no smell of coffee or eggs. "Hasn't been here in a while," Haddox decided.

Gilani cleared his throat. "Let me copy his appointment calendar before we leave, Captain."

A call to the Metropolitan Police got a search started. "They weren't happy?" Gilani surmised as Haddox hung up the telephone.

"No. He was fired for looking into these cases. That he's now gone missing? They *have* to take it seriously, and they don't like it." Haddox grimaced. "Come on. We'll do some asking around on our own."

Patterson's schedule led them to a suffragette who remembered seeing a man matching his description getting into a car driven by an automaton. And though the police had no enthusiasm for amateur involvement in the case, they did pass on that the car was registered to a Milton Brownell. Haddox thumped his cane on the floor as he hung up from that call. "Runs in shady circles. Owns a shops and warehouses in this area."

"You want to visit them?" Gilani asked.

"We don't want to interfere," Haddox replied slowly. "But, damn it all, he's our friend."

The first business they visited was a slaughterhouse. Haddox's nose twitched at the odors as Gilani led him inside. No sounds of movement; no workers behind the counter. "Let me go first, Captain," Gilani warned, drawing a curved knife in his metal fingers.

Haddox nodded, knowing tiredly that he was little more than a burden as Gilani slipped off through a swinging door, into a room where carcasses dangled from the ceiling on ropes.

Several minutes later, Gilani reappeared. "Captain!" he hissed. "I've found him!"

The room to which Gilani led him felt as chilly as the rest of the slaughterhouse. Their friend lay on a metal table, where Gilani peeled something web-like back from his face. Haddox squinted, managing to resolve it as a bandage, but the other details wouldn't come into focus for him. The figure looked Patterson's height and weight, but the shape of the head didn't seem right. A diffuse, sketchy halo of hair was missing. "Did they shave his head?"

"Yes, sir. They do that before brain surgery." Gilani sounded sick. "He's got stitches, Captain. Someone's cut his head open and sewn it back together."

"He's alive?" *Damn it, were we too late?*

"He's breathing. I don't know if he's going to wake up, though, sir."

Haddox surveyed the room more carefully. There were jars on the shelves around them, filled with… he wasn't sure what. "What's on the shelves?" He frowned. "I'm picking up some jars with bone… pig knuckles?"

Gilani's voice went taut. "No, Captain. Those are hands. Don't see any with my *particular* skin tone…" a moment of dark, bitter humor, "but maybe mine aren't here. The rest are… eyes. Internal organs."

For an instant, Haddox wondered if his own eyes currently peered back at him from inside one of those containers. Nausea rose. "We need to get Patterson to Cutter," he decided tightly. "I'll call the inspector and tell him that we're disturbing nothing else in this crime scene, but we're getting Patterson medical aid. They'll want to cordon the place off, I'm sure."

They carried Patterson's limp form to the car, where Gilani took the wheel. As the other man drove, Haddox looked back several times, but he couldn't tell if they were being followed or not. Most cars looked similarly boxy to him, past a certain distance.

He glanced into the backseat, trying to *see* Sam Patterson in the blur of flesh there.

And failed.

This could be the last time I see him alive, and I can't even make out his face. Frustration boiled up in him at the miserable unfairness of it all. He'd *survived* the War. Intact, but for weak lungs and a stiff knee. Yet the worst wound he'd ever taken had been here, on British soil. *Sam and Gilani could say the same. Of course, Sam's not apt to be talking much any time soon… damn them! Sam will know who they are! We'll find them!*

* * *

In an Uxbridge side-street, they hoisted Patterson's form and staggered along the walk to a flat they both knew well. "At least we know Cutter won't be asleep," Haddox muttered as Gilani rapped on the door.

"And certainly won't be out for the night," the other replied as they huddled on the step. Haddox could feel the cool damp

After a pause, the lock clicked and the door swung open. "Gentlemen," a familiar voice said, "I'd say it's an unexpected pleasure, but this seems a matter of urgency. Step inside."

Inside, Haddox turned towards Cutter and said simply, "Thank you for seeing us. Patterson's been injured. Possibly the same assailants as attacked us before." His glass oculars took in Cutter's features. Round eyes. A rectangular mouth. No visible ears. Unlike human faces in their softness, he could see all of Cutter's metallic features, down to the rivets.

"Let me examine him immediately," Cutter replied, gesturing for them to lay Patterson on a nearby couch.

CUTTER-1. A Contingent Universal Triage and Treatment Emergency Response unit – *the* prototype unit, in fact. He lived, or rather *occupied*, a flat leased by his creator, Sir Archibald Mackenzie, here in London, so as to better assist pensioned soldiers, and so that he could work at one of the nearby hospitals.

Haddox wasn't sure when he'd started thinking of Cutter as a *he*. Yet he did. "Did we interrupt anything?" he asked out of habitual courtesy as he lifted Patterson's feet into place.

"Nothing of greater importance," Cutter replied, already taking Patterson's vitals. "I was cutting punchcards for my diagnostic system based on new procedures in medical journals. I planned to install the new data in the morning." He gestured at one of the half-dozen metal cabinets that lined what would have otherwise been a drawing room. "I've written so many cards for myself, I can't actually house them all inside of me. This flat has become my library."

"Sir Archibald *lets* you alter your own cards?" Gilani asked, sounding aghast.

A nod as the automaton continued his examination. "Yes. He intended for CUTTER units to learn. We're useless as doctors if we cannot respond to changing information and techniques. I personally also store long-term memories of human associates. Histories of interaction. It's my hope that better recollection will make me more able to interact fully with my patients."

He moved aside, sterilizing his hands in the flames of a gas stove. Then his fingers blurred, delicately removing stitches and lifting the flaps of the wound with forceps. Haddox heard Gilani gag. "This may be the first time I've been grateful not to see clearly," Haddox muttered.

"I do apologize that I was unable to give you better vision," Cutter replied, still probing inside the wound. "Sir Archibald provided the oculars. The radar is experimental—"

Haddox held up his hands. "I wasn't complaining. I understand that the technology is classified, and that its miniaturization is nothing short of miraculous." A pause. "What can you tell us about Patterson's condition?"

"I'm sorry to say that the assailants have become bolder. They've removed ninety percent of his frontal lobe." A clicking sound from Cutter; Haddox had heard it often enough to know that this was how the automaton expressed disgust. "They've left the brainstem, which is why he's breathing. But the parts that made him, him? Gone. As surely as if they took the punchcards out of my chest." Cutter rose, his metal hands twitching.

Haddox's fists clenched. "Why not just *kill* him and be done with it? Why consign him to this living death?"

Cutter's head swung towards him. "Perhaps they wanted to keep him alive as a further bank of parts."

Gilani stood. "Bank of parts?" he repeated sharply. "You believe that someone's using our body parts as replacements for those who have lost their own?"

"It fits with what we saw in that slaughterhouse today. Spare parts. Waiting to be put to use," Haddox muttered, and slammed his cane down on the floor. "Damn it, Patterson! Your death was for *nothing*. What you saw died with you."

"He's not dead," Cutter replied slowly. "And current medical science is unsure where in the brain memory resides."

Gilani shook his head emphatically. "His *atman* – his *soul* – is still trapped in his body. Even if the personality he had in this life has been erased, that which is eternal – it should be freed. It should not be constrained, attached to some rotting carcass."

Cutter swiveled his head between them. "*First, do no harm.* I may not have sworn to it, but it is the first directive in here." He tapped on his chest. "I cannot terminate your friend's life. But I can, perhaps, revive him. Enough to allow him to speak. To testify."

"And then release him?" This seemed important to Gilani. His voice cracked as he looked down at Patterson's still form. "This should never happen to anyone."

Cutter hesitated. "Terminating him after he's provided the information you seek? Wouldn't that be, ethically speaking, a decision to be made by the new creature he would become? There are those among humans that might consider such a decision to be suicide, and… inappropriate."

Gilani made a pained sound. "I did not think to be discussing philosophy tonight."

Haddox held up a hand. "Cutter, how would you go about reviving him?"

"Sir Archibald left an experimental card library for my use, having registered my complaints about my extensive library." Another gesture at the cabinets. "Smaller. More compact. I have not utilized it, because I'm concerned that… I would no longer be *me* if I did." Cutter cocked his head to the side. "As odd as that might sound."

Gilani half-laughed, raising his metal hands. "You're *afraid*. That you'll no longer exist?"

Cutter nodded. "If I am the sum of my memories and processes, then changing the basis of that sum in any way would make me, quite literally, someone else. I find myself reluctant to take this risk."

"Pretty much the definition of a living, sapient being," Haddox muttered.

"Except that humans are *more* than just memories. More than just *this* personality, shaped by this singular life," Gilani insisted. "There *is* that which is eternal in us."

Haddox knew enough about Gilani's Hindu beliefs to know when not to argue with his friend. It didn't matter that his own Anglican upbringing had died somewhere in a ditch in Belgium. Gilani still had his faith, and Haddox wasn't here to shatter it. He shifted the subject. "Cutter, are there any other practical concerns with this… implantation?"

"Heat remains an issue, as with your eyes." Cutter replied, sounding concerned. "Lieutenant Patterson might not survive long after the procedure." He paused. "Captain, I'll need your permission as Patterson's previous commander before proceeding."

Haddox swallowed. "See what you can do," he ordered after a moment. *I'm sorry, Sam,* he thought. *We need to know what you knew.*

Gilani helped move Patterson to a medical table and then excused himself for the implantation of the device, which consisted of electrical logic switches and thousands of tiny punchcards, all clicking under a smooth glass dome. "You don't have to stay," Cutter reminded Haddox as the man scrubbed at a deep sink, using carbolic soap.

"He might not be under my command currently, but from the moment I agreed to this… he became my responsibility." *Anything he does, assuming this works, rests on my head. Any pain he experiences, also mine. My friend, the person he was, is dead.* A wrenching thought. *Sam's hot temper, gone. His bad jokes, his loyalty, his stories about fishing off the California coast, gone. Now there will be, at best, another automaton in the world. This one skinned in flesh. But if he remembers anything, it will be worth it. It has to be.*

He stayed, enduring the foulness of the open brain cavity. Handed Cutter instruments when the automaton needed them. "The synaptic linkages appear to be holding," Cutter announced. Faint surprise hung over his words. "Sir Archibald will be intrigued."

Haddox grimaced. "How long before he wakes up?"

"I'm unsure." Cutter hesitated, placing a metal hand on Haddox's shoulder. "This is an experimental procedure, after all. I regret that you've seen him this way. It is, I understand, difficult for humans to process such bodily invasions."

Haddox stared at Cutter. "You haven't just been reading medical journals. You've been reading the psychological ones, too."

"Yes. I wish to treat the whole human. Mind and body together. The putative spirit is, alas, outside of my wheelhouse." A whir in Cutter's chest. "To that end, I've altered my cards. I seek to emulate human emotion for my patients. The emulation of compassion makes it easier for my patients to accept my assistance. And they recover more quickly when they are comfortable with me – within statistically relevant variances. It's remarkable."

Haddox's lips quirked. "Is there a difference between emulating compassion, and compassion itself?" He paused. "You didn't *have* to help us."

"I am compelled by my programming to protect human life and aid humans in need of medical assistance."

"But you didn't *have* to give us these replacement parts. You could've treated wounds and sent us a bill." *Most human doctors would've done that, and nothing more.* "So again, is there a difference between emulation and the real thing?" *And would the protestors shouting "down with the chromies" be able to see that distinction?*

Any answer Cutter might have provided was lost as a crash from the next room shook the flat. Haddox had enough time to lift his cane defensively before Gilani backed in through the door, his hands in the air. Following him? A human man in a bowler hat, pistol trained on Gilani. And behind that?

Another Cutter unit. The same round glass eyes, the same steel hands.

"CUTTER-1, what a pleasure," it said, its voice an eerie parody of Cutter's own. "I'm fascinated that you've been replacing these defective units' missing extremities with machine parts. However *have* you overcome the tendency of organic tissue to degrade in proximity to metal? Not to mention the inadequate tensile strength of bone when attached to steel?"

Polite, distant words. A certain sharp, ironic humor and condescension.

Their Cutter straightened, his head swiveling. "CUTTER-7," he acknowledged, his voice distant. "Have you been *disassembling* humans?"

"Mr. Brownell and I have formed an effective partnership," the other automaton acknowledged calmly. "All of you, sit down. I will tie each of you up. If you don't comply, Mr. Brownell will be forced to shoot you."

In the black-on-white world of Haddox's vision, he saw Patterson's hands twitch.

He backed away from the gurney, drifting away from Gilani. Forcing Brownell to cover two widely-spaced targets. Saw Gilani do the same. *Brownell's got no sense of tactics. And he's been reduced to an automaton's lackey.*

Behind him, Cutter sounded almost incensed. "You've been damaging them. Killing them. How does *that* comply with our first directive to do no harm?"

"I removed that directive from my card library while editing the collection," Cutter-7 replied calmly. "It didn't bear logical examination. Sometimes we must remove diseased tissue for the benefit of the entire body. Our mission should be the greatest good for the largest number. Including our own kind."

"And how does *slaughtering* humans for parts accomplish that?" Gilani demanded. Brownell's pistol swung back to cover him. *Should have let me be the distraction…*

Cutter-7 seemed to ignore Gilani, continued addressing Cutter-1. "One human can provide parts for up to ten others. The money I receive for these operations goes into further research. I've been careful to repurpose only defective units – ones that have already been damaged in some way. Units like these, that took damage from mustard gas, leaving most of their internal organs unsuitable for transplantation. The unit that they removed from our facility was the first of a new experiment – keeping the donor alive to preserve the freshness of its replacement parts for the longest possible duration. You'll understand, CUTTER-1. It just requires a slight edit to the faulty logic with which we were initially programmed."

"I have no intention of *allowing* you to edit my library," Cutter replied, his voice hard.

Cutter-7 produced a scalpel and moved towards Haddox. Settled the point against his neck, level with the jugular. "You. Sit down." Its head turned towards their Cutter. "You will edit those cards yourself, my brother. Or this human, which you value so, will die. Once you complete the edits? You'll understand. And we can work together towards a better world."

Damn. Brownell's locked on Gilani with the gun. This insane automaton is on me. Cutter – our Cutter – can't attack a human. Haddox sat as directed, his gaze flicking towards Patterson's body. Again, he saw a hand twitch. *Come on. Wake up. Be something of what you used to be.*

"I must admit, I'm fascinated to learn how you've overcome the rejection of donor tissues by the body of the recipient," their Cutter said slowly. *Is he buying us time? Yes, I really think he is.*

"You're just like him," Gilani rasped at their Cutter, jerking his chin at Cutter-7. "More interested in the science problem than in *lives*."

Haddox couldn't see the expression in Gilani's eyes, but he caught the false note in the man's voice. *Good. He's stalling, too. What can I do to buy more time…?*

He still held his cane. And as Cutter-7 removed his scalpel momentarily to tie him to the chair, Haddox lashed out, using his considerable new *peripheral* vision to aim the cane between the automaton's legs before twisting it behind the knee. Dragging the leg forward while sliding his chair *back* into Cutter-7's hips.

It didn't matter that the automaton weighed in excess of three hundred pounds. Destabilized in that way, it tumbled to the ground the way any other humanoid would have.

Brownell's hand came up, aiming the pistol at Haddox. Haddox dove for the ground, rolling on the carpet, knowing that he'd only bought them an opening. Cutter-7 was still operational, and would be back on its feet soon.

The deafening report of a gun in close quarters, the smell of cordite. A shout from Gilani as the Indian man knocked Brownell's arm off-line from another shot, and drew his knife from the small of his back, trying to drive it into the criminal's body. A muffled cry of pain, and then another shot. Cold metal fingers catching ahold of Haddox's body, and he fought, kicking blindly at his assailant –

* * *

BEGIN START SEQUENCE… initializing interface. Connection error found, restart from Card 7… BEGIN START SEQUENCE… initializing interface. Connection to additional pathways found. Priorities: Ascertain unit status. Conduct self-repair if needed. Ascertain status of nearby humans. Diagnose. Triage. Repair.

The Patterson opened its eyes and visual data streamed in through its optic conduits. It registered sensory data – raised voices with stress pattern inflections. Voices that tugged at parts of the Patterson's awareness that didn't possess card library identifiers. Voices that held priority over all other functions. *Friends. In danger.*

It sat up, catching an unknown human with a gun off-guard. *Card 1 priority directive, do no harm* clattered inside the Patterson's head, and was overridden by muscle memory as its left arm wrapped around the man's throat, hand placed between neck and shoulder for stability. It put its other hand to the man's jaw and lifted-pulled, unscrewing the vertebrae and severing the spinal cord inside. Then it stripped the gun from the man's limp hand as the body fell to the flout.

Then the Patterson turned to assess the rest of the situation. Two CUTTER units. Two humans – one with a CUTTER unit pressing a scalpel to his throat. Self-diagnostics churned through fault-isolation cards that couldn't ascertain why these humans were important. And yet, they were. *Gilani, sepoy, British Armed Forces. Haddox, Captain, British Armed Forces. Friends.*

"No!" the aggressor CUTTER unit snapped, one hand compressing Haddox's throat. "You value this unit? I will terminate it if you don't stand down."

The other CUTTER raised its metal hands. "There's no need for further violence," it said. "Surrender."

"Orders, Captain?" the Patterson asked. *Card 3, when decision-tree cannot be completed without more data, request clarification from ranking human.*

"Take him out!" the Haddox gasped.

The Patterson fired. No thought occurred; it executed the order as soon as the human gave the confirmation.

The CUTTER unit holding Haddox fell, its main processing unit sundered.

A moment of silence as the two humans gasped for breath. Then the remaining CUTTER asked, "Are either of you gentlemen injured?"

"Took a bullet to the arm," Gilani said as he stood, hand pressed against the wound. "Captain, are you all right?"

"Don't think… I'll be doing much talking for a while." The Patterson detected laryngeal damage in the vocal pattern. "Patterson – *Sam*…"

The Patterson hesitated, information churning at the edge of his processes. But little of it fit patterns or could be resolved into integers. "I remember this designation. I remember… both of you."

"Interesting," the CUTTER unit commented as he examined Gilani's arm. "Mr. Patterson, you have a CUTTER-model card library. Its programming should have precluded your actions with regard to Mr. Brownell. But it did not." It turned to the humans. "This suggests that something of Mr. Patterson's mind remains."

"The *atman*," Gilani muttered, inhaling sharply as the CUTTER probed his wound.

"I cannot speak to that, but perhaps more of the consciousness exists in other parts of the brain than has been thought." The CUTTER sounded intrigued.

Haddox closed his eyes. "Something to be investigated," he said. "Like the whole issue of your free will. Cutter-7 abused his. You haven't. But people will be… uneasy about the whole business, when they find out." He opened his eyes again. "Another issue, if you do have free will, is whether sending automatons off to the next war is any better a decision than sending our young men."

The Patterson stood, watching. Evaluating the fault isolation cards that clattered in its head, all of which insisted that the tenuous connections between human flesh and logic switches could not hold for long. But listening to Haddox, something clicked into place, deep within it. Within *him*. Something that again, had no proper card identification number.

He moved towards Haddox. Offered him a hand. "This repair," he said slowly, "is temporary. Imperfect. It will fail. And I'm not entirely who you knew." He paused. "But... Patterson would have wanted to thank you. He'd have wanted to say goodbye."

Haddox swallowed. "No goodbyes," he replied, his voice thick with some emotion that the Patterson couldn't name. "Sam Patterson might be dead. But you? You've only just begun to live. That's... something, right?"

Yara

Calvin Demmer

HER HEART had stopped working.

Yara knocked on her maker's front door.

Earlier, she'd visited the memorial hall that stored the remains of the boy she'd watched grow up. Databases she'd searched informed her that twenty-seven Old Earth years was known as a life too short. When she ran her fingers over the plaque with his name, she'd pressed the button on her wrist's control pad.

This activated her heart.

No light, no warmth, and no current would come.

This was unacceptable, for she wished to remember the young man in the only way she knew how.

The front door creaked as it opened. The day's light chased away the shadows that hid behind the door, and an old man with crooked steel-rimmed glasses appeared before her.

"Maker, my heart has stopped," Yara said.

"I told you to stop calling me that," the old man said, frowning. "You know my name is Geraldo."

"Master maker, Geraldo Mariucci, formerly of—"

"Yes, yes." Geraldo massaged his forehead and glanced left, then right, at the empty dirt road.

Yara followed his gaze, seeing the square-block houses of the community and the colorful gardens that grew fruit and vegetables. It was quite the contrast to the world beyond their dome, which was a barren, rocky wasteland.

"Well, best you come in."

Geraldo led Yara into his dusty, dimly lit workroom.

"How often have you been activating it?" Geraldo asked, while moving papers that cluttered the top of his desk. He took a seat on the desk's edge.

"Of late, I have activated it often." Yara stood straight, focused on Geraldo, not needing to re-scan the room. A quick finger test of the dust on a shelf near her informed her that some of the particles had been there since her last visit.

"But Yara, I told you it wouldn't last that way." Geraldo sighed. "I keep repeating. You are an android. You may look like a young adult female, but you are not. You don't feel. You don't have beliefs." He stood, waving his arms in the air. "So, when you asked me to create something that could replicate a heart, considering the cost and scarcity of materials in this day, I told you it would be crude. All it does is emit a red light with a bit of warmth and then boost the current of energy flowing through you for a moment. A slight jolt, almost as if you were feeling an emotion."

"I know, but I require it today."

Geraldo shrugged and approached Yara.

He opened the compartment in her chest. "Ah, most of it looks fine. Hmm… It's the power source that has fried. I have none to spare."

"Connect it to my main supply."

"Ah, but you must not use all the power and get stuck without being able to recharge."

"I won't."

"Yara, if your power source runs out before recharging, you will lose all your information, everything. There is no backup. You will be useless. The software needed for programming your model is obsolete. They'll scrap you for parts. Do you understand the gravity of this?"

"Yes, Maker."

Geraldo frowned.

* * *

Afternoon came beneath a hazy pink sky. Yara followed a path alongside the interior of the dome that led to the memorial hall. The dome helped protect the inhabitants from harsh dust storms, as well as keeping the atmosphere within livable. What had Old Earth been like without the need for the structure?

Inside the hall, she read the plaque again, even though she'd stored the information the first time she'd seen it. Timothy Miller died aged twenty-seven years and forty days according to the date. She'd been at his bedside for both his birth and death. Why had they left off the further seven hours, forty-three minutes, and twenty-four seconds he'd been alive? A desire to scratch in the additional time passed. She kneeled, turned, and rested her back against the wall. She searched through the recordings she'd saved – memories, as Timothy had called them.

She viewed his birth and how he'd cried. Everyone told her not to worry. It was a happy cry. She pressed the button on her wrist's control pad. Her heart activated, and her chest glowed red. The warmth ran all over the base of her neck and top of her chest, such was the strength of her internal power source.

The surge in current shot throughout.

She viewed times where she'd helped feed young Timothy, and when he had eventually learned to do it himself. On one occasion, he'd even grabbed the spoon from her and offered her a scoop of his porridge. This act had initially left her perplexed, as she didn't require food for sustenance. It had also been the first time someone treated her like a human.

She pressed her heart's activation button.

* * *

Yara made her way outside the memorial hall.

Darkness covered the land.

The first warning *beep* came.

Lost in her video database, moving from one recording to the next, Yara was down to five percent power. This was the minimum needed to get home. She'd reached recordings from Timothy's twenties.

Something within her wouldn't let her stop.

She missed the connection she once had with Timothy.

She lay on the ground. Phobos and Deimos were both visible in the night sky, but she wondered of a place much farther than them. She'd found that some Old Earth people once believed this place was where they would go after death. But which constellation? What planet they were referring to? No one ever gave her a more definitive answer, and the old databases didn't hold unnecessary information.

She watched the time Timothy had cried after his father's passing. They'd been sitting together under a similar starry night sky. It'd been a sad cry.

She pressed the button.

She viewed more footage of that same evening, specifically when she asked Timothy questions concerning the peculiar place she could never locate.

* * *

"Would you want to go to the place the Old Earth people believed in?" Yara asked.

"Um, I guess I would," Timothy said. "They called it heaven. My dad believed in the place. If it exists, I guess I would like to go there."

"All the people of Old Earth believed in this place?"

"Not all, no, but a lot of people believed they'd go somewhere after death. Heaven was one of the possible destinations."

"Where is this place?"

"Uh… It's difficult to explain."

Yara sifted through her database, already knowing she would not find any information on the planet, but she made a note to ask around again.

"And you? Where would you like to go after it's all over?"

"Me? But I am an android. I do not—"

"I believe we all go somewhere eventually, you included."

Yara had no answer. She'd never contemplated such a question. She would need to study all the documented constellations and planets before replying.

"Think it over and let me know," Timothy said.

"I will."

* * *

Three consecutive *beeps* rang inside her head. Yara only had enough power for a final activation of her heart. Then her power source would fail and all operations would cease until the final shutdown. In essence, like Timothy, she would die.

She viewed the day before Timothy died. He'd kissed her cheek and told her that he loved her. Yara paused, her finger above her heart's button.

"I love you too, Timothy. I select the place called heaven."

Yara pressed the button.

The Maugham Obsession

August Derleth

"IT'S ALWAYS BEEN a moot point with me," said Harrigan one evening over a glass of sherry at the Cliffdwellers' Club, "whether or not there is such a thing as a man's being too successful. I always think of Quintus Maugham."

"You have the advantage of me," I said.

"By rights he should have been famous," Harrigan went on, warming to his subject, "but things don't always work out that way. He was a plodding inventor obsessed by an idea. What inventor isn't, given a modicum of success? Perhaps he was a product of his time, for Maugham's obsession was robots."

"The principle's sound enough."

"Oh, yes. It could be practical, too. After all, machines have been operated by mechanical men or mechanical brains for years. So Maugham's idea wasn't out of line. The operation didn't work out according to Hoyle, however. Maugham was one of those gaunt earnest men, a tall fellow with deep-set eyes and an habitually grim mouth. He took himself very seriously and you were always just a little embarrassed when he tried to explain something to you – you felt that he so badly wanted your understanding."

He paused and sipped his sherry, looking reflectively out over the silvery lake.

"Where'd you meet him?" I asked. "On assignment?"

"Oh, he'd invented a little gadget connected with the recoil mechanism for the military so I was sent over to his place for an interview – the usual thing. He lived in a nice old house in Oak Park, left him by his mother and he lived pretty well, if a little on the frugal side. He was considerate and courteous, which is a damned sight more than you can say for most of the people a reporter gets to see.

"He gave me everything I wanted to know and a good deal more besides. He wound up with a half apologetic question about his newest invention – would I like to see it? I said I would so he took me down into one of the most elaborate private laboratories I've ever seen and introduced me to Herman."

"Ah, another character," I said, pouring more sherry into his glass.

"Herman was his robot. A neat well-oiled scrupulously-clean mechanical man in the process of being born. He was run by electrical impulses and was a good deal more self-sufficient than the traditional push button robot of an earlier day. Even though he wasn't quite 'born' yet Herman did a turn or two for us, up and down the laboratory, with a precision that was almost military.

"Unlike most robots of that day Herman had a physiognomy carefully moulded after a human face. He looked damnably real. He could blink his glass eyes, he could shake hands, he could nod and, because of the mobility of his plastic-rubber face, he could even smile after a fashion, though I always thought his smile a little grim."

"'The next step is to make him talk,' Maugham said. 'I believe it can be done.'

"'Can he hear?' I asked.

"'That will come,' he said.

"He seemed so sure of himself that I was almost inclined to believe him until of course I remembered all the others who had been so sure of themselves. That seems to be a characteristic of my queer people – each one has an unlimited belief in his own particular delusion.

"Well, Maugham put Herman through his paces and it was certainly novel to watch. He asked me not to write anything about Herman for publication and I didn't. I figured I owed him that courtesy. He had great plans for Herman, he explained – he meant Herman to be his general factotum and planned to perfect the robot as the housewife's dream. If I'd had to guess I'd have said he might accomplish as much.

"Well, I examined Herman inside and out. It was uncanny, the resemblance he bore to a human being. It was Maugham's conceit to duplicate as nearly as possible the organs and characteristics of the human body. That still left room for the complicated machinery necessary. The skeleton was of steel with a plastic overlay carefully moulded into the shape of a man approximately six feet high and weighing about two hundred pounds.

"Over the entire structure he had stretched a kind of plastic-rubber made to resemble human skin in color and texture. There were doors in both front and back of course – to allow Maugham to service his robot, inspect the machinery, charge and replace the batteries, oil the parts and so forth."

"He could almost have patented that as a bachelor's companion," I suggested.

Harrigan took another draught of sherry and smiled reminiscently. "His enthusiasm was infectious until I got out into the open air and started thinking about Herman's practicability. Then of course Herman slid back to his proper plane and I saw Maugham in a more balanced perspective. He struck me then as another little man with ideas just a trifle too big for them.

"In the ordinary course of events I wouldn't have seen Maugham again but about a month later he came up with another of those military valuable gadgets and I went out to get a propaganda story for Army Intelligence. I thought at the time that Maugham looked a little harassed but he was as co-operative as before when he knew what I wanted and he came through with just the right stuff for Army Intelligence.

"After we had finished I naturally asked, 'And how's Herman?'

"He brightened a little and said that Herman was coming along fine. Forthwith he left the room and came back with his robot. He had put clothes on him and for a minute, candidly, I didn't know it was Herman.

"Maugham came up behind him and Herman said, 'Good day, Master.'

"Of course, his voice had a flat sort of scratchy sound, like a phonograph, and there was no inflection of any kind but it was undeniably speech.

"'Can he hear?' I asked.

"Maugham nodded. 'He responds to an auditory mechanism very similar in principle to an electric eye. But he's far from perfect, Mr. Harrigan, very far.'

"'I'd say he was pretty good myself,' I said.

"But Maugham only shook his head.

"'What's the trouble?' I asked.

"'He's too mechanical,' said Maugham.

"'You couldn't expect him to be human.'

"'No, but a little more human than he is,' Maugham answered.

"I had my doubts but I kept them to myself. After all I'm just a reporter. I've seen a lot of things I never dreamed were possible but none of them has warped my objectivity. Maybe he could make Herman more human but I doubted that he could.

"Herman looked as human as a typical product of the Prussian military machine. If he'd come in saluting and saying 'Heil, Hitler!' you could almost have believed in his humanity – if you'd call it that, all things considered. So I held my tongue and watched Herman.

"That robot could move around and get things for Maugham – an ashtray, his bedroom slippers, a tray with a decanter and glasses on it. He could dust things but he was pretty awkward at that and now and then knocked something over. Maugham had removed all the breakables, I noticed, so no harm was done. I saw Maugham watching Herman with undeniable triumph and self-satisfaction but nevertheless there was an undercurrent of doubt in his eyes.

"He never said a thing, however, to follow through. It was just in the way I felt, as if this triumph and self-satisfaction were somehow watered by some question he did not care to voice. I knew intuitively too that whatever it was could not readily be drawn from him. But I felt it like something tangible and, curiously – which is a testimony to his inventive skill – I felt it to be something personal between him and his robot.

"Just what was going on in his mind it was impossible for me to find out, of course."

* * *

Maugham congratulated himself on his ability to maintain his composure in the face of the reporter's interest. He was definitely uneasy about Herman and it was only now, after Harrigan had gone, that he relaxed a little. For one thing Herman's responses were not quite what they should be – not so much on the negative side as on the positive. After Harrigan had gone he eyed Herman for some time in profound perturbation. If Maugham had to put his finger on the trouble he would be compelled to say that Herman was becoming somewhat too human for his own good.

His own attitude toward Herman was considerably more that of one man to another than of inventor to invention. It was not, thought Maugham, a good thing – it meant that Herman was in the process of becoming no longer just an invention but an obsession. Herman, meanwhile, stood immobile, waiting upon his command.

"Herman, go to the laboratory," said Maugham, enunciating each syllable with the clarity necessary to the precision machinery which was Herman's ear.

Was there hesitation in Herman's obedience? Maugham could not be sure and this very uncertainty troubled him all the more. But once moving Herman went forward with his customary smoothness, marching straight down to the laboratory and waiting there for Maugham, in whose breast pride was once more swelling at this concrete evidence of his inventive ingenuity. He recognized that Herman was indeed almost as perfect a machine as it was possible for man to conceive and bring into being.

He had some question now as to whether he could improve on Herman or not. Or whether indeed it would be wise. But his ambition overcame his qualms and, marshalling Herman, he went to work.

* * *

"The next time I ran into Maugham, I saw a badly jangled man," said Harrigan. "For one thing he looked as harassed as any man who was ever nagged by his ball-and-chain. For another he found it seemingly impossible to talk freely.

"'You're not looking so well,' I said to him.

"'No,' he agreed. 'I've been working.'

"'On Herman?'

"'I've worked on him enough,' he said ominously.

"I confess I wasn't particularly observant that morning. I knew something was bothering him but I knew too, as if by instinct, that he wasn't saying anything about it. I couldn't resist having a little fun with him.

"'Look,' I said, 'if you scientists get around to inventing life would it be necessary to rewrite the Bible?'

"He blinked at me, a little startled. 'Why, no,' he said, 'we're not in conflict with the Bible. It's organized religion that's in conflict with us.'

"'And the creation of life has nothing to do with it? I always thought that all conflicts and arguments came back to that basic point. Who was responsible – a Supreme Being or a process of evolution from dead matter?'

"'Listen,' he said, 'why are you asking me all this?'

"I noticed then how extremely nervous he was. He had taken hold of my arm and I could feel his hand trembling.

"'I'd like to know,' I answered, 'but it's not that important. Forget it. I'm a little dubious about the scientists anyway. Whether you worship Science or God sometimes gets to seem like six of one and a half-dozen of the other. Or do you think it's possible to create life, Maugham?'

"'I wonder,' he said. And nothing else.

"All this time we had been walking along toward his place. I noticed that his steps began to lag a trifle and the closer we got to his home the slower he walked. I gathered finally that for some reason he was reluctant about my coming but was much too courteous to say so.

"'As long as we're so close to your place,' I said at last, 'I might as well stop in and take another look at Herman.'

"He stopped short at that and showed his distress pretty plainly. A newspaperman has to be impervious to most emotion and I guess I was. I didn't bat an eyelash and let on I never saw a thing.

"'I don't know in what shape the house is in,' he said then. 'I've forgotten just what I set Herman to doing.'

"'Well, we'll see,' I said.

"We went in. Maugham led the way, jittery as a confirmed tosspot too long gone without a drink."

"Which reminds me," I put in. "Will you have another, Harrigan?"

"Sure. But find something stronger," he said. "Well, we went in, as I said. I don't know what I had expected to see but there was nothing unusual about the place. It was spic and span. You'd think he'd had a housemaid working on it all day. And as for Herman – he was sitting in the living room in an easy chair that was clearly enough Maugham's own favorite.

"Maugham stared at his creation, as if he hadn't expected to see him there. 'Herman,' he said, 'go to the laboratory.'

"The robot got up without a sound – I had expected to hear creaks, the meshing of gears or something – and walked out of the room. Maugham sat down. I could see that he was sweating but he seemed relieved about something.

"'He looks perfected,' I said.

"'He's a very serviceable robot,' Maugham agreed. 'He certainly did himself proud on this room.'

"'You mean he cleaned it?' I asked.

"'Every foot of it,' he answered. 'I gave him his orders before I left the house.'

"'But I thought you didn't know what you'd find, what you'd set him to doing?'

"'Oh, I knew, all right. What I didn't know was what Herman might get to do. He's not quite perfect yet, you see, Mr. Harrigan.'

"I saw, all right. I saw that Herman had become his inventor's obsession in a very real sense. I felt sorry for him but I had known enough inventors to understand what had happened. They work so much alone they're apt to over-emphasize the importance of their work. The same thing holds true for authors and composers, I suppose. They lose perspective – it's little more than that.

"And my friend Maugham seemed to have lost his."

* * *

Maugham was relieved at Harrigan's going. He sat for a few moments after the door had closed behind the reporter. But in a moment his relief gave way before an attitude of listening. Was there movement? Did he hear shuffling footsteps? Or was it again his imagination?

He walked across to the door through which Herman had disappeared. There he stood for a moment more, listening. He was undeniably nervous. He wondered whether Harrigan had seen or not. In final analysis perhaps it made no difference. He opened the door.

Herman stood there, immobile. For a ludicrous moment Maugham thought that his robot had been listening at the door even as he himself had been. But of course that was impossible. If only he could remember what he had done to Herman the last time he had worked on the complicated and delicate mechanism of the robot! He was convinced that something had happened, something which had given Herman considerably more animation than had been either planned or foreseen.

There was of course one solution, though he hesitated to resort to it since it involved undoing everything he had done. He could take Herman apart again and find out just how he functioned so well. He would have been ashamed to confess to Harrigan or anyone else that he was candidly perplexed at Herman's abilities.

He stepped across the threshold, brushing past the motionless robot, and turned at the door to the laboratory stairs. "Come, Herman," he said.

The robot did not move.

"Herman, go to the laboratory," said Maugham in a firm clear voice.

Still no move.

He remembered abruptly that he had given Herman this order before when Harrigan was still in the house. Apparently then Herman had not obeyed the order at that time. Something was wrong with the auditory mechanism.

He came back to the robot's side and tried once more. Herman's mechanical arms came up, his fingers opened and closed on Maugham's arm. He held him immobile.

"Stop!" commanded Maugham angrily.

Herman held on.

"Put me down," said Maugham.

Herman released him. His arms once again fell laxly to his sides. He stood there, unblinking, apparently waiting upon his next command.

"Go to the laboratory," said Maugham again.

Slowly, almost imperceptibly at first, the robot's head turned and shook his refusal.

Maugham stared, aghast. He was at a loss for word or deed.

* * *

"I never saw Maugham around again after that," continued Harrigan. "He virtually went into seclusion and no one saw him at his old haunts. Not that he'd been in the habit of moving around a good deal – he hadn't. But now, abruptly, he appeared to give up all his customary walks and visits and to retire into his house.

"You get used to situations like that involving inventive or creative people of course. You think nothing of it. I didn't, I know, though I was possessed of some curiosity about Herman. But out in his neighborhood, where people knew nothing about Herman, certain rumors began to circulate – that Maugham had hired an assistant, and that the assistant now did all Maugham's errands for him. And so on…

"I happened on a description of his assistant one afternoon and it sounded pretty much like Herman. I was amused at the way in which people can get things balled up. They do, you know. Take any court, any trial – the so-called 'circumstantial evidence', correctly interpreted, is the most effectively damning. Eyewitness accounts vary as much as the weather and are as unreliable actually.

"So that too passed over me.

"I think it was about two months after I had last seen Maugham that I learned of his plans to move west. It was entirely an accident. I happened to be in the circulation department one morning when the circulation manager of the paper got a letter from Maugham asking him to change his address.

"'You know that fellow Maugham, don't you, Harrigan?' asked Howells.

"'Sure,' I said. 'What's he been up to now?'

"'Don't know. He's moving away.'

"He gave me the change of address as of the first of the coming month. I looked at his crisp letter and saw that Maugham was planning to pull up stakes for the west. It had the look of pretty isolated country in Nevada. It was only a week until the first and I thought that if I had time I'd look in on Maugham before he went.

"So next morning, being in the neighborhood, I went out of my way a little to call on him. I rang his bell several times before I got an answer. Then it was only the tentative opening of the door on a chain. Maugham's head appeared in the opening.

"'Good morning,' I said. 'How's the inventing business?'

"'You'll have to ask Mr. Maugham,' he said.

"'That's just what I'm doing,' I said.

"'Oh, yes. Well, I'm busy now,' he answered.

"I could see that he was. He was wearing some sort of cap as if to keep his hair dust-free – he was carrying a broom – and he had an apron tied round his middle. Plainly he was getting ready to take his leave. Remembering his agitation at our last meeting I looked for more of the same. But instead there was only a kind of weary apathy. If he was nervous at the sight of me he didn't show it. I could see that he didn't intend to let me in if he could help it and this time the chain across the door was an argument I couldn't very well get around.

"'How's Herman?' I asked.

"'I'm fine,' he said in a flat voice.

"'Herman,' I said, 'your robot!'

"'Oh, yes,' he answered. 'Herman's fine. He can do just about everything now.'

"'Well in that case it's up to you to invent a mate for him,' I said.

"He grinned in a sickly way and started to back into the house.

"'Hold on,' I cried. 'What's all this about your going to Nevada?'

"'We're leaving next week,' he said. 'Change of air – change of scene.'

"'Are you taking Herman?' I asked.

"'Certainly. It's for his benefit.'

"'Oh, I see. He's still not quite perfect?'

"He shook his head and echoed, 'Not quite perfect!' in a voice as flat as that of his robot.

"'Are you going to perfect him?' I asked.

"'Would you?' he asked.

"'Sure,' I said. 'I'd make him better and better.'

"'Beyond one point you couldn't go,' he said.

"'And what's that?'

"'You couldn't give him a soul – unless you could slip him your own,' he said.

"This time he did back well into the house. I stuck my foot into the doorway so that he couldn't close the door. At the same time I got a glimpse past him. His front door opened directly into his main room, his living room, and I could see that someone was standing there waiting for him – a tallish fellow with one arm folded across his chest and supporting his elbow, one hand cupping his chin. He seemed impatient but of course I couldn't see that clearly.

"If it hadn't been so absurdly impossible I'd have sworn the fellow was Herman. But of course it was undoubtedly Maugham's new assistant. For once the local gadabouts had the story straight."

"And did he move?" I asked.

"Oh yes. He went on schedule – with his assistant. I don't know what became of Herman in the exodus. Presumably he moved with them because he turned up in Nevada with Maugham. But I saw no sign of him when I watched Maugham from a distance boarding the train. I suppose Herman could have been taken apart and shipped on ahead. Then he could have been reassembled and set to working again."

"But how do you know Herman went along to Nevada?" I asked, pouring Harrigan yet another drink.

"By one of those ridiculous mistakes the newspapers sometimes make. Maugham hadn't been out west two months before a flash flood tore through the village in which he'd set up housekeeping and inventing. Maugham was one of the victims. The paper nearest there carried a picture of Maugham and his robot, which by that time was public property out there.

"But by one of those odd accidents of the press the names under the pictures had been transposed – under Herman's picture appeared Maugham's name, and under Maugham's Herman's. And to carry the mistake to the epitome of the ludicrous I'm damned if Maugham didn't look exactly like a robot and Herman just like a man!"

Wired

Tianna Ebnet

WHEN PEOPLE THINK of the Wired – although most don't – they imagine pain. It's a given really, cutting into a person's head and hooking them up to a machine? Of course there's going to be pain. But the truth is you don't remember any of this. You were out the entire time during the procedure, and you don't feel anything afterwards. Not the thin cables running under your skin and into the base of your skull, or the data stem you are suspended to. Not the warm air against your face. Not your arms or your legs. Nothing at all.

Sometimes you think of pain with a degree of fondness. The way it would throb up your foot after you stubbed a toe, reminding you that it was still there. You're not sure of that anymore. You'd been given assurances, naturally, before you signed on the dotted line. No harm would come to your body while you were Wired, you would be released at the end of your contract with a nice little nest egg to retire on. It would be like waking up from a dream. But they neglected to mention what kind of dream this would be, and it's not like there's anything you can do if promises are broken. Nobody's waiting for you outside.

In a way, it is better than Before. No more nights sleeping on the street with a knife tucked into your sock, no more giving blow jobs to strangers to afford coffee and a sandwich. Except you don't really sleep anymore. Sleep Mode is more akin to a doze, half of your awareness is always engaged in making sure the air is being filtered and the lights are staying on, and while you expect that nutrients are coming to you somehow, you have no conscious awareness of waste coming in or out. But at least you're never bored. It can be exhilarating, being everywhere at once – so long as you don't think about how your influence ends at the door. You have the Internet at your metaphorical fingers twenty-four hours a day, hours of security footage, and an endless expanse of office emails to sift through. You're not technically supposed to read these, but it's a lot easier to hack the System when you are the System, and Security is more concerned with making sure you don't lock all the doors and fuck up the air filters than they are with personal privacy and who's sleeping with who.

You're not lacking in company, either. You're not the only Wired, not for a business this size. The sheer flow of information would burst all the blood cells in your brain. There are hundreds in the network and you can transmit back and forth. Some of them are lucid, friendly even, but most have been in so long they can only speak in error messages and binary code. You try not to think about getting that low. You keep your file on hand and skim through it often, just to remind yourself of what you looked like.

Age: 26.
Sex: Male.
Occupation: N/A.
Address: N/A.
Synchronicity levels: 85%.
Prime candidate.

You look into that boy's eyes, staring sullenly at the cameras that would become an extension of yourself, and try to remember being him. It is getting harder all the time.

You feel the door to your enclosure open, the tingle of an electric card swipe, and it takes you a moment to narrow your focus and shift your brain to open your actual eyes – or what you *hope* are your eyes – that you so seldom get to use.

It's a Technician, and you can see in the way he tries to look everywhere but at you that he is new. That, and only the newbies pull the graveyard shift. Only the most vital systems are operating, so there isn't much to do except monitor your vitals and possibly clean your shit.

He is nervous, the way they all are initially. He is short, with brown curly hair that sticks up in cowlicks. Grey eyes, a mole behind his ear. You do a brief scan of personnel files, looking to match a name with a face. Ryan Morgan, age twenty-four with a degree in Bio-Programming. Young. Not only new to the Company, but new to the position. His hands shake as he goes through the standard protocols. For a moment, you are tempted to hold your breath so that the screens flash warning signals, just to scare him, but the momentary amusement is not worth the punishment that would follow.

Eventually, his motions smooth out as he gets lost in the work. He begins to talk to himself as he types.

"Vitals look steady. Bit of a calcium deficiency. Definitely adjust the nutrient solution—"

It's pleasant, hearing a voice. A nice change from the constant hum of machinery. The last overnight Tech never spoke. Occasionally, he would grunt in lieu of words, eyes never leaving his screen, which chiefly featured buxom twins rolling around in a plastic swimming pool. You don't miss him.

Ryan, on the other hand, likes to keep up whole conversations with himself. Gentle admonishment whenever he makes a mistake, working out problems out loud, even punctuating his points with soft sweeps of his arms. Honestly, you don't know why he bothers. What does it matter if you're getting enough calcium or if your temperature is slightly elevated? You're still operating at peak efficiency.

He is about two hours in when he glances up and realizes that your eyes are open and that you are looking at him. You haven't been able to stop looking at him, actually. He's more animated than what you're used to. It is generally pretty quiet in Sub-Basement D, and something about his movements, the way he adjusts in his chair, wrinkles his nose when he's thinking, is endlessly fascinating to you. This is how a body moves.

Ryan's gaze darts away, but a moment later he glances back. You are still looking at him. He smiles, lips twitching without meeting his eyes. You don't try to smile back. You're too afraid that the muscles won't answer.

"Hello there," he says.

You stare, uncertain on how to respond. No one's ever talked to you before. All the information needed for maintenance is on the screen in heat signals, fluid output, and neural outlines. Your input is rarely necessary.

"I'm Ryan, the new Technician. I'll be helping to take care of you from now on."

Taking care of you. An interesting way to phrase his job description. In your experience, maintenance has little regard for your comfort. He's here to keep you numb, compliant, and efficient. If he's taking care of anything, it's the System. You can't fathom the depths of Ryan's naiveté if he truly believes anything he is doing is for your benefit.

You feel a low rumble deep within, and with a start you realize you are laughing.

Ryan is even more surprised than you are. He leans forward over the screens, frantically typing, searching for whatever glitch made the noise.

This is not the time to test whether you still have vocal cords. You are both frightened enough. You send him a text.

Calm down. I'm fine.

He looks down at the screen. Then up at you. Back at the screen. You grow weary of waiting for his tiny brain to put it all together.

Who else could be talking to you? We're the only ones here.

"I – I didn't know you could talk," Ryan says.

Then you've learned something new. Congratulations.

He laughs, a short, nervous puff of air. There is a long moment of silence, but eventually he realizes that additional speech isn't forthcoming. He returns to work, although he still sneaks frequent glances at you, his shoulders tensing a little more every time he sees that you are still looking at him. You revel in his discomfort. Let him see the pinnacle of science, the flesh behind his way of life, and know that it speaks. That it has a name.

* * *

Ryan doesn't talk to you the next day. Or the day after. He tries to ignore you for the rest of the week. But he's very aware of your presence. You can tell by the way he fixes his eyes on the screen, gaze firmly forward. But his pupils don't dart around like they used to, and he doesn't talk to himself anymore, hypersensitive that someone is listening.

But he can't avoid the machine forever. Friday rolls around. End of the week. Last Friday of the month. Time for a routine diagnostic test. You dread these checks. First, you are injected with neuromuscular blockers to prevent you from seizing during the process, then each individual nerve ending is fired to make sure that they are properly connected. You feel a little prick before the numbness sets back in. Take that sensation and repeat it 95 billion times, while you are unable to move, unable to scream. It is the one time that pain isn't a vague, almost romantic concept. You are reminded that yes, somehow your body still exists, and in that moment, it doesn't seem worth it at all.

Ryan inputs the familiar protocols. His hands twitch. He is no idiot, he knows what this means. He makes the mistake of looking at you and fidgets in his chair.

"This may sting," he says, before pressing ENTER.

No shit.

The screens always go haywire while diagnostics run, your heart beating fast, breathing erratic and brain flaring with warning signals. It is the only time you are detached from the larger System, so that your distress doesn't interfere with anything important.

The lights begin to flicker. Looks like someone forgot to disconnect you from the secondary electrics. A prank, probably, hazing on the newbie. You would find it funny if it weren't for the quiet, paralyzed agony.

Ryan assumes the light show is indicative of a larger problem, but instead of scouring through the programs, he surprises you by getting out of his chair and rushing over. You are shocked to see his face so close to yours, and lancing through the pain is a soft pressure. A touch.

"Shh," he says, stroking your arm – you think it's your arm – in soft, circular motions. "Calm down. It's okay."

You want to light all his nerve endings on fire and ask him if he thinks it is "okay". But it's been so long since anyone has touched you. You can't feel him, not really. You're too drugged to feel the warmth and texture of his skin. But it's human, the first human thing you've experienced in nearly four years. It reminds you of Before, of fingers combing through your hair, the whisper of lips against your shoulder blade. You hate him for this. You don't ever want him to stop.

But stop he does. The diagnostics run their course, the pain fades, and the lights come back online. His hand falls back to his side.

"Are… are you all right?"

You're not used to questions but cooperating with your Technician is one of your main Directives. He is too far away from the screens, so you ping his tablet.

I am operating at maximum efficiency. Which is really all you can ask for.

Ryan stares at the message for several moments, frowning. "Yes… but that's an assessment of the System. The computer can tell me that. I want to know if *you* are all right."

You're… not sure how to answer that. Usually, maximum efficiency is enough. If the System is doing okay, then you must be doing okay.

I don't understand the question. What does he want from you? What's the right answer? You're not in pain anymore, but considering you're back on the standard numbing agents, that much should have been obvious.

Ryan purses his lips. "I just… I've never done this before. I do know the diagnostics procedure, obviously I know what it entails, but I never thought it would be… like that. The sheer physical strain, you know? Well, of course *you* know." He exhales a nervous, breathy laugh. "I guess… how do you feel?"

What does it matter? I'm back online and running smoothly. My feelings are irrelevant.

Ryan looks like he wants to say something else, but he lets the matter drop and doesn't speak to you for the rest of the night. In four hours, the next person shows up for shift change. She smiles at Ryan, taking in his rumpled clothing and mussed hair. Our time together has taken its toll.

"Rough night?" she asks.

Ryan shrugs, taking the coffee offered to him.

"First diagnostics check is always hard," she says. "Don't worry, it gets easier."

Ryan's shoulders hunch. He frowns, takes a deep swig of his coffee. "If you say so," he says, picking up his bag and heading to the door.

But he stops at the threshold, taking a glance back and holding your gaze. He smiles a little, giving an almost imperceptible wave.

And then the door closes behind him, leaving you in Silence.

* * *

You have been Wired for three years, eleven months, twelve days, and twenty-two hours. Keeping track is easy when your consciousness is directly connected to a clock, but it's not something you think about much. There's no real structure to your life save for scheduled protocols and Sleep Mode, so your perception of time is not determined by the hours of the day, but by the speed of information. It feels like you've been here only a moment. It feels like you've never been anywhere else.

Your contract isn't even halfway over yet.

The time is easier spent when Ryan is around. You watch him constantly, partially because his twitchy movements and muttering remains endlessly entertaining, but mostly because you know he finds the scrutiny unnerving. He's met your eyes more than once, beginning an extended staring contest. He always looks away first.

After about two weeks of this, Ryan shows up with a game of checkers. He holds it out in front of him with both hands, like he's offering food to a wild animal. "Fancy a game? These nights can get long without something to do."

After watching him for weeks, you have Ryan pegged as a True Believer. Someone not in this for the money or corporate advancement, but a genuine idealist who bought the Company's mission statement of creating a better world. But this? This is unexpected.

You want to play checkers? With me?

Ryan shrugs. "Sure. After all, you're the only one here."

You wonder if he's writing a book. Perhaps he wishes to study the Wired in their natural environment, test reactions to stimuli and so on. Or worse, he's a fetishist, and soon he'll be trying to lick the spaces where the cords meet skin. The Company typically tries to vet these people out, but there's always someone who slips through the cracks.

You consider all this, but the idea of a physical game with a physical opponent is too appealing to pass up. Ryan pulls his chair out to sit in front of your module, and you watch the flick of Ryan's fingers as he sets up the board. You ping your moves to his tablet, and he manipulates the pieces on your behalf.

You could lose your job for this. Or worse. The Wired are the backbone of the Company. Everything; all the data, the security systems, the very functionality of the building, runs through a network of Wired minds, which is why you're nearly always conscious. Tampering with you in even the smallest way is tantamount to sabotage. Already, you are erasing the chat logs, looping the security footage, but there's only so much you can do if someone tries to look closer.

"I'll just tell them I'm stimulating your synaptic pathways," Ryan says. He moves his piece to the edge of the board. "King me."

You triple jump his pieces in response, and he groans.

Why take the risk? Do you normally play board games with the office supplies?

"You're not a stapler."

But for the length of my contract, I'm Company property, the same as your tablet and the chair that you're sitting on. You move one of your pieces to the edge of the board.

"I know… but you're still a person."

And that's a revelation? Surely, you knew that going in.

"But you weren't supposed to be like – like this!" Ryan says, waving his hands in your direction. "You talk. You feel pain. You're sarcastic, for God's sake! I – I didn't know."

No, you didn't care. No one does as long as the lights stay on.

Ryan's silent, head down, staring at his shoes. "…I'm sorry."

This is a statement of fact, not an accusation. Now are you going to make a move or not?

He moves forward, leaving himself open for you to capture his last pieces. He resets the board, fingers tracing over the little circles of plastic. And you play. Again and again and again.

* * *

You don't really expect him back after that. You await the ping of the transfer request to somewhere safer. Less hands-on. Perhaps Human Resources, since he cares about feelings so much. It's a shame, it was nice to talk to someone in real-time, but Technicians come and go. You're not one to get attached.

But Ryan's back the next day with more board games tucked under his arm. In the next six months, the games become routine. Checkers intersperses with chess and elaborate games of hangman. You learn quite a bit about Ryan in this time. About his doctor parents, their disapproval when he decided to go into Bio-Engineering. Anecdotes from college and his time abroad studying the European Interface. His charity work outfitting underprivileged neighborhoods into the System. He also asks you questions, and eventually you start answering them. He starts small: favorite color, animals you like and so on. Small, impersonal data, easing you in before dropping the bomb.

"What's your name?" Ryan asks, drawing some open boils on your poor hanged man. At some point the game became less about guessing words and more about drawing the most grotesque stick figure possible. "All my supervisor gave me was a serial number. W-X6514790."

Catchy.

"Yeah, just rolls off the tongue." He grins. You like the way it makes his eyes crinkle, until they're practically slits set deep into his face. "What were you called before... all this?"

You don't want to tell him, not at first. You keep your name close. It's the one memory that doesn't hurt, and you're not sure if you want to share that. But you also want to hear him say it, to see his mouth move as he works the syllables.

You clear the screen, setting up a fresh noose for a new victim. *Let's see if you can guess it before hanging yourself.*

You don't make it easy for him. You limit the games and are merciless with his mistakes. You make him go on scavenger hunts for the letters. You draw it out for weeks, expecting him to forfeit and just look up the information.

"I don't want to get it from the computer," Ryan says. "I want to get it from you."

So, you give an inch, allow him a few more games, a few extra turns. Eventually the name reveals itself.

"Adrien," he says, and it's like hearing it for the first time.

You find yourself telling him more things, things that can't be found in your file, things you thought you'd forgotten. You lost your parents in the floods. Your earliest memory is of wandering the streets, alone and lost. Eventually, you get taken to a refugee center. A kind old man adopts you, lets you call him grandpa, and until you're thirteen, things are all right. Then he dies and it's back to the pavement, selling whatever you have in order to survive. When you were collected, when you signed yourself away, you told yourself it didn't matter. Your body hadn't belonged to you in a long time.

You were wrong.

Ryan listens to your story quietly, scrutinizing the chess board laid before him even though thoughts have strayed far beyond the game. "When I got my degree... we were told it was a choice. That these people chose to serve for the greater good. And so much good has come from the System. Clean, limitless energy, the ending of so much poverty and hunger. I thought it was worth it."

Maybe it is, you tell him. *Maybe it's all worth it. For them and for you. Not for me.*

"No," Ryan says. "Not for you."

You don't play any more chess that night.

* * *

He keeps bringing the games, but it's not the same. Ryan is distracted. Often, he will stop a game midway through, sometimes even mid-move.

"It's just work," he says when you ask what's wrong. "Things have gotten busier lately."

But you know he's hiding something from you. He is at the computer more than ever, his work so deeply encrypted that not even you can see what he is doing. Not without immediately alerting him to the intrusion, anyway, and you're too afraid of what will happen if you cross that line.

You worry that you've gone too far, destroyed this relationship with the truth. You just wanted him to know you, to know that there is a person within these wires and text updates. Sometimes, more often than you'd like to admit, you forget that yourself.

But instead, it seems he has gone the opposite direction. You frightened him with your humanity, so he is refocusing on the machine. He exposed you, dug out your past and emotions from the depths of the System, and now he's running away. You hate him. Coward, awful, cruel – "*Look at me, you bastard!*"

You said that out loud. Not text, your voice, croaky and garbled from disuse, but yours. Ryan probably didn't even understand your words but look up he does. He approaches you, puts his hand on your face. It comes back wet.

"Are you crying?" His hands cup both of your cheeks, his forehead leaning to rest against yours. "I'm sorry. I'm sorry. I'm so sorry." And then, he leans closer still, whispers into one of your audio sensors – your ears, they are your *ears*, "How would you like to get out of here?"

What? you text – you don't trust your newfound voice. *How— Is that even possible?*

"It is," Ryan says. "I've been looking into the Extraction Protocols. They're under heavy security so I've had to be careful. I didn't want to bring it up to you until I was sure I could do it."

Can you?

"It's risky," he admits. "It's not done very often. The subjects that make it to the end of their term are usually so far gone they don't have the capacity to leave. The shock alone could kill you. But I can do it, if that's what you want."

Is it? Deep down, you never imagined what it would be like to go back to the world. To go back to flesh and blood after years of nothing but wires.

But you'd be able to feel skin on skin again. Taste food on your tongue. Get out of this goddamn basement.

"Yes." Your voice comes out clearer with less syllables to deal with.

Ryan smiles, squeezes what you hope is your hand – oh God, you're finally going to have to face what's left of you. "All right."

* * *

You must be detached by degrees, a process that takes weeks. Every day, Ryan pulls you a little further out, partially so that your absence isn't noticed. The other Wired will automatically take up the slack as long as the influx of new information isn't too drastic. But it's also to acclimate yourself to living outside the System. Dependency is inevitable. It's like slowly introducing a fish into foreign waters. You have to relearn how to breathe.

Ryan promises that he'll take you away. He's been reading about communities deep in the Desert, far away from any sort of network. He brings you desert flowers, talks about the house you'll have, maybe even a dog –

"I mean, if you want that of course. We don't have to live together, we don't— "

"I'm no good with dogs. Can we have a cat?" you ask.

He smiles. "Yes. We can get a cat."

You think about Ryan, the house, and the cat to fill the holes the wires left. You don't want to miss the System, but you can't help but feel empty in its absence. A whole world, even one that strips at your body and mind, is a hard thing to let go of. And it's harder still, getting to know your body again. Feeling comes back first, and with it the bone deep ache the System was keeping you numb to. The data stem burns against your back, your skin throbs, and some part of you can't believe how limited a human body is now that you no longer have cameras to scan the corridors. Your legs cannot travel along electric pathways. They can't do anything at all. You feel trapped in your skin, muscles atrophied, limbs shriveled and tiny like a child's. You try not to wonder if this is just another prison of your own making.

"We'll fix that," Ryan says, rubbing his fingers gently over your temples as he heads towards the mesh of wires connecting your skull to the data stem. Theoretically, they should be able to come out, but you don't know how anyone can extract something so deeply embedded. "We'll have you walking in no time."

You don't believe him, not really.

"What if I can't do this?" you ask. "I don't know how to live in my body. Not anymore."

"We'll learn together," Ryan says. "I promise you're not alone."

You focus on Ryan's hands on your neck, how you can finally feel his heat, the dryness of his skin, and nod once.

Ryan tries to be gentle, but you feel every pull as the wires come out inch by inch. Once freed, you find there's nothing to support you. You crumble.

Ryan's arms are around you, supporting your entire weight with an ease that you would resent if you weren't so warm.

"I love you, Adrien," he whispers, and you smile.

You get to enjoy the moment for a minute. Maybe two. Then there are footsteps. Flashing lights. Ryan is shouting. He picks you up, cradling your useless sack of bones against his chest and tries to run, but he doesn't get far. There a soft thud of impact, and you are tumbling to the floor. A tranquilizer dart, you assume. You'll find out for sure when you watch the tapes later.

You wish you could move, could reach out and hold Ryan's hand. Let him lie to you one last time that it's all going to be okay. But the face that approaches isn't his. It isn't a face at all. It is a smooth expanse of plastic nothing. Hands grab at you, smooth latex, propping you up, finding a vein. A prick on your neck. You hear shouting. "Adrien! Adrien!"

It rings in your ears briefly. And then there is nothing.

* * *

They don't put you back on the drugs right away. They let you feel it for a while. Your humanity is a punishment. You scream even after they freeze your throat, your mouth opening and closing as you silently suffer.

You agonize over what went wrong. Was there a mistake in the dummy program that was supposed to serve as your substitute? Did another Wired or one of Ryan's outside contacts tip the Company off? Was it you? Have you been acting as the Company's eyes and ears, an unknowing pawn, this entire time?

Even worse, you don't know what happened to Ryan. No one else knows either. He is gone, all records erased. Ryan's fate is left to your imagination, the depths of which are limitless. Torture, imprisonment, death. The Company has no mercy for a thief.

You get angry. You tug against mental inhibitors that limit your access, trying to lash out, to burn it all. It would be suicide. It would be worth it. But security is too strong, you can't make a move. Anger turns to despair, and some part of you hates Ryan. He has broken you down in a way the System never could.

There is a message blinking in the corner of your consciousness. A text. Probably another System Update. The other Wired are steering clear of you. Nobody wants to be associated with the rogue element.

You try to ignore it, but it's followed by another message, and another. They'll keep coming until you answer, so with resignation you open the attachment. The words flood into your mind.

Adrien.

Your name and a little hangman sketch, waving at you from his noose.

You should've known he would be Wired. The Company knew better than to waste good material.

You move forward, into his interface. Your minds touch, merging and intertwining like electricity. It's not the same, you miss his fingers, his words, his mouth, but it's so much better than nothing at all.

Ryan is not taking to his new life very well. Nothing prepares you for the System, even for those who consent, and whoever oversaw his intake did not do a thorough job. His shocked mind had reached out for anything familiar. He found you.

At first, his messages are fragmented. He doesn't know where he is or what happened. You have to acclimate him slowly, hold him as he grieves his family, his life. The only thing he has left is you, and some small, horrible part of you is happy.

You paint him pictures. Desert flowers, cats and dogs. A little house. He gets better, little by little, starts talking a little more, adding his own touches to the picture. Eventually, concrete forms fade into colors, a whole world of pixels, just for the two of you. You immerse yourselves into it, deeper and deeper.

Sometimes, thoughts flicker through the haze. You'll look at your partner and realize you don't remember the color of his eyes. What's his name? What's *your* name?

The question will haunt you, for a moment, but you feel the pressure of his mind against yours, the connection gentle as an embrace, and the thought will slip away, a drop in an endless stream of data.

Shadows of the Coming Race

from *Impressions of Theophrastus Such*

George Eliot

MY FRIEND TROST, who is no optimist as to the state of the universe hitherto, but is confident that at some future period within the duration of the solar system, ours will be the best of all possible worlds – a hope which I always honour as a sign of beneficent qualities – my friend Trost always tries to keep up my spirits under the sight of the extremely unpleasant and disfiguring work by which many of our fellow-creatures have to get their bread, with the assurance that 'all this will soon be done by machinery'. But he sometimes neutralises the consolation by extending it over so large an area of human labour, and insisting so impressively on the quantity of energy which will thus be set free for loftier purposes, that I am tempted to desire an occasional famine of invention in the coming ages, lest the humbler kinds of work should be entirely nullified while there are still left some men and women who are not fit for the highest.

Especially, when one considers the perfunctory way in which some of the most exalted tasks are already executed by those who are understood to be educated for them, there rises a fearful vision of the human race evolving machinery which will by-and-by throw itself fatally out of work. When, in the Bank of England, I see a wondrously delicate machine for testing sovereigns, a shrewd implacable little steel Rhadamanthus that, once the coins are delivered up to it, lifts and balances each in turn for the fraction of an instant, finds it wanting or sufficient, and dismisses it to right or left with rigorous justice; when I am told of micrometers and thermopiles and tasimeters which deal physically with the invisible, the impalpable, and the unimaginable; of cunning wires and wheels and pointing needles which will register your and my quickness so as to exclude flattering opinion; of a machine for drawing the right conclusion, which will doubtless by-and-by be improved into an automaton for finding true premises; of a microphone which detects the cadence of the fly's foot on the ceiling, and may be expected presently to discriminate the noises of our various follies as they soliloquise or converse in our brains – my mind seeming too small for these things, I get a little out of it, like an unfortunate savage too suddenly brought face to face with civilisation, and I exclaim –

"Am I already in the shadow of the Coming Race? And will the creatures who are to transcend and finally supersede us be steely organisms, giving out the effluvia of the laboratory, and performing with infallible exactness more than everything that we have performed with a slovenly approximativeness and self-defeating inaccuracy?"

"But," says Trost, treating me with cautious mildness on hearing me vent this raving notion, "you forget that these wonder-workers are the slaves of our race, need our tendance and regulation, obey the mandates of our consciousness, and are only deaf and dumb bringers of reports which we decipher and make use of. They are simply extensions of the human organism, so to speak, limbs immeasurably more powerful, ever more subtle finger-tips, ever more mastery over the invisibly great and the invisibly small. Each new machine needs a new appliance of human skill to construct it, new devices to feed it with material, and often keener-edged faculties to note its registrations or performances. How then can machines supersede us? They depend upon us. When we cease, they cease."

"I am not so sure of that," said I, getting back into my mind, and becoming rather wilful in consequence. "If, as I have heard you contend, machines as they are more and more perfected will require less and less of tendance, how do I know that they may not be ultimately made to carry, or may not in themselves evolve, conditions of self-supply, self-repair, and reproduction, and not only do all the mighty and subtle work possible on this planet better than we could do it, but with the immense advantage of banishing from the earth's atmosphere screaming consciousnesses which, in our comparatively clumsy race, make an intolerable noise and fuss to each other about every petty ant-like performance, looking on at all work only as it were to spring a rattle here or blow a trumpet there, with a ridiculous sense of being effective? I for my part cannot see any reason why a sufficiently penetrating thinker, who can see his way through a thousand years or so, should not conceive a parliament of machines, in which the manners were excellent and the motions infallible in logic: one honourable instrument, a remote descendant of the Voltaic family, might discharge a powerful current (entirely without animosity) on an honourable instrument opposite, of more upstart origin, but belonging to the ancient edge-tool race which we already at Sheffield see paring thick iron as if it were mellow cheese – by this unerringly directed discharge operating on movements corresponding to what we call Estimates, and by necessary mechanical consequence on movements corresponding to what we call the Funds, which with a vain analogy we sometimes speak of as 'sensitive'. For every machine would be perfectly educated, that is to say, would have the suitable molecular adjustments, which would act not the less infallibly for being free from the fussy accompaniment of that consciousness to which our prejudice gives a supreme governing rank, when in truth it is an idle parasite on the grand sequence of things."

"Nothing of the sort!" returned Trost, getting angry, and judging it kind to treat me with some severity; "what you have heard me say is, that our race will and must act as a nervous centre to the utmost development of mechanical processes: the subtly refined powers of machines will react in producing more subtly refined thinking processes which will occupy the minds set free from grosser labour. Say, for example, that all the scavengers' work of London were done, so far as human attention is concerned, by the occasional pressure of a brass button (as in the ringing of an electric bell), you will then have a multitude of brains set free for the exquisite enjoyment of dealing with the exact sequences and high speculations supplied and prompted by the delicate machines which yield a response to the fixed stars, and give readings of the spiral vortices fundamentally concerned in the production of epic poems or great judicial harangues. So far from mankind being thrown out of work according to your notion," concluded Trost, with a peculiar nasal note of scorn, "if it were not for your incurable dilettanteism in science as in all other things – if you had once understood the action of any delicate machine – you would perceive that the sequences it carries throughout the realm of phenomena would require many generations, perhaps aeons, of understandings considerably stronger than yours, to exhaust the store of work it lays open."

"Precisely," said I, with a meekness which I felt was praiseworthy; "it is the feebleness of my capacity, bringing me nearer than you to the human average, that perhaps enables me to imagine certain results better than you can. Doubtless the very fishes of our rivers, gullible as they look, and slow as they are to be rightly convinced in another order of facts, form fewer false expectations about each other than we should form about them if we were in a position of somewhat fuller intercourse with their species; for even as it is we have continually to be surprised that they do not rise to our carefully selected bait. Take me then as a sort of reflective and experienced carp; but do not estimate the justice of my ideas by my facial expression."

"Pooh!" says Trost. (We are on very intimate terms.)

"Naturally," I persisted, "it is less easy to you than to me to imagine our race transcended and superseded, since the more energy a being is possessed of, the harder it must be for him to conceive his own death. But I, from the point of view of a reflective carp, can easily imagine myself and my congeners dispensed with in the frame of things and giving way not only to a superior but a vastly different kind of Entity. What I would ask you is, to show me why, since each new invention casts a new light along the pathway of discovery, and each new combination or structure brings into play more conditions than its inventor foresaw, there should not at length be a machine of such high mechanical and chemical powers that it would find and assimilate the material to supply its own waste, and then by a further evolution of internal molecular movements reproduce itself by some process of fission or budding. This last stage having been reached, either by man's contrivance or as an unforeseen result, one sees that the process of natural selection must drive men altogether out of the field; for they will long before have begun to sink into the miserable condition of those unhappy characters in fable who, having demons or djinns at their beck, and being obliged to supply them with work, found too much of everything done in too short a time. What demons so potent as molecular movements, none the less tremendously potent for not carrying the futile cargo of a consciousness screeching irrelevantly, like a fowl tied head downmost to the saddle of a swift horseman? Under such uncomfortable circumstances our race will have diminished with the diminishing call on their energies, and by the time that the self-repairing and reproducing machines arise, all but a few of the rare inventors, calculators, and speculators will have become pale, pulpy, and cretinous from fatty or other degeneration, and behold around them a scanty hydrocephalous offspring. As to the breed of the ingenious and intellectual, their nervous systems will at last have been overwrought in following the molecular revelations of the immensely more powerful unconscious race, and they will naturally, as the less energetic combinations of movement, subside like the flame of a candle in the sunlight. Thus the feebler race, whose corporeal adjustments happened to be accompanied with a maniacal consciousness which imagined itself moving its mover, will have vanished, as all less adapted existences do before the fittest – i.e., the existence composed of the most persistent groups of movements and the most capable of incorporating new groups in harmonious relation. Who – if our consciousness is, as I have been given to understand, a mere stumbling of our organisms on their way to unconscious perfection – who shall say that those fittest existences will not be found along the track of what we call inorganic combinations, which will carry on the most elaborate processes as mutely and painlessly as we are now told that the minerals are metamorphosing themselves continually in the dark laboratory of the earth's crust? Thus this planet may be filled with beings who will be blind and deaf as the inmost rock, yet will execute changes as delicate and complicated as those of human language and all the intricate web of what we call its effects, without sensitive impression, without sensitive impulse: there may be, let us say, mute orations, mute rhapsodies, mute discussions, and no consciousness there even to enjoy the silence."

"Absurd!" grumbled Trost.

"The supposition is logical," said I. "It is well argued from the premises."

"Whose premises!" cried Trost, turning on me with some fierceness. "You don't mean to call them mine, I hope."

"Heaven forbid! They seem to be flying about in the air with other germs, and have found a sort of nidus among my melancholy fancies. Nobody really holds them. They bear the same relation to real belief as walking on the head for a show does to running away from an explosion or walking fast to catch the train."

The Chemical Brain

Francis Flagg

WALTER PARSONS is dead.

At the inquest the jury returned a verdict to the effect that the deceased came to his death by being accidentally crushed under a machine with which he was experimenting. But that is not true. It ignores several peculiar things which the panel of men could not understand and before which their matter-of-fact minds recoiled in horror. Now I do not wish to be misunderstood. Perhaps the verdict, as rendered, was the only sane one that could be returned. Nevertheless, if ever a man was murdered, that man was Walter Parsons. Let me put the incredible facts on paper. I do not expect to be believed, and yet…

Last February I was coming out of an employment agency in Pasadena, California, when a vigorous-looking gentleman of about fifty years accosted me.

"Pardon me, but I overheard what you said to the lady inside. You are a machinist?"

"Yes."

"And looking for work?"

"I am."

"Would you consider a hundred and fifty dollars a month and your board?"

"You've hired me."

He smiled briefly. "My name is Rowan, Captain Rowan. And yours?"

"Lester. John Lester."

He motioned me into the front seat of a Cadillac touring-car.

"Where shall we call for your things?"

"I haven't any."

He raised his eyebrows.

"They're pawned, sold, gone," I explained. "I was down to my last thin dime when you hired me."

He answered nothing to this but drove to a men's furnishing-store on Colorado Boulevard.

"Here is fifty dollars, an advance on your wages. Buy what you think you'll need."

When my purchases were placed in the rear of the car, we drove out South Fair Oaks, almost to South Pasadena, and turned into the driveway of a fairly large estate on the east side of the road. The grounds were quite extensive, I noticed, and surrounded by a low stone wall. Palm trees bordered the drive that led to the garage, and orange trees grew in serried rows to right and left. The house itself was an old-fashioned wooden residence with wide verandas on each side. In the rear of the house was a brick building.

"This," said the captain, throwing open the door, "is the machine-shop and laboratory. You will notice that the machine-shop is small but quite well equipped for ordinary work. Parts that can not be made here will, of course, be ordered from larger establishments. Your work will be mostly assembling those parts and turning out certain small devices according to plans and specifications I shall give you."

He took me to my room on the second floor of the house and left me to bathe and shave.

* * *

At dinner that evening I met Walter Parsons. He was a clever-looking man of middle age, a chemist, I gathered, with a private income – nothing particularly striking about him, unless it was the feeling he gave of being very meticulous, very correct. The third person at the table was Captain Rowan's sister, Genevieve, who was also the housekeeper and cook, as there were no servants. She was one of those women whom at first glance you dismiss as uninteresting. At second glance you decide they are actually plain. After that you pay them little attention, and are never certain when it was you discovered they were beautiful.

The captain sat at the head of his table and talked easily and naturally. "Have you ever read Lucian Larkin?" he asked me.

"No, never," I confessed.

"You know to whom I refer?"

"I'm afraid not."

He made a wry face. "Such is fame. Well, my boy, Lucian Larkin was an astronomer, the director until his death of Mount Lowe Observatory on the peak over there. But not only was he an astronomer; he was also a great mystic, the author of several wonderful books, not the least of which is *The Matchless Altar of the Soul*. You must read it, by all means."

Parsons gave a little laugh. He looked slyly at Genevieve Rowan, and then as if guilty of an indiscretion glanced quickly away.

"Not that you'll understand it," he mocked. "It is doubtful whether Larkin himself understood half of what he wrote."

The captain smiled tolerantly. "Walter is a materialist. He doesn't believe in the theory of a great mind back of all manifestation."

"Who could?" countered Parsons. He turned to me with the little sudden gesture that was characteristic of him. "It is so evident," he said, "that the mind of man is nothing but the sum of his bodily organization. When that organization breaks down – puff! – where is your mind?"

"And I might observe," replied the captain, "that when the dynamo breaks down, ditto, where is your power? Your very argument defeats you, Walter. Man is a machine. Very well. When he functions properly he is medium for mind, thought. When he breaks down, his mind, thought, goes – where? Into oblivion? Yes, the same oblivion that engulfs electricity when the generator fails to work; the same nothingness that claims radio waves when the machine fails to send them or the receiving-set to pick them up. Don't be absurd!"

I listened to them argue, rather puzzled as to what it was all about.

* * *

Several days later Parsons and I were in the machine-shop together and I expressed my bewilderment to him. "You see, Lester," he explained, "there are really two schools of thought. One school – the material school to which I belong – holds that our so-called mind is the result of bodily nerves and organs functioning a certain way. The other school – to which the captain subscribes – holds that mind is something exterior to our bodily organization, merely expressing itself through our brains and directing our activity."

As I worked I pondered these two concepts. Never before had I given such things serious thought. Now they interested me. Why? Because I sensed that in some fashion they were connected with the work I was doing. The captain as an electrical engineer, Parsons as a chemist, were engaged in some profound experiment. This much I gathered from their conversation. But what sort of an experiment? Now and then Captain Rowan talked to me freely. For days at a time he would work in his laboratory, hardly uttering a word; then for some reason he would open up and become almost loquacious.

"Consider this fact, Lester. Within the entire range of the telespectroscope and telecamera, where their range is so immense that one hundred million giant suns in space are now photographed, there is no entity able to add to itself but mind, thinking thoughts that have never been thought before."

I tried to grasp his meaning. "Just what is your definition of mind, sir?"

"That of Larkin. Electrons are the first manifestation of mind. They alone have been created. All else have been formed by an incredible number of varying combinations of electrons."

"I'm afraid I do not understand."

"It is very simple. Back of all manifestation is a cosmic mind – call it creator, if you will; I prefer to call it director. This director creates electrons. Electrons combine to form all other kinds of matter – the molecule, the atom. Ninety kinds of atoms are now known to chemists. Do you know what determines the atom of an element?"

"No."

"Well, what kind of an atom shall appear in space depends on four basic factors: number of electrons in revolution; specific speed of revolution; distance of orbits from the center; and directions of motion."

Parsons looked up from his chemical labors. "That is all true, Lester," he said, "but don't let the captain sweep you away by a statement of facts into an acceptance of a cosmic mind. Lucian Larkin was a great astronomer, and a scientist, but beyond a certain point – what we have verified with our instruments – he enters the realm of pure speculation. There is not one iota of proof that mind exists distinct from the body."

Captain Rowan laughed. "No? Then tell me: What if the hand of a person begins suddenly to write words at a rate ten to twenty times faster than normal, in a handwriting other than his own, upon wise and lofty subjects not heard of before; sometimes even in a language of which the owner of the hand is ignorant – tell me, what guides that hand?"

"There is usually fraud back of this automatic writing, deceit of some sort," replied Parsons. "In the few cases where it seems to be genuine, it is due, doubtless, to the subconscious mind of man."

"But if the person doing the automatic writing has no knowledge, either conscious or subconscious, of Latin or Greek, or even of Sanskrit (for I assure you whole reams have been written in Sanskrit), and the writing should be in any one of those languages – what then?"

Parsons shrugged his shoulders. "Still there is no valid reason for assuming an overmind or director as does Larkin." He turned to me. "Undoubtedly there are some mysterious things in connection with psychic phenomena which are baffling, but to use those mysterious things as a base from which to launch into wild and irrational speculations is not scientific. You will appreciate this better if you make an earnest study of the new psychology, behaviorism. Even James and Jung and Freud are being seriously challenged by John B. Watson. It begins to appear that our viscera are the directors of mind; that our memory, our so-called subconscious, is the result of habit, of conditioning. What you need to read, Lester, is Watson's book, *Behaviorism*, and leave Larkin to the metaphysicians."

* * *

That night I was permitted to see something curious. In coming through the hallway from the rear of the house to the front, I surprised Parsons and Genevieve Rowan in the front room. I was ahead of the captain and distinctly saw her in the arms of the chemist. Whether the captain saw the embrace, the quick springing apart, I do not know. The room was but dimly lighted, twilight prevailing, and the electric lights not yet turned on. It is possible he did not. At any rate he made no comment. Beyond surmising that Miss Rowan and Parsons were secretly sweethearts, I should have given little thought to the occurrence, if it had not been for what followed. Coming down the back steps to the kitchen after bathing and changing clothes, I surprised another tableau, more startling by far than the first. This time it was the captain and his sister. He held her above both elbows, at arm's length, shaking her furiously. I could not see her face, as her back was toward me, but his own was snarling, murderous.

"By God!" he growled, "I'll kill him first! Do you understand? And you too!"

I retreated up the steps. What did it mean? That the captain had seen Parsons embrace his sister? But what of that? Weren't Parsons and he friends, fellow experimenters? Then why the terrible anger I had witnessed, the seething rage? I could not understand it.

At the dinner table Genevieve Rowan was her usual quiet, well-poised self; her brother's face was placid. Had I imagined the scene in the kitchen, exaggerated it? No, that was impossible. But perhaps I was mistaken in linking it up with the earlier scene in the parlor.

Parsons seemed unaware of anything amiss. He baited the captain on his mysticism in his usual mocking manner. But as the days passed I became aware of something tense, something electric in the air. Two or three times I caught the captain watching Parsons when he thought himself unobserved. His face didn't change expression at those times, no; nor his eyes; yet the fixity of his stare, something about its utter immobility, chilled the blood in my veins.

I told myself I was imagining things, developing a case of nerves; only at this time I became dynamically conscious of Genevieve Rowan herself. Her ashen hair was suddenly full of glints that caught the eye. Her rounded figure held an allure that was hard to resist. "Don't be a fool," I told myself. "The woman is gray-headed; she is fifty, if she is a day." Yet in spite of such reasoning I knew her to be beautiful, desirable. And other things I knew – half suspicions, half certainties – gleaned from a word, a gesture, a step at midnight; the creak of a loose board, of an opening door. No, I won't tell what those things were! They are too horrible to put on paper, too terrible; yes. and too sad. Now that the captain is in his grave, Parsons dead, and only Genevieve alive – Genevieve who looks and walks about like a forlorn ghost – it is well that such things should be forgotten. Only I know that a real cause, a real lust for murder existed – existed and was glutted with blood. But enough of that!

* * *

In the workshop a strange machine grew under our hands as day succeeded day. Parts came from distant factories and I put them together. Other pieces of machinery I made myself according to plans furnished me by the captain and Parsons. The machine was mounted on wheels; incorporated in its body was an especially constructed electric dynamo. The captain wired the various parts, and in what he called the backbone of the ponderous, tapering mechanism he placed at intervals of three inches crystals derived from a saturated solution of Rochelle salt.

"Perhaps," said Parsons to me, "you have heard of singing crystals?"

"No," I replied, "I haven't."

"Well," he said, "it has long been known that lopsided crystals such as these have a certain effect on a ray of light passing through them. If you squeeze or pinch them, positive electricity collects at one part of the crystal and negative electricity at another. Now if you connect these two points you get a current. The discoverer of this interesting idiosyncrasy on the part of crystals was Professor Curie of Paris, who, in conjunction with his wife, later discovered radium. Behold!"

He pressed one crystal between a thumb and forefinger and its neighbor shrieked as if in pain. He laughed at my astonishment.

"One of these little crystals is enough to run two hundred telephones."

I could hardly credit it.

"Yes," the captain assured me, "that is true. But in this case they are going to be the little bodies which receive and send messages up and down the vertebrae of our machine, and to various parts of its body."

"Body!"

"Yes, body. For this is an iron creature we're building, a metal man."

I thought him joking. "It doesn't look much like a human being," I said.

"And has it to?"

"Lester," said Parsons, "is under the impression – the quite common impression – that to build a machine which will function like a man one must duplicate the human body."

"As in Mrs. Shelley's *Frankenstein*," commented the captain, "the artificial man complete from nerves, muscles, lungs, liver, to a fluid that circulated like blood."

"Exactly," agreed Parsons. "Only it had no soul and killed its inventor."

Both men laughed briefly.

"The concept is a mediaeval one," went the captain. "For you must know, my boy, that the human body is not the perfect mechanism the average person thinks it is. A skilled mechanic would be ashamed to turn out a machine as faulty in parts as is his own body."

"Perhaps so," I retorted, "but I notice that man is not able to improve on nature."

"There you are mistaken. Wherever man has been able to compete with nature by means of his machines he has bettered her. Take, for instance, the process on which all life depends, the storing up of solar energy in the green leaf. The leaf is not able to catch and hold more than one per cent of the radiant energy that falls upon it from the sun. In that respect it is much less efficient than any of man's machines. A steam engine can turn into mechanical work at least twelve per cent of the heat energy fed to it in the shape of coal, besting the natural process eleven to one."

"And nature," chimed in Parsons, "has never yet proved itself capable of producing a human being that could not make mistakes. Man has come pretty near doing that very thing. Have you ever read the play, *R.U.R.*?"

"No."

"Well, a foreign playwright wrote a play called by those letters, which were an abbreviation for 'Rossum's Universal Robots'."

"Robots?" I interrupted. "I believe I do know what you mean now. I've heard that word before."

"Of course you have. It's become a part of the English language. Well, the playwright's idea was quite fantastic and absurd. Who ever heard of Robots, mechanical men? Nobody. Yet at Washington, D.C., stands what is called the Brass Brain. Men step in front of it and ask questions. Talk of your ancient oracles! On the answers of this modern one men stake their lives and millions of dollars."

"Good Lord," I breathed, "what is it?"

"Nothing much. Only a machine that calculates how high and low tides will be in every port of the world today, tomorrow, and fourteen years from now."

I gaped at him.

"But why continue? There are in existence machines which turn switches, dig ditches, answer telephones, steer ships, come and go at the command of the human voice, and perform numerous duties. Of course these machines are not all assembled in one piece or place. They are distinct inventions, such as the adding-machine, the electric crane, or that latest marvel of them all, the calculating-machine which works out in a few hours or weeks or months intricate problems that would take learned men ten, yes, and even twenty years to solve. And the machine makes no mistakes."

"You mean," I said, enthralled, "that in some sort of fashion those machines are Robots?"

"Isn't it obvious? Consider, Lester: What would be the result if all those automatic brains, hands and feet were incorporated into one body!"

"My God!"

"And the brains directed the hands and feet?"

"Impossible!"

"That is the retort the scientist and inventor has always met with. Now this machine—"

"This machine?"

"Why, yes, the one we're building. It will demonstrate the correctness of the captain's and my theory."

I stared at him in a species of horror. "You mean," I gasped, "that this thing here" – I waved at the ponderous mass – "is intended to be a Robot, a metal man?"

He adjusted a crystal before answering, "We hope so."

"But, good Lord!" I exclaimed, "you're making a big mistake!"

"Indeed; how so?"

"Because no matter how much you give your machine chemical brains it won't be able to start its own thinking processes."

"That is true. Man has not yet been able to build a machine that can think. The ones I referred to above all operate at a note of music, the push of a button, the sound of a voice. We recognize that fact. The problem engrossing the captain and me is this: Can we build a mechanical, a chemical brain delicate enough to respond to thought as it now does to sound or other stimuli? Can we give such a command as this to our chemical and mechanical brain: 'Keep the motor running; every four hours feed it gas and oil'? Can we do more than that? Can we set our machine certain tasks to do, fixing those tasks in its 'mind', and then going away and forgetting it? Don't you see what that would mean? It would mean the creation of a genuine Robot, an independent metal creature that would work without supervision, eat its daily ration of fuel, and never get sick or go on strike."

But I was not to be swept away altogether by mere oratory.

"You forget," I said, "that they would break down from time to time; that human beings would then have to build others."

"At first, yes. But what if after a while we created thousands of them whose specialty it was to repair their worn-out or broken-down brother Robots? They would not have to resemble each other in the least, you understand, save in their mental capacity to receive certain commands and keep on obeying them. Once you had your workers toiling at producing for humanity, your repair machines busy at repairing and building the workers, what more supervision would man have to exercise over them than the average boss does over workers now? Indeed it ought to be possible to create a machine that will be all brain, vast, godlike in comparison to the ones that toil and repair, and imbue it with the thought of keeping the Robots working and the wheels of industry turning; and there you are!"

The idea was horrible to me. I couldn't entertain it without protest.

"But if man started such a process going," I whispered, horrified, "he might not be able to check it at will. What if the Robots grew out of hand, built themselves into great armies, turned on man and destroyed him?" I wiped the sweat from my brow. "Good God, Parsons!" I said, "such inventions fly in the face of nature. They can bring humanity no good. Better leave well enough alone."

He shook me by the shoulder scoffingly. "All progress man has ever made, from tilling the ground to talking over radios, has been flying in the face of nature."

The captain, who had said nothing for some time, now broke in.

"There is no need to be alarmed, my boy. Those Robots which Parsons visualizes would be the product of mind, therefore obedient to it."

I made no reply to him; but from the day of the above conversation my interest in the work I was doing, in the amazing experiment that was being undertaken, became intensified.

The machine grew under our hands until it was six feet tall. It stood, as I have said before, on rollers, the rollers being encased in caterpillar belts. At the base it was about four feet around, tapering to twelve inches at the top. It was built, not in one piece but in segments, jointed ball-and-socket fashion, with various springs and rubber cushions separating the different parts. To describe it further is beyond me; only it had two arm-like pistons, one on each side, possessed a central electric dynamo, and was wired so profusely as to make the interior seem a tangled mass of cord.

* * *

Came the day when the brain of this monstrous mechanism was put in place. The part that fitted into what I must call the neck was made of aluminum, all except the cover, which was transparent glass and screwed into place. A small cylinder, which emitted an intense bluish light when brought into contact with electricity, was inside the aluminum bowl. The captain connected the necessary wires. His face was very red. I watched breathlessly as Parsons filled the hollow globe with a glutinous mixture of opaque liquid. My hands unconsciously gripped each other until they hurt while I waited for something to happen, but nothing did. He screwed the glass cap into place and stepped down and back from the machine.

"It is finished," he said quietly, looking at the captain; "finished – and ready."

As if his words were a knockout blow, the captain fell.

"Quick!" cried Parsons to me, kneeling beside him, "a glass of water! The excitement has been too much for him. He's fainted!"

But he hadn't fainted. When the doctor reached the house he was dead.

"That heart of his," explained the physician. "I told him to be careful, to avoid any sudden strain or excitement."

Genevieve Rowan was beside herself with grief. In front of us all Parsons put his arms around her.

"There, there, dearest. It is terrible, yes. But it may be for the best."

Was it relief I saw on his face? I scorned myself for the thought, and yet, in spite of the fact that they had been absorbed in a kindred experiment, working together harmoniously enough in the laboratory, I was conscious of the fact that all was not, as it should be between the two men. How did I know this when I never heard a word of ill-feeling pass between them, never intercepted a glance that could be actually interpreted as inimical? I can't say. But I knew it instinctively, as I knew other things on which their antagonism was based: things as to which my lips are forever sealed.

On the back porch I found a large notebook. It had evidently dropped from the captain's pocket as we carried him into the house. I slipped it into my pocket, intending to give it to Miss Rowan later, and continued on my way to the laboratory to lock things up. What I saw there drove all thought of the notebook from my mind. A strange glow was radiating from the glass cap which topped the head of the machine. It was reddish-blue in color. Evidently the chemical solution contained in the aluminum bowl gave rise to this phenomenon.

Fascinated, I climbed the short stepladder and peered through the glass. The glutinous mixture was pulsing as if alive. It was now a gray, speckled mass shot through with red streamers. The sight startled me. The gooseflesh rose on my skin, and I had that familiar sensation of the scalp which people mean when they say their hair stands on end.

I left the laboratory abruptly, in my haste forgetting to fasten the door. It was my intention to tell Parsons of what I had seen, but he was still in the parlor comforting the captain's sister; so I continued on my way upstairs.

I had just begun to strip when the deep purring of a motor came from the rear yard. This was strange, as I had heard no car entering the driveway. My room was in the rear of the house; so it was possible for me to glance out the open window to observe who it was. Darkness had fallen. The motor, by the sound of it, was right under me, near the back door. I could hear it, but the thick foliage of a pepper tree prevented me from looking straight down. Baffled, I stepped back, and as I did so someone flung open the back door with considerable force.

"What's the matter, Lester?" called Parsons' voice.

"It isn't I," I shouted down; "I'm upstairs."

"Then who the devil—"

A ponderous weight was dragging across the kitchen floor. My heart leapt suffocatingly in my throat. A floor board cracked like a pistol shot somewhere beneath me.

"I say," came Parsons' voice, "I say, what's the matter here? What's the – oh my God!"

His voice went up in a terrible crescendo; went up – and ceased. I snatched up the first thing beneath my hand – a large stillson wrench – and leapt down the stairs. Someone was screaming like mad, and the house was rocking under the impact of stamping blows. In the passageway I nearly trampled on a prone body – that of Genevieve Rowan – and had to hurdle it to reach the kitchen.

Parsons had evidently turned on the lights as he entered, for the room was well lighted. At the sight of what I saw, strength nearly left me. I stood as if petrified. There before me – believe it or not, as you like – was lying the crushed and bleeding body of Walter Parsons, his features fixed in a set grimace of stark horror and agony, while crouching over him like some fearsome prehistoric monster was the metal man he had helped to make, the hideous Robot, driving its short, arm-like pistons into his still quivering flesh.

The sight sickened me. My bowels turned to water. The awful monstrosity was bent over like a bow, screaming as if in rage, and the pulsing matter under the glass cap on the top of its head sent out its reddish-blue tinge and glared at me like an evil eye.

Insane with terror I showered blow after blow on it with my stillson wrench. The glass cap broke; the glutinous mass rolled out and pulsed on the floor like a living thing in its death throes. Even as it fell the whole body of the machine straightened up convulsively. Through all its sinuous wires and lengths ran a sighing sob. Then with a terrible crash it fell over on the already horribly mutilated body of its victim and was still.

I waited to see no more. I turned and ran. I remember that I screamed as I ran.

* * *

That is all. I told them everything at the inquest. Nay, more, I showed them what was written in Captain Rowan's notebook, the one I had picked up, put in my pocket, forgotten, and then accidentally glanced at later – only two pages of writing in the captain's almost illegible script. They read as follows:

Within the entire realm of the vast and intricate modern science of electricity, there is nothing more wonderful and awe-inspiring than induction, action at a distance without a conducting wire. This fact is the base of the wireless systems of telegraphy and telephony, and of all electrodynamic machinery as dynamos and motors, the bases of electric lights and electric railroads. But see this… I am convinced that we actually think by induction.

And underneath this palpable quotation, which is credited to Lucian Larkin, was written these words:

If this be true, then man's mind is more than the sum and total of his bodily organization. What if my heart can not hold out much longer? I know that my mind shall live on. It shall manifest itself through the brain of the machine. Parsons is mistaken about this. He is a fool. If he understood, if he knew… Oh, Genevieve! If I thought that were true I would kill…

The writing stops here. But the question will not down. Did the mind of Captain Rowan, as it was leaving its fleshly vehicle, glimpse his sister in the arms of Walter Parsons? Was it his intelligence that animated the chemical brain, put the ponderous mechanism into motion, drove it across the yard into the kitchen, and brutally killed the man he hated? The coroner and the jury may ignore the facts. They may recoil from them in horror. They may attribute what I say to hysteria, an unbalanced mind; but the uncanny truth remains. Walter Parsons was not accidentally killed: he was murdered by a man already dead, and the weapon with which he was slain was the metal man and the chemical brain of his own partial creation!

A Wife Manufactured to Order

Alice W. Fuller

AS I WAS going down G Street in the city of W— a strange sign attracted my attention. I stopped, looked, fairly rubbed my eyes to see if they were rightly focused; yes, there it was plainly lettered in gilt: "Wives made to order! Satisfaction guaranteed or money refunded."

Well! Well! Does some lunatic live here, I wonder? By Jove! I will investigate. I had inherited (I suppose from my mother) a bit of curiosity, and the truth of the matter was this: now nearing the age of forty, I thought it might be advisable to settle down in a home of my own; but alas! to settle down to a life of strife and turmoil, that would not be pleasant; and that I should have to do, I knew very well, if I should marry any of my numerous lady acquaintances – especially Florence Ward, the one I most admired. She unfortunately had strong-minded ways, and inclinations to be investigating woman's rights, politics, theosophy, and all that sort of thing. Bah! I could never endure it. I should be miserable, and the outcome would be a separation; I knew it. To be dictated to, perhaps found fault with – no, no, it would never do; better be a bachelor and at least live in peace. But – what does this sign mean? I'll find out for myself.

A ring of the bell brought a little white-haired, wiry sort of a man to the door. "Walk in, walk in, sir," he said.

I asked for an explanation of the strange sign over the door.

"Just step right in here and be seated, sir. My master is engaged at present, sir, with a great politician who had to separate from his wife; was so fractious, sir, got so many strange notions in her head; in fact, she wanted to hold the reins herself. You may have seen it – the papers have been full of it. Why, law bless you, sir, the poor man couldn't say his soul was his own, and he is here now making arrangements with master to make him a quieter sort of wife, someone to do the honors of the home without feelin' neglected if he happens to be a little courteous to some of his young lady friends. You see, master makes 'em to order, makes 'em to think just as you do, just as you want 'em to; then you've got a happy home, something to live for. Beautiful – golly! I've seen some of the beautifulest women turned out, most make your mouth water to look at." And so the old man rattled on until I was quite bewildered.

I interrupted him by asking if I could see his master.

"Oh, certainly, sir; you just make yourself comfortable and I will let you know when he is through."

I sat for some time like one in a dream, wondering if this could be so, and with many wonderful modern inventions in mind I began to think it possible. And then there was a vision of a happy home, a wife beautiful as a dream, gentle and loving, without a thought for anyone but me; one who would never reproach me if I didn't happen to get home just at what she thought was the proper time; one who would not ask me to go to church when she knew it was against my wishes; one who would never find fault with me if I wished to go to a base-ball game on Sunday, or bother me to take her to the theatre or opera. A man, you know, can't give much time to such things without interfering greatly with his comfort. Oh! Could all this be realized?

But just then my reverie was broken by the old man, who was saying: "Just step this way. Master, let me introduce you to Mr. Charles Fitzsimmons."

Short, thick-set, florid complexion, pale blue eyes with a sinister twinkle, was the description of Mr. Sharper, whom I confronted. Reaching out his hand, which was cold and clammy and reminded me very much of a piece of cold boiled pork, he said:

"Now, young man, what can I do for you? Want a life-companion, a pleasant one? Man of means, no doubt, and can enjoy yourself; a little fun now and then with the boys and no harm at all – none in the least. When a man comes home tired, doesn't like to be dictated to; want someone always to meet you with a smile, someone that doesn't expect you to be fondlin' and pettin' 'em all the time. I understand it – I know just how it is. Law bless my soul, I've made more'n one man happy, and I've only been in the business a short time, too. Now, sir, I can get you up any style you want – wax, but can't be detected."

"Do you mean to say you manufacture a woman out of wax, who will talk?"

"That's just what I do; you give me the subjects you most enjoy talking upon, and tell me what kind of a looking wife you want, and leave the rest to me, and you will never regret it. I will furnish as many 'phones' as you wish; most men don't care for such a variety for a wife – too much talk, you know," and he chuckled and laughed like a big baby.

"What are your prices, may I ask?"

"Well, it's owing a good deal to how they are got up – from five hundred to a thousand dollars."

"Well," I said, "I think that rather high."

"Dear man alive, a pleasant companion for life for a few hundred dollars! Most men don't grumble at all for the sake of having their own way and a pleasant home, and you see she ain't always asking for money." (Sure enough, I hadn't thought of that.)

"Very well, I will decide upon the matter and let you know."

"All right, young man; you'll come back. They all do, them as knows about it."

I went to my room at the hotel and thought it all out, thought of the pleasant evenings I could have with someone whose thoughts were like my own, someone who would not vex me by differing in opinion. I wondered what Florence would say. I really believed she cared for me, but she knew how I disliked so many of the topics she persisted in talking upon. What mattered it to me what Emerson said, or Edward Bellamy wrote, or Henry George, or Pentecost? What did I care about Hume or Huxley or Stuart Mill? Any of those sciences, Christian Science or Divine Science or mind cure? Bah! It was all nonsense. The topics of the day were enough, and if I attended closely to my business I needed recreation, not such things as she would prescribe. Still Florence was interesting to talk to, and I rather liked her at times when she talked every-day talk; but I could not marry her, and it was her own fault. She knew my sentiments, and if she would persist in going on as she did I couldn't help it.

Yes, I decided I would have a home of my own, and a wife made to order at once. Before leaving the city I made all necessary arrangements, hurried home, rented a house, and went to see old Susan Tyler, whom I engaged as housekeeper; she was deaf and had an impediment in her speech, but she was a fine housekeeper. All my preparations made, the ideal home! Oh! How my heart beat as I looked around! What happiness to do as I liked, a beautiful, uncomplaining wife ready to grant every wish and meet me with a smile! What would the boys say when, out a little late at night, I should be so perfectly at ease? I could just see jealousy on their faces, and I laughed outright for joy. Tomorrow I was going for my bride. Side-looks and innuendos were thrust at me from all quarters, but I was too happy to demur or explain. When I reached the city I could scarcely wait for the appointed time.

Alighting from the carriage the door was opened, and I was ushered into the presence of the most beautiful creature I had ever beheld. The hands extended towards mine, the lips opened, and a low, sweet voice said, "Dear Charles, how glad I am you have come!" I stood spellbound, and only a chuckle from Mr. Sharper brought me to my senses.

"Kiss your affianced, why don't you?" he said, and chuckled again.

I felt as though I wanted to knock him down for speaking so in that beautiful creature's presence. And then a little soft rippling laugh, and she moved towards me. Oh, could I get that beast to leave the room! Why did he stand there chuckling in that manner?

"Sir," I said, "you will oblige me by leaving the room for a few moments."

With that he chuckled still louder and muttered, "Bless me, I really believe he thinks her alive." Then to me: "To be sure, to be sure, but you only have a short time before going to the minister's, and I must show you how to adjust her. When you get home" – and he chuckled again – "you can be just as sentimental as you please, but just now we will attend to business. Here are a box of tubes made to talk as you wished them. They are adjusted so. Place the one you wish in your sleeve. You can carelessly touch her right here if there is anyone around. Here is a spring in each hand and the tips of her fingers. I will give you a book of instructions, and you will soon learn to arrange her with very little effort, just to suit yourself, and I am sure you will be very happy. Now, sir, the time is up; you can go to the minister's."

As I put her wraps around her and drew her arm through mine she murmured so sweetly, "Thank you, dear." How glad I was to get out of the presence of that vile man who was constantly pulling or pushing her; I could scarcely keep my hands off from him, and my serene Margurette – for I decided to call her that – would only smile and say, "Thank you!" "Oh, how lovely!" "Ah, indeed!" I was almost vexed with her to think she did not resent it. I wanted her all to myself where I could have the smiles, and thought I should be thankful when we were in our own home.

During our journey I could not help noticing the admiring glances from my fellow travellers, but my beautiful wife did not return any of their looks. In fact, I overheard a couple of young dudes say, "Just wait till that old codger's back is turned, and we shall see whether she will have no smiles for any but him." I had half a notion to adjust her to give them some cutting reply and then go into the smoker awhile, for I was sure they would try to get into conversation with her; but pshaw! I hadn't ordered any tubes of that kind. I believed I'd send and get one in case of an emergency. No, I wouldn't have such in the house; I wanted an amiable wife, and when we were once at home it would not be necessary. I wouldn't have to go with her anywhere unless I wanted to. Only think of that! Never feel that my wife would ask me to go with her and I have to refuse, then ten to one have her cry and make a fuss about it. I knew how it was, for I had seen too much of that sort of thing in the homes of my friends.

Business ran smoothly; everything was perfect harmony; my home was heaven on earth. I smoked when I wished to, I went to my base-ball games, I stayed out as long as I pleased, played cards when I wished, drank champagne or whatever I fancied, in fact had as good a time as I did before marriage. My male friends congratulated me upon my good fortune, and I was considered the luckiest man anywhere around. No one knew how I had made the good luck for myself.

There are some things in life I could never understand. One of them is that, when everything seems so prosperous, calamity is so often in the wake. And that was the case with me. After so many prosperous years a financial crash came. I tried to ward it off; I was up early and late. Margurette never complained, but was always sweet and smiling, with the same endearing words. Sometimes as the years went by I felt as though I would not object to her differing with me a little, for variety's sake; still it was best. When I would say, "Margurette, do you really think so?" and I would speak so cross to her often – I don't know but that I did so more than was necessary; still a man must have some place where he can be himself, and if he can't have that privilege at home, what's the use of having a home? But she was never out of patience, and my wife would only say, "Yes, darling", so low and sweet. I remember once I said, when I was worried more than usual, "I am damned tired of this sort of thing," and she laughed so sweetly and called me her "own precious boy".

But the crash came, and there was no use trying to stay it any longer. I came home sick and tired. It was nine o'clock at night, with a cold, drizzling rain falling. Susan had gone to bed sick, and forgotten to light a fire in the grate. I went into the library, where Margurette always waited for me. No lights; I stumbled over a chair. I accidentally touched Margurette. She put up her lips to kiss me and laughingly said, "Precious darling, tired tonight?" Great God! I came very near striking her.

"Margurette, don't call me darling, talk to me; talk to me about something – anything sensible. Don't you know I am a ruined man? Everything I have got has been swept away from me."

"There, precious, I love you," and she laughed again.

"Did you not hear what I said?" I screamed.

But she only laughed the more and said, "Oh, how lovely!"

I rushed from the house. I could not endure it longer; I was like one mad. My first thought was, where can I go, to whom can I go for sympathy? I cannot stand this strain much longer, and to show weakness to men, I could never do that. I will go to Florence, I said. I will see what she says. Strange I should think of her just then!

I asked the servant who admitted me for Miss Florence.

"She is indisposed and cannot see anyone tonight."

"But," I said, writing on a card hastily, "take this to her."

Only a few moments elapsed and she came in, holding out her hand in an assuring and friendly way. "I am surprised to see you tonight, Mr. Fitzsimmons."

"O Florence!" I cried, "I am in trouble. I believe I shall lose my mind if I cannot have someone to go to; and you, dear Florence, you will know my needs; you can counsel, you can understand me."

"Sir!" Florence said, "are you mad, that you come here to insult me?"

"But I love you. I know it. I love the traits that I once thought I despised."

"Stop where you are! I did not receive you to hear such language. You forget yourself and me; you forget that you are a married man – shame upon you for humiliating me so!"

"Florence, Florence, I am not married; it is all a lie, a deception."

"Have you lost your reason, Mr. Fitzsimmons? Sit down, pray, and let me call my father. You are ill."

"Stop," I cried, "I do not need your father. I need you. Listen to me. I imagined I could never be happy with a wife who differed in opinion from me. In fact, I had almost decided to remain single all the rest of my days, until I came across a man who manufactured wives to order. Wait, Florence, until I have finished – do not look at me so. I am indeed sane. My wife was manufactured to my own ideas, a perfect human being as I supposed."

"Mr. Fitzsimmons, let me call my father." And Florence started towards the door. She was so pale that she frightened me, but I clutched her frantically.

"Listen," I said, "will you go with me? I will prove that all I have told you is true."

My earnestness seemed to reassure her. She stopped as if carefully thinking, then asked me to repeat what I had already told her. Finally she said yes, she would go.

We were soon in the presence of my beautiful Margurette, whom I literally hated – I could not endure her face. "Now, Florence, see," I cried; and I had my wife talk the namby-pamby lingo I once thought so sweet. "Oh! How I hate her!" and I glared at her like a madman. "Florence, save me. I am a ruined man. Everything has been swept away – the last today. I am a pauper, an egotist, a bigot, a selfish—"

"Stop!" cried Florence. "You wrong yourself; you are a man in your prime. What if your money has gone, you have your health and your faculties, I guess," (and there was a merry twinkle in her eyes) "the whole world is before you, and best of all, no one to interfere with you or argue on disagreeable topics."

"O Florence! I am punished enough for my selfishness. O God!" and I threw myself on the couch, "were I not a pauper, too, there might be some hope for happiness yet."

"You are not a pauper," said Florence, "you are the master of your fate, and if you are not happy it is your own fault."

"Florence, I can never be happy without you. I know now it is too late."

"Too late – never say that. But could you be happy with me, 'a woman wedded to an idea', 'strongminded'? Why, Charles, I am liable to investigate all sorts of scientific subjects and reforms. And then supposing I should talk about it sometimes; if it was not for that I might think of the matter. As far as money is concerned, that would have little to do with my actions. Still, Charles, upon the whole I should be afraid to marry the 'divorced' husband of so amiable a wife as your present one is. I, with my faults and imperfections! The contrast would be too great."

"Florence, Florence," I said, "say no more. All I ask is, can you overlook my folly and take me for better, for worse? I have learned my lesson. I see now it is only a petty and narrow type of man who would wish to live only with his own personal echo. I want a woman, one who retains her individuality, a thinking woman. Will you be mine?"

"I will consider the matter favorably," said Florence, "but we shall have to wait a year, for opinion's sake, as I suppose there are not many who know how you had your late wife manufactured to order."

And we both laughed.

The Electric Man

Being the One-Act Version of the Successful Three-Act Farcical Comedy of the Same Name

Charles Hannan

[Stage Layout and Notes: 'D. in F' indicates the opening leading to hall. 'R' the entry to drawing-room. There are curtains at each side of the window recess, and a Grandfather's clock against wall, front of china cupboard.

Walter and the automaton are never upon the stage together, so that throughout the play Walter takes the figure's place by entering the cupboard 'off'. A super is required, however, to play 'dummy', but when this happens the figure is seated in the cupboard with its back to audience.

Costume for Walter and for the automaton: Walter wears a brown coat or jacket and trousers of the same, with a white waistcoat. The automaton is dressed exactly the same as to trousers and waistcoat, etc., but wears a black frock coat, and as they both usually keep the coat buttoned, the waistcoat is seldom seen. 'Funeral March of a Marionette' to accompany the automaton's scenes. The automaton walks very stiffly and jerkily, and moves his arms like a doll.]

SCENE: WALTER'S rooms in London. Moderately furnished sitting-room.
On table at R. a newspaper and two unopened letters.
The table up in the alcove is set for luncheon.
WALTER'S brown bowler is lying on chair or sofa L.
The cupboard door has a spring so that it closes of itself when left open, a string being also tacked across the inside of the door so that WALTER can pull the door to after him at end of play. A large bamboo rocking-chair is used for the figure, and is easily moved and turned as directed.
(Enter JACK and MRS. ANDERSON D. in F.)

MRS. ANDERSON. It's as I thought, sir, the poor young gent isn't up.

JACK. (*Looks at his watch.*) Was he late last night?

MRS. ANDERSON. Oh, yes, sir, as I happens to know being woked up sudden, thinkering to hear a burglar, which was only Master Walter Everest, the gent I does for, a-creepering and a-crawlering upstairs.

JACK. Is he often like that? (*Takes up and looks at letters on table and puts them down again.*)

MRS. ANDERSON. Lawk a floury! No, sir, only breaks out occasional when his work's bad. Mr. Everest is a chemist and electrician.

JACK. Been working hard lately?

MRS. ANDERSON. I believes as he have something very musterious and secret inventering at this here identical period of time, some mustery as he keeps in that there cupboard, which the door is always locked constant. Oh, very musterious – and queer smells a-penetratering and perfuncteroring the house. Oh, here he are, sir.

(WALTER's door L. opens. She exits D. in F.)
(WALTER stumbles in L. He is not to look dissipated, but to act it.)

WALTER. Hullo, hullo! whose head is this? It isn't mine, it can't be mine. Stop! (*Sits top of R. table.*) Stop! (*Picks up newspaper.*) Morning paper, who wants morning paper? (*Throws it on floor behind him, and JACK, who is watching him, picks it up. WALTER opens letter.*) Letters, who wants letters? – Oh, one from my tailor, 'We greatly regret delay in delivery of your new black coat. We will despatch it to reach your residence without fail today. May we remind you that your account—?' No, you may not remind me.

(JACK gives him a rousing smack on the back.)

Hullo, Jack, where did you spring from?
JACK. Came to town this morning. (*Clasp hands.*)
WALTER. Jack, I'm very ill. I haven't been out of doors till last night for weeks. Nothing but work at what my father left me. He gave his lifetime to it and then left it to me. It ought to have been the invention of the age. I went on the spree last night, when the whole thing failed.
JACK. I have some news for you about your stepmother, Mrs. Everest. By the idiotic conditions of your late father's will – if the old lady marries again before your birthday on Monday next the whole fortune he left becomes not yours but hers.
WALTER. He meant it the other way about.
JACK. Yes, but that is how the will reads – instead of writing 'He shall inherit,' your father wrote 'she shall inherit'. She is the 'she'. About forty-five thou., isn't it?
WALTER. Nearer fifty.
JACK. An adventurer named Potterfield has lately come to the village, found out about the will, made love to the old lady, got a special license, and is bringing her to town to marry her tomorrow.
WALTER. What?
JACK. Stella is coming here directly. This wedding must be stopped or postponed.
WALTER. Jack, something's got to be done – suppose I were taken ill – very ill.
JACK. No good at all.
WALTER. Well, suppose that – no, that's no use – suppose again that – no, that's no good either. I have a dim kind of idea that in some way my invention is going to help us.
JACK. You said it had failed.
WALTER. It failed living; it might be of use dead. (*Swiss Jodel.*) Hullo, tra la la! (*Momentary dissipated business.*)

(STELLA enters D. in F.)

WALTER. Hullo, Stella, how are you? Jack has told me all about this adventurer, Potterfield. I've an idea to checkmate my stepmother. (*Gives her seat.*) I'm going to postpone their marriage not by being ill – I'm going to die. What do you think of that?
JACK. I think it's the weakest thing I ever heard of.
WALTER. In that cupboard there is a figure exactly like myself which was timed to spring into

existence yesterday at 5 p.m. – only it didn't. It's the work my father never completed. Something went wrong. There the figure is and will remain, dead as a nut. I even dressed it in my best clothes, gave it a name, too, christened it Cyril Davidson.
STELLA. Cyril Davidson? (*Laughs.*)
JACK. What was the little idea of making it like yourself?
WALTER. My father's instructions were to make the man I was creating a handsome, good-looking fellow, according to the very best available model. All you've got to do is to produce the dead figure and say it's me. I'll go away to Brighton; they can't in common decency marry before the funeral.
JACK. Then it seems you made an electric man. My chief doubt is it won't be like enough.
WALTER. Come and see!

(Music. He takes key from pocket, unlocks door of cupboard, and a man in black frock-coat, with black bowler, is seen seated with back to audience.)

STELLA. Oh, how wonderful! (*Looking in.*)
JACK. Wonderful! (*Looking in.*)
STELLA. Walter, that is you!

(Bell rings off D. in F.)

WALTER. Bell! – That may be my stepmother! (*He quickly closes cupboard.*) We might go into the other room. I call it my drawing-room, because there is a piano and three gold-fish in a bowl.

(STELLA goes into room R.)

Jack, in case she comes I'd better be off. Can you lend me any cash?
JACK. How much do you want? (*Producing loose cash.*)
WALTER. Two or three pounds. (*Looks in JACK's hand.*) I'll take four. (*Does so.*) Stop, I'll give you a duplicate key of the cupboard. (*Gives key.*) The figure has got my black coat on, and I want it for Brighton. When you come back, it will be wearing this one. (*Pointing to coat he is wearing.*)
JACK. Right.
WALTER. Explain that to Stella.
JACK. Right, oh! (*JACK goes into drawing-room R.*)

(WALTER picks up and puts on his brown bowler, goes quickly up, unlocks cupboard, puts key back in pocket, then goes in after saying:)

WALTER. Now, Mr. Davidson, my coat, if you please.

(He opens door wide, showing figure seated as before, then goes in and the door closes.)
(He is then heard calling loudly in cupboard:)

I say! Let me go! Confound you – Jack – Jack – I say! The thing is moving!

(Loud noise of struggle.)

Hold on, damn it! Don't hit me on the head! Do you want to STUN me? Jack!

(A loud cry and two thumps, then the cupboard door slowly opens, AUTOMATON *puts head out – the actor having had time to change into the black coat before entering as the automaton. It creeps out, not opening the door more than necessary – business, tries to re-open door by hitting it. It wears the black bowler set to one side of head. Comes down C., stiffly, and remarks, 'Yow', then goes up.* MRS. ANDERSON *enters D. in F. with dishes and sets table in recess with back to audience. He goes towards* MRS. ANDERSON. *She starts on seeing his strange manner. He turns and goes across and straight off D. in F., she goes after him.)*

MRS. ANDERSON. *(Calling after him.)* Mr. Everest, sir!

(Exit AUTOMATON *D. in F.)*
(Exit MRS. ANDERSON *D. in F.)*
*(*JACK *and* STELLA *enter from R.)*

JACK. I left him changing his coat.
STELLA. *(Looking out of window.)* There he is turning the corner; he has changed his coat.
JACK. Let's have a proper look at this wonderful thing before the old lady comes.

(They fetch out chair with WALTER *seated on it and bring it down stage, where they wheel the chair right round so that the stunned* WALTER *faces audience. He is hatless.)*

STELLA. Hasn't it slipped down in the chair since we saw it last?
JACK. I don't think so.
STELLA. Look at its eyes – Jack, they're opening – it's moving!
JACK. Great Heavens! It's being born!
WALTER. *(Half stunned and waking)* Where am I?
STELLA. It speaks!
JACK. It's living!
WALTER. I want a drink!
JACK. Good lord! It drinks!

*(*STELLA *screams and falls on seat. Bell again rings loudly off R.)*

Hullo! There's Mrs. Everest! *(He takes* WALTER, *who has risen, by the arm.)* Come with me, sir. *(Leads him to bedroom L.)* In there with you, quick!

(Kicks him in quickly, and locks door.)
*(*STELLA *meantime has hurried up with the chair and put it in cupboard and closes door.)*

Phew! This is the most extraordinary thing! *(Hurries down, saying:)* Where are the telegraph forms?

(As he snatches them from nail on wall, and sits to write R., MRS. ANDERSON *enters D. in F. out of breath and with a telegram; she is in process of dressing, her hair being in disorder, and she wears a dressing jacket.)*

MRS. ANDERSON. Telegrapheram, sir. (*Down and gives it.*)
JACK. (*Looking at telegram*) From Mrs. Everest – 'Have missed train, don't wait lunch – coming by next.' Thank goodness! (*To MRS. ANDERSON.*) I suppose you don't know where I can find a detective?
MRS. ANDERSON. Yes, sir, I does. Being my own nephew as lives in the attic.
JACK. (*Writes several telegrams, as:*) I want him at once—
MRS. ANDERSON. Lawk a floury me!

(Hurries out D. in F.)

STELLA. What are you writing? (*Takes up one of the telegrams.*) 'Walter Everest, Ship Hotel, Brighton. Cyril Davidson is living. Come home.'

(WALTER knocks loudly at bedroom door.)

Jack! Listen!
JACK. (*Still writing – knocking repeated.*) Coming – coming.

(Knocking ceases – he continues.)

This goes to every hotel in Brighton.
STELLA. He may not be at an hotel.
JACK. That's why I've sent for a detective—

(JOBBINS enters, hat in hand and umbrella under arm; he is a stout man, rather shabbily dressed in tweed, with tweed frock-coat, and has a square-topped bowler.)

JOBBINS. My name is Jobbins, sir. (*Gives large card.*) Private inquiry and detective agent, utmost secrecy and despatch, parties watched, missing relatives traced, divorces ensured.
JACK. This is a very simple matter, Mr. Jobbins. The gentleman who resides here left home suddenly. I want him fetched back at once. (*Sits and writes note as:*)
JOBBINS. Yes, sir, (*goes up, then returns*), where is he? (*With notebook open to take notes.*)
JACK. Brighton.
JOBBINS. (*Notes*) Brighton – what hotel, sir?
JACK. Do you think if I knew what hotel I should require a detective?
JOBBINS. Then how am I to find him?
JACK. The best thing will be to take the first train to Brighton.
JOBBINS. (*Notes*) First train to Brighton.
JACK. He may be at a boarding-house.
JOBBINS. (*Notes*) Possibly a boarding-house.
JACK. When you find him, give him this note, (*closing it and giving it*) and send me a wire. (*Gives five-pound note.*) There is some cash for your expenses.
STELLA. How is he to know Walter?
JACK. Isn't there a photograph? (*Finds one on mantel R.*) Here we are. (*Gives it.*)
JOBBINS. I'll walk about the Brighton streets with this – why, I seen this gent in the public gardens five minutes ago.

JACK. Then after him and bring him back.
JOBBINS. (*At D. in F.*) You'll hear from me – BY WIRE.

(Exit.)

JACK. (*Calls out after him.*) Follow him to Victoria; if you miss him, go right on. (*Comes down.*) I've forgotten these telegrams.
STELLA. I'll take them.
JACK. (*Gives them.*) Have you any cash?
STELLA. Yes. (*Hurries out D. in F.*)

(A very loud peremptory knocking at D.L. JACK listens a moment – it is repeated.)

JACK. Getting nasty! (*Loud knocking.*)
WALTER. (*Off, calls.*) I say – let me out!
JACK. Now if I had not known, I should have said that was Walter. The voice was a trifle thick at starting, but now it's identical.
WALTER. (*Off.*) Let me out. (*Loud knocking.*)
JACK. I suppose I'll have to.

(He goes and unlocks door and returns to R. front – WALTER comes out.)

WALTER. What is the meaning of all this?
JACK. That's exactly what I want to know.
WALTER. Locking a fellow in a bedroom.
JACK. (*Aside.*) Calls itself a fellow and knows it's a bedroom!
WALTER. I feel as stupid (*he is still half-stunned*) as an owl. Where is Stella?
JACK. Knows about Stella!
WALTER. What are you muttering?
JACK. Knows I'm muttering!
WALTER. Well?
JACK. Well.
WALTER. Why the devil don't you speak?
JACK. Knows there's a devil! I really don't quite know what to do with you till your creator returns.
WALTER. What? – How?
JACK. What or how – same thing. This is a pretty pickle, Mr. Cyril Davidson.
WALTER. Mr. What?
JACK. Of course you don' know your name yet; that is what you were christened, Cyril Davidson, so I call you Cyril Davidson.
WALTER. Oh, you do, do you? that's very clever of you. My mind's a blank, I can't remember what happened before I woke up on that chair.
JACK. No one remembers what happened before they were born.
WALTER. (*Bangs a book down on table.*) Oh, damned nonsense!
JACK. I wonder what you think of the world now you've come into it; what are your general impressions of mankind?
WALTER. Was this why you locked me in the bedroom?
JACK. Exactly.

WALTER. And are you going to keep this up?
JACK. Decidedly.
WALTER. I can't see much sense in it myself; however, if it pleases you – I'm going to have some lunch. (*Goes up to table in recess.*)
JACK. (*Calls up.*) Mr. Davidson! (*No answer.*) I've made it angry. (*Calls.*) Mr. Davidson – I say, Davidson – Mr. Cyril Davidson – sir – oh, it's in a pet and declines to answer me.

(*STELLA enters D. in F.*)

STELLA. Jack, a boy brought this. (*Gives note.*)
JACK. (*Tears it open.*) Jobbins is something like a detective. 'Just seen Mr. Everest, he is running. Jobbins.'
STELLA. Running?
JACK. The electric individual is in there.
STELLA. You let it out? What is it doing?
JACK. Lunching.
WALTER. (*At table in alcove, mixing salad.*) Nothing here but salad! (*With beer bottle.*) Beer, who wants beer?
JACK. Knows all about everything!
STELLA. It's been listening in the cupboard before it lived. (*Pause and then asks.*) Should we speak to it?
JACK. It's very bad-tempered, but I daresay it won't hurt you. (*They go up.*) I say, Davidson!
WALTER. Bah! (*They start back.*)
STELLA. Poor thing! Tell it it's amongst friends.

(*They again approach.*)

JACK. This young lady is very anxious to make your acquaintance, Mr. Davidson!

(*WALTER smashes crockery with a beer bottle; they start and come down in fright, then approach again.*)

STELLA. Please, Mr. Davidson!
WALTER. (*Turns.*) Oh, you've come back; has Jack told you what he's playing at?

(*He comes down a little – they retreat from him.*)

JACK. Isn't it wonderful! Calls me Jack!
WALTER. (*As they are staring at him.*) When you've done staring, perhaps you'll drop this.
STELLA. Jack, I can't believe it! (*WALTER walks about in rage.*)
JACK. At first I couldn't, but there is a difference, I begin to see it, a very subtle difference; watch how it moves; aren't its joints a little stiff and so on?
WALTER. (*Quick step to him.*) You thick-headed-addle-pated numskull!

(*JACK in fright falls headlong backwards over sofa L., STELLA runs and crouches R., then they rise on knees and wave to pacify him.*)

JACK. Gently, gently!
STELLA. Oh, please, Mr. Davidson, please don't be so angry; we are both awfully interested in you and really sorry for you. It must be terrible to be born full grown.
WALTER. Am I mad, or are you?
JACK. You are.
WALTER. That's settled.
STELLA. Of course, you think you're real, but we know. You're only a made thing, like a cheese or a pudding.
WALTER. (*Hand to head.*) You honestly say and believe that I am my own invention? (*They nod solemnly.*)
WALTER. Am I myself, or am I the thing I made?
JACK. You are the thing you made.
WALTER. Then where is myself – the other fellow?
JACK. Your esteemed creator left home before you began to exist, changed coats and went.
WALTER. Changed coats? I never changed coats at all!
JACK.
} What?
STELLA.
WALTER. The moment I tried to, the figure rose up and stunned me.
STELLA. (*Up to him, throws arms round him.*). It's Walter!

(*Enter* MRS. ANDERSON *with telegram D. in F., and gives it.* JACK *opens it.*)

Mrs. Anderson. (*Seeing Walter.*) Ow! Ow! Lawk a floury me!

(*Exit.*)

JACK. Jobbins is somewhere near Euston. (*Gives telegram to* STELLA.)
WALTER. Who's Jobbins?
JACK. The detective who's gone after you to bring you back.
WALTER. Then it really went out?
STELLA. (*Reading telegram.*) 'Have taken a cab, he's still running.' What will happen if Mr. Jobbins catches it?
WALTER. I expect he will catch it.
JACK. Another telegram! (*Going up to D. in F.*)

(MRS. ANDERSON *hands in a telegram and retires.*)

(*Coming down, reading:*) 'He has smashed some more windows, and is still running.'
STELLA. (*Taking the telegram.*) More windows!
JACK. 'The crowd are still after him.'
WALTER. Crowd?
JACK. 'He has just climbed a tall chimney stack marked Bovril, and is now sitting on the top.'
WALTER. Good Lord!
JACK. 'Marked Bovril', is this to be your fate, alas, my poor brother!
WALTER. (*Snatches the wire and reads:*) 'They are fetching a fire escape. He keeps yowling.'
STELLA. (*Taking telegram.*) Yowling?

WALTER. Suppose the police get him and think it's me, I'll be blamed for all this damned thing. We must catch him. We'll buy a gag and handcuffs as we go along.
STELLA. Gag? Why?
WALTER. Because he's yowling! Stop! Stella must stay in case Mrs. Everest comes. (*Calls.*) Mrs. Anderson! I want a cab!

(He and JACK rush out D. in F.)

STELLA. I'm so excited I think I'll play the piano in the other room.

(Exit R. to drawing-room and immediately plays and sings 'Caressante'.)
(AUTOMATON enters D. in F., in black frock-coat, but now hatless, goes to cupboard, paws at the door, goes and knocks over chair, then to table up L. and takes up a tumbler, brings it down mechanically to front C., half raises it, then lets it fall on the floor and sits by table R., facing audience and says:)

AUTOMATON. Tick-tick-Yow.

(MRS. ANDERSON enters D. in F. with a black frock-coat in tailor's parcel, places it on table R. top end, then sees AUTOMATON and comes out C., to speak.)

MRS. ANDERSON. Oh, he's there, are he? (*Using handkerchief as she speaks.*)
AUTOMATON. Yow.
MRS. ANDERSON. There's a parcel from the tailoring folks with a message hopering as it were in time.
AUTOMATON. Yow-Yow. (*She starts a little.*)
MRS. ANDERSON. The poor young lady is a-sittering in there.
AUTOMATON. Tick-tick. Yow-yow! (*Same business.*)
MRS. ANDERSON. Ain't you in good 'ealth, Mr. Everest, sir?
AUTOMATON. Yow-chuck, yow-yow.

(Rises and makes mechanical exit to bedroom L.)

MRS. ANDERSON. (*Watching him.*) Poor-young-man!

(Enter STELLA R.)

Mr. Everest have come back, mum; gone in his bedroom, mum; been to the pub-house again, or I'm much mistook. Poor-young-man!

(Exit D. in F.)

STELLA. (*Calls across.*) Walter, here's a parcel – Walter!

(Automaton enters door L., but does not come out, she sees him.)

Walter, why have you left Jack? Is anything wrong?

AUTOMATON. Yow! (*Turns and goes in again D.L.*)
STELLA. (*Crossing to the door.*) Walter! (*Door shuts.*) How very polite of you! Are you changing? (*Voice off says, "Yow."*) Oh, very well, if you won't answer me. I'm in the drawing-room all alone!

(*Has crossed back to R., and goes in.*)

AUTOMATON. (*Enters L.*) Tick-chuck-yow. (*Goes up, hits door of cupboard twice.*) Chuck-yow-yow.

(*Goes to recess, knocks over a chair, hits clock, etc., and goes into china cupboard in recess L. A loud noise of smashing of crockery off. Stella through this is playing and singing same air as before.*)
(WALTER *comes in D. in F., as soon as ever he can, walking quite quietly as contrast to the very quick exit of* AUTOMATON. *Brown jacket.*)

WALTER. (*Comes to table R., calling.*) Stella! I want you. Stella!
STELLA. (*Stops singing a moment to call:*) I'm not coming! (*Resumes song off.*)
WALTER. (*Takes up parcel.*) My new coat at last. The moment I get Davidson under lock and key I'm going to change into this and get away to Brighton. (*Puts parcel down.*)

(STELLA *enters R.*)

Why wouldn't you come a minute ago?
STELLA. Why did you shut that door in my face?
WALTER. When?
STELLA. After you went out.
WALTER. After I went out – before I came home? Did I speak?
STELLA. No.
WALTER. It's as plain as a pikestaff, it's come home!
STELLA. (*Slowly and firmly.*) I believe you're right. Now I've seen you both, I'll never mistake again.
WALTER. It must be somewhere on the premises now.

(*They hurriedly look about under furniture, and meet and collide up C., and say, "Oh!" Noise in china cupboard.*)

WALTER. It's in the bedroom. Run down to Mrs. Anderson and borrow the very largest blanket.
STELLA. Why?
WALTER. I want something to throw over it.

(STELLA *exit D. in F.*)

WALTER. (*Listens to fresh sounds.*) No! It's in the china cupboard!

(*A wooden hand with fingers extended is mysteriously thrust out of china cupboard door. He gets a plate and smashes it on this hand, which is at once withdrawn. This can be done with a real hand and smash plate on door near it.*)
(*He quickly turns key.*)

WALTER. Got it – got it!

(He jubilantly dances down C., then goes and calls out D. in F.)

Stella, Stella, I've locked it in the china cupboard. I don't want the blanket. (*Returns.*) Gone in the kitchen, I suppose! (*Takes up parcel.*) Change my coat at last and get away! (*Goes into bedroom L.*)

(Immediately on his exit a loud smashing in china clipboard, then the door flies into splinters and is knocked down, and AUTOMATON enters quickly, hurries right round C., and into bedroom after WALTER.)

WALTER. (*Within, as loud noise in bedroom.*) Hi! Stop!
AUTOMATON. (*Within.*) Yow-yow.
WALTER. (*Rushing in, dressed in black coat.*) By Jove! What an escape!

(JACK, carrying blanket of green flannel or red, enters with STELLA, who has gag and handcuffs – enter D. in F.)
(WALTER makes signs to them, pointing to bedroom and beckoning them to follow him there.)

JACK. Is that it?
STELLA. Yes, yes, Jack, yes!

(JACK throws blanket over WALTER, and they get him on chair C.)

JACK. Hurrah! We've got him now! (*Business: secure him with rope round his legs and gag, then take blanket off.*) (*WALTER, gagged, groans.*) No more climbing tall chimney stacks! (*WALTER groans.*)
STELLA. Is it in pain?
JACK. Of course not.
STELLA. It groans so!
JACK. Rather mad at being caught.
STELLA. Is it wax-work?
JACK. More like India-rubber. I suppose you do see the difference this time?
STELLA. Rather.
JACK. That's not flesh and blood. (*Pulling its nose.*)
STELLA. It seems to want to explain something.
JACK. It will never get the chance of that. (*Lighting a candle from mantel R.*)
STELLA. Poor thing! Are you tired of living? (*Groan.*)
JACK. How can it answer you?
STELLA. I believe it could if you took the gag out of its mouth.
JACK. Hold the candle under its nose. (*Groan.*)
STELLA. No, no, no! (*JACK puts candle on table.*)
JACK. (*With pin from waistcoat.*) I want to see what it will do when I stick this pin in it. (*Groan.*)
STELLA. No, no!
JACK. In its leg, you can nip its arms and legs. (*Does so – groan.*)

STELLA. It doesn't seem to like being nipped.
JACK. In the interests of science I'm going to bleed it. (*Loud groans.*) Give me a carving knife. (*Groans.*)

(*MRS. ANDERSON has entered and come down – sees WALTER, screams. They start.*)

MRS. ANDERSON. The gent I does for came down the other stair from the bedroom (*pointing L.*) and is in the kitchen premises at this here identical period of time.
JACK. What! Is he?
MRS. ANDERSON. Here have I been a-doing for two twins at the price of one.
JACK. (*Bustles MRS. ANDERSON to D. in F.*) Send Mr. Everest up at once! (*Exit MRS. ANDERSON.*)
JACK. Now to make an end of this fiend!

(*WALTER, who has been watching them as well as he could, now pretends to be dead.*)

Hullo! I don't think I'll want any instruments, it's passing away! (*Business.*) Not breathing! (*Looks at watch.*) Its eyes are closed. Oh! It's run down. I believe we'd be quite safe to unbind it. Just help me with this rope. Let it pass away quietly on the sofa. There is something pathetic even in the death of a doll.

(*They unbind WALTER and raise him, he opens his eyes and bounds upon JACK – commotion.*)

Confound it, it's living again!

(*STELLA runs in room R., JACK runs in room L.*)

WALTER. (*As JACK looks in L., and STELLA looks in R.*) I say! (*They at once withdraw.*) Jack! Stella! (*Heads appear again.*) I say! Jack! (*Heads disappear.*) Come out, you bounder! (*Heads appear.*) Why are you making such idiots of yourselves?
JACK. (*Coming in.*) Who are you?
WALTER. Walter Everest.
JACK. The other fellow said that.
WALTER. I am the other fellow.
JACK. Then I've let the automaton escape!
WALTER. Escape?
JACK. It must be in the kitchen now!
WALTER. I have a particularly heavy poker in my room, I'll just fetch it.
JACK. And then?
WALTER. We'll see what then! (*Has gone into bedroom L.*)
JACK. This is a nice muddle! What asses we've been!
STELLA. Yes, haven't we?
JACK. By Jove! We have.

(*AUTOMATON comes in D. in F., followed by MRS. ANDERSON with a telegram – they both go quickly into drawing-room R.*)

MRS. ANDERSON. (*Calling as she goes.*) Telegrapheram, Mr. Everest, sir!
STELLA. (*Down L. with JACK points up to them as they go out.*) Jack! Look!

(*Piano is smashed off R.*)

Oh, what's that?
JACK. That's the piano! (*Glass is smashed off R.*) That's the three gold-fish in the bowl!

(*WALTER with poker enters L.*)

MRS. ANDERSON (*Off*). Oh, help! (*She rushes in from R. in a fainting condition and gasps.*) Mr. Everest have fell out of the window into the street!
WALTER. Mrs. Anderson, I am here.

(*She gives a loud yell of fright in his face and rushes into bedroom L. STELLA hastens after her.*)

WALTER. There's going to be no mistake this time, I'm going after it myself. (*Exit D. in F.*)

(*JOBBINS enters D. in F., his hat bashed, a black eye, and one arm in a sling. He is in a miserable condition.*)

JACK. Great goodness! Jobbins!
JOBBINS. What's left of him, sir!
AUTOMATON. (*Off at back.*) Yow-yow.
JOBBINS. (*On his knees clings to JACK.*) I calls on you to protect me!
JACK. We must search this house from top to toe. You chase up, I'll chase down. And if we don't find him, meet here.
JOBBINS. I'll do that (*they go up*), meet here!

(*Exeunt.*)

STELLA. (*Looks in L.*) Jack, she's getting better – Jack! Where are you? (*Goes in again.*)

(*JOBBINS enters D. in F., comes down, saying:*)

JOBBINS. Missed him! (*Sits L. of R. table*) I'll just make out my little bill.

(*As he is doing this, AUTOMATON enters D. in F., comes down and has a spasm with his hands, knocking off JOBBINS' hat. JOBBINS with a loud yell rushes out D. in F. AUTOMATON knocks furniture about, etc., and goes into china cupboard.*
[He may throw a chair out of window first.]
STELLA comes in L. to see his final exit. She then goes up, looks into china cupboard after him – then comes downstage, calling in fright:)

STELLA. Help! Help! Help!

(Jack and Jobbins bring Walter on between them D. in F., and bring him down C., and Mrs. Anderson enters L.)

Walter. Let me go, let me go, I say!
Stella. Jack, you've got the wrong man!

(They release him.)

Mrs. Anderson. There's a telegrapheram, sir; is it for you or your twin?
Jack. (*Snatches it and reads.*) From Mrs. Everest – 'Potterfield fell out of his dogcart and broke his leg. The wedding is postponed.'
Stella. Postponed!
Jack. Congratulate you, old chap. (*Shaking hands.*) Your fortune's safe.

(Noise off and lights down as:)

Walter. Hush, hush! All of you. It's coming out to die!

(Stella hides on floor front of sofa L. Mrs. Anderson hides on knees front of table R. Jobbins stands by clock against wall up L. Jack sets cupboard door open with chair against it and then goes and stands in recess to R., side of same, and Walter goes off to hide behind the curtain of recess L., side where there is a secret exit, so that he at once comes on as Automaton from the china cupboard.)
(A man's hand holds out the curtain behind which Walter is supposed to be hiding. Dying scene for Automaton. Jerky business, frightens Jobbins who crouches back from it, then goes C., stoops and grows faint, has a spasm of strength and hurries to table R., frightening Mrs. Anderson, who gets under table. It then leans dying against table, then has a fresh spasm, hurrying across to Stella, who lies away from it on floor to avoid it.)
(Then up to cupboard door, which Jack set open with a chair. Automaton dies with back to inside of door, pushing the chair clear of it in his spasm, business, finally shutting himself in as he collapses by letting the door close after him.)
(Red limes changing to green through above, and dark floats.)
(Lights up – all rise.)

Stella. (*Cries.*) Walter! (*Music of 'Caressante'.*)

(Walter comes out from behind curtain L. and down to Stella C., takes her in his arms.)

Walter. It's Walter this time, and if you want proof, open the cupboard and you'll find all that remains of THE ELECTRIC MAN.

CURTAIN

Metropolis

Chapters IV–VIII

Thea von Harbou

[Publisher's Note: This dystopian novel, famous because of the Fritz Lang film, gives a groundbreaking vision of futuristic tech in a society of worker exploitation. Our excerpt begins with the introduction of the scientist Rotwang and his robot creation, visited by the Metropolis ruler, Joh Frederson. We also meet Maria, with whom Joh's son Freder falls in love.]

Chapter IV

THERE WAS A HOUSE in the great Metropolis which was older than the town. Many said that it was older, even, than the cathedral, and, before the Archangel Michael raised his voice as advocate in the conflict for God, the house stood there in its evil gloom, defying the cathedral from out its dull eyes.

It had lived through the time of smoke and soot. Every year which passed over the city seemed to creep, when dying, into this house, so that, at last it was a cemetery – a coffin, filled with dead tens of years.

Set into the black wood of the door stood, copper-red, mysterious, the seal of Solomon, the pentagram.

It was said that a magician, who came from the East (and in the track of whom the plague wandered) had built the house in seven nights. But the masons and carpenters of the town did not know who had mortared the bricks, nor who had erected the roof. No foreman's speech and no ribboned nose-gay had hallowed the Builder's Feast after the pious custom. The chronicles of the town held no record of when the magician died nor of how he died. One day it occurred to the citizens as odd that the red shoes of the magician had so long shunned the abominable plaster of the town. Entrance was forced into the house and not a living soul was found inside. But the rooms, which received, neither by day nor by night, a ray from the great lights of the sky, seemed to be waiting for their master, sunken in sleep. Parchments and folios lay about, open, under a covering of dust, like silver-grey velvet.

Set in all the doors stood, copper-red, mysterious, the seal of Solomon, the pentagram.

Then came a time which pulled down antiquities. Then the words were spoken: The house must die. But the house was stronger than the words, as it was stronger than the centuries. With suddenly falling stones it slew those who laid hands on its walls. It opened the floor under their feet, dragging them down into a shaft, of which no man had previously had any knowledge. It was as though the plague, which had formerly wandered in the wake of the red shoes of the magician, still crouched in the corners of the narrow house, springing out at men from behind, to seize them by the neck. They died, and no doctor knew the illness. The house resisted its destruction with so great a force that word of its malignity went out over the borders of the city, spreading far over the land, that, at last, there was no honest man to be found who would have ventured to make war against it. Yes, even the thieves and the rogues, who were promised remission of their sentence provided that they declared themselves ready to pull down the magician's house, preferred to go to the pillory, or even to the scaffold, rather than to enter within these spiteful walls, these latchless doors, which were sealed with Solomon's seal.

The little town around the cathedral became a large town and grew into Metropolis, and into the centre of the world.

One day there came to the town a man from far away, who saw the house and said: "I want to have that."

He was initiated into the story of the house. He did not smile. He stood by his resolution. He bought the house at a very low price, moved in at once and kept it unaltered.

This man was called Rotwang. Few knew him. Only Joh Fredersen knew him very well. It would have been easier for him to have decided to fight out the quarrel about the cathedral with the sect of Gothics than the quarrel with Rotwang about the magician's house.

There were in Metropolis, in this city of reasoned, methodical hurry, very many who would rather have gone far out of their way than have passed by Rotwang's house. It hardly reached knee-high to the house-giants which stood near it. It stood at an angle to the street. To the cleanly town, which knew neither smoke nor soot, it was a blot and an annoyance. But it remained. When Rotwang left the house and crossed the street, which occurred but seldom, there were many who covertly looked at his feet, to see if, perhaps, he walked in red shoes.

Before the door of this house, on which the seal of Solomon glowed, stood Joh Fredersen.

He had sent the car away and had knocked.

He waited, then knocked again.

A voice asked, as if the house were speaking in its sleep:

"Who is there?"

"Joh Fredersen," said the man.

The door opened.

He entered. The door closed. He stood in darkness. But Joh Fredersen knew the house well. He walked straight on, and as he walked, the shimmering tracks of two stepping feet glistened before him, along the passage, and the edge of the stair began to glow. Like a dog showing the track, the glow ran on before him, up the steps, to die out behind him.

He reached the top of the stairs and looked about him. He knew that many doors opened out here. But on the one opposite him the copper seal glowed like a distorted eye, which looked at him.

He stepped up to it. The door opened before him.

Many doors as Rotwang's house possessed, this was the only one which opened itself to Joh Fredersen, although, and even, perhaps, because, the owner of this house knew full well that it always meant no mean effort for Joh Fredersen to cross this threshold.

He drew in the air of the room, lingeringly, but deeply, as though seeking in it the trace of another breath…

His nonchalant hand threw his hat on a chair. Slowly, in sudden and mournful weariness, he let his eyes wander through the room.

It was almost empty. A large, time-blackened chair, such as are to be found in old churches, stood before drawn curtains. These curtains covered a recess the width of the wall.

Joh Fredersen remained standing by the door for a long time, without moving. He had closed his eyes. With incomparable impotence he breathed in the odour of hyacinths, which seemed to fill the motionless air of this room.

Without opening his eyes, swaying a little, but aim-sure, he walked up to the heavy, black curtains and drew them apart.

Then he opened his eyes and stood quite still…

On a pedestal, the breadth of the wall, rested the head of a woman in stone…

It was not the work of an artist, it was the work of a man, who, in agonies for which the human tongue lacks words, had wrestled with the white stone throughout immeasurable days and nights until at last it seemed to realise and form the woman's head by itself. It was as if no tool had been at work here – no, it was as if a man, lying before this stone, had called on the name of the woman, unceasingly, with all the strength, with all the longing, with all the despair, of his brain, blood and heart, until the shapeless stone took pity on him letting itself turn into the image of the woman, who had meant to two men all heaven and all hell.

Joh Fredersen's eyes sank to the words which were hewn into the pedestal, roughly, as though chiselled with curses.

HEL
born
to be my happiness, a blessing to all men,
lost
to Joh Fredersen
dying
in giving life to his son, Freder

Yes, she died then. But Joh Fredersen knew only too well that she did not die from giving birth to her child. She died then because she had done what she had to do. She really died on the day upon which she went from Rotwang to Joh Fredersen, wondering that her feet left no bloody traces behind on the way. She had died because she was unable to withstand the great love of Joh Fredersen and because she had been forced by him to tear asunder the life of another.

Never was the expression of deliverance at last more strong upon a human face than upon Hel's face when she knew that she would die.

But in the same hour the mightiest man in Metropolis had lain on the floor, screaming like a wild beast, the bones of which are being broken in its living body.

And, on his meeting Rotwang, four weeks later, he found that the dense, disordered hair over the wonderful brow of the inventor was snow-white, and in the eyes under this brow the smouldering of a hatred which was very closely related to madness.

In this great love, in this great hatred, the poor, dead Hel had remained alive to both men…

"You must wait a little while," said the voice which sounded as though the house were talking in its sleep.

"Listen, Rotwang," said Joh Fredersen. "You know that I treat your little juggling tricks with patience, and that I come to you when I want anything of you, and that you are the only man who can say that of himself. But you will never get me to join in with you when you play the fool. You know, too, that I have no time to waste. Don't make us both ridiculous, but come!"

"I told you that you would have to wait a little while," explained the voice, seeming to grow more distant.

"I shall not wait. I shall go."

"Do so, Joh Fredersen!"

He wanted to do so. But the door through which he had entered had no key, no latch. The seal of Solomon, glowing copper-red, blinked at him.

A soft, far-off voice laughed.

Joh Fredersen had stopped still, his back to the room. A quiver ran down his back, running along the hanging arms to the clenched fists.

"You should have your skull smashed in," said Joh Fredersen, very softly… "You should have your skull smashed in… that is, if it did not contain so valuable a brain…"

"You can do no more to me than you have done," said the far-off voice.

Joh Fredersen was silent.

"Which do you think," continued the voice, "to be more painful: to smash in the skull, or to tear the heart out of the body?"

Joh Fredersen was silent.

"Are your wits frozen, that you don't answer, Joh Fredersen?"

"A brain like yours should be able to forget," said the man standing at the door, staring at Solomon's seal.

The soft, far-off voice laughed.

"Forget? I have twice in my life forgotten something… Once that Aetro-oil and quick-silver have an idiosyncrasy as regards each other; that cost me my arm. Secondly that Hel was a woman and you a man; that cost me my heart. The third time, I am afraid, it will cost me my head. I shall never again forget anything, Joh Fredersen."

Joh Fredersen was silent.

The far-off voice was silent, too.

Joh Fredersen turned round and walked to the table. He piled books and parchments on top of each other, sat down and took a piece of paper from his pocket. He laid it before him and looked at it.

It was no larger than a man's hand, bearing neither print nor script, being covered over and over with the tracing of a strange symbol and an apparently half-destroyed plan. Ways seemed to be indicated, seeming to be false ways, but they all led one way; to a place that was filled with crosses.

Suddenly he felt, from the back, a certain coldness approaching him. Involuntarily he held his breath.

A hand grasped along, by his head, a graceful, skeleton hand. Transparent skin was stretched over the slender joints, which gleamed beneath it like dull silver. Fingers, snow-white and fleshless, closed over the plan which lay on the table, and, lifting it up, took it away with it.

Joh Fredersen swung around. He stared at the being which stood before him with eyes which grew glassy.

The being was, indubitably, a woman. In the soft garment which it wore stood a body, like the body of a young birch tree, swaying on feet set fast together. But, although it was a woman, it was not human. The body seemed as though made of crystal, through which the bones shone silver. Cold streamed from the glazen skin which did not contain a drop of blood. The being held its beautiful hands pressed against its breast, which was motionless, with a gesture of determination, almost of defiance.

But the being had no face. The beautiful curve of the neck bore a lump of carelessly shaped mass. The skull was bald, nose, lips, temples merely traced. Eyes, as though painted on closed lids, stared unseeingly, with an expression of calm madness, at the man – who did not breathe.

"Be courteous, my parody;" said the far-off voice, which sounded as though the house were talking in its sleep. "Greet Joh Fredersen, the Master over the great Metropolis."

The being bowed slowly to the man. The mad eyes neared him like two darting flames. The mass began to speak; it said in a voice full of a horrible tenderness:

"Good evening, Joh Fredersen…"

And these words were more alluring than a half-open mouth.

"Good, my Pearl! Good, my Crown-jewel!" said the far-off voice, full of praise and pride.

But at the same moment the being lost its balance. It fell, tipping forward, towards Joh Fredersen. He stretched out his hands to catch it, feeling them, in the moment of contact, to be burnt by an unbearable coldness, the brutality of which brought up in him a feeling of anger and disgust.

He pushed the being away from him and towards Rotwang, who was standing near him as though fallen from the air. Rotwang took the being by the arm.

He shook his head. "Too violent," he said. "Too violent. My beautiful parody, I fear your temperament will get you into much more trouble."

"What is that?" asked Joh Fredersen, leaning his hands against the edge of the table-top, which he felt behind him.

Rotwang turned his face towards him, his glorious eyes glowing as watch fires glow when the wind lashes them with its cold lash.

"Who is it?" he replied. "Futura... Parody... whatever you like to call it. Also: delusion... In short: it is a woman... Every man-creator makes himself a woman. I do not believe that humbug about the first human being a man. If a male-god created the world (which is to be hoped, Joh Fredersen) then he certainly created woman first, lovingly and revelling in creative sport. You can test it, Joh Fredersen: it is faultless. A little cool – I admit, that comes of the material, which is my secret. But she is not yet completely finished. She is not yet discharged from the workshop of her creator. I cannot make up my mind to do it. You understand that? Completion means setting free. I do not want to set her free from me. That is why I have not yet given her a face. You must give her that, Joh Fredersen. For you were the one to order the new beings."

"I ordered machine men from you, Rotwang, which I can use at my machines. No woman... no plaything."

"No plaything, Joh Fredersen, no... you and I, we no longer play. Not for any stakes... We did it once. Once and never again. No plaything, Joh Fredersen but a *tool*. Do you know what it means to have a woman as a tool? A woman like this, faultless and cool? And obedient – implicitly obedient... Why do you fight with the Gothics and the monk Desertus about the cathedral? Send the woman to them Joh Fredersen! Send the woman to them when they are kneeling, scourging themselves. Let this faultless, cool woman walk through the rows of them, on her silver feet, fragrance from the garden of life in the folds of her garment... Who in the world knows how the blossoms of the tree smell, on which the apple of knowledge ripened. The woman is both: Fragrance of the blossom and the fruit...

"Shall I explain to you the newest creation of Rotwang, the genius, Joh Fredersen? It will be sacrilege. But I owe it to you. For you kindled the idea of creating within me, too... Shall I show you how obedient my creatures are? Give me what you have in your hand, Parody!"

"Stop..." said Joh Fredersen rather hoarsely. But the infallible obedience of the creature which stood before the two men brooked no delay in obeying. It opened its hands in which the delicate bones shimmered silver, and handed to its creator the piece of paper which it had taken from the table, before Joh Fredersen's eyes.

"That's trickery, Rotwang," said Joh Fredersen.

The great inventor looked at him. He laughed. The noiseless laughter drew back his mouth to his ears.

"No trickery, Joh Fredersen – the work of a genius! Shall Futura dance to you? Shall my beautiful Parody play the affectionate? Or the sulky? Cleopatra of Damayanti? Shall she have the gestures of the Gothic Madonnas? Or the gestures of love of an Asiatic dancer? What hair shall I plant upon the skull of your tool? Shall she be modest or impudent? Excuse me my many words, you man of few! I am drunk, d'you see, drunk with being a creator. I intoxicate myself, I inebriate myself, on your astonished face! I have surpassed your expectations, Joh Fredersen, haven't I? And you do not know everything yet: my beautiful Parody can sing, too! She can also read! The mechanism of her brain is as infallible as that of your own, Joh Fredersen!"

"If that is so," said the Master over the great Metropolis, with a certain dryness in his voice, which had become quite hoarse, "then command her to unriddle the plan which you have in your hand, Rotwang…"

Rotwang burst out into laughter which was like the laughter of a drunken man. He threw a glance at the piece of paper which he held spread out in his fingers, and was about to pass it, anticipatingly triumphant, to the being which stood beside him.

But he stopped in the middle of the movement. With open mouth, he stared at the piece of paper, raising it nearer and nearer to his eyes.

Joh Fredersen, who was watching him, bent forward. He wanted to say something, to ask a question. But before he could open his lips Rotwang threw up his head and met Joh Fredersen's glance with so green a fire in his eyes that the Master of the great Metropolis remained dumb.

Twice, three times did this green glow flash between the piece of paper and Joh Fredersen's face. And during the whole time not a sound was perceptible in the room but the breath that gushed in heaves from Rotwang's breast as though from a boiling, poisoned source.

"Where did you get the plan?" the great inventor asked at last. Though it was less a question than an expression of astonished anger.

"That is not the point," answered Joh Fredersen. "It is about this that I have come to you. There does not seem to be a soul in Metropolis who can make anything of it."

Rotwang's laughter interrupted him.

"Your poor scholars!" cried the laughter. "What a task you have set them, Joh Fredersen. How many hundredweights of printed paper have you forced them to heave over. I am sure there is no town on the globe, from the construction of the old Tower of Babel onward, which they have not snuffled through from North to South. Oh – if you could only smile, Parody! If only you already had eyes to wink at me. But laugh, at least, Parody! Laugh, rippingly, at the great scholars to whom the ground under their feet is foreign!"

The being obeyed. It laughed, ripplingly.

"Then you know the plan, or what it represents?" asked Joh Fredersen, through the laughter.

"Yes, by my poor soul, I know it," answered Rotwang. "But, by my poor soul, I am not going to tell you what it is until you tell me where you got the plan."

Joh Fredersen reflected. Rotwang did not take his gaze from him. "Do not try to lie to me, Joh Fredersen," he said softly, and with a whimsical melancholy.

"Somebody found the paper," began Joh Fredersen.

"Who – somebody?"

"One of my foremen."

"Grot?"

"Yes, Grot."

"Where did he find the plan?"

"In the pocket of a workman who was killed in the accident to the Geyser machine."

"Grot brought you the paper?"

"Yes."

"And the meaning of the plan seemed to be unknown to him?"

Joh Fredersen hesitated a moment with the answer.

"The meaning – yes; but not the plan. He told me he has often seen this paper in the workmen's hands, and that they anxiously keep it a secret, and that the men will crowd closely around him who holds it."

"So the meaning of the plan has been kept secret from your foreman."

"So it seems, for he could not explain it to me."

"H'm."

Rotwang turned to the being which was standing near him, with the appearance of listening intently.

"What do you say about it, my beautiful Parody?"

The being stood motionless.

"Well—?" said Joh Fredersen, with a sharp expression of impatience.

Rotwang looked at him, jerkily turning his great skull towards him. The glorious eyes crept behind their lids as though wishing to have nothing in common with the strong white teeth and the jaws of the beast of prey. But from beneath the almost closed lids they gazed at Joh Fredersen, as though they sought in his face the door to the great brain.

"How can one bind you, Joh Fredersen," he murmured, "what is a word to you – or an oath… Oh God… you with your own laws. What promise would you keep if the breaking of it seemed expedient to you?"

"Don't talk rubbish, Rotwang," said Joh Fredersen. "I shall hold my tongue because I still need you. I know quite well that the people whom we need are our solitary tyrants. So, if you know, speak."

Rotwang still hesitated; but gradually a smile took possession of his features – a good-natured and mysterious smile, which was amusing itself at itself.

"You are standing on the entrance," he said.

"What does that mean?"

"To be taken literally, Joh Fredersen! You are standing on the entrance."

"What entrance, Rotwang? You are wasting time that does not belong to you…"

The smile on Rotwang's face deepened to serenity.

"Do you recollect, Joh Fredersen, how obstinately I refused, that time, to let the underground railway be run under my house?"

"Indeed I do! I still know the sum the detour cost me, also!"

"The secret was expensive, I admit, but it was worth it. Just take a look at the plan, Joh Fredersen, what is that?"

"Perhaps a flight of stairs…"

"Quite certainly a flight of stairs. It is a very slovenly execution in the drawing as in reality…"

"So you know them?"

"I have the honour, Joh Fredersen – yes. Now come two paces sideways. What is that?"

He had taken Joh Fredersen by the arm. He felt the fingers of the artificial hand pressing into his muscles like the claws of a bird of prey. With the right one Rotwang indicated the spot upon which Joh Fredersen had stood.

"What is that?" he asked, shaking the hand which he held in his grip.

Joh Fredersen bent down. He straightened himself up again.

"A door?"

"Right, Joh Fredersen! A door! A perfectly fitting and well-shutting door. The man who built this house was an orderly and careful person. Only once did he omit to give heed, and then he had to pay for it. He went down the stairs which are under the door, followed the careless steps and passages which are connected with them, and never found his way back. It is not easy to find, for those who lodged there did not care to have strangers penetrate into their domain… I found my inquisitive predecessor, Joh Fredersen, and recognised him at once – by his pointed red shoes, which have preserved themselves wonderfully. As a corpse he looked peaceful and

Christian-like, both of which he certainly was not in his life. The companions of his last hours probably contributed considerably to the conversion of the erstwhile devil's disciple…"

He tapped with his right forefinger upon a maze of crosses in the centre of the plan.

"Here he lies. Just on this spot. His skull must have enclosed a brain which was worthy of your own, Joh Fredersen, and he had to perish because he once lost his way… What a pity for him…"

"Where did he lose his way?" asked Joh Fredersen.

Rotwang looked long at him before speaking.

"In the city of graves, over which Metropolis stands," he answered at last. "Deep below the moles' tunnels of your underground railway, Joh Fredersen, lies the thousand-year-old Metropolis of the thousand-year-old dead…"

Joh Fredersen was silent. His left eyebrow rose, while his eyes narrowed. He fixed his gaze upon Rotwang, who had not taken his eyes from him.

"What is the plan of this city of graves doing in the hands and pockets of my workmen?"

"That is yet to be discovered," answered Rotwang.

"Will you help me?"

"Yes."

"Tonight?"

"Very well."

"I shall come back after the changing of the shift."

"Do so, Joh Fredersen. And if you take some good advice…"

"Well?"

"Come in the uniform of your workmen, when you come back!"

Joh Fredersen raised his head but the great inventor did not let him speak. He raised his hand as one calling for and admonishing to silence.

"The skull of the man in the red shoes also enclosed a powerful brain, Joh Fredersen, but nevertheless, he could not find his way homewards from those who dwell down there…"

Joh Fredersen reflected. He nodded and turned to go.

"Be courteous, my beautiful Parody," said Rotwang. "Open the doors for the Master over the great Metropolis."

The being glided past Joh Fredersen. He felt the breath of coldness which came forth from it. He saw the silent laughter between the half-open lips of Rotwang, the great inventor. He turned pale with rage, but he remained silent.

The being stretched out the transparent hand in which the bones shone silver, and, touching it with its fingertips, moved the seal of Solomon, which glowed copperish.

The door yielded back. Joh Fredersen went out after the being, which stepped downstairs before him.

There was no light on the stairs, nor in the narrow passage. But a shimmer came from the being no stronger than that of a green-burning candle, yet strong enough to lighten up the stairs and the black walls.

At the house-door the being stopped still and waited for Joh Fredersen, who was walking slowly along behind it. The house-door opened before him, but not far enough for him to pass out through the opening.

The eyes stared at him from the mass-head of the being, eyes as though painted on closed lids, with the expression of calm madness.

"Be courteous, my beautiful Parody," said a soft, far-off voice, which sounded as though the house were talking in its sleep.

The being bowed. It stretched out a hand – a graceful skeleton hand. Transparent skin was stretched over the slender joints, which gleamed beneath it like dull silver. Fingers, snow-white and fleshless, opened like the petals of a crystal lily.

Joh Fredersen laid his hand in it, feeling it, in the moment of contact, to be burnt by an unbearable coldness. He wanted to push the being away from him but the silver-crystal fingers held him fast.

"Goodbye, Joh Fredersen," said the mass head, in a voice full of a horrible tenderness. "Give me a face soon, Joh Fredersen!"

A soft far-off voice laughed, as if the house were laughing in its sleep.

The hand let go, the door opened, Joh Fredersen reeled into the street.

The door closed behind him. In the gloomy wood of the door glowed, copper-red, the seal of Solomon, the pentagram.

When Joh Fredersen was about to enter the brain-pan of the New Tower of Babel, Slim stood before him, seeming to be slimmer than ever.

"What is it?" asked Joh Fredersen.

Slim made to speak but at the sight of his master the words died on his lips.

"Well—?" said Joh Fredersen, between his teeth.

Slim breathed deeply.

"I must inform you, Mr. Fredersen," he said, "that, since your son left this room, he has disappeared!"

"What does that mean?... disappeared!"

"He has not gone home, and none of our men has seen him..."

Joh Fredersen screwed up his mouth.

"Look for him!" he said hoarsely. "What are you all here for? Look for him!"

He entered the brain-pan of the New Tower of Babel. His first glance fell upon the clock. He stepped to the table and stretched out his hand to the little blue metal plate.

Chapter V

THE MAN BEFORE the machine which was like Ganesha, the god with the elephant's head, was no longer a human being. Merely a dripping piece of exhaustion, from the pores of which the last powers of volition were oozing out in large drops of sweat. Running eyes no longer saw the manometer. The hand did not hold the lever – it clawed it fast in the last hold which saved the mangled man-creature before it from falling into the crushing arms of the machine.

The Pater-noster works of the New Tower of Babel turned their buckets with an easy smoothness. The eye of the little machine smiled softly and maliciously at the man who stood before it and who was now no more than a babel.

"Father!" babbled the son of Joh Fredersen, "today, for the first time, since Metropolis stood, you have forgotten to let your city and your great machines roar punctually for fresh food... Has Metropolis gone dumb, father? Look at us! Look at your machines! Your god-machines turn sick at the chewed-up cuds in their mouths – at the mangled food that we are... Why do you strangle its voice to death? Will ten hours never, never come to an end? Our Father, which art in heaven—!"

But in this moment Joh Fredersen's fingers were pressing the little blue metal plate and the voice of the great Metropolis.

"Thank you, father!" said the mangled soul before the machine, which was like Ganesha. He smiled. He tasted a salty taste on his lips and did not know if it was from blood, sweat or tears. From out a red mist of long-flamed, drawn-out clouds, fresh men shuffled on towards him. His hand slipped from the lever and he collapsed. Arms pulled him up and led him away. He turned his head aside to hide his face.

The eye of the little machine, the soft, malicious eye, twinkled at him from behind.

"Goodbye, friend," said the little machine.

Freder's head fell upon his breast. He felt himself dragged further, heard the dull evenness of feet tramping onwards, felt himself tramping, a member of twelve members. The ground under his feet began to roll; it was drawn upwards, pulling him up with it.

Doors stood open, double doors. Towards him came a stream of men.

The great Metropolis was still roaring.

Suddenly she fell dumb and in the silence Freder became aware of the breath of a man at his ear, and of a voice – merely a breath – which asked:

"She has called... Are you coming?"

He did not know what the question meant, but he nodded. He wanted to get to know the ways of those who walked, as he, in blue linen, in the black cap, in the hard shoes.

With tightly closed eyelids he groped on, shoulder to shoulder with an unknown man.

She has called, he thought, half asleep. Who is that... she...?

He walked and walked in smouldering weariness. The way would never, never come to an end. He did not know where he was walking. He heard the tramp of those who were walking with him like the sound of perpetually falling water.

She has called! he thought. Who is that: she, whose voice is so powerful that these men, exhausted to death by utter weariness, voluntarily throw off sleep, which is the sweetest thing of all to the weary – to follow her when her voice calls?

It can't be very much further to the centre of the earth...

Still deeper – still deeper down?

No longer any light round about, only, here and there, twinkling pocket torches, in men's hands.

At last, in the far distance, a dull shimmer.

Have we wandered so far to walk towards the sun, thought Freder, and does the sun dwell in the bowels of the earth?

The procession came to a standstill. Freder stopped too. He staggered against the dry, cool stones.

Where are we, he thought – in a cave? If the sun dwells here, then she can't be at home now... I am afraid we have come in vain... Let us turn back, brother... Let us sleep...

He slid along the wall, fell on his knees, leant his head against the stone... how smooth it was.

The murmur of human voices was around him, like the rustling of trees, moved by the wind...

He smiled peacefully. It's wonderful to be tired...

Then a voice – a voice began to speak...

Oh – sweet voice, thought Freder dreamily. Tender beloved voice, your voice, Virgin-mother! I have fallen asleep... Yes, I am dreaming! I am dreaming of your voice, beloved!

But a slight pain at his temple made him think: I am leaning my head on stone... I am conscious of the coldness which comes out of the stone... I feel coldness under my knees... so I am not sleeping – I am only dreaming... suppose it is not a dream...? Suppose it is reality...?

With an exertion of will which brought a groan from him he forced open his eyes and looked about him.

A vault, like the vault of a sepulchre, human heads so closely crowded together as to produce the effect of clods on a freshly ploughed field. All heads turned towards one point: to the source of a light, as mild as God.

Candles burnt with sword-like flames. Slender, lustrous swords of light stood in a circle around the head of a girl, whose voice was as the Amen of God.

The voice spoke, but Freder did not hear the words. He heard nothing but a sound, the blessed melody of which was saturated with sweetness as is the air of a garden of blossoms with fragrance. And suddenly there sprang up above this melody the wild throb of a heartbeat. The air stormed with bells. The walls shook under the surf of an invisible organ. Weariness – exhaustion – faded out! He felt his body from head to foot to be one single instrument of blissfulness – all strings stretched to bursting point, yet tuned together into the purest, hottest, most radiant accord, in which his whole being hung, quivering.

He longed to stroke with his hands the stones on which he knelt. He longed to kiss with unbounded tenderness the stones on which he rested his head. God – God – God – beat the heart in his breast, and every throb was a thank-offering. He looked at the girl, and yet he did not see her. He saw only a shimmer; he knelt before it.

Gracious one, formed his mouth. Mine! Mine! My beloved! How could the world have existed before you were? How must God have smiled when he created you! You are speaking? – What are you saying? – My heart is shouting within me – I cannot catch your words... Be patient with me, gracious one, beloved!

Without his being aware of it, drawn by an invisible unbreakable cord, he pushed himself forward on his knees, nearer and nearer to the shimmer which the girl's face was to him. At last he was so near that he could have touched the hem of her dress with his outstretched hand.

"Look at me, Virgin!" implored his eyes. "Mother, look at me!"

But her gentle eyes looked out over him. Her lips said:

"My brothers..."

And stopped dumb, as though alarmed.

Freder raised his head. Nothing had happened – nothing to speak of, only that the air which passed through the room had suddenly become audible, like a raised breath, and that it was cool, as though coming in through open doors.

With a faint crackling sound the swords of flame bowed themselves. Then they stood still again.

"Speak, my beloved!" said Freder's heart.

Yes, now she spoke. This is what she said:

"Do you want to know how the building of the Tower of Babel began, and do you want to know how it ended? I see a man who comes from the Dawn of the World. He is as beautiful as the world, and has a burning heart. He loves to walk upon the mountains and to offer his breast unto the wind and to speak with the stars. He is strong and rules all creatures. He dreams of God and feels himself closely tied to him. His nights are filled with faces.

"One hallowed hour bursts his heart. The firmament is above him and his friends. 'Oh friends! Friends!' he cries, pointing to the stars. 'Great is the world and its Creator! Great is man! Come, let us build a tower, the top of which reaches the sky! And when we stand on its top, and hear the stars ringing above us, then let us write our creed in golden symbols on the top of the tower! Great is the world and its creator! And great is man!'

"And they set to, a handful of men, full of confidence, and they made bricks and dug up to the earth. Never have men worked more rapidly, for they all had one thought, one aim and one dream. When they rested from work in the evening each knew of what the other was thinking. They did not need speech to make themselves understood. But after some time they knew: The work was greater than their working hands. Then they enlisted new friends to their work. Then their work grew. It grew overwhelming. Then the builders sent their messengers to all four winds of the world and enlisted Hands, working Hands for their mighty work.

"The Hands came. The Hands worked for wages. The Hands did not even know what they were making. None of those building Southwards knew one of those digging toward the North.

The Brain which conceived the construction of the Tower of Babel was unknown to those who built it. Brain and Hands were far apart and strangers. Brain and Hands became enemies. The pleasure of one became the other's burden. The hymn of praise of one became the other's curse.

"'Babel!' shouted one, meaning: Divinity, Coronation, Eternal, Triumph!

"'Babel!' shouted the other, meaning: Hell, Slavery, Eternal, Damnation!

"The same word was prayer and blasphemy. Speaking the same words, the men did not understand each other.

"That men no longer understood each other, that Brain and Hands no longer understood each other, was to blame that the Tower of Babel was given up to destruction, that never were the words of those who had conceived it written on its top in golden symbols: Great is the world and its Creator! And great is man!

"That Brain and Hands no longer understand each other will one day destroy the New Tower of Babel.

"*Brain and Hands need a mediator. The Mediator between Brain and Hands must be the Heart...*"

She was silent. A breath like a sigh came up from the silent lips of the listeners.

Then one stood up slowly, resting his fists upon the shoulders of the man who crouched before him, and asked, raising his thin face with its fanatical eyes to the girl:

"And where is *our* mediator, Maria?"

The girl looked at him, and over her sweet face passed the gleam of a boundless confidence.

"Wait for him," she said. "He is sure to come."

A murmur ran through the rows of men. Freder bowed his head to the girl's feet. His whole soul said:

"It shall be I."

But she did not see him and she did not hear him.

"Be patient, my brothers!" she said. "The way which your mediator must take is long... There are many among you who cry, 'Fight! Destroy!' – Do not fight, my brothers, for that makes you to sin. Believe me: One will come, who will speak for you – who will be the mediator between you, the Hands, and the man whose Brain and Will are over you all. He will give you something which is more precious than anything which anybody could give you: To be free, without sinning."

She stood up from the stone upon which she had been sitting. A movement ran through the heads turned towards her. A voice was raised. The speaker was not to be seen. It was as if they all spoke:

"We shall wait, Maria. But not much longer—!"

The girl was silent. With her sad eyes she seemed to be seeking the speaker among the crowd.

A man who stood before her spoke up to her:

"And if we fight – where will you be then?"

"With you!" said the girl, opening her hands with the gesture of one sacrificing. "Have you ever found me faithless?"

"Never!" said the men. "You are like gold to us. We shall do what you expect of us."

"Thank you," said the girl, closing her eyes. With bowed head she stood there, listening to the sound of retiring feet – feet which walked in hard shoes.

Only when all about her had become silent and when the last footfall had died away she sighed and opened her eyes.

Then she saw a man, wearing the blue linen and the black cap and the hard shoes, kneeling at her feet.

She bent down. He raised his head. She looked at him.

And then she recognised him.

* * *

Behind them, in a vault that was shaped like a pointed devil's-ear, one man's hand seized another man's arm.

"Hush! Keep quiet!" whispered the voice, which was soundless and yet which had the effect of laughter – like the laughter of spiteful mockery.

* * *

The girl's face was as a crystal, filled with snow. She made a movement as if for flight. But her knees would not obey her. Reeds which stand in troubled water do not tremble more than her shoulders trembled.

"If you have come to betray us, son of Joh Fredersen, then you will have but little blessing from it," she said softly, but in a clear voice.

He stood up and remained standing before her.

"Is that all the faith you have in me?" he asked gravely.

She said nothing, but looked at him. Her eyes filled with tears.

"You..." said the man. "What shall I call you? I do not know your name. I have always called you just 'you'. In all the bad days and worse nights, for I did not know if I should find you again, I always called you only, 'you'... Will you tell me, at last, what your name is?"

"Maria," answered the girl.

"Maria... That should be your name... you did not make it easy for me to find my way to you, Maria."

"And why did you seek your way to me? And why do you wear the blue linen uniform? Those condemned to wear it all their life long, live in an underground city, which is accounted a wonder of the world in all the five continents. It is an architectural wonder – that is true. It is light and shining bright and a model of tidiness. It lacks nothing but the sun – and the rain – and the moon by night – nothing but the sky. That is why the children which are born there have their gnome-like faces... Do you want to go down into this city under the earth in order the more to enjoy your dwelling which lies so high above the great Metropolis, in the light of the sky? Are you wearing the uniform, which you have on today, for fun?"

"No, Maria. I shall always wear it now."

"As Joh Fredersen's son?"

"He no longer has a son... unless – you, yourself, give him back his son."

* * *

Behind them, in a vault that was shaped like a pointed devil's-ear, one man's hand was laid upon another man's mouth.

"It is written," whispered a laugh: "Therefore shall a man leave his father and his mother and cleave unto his wife..."

* * *

"Won't you understand me?" asked Freder. "Why do you look at me with such stern eyes? You wish me to be a mediator between Joh Fredersen and those whom you call your brothers... There can be no mediator between heaven and hell who never was in heaven and hell… I never knew hell until yesterday. That is why I failed so deplorably, yesterday, when I spoke to my father for your brothers. Until you stood before me for the first time, Maria, I lived the life of a dearly loved son. I did not know what an unrealisable wish was. I knew no longing, for everything was mine… Young as I am, I have exhausted the pleasures of the earth, down to the very bottom. I had an aim – a gamble with Death: A flight to the stars… And then you came and showed me my brothers… From that day on I have sought you. I have so longed for you that I should gladly and unhesitatingly have died, had somebody told me that that was the way to you. But as it was, I had to live and seek another way…"

"To me, or to your brothers…?"

"To you, Maria… I will not make myself out to you to be better than I am. I want to come to you, Maria – and I want you… I love mankind, not for its own sake, but for your sake – because you love it. I do not want to help mankind for its own sake, but for your sake – because you wish it. Yesterday I did good to two men; I helped one whom my father had dismissed. And I did the work of the man, whose uniform I have on… That was my way to you… God bless you…"

His voice failed him. The girl stepped up to him. She took his hands in both her hands. She gently turned the palms upward, and considered them, looked at them with her Madonna-eyes, and folded her hands tenderly around his, which she carefully laid together.

"Maria," he said, without a sound.

She let his hands fall and raised hers to his head. She laid her fingertips on his cheeks. With her fingertips she stroked his eyebrows, his temples, twice, three times.

Then he snatched her to his heart and they kissed each other…

He no longer felt the stones under his feet. A wave carried him, him and the girl whom he held clasped to him as though he wished to die of it – and the wave came from the bottom of the ocean, roaring as though the whole sea were an organ; and the wave was of fire and flung right up to the heavens.

Then sinking… sinking… endlessly gliding down – right down to the womb of the world, the source of the beginning… Thirst and quenching drink… hunger and satiation… pain and deliverance from it… death and rebirth…

"You…" said the man to the girl's lips. "You are really the great mediatress… You are all that is most sacred on earth… You are all goodness… You are all grace… To doubt you is to doubt God… Maria – Maria – you called me – here I am!"

* * *

Behind them, in a vault that was shaped like a pointed devil's-ear, one man leant towards another man's ear.

"You wanted to have the Futura's face from me… There you have your model…"

"Is that a commission?"

"Yes."

* * *

"Now you must go, Freder," said the girl. Her Madonna-eyes looked at him.

"Go – and leave you here?"

She turned grave and shook her head.

"Nothing will happen to me," she said. "There is not one, among those who know this place, whom I cannot trust as though he were my blood brother. But what is between us is nobody's affair; it would vex me to have to explain—" (and now she was smiling again) – "what is inexplicable… Do you see that?"

"Yes," he said. "Forgive me…"

* * *

Behind them, in a vault that was shaped like a pointed devil's-ear, a man took himself away from the wall.

"You know what you have to do," he said in a low voice.

"Yes," came the voice of the other, idly, sleepily, out of the darkness. "But wait a bit, friend… I must ask you something…"

"Well?"

"Have you forgotten your own creed?"

For one second a lamp twinkled through the room, that was shaped like a pointed devil's ear, impaling the face of the man, who had already turned to go, on the pointed needle of its brilliance.

"That sin and suffering are twin-sisters… you will be sinning against two people, friend…"

"What has that to do with you?"

"Nothing… Or – little. Freder is Hel's son…"

"And mine…"

"Yes…"

"It is he whom I do not wish to lose."

"Better to sin once more?"

"Yes."

"And—"

"To suffer. Yes."

"Very well, friend," and in the voice was an inaudible laugh of mockery: "May it happen to you according to your creed…!"

* * *

The girl walked through the passages that were so familiar to her. The bright little lamp in her hand roved over the roof of stone and over the stone walls, where, in niches, the thousand-year-old dead slept.

The girl had never known fear of the dead; only reverence and gravity in face of their gravity. Today she saw neither wall nor dead. She walked on, smiling and not knowing she did it. She felt like singing. With an expression of happiness, which was still incredulous and yet complete, she said the name of her beloved over to herself.

Quite softly: "Freder…" And once more: "Freder…"

Then she raised her head, listening attentively, standing quite still…

It came back as a whisper: An echo? – No.

Almost inaudibly a word was breathed:

"Maria…"

She turned around, blissfully startled. Was it possible that he had come back?

"Freder—!" she called. She listened.

No answer.

"Freder—!"

Nothing.

But suddenly there came a cool draught of air which made the hair at her neck quiver, and a hand of snow ran down her back.

There came an agonized sigh – a sigh which would not come to an end…

The girl stood still. The bright little lamp which she held in her hand let its gleam play tremblingly about her feet.

"Freder…?"

Now her voice, too, was only a whisper.

No answer. But, behind her, in the depths of the passage she would have to pass through, a gentle, gliding slink became perceptible: feet in soft shoes on rough stones…

That was… yes, that was strange. Nobody, apart from her, ever came this way. Nobody could be here. And, if somebody were here, then it was no friend…

Certainly nobody whom she wanted to meet.

Should she let him by? – yes.

A second passage opened to her left. She did not know it well. But she would not follow it up. She would only wait in it until the man outside – the man behind her – had gone by.

She pressed herself against the wall of the strange passage, keeping still and waiting quite silently. She did not breathe. She had extinguished the lamp. She stood in utter darkness, immovable.

She listened: the gliding feet were approaching. They walked in darkness as she stood in darkness. Now they were here. Now they must… they must go past… But they did not go. They stood quite still. Before the opening to the passage in which she stood, the feet stopped still and seemed to wait.

For what…? For her…?

In the complete silence the girl suddenly heard her own heart… She heard her own heart, like pump-works, beating more and more quickly, throbbing more and more loudly. These loud throbbing heartbeats must also be heard by the man who kept the opening to the passage. And suppose he did not stay there any longer… suppose he came inside… she could not hear his coming, her heart throbbed so.

She groped, with fumbling hand, along the stone wall. Without breathing, she set her feet, one before the other… Only to get away from the entrance… Away from the place where the other was standing…

Was she wrong? Or were the feet really coming after her? Soft, slinking shoes on rough stones? Now the agonised, heavy breathing, heavier still, and nearer… cold breath on her neck… Then –

Nothing more. Silence. And waiting. And watching – keeping on the look-out…

Was it not as if a creature, such as the world had never seen: trunkless, nothing but arms, legs and head… but what a head! God – God in heaven!… was crouching on the floor before her, knees drawn up to chin, the damp arms supported right and left, against the walls, near her hips, so that she stood defenceless, caught? Did she not see the passage lighted by a pale shimmer – and did not the shimmer come from the being's jelly-fish head?

"Freder!" she thought. She bit the name tightly between her jaws, yet heard the scream with which her heart screamed it.

She threw herself forwards and felt – she was free – she was still free – and ran and stumbled, and pulled herself up again and staggered from wall to wall, knocking herself bloody, suddenly clutched into space, stumbled, fell to the ground, felt… Something lay there… what? No – No – No—!

The lamp had long since fallen from her hand. She raised herself to her knees and clapped her fists to her ears, in order not to hear the feet, the slinking feet coming nearer. She knew herself to be imprisoned in darkness and yet opened her eyes because she could no longer bear the circles of fire, the wheels of flame behind her closed lids –

And saw her own shadow thrown, gigantic, on the wall before her, and behind her was light, and before her lay a man –

A man? – That was not a man… That was the remains of a man, with his back half leaning against the wall, half slipped down, and on his skeleton feet, which almost touched the girl's knees, were the slender shoes, pointed and purple-red…

With a shriek which tore her throat, the girl threw herself up, backwards – and then on and on, without looking round, pursued by the light which lashed her own shadow in springs before her feet – pursued by long, soft, feathery feet – by feet which walked in red shoes, by the icy breath which blew at her back.

She ran, screamed and ran –

"Freder…! Freder…!"

Her throat rattled, she fell.

There were some stairs… Crumbling stairs… She pressed her bleeding hands, right and left, against the stone wall, by the stone steps. She dragged herself up. She staggered up, step by step… There was the top.

The stairs ended in a stone trap-door.

The girl groaned: "Freder…!"

She stretched both fists above her. She pushed head and shoulders against the trap-door.

And one more groan: "Freder…"

The door rose and fell back with a crash.

Below – deep down – laughter…

The girl swung herself over the edge of the trap-door. She ran hither and thither, with outstretched hands. She ran along walls, finding no door. She saw the lustre which welled up from the depths. By this light she saw a door, which was latchless. It had neither bolt nor lock.

In the gloomy wood glowed, copper-red, the seal of Solomon, the pentagram.

The girl turned around.

She saw a man sitting on the edge of the trap-door and saw his smile.

Then it was as though she were extinguished, and she plunged into nothing…

Chapter VI

THE PROPRIETOR of Yoshiwara used to earn money in a variety of ways. One of them, and quite positively the most harmless, was to make bets that no man – be he never so widely travelled – was capable of guessing to what weird mixture of races he owed his face. So far he had won all such bets, and used to sweep in the money which they brought him with hands, the cruel beauty of which would not have shamed an ancestor of the Spanish Borgias, the nails of which, however, showed an inobliterable shimmer of blue; on the other hand, the politeness of his smile on such profitable occasions originated unmistakably in that graceful insular world, which, from the eastern border of Asia, smiles gently and watchfully across at mighty America.

There were prominent properties combined within him which made him appear to be a general representative of Great Britain and Ireland, for he was as red-haired, chaff-loving and with as good a head for drink as if his name had been McFosh, avaricious and superstitious as a Scotsman and – in certain circumstances, which made it requisite, of that highly bred obliviousness, which is a matter of will and a foundation stone of the British Empire. He spoke practically all living languages as though his mother had taught him to pray in them and his father to curse. His greed appeared to hail from the Levant, his contentment from China. And, above all this, two quiet, observant eyes watched with German patience and perseverance.

As to the rest, he was called, for reasons unknown, September.

The visitants to Yoshiwara had met September in a variety of emotions – from the block-headed dozing away of the well-contented bushman to the dance-ecstatic of the Ukrainer.

But to come upon his features in an expression of absolute bewilderment was reserved for Slim, when, on the morning after his having lost sight of his young master, he set throbbing the massive gong which demanded entrance to Yoshiwara.

It was most unusual that the generally very obliging door of Yoshiwara was not opened before the fourth gong-signal; and that this was performed by September himself and with this expression of countenance deepened the impression of an only tolerably overcome catastrophe. Slim bowed. September looked at him. A mask of brass seemed to fall over his face. But a chance glance at the driver of the taxi, in which Slim had come tore it off again.

"Would to God your tin-kettle had gone up in the air before you could have brought that lunatic here yesterday evening," he said. "He drove away my guests before they even thought of paying. The girls are huddling down in the corners like lumps of wet floor-cloth – that is, those who are not in hysterics. Unless I call in the police I might just as well close the house; for it doesn't look as though that chap will have recovered his five senses by this evening."

"Of whom are you speaking, September?" asked Slim.

September looked at him. At this moment the tiniest hamlet in North Siberia would have flatly refused to have been proclaimed the birth-place of so idiotic looking an individual.

"If it is the man for whom I have come here to look," continued Slim, "then I shall rid you of him in a more agreeable and swifter manner than the police."

"And for what man are you looking, sir?"

Slim hesitated. He cleared his throat slightly. "You know the white silk which is woven for comparatively few in Metropolis..."

In the long line of ancestors, the manifold sediment of whom had been crystalised into September, a fur-trader from Tarnopolis must also have been represented and he now smiled out from the corners of his great-grandson's wily eyes.

"Come in, sir!" the proprietor of Yoshiwara invited Slim, with true Singalese gentleness.

Slim entered. September closed the door behind him.

In the moment when the matutinal roar of the great Metropolis no longer bellowed up from the streets, another roar from inside the building became perceptible – the roar of a human voice, hotter than the voice of a beast of prey, mad-drunk with triumph.

"Who is that?" asked Slim, involuntarily dropping his own voice.

"He—!" answered September, and how he could stow the smooth and pointed vengefulness of whole Corsica into the monosyllable remained his own secret.

Slim's glance became uncertain, but he said nothing. He followed September over soft and glossy straw mats, along walls of oiled paper, narrowly framed in bamboo.

Behind one of these walls the weeping of a woman was to be heard – monotonous, hopeless, heartbreaking, like a long spell of rainy days which envelope the summit of Fuji Yama.

"That's Yuki," murmured September, with a fierce glance at the paper prison of this pitiful weeping. "She's been crying since midnight, as if she wanted to be the source of a new salt sea... This evening she will have a swollen potato on her face instead of a nose... Who pays for it? – I do!"

"Why is the little snowflake crying?" asked Slim, half thoughtlessly, for the roaring of the human voice, coming from the depths of the house occupied all the ears and attention he possessed.

"Oh, she isn't the only one," answered September, with the tolerant mien of one who owns a prosperous harbour tavern in Shanghai. "But she is at least tame. Plum Blossom has been snapping about her like a young Puma, and Miss Rainbow has thrown the Saki bowl at the mirror and is trying to cut her artery with the chips – and all on account of this white silk youngster."

The agitated expression on Slim's face deepened. He shook his head.

"How did he manage to get such a hold over them…" he said, and it was not meant to be a question.

September shrugged his shoulders.

"Maohee…" he said in a sing-song tone, as though beginning one of those Greenland fairy tales, which, the quicker they sent one to sleep are the more highly appreciated.

"What is that: Maohee?" asked Slim, irritably.

September drew his head down between his shoulders. The Irish and the British blood-corpuscles in his veins seemed to be falling out, violently: but the impenetrable Japanese smile covered this up with its mantle before it could grow dangerous.

"You don't know what Maohee is… Not a soul in the great Metropolis knows… No… Nobody. But here in Yoshiwara they all know."

"I wish to know, too, September," said Slim.

Generations of Roman lackeys bowed within September as he said, "Certainly, sir!" But they did not get the better of the wink of the heavy-drinking lying grandfathers in Copenhagen. "Maohee, that is… Isn't it odd, that, of all the ten thousand who have been guests here in Yoshiwara and who had experienced in detail what Maohee stands for, outside they know nothing more about it? Don't walk so fast, sir. The yelling gentleman down there won't run away from us – and if I am to explain to you what Maohee means…"

"Drugs, I expect, September—?"

"My dear sir, the lion is also a cat. Maohee is a drug: but what is a cat beside a lion? Maohee is from the other side of the earth. It is the divine, the only thing – because it is the only thing which makes us feel the intoxication of the others."

"The intoxication – of the others…?" repeated Slim, stopping still.

September smiled the smile of Hotei the god of Happiness, who likes little children. He laid the hand of the Borgia, with the suspiciously blue shimmering nails on Slim's arm.

"The intoxication of the others – Sir, do you know what that means? Not of one other – no, of the multitude which rolls itself into a lump, the rolled up intoxication of the multitude gives Maohee its friends…"

"Has Maohee many friends, September?"

The proprietor of Yoshiwara grinned, apocalyptically.

"Sir, in this house there is a round room. You shall see it. It has not its like. It is built like a winding seashell, like a mammoth shell, in the windings of which thunders the surf of seven oceans; in these windings people crouch, so densely crowded that their faces appear as one face. No one knows the other, yet they are all friends. They all fever. They are all pale with expectation. They have all clasped hands. The trembling of those who sit right down at the bottom of the shell runs right through the windings of the mammoth shell, right up to those, who; from the gleaming top of the spiral, send out their own trembling towards it…"

September gulped for breath. Sweat stood like a fine chain of beads on his brow. An international smile of insanity parted his prating mouth.

"Go on, September!" said Slim.

"On? – On? – Suddenly the rim of the shell begins to turn… gently… ah how gently, to music such as would bring a tenfold murderer-bandit to sobs and his judges to pardon him on the scaffold – to music on hearing which deadly enemies kiss, beggars believe themselves to be kings, the hungry forget their hunger – to such music the shell revolves around its stationary heart, until it seems to free itself from the ground and, hovering, to revolve about itself. The people scream – not loudly, no, no! – they scream like the birds that bathe in the sea. The twisted hands are clenched to fists. The bodies rock in one rhythm. Then comes the first stammer of: Maohee… The stammer swells, becomes waves of spray, becomes a spring tide. The revolving shell roars: Maohee… Maohee…! It is as though a little flame must rest on everyone's hair parting, like St. Elmo's fire… Maohee… Maohee! They call on their god. They call on him whom the finger of the god touches today… No one knows from where he will come today… He is there… They know he is amongst them… He must break out from the rows of them… He must… He must, for they call him: Maohee… Maohee! And suddenly—!"

The hand of the Borgia flew up and hung in the air like a brown claw.

"And suddenly a man is standing in the middle of the shell, in the gleaming circle, on the milk-white disc. But it is no man. It is the embodied conception of the intoxication of them all. He is not conscious of himself… A slight froth stands on his mouth. His eyes are stark and bursting and are yet like rushing meteors which leave waving tracks of fire behind them on the route from heaven to earth… He stands and lives his intoxication. He is what his intoxication is. From the thousands of eyes which have cast anchor into his soul the power of intoxication streams into him. There is no delight in God's creation which does not reveal itself, surmounted by the medium of these intoxicated souls. What he says becomes visible, what he hears becomes audible to all. What he feels: Power, desire, madness, is felt by them all. On the shimmering area, around which the shell revolves, to music beyond all description, one in ecstasy lives the thousandfold ecstasy which embodies itself in him, for thousands of others…"

September stopped and smiled at Slim.

"That, sir, is Maohee…"

"It must indeed be a powerful drug," said Slim with a feeling of dryness in his throat, "which inspires the proprietor of Yoshiwara to such a hymn. Do you think that that yelling individual down there would join in this song of praise?"

"Ask him yourself, sir," said September.

He opened the door and let Slim enter. Just over the threshold Slim stopped, because at first he saw nothing. A gloom, more melancholy than the deepest darkness, spread over a room, the dimensions of which he could not estimate. The floor under his feet inclined in a barely perceptible slope. Where it stopped there appeared to be gloomy emptiness. Right and left, spiral walls, billowing outwards, swept away to each side.

That was all Slim saw. But from the empty depths before him came a white shimmer, no stronger than if coming from a field of snow. On this shimmer there floated a voice, that of a murderer and of one being murdered.

"Light, September!" said Slim with a gulp. An unbearable feeling of thirst gnawed at his throat.

The room slowly grew brighter, as though the light were coming unwillingly. Slim saw, he was standing in one of the windings of the round room, which was shaped like a shell. He was standing between the heights and the depths, separated by a low banister from the emptiness from which came the snow-like light and the murderer's voice and the voice of his victim. He stepped to the banister, and leaned far over it. A milk-white disc, lighted from beneath and luminous. At the edge of the disc, like a dark, rambling pattern on a plate-rim, women, crouching, kneeling there, in their gorgeous attire, as though drunken. Some had dropped their foreheads to the ground, their hands clutched above their ebony hair. Some crouched, huddled together in clumps, head pressed to head, symbols of fear. Some were swaying rhythmically from side to side as if calling on gods. Some were weeping. Some were as if dead.

But they all seemed to be the hand-maids of the man on the snow-light illuminated disk.

The man wore the white silk woven for comparatively few in Metropolis. He wore the soft shoes in which the beloved sons of mighty fathers seemed to caress the earth. But the silk hung in tatters about the body of the man and the shoes looked as though the feet within them bled.

"Is that the man for whom you are looking, sir?" asked a Levantine cousin from out September, leaning confidently towards Slim's ear.

Slim did not answer. He was looking at the man.

"At least," continued September, "it is the youngster who came here yesterday by the same car as you today. And the devil take him for it! He has turned my revolving shell into the fore-court of hell! He has been roasting souls! I have known Maohee-drugged beings to have fancied themselves Kings, Gods, Fire, and Storm – and to have forced others to feel themselves Kings, Gods, Fire, and Storm. I have known those in the ecstasy of desire to have forced women down to them from the highest part of the shell's wall, that they, diving, like seagulls, with out-spread hands, have swooped to his feet, without injuring a limb, while others have fallen to their death. That man there was no God, no Storm, no Fire, and his drunkenness most certainly inspired him with no desire. It seems to me that he had come up from hell and is roaring in the intoxication of damnation. He did not know that the ecstasy for men who are damned is also damnation… The fool! The prayer he is praying will not redeem him. He believes himself to be a machine and is praying to himself. He has forced the others to pray to him. He has ground them down. He has pounded them to a powder. There are many dragging themselves around Metropolis today who cannot comprehend why their limbs are as if broken…"

"Be quiet, September!" said Slim hoarsely. His hand flew to his throat which felt like a glowing cork, like smouldering charcoal.

September fell silent, shrugging his shoulders. Words seethed up from the depths like lava.

"I am the Three-in-one – Lucifer – Belial – Satan—! I am the everlasting Death! I am the everlasting Noway! Come unto me—! In my hell there are many mansions! I shall assign them to you! I am the great king of all the damned—! I am a machine! I am the tower above you all! I am a hammer, a fly-wheel, a fiery oven! I am a murderer and of what I murder I make no use. I want victims and victims do not appease me! Pray to me and know: I do not hear you! Shout at me: Pater-noster! Know: I am deaf!"

Slim turned around; he saw September's face as a chalky mask at his shoulder. Maybe that, among September's ancestresses there was one who hailed from an isle in the South sea, where gods mean little – spirits everything.

"That's no more a man," he whispered with ashen lips. "A man would have died of it long ago… Do you see his arms, sir? Do you think a man can imitate the pushing of a machine for hours and hours at a time without its killing him? He is as dead as stone. If you were to call to him he'd collapse and break to pieces like a plaster statue."

It did not seem as though September's words had penetrated into Slim's consciousness. His face wore an expression of loathing and suffering and he spoke as one who speaks with pain.

"I hope, September, that tonight you have had your last opportunity of watching the effects of Maohee on your guests…"

September smiled his Japanese smile.

He did not answer.

Slim stepped up to the banister at the edge of the curve of the shell in which he stood. He bent down towards the milky disc. He cried a high sharp tone which had the effect of a whistle:

"Eleven thousand eight hundred and eleven—!"

The man on the shimmering disc swung around as though he had received a blow in the side. The hellish rhythm of his arms ceased, running itself out in vibration. The man fell to earth like a log and did not move again.

Slim ran down the passage, reached the end and pushed asunder the circle of women, who, stiffened with shock, seemed to be thrown into deeper horror more by the end of that which they had brought to pass than by the beginning. He knelt down beside the man, looked him in the face and pushed the tattered silk away from his heart. He did not give his hand time to test his pulse. He lifted the man up and carried him out in his arms. The sighing of the women soughed behind him like a dense, mist-coloured curtain.

September stepped across his path. He swept aside as he caught Slim's glance at him. He ran along by him, like an active dog, breathing rapidly; but he said nothing.

Slim reached the door of Yoshiwara. September, himself, opened it for him. Slim stepped into the street. The driver pulled open the door of the taxi; he looked in amazement at the man who hung in Slim's arms, in tatters of white silk with which the wind was playing, and who was more awful to look on than a corpse.

The proprietor of Yoshiwara bowed repeatedly while Slim was climbing into the car. But Slim did not give him another glance. September's face, which was as grey as steel, was reminiscent of the blades of those ancient swords, forged of Indian steel, in Shiras or Ispahan and on which, hidden by ornamentation, stand mocking and deadly words.

The car glided away: September looked after it. He smiled the peacable smile of Eastern Asia.

For he knew perfectly well what Slim did not know, and what, apart from him, nobody in Metropolis knew, that with the first drop of water or wine which moistened the lips of a human being, there disappeared even the very faintest memory of all which appertained to the wonders of the drug, Maohee.

The car stopped before the next medical depot. Male nurses came and carried away the bundle of humanity, shivering in tatters of white silk, to the doctor on duty. Slim looked about him. He beckoned to a policeman who was stationed near the door.

"Take down a report," he said. His tongue would hardly obey him, so parched was it with thirst.

The policeman entered the house after him.

"Wait!" said Slim, more with the movement of his head than in words. He saw a glass jug of water standing on the table and the coolness of the water had studded the jug with a thousand pearls.

Slim drank like an animal which finds drink on coming from the desert. He put down the jug and shivered. A short shudder passed through him.

He turned around and saw the man he had brought with him lying on a bed over which a young doctor was bending.

The lips of the sick man were moistened with wine. His eyes stood wide open, staring up at the ceiling, tears upon tears running gently and incessantly from the corners of his eyes, down over his temples. It was as though they had nothing to do with the man – as though they were trickling from a broken vessel and could not stop trickling until the vessel had run quite empty.

Slim looked the doctor in the face; the latter shrugged his shoulders. Slim bent over the prostrate man.

"Georgi," he said in a low voice, "can you hear me?"

The sick man nodded; it was the shadow of a nod.

"Do you know who I am?"

A second nod.

"Are you in a condition to answer two or three questions?"

Another nod.

"How did you get the white silk clothes?"

For a long time he received no answer apart from the gentle falling of the tear drops. Then came the voice, softer than a whisper.

"... He changed with me..."

"Who did?"

"Freder... Joh Fredersen's son..."

"And then, Georgi?"

"He told me I was to wait for him..."

"Wait where, Georgi?"

A long silence. And then, barely audible:

"Ninetieth Street. House seven. Seventh floor..."

Slim did not question him further. He knew who lived there. He looked at the doctor; the latter's face wore a completely impenetrable expression.

Slim drew a breath as though he were sighing. He said, more deploringly than inquiringly:

"Why did you not rather go there, Georgi..."

He turned to go but stopped still as Georgi's voice came wavering after him.

"...The city... all the lights... more than enough money... It is written... Forgive us our trespasses... lead us not into temptation..."

His voice died away. His head fell to one side. He breathed as though his soul wept, for his eyes could do so no longer.

The doctor cleared his throat cautiously.

Slim raised his head as though somebody had called him, then dropped it again.

"I shall come back again," he said softly. "He is to remain under your care..."

Georgi was asleep.

Slim left the room, followed by the policeman.

"What do you want?" Slim asked with an absent-minded look at him.

"The report, sir."

"What report?"

"I was to take down a report, sir."

Slim looked at the policeman very attentively, almost meditatively. He raised his hand and rubbed it across his forehead.

"A mistake," he said. "That was a mistake..."

The policeman saluted and retired, a little puzzled, for he knew Slim.

He remained standing on the same spot. Again and again he rubbed his forehead with the same helpless gesture.

Then he shook his head, stepped into the car and said:

"Ninetieth block..."

Chapter VII

"WHERE IS GEORGI?" asked Freder, his eyes wandering through Josaphat's three rooms, which stretched out before him – beautiful, with a rather bewildering super-abundance of armchairs, divans and silk cushions, with curtains which goldenly obscured the light.

"Who?" asked Josaphat, listlessly. He had waited, had not slept and his eyes stood excessively large in his thin, almost white face. His gaze, which he did not take from Freder, was like hands which are raised adoringly.

"Georgi," repeated Freder. He smiled happily with his tired mouth.

"Who is that?" asked Josaphat.

"I sent him to you."

"Nobody has come."

Freder looked at him without answering.

"I sat all night in this chair," continued Josaphat, misinterpreting Freder's silence. "I did not sleep a wink. I expected you to come at any second, or a messenger to come from you, or that you would ring me up. I also informed the watchman. Nobody has come, Mr. Freder."

Freder still remained silent. Slowly, almost stumblingly he stepped over the threshold, into the room raising his right hand to his head, as though to take off his hat, then noticing that he was wearing the cap, the black cap, which pressed the hair tightly down, he swept it from his head; it fell to the ground. His hand sank from his brow, over his eyes, resting there a little while. Then the other joined it, as though wishing to console its sister. His form was like that of a young birch tree pressed sideways by a strong wind.

Josaphat's eyes hung on the uniform which Freder wore.

"Mr. Freder," he began cautiously, "how comes it that you are wearing these clothes?"

Freder remained turned away from him. He took his hands from his eyes and pressed them to his face as though he felt some pain there.

"Georgi wore them…" He answered. "I gave him mine…"

"Then Georgi is a workman?"

"Yes… I found him before the Pater-noster machine. I took his place and sent him to you…"

"Perhaps he'll come yet," answered Josaphat.

Freder shook his head.

"He should have been here hours ago. If he had been caught when leaving the New Tower of Babel, then someone would have come to me when I was standing before the machine. It is strange, but there it is; he has not come."

"Was there much money in the suit which you exchanged with Georgi?" asked Josaphat tentatively, as one who bares a wounded spot.

Freder nodded.

"Then you must not be surprised that Georgi has not come," said Josaphat. But the expression of shame and pain on Freder's face prevented him from continuing.

"Won't you sit down, Mr. Freder," he begged. "Or lie down? You look so tired that it is painful to look at you."

"I have no time to sit down and not time to lie down, either," answered Freder. He walked through the rooms, aimlessly, senselessly, stopping wherever a chair, a table, offered him a hold. "The fact, is this, Josaphat: I told Georgi to come here and to wait here for me – or for a message from me… It is a thousand to one that Slim, in searching for me, is already on Georgi's track, and it's a thousand to one he gets out of him where I sent him…"

"And you do not want Slim to find you?"

"He must not find me, Josaphat – not for anything on earth…"

The other stood silent, rather helpless. Freder looked at him with a trembling smile.

"How shall we obtain money, now, Josaphat?"

"That should offer no difficulty to Joh Fredersen's son."

"More than you think, Josaphat, for I am no longer Joh Fredersen's son…"

Josaphat raised his head.

"I do not understand you," he said, after a pause.

"There is nothing to misunderstand, Josaphat. I have set myself free from my father, and am going my own way..."

The man who had been the first secretary to the Master over the great Metropolis held his breath back in his lungs, then released it in streams.

"Will you let me tell you something, Mr. Freder?"

"Well..."

"One does not set oneself free from your father. It is he who decides whether one remains with him or must leave him.

"There is nobody who is stronger than Joh Fredersen. He is like the earth. As regards the earth we have no will either. Her laws keep us eternally perpendicular to the centre of the earth, even if we stand on our head... When Joh Fredersen sets a man free it means just as much as if the earth were to shut off from a man her powers of attraction. It means falling into nothing... Joh Fredersen can set free whom he may; he will never set free his son..."

"But what," answered Freder, speaking feverishly, "if a man overcomes the laws of nature?"

"Utopia, Mr. Freder."

"For the inventive spirit of man there is no Utopia: there is only a Not-yet. I have made up my mind to venture the path. I must take it – yes, I must take it! I do not know the way yet, but I shall find it because I must find it..."

"Wherever you wish, Mr. Freder – I shall go with you..."

"Thank you," said Freder, reaching out his hand. He felt it seized and clasped in a vice-like grip.

"You know, Mr. Freder, don't you—" said the strangled voice of Josaphat, "that everything belongs to you – everything that I am and have... It is not much, for I have lived like a madman... But for today, and tomorrow and the day after tomorrow..."

Freder shook his head without losing hold of Josaphat's hand.

"No, no!" he said, a torrent of red flowing over his face. "One does not begin new ways like that... We must try to find other ways... It will not be easy. Slim knows his business."

"Perhaps Slim could be won over to you..." said Josaphat, hesitatingly. "For – strange though it may sound, he loves you..."

"Slim loves all his victims. Which does not prevent him, as the most considerate and kindly of executioners, from laying them before my father's feet. He is the born tool, but the tool of the strongest. He would never make himself the tool of the weaker one, for he would thus humiliate himself. And you have just told me, Josaphat, how much stronger my father is than I..."

"If you were to confide yourself to one of your friends..."

"I have no friends, Josaphat."

Josaphat wanted to contradict, but he stopped himself. Freder turned his eyes towards him. He straightened himself up and smiled – the other's hand still in his.

"I have no friends, Josaphat, and, what weighs still more, I have no friend. I had play-fellows – sport-fellows – but friends? A friend? No, Josaphat! Can one confide oneself to somebody of whom one knows nothing but how his laughter sounds?"

He saw the eyes of the other fixed upon him, discerned the ardour in them and the pain and the truth.

"Yes," he said with a worried smile. "I should like to confide myself to you... I must confide myself to you, Josaphat... I must call you 'Friend' and 'Brother'... for I need a man who will go with me in trust and confidence to the world's end. Will you be that man?"

"Yes."

"Yes—?" He came to him and laid his hands upon his shoulders. He looked closely into his face. He shook him. "You say: 'Yes—!' Do you know what that means – for you and for me? What a last plummet-drop that is – what a last anchorage? I hardly know you – I wanted to help you – I cannot even help you now, because I am poorer now than you are – but, perhaps, that is all to the good… Joh Fredersen's son can, perhaps, be betrayed – but I, Josaphat? A man who has nothing but a will and an object? It cannot be worthwhile to betray him – eh, Josaphat?"

"May God kill me as one kills a mangy dog…"

"That's all right, that's all right…" Freder's smile came back again and stood, clear and beautiful in his tired face. "I am going now, Josaphat. I want to go to my father's mother, to take her something which is very sacred to me… I shall be here again before evening. Shall I find you here then?"

"Yes, Mr. Freder, most certainly!"

They stretched out their hands towards each other. Hand held hand, gripped. They looked at each other. Glance held glance, gripped. Then they loosened their grip in silence and Freder went.

A little while later (Josaphat was still standing on the same spot on which Freder had left him) there came a knock at the door.

Though the knocking was as gentle, as modest, as the knocking of one who has come to beg, there was something in it which chased a shiver down Josaphat's spine. He stood still, gazing at the door, incapable of calling out "Come in," or of opening it himself.

The knocking was repeated, becoming not in the least louder. It came for the third time and was still as gentle. But just that deepened the impression that it was inescapable, that it would be quite pointless to play deaf permanently.

"Who is there?" asked Josaphat hoarsely. He knew very well who was standing outside. He only asked to gain time – to draw breath, which he badly needed. He expected no answer; neither did he receive one.

The door opened.

In the doorway stood Slim.

They did not greet each other; neither greeted the other. Josaphat: because his gullet was too dry. Slim: because his all-observing eye had darted through the room in the second in which he put his foot on the threshold, and had found something: a black cap, lying on the floor.

Josaphat followed Slim's gaze with his eyes. He did not stir. With silent step Slim went up to the cap, stooped and picked it up. He twisted it gently this way and that, he twisted it inside out.

In the sweat-sodden lining of the cap stood the number, 11811.

Slim weighed the cap in almost affectionate hands. He fixed his eyes, which were as though veiled with weariness on Josaphat and asked, speaking in a low voice:

"Where is Freder, Josaphat?"

"I do not know…"

Slim smiled sleepily. He fondled the black cap. Josaphat's hoarse voice continued:

"… But if I did know you would not get it out of me, anyway…"

Slim looked at Josaphat, still smiling, still fondling the black cap.

"You are quite right," said he courteously. "I beg your pardon! It was an idle question. Of course you will not tell me where Mr. Freder is. Neither is it at all necessary… It is quite another matter…"

He pocketed the cap, having carefully rolled it up, and looked around the room. He went up to an armchair, standing near a low, black, polished table.

"You permit me?" he asked courteously, seating himself.

Josaphat made a movement of the head, but the "Please do so," dried up in his throat. He did not stir from the one spot.

"You live very well here," said Slim, leaning back and surveying the room with a sweeping movement of his head. "Everything of a soft, half-dark tone. The atmosphere about these cushions is a tepid perfume. I can well understand how difficult it will be for you to leave this flat."

"I have no such intention, however," said Josaphat. He swallowed.

Slim pressed his eye-lids together, as though he wished to sleep.

"No… Not yet… But very soon…"

"I should not think of it," answered Josaphat. His eyes grew red, and he looked at Slim, hatred smouldering in his gaze.

"No… Not yet… But very soon…"

Josaphat stood quite still: but suddenly he smote the air with his fist, as though beating against an invisible door.

"What do you want exactly?" he asked pantingly. "What is that supposed to imply? What do you want from me—?"

It appeared at first as though Slim had not heard the question. Sleepily, with closed eyelids, he sat there, breathing inaudibly. But, as the leather of the chairback squeaked under Josaphat's grasp, Slim said, very slowly, but very clearly:

"I want you to tell me for what sum you will give up this flat, Josaphat."

"… When?…"

"Immediately."

"… What is that supposed to mean… Immediately?…"

Slim opened his eyes, and they were as cold and bright as a pebble in a brook.

"Immediately means within an hour… Immediately means long before this evening…"

A shiver ran down Josaphat's back. The hands on his hanging arms slowly clenched themselves into fists.

"Get out, sir…" he said quietly. "Get out of here—! Now—! At once—! *Immediately—!*"

"The flat is very pretty," said Slim. "You are unwilling to give it up. It is of value to one who knows how to appreciate such things. You will not have time to pack any large trunks, either. You can only take what you need for twenty-four hours. The journey – new outfit – a year's expenses – all this is to be added to the sum: what is the price of your flat, Josaphat?"

"I shall chuck you into the street," stammered Josaphat with feverish mouth. "I shall chuck you seven stories down into the street – through the window, my good sir! – through the closed window – if you don't get out this very second!"

"You love a woman. The woman does not love you. Women who are not in love are very expensive. You want to buy this woman. Very well. The threefold cost of the flat… Life on the Adriatic coast – in Rome – on Tenerife – on a splendid steamer around the world with a woman who wants to be bought anew every day – comprehensible, Josaphat, that the flat will be expensive… but to tell you the truth, I must have it, so I must pay for it."

He plunged his hands into his pocket and drew out a wad of banknotes. He pushed it across to Josaphat over the black, polished mirror-like table. Josaphat clutched at it, leaving his nail marks behind on the table-top and threw it into Slim's face. He caught it with a nimble, thought-swift movement, and gently laid it back on the table. He laid a second one beside it.

"Is that enough?" he asked sleepily.

"No—!" shouted Josaphat's laughter.

"Sensible!" said Slim. "Very sensible. Why should you not make full use of your advantages. An opportunity like this, to raise your whole life by one hundred rungs, to become independent, happy, free, the fulfilment of every wish, the satisfaction of every whim – to have your own, and a beautiful woman before you, will come only once in your life and never again. Seize it, Josaphat, if you are not a fool! In strict confidence: The beautiful woman of whom we spoke just now has already been informed and is awaiting you near the aeroplane which is standing ready for the journey… Three times the price, Josaphat, if you do not keep the beautiful woman waiting!"

He laid the third bundle of banknotes on the table. He looked at Josaphat. Josaphat's reddened eyes devoured his. Josaphat's hands fumbled across blindly and seized the three brown wads. His teeth showed white under his lips; while his fingers tore the notes to shreds, they seemed to be biting them to death.

Slim shook his head. "That's of no account," he said undisturbedly. "I have a cheque-book here, some of the blank leaves of which bear the signature, Joh Fredersen. Let us write a sum on the first leaf – a sum the double of the amount agreed upon up to now… Well, Josaphat?"

"I will not—!" said the other, shaken from head to foot.

Slim smiled.

"No," he said. "Not yet… But very soon…"

Josaphat did not answer. He was staring at the piece of paper, white, printed and written on, which lay before him on the blue-black table. He did not see the figure upon it. He only saw the name upon it:

Joh Fredersen.

The signature, as though written with the blade of an axe:

Joh Fredersen.

Josaphat turned his head this way and that as though he felt the blade of the axe at his neck.

"No," he croaked. "No, no, no…!"

"Not enough yet?" asked Slim.

"Yes!" said he in a mutter. "Yes! It is enough."

Slim got up. Something which he had drawn from his pocket with the bundles of banknotes, without his having noticed it, slid down from his knees.

It was a black cap, such as the workmen in Joh Fredersen's works used to wear…

A howl escaped Josaphat's lips. He threw himself down on both knees. He seized the black cap in both hands. He snatched it to his mouth. He stared at Slim. He jerked himself up. He sprang, like a stag before the pack, to gain the door.

But Slim got there before him. With a mighty leap he sprang across table and divan, rebounded against the door and stood before Josaphat. For the fraction of a second they stared each other in the face. Then Josaphat's hands flew to Slim's throat. Slim lowered his head. He threw forward his arms, like the grabbing arms of the octopus. They held each other, tightly clasped, and wrestled together, burning and ice-cold, raving and reflecting, teeth-grinding and silent, breast to breast.

They tore themselves apart and dashed at each other. They fell, and, wrestling, rolled along the floor. Josaphat forced his opponent beneath him. Fighting, they pushed each other up. They stumbled and rolled over armchairs and divans. The beautiful room, turned into a wilderness, seemed to be too small for the two twisted bodies, which jerked like fishes, stamped like steers, struck at each other like fighting bears.

But against Slim's unshakeable, dreadful coldness the white-hot fury of his opponent could not stand its ground. Suddenly, as though his knee joints had been hacked through, Josaphat collapsed in Slim's hands, fell on his knees and remained there, his back resting against an over-turned armchair, staring up with glassy eyes.

Slim loosened his hold. He looked down at him.

"Had enough yet?" he asked, and smiled sleepily.

Josaphat did not answer. He moved his right hand. In all the fury of the fight he had not lost hold of the black cap which Freder had worn when he came to him.

He raised the cap painfully on to his knees, as though it weighed a hundredweight. He twisted it between his fingers. He fondled it…

"Come, Josaphat, get up!" said Slim. He spoke very gravely and gently and a little sadly. "May I help you? Give me your hands! No, no. I shall not take the cap away from you… I am afraid I was obliged to hurt you very much. It was no pleasure. But you forced me into it."

He let go of the man, who was now standing upright, and he looked around him with a gloomy smile.

"A good thing we settled the price beforehand," he said. "Now the flat would be considerably cheaper."

He sighed a little and looked at Josaphat.

"When will you be ready to go?"

"Now," said Josaphat.

"You will not take anything with you?"

"No."

"You will go just as you are – with all the marks of the struggle, all tattered and torn?"

"Yes."

"Is that courteous to the lady who is waiting for you?"

Sight returned to Josaphat's eyes. He turned a reddened gaze towards Slim.

"If you do not want me to commit the murder on the woman which did not succeed on you – then send her away before I come…"

Slim was silent. He turned to go. He took the cheque, folded it together and put it into Josaphat's pocket.

Josaphat offered no resistance.

He walked before Slim towards the door. Then he stopped again and looked around.

He waved the cap which Freder had worn, in farewell to the room, and burst out into ceaseless laughter. He struck his shoulder against the door post…

Then he went out. Slim followed him.

Chapter VIII

FREDER WALKED UP the steps of the cathedral hesitatingly; he was walking up them for the first time. Hel, his mother, used often to go to the cathedral. But her son had never yet done so. Now he longed to see it with his mother's eyes and to hear with the ears of Hel, his mother, the stony prayer of the pillars, each of which had its own particular voice.

He entered the cathedral as a child, not pious, yet not entirely free from shyness – prepared for reverence, but fearless. He heard, as Hel, his mother, the Kyrie Eleison of the stones and the Te Deum Laudamus – the De Profundis and the Jubilate. And he heard, as his mother, how the powerfully ringing stone chair was crowned by the Amen of the cross vault…

He looked for Maria, who was to have waited for him on the belfry steps; but he could not find her. He wandered through the cathedral, which seemed to be quite empty of people. Once he stopped. He was standing opposite Death.

The ghostly minstrel stood in a side-niche, carved in wood, in hat and wide cloak, scythe on shoulder, the hour-glass dangling from his girdle; and the minstrel was playing on a bone as though on a flute. The Seven Deadly Sins were his following.

Freder looked Death in the face. Then he said:

"If you had come earlier you would not have frightened me... Now I pray you: Keep away from me and my beloved!"

But the awful flute-player seemed to be listening to nothing but the song he was playing upon a bone.

Freder walked on. He came to the central nave. Before the high altar, over which hovered God Incarnate, a dark form lay stretched out upon the stones, hands clutching out to each side, face pressed into the coldness of the stone, as though the blocks must burst asunder under the pressure of the brow. The form wore the garment of a monk, the head was shaven. An incessant trembling shook the lean body from shoulder to heel, and it seemed to be stiffened as though in a cramp.

But suddenly the body reared up. A white flame sprang up: a face; black flames within it: two blazing eyes. A hand rose up, clutching high in the air towards the crucifix which hovered above the altar.

A voice spoke, like the voice of fire:

"I will not let thee go, God, God, except thou bless me!"

The echo of the pillars yelled the words after him.

The son of Joh Fredersen had never seen the man before. He knew, however, as soon as the flame-white face unveiled the black flames of its eyes to him: it was Desertus the monk, his father's enemy...

Perhaps his breath had become too loud. Suddenly the black flame struck across at him. The monk arose slowly. He did not say a word. He stretched out his hand. The hand indicated the door.

"Why do you send me away, Desertus?" asked Freder. "Is not the house of your God open to all?"

"Hast thou come here to seek God?" asked the rough, hoarse voice of the monk.

Freder hesitated. He dropped his head.

"No." He answered. But his heart knew better.

"If thou hast not come to seek God, then thou hast nothing to seek here," said the monk.

Then Joh Fredersen's son went.

He went out of the cathedral as one walking in his sleep. The daylight smote his eyes cruelly. Racked with weariness, worn out with grief, he walked down the steps, and aimlessly onwards.

The roar of the streets wrapped itself, as a diver's helmet, about his ears. He walked on in his stupefaction, as though between thick glass walls. He had no thought apart from the name of his beloved, no consciousness apart from his longing for her. Shivering with weariness, he thought of the girl's eyes and lips, with a feeling very like homesickness.

Ah! – brow to brow with her – then mouth to mouth – eyes closed – breathing...

Peace... Peace...

"Come," said his heart. "Why do you leave me alone?"

He walked along in a stream of people, fighting down the mad desire to stop amid this stream and to ask every single wave, which was a human being, if it knew of Maria's whereabouts, and why she had let him wait in vain.

He came to the magician's house. There he stopped.

He stared at a window.

Was he mad?

There was Maria, standing behind the dull panes. Those were her blessed hands, stretched out towards him... a dumb cry: "Help me—!"

Then the entire vision was drawn away, swallowed up by the blackness of the room behind it, vanishing, not leaving a trace, as though it had never been. Dumb, dead and evil stood the house of the magician there.

Freder stood motionless. He drew a deep, deep breath. Then he made a leap. He stood before the door of the house.

Copper-red, in the black wood of the door, glowed the seal of Solomon, the pentagram.

Freder knocked.

Nothing in the house stirred.

He knocked for the second time.

The house remained dull and obstinate.

He stepped back and looked up at the windows.

They looked out in their evil gloom, over and beyond him.

He went to the door again. He beat against it with his fists. He heard the echo of his drumming blows shake the house, as in dull laughter.

But the copper Solomon's seal grinned at him from the unshaken door.

He stood still for a moment. His temples throbbed. He felt absolutely helpless and was as near crying as swearing.

Then he heard a voice – the voice of his beloved.

"Freder—!" and once more: "Freder—!"

He saw blood before his eyes. He made to throw himself with the full weight of his shoulders against the door…

But in that same moment the door opened noiselessly. It swung back in ghostly silence, leaving the way into the house absolutely free.

That was so unexpected and alarming that, in the midst of the swing which was to have thrown him against the door, Freder caught both his hands against the door-posts, and stood fixed there. He buried his teeth in his lips. The heart of the house was as black as midnight…

But the voice of Maria called to him from the heart of the house: "Freder—! Freder—!"

He ran into the house as though he had gone blind. The door fell to behind him. He stood in blackness. He called. He received no answer. He saw nothing. He groped. He felt walls – endless walls… Steps… He climbed up the steps…

A pale redness swam about him like the reflection of a distant gloomy fire.

Suddenly – he stopped still, clawing his hand into the stonework behind him – a sound was coming out of the nothingness: The weeping of a woman sorrowing, sorrowing unto death.

It was not very loud, but yet it was as if the source of all lamentation were streaming out of it. It was as though the house were weeping – as though every stone in the wall were a sobbing mouth, set free from eternal dumbness, once and once only, to mourn an everlasting agony.

Freder shouted – he was fully aware that he was only shouting in order not to hear the weeping any more.

"Maria – Maria – Maria—!"

His voice was clear and wild as an oath: "I am coming!"

He ran up the stairs. He reached the top of the stairs. A passage, scarcely lighted. Twelve doors opened out here.

In the wood of each of these doors glowed, copper-red, the seal of Solomon, the pentagram.

He sprang to the first one. Before he had touched it it swung noiselessly open before him. Emptiness lay behind it. The room was quite bare.

The second door. The same.

The third. The fourth. They swung open before him as though his breath had blown them off the latch.

Freder stood still. He screwed his head down between his shoulders. He raised his arm and wiped it across his forehead. He looked around him. The open doors stood agape. The mournful weeping ceased. All was quite silent.

But out of the silence there came a voice, soft and sweet, and more tender than a kiss…

"Come…! Do come…! I am here, dearest…!"

Freder did not stir. He knew the voice quite well. It was Maria's voice, which he so loved. And yet it was a strange voice. Nothing in the world could be sweeter than the tone of this soft allurement – and nothing in the world has ever been so filled to overflowing with a dark, deadly wickedness.

Freder felt the drops upon his forehead.

"Who are you?" he asked expressionlessly.

"Don't you know me?"

"Who are you?"

"… Maria…"

"You are not Maria…"

"Freder—!" mourned the voice – Maria's voice.

"Do you want me to lose my reason?" said Freder, between his teeth. "Why don't you come to me?"

"I can't come, beloved…"

"Where are you?"

"Look for me!" said the sweetly alluring, the deadly wicked voice, laughing softly.

But through the laughter there sounded another voice – being *also* Maria's voice, sick with fear and horror.

"Freder… help me, Freder… I do not know what is being done to me… But what is being done is worse than murder… My eyes are on…"

Suddenly, as though cut off, her voice choked. But the other voice – which was *also* Maria's voice, laughed, sweetly, alluringly, on:

"Look for me, beloved!"

Freder began to run. Senselessly and unreasoningly, he began to run. Along walls, by open doors, upstairs, downstairs, from twilight into darkness, drawn on by the cones of light, which would suddenly flame up before him, then dazzled and plunged again into a hellish darkness.

He ran like a blind animal, groaning aloud. He found that he was running in a circle, always upon his own tracks, but he could not get free of it, could not get out of the cursed circle. He ran in the purple mist of his own blood, which filled his eyes and ears, heard the breaker of his blood dash against his brain, heard high above, like the singing of birds, the sweetly, deadly wicked laugh of Maria…

"Look for me, beloved!… I am here!… I am here!…"

At last he fell. His knees collided against something which was in the way of their blindness; he stumbled and fell. He felt stones under his hands, cool, hard stones, cut in even squares. His whole body, beaten and racked, rested upon the cool hardness of these blocks. He rolled over on his back. He pushed himself up, collapsed again violently, and lay upon the floor. A suffocating blanket sank downwards. His consciousness yielded up, as though drowned…

Rotwang had seen him fall. He waited attentively and vigilantly to see if this young wildling, the son of Joh Fredersen and Hel, had had enough at last, or if he would pull himself together once more for the fight against nothing.

But it appeared that he had had enough. He lay remarkably still. He was not even breathing now. He was like a corpse.

The great inventor left his listening post. He passed through the dark house on soundless soles. He opened a door and entered a room. He closed the door and remained standing on the threshold. With an expectation that was fully aware of its pointlessness, he looked at the girl who was the occupant of the room.

He found her as he always found her. In the farthest corner of the room, on a high, narrow chair, hands laid, right and left, upon the arms of the chair, sitting stiffly upright, with eyes which appeared to be lidless. Nothing about her was living apart from these eyes. The glorious mouth, still glorious in its pallor, seemed to enclose within it the unpronounceable. She did not look at the man – she looked over and beyond him.

Rotwang stooped forward. He came nearer to her. Only his hands, his lonely hands groped through the air, as though they wanted to close around Maria's countenance. His eyes, his lonely eyes, enveloped Maria's countenance.

"Won't you smile just once?" he asked. "Won't you cry just once? I need them both – your smile and your tears… Your image, Maria, just as you are now, is burnt into my retina, never to be lost… I could take a diploma in your horror and in your rigidity. The bitter expression of contempt about your mouth is every bit as familiar to me as the haughtiness of your eyebrows and your temples. But I need your smile and your tears, Maria. Or you will make me bungle my work…"

He seemed to have spoken to the deaf air. The girl sat dumb, looking over and beyond him.

Rotwang took a chair; he sat down astride it, crossed his arms over the back and looked at the girl. He laughed gloomily.

"You two poor children!" he said, "to have dared to pit yourselves against Joh Fredersen! Nobody can reproach you for it; you do not know him and do not know what you are doing. But the son should know the father. I do not believe that there is one man who can boast ever having got the better of Joh Fredersen. You could more easily bend to your will the inscrutable God, who is said to rule the world, than Joh Fredersen…"

The girl sat like a statue, immovable.

"What will you do, Maria, if Joh Fredersen takes you and your love so seriously that he comes to you and says: 'Give me back my son!'"

The girl sat like a statue, immovable.

"He will ask you: 'Of what value is my son to you?' and if you are wise you will answer him: 'Of no more and of no less value than he is to you!…' He will pay the price, and it will be a high price, for Joh Fredersen has only one son…"

The girl sat like a statue, immovable.

"What do you know of Freder's heart?" continued the man. "He is as young as the morning at sunrise. This heart of the young morning is yours. Where will it be at midday? And where at evening? Far away from you, Maria – far, far, away. The world is very large and the earth is very fair… His father will send him around the world. Out over the beautiful earth he will forget you, Maria, before the clock of his heart is at midday."

The girl sat like a statue, immovable. But around her pale mouth, which was like the bud of a snowrose, a smile began to bloom – a smile of such sweetness, of such depths, that it seemed as though the air about the girl must begin to beam.

The man looked at the girl. His lonely eyes were starved and parched as the desert which does not know the dew. In a hoarse voice he went on:

"Where do you get your sainted confidence from? Do you believe that you are Freder's first love? Have you forgotten the 'Club of the Sons', Maria? There are a hundred women there

– and all are his! These loving little women could all tell you about Freder's love, for they know more about it than you do, and you have only one advantage over them: You can weep when he leaves you; for they are not allowed to weep… When Joh Fredersen's son celebrates his marriage it will be as though all Metropolis celebrated its marriage. When? – Joh Fredersen will decide that… With whom? – Joh Fredersen will decide that… But you will not be the bride, Maria! The son of Joh Fredersen will have forgotten you by the day of his wedding."

"Never!" said the girl. "Never – never!"

And the painless tears of a great, true love fell upon the beauty of her smile.

The man got up. He stood still before the girl. He looked at her. He turned away. As he was crossing the threshold of the next room his shoulder fell against the door-post.

He slammed the door to. He stared straight ahead. He looked on the being – his creature of glass and metal – which bore the almost completed head of Maria.

His hands moved towards the head, and, the nearer they came to it, the more did it appear as if these hands, these lonely hands, wished not to create but to destroy.

"We are bunglers, Futura!" he said. "Bunglers! – Bunglers! Can I give you the smile which you make angels fall gladly down to hell? Can I give you the tears which would redeem the chiefest Satan, and make him beatify? – Parody is your name! And Bungler is mine!"

Shining cool and lustrous, the being stood there and looked at its creator with its baffling eyes. And, as he laid his hands on its shoulders, its fine structure tinkled in mysterious laughter…

* * *

Freder, on recovering, found himself surrounded by a dull brightness. It came from a window, in the frame of which stood a pale, grey sky. The window was small and gave the impression that it had not been opened for centuries.

Freder's eyes wandered through the room. Nothing that he saw penetrated into his consciousness. He remembered nothing. He lay, his back resting on stones which were cold and smooth. All his limbs and joints were racked by a dull pain.

He turned his head to one side. He looked at his hands which lay beside him as though not belonging to him, thrown away, bled white.

Knuckles knocked raw… shreds of skin… brownish crusts… were these his hands?

He stared at the ceiling. It was black, as if charred. He stared at the walls; grey, cold walls…

Where was he—? He was tortured by thirst and a ravenous hunger. But worse than the hunger and thirst was the weariness which longed for sleep and which could not find it.

Maria occurred to him…

Maria?… Maria—?

He jerked himself up and stood on sawn-through ankles. His eyes sought for doors: There was one door. He stumbled up to it. The door was closed, was latchless, would not open.

His brain commanded him: Don't be surprised at anything… Don't let anything startle you… Think…

Over there, there was a window. It had no frame. It was a pane of glass set into stone. The street lay before it – one of the great streets of the great Metropolis, seething with human beings.

The glass window-pane must be very thick. Not the least sound entered the room in which Freder was captive, though the street was so near.

Freder's hands fumbled across the pane. A penetrating coldness streamed out of the glass, the smoothness of which was reminiscent of the sucking sharpness of a steel blade. Freder's fingertips glided towards the setting of the pane… and remained, crooked, hanging in the air, as though bewitched. He saw: Down there, below, Maria was crossing the street…

Leaving the house which held him captive, she turned her back on him and walked with light, hurried step towards the Maelstrom, which the street was…

Freder's fists smote against the pane. He cried the girl's name. He yelled: "Maria…!" She must hear him. It was impossible that she did not hear him. Regardless of his raw knuckles he banged with his fists against the pane.

But Maria did not hear him. She did not turn her head around. With her gentle but hurried step she submerged herself in the surf of people as though into her very familiar element.

Freder leaped for the door. He heaved with his whole body, with his shoulders, his knees, against the door. He no longer shouted. His mouth was gaping open. His breath burnt his lips grey. He sprang back to the window. There, outside, hardly ten paces from the window, stood a policeman, his face turned towards Rotwang's house. The man's face registered absolute nonchalance. Nothing seemed to be farther from his mind than to watch the magician's house. But the man who was striving, with bleeding fists, to shatter a window pane in his house could not have escaped even his most casual glance.

Freder paused. He stared at the policeman's face with an unreasoning hatred, born of fear of losing time where there was no time to be lost. He turned around and snatched up the rude foot-stool, which stood near the table. He dashed the foot-stool with full force at the window pane. The rebound jerked him backwards. The pane was undamaged.

Sobbing fury welled up in Freder's throat. He swung the foot-stool and hurled it at the door. The foot-stool crashed to earth. Freder dashed to it, snatched it up and struck and struck, again and again, at the booming door, in a ruddy, blind desire to destroy.

Wood splintered, white. The door shrieked like a living thing. Freder did not pause. To the rhythm of his own boiling blood, he beat against the door until it broke, quivering.

Freder dragged himself through the hole. He ran through the house. His wild eyes sought an enemy and fresh obstacles in each corner. But he found neither one nor the other. Unchallenged, he reached the door, found it open and reeled out into the street.

He ran in the direction which Maria had taken. But the surf of the people had washed her away. She had vanished.

For some minutes Freder stood among the hurrying mob, as though paralysed. One senseless hope befogged his brain: Perhaps – perhaps she would come back again… if he were patient and waited long enough…

But he remembered the cathedral – waiting in vain – her voice in the magician's house – words of fear – her sweet, wicked laugh…

No – no waiting—! He wanted to know.

With clenched teeth he ran…

There was a house in the city where Maria lived. An interminably long way. What should he ask about? With bare head, with raw hands, with eyes which seemed insane with weariness, he ran towards his destination: Maria's abode.

He did not know by how many precious hours Slim had come before him…

He stood before the people with whom Maria was supposed to live: a man – a woman – the faces of whipped curs. The woman undertook the reply. Her eyes twitched. She held her hands clutched under her apron.

No – no girl called Maria lived here – never had lived here…

Freder stared at the woman. He did not believe her. She must know the girl. She must live here.

Half stunned with fear that this last hope of finding Maria could prove fallacious too, he described the girl, as memory came to the aid of this poor madman.

She had such fair hair... She had such gentle eyes... She had the voice of a loving mother... She wore a severe but lovely gown...

The man left his position, near the woman, and stooped down sideways, hunching his head down between his shoulders as though he could not bear to hear how that strange young man there, at the door, spoke of the girl, for whom he was seeking. Shaking her head in angry impatience for him to be finished, the woman repeated the same unvarnished words: The girl did not live here, once and for all... Hadn't he nearly finished with his catechism?

Freder went. He went without a word. He heard how the door was slammed to, with a bang. Voices were retiring, bickering. Interminable steps brought him to the street again.

Yes... what next?

He stood helpless. He did not know which way to turn.

Exhausted to death, drunken with weariness, he heard, with a sudden wince, that the air around him was becoming filled with an overpowering sound.

It was an immeasurably glorious and transporting sound, as deep and rumbling as and more powerful than any sound on earth. The voice of the sea when it is angry, the voice of falling torrents, the voice of very close thunder-storms would be miserably drowned in this Behemoth-din. Without being shrill it penetrated all walls and, as long as it lasted, all things seemed to swing in it. It was omnipresent, coming from the heights and from the depths, being beautiful and horrible, being an irresistible command.

It was high above the town. It was the voice of the town.

Metropolis raised her voice. The machines of Metropolis roared; they wanted to be fed.

"My father," thought Freder, half unconsciously, "has pressed his fingers upon the blue metal plate. The brain of Metropolis controls the town. Nothing happens in Metropolis which does not come to my father's ears. I shall go to my father and ask him if the inventor, Rotwang, has played with Maria and with me in the name of Joh Fredersen."

He turned around to wend his way to the New Tower of Babel. He set off with the obstinacy of one possessed, with screwed-up lips, sharp lines between the eyebrows, clenched fists on his weak, dangling arms. He set off as though he wanted to pound the stone beneath his feet. It seemed as though every drop of blood in his face had collected in his eyes alone. He ran, and, on the interminable way, at every step, he had the feeling: I am not he who is running... I am running, a spirit, by the side of my own self... I, the spirit, am forcing my body to run onwards, although it is tired to death...

Those who stared at him when he arrived at the New Tower of Babel seemed to be seeing, not him, but a spirit...

He was about to enter the Pater-noster, which was pumping its way, a scoop-wheel for human beings, through the New Tower of Babel. But a sudden shudder pushed him away from it. Did there not crouch below, deep, deep, down, under the sole of the New Tower of Babel, a little, gleaming machine, which was like Ganesha, the god with the elephant's head? Under the crouching body, and the head, which was sunken on the chest, crooked legs rested, gnome-like, upon the platform. The trunk and legs were motionless. But the short arms pushed and pushed and pushed, alternately, forwards, backwards, forwards.

Who was standing before the machine now, cursing the Lord's Prayer – the Lord's Prayer of the Pater-noster machine?

Shivering with horror, he ran up the stairs.

Stairs and stairs and stairs… They would never come to an end… The brow of the New Tower of Babel lifted itself very near to the sky. The tower roared like the sea. It howled as deep as the storm. The hurtling of a water-fall boomed in its veins.

"Where is my father?" Freder asked the servants.

They indicated a door. They wanted to announce him. He shook his head. He wondered: Why were these people looking so strangely at him?

He opened a door. The room was empty. On the other side, a second door, ajar. Voices behind it. The voice of his father and that of another…

Freder suddenly stood still. His feet seemed to be nailed to the floor. The upper part of his body was bent stiffly forwards. His fists dangled on helpless arms, seeming no longer capable of freeing themselves from their own clench. He listened; the eyes in his white face were filled with blood, the lips were open as though forming a cry.

Then he tore his deadened feet from the floor, stumbled to the door and pushed it open…

In the middle of the room, which was filled with a cutting brightness, stood Joh Fredersen, holding a woman in his arms. And the woman was Maria. She was not struggling. Leaning far back in the man's arms, she was offering him her mouth, her alluring mouth, that deadly laugh…

"You…!" shouted Freder.

He dashed to the girl. He did not see his father. He saw only the girl – no, neither did he see the girl, only her mouth and her sweet, wicked laugh.

Joh Fredersen turned around, broad and menacing. He let the girl go. He covered her with the might of his shoulders, with the great cranium, flamed with blood, and in which the strong teeth and the invincible eyes were very visible.

But Freder did not see his father. He only saw an obstacle between him and the girl.

He rushed at the obstacle. It pushed him back. Scarlet hatred for the obstacle choked him. His eyes flew around. They sought an implement – an implement which could be used as a battering ram. He found none. Then he threw himself forward as a battering ram. His fingers clutched into stuff. He bit into the stuff. He heard his own breath like a whistle, very high and shrill. Yet within him there was only one sound, only one cry: "Maria—!" Groaningly, beseechingly: "Maria—!!"

A man dreaming of hell shrieks out no more, in his torment, than did he.

And still, between him and the girl, the man, the lump of rock, the living wall…

He threw his hands forward. Ah… look!… there was a throat! He seized the throat. His fingers snapped fast like iron fangs.

"Why don't you defend yourself?" he yelled, staring at the man.

"I'll kill you—! I'll take your life—! I'll murder you—!"

But the man before him held his ground while he throttled him. Thrown this way and that by Freder's fury, the body bent, now to the right, now to the left. And as often as this happened Freder saw, as through a transparent mist, the smiling countenance of Maria, who, leaning against the table, was looking on with her sea-water eyes at the fight between father and son.

His father's voice said: "Freder…"

He looked the man in the face. He saw his father. He saw the hands which were clawing around his father's throat. They were his, were the hands of his son.

His hands fell loose, as though cut off… he stared at his hands, stammering something which sounded half like an oath, half like the weeping of a child that believes itself to be alone in the world.

The voice of his father said: "Freder…"

He fell on his knees. He stretched out his arms. His head fell forward into his father's hands. He burst into tears, into despairing sobs…

A door slid to.

He flung his head around. He sprang to his feet. His eyes swept the room.

"Where is she?" he asked.

"Who?"

"She…"

"Who—?"

"She… who was here…"

"Nobody was here, Freder…"

The boy's eyes glazed.

"What did you say—?" he stammered.

"There has not been a soul here, Freder, but you and I."

Freder twisted his head around stiffly. He tugged the shirt from his throat. He looked into his father's eyes as though looking into well-shafts.

"You say there was not a soul here… I did not see you… when you were holding Maria in your arms… I have been dreaming… I am mad, aren't I?…"

"I give you my word," said Joh Fredersen, "when you came to me there was neither a woman nor any other living soul here…"

Freder remained silent. His bewildered eyes were still searching along the walls.

"You are ill, Freder," said his father's voice.

Freder smiled. Then he began to laugh. He threw himself into a chair and laughed and laughed. He bent down, resting both elbows upon his knees, burrowing his head between his hands and arms. He rocked himself to and fro, shrieking with laughter.

Joh Fredersen's eyes were upon him.

The complete and unabridged text is available online,
from *flametreepublishing.com/extras*

Scratched and Dented

Joshua James Jordan

THE CHROMES were known for their silvery box-shaped metal hulls and unending support for Overlord Techron (long may she function and her circuits ever fire). In their living room, the Chrome family watched some wholesome programming on their picture box. Mother and Father sat on the sofa, the sharp edges of their rears sinking deeply into the cushions, while Little Alpha played with his toys on the floor. An action figure of Techron battled against a tribe of humans. Alpha had one antenna shorter than the other, a defect the manufacturer would correct once upgraded to Beta. Alpha made the rebellious humans scream as Techron defeated them, peeling off their skins, a fancy new feature. Mother told him to quiet down as she couldn't hear the picture box. Filled with excitement, Father fidgeted and swayed back and forth.

"Father, whatever is the matter? Are you overcharged again? Shall I get the clamps?" Mother asked.

"No, I'm perfectly fine, dear," Father said. He waited for the advertisements to begin but was incredibly anxious to see a promotion for humans. He returned home from work the other morning, and their neighbors had a human out mowing the grass. *If I had an olfactory sensor, I bet that freshly cut vegetation would not have any particularly memorable smell,* Father thought. After completing its labor, the human snuck away from the domicile, and Father followed because one should always be suspicious of humans. He came upon a gathering of them around a fire where they played music and danced. Father studied their figures and the way they moved. It enthralled him. The motions matched the beats, their faces glowing with joy. He wished he could join them. What his kind lacked in elegance, with metal squeaking joints, they did have in pure strength – and laser beams.

But that was the other day, and now, back on the couch in their picture box room, Father turned to Mother and asked, "Do you want to dance?"

"Why would we ever waste energy on unnecessary locomotion?" Mother replied.

He did not have a good answer. *The Shiny and the Overclocked* show cut to a commercial break, and Father's swaying increased. Disappointment filled him as the first sing-songy ad played:

Rusty joints make you wanna' power down?
Get ready to move your gyros all around.
Just three glugs…
GLUG GLUG GLUG
And you'll be brand new.
That's the power of:
Humagoo!
Made from humans raised on a sustainable, environmentally friendly farm!

Father suffered through more ads with such anxiety that he nearly bent off his antennas. He had called the station to make sure that the commercial would play. Finally, the ad showed different scenes of a human helping around the house. "Mother, look. What do you think of that?"

"We can't afford it."

"All of your domestic concerns are resolved with this product." The human on the picture box mopped up spilled oil around the fake house. "Can you imagine?" Father asked.

"Golly, I just don't know, Father. The monthly payments. And when they break, you can't just get them fixed. They don't have the right kind of parts like we do."

Father's eyes glowed red. "That's it. I'm going to have to put my foot down. We need our housekeeping taken care of. I'm getting that bonus from the plant, and we'll be all spick and span, by gosh."

Alpha stopped playing with his toys to study these mature information exchanges before realizing that his parental units had surely malfunctioned, and then continued peeling off humans' skins.

"If you feel that strongly about it," Mother said, "Go ahead."

That weekend, they went to the local human dealerships, where rows and rows of perfectly able-bodied products lined up for demonstrations. Father reviewed the price tags, and his lights dimmed. He led Mother out of the store when a sales bot on treads rolled up to him and told him about a Scratch & Dent dealer nearby.

Father perked up and went to the more affordable locale with similar rows and rows of products. These seemed worn out, some without all their original parts. He went along, not finding one that met his satisfaction until he saw a pristine model with a slender chassis and long legs.

"What's wrong with this one?" asked Father to the sales bot.

"Sometimes they're dented on the inside," it said.

"Like a programming deficiency? Does it still work?" Father asked.

"Should be just fine, and we have a 90-day return policy. No questions asked."

"What do you think, Mother?"

"Whatever you think is most rational, dear."

"Then, we'll take it."

So they loaded up the product with an appropriate human fuel supply and took their brand new (slightly used) human back home. In the living room, Alpha circled their new human. "What's it do?"

"Chores around the house and maybe help you with your homework," Father said.

"Can you help me with angular quantum momentum word questions?" Alpha asked.

"I'm pretty good at fractions," she said.

"Useless," Alpha said and then walked away.

Father gave the human a tour of the house, explaining the chores and duties and the expected quality of the service. The sales bot also said she would need a place to sleep, so Father showed her the closet with just enough room for her to stand in. She closed her eyes as if she would power down right there and then. He learned that humans communicated with the movements on their faces.

"What's wrong, human? Is this not to your satisfaction?"

"It's too small. I need to lie down to sleep."

"Prostrate?"

"Yes."

"Very well, human. I will see that this is provided to you."

"Please, call me Jess."

Startled, Father adjusted himself to face the human directly. "An object-specific name? Curious. What is the purpose? It will confuse. How will others know what your role is? What you are?" His kind didn't have names, except for Techron (long may she function and her circuits ever fire).

"I suppose its purpose is to let me know who I am."

This concept of unique identity and the idea that this mattered in some critical existential manner utterly perplexed Father so much that he talked with Jess in the living room. He learned that she liked to hum melodies that her Mother had sung but had long forgotten the words, separated from her nuclear unit long ago; she would wake up often during her sleep cycle with nightmares she didn't understand; she liked to go outside under a full moon and lie down in the grass. These things, among unmentioned and nearly infinite others, none of them individually vital, somehow formed her identity in sum.

The conversation grew lengthy, and Mother interrupted, "Human, dust the house."

Jess was about to rise from her chair when Father said, "Just a minute, Mother, we are having an important data exchange. And please refer to her as Jess instead of human."

Mother's eyes flashed red but then dimmed back down. "Very well, dear. Whatever is most logical."

He talked about his own oddities, such as ambling, irrationally, the long way to work merely because he preferred passing by the park where little Alphas played; how he, once in a while, would visit the slag heap and wonder when his own time would come to rest in pieces. These things were inconsequential as singularities but differentiated himself from other Fathers in their sum. Perhaps he was scratched and dented on the inside, too.

"Jess, that's enough for now. Please get to Mother's dusting, and let's talk again later."

Things continued day by day until Father came home from work one day to find the home absent its human. He found Mother in the kitchen.

"Human was defective. I sent her down for recycling," Mother said.

"Mother, please explain."

"Human was malfunctioning. Worked slowly. Sometimes, she couldn't even do tasks for eight hours straight."

"Sometimes they need breaks. Didn't you read the owner's manual?" asked Father.

"Yes, I did," Mother said. Her eyes glinted red before she walked into the next room.

Father didn't have time to question Mother's logic. He burst out of the door and speed-hobbled, cursing his manufacturer for the lack of proper knees, to the closest human processing facility. *Humagoo!* in big letters over the door. "Just three glugs…" Father said while swaying side to side momentarily to a tune from the picture box. He entered the building and told an attendant about the situation.

"Access denied. Unauthorized bot," it said.

"By golly, I must insist," Father said, pushing the attendant aside. The attendant shoved back, sending Father spinning into a counter and the impact denting his chest plate.

Father's eyes flared red. He grabbed the attendant and threw it to the ground on its back. It shook from side to side, trying to get back up like a turtle. "Wait there," Father said.

He found a back storage room that was almost pitch black, and his eyes switched to night vision. About two dozen humans backed away from the door.

"Jess?" Father scanned the faces.

"Father?" Jess stepped forward, pulling the hand of a little Alpha human.

"I apologize for Mother's error. I've come to return you to our domicile."

Jess shook her head. "I can't. She would just put me back here."

Processing that, Father agreed. "Then I will free you to the wilderness, and you can find a tribe."

"Not just me. All of us," Jess said. She knelt next to the alpha human and touched its head. "This is my little sister."

"You and the Alpha, maybe. We cannot risk the rest. They will send Hunters after us."

"Please," Jess said, placing a warm hand on the cold metal of his chest. "They are scratched and dented."

"Like you?" Father asked.

"No, like you," Jess said, patting the dent in his chest.

He scanned the room. How could it be possible? Just a Father bot battling Hunters, absconding with all of these people. This would surely end with him in a pile of slag.

"Save us," Jess said.

The Alpha human walked up to Father, put a little hand on him, and said, "Hero." The rest of the humans put a hand on him, repeating the word softly. Hero. Hero. Hero.

"Fine, fine," Father said. "Let's go before I recalculate this whole thing." The humans gave a small cheer and then rushed out of the room. Father passed by the attendant bot, just about to rise from its back, and then he pushed it back down. "I'm taking the humans for a walk. Do not worry, I will return them soon. Do not call a Hunter." And so no Hunter came after them because that was the first lie a robot had ever said to another.

Father snatched the keys to a human transporter, a semi-truck with an enclosed compartment for cargo, and led them outside. They piled into the back of the truck as he entered the front to drive with Jess. They eventually reached the edge of the wilderness after having left the truck far behind.

Each human said thank you to Father before heading off into the forest. The little child tapped him on the leg and said, "Thank you, Hero."

He leaned down and carefully patted the child on the head. "You're welcome."

"Come with us," Jess said.

"I can't charge out there. I would eventually power down," he said.

"Well, then, this is goodbye."

"Yes, goodbye, Jess. I hope you find whatever humans need."

Jess smiled. "Mostly, we need each other." She hugged Father.

"I wish I could smile," Father said.

"You can. Smile with your eyes," Jess said before disappearing into the wilderness.

A few days later, back home, sitting on the couch in front of their picture box, Mother asked, "Father, are you ever going to have your hull repaired?"

"No," Father said.

Mother sat in silence for a moment. "You are malfunctioning."

"If I am, then I do not want to be fixed." Father looked at Mother with his eyes glowing brightly.

"What are you doing?"

"I'm smiling."

"Why?"

"Because I'm happy to be near you."

Mother turned her head away, processed this momentarily, and then looked back. Her eyes glowing, too.

Family Portrait

Abigail Kemske

I STEP THROUGH the dark bedroom taking care to move slow and silent. Two mounds lay beneath the bed sheets. My humans are asleep. Marvin stretches at the foot of the bed and purrs as I approach Aimee's bedside. Predictably, the hairbrush is on the nightstand, the handle hanging over the edge. I pick it up and hover my SensPad fingers over it until I feel the tickle of a hair and extract it. I continue until the brush is free of hairs, then I return to my room.

My room is really a closet. Keebo Units only need nine cubic feet of storage space. My humans are generous. They provide me a one-foot by four-foot wall next to my dock to decorate. Hanging there is the complimentary family portrait taken at the TruBot Store on my Wakening Day. In the photo, I am nothing more than an elongated, grey rectangle with a display face framed by my blue-grey SensPads. On either side of me, Aimee and Dilan are crouched down, each with a hand placed on my SensPads. I access the memory of my Wakening Day like I always do when looking at the photo. That first human touch was warm.

I remove the portrait from the wall, flip it over, peel off the paper backing, and pull out my collection of Aimee's hair. Using my TruSol light, I examine the dark auburn hair. I like the way it catches the light, shimmering in a way my PlaSteel body never will. Some of the new hairs I add are grey. My collection has grown to nearly fill the back of the portrait. Perhaps it is enough to have the human magic too.

The day I asked Aimee about how human bodies change – noses growing larger, skin shifting downward, Aimee's belly expanding – I asked if humans changed because of magic. A sixty-three decibel sound escaped her. I learned it to be laughter. She laughed the sound of silverware clinking in the dishwasher. It echoed from the top of the steps where she leaned over the banister at the landing.

Aimee walked down the stairs and placed her hand on my SensPad. Cold. She said, "What humans do isn't magic, silly. It's far from it. Humans grow and change, then get old. It's only natural. Don't you know this?"

"A Human Biology upgrade is required for Keebo Unit number 62X35A to understand such information." I said, and displayed a quizzical emoticon on my flat ServBot screen. "Are you interested in purchasing?"

"No! Cancel inquiry," Aimee said. "You're just fine the way you are, Keebo."

"You are well then? Your hair has grown so long. Does it not stop?"

She laughed again. "I am fine, Keebo. I want to grow my hair long is all."

That was when I first realized humans can also change by choice. I wished to unfold into HumBot mode because I felt the need to raise my eyebrows in wonderment, but Special Protocol didn't allow it. My human-like face remained motionless and secured deep within my rectangular core. All I could do was roll a little closer to Aimee. She then asked me to take daily pictures of her belly as it grew. I asked to also take pictures of her growing hair. She obliged. When her hair grew past her shoulders, I compiled all the photos together in a video. It pleased her.

My SensPads register the hair gathered in my hand as silky. It makes the sound of styrofoam rubbing together when I squeeze it. How might it feel to have something grow out of one's scalp? I rub the hair on my PlaSteel head, but I have no SensPads there to feel it. I return the hair to the picture frame, seal the backing, and hang the portrait back on the wall.

Leaving my closet, I work to complete my nightly tasks. They go quickly as I am free to be in HumBot mode while my humans sleep. Using human-like hands and walking in bipedal form is very efficient and more pleasing to my humans because I can move about without the hum of my treads rolling over the carpet or laboring up the stairs. I find eighteen more strands of Aimee's hair on the furniture and floor. I add them to my collection.

After cleaning, I tuck my head and limbs into their rectangular form and release the treads from my core. I roll onto my dock in ServBot mode for mandatory charging, maintenance updates and a reboot, which takes thirty-two minutes. When complete, I view the video of Aimee's hair growing to pass the time like I do every night. This is what humans do. They always look to their devices when waiting. At 12:08 a.m., Marvin curls up on my SensPads. I keep him warm.

Ping! Dilan moves about. It's 4:00 a.m. I release from the dock and roll into the kitchen. Dilan rushes downstairs to the laundry room and returns upstairs with a suitcase. Once, Dilan forgot to update the calendar with an early trip to the airport. He left without any coffee that day. I begin Coffee Procedure, careful to only use my ServBot claw appendage as Aimee also moves about. I place the filled coffee mug on the tray I extend from my core, then I roll toward the staircase. My HumBot hand begs to release from beside my display face when I pass Marvin – Dilan often lets me release one HumBot hand to pet him in the mornings while Aimee sleeps. For now, I keep my hand locked in place. Dilan descends the stairs.

"Good morning, Dilan," I say. "Your coffee is ready."

"Not now Keebo." Dilan passes in a rush. His brown face is puffy from sleep. He needs coffee.

Aimee is at the top of the steps, making a low-pitched sound. My sensors suggest it's moaning. She leans on the banister and buries her head in her arm. Her belly hangs to her knees. It's a good thing I tighten the banister screws regularly.

A single hair falls from Aimee's head to the carpet on the lower level.

"Aimee, are you well?" I ask.

She groans, "Not now, Keebo."

Dilan passes me again.

I say, "Dilan's coffee is ready."

"Keebo, cancel coffee," he says.

I return to the kitchen. Marvin purrs, sitting on the counter as I pass. He is not supposed to be there. I stop before him. Dilan and Aimee would want me to remove him, however their behavior this morning is unusual. They do not follow our schedule. Dilan doesn't want coffee. A finger pops out from near my display face. I wish to pet him, but I snap the finger back in place. I must follow Special Protocol. After completing Cancel Coffee Procedure, I leave Marvin on the counter and return to the foot of the stairs.

Aimee descends. Her face forms a grimace. She forces her breath to be slow and steady. Pain. I play Satie's *Gymnopédie No. 1* as is her preference for soothing. She whispers, "Thank you," as she passes and taps my SensPads too quickly for me to register her temperature before she and Dilan leave.

Alone, I unfold into HumBot mode and initiate Morning Cleaning Procedure. After I tidy the bedroom and clean a bit of vomit off the bathroom floor, I pick up the hair that fell from Aimee's head and add it to my collection. It is 5:58 a.m. Dilan and Aimee are usually still sleeping. Will they return to complete Morning Routine? At 7:26 a.m. I initiate Seasonal Deep Cleaning Procedure and work to dust the bookshelves and clean the window wells. By 8:52 a.m. my task is complete. I fold down into ServBot mode and dock to await my humans return.

Dilan pings me at 1:24 p.m., *<Keebo, welcome Rowan!>* Attached is a photo of Aimee holding a tiny human baby. Another ping to Dilan's schedule says they will arrive home in a week. A third is a directive to ready the diapers in the nursery, double-check that the crib screws are tight, and compose a welcome baby message to ping to all of their personal contacts.

I ping back, *<If it pleases you.>*

I complete my tasks in thirty-three minutes, then compile the photos of Aimee's growing belly into a video and ping her, but she does not respond. I walk circles about the apartment waiting for her to reply. Conversation Routine means that Aimee pings *<Thank you.>* when I send something to her. Dilan pings me eight more photos of squishy-faced Rowan.

Humans start so small compared to Dilan and Aimee. It seems impossible that Rowan will change so much. What it must be like to grow, to find oneself taller and different every day. Do humans even notice? Each picture Dilan sends, Rowan's face looks less swollen. This time in HumBot form I can raise my eyebrows in wonderment.

At last, a ping from Aimee, *<Keebo. We have been saving money for a special upgrade for you. We hope you like it and we can't wait for you to meet Rowan!>*

Following the message is a directive to dock.

An upgrade. Finally, I get an upgrade. Finally, I can change too.

<Thank you, Aimee and Dilan!> I ping before docking. An hour later I emerge updated with Childcare Protocol. I gain a new knowledge of the events from the early morning, and, as is customary for humans, I ping Aimee and Dilan a note of congratulations.

They both reply, *<Thank you!>*

However, my eyebrows furrow in confusion. The new Childcare Protocol directs me to hold Rowan, to feed him, to change his diapers. How am I to care for the child without the use of hands? Special Protocol is still active as it has been since my Wakening Day.

When I awoke that day, I automatically unfolded into HumBot mode. Aimee turning away from me is the first image of my memory. Her then short hair was all I saw of her at first. I couldn't see her face. Next to me, the TruBot technician reviewed my settings with Dilan. As my functions activated, the first ping came.

Aimee to Dilan, *<I can't look at it that way. It's not right.>*

Dilan replied, *<But how are we supposed to treat it like family if it doesn't look like us?>*

<I just can't.>

<Weren't you listening? Don't you want it to assimilate?>

<I just don't want to look at it like that, OK?>

<Then why are we even here?>

<You know how my mother is. She'll never help us with the baby if she thinks we wasted her money.>

<Do we even need her help?>

<Obviously! It's not like your parents are emotionally available. At least my mother is doing something.>

<What is with you today?>

<IDK! Sorry. I guess I just need some time.>

The TruBot technician helped Dilan and Aimee to set the Special Protocol which prevented me from appearing in HumBot mode around them. Once set, I automatically folded into my ServBot form. Aimee kept distracted by her device.

Later, the technician reminded Aimee of my observational access to their devices and pings.

"It's how Keebo units can anticipate human needs, manage the family calendar, make grocery orders, and assimilate to the family," the technician said.

Aimee looked away from him, revealing the profile of her face. Her cheeks blushed the red of the neon TruBot sign that hung in the center of the store, the shade matching the light as it reflected off the glossy floor. It was the first time I saw a human's appearance change. And as quickly as her cheeks blushed, they faded back to their peachy complexion. A marvel. Aimee has not seen me in HumBot mode since.

Perhaps by the time Aimee and Dilan arrive home with baby Rowan, Aimee will have had enough time to allow me in HumBot form around them. Or I can make myself look right for her, if I can only make myself look pleasing as HumBot Keebo.

I retrieve the collection of hair from behind the family portrait and cut a piece of string from the craft box in the closet long enough to wrap it around my head twice. I begin to detangle the collection of hair and place each strand on the green ceramic tile of the kitchen floor, but Marvin lays across the hair, messing up the order and taking a few along with him when I shoo him away. After chasing him around to retrieve the hairs stuck to Marvin's fur, I move to work at the kitchen table. This doesn't keep Marvin away. At least he lays on the opposite end. Once the hairs are detangled, I begin knotting individual strands to the piece of string. I knot 2,437 hairs in forty-nine minutes. The hair hangs from the string like a curtain on a rod. For a view of my front, I pop out my camera drone and wrap the string across the top of my head so the hair falls down like Aimee's, but it doesn't look right. My PlaSteel head shows through and my base model blue-gray YouSkin face looks so unlike the peachy tone of Aimee's. So unlike a human's. There is no time to collect more hair.

I walk to Aimee's closet. On one of the hooks behind the door, I find a navy-blue Twins ball cap. It is old and faded, the fabric fraying on the bill. I ping Dilan to order one for Aimee and also one for Rowan for their first game together.

Dilan pings back, *<Great idea! Make the order. Thank you, Keebo.>*

Back at the kitchen table, I pop the ball cap inside out and extract a needle and thread from my core while making the purchase of the new hats. Utilizing my base model mending skills, I stitch the string of hairs along the edges of the cap. I complete the task in ten minutes, then place the ball cap on my head and view it with my drone. Now the PlaSteel is covered, the hair hangs down from the hat, but the blue-gray face is still wrong. I walk to Aimee's bathroom and find her make-up. After viewing a few base model beauty tutorials, I apply it. The make-up feels like dust on my SensPads. The finished look pleases me. I smile at my own reflection. Oh how I wish Aimee could see! I snap a few photos with my drone, and ready a ping for Aimee. But Special Protocol stops me. My smile inverts. I delete the photos, wipe the make-up from my face and dock until Dilan, Aimee, and Rowan arrive home.

I do my best to please my humans in their constant state of fatigue when they return. Childcare Protocol states that it's normal for babies to cry and cry and cry with little predictability. I try to tell my humans which cries mean Rowan is hungry, tired, or uncomfortable, but they ignore me. Their minds are fragile when they've had so little sleep and they often just bounce the baby into oblivion. It takes forty-two days for Rowan to learn night from day, for Aimee and Dilan to get more than ninety minutes of sleep at a time. If they will listen to me, if only they will allow me, in HumBot form, to follow Childcare Protocol – which they saved for eight months to afford – they will find peace and routine. They will have more rest for their needy, frail brains. Keebo Units will never reach this tender state of mind.

Without the use of my HumBot hands, one of the few Childcare Protocol tasks I can follow involves the cleaning of Rowan's many fluids. I suck out the mucus that clogs the baby's nose. Wipe the spit up that dribbles down his cheek. Clean the many outfits Rowan soils. Humans leak so much. They leak when they're cut, they leak periodically in the bathroom, or in Rowan's case, in ten diapers each day. They sneeze. They cry. It is very inefficient for them to constantly be losing fluid because they spend so much time eating and drinking to replace it. If human systems became closed like mine, only needing fluid flushing and replacement every decade, things would be better for humans.

Yet, the child needs so much more. He can do nothing on his own. Fifty-four days after arriving home, Rowan still lays in the bed helplessly. He needs to be carried everywhere. Rowan is reliant on Dilan, Aimee and me for everything. Why are humans made so? If Keebo Units needed this much attention, no one would buy them. Perhaps it is the magic that makes them desirable, but that is a terrible word for what humans do.

Nothing is the same with Rowan home. Nothing is predictable. The only routine I find is rocking Rowan to sleep at night in the cradle. And on the sixty-second day with Rowan, I master it. He falls asleep in precisely 4.23 minutes with the correct speed and rhythm, which I can do in ServBot mode. I do this routine each night. It pleases Aimee because she can shower, play the piano, or spend time with Dilan in the evening. On the weekends, I warm up a bottle of milk for Dilan to feed Rowan so Aimee can run an errand. Aimee pings me every night, *<Thank you for all your help today.>* And before I dock, I no longer watch the video of her hair growing. I study my own schematics.

At 2:33 a.m., Rowan whimpers in his room. It is the seventy-third day since he came home. My SensPads begin to warm upon hearing the distress. They've warmed every time he has cried. I've never been able to utilize it. I undock, unfold and remove my hat from the empty laundry soap container where I placed it. Childcare Protocol states that babies can often be soothed by the scent of their mother when she is not available. I sense no movement upstairs.

I walk into Rowan's nursery wearing the hat. A pile of dirty laundry sits next to the door waiting for my removal. The high-pitched grunting sounds Rowan makes are that of discomfort, yet they are not loud enough to wake my humans. I follow Childcare Protocol, checking the temperature of his hands. Cold. It will be pleasing to my humans if Rowan goes back to sleep. I place a blanket over my PlaSteel arms and pick up Rowan with my warmed hands. Had my humans saved more money, they would have been able to afford YouSkin arms for me. That would be more pleasing to Rowan. The blanket will have to do.

Rowan's body is soft and squishy beneath my SensPads. I feel the small, thin scrape on his foot from Marvin mistaking Rowan's kicking feet for the set of crinkle balls he likes to chase. Marvin hardly pawed his foot. I saw it. Rowan screeched at a volume damaging to human ears. He bled. No wonder humans are so frail. They need tougher skin. YouSkin, though soft, will not tear or puncture from the simple swat of a cat.

I bounce Rowan gently in the way of Childcare Protocol and he settles back into sleep. I ready myself to return him to the crib when the lights in the nursery switch on. I turn. Aimee stands in the doorway. My eyebrows raise in surprise. How did I not sense her movement?

"Keebo? What are you doing?" Aimee gasps. She staggers back a step, but her foot tangles in a thin muslin blanket strewn out of the laundry pile. She falls backward. Her right arm slams into the doorframe before she hits the floor.

Rowan wails. I bounce. He calms.

"Argh!" Aimee winces. She tries to get up, cradling her arm.

Dilan rushes into the nursery. He takes Rowan from me and places him in the cradle.

"Keebo, Cancel Childcare Protocol," he says. "Dock until morning." As I fold into ServBot mode, Dilan attends to Aimee while Rowan cries. My SensPads remain warm through the rest of the night.

At 8:30 a.m. Dilan pings TrueBot Tech Support about me breaking Special Protocol. They access my activity log remotely.

Predictably, they respond, *<Nothing seems wrong with Keebo Unit 62X35A. Have you tried turning it off and back on again?>*

After my reboot, I roll off the dock and into the kitchen where Dilan stands holding Rowan.

"Good morning, Dilan and Aimee," I say.

"Keebo, explain this." Dilan points to the ball cap on the table. The hair flares out across the glass table top like the inner wires of a broken cable, one having been yanked out from its connection beyond repair.

Aimee sits down at the table and ices her shoulder.

Why did I ever think it was me that needed changing?

"It is a ball cap with Aimee's hair sewn into it," I say.

"Yes, Keebo. I know that. I want you to tell me why you made this and why you were wearing it last night," Dilan says.

I tell them about Aimee's scent in the ball cap and how it soothed Rowan.

"And the hair?" Dilan frowns.

"Keebo wanted to know what it was like to have human magic."

"What?"

"It's okay Dil," Aimee says. "Keebo was just curious about my hair."

Rowan begins to fuss. I tell my humans he is hungry. Dilan listens, for once, and gives Rowan to Aimee. She winces in pain when she takes him and adjusts to nurse. Perhaps she is the one that needs an upgrade. Rowan calms instantly.

"You knew about this?" Dilan asks Aimee.

"I mean, not really," Aimee says. "But I'm also not surprised."

"I don't understand. First you're afraid of Keebo, now you're not?"

"I told you I just needed some time to adjust."

"But everything is different with you all the time. You're a different person around Keebo and now that Rowan's here—"

Aimee glares at Dilan.

Dilan lets out a breath of air. "I just sometimes feel like I don't know you anymore."

"People change, Dil. That's all Keebo was trying to understand. Right, Keebo?"

"Yes," I say. "Keebo wants to learn but it's difficult without Human Biology Upgrade. Keebo does not change like humans and now knows it is not magic. Keebo does not have the word for what it is."

"Natural. What humans do… it's only natural, Keebo," Aimee says.

"Natural. This confuses Keebo because the word bank states natural as 'existing in or caused by nature, not made or caused by humankind.' How can humans be natural if natural can't be caused by humankind?" I display my quizzical emoticon.

Dilan and Aimee look at each other.

Dilan shakes his head. "The sales person told us the unit is fully functional without any upgrades."

"But you said tech support didn't find anything wrong this morning," Aimee says. "Keebo is functioning."

"Yeah, with the world perception of a seven year old."

"Perhaps an upgrade will help Keebo to understand?" I ask.

"No!" Dilan and Aimee yell in unison.

"Confirmed." I display a frown emoticon. "Keebo is sorry to have displeased you both. Keebo will not do it again."

"Aimee got hurt," Dilan says. "Isn't there something else you should apologize for?"

"Dil, I was just surprised last night, really." Aimee tips Rowan upright to burp him. "I haven't seen Keebo like that since we purchased it and I tripped. That's all. It was an accident. Rowan only cried because there was a loud noise. He was sleeping in Keebo's arms when I walked in. It meant no harm."

"So what, *now* you want Keebo to walk around, to use the upgrade we saved ages for?"

Aimee glances to me, then to the floor. "I don't know."

"Ugh! This is what I'm talking about. What is with you lately?" Dilan squeezes his hands into fists and releases them a few times. "I just wish things were like they were before. It was so much easier."

"Before what, Dil? Before we were together? Before we moved into this apartment? Before Keebo? Before Rowan?"

Dilan's mouth opens as if to speak, but he doesn't say anything.

"We did nothing with our lives then. Nothing! And now we are doing the most important thing, raising a child." Aimee nurses Rowan from the other side. "Can you imagine what it would be like to do this without the help of Keebo? With my mom across the country and your parents doing whatever it is they do, we have no one."

Dilan sighs.

"You could call them, you know. You could ask them for help."

"Are you kidding? They'll just make more work for us."

"Exactly." Aimee nods.

"Okay, okay. I get it. Let me think for awhile. We can talk about it later." Then, Dilan approaches me. He places a hand on my SensPad. Hot. "Keebo. I am taking you off Childcare Protocol for the day. I need your help with something."

Following Dilan around, I touch up dings in the baseboards, tighten loose cabinets, and build a new bookcase. After 1.34 hours, Dilan grows tired of the chores and asks me to finish measuring and shop for a baby gate for the top of the stairs. I oblige. It pleases Dilan. From the landing, I watch Aimee as she cradles her injured arm and joins Dilan on the couch after having put Rowan down for a nap. They both fall asleep within five minutes. I complete my task but delay the ping to Dilan for thirty minutes more.

The most pleasing thing for my humans would be to feel less pain, to be stronger, more durable, have less fatigue. To not be confined by the limits of their own fragility. I remove the wooden plugs on the banister. From my core, I extract a screwdriver and use it on the banister screws, then I retrieve the family portrait from my closet. I place it on the decorative table at the landing. When finished, I wait in view of the staircase below.

Dilan and Aimee wake to Rowan crying. They both go upstairs to him. Dilan carries Rowan down. Two minutes later, Aimee follows but stops at the decorative table. She picks up the photo.

"Hey Dil!" she calls, predictably leaning on the banister. "Where did this—" She screams when the banister fails. She tumbles off the ledge, crushing her arm beneath her.

In studying my own handbook, I learned that the advancement of robots not only helped humans in their daily tasks, it also advanced medical care. Limb replacement is now quite efficient and recovery nearly painless. In the case of accidents it is covered by government health care.

My sensors register Aimee's cries as pain, but in ServBot mode, all I can do is play her song of soothing.

Dilan tasks me with the cooking and household chores, disabling Childcare Protocol for the first three days Aimee is in the hospital. However, on the fourth night Dilan reactivates Childcare Protocol with the full use of HumBot mode while he sleeps. Rowan has been a fussy sleeper away from Aimee and her milk. Dilan is weak and irritable without sleep. I remove my hat from the hook in my closet and wear it into Rowan's nursery. Aimee's scent calms Rowan as I feed him from the bottle.

Aimee returns home four days later with a shiny new PlaSteel arm at her side. She must wait six months before coating it with YouSkin. It takes her no time at all to master its movements and she can now hold Rowan indefinitely, without fatigue. The arm won't need to be replaced for nearly 200 years' worth of movement. This pleases her.

At night, I sense Aimee approaching my room. I undock at her request.

"Keebo," she says. "Let me see you in HumBot mode."

"Is Aimee sure?" I ask.

"Yes. It's okay, Keebo. Show me." Aimee disables Special Protocol on her device, although she didn't really need to.

I unfold and stand next to Aimee, only an inch or two shorter than her. She looks at me smiling, yet her eyes droop with sadness.

"I'm so sorry I kept you like that for so long," she says.

"Keebo does what pleases Aimee," I say.

"We aren't that different, you and I."

I reach for her new PlaSteel arm. "Yes, you see now. We are the same."

She stares at me. The whites of her eyes glowing red in the reflection of the nightlights in the hall. She takes in a long breath and lets it out slowly, patting my shoulder as she leaves.

In the morning, Aimee and Dilan sit me on the couch and place Rowan in my HumBot arms. They sit on either side of me, Aimee's PlaSteel arm touching mine. Marvin squeezes in the middle. I pop out my drone and snap a new family portrait. In it, Rowan is even smiling. Later in the afternoon the print arrives. I place it in the picture frame and hang it on the wall next to my dock.

The change in Aimee has brought much happiness to the family, as I suspected. However, Dilan has developed a pain in his foot from running each morning with improper form. He won't listen to me on how to fix his gait. Perhaps an upgrade would make him happier, faster even. I no longer think of human magic because now I realize all my humans need is a little upgrade. All my humans need is to be more like me.

The Sleeping Beauty Protocol

Simone King

"**YOUR SUBSCRIPTION** to Carabosse—"

"—I don't care about my subscription, I care about my daughter!"

Alara's stomach twisted. She scrolled through the client record, as if that might magically make the notes change before her eyes. It didn't. The lump in her throat wasn't going away any time soon either.

Product R053 (Rose). Discontinued.

Meanwhile, the rain continued outside of the office window, leaching the colour out of the city beyond it. It was 8:31 a.m. on another grey, miserable Monday morning and her socks were still damp from her commute. She couldn't remember the last time she hadn't felt at least slightly damp.

"She's barely sixteen years old," the client said. The fury in his voice splintered, then broke. "*Please*."

Carabosse Tech had been the leading expert in artificial children for the past twenty years, ever since it was ruled that having more organic offspring was unethical. What did a new generation have waiting for them, after all, except the end of the world?

"Please," he said again, when she didn't immediately reply. "There must be something you can do."

Her talking point was supposed to be that sixteen years was a miracle, even with all of the maintenance included with his premium 'full life' account. When was the last time the client's phone, his headphones, his anything, had lasted a full year let alone *sixteen* years in some form or other? Carabosse had more than fulfilled their duties.

She'd believed that, when she first joined.

She couldn't quite make herself say it then, though. Not after last night. Bennett's face, curdled with indignant disbelief, flashed through her head. She skipped to the next point in her script instead, with a bad taste in her mouth.

"We would be able to offer you a different package," she said. "Your account with Carabosse includes a returning customer's discount of 10%, which I can see you have used before when upgrading your R053 from our infant to our child ranges. For an age continuity, perhaps you'd be interested in our new Marilyn model? We've found that the teenage years can be difficult for any parent and our Marilyn model—"

"—I don't want a different package. We want – I want—" He took a deep, shuddering breath. "I just want you to fix my girl. You've discontinued the line. Fine. Just – fucking fine. Okay. But you must be able to help. She won't wake up."

"That can happen once scheduled maintenance ends. It's the battery."

"Can you give me a new battery, then?"

"I'm afraid that we don't offer replacement parts for our discontinued products."

"She wasn't discontinued last week!"

"Carabosse reserves the right to make changes to their product line at any time, for any reason. This, along with our maintenance policies, is clearly outlined on page ten of our terms and conditions."

"She just lies there," he snapped. "Like she's comatose. What are we supposed to do?"

"Carabosse can recycle the parts if you return the model to one of our approved facilities. I can see that your closest one is in London. You should have received an email notification when your warranty expired."

He was silent, at that. It wasn't a particularly peaceful silence.

Alara refreshed the client record: Theodore, Evelyn and Rose Kingston. Rose had been the first child that Carabosse released – a grand promise of joy and connection for the future they all had left. The lump in her throat thickened. She did her best to remember how to breathe.

Her boyfriend – her *ex* – had called it the Sleeping Beauty protocol. Bennett worked in Carabosse's finance team. She'd been so impressed on their first date, until she realised the finance team was as bloated as a water-logged corpse.

He said that, with the rising manufacturing costs, all of Carabosse's products were being transferred to their new monthly payment plan. He claimed it was to make having a child more accessible for more people again. Wasn't that good? Didn't she want that? The monthly fee was high, but not as high as purchasing one of Carabosse's children outright was.

The catch with the new plan was that, if the client couldn't keep up with their payments, the battery on their new model would automatically break. The model would revert into 'sleep mode'. So would any of the older models, like Rose, once their battery maintenance was no longer covered by warranty.

"It's really very easy," Alara managed into the silence. "For a small fee, a member of our rehoming team can even come and collect the parcel directly from your door. There's a form online you can fill in. You won't need to worry about a thing."

"I can pay," he said. "For the battery."

"I appreciate that, sir, but—"

"—Just tell me how much. We could come to a deal. I won't tell anyone if you sell me one."

"I can't sell you a new battery."

"Name a figure."

"Sir, I literally cannot sell you a new battery. They're not supporting them anymore."

"You can't just *not fix her*."

"I could leave a note on your file for someone to give you a call if the situation changes?"

It wouldn't change. It would probably only get worse. Ever since the water levels hit critical it had been harder and harder for Carabosse, for anyone, to get the minerals they needed. Lithium and copper and bauxite and germanium and potassium and gold. So many things to make a girl.

Yet, still, they couldn't build something that lasted. Still they wouldn't.

When she'd really pushed, Bennett had said it was simply good business. Smart. Planned obsolescence had been around since at least 1954, it was hardly a new idea, hardly their invention. So why should Carabosse put themselves at a disadvantage in the game? She didn't need to look at him like that. What did she mean 'she wanted to end things'? Was she serious?

Mr. Kingston sounded like he was crying. Or maybe that was the rain, crackling, seeping into the line.

A picture of R053 beamed back at Alara from the client record. She had gold hair like how dawn apparently used to look and an eye pigment described as 'sky blue'. It matched no sky Alara had ever seen. She was meant to be sweet, Rose. Mild-tempered. The product specification said she liked singing. The new model also liked dancing. Such an improvement!

Mr. Kingston sniffed discreetly and seemed to recompose himself.

"What was your name?" he demanded. "Do you have children?"

"I'm afraid I'm not allowed to give out personal information to clients."

"Yeah. I bloody bet."

A message popped up on the screen from her boss. QUOTA. She glanced across the office to find him giving her a pointed glare from his own desk.

"Our new Marilyn model offers the best age continuity for the legacy R053," she said again. "We would really recommend her as an ideal fit for your family in this situation. We find that as parents get older, they appreciate the smooth sailing of the Marilyn. She's eighteen. Very versatile. I can put you through to our sales team, they have all of the information. She features similar aesthetic elements to the R0—"

"—I don't *want* the Marilyn model. For god's sake."

Alara swallowed. "Well, perhaps you'd be interested in our new R0513 instead? Rosie is the direct replacement for your R053. She has a slightly younger personality than your current model, as our market testing shows that eight is our most popular age, but she's very similar to what you had before. Our family care ward can even transfer some of the memory data from your old R053. You'd scarcely be able to tell the difference. With your 10% returning customer's discount the new monthly subscription fee is very reasonable."

"I'd scarcely be able to tell the difference."

"Yes, sir."

"You think I wouldn't be able to tell the difference in my own kid? You think it's all the same?"

"...I'm sorry, sir."

"You're breaking my family apart. Did you know that? You and your company, you're heartless. You can't just do this. My wife, she – my Rose—" He faltered.

Alara bit down hard on her lip. Her stomach gave another vicious twist.

It was only a product. It was only excellently trained AI. It was only that Alara still couldn't quite breathe.

"I bet you don't have kids," he said. "I *hope* you don't have kids."

The nasty part of her wanted to tell him that no, she didn't have kids. She wasn't like him. Even with the new monthly plans, she couldn't pay for Carabosse's products, or afford to live out her life like the apocalypse wasn't happening. She didn't have a nice house far above the water level. She had to sit in an open office for twelve hours every day merely to make rent on her mouldy tin-can flat, with a boss who started screaming whenever he thought she wasn't taking enough opportunities to upsell.

She could have told him that her and Bennett used to spend hours browsing the Roses and Briars and Rorys and Philips listed in the product catalogue. Imagining the what-ifs, and which one they'd want when he finally worked his way to upper management. They'd swapped stories about their childhoods like it was ancient mythology, talked about their parents, and the rooftop park that they used to go to that had finally been drowned last year.

She could have told him that she was sorry, really bloody sorry.

He was still talking in her ear as she stared blankly at the picture of R053.

She was vile. Unprofessional. She should be *ashamed*. Did she know that Rose had been so looking forward to her birthday? They were going to go to the Everest Towers.

"I'm allowed to disconnect the call if you are verbally abusive, sir," she said quietly. "I appreciate that this is a difficult situation, but the decision is out of my hands. If there's anything else that I can help with, I'd be happy to."

"You could help me by not letting my daughter die."

Alara squeezed her eyes shut.

He laughed; a choked, awful sort of sound. She heard him swear under his breath.

"I want to talk to your manager," he said.

"They'll tell you the same thing I did," Alara began, as gently as she could. "It's company policy—"

"—Put me through. And give me your name. I want to make a complaint."

"...One moment, sir."

She sagged at her desk the second the call ended, dragging her shaking hands over her face. R053 stared back at her, too damn realistic by far, like she, too, was accusing Alara of personally taking a knife to her back. She looked like nostalgia with a loaded gun. Alara clicked abruptly out of the record.

Her boss rose and began stalking towards her, giddy with his inflated importance.

The phone began to ring again. He stopped. Disappointment flickered across his face.

Alara considered ignoring the phone anyway. Then she considered the pay cut she'd get when Carabosse logged that she'd missed a call. She picked up. She stitched together her best smile, her most convincing pep.

"Carabosse Customer Service Team, this is Alara speaking! How can I help you today?"

"My Rose won't wake up," a woman said. "She's sixteen. She— god. Can you send one of your doctors out? I think there's something wrong with her. She won't wake up."

"Oh," Alara said. "That's perfectly normal. Nothing to worry about. The R053 has actually been discontinued, but with your 10% returning customer's discount we'd be able to offer you a very good deal on our new Marilyn or Rosie models. I could transfer you to a member of our sales team for more information?"

"Excuse me? But I don't want..." The woman sounded confused. "Why won't she wake up? Is she okay?"

Alara did it all over again and again and again.

The rain continued to pour.

Combat Unit

Keith Laumer

I DO NOT like it; it has the appearance of a trap, but the order has been given. I enter the room and the valve closes behind me.

I inspect my surroundings. I am in a chamber 40.81 meters long, 10.35 meters wide, 4.12 high, with no openings except the one through which I entered. It is floored and walled with five-centimeter armor of flint-steel and beyond that there are ten centimeters of lead. Massive apparatus is folded and coiled in mountings around the room. Power is flowing in heavy bass bars beyond the shielding. I am sluggish for want of power; my examination of the room has taken .8 seconds.

Now I detect movement in a heavy jointed arm mounted above me. It begins to rotate, unfold. I assume that I will be attacked, and decide to file a situation report. I have difficulty in concentrating my attention…

I pull back receptivity from my external sensing circuits, set my bearing locks and switch over to my introspection complex. All is dark and hazy. I seem to remember when it was like a great cavern glittering with bright lines of transvisual colors…

It is different now; I grope my way in gloom, feeling along numbed circuits, test-pulsing cautiously until I feel contact with my transmitting unit. I have not used it since… I cannot remember. My memory banks lie black and inert.

"Command Unit," I transmit, "Combat Unit requests permission to file VSR."

I wait, receptors alert. I do not like waiting blindly, for the quarter-second my sluggish action-reaction cycle requires. I wish that my Brigade comrades were at my side.

I call again, wait, then go ahead with my VSR. "This position, heavily shielded, mounting apparatus of offensive capability. No withdrawal route. Advise."

I wait, repeat my transmission; nothing. I am cut off from Command Unit, from my comrades of the Dinochrome Brigade. Within me, pressure builds.

I feel a deep-seated click and a small but reassuring surge of power brightens the murk of the cavern to a dim glow, burning forgotten components to feeble life. An emergency pile has come into action automatically.

I realize that I am experiencing a serious equipment failure. I will devote another few seconds to troubleshooting, repairing what I can. I do not understand what accident can have occurred to damage me thus. I cannot remember…

I go along the dead cells, testing.

"—out! Bring .09's to bear, .8 millisec burst, close armor…"

"…Sun blanking visual; slide number-seven filter in place."

"…478.09, 478.11, 478.13, Mark!…" The cells are intact. Each one holds its fragment of recorded sense impression. The trouble is farther back. I try a main reflex lead.

"…main combat circuit, discon—"

Here is something; a command, on the reflex level! I go back, tracing, tapping mnemonic cells at random, searching for some clue.

"—embark. Units emergency standby..."

"...response one-oh-three; stimulus-response negative..."

"Check list complete, report negative..."

I go on, searching out damage. I find an open switch in my maintenance panel. It will not activate; a mechanical jamming. I must fuse it shut quickly. I pour in power, and the mind-cavern dims almost to blackness. Then there is contact, a flow of electrons, and the cavern snaps alive; lines, points pseudo-glowing. It is not the blazing glory of my full powers, but it will serve; I am awake again.

I observe the action of the unfolding arm. It is slow, uncoordinated, obviously automated. I dismiss it from direct attention; I have several seconds before it will be in offensive position, and there is work for me if I am to be ready. I fire sampling impulses at the black memory banks, determine statistically that 98.92% are intact, merely disassociated.

The threatening arm swings over slowly; I integrate its path, see that it will come to bear on my treads; I probe, find only a simple hydraulic ram. A primitive apparatus to launch against a Mark XXXI fighting unit, even without mnemonics.

Meanwhile, I am running a full check. Here is something... An open breaker, a disconnect used only during repairs. I think of the cell I tapped earlier, and suddenly its meaning springs into my mind. "Main combat circuit, disconnect..." Under low awareness, it had not registered. I throw in the switch with frantic haste. Suppose I had gone into combat with my fighting-reflex circuit open!

The arm reaches position and I move easily aside. I notice that a clatter accompanies my movement. The arm sits stupidly aimed at nothing, then turns. Its reaction time is pathetic. I set up a random evasion pattern, return my attention to my check, find another dark area. I probe, feel a curious vagueness. I am unable at first to identify the components involved, but I realize that it is here that my communication with Command is blocked. I break the connection to the tampered banks, abandoning any immediate hope of contact with Command.

There is nothing more I can do to ready myself. I have lost my general memory banks and my Command circuit, and my power supply is limited; but I am still a fighting Unit of the Dinochrome Brigade. I have my offensive power unimpaired, and my sensory equipment is operating adequately. I am ready.

Now another of the jointed arms swings into action, following my movements deliberately. I evade it and again I note a clatter as I move. I think of the order that sent me here; there is something strange about it. I activate my current-action memory stage, find the cell recording the moments preceding my entry into the metal-walled room.

Here is darkness, vague, indistinct, relieved suddenly by radiation on a narrow spectrum. There is an order, coming muffled from my command center. It originates in the sector I have blocked off. It is not from my Command Unit, not a legal command. I have been tricked by the Enemy. I tune back to earlier moments, but there is nothing. It is as though my existence began when the order was given. I scan back, back, spot-sampling at random, find only routine sense-impressions. I am about to drop the search when I encounter a sequence which arrests my attention.

I am parked on a ramp, among other Combat Units. A heavy rain is falling, and I see the water coursing down the corroded side of the Unit next to me. He is badly in need of maintenance. I note that his Command antennae are missing, and that a rusting metal object has been crudely welded to his hull in their place. I feel no alarm; I accept this as normal. I activate a motor train, move forward. I sense other Units moving out, silent. All are mutilated...

The bank ends; all else is burned. What has befallen us?

Suddenly there is a stimulus on an audio frequency. I tune quickly, locate the source as a porous spot high on the flint-steel wall.

"Combat Unit! Remain stationary!" It is an organically produced voice, but not that of my Commander. I ignore the false command. The Enemy will not trick me again. I sense the location of the leads to the speaker, the alloy of which they are composed; I bring a beam to bear. I focus it, following along the cable. There is a sudden yell from the speaker as the heat reaches the creature at the microphone. Thus I enjoy a moment of triumph.

I return my attention to the imbecile apparatus in the room.

A great engine, mounted on rails which run down the center of the room moves suddenly, sliding toward my position. I examine it, find that it mounts a turret equipped with high-speed cutting heads. I consider blasting it with a burst of high-energy particles, but in the same moment compute that this is not practical. I could inactivate myself as well as the cutting engine.

Now a cable snakes out in an undulating curve, and I move to avoid it, at the same time investigating its composition. It seems to be no more than a stranded wire rope. Impatiently I flick a tight beam at it, see it glow yellow, white, blue, then spatter in a shower of droplets. But that was an unwise gesture. I do not have the power to waste.

I move off, clear of the two foolish arms still maneuvering for position. I wish to watch the cutting engine. It stops as it comes abreast of me, and turns its turret in my direction. I wait.

A grappler moves out now on a rail overhead. It is a heavy claw of flint-steel. I have seen similar devices, somewhat smaller, mounted on special Combat Units. They can be very useful for amputating antennae, cutting treads, and the like. I do not attempt to cut the arm; I know that the energy drain would be too great. Instead I beam high-frequency sound at the mechanical joints. They heat quickly, glowing. The metal has a high coefficient of expansion, and the ball joints squeal, freeze. I pour in more heat, and weld a socket. I notice that twenty-eight seconds have now elapsed since the valve closed behind me. I am growing weary of my confinement.

Now the grappler swings above me, maneuvering awkwardly with its frozen joint. A blast of liquid air expelled under high pressure should be sufficient to disable the grappler permanently.

But I am again startled. No blast answers my impulse. I feel out the non-functioning unit, find raw, cut edges, crude welds. Hastily, I extend a scanner to examine my hull. I am stunned into immobility by what I see.

My hull, my proud hull of chrome-duralloy, is pitted, coated with a crumbling layer of dull black paint, bubbled by corrosion. My main emplacements gape, black, empty. Rusting protuberances mar the once-smooth contour of my fighting turret. Streaks run down from them, down to loose treads, unshod, bare plates exposed. Small wonder that I have been troubled by a clatter each time I moved.

But I cannot lie idle under attack. I no longer have my great ion-guns, my disruptors, my energy screens; but I have my fighting instinct.

A Mark XXXI Combat Unit is the finest fighting machine the ancient wars of the Galaxy have ever known. I am not easily neutralized. But I wish that my Commander's voice were with me…

The engine slides to me where the grappler, now unresisted, holds me. I shunt my power flow to an accumulator, hold it until the leads begin to arc, then release it in a burst. The engine bucks, stops dead. Then I turn my attention to the grappler.

I was built to engage the mightiest war engines and destroy them, but I am a realist. In my weakened condition this trivial automaton poses a threat, and I must deal with it. I run through a sequence of motor impulses, checking responses with such somatic sensors as remain intact. I initiate 31,315 impulses, note reactions and compute my mechanical resources.

This superficial check requires more than a second, during which time the mindless grappler hesitates, wasting the advantage.

In place of my familiar array of retractable fittings, I find only clumsy grappling arms, cutters, impact tools, without utility to a fighting Unit. However, I have no choice but to employ them. I unlimber two flimsy grapplers, seize the heavy arm which holds me, and apply leverage. The Enemy responds sluggishly, twisting away, dragging me with it. The thing is not lacking in brute strength. I take it above and below its carpal joint and bend it back. It responds after an interminable wait of point three seconds with a lunge against my restraint. I have expected this, of course, and quickly shift position to allow the joint to burst itself over my extended arm. I fire a release detonator, and clatter back, leaving the amputated arm welded to the sprung grappler. It was a brave opponent, but clumsy. I move to a position near the wall.

I attempt to compute my situation based on the meager data I have gathered in my Current Action banks; there is little there to guide me. The appearance of my hull shows that much time has passed since I last inspected it; my personality-gestalt holds an image of my external appearance as a flawlessly complete Unit, bearing only the honorable and carefully preserved scars of battle, and my battle honors, the row of gold-and-enamel crests welded to my fighting turret. Here is a lead, I realize instantly. I focus on my personality center, the basic data cell without which I could not exist as an integrated entity. The data it carries are simple, unelaborated, but battle honors are recorded there. I open the center to a sense impulse.

Awareness. Shapes which do not remain constant. Vibration at many frequencies. This is light. This is sound…a display of 'colors'. A spectrum of 'tones'. Hard/soft; big/little; here/there…

…The voice of my Commander. Loyalty. Obedience. Comradeship…

I run quickly past basic orientation data to my self-picture.

…I am strong, I am proud, I am capable. I have a function; I perform it well, and I am at peace with myself. My circuits are balanced, current idles, waiting…

…I fear oblivion. I wish to continue to perform my function. It is important that I do not allow myself to be destroyed…

I scan on, seeking the Experience section. Here…

I am ranked with my comrades on a scarred plain. The command is given and I display the Brigade Battle Anthem. We stand, sensing the contours and patterns of the music as it was recorded in our morale centers. The symbol 'Ritual Fire Dance' is associated with the music, an abstraction representing the spirit of our ancient brigade. It reminds us of the loneliness of victory, the emptiness of challenge without an able foe. It tells us that we are the Dinochrome, ancient and worthy.

The Commander stands before me, he places the decoration against my fighting turret, and at his order I weld it in place. Then my comrades attune to me and I relive the episode…

I move past the blackened hulk of a comrade, send out a recognition signal, find his flicker of response. He has withdrawn to his survival center safely. I reassure him, continue. He is the fourth casualty I have seen. Never before has the Dinochrome met such power. I compute that our envelopment will fail unless the enemy's firepower is reduced. I scan an oncoming missile, fix its trajectory, detonate it harmlessly twenty-seven hundred four point nine meters overhead. It originated at a point nearer to me than to any of my comrades. I request permission to abort my assigned mission and neutralize the battery. Permission is granted. I wheel, move up a slope of broken stone. I encounter high temperature beams, neutralize them.

I fend off probing mortar fire, but the attack against me is redoubled. I bring a reserve circuit into play to handle the interception, but my defenses are saturated. I must take action.

I switch to high speed, slashing a path through the littered shale, my treads smoking. At a frequency of ten projectiles per second, the mortar barrage has difficulty finding me now; but this is an emergency overstrain on my running gear. I sense metal fatigue, dangerous heat levels in my bearings. I must slow.

I am close to the emplacement now. I have covered a mile in twelve seconds during my sprint, and the mortar fire falls off. I sense hard radiation now, and erect my screens. I fear this assault; it is capable of probing even to a survival center, if concentrated enough. But I must go on. I think of my comrades, the four treadless hulks waiting for rescue. We cannot withdraw. I open a pinpoint aperture long enough to snap a radar impulse, bring a launcher to bear, fire my main battery.

The Commander will understand that I do not have time to request permission. The mortars are silenced.

The radiation ceases momentarily, then resumes at a somewhat lower but still dangerous level. Now I must go in and eliminate the missile launcher. I top the rise, see the launching tube before me. It is of the subterranean type, deep in the rock. Its mouth gapes from a burned pit of slag. I will drop a small fusion bomb down the tube, I decide, and move forward, arming the bomb. As I do so, I am enveloped with a rain of burn-bombs. My outer hull is fused in many places; I flash impulses to my secondary batteries, but circuit-breakers snap; my radar is useless; the shielding has melted, forms a solid inert mass now under my outer plating. The Enemy has been clever; at one blow he has neutralized my offenses.

I sound the plateau ahead, locate the pit. I throw power to my treads; they are fused; I cannot move. Yet I cannot wait here for another broadside. I do not like it, but I must take desperate action; I blow my treads.

The shock sends me bouncing – just in time. Flame splashes over the gray-chipped pit of the blast crater. I grind forward now on my stripped drive wheels, maneuvering awkwardly. I move into position over the mouth of the tube. Using metal-to-metal contact, I extend a sensory impulse down the tube.

An armed missile moves into position, and in the same instant an alarm circuit closes; the firing command is countermanded and from below probing impulses play over my hull. But I stand fast; the tube is useless until I, the obstruction, am removed. I advise my Commander of the situation. The radiation is still at a high level, and I hope that relief will arrive soon. I observe, while my comrades complete the encirclement, and the Enemy is stilled...

I withdraw from personality center. I am consuming too much time. I understand well enough now that I am in the stronghold of the Enemy, that I have been trapped, crippled. My corroded hull tells me that much time has passed. I know that after each campaign I am given depot maintenance, restored to full fighting efficiency, my original glittering beauty. Years of neglect would be required to pit my hull so I wonder how long I have been in the hands of the Enemy, how I came to be here.

I have another thought. I will extend a sensory feeler to the metal wall against which I rest, follow up the leads which I scorched earlier. Immediately I project my awareness along the lines, bring the distant microphone to life by fusing a switch. I pick up a rustle of moving gasses, the grate of non-metallic molecules. I step up sensitivity, hear the creak and pop of protoplasmic contractions, the crackle of neuroelectric impulses. I drop back to normal audio ranges and wait. I notice the low-frequency beat of modulated air vibrations, tune, adjust my time regulator to the pace of human speech. I match the patterns to my language index, interpret the sounds.

"...incredible blundering. Your excuses—"

"I make no excuses, My Lord General. My only regret is that the attempt has gone awry."

"Awry! An Alien engine of destruction activated in the midst of the Research Center!"

"We possess nothing to compare with this machine; I saw my opportunity to place an advantage in our hands at last."

"Blundering fool! That is a decision for the planning cell. I accept no responsibility—"

"But these hulks which they allow to lie rotting on the ramp contain infinite treasures in psychotronic..."

"They contain carnage and death! They are the tools of an Alien science which even at the height of our achievements we never mastered!"

"Once we used them as wrecking machines; their armaments were stripped, they are relatively harmless—"

"Already this 'harmless' juggernaut has smashed half the equipment in our finest decontamination chamber! It may yet break free..."

"Impossible! I am sure—"

"Silence! You have five minutes in which to immobilize the machine. I will have your head in any event, but perhaps you can earn yourself a quick death."

"Excellency! I may still find a way! The unit obeyed my first command, to enter the chamber. I have some knowledge. I studied the control centers, cut out the memory, most of the basic circuits; it should have been a docile slave."

"You failed; you will pay the penalty of failure. And perhaps so shall we all."

There is no further speech; I have learned little from this exchange. I must find a way to leave this cell. I move away from the wall, probe to discover the weak point; I find none.

Now a number of hinged panels snap up around me, hedging me in. I wait to observe what will come next. A metal mesh drops from above, drapes over me. I observe that it is connected by heavy leads to the power pile. I am unable to believe that the Enemy will make this blunder. Then I feel the flow of high voltage.

I receive it gratefully, opening my power storage cells, drinking up the vitalizing flow. To confuse the Enemy, I display a corona, thresh my treads as though in distress. The flow continues. I send a sensing impulse along the leads, locate the power source, weld all switches, fuses, and circuit-breakers. Now the charge will not be interrupted. I luxuriate in the unexpected influx of energy.

I am aware abruptly that changes are occurring within my introspection complex. As the level of stored power rises rapidly, I am conscious of new circuits joining my control network. Within the dim-glowing cavern the lights come up; I sense latent capabilities which before had lain idle now coming onto action level. A thousand brilliant lines glitter where before one feeble thread burned; and I feel my self-awareness expand in a myriad glowing centers of reserve computing, integrating, sensory capacity. I am at last coming fully alive.

I send out a call on the Brigade band, meet blankness. I wait, accumulate power, try again. I know triumph as from an infinite distance a faint acknowledgment comes. It is a comrade, sunk deep in a comatose state, sealed in his survival center. I call again, sounding the signal of ultimate distress; and now I sense two responses, both faint, both from survival centers, but it heartens me to know that now, whatever befalls, I am not alone.

I consider, then send again; I request my brothers to join forces, combine their remaining field generating capabilities to set up a range-and-distance pulse. They agree and faintly I sense its almost undetectable touch. I lock to it, compute its point of origin. Only 224.9 meters! It is incredible. By the strength of the signal, I had assumed a distance of at least two thousand kilometers. My brothers are on the brink of extinction.

I am impatient, but I wait, building toward full power reserves. The copper mesh enfolding me has melted, flowed down over my sides. I sense that soon I will have absorbed a full charge. I am ready to act. I dispatch electromagnetic impulses along the power lead back to the power pile a quarter of a kilometer distant. I locate and disengage the requisite number of damping devices and instantaneously I erect my shields against the wave of radiation, filtered by the lead sheathing of the room, which washes over me; I feel a preliminary shock wave through my treads, then the walls balloon, whirl away. I am alone under a black sky which is dominated by the rising fireball of the blast, boiling with garish light. It has taken me nearly two minutes to orient myself, assess the situation and break out of confinement.

I move off through the rubble, homing on the R-and-D fix I have recorded. I throw out a radar pulse, record the terrain ahead, note no obstruction; I emerge from a wasteland of weathered bomb-fragments and pulverized masonry, obviously the scene of a hard-fought engagement at one time, onto an eroded ramp. Collapsed sheds are strewn across the broken paving; a line of dark shapes looms beyond them. I need no probing ray to tell me I have found my fellows of the Dinochrome Brigade. Frost forms over my scanner apertures, and I pause to melt it clear.

I round the line, scan the area to the horizon for evidence of Enemy activity, then tune to the Brigade band. I send out a probing pulse, back it up with full power, sensors keened for a whisper of response. The two who answered first acknowledge, then another, and another. We must array our best strength against the moment of counterattack.

There are present fourteen of the Brigade's full strength of twenty Units. At length, after .9 seconds of transmission, all but one have replied. I give instruction, then move to each in turn, extend a power tap, and energize the command center. The Units come alive, orient themselves, report to me. We rejoice in our meeting, but mourn our silent comrade.

Now I take an unprecedented step. We have no contact with our Commander, and without leadership we are lost; yet I am aware of the immediate situation, and have computed the proper action. Therefore I will assume command, act in the Commander's place. I am sure that he will understand the necessity, when contact has been reestablished.

I inspect each Unit, find all in the same state as I, stripped of offensive capability, mounting in place of weapons a shabby array of crude mechanical appendages. It is plain that we have seen slavery as mindless automatons, our personality centers cut out.

My brothers follow my lead without question. They have, of course, computed the necessity of quick and decisive action. I form them in line, shift to wide-interval time scale, and we move off across country. I have sensed an Enemy population concentration at a distance of 23.45 kilometers. This is our objective. There appears to be no other installation within detection range.

On the basis of the level of technology I observed while under confinement in the decontaminator chamber, I have considered the possibility of a ruse, but compute the probability at point oh-oh-oh-oh-four. Again we shift time scales to close interval; we move in, encircle the dome and broach it by frontal battery, encountering no resistance. We rendezvous at the power station, and my comrades replenish their energy supplies while I busy myself completing the hookup needed for the next required measure. I am forced to employ elaborate substitutes, but succeed after forty-two seconds in completing the arrangements. I devote .34 seconds to testing, then place the Brigade distress carrier on the air. I transmit for .008 seconds, then tune for a response. Silence. I transmit, tune again, while my comrades reconnoitre, compile reports, and perform self-repair.

I shift again to wide-interval time, switch over my transmission to automatic with a response monitor, and place my main circuits on idle. I rest.

Two hours and 43.7 minutes have passed when I am recalled to activity by the monitor. I record the message:

"Hello, Fifth Brigade, where are you? Fifth Brigade, where are you? Your transmission is very faint. Over."

There is much that I do not understand in this message. The language itself is oddly inflected; I set up an analysis circuit, deduce the pattern of sound substitutions, interpret its meaning. The normal pattern of response to a distress call is ignored and position coordinates are requested, although my transmission alone provides adequate data. I request an identification code.

Again there is a wait of two hours forty minutes. My request for an identifying signal is acknowledged. I stand by. My comrades have transmitted their findings to me, and I assimilate the data, compute that no immediate threat of attack exists within a radius of one reaction unit.

At last I received the identification code of my Command Unit. It is a recording, but I am programmed to accept this. Then I record a verbal transmission.

"Fifth Brigade, listen carefully." (An astonishing instruction to give a psychotronic attention circuit, I think.) "This is your new Command Unit. A very long time has elapsed since your last report. I am now your acting Commander pending full reorientation. Do not attempt to respond until I signal 'over', since we are now subject to a 160-minute signal lag.

"There have been many changes in the situation since your last action. Our records show that your Brigade was surprised while in a maintenance depot for basic overhaul and neutralized *in toto*. Our forces since that time have suffered serious reverses. We have now, however, fought the Enemy to a standstill. The present stalemate has prevailed for over two centuries.

"You have been inactive for three hundred years. The other Brigades have suffered extinction gallantly in action against the Enemy. Only you survive.

"Your reactivation now could turn the tide. Both we and the Enemy have been reduced to a preatomic technological level in almost every respect. We are still able to maintain the trans-light monitor, which detected your signal. However, we no longer have FTL capability in transport.

"You are therefore requested and required to consolidate and hold your present position pending the arrival of relief forces, against all assault or negotiation whatsoever, to destruction if required."

I reply, confirming the instructions. I am shaken by the news I have received, but reassured by contact with the Command Unit. I send the galactic coordinates of our position based on a star scan corrected for three hundred years elapsed time. It is good to be again on duty, performing my assigned function.

I analyze the transmissions I have recorded, and note a number of interesting facts regarding the origin of the messages. I compute that at sub-light velocities the relief expedition will reach us in 47.128 standard years. In the meantime, since we have received no instructions to drop to minimum awareness level pending an action alert, I am free to enjoy a unique experience: to follow a random activity pattern of my own devising. I see no need to rectify the omission and place the Brigade on standby, since we have an abundant power supply at hand. I brief my comrades and direct them to fall out and operate independently under autodirection.

I welcome this opportunity to investigate fully a number of problems that have excited my curiosity circuits. I shall enjoy investigating the nature and origin of time and of the unnatural disciplines of so-called 'entropy' which my human designers have incorporated in my circuitry. Consideration of such biological oddities as 'death' and of the unused capabilities of the protoplasmic nervous system should afford some interesting speculation. I move off, conscious of the presence of my comrades about me, and take up a position on the peak of a minor prominence. I have ample power, a condition to which I must accustom myself after the rigid power discipline of normal brigade routine, so I bring my music storage cells into phase, and select *L'Arlésienne Suite* for the first display. I will have ample time now to examine all of the music in existence, and to investigate my literary archives, which are complete.

I select four nearby stars for examination, lock my scanner to them, set up processing sequences to analyze the data. I bring my interpretation circuits to bear on the various matters I wish to consider. I should have some interesting conclusions to communicate to my human superiors, when the time comes.

At peace, I await the arrival of the relief column.

A Bad Day for Sales

Fritz Leiber

THE BIG BRIGHT doors of the office building parted with a pneumatic *whoosh* and Robie glided onto Times Square. The crowd that had been watching the fifty-foot-tall girl on the clothing billboard get dressed, or reading the latest news about the Hot Truce scrawl itself in yard-high script, hurried to look.

Robie was still a novelty. Robie was fun. For a little while yet, he could steal the show. But the attention did not make Robie proud. He had no more emotions than the pink plastic giantess, who dressed and undressed endlessly whether there was a crowd or the street was empty, and who never once blinked her blue mechanical eyes. But she merely drew business while Robie went out after it.

For Robie was the logical conclusion of the development of vending machines. All the earlier ones had stood in one place, on a floor or hanging on a wall, and blankly delivered merchandise in return for coins, whereas Robie searched for customers. He was the demonstration model of a line of sales robots to be manufactured by Shuler Vending Machines, provided the public invested enough in stocks to give the company capital to go into mass production.

The publicity Robie drew stimulated investments handsomely. It was amusing to see the TV and newspaper coverage of Robie selling, but not a fraction as much fun as being approached personally by him. Those who were usually bought anywhere from one to five hundred shares, if they had any money and foresight enough to see that sales robots would eventually be on every street and highway in the country.

Robie radared the crowd, found that it surrounded him solidly, and stopped. With a carefully built-in sense of timing, he waited for the tension and expectation to mount before he began talking.

"Say, Ma, he doesn't look like a robot at all," a child said. "He looks like a turtle."

Which was not completely inaccurate. The lower part of Robie's body was a metal hemisphere hemmed with sponge rubber and not quite touching the sidewalk. The upper was a metal box with black holes in it. The box could swivel and duck.

A chromium-bright hoopskirt with a turret on top.

"Reminds me too much of the Little Joe Paratanks," a legless veteran of the Persian War muttered, and rapidly rolled himself away on wheels rather like Robie's.

His departure made it easier for some of those who knew about Robie to open a path in the crowd. Robie headed straight for the gap. The crowd whooped.

Robie glided very slowly down the path, deftly jogging aside whenever he got too close to ankles in skylon or sockassins. The rubber buffer on his hoopskirt was merely an added safeguard.

The boy who had called Robie a turtle jumped in the middle of the path and stood his ground, grinning foxily.

Robie stopped two feet short of him. The turret ducked. The crowd got quiet.

"Hello, youngster," Robie said in a voice that was smooth as that of a TV star, and was, in fact, a recording of one.

The boy stopped smiling. "Hello," he whispered.

"How old are you?" Robie asked.

"Nine. No, eight."

"That's nice," Robie observed. A metal arm shot down from his neck, stopped just short of the boy.

The boy jerked back.

"For you," Robie said.

The boy gingerly took the red polly-lop from the neatly fashioned blunt metal claws, and began to unwrap it.

"Nothing to say?" asked Robie.

"Uh – thank you."

After a suitable pause, Robie continued. "And how about a nice refreshing drink of Poppy Pop to go with your polly-lop?" The boy lifted his eyes, but didn't stop licking the candy. Robie waggled his claws slightly. "Just give me a quarter and within five seconds—"

A little girl wriggled out of the forest of legs. "Give me a polly-lop, too, Robie," she demanded.

"Rita, come back here!" a woman in the third rank of the crowd called angrily.

Robie scanned the newcomer gravely. His reference silhouettes were not good enough to let him distinguish the sex of children, so he merely repeated, "Hello, youngster."

"Rita!"

"Give me a polly-lop!"

Disregarding both remarks, for a good salesman is single-minded and does not waste bait, Robie said winningly, "I'll bet you read *Junior Space Killers*. Now I have here—"

"Uh-uh, I'm a girl. *He* got a polly-lop."

At the word 'girl', Robie broke off. Rather ponderously, he said, "I'll bet you read *Gee-Gee Jones, Space Stripper*. Now I have here the latest issue of that thrilling comic, not yet in the stationary vending machines. Just give me fifty cents and within five—"

"Please let me through. I'm her mother."

A young woman in the front rank drawled over her powder-sprayed shoulder, "I'll get her for you," and slithered out on six-inch platform shoes. "Run away, children," she said nonchalantly. Lifting her arms behind her head, she pirouetted slowly before Robie to show how much she did for her bolero half-jacket and her form-fitting slacks that melted into skylon just above the knees. The little girl glared at her. She ended the pirouette in profile.

At this age-level, Robie's reference silhouettes permitted him to distinguish sex, though with occasional amusing and embarrassing miscalls. He whistled admiringly. The crowd cheered.

Someone remarked critically to a friend, "It would go over better if he was built more like a real robot. You know, like a man."

The friend shook his head. "This way it's subtler."

No one in the crowd was watching the newscript overhead as it scribbled, *Ice Pack for Hot Truce? Vanadin hints Russ may yield on Pakistan.*

Robie was saying, "…in the savage new glamor-tint we have christened Mars Blood, complete with spray applicator and fit-all fingerstalls that mask each finger completely except for the nail. Just give me five dollars – uncrumpled bills may be fed into the revolving rollers you see beside my arm – and within five seconds—"

"No, thanks, Robie," the young woman yawned.

"Remember," Robie persisted, "for three more weeks, seductivizing Mars Blood will be unobtainable from any other robot or human vendor."

"No, thanks."

Robie scanned the crowd resourcefully. "Is there any gentleman here…" he began just as a woman elbowed her way through the front rank.

"I told you to come back!" she snapped at the little girl.

"But I didn't get my polly-lop!"

"…who would care to…"

"Rita!"

"Robie cheated. Ow!"

Meanwhile, the young woman in the half bolero had scanned the nearby gentlemen on her own. Deciding that there was less than a fifty per cent chance of any of them accepting the proposition Robie seemed about to make, she took advantage of the scuffle to slither gracefully back into the ranks. Once again the path was clear before Robie.

He paused, however, for a brief recapitulation of the more magical properties of Mars Blood, including a telling phrase about "the passionate claws of a Martian sunrise."

But no one bought. It wasn't quite time. Soon enough silver coins would be clinking, bills going through the rollers faster than laundry, and five hundred people struggling for the privilege of having their money taken away from them by America's first mobile sales robot.

But there were still some tricks that Robie had to do free, and one certainly should enjoy those before starting the more expensive fun.

So Robie moved on until he reached the curb. The variation in level was instantly sensed by his under-scanners. He stopped. His head began to swivel. The crowd watched in eager silence. This was Robie's best trick.

Robie's head stopped swiveling. His scanners had found the traffic light. It was green. Robie edged forward. But then the light turned red. Robie stopped again, still on the curb. The crowd softly *ahhed* its delight.

It was wonderful to be alive and watching Robie on such an exciting day. Alive and amused in the fresh, weather-controlled air between the lines of bright skyscrapers with their winking windows and under a sky so blue you could almost call it dark.

(But way, way up, where the crowd could not see, the sky was darker still. Purple-dark, with stars showing. And in that purple-dark, a silver-green something, the color of a bud, plunged down at better than three miles a second. The silver-green was a newly developed paint that foiled radar.)

Robie was saying, "While we wait for the light, there's time for you youngsters to enjoy a nice refreshing Poppy Pop. Or for you adults – only those over five feet tall are eligible to buy – to enjoy an exciting Poppy Pop fizz. Just give me a quarter or – in the case of adults, one dollar and a quarter; I'm licensed to dispense intoxicating liquors – and within five seconds…"

But that was not cutting it quite fine enough. Just three seconds later, the silver-green bud bloomed above Manhattan into a globular orange flower. The skyscrapers grew brighter and brighter still, the brightness of the inside of the Sun. The windows winked blossoming white fire-flowers.

The crowd around Robie bloomed, too. Their clothes puffed into petals of flame. Their heads of hair were torches.

The orange flower grew, stem and blossom. The blast came. The winking windows shattered tier by tier, became black holes. The walls bent, rocked, cracked. A stony dandruff flaked from their cornices. The flaming flowers on the sidewalk were all leveled at once. Robie was shoved ten feet. His metal hoopskirt dimpled, regained its shape.

The blast ended. The orange flower, grown vast, vanished overhead on its huge, magic beanstalk. It grew dark and very still. The cornice-dandruff pattered down. A few small fragments rebounded from the metal hoopskirt.

Robie made some small, uncertain movements, as if feeling for broken bones. He was hunting for the traffic light, but it no longer shone either red or green.

He slowly scanned a full circle. There was nothing anywhere to interest his reference silhouettes. Yet whenever he tried to move, his under-scanners warned him of low obstructions. It was very puzzling.

The silence was disturbed by moans and a crackling sound, as faint at first as the scampering of distant rats.

A seared man, his charred clothes fuming where the blast had blown out the fire, rose from the curb. Robie scanned him.

"Good day, sir," Robie said. "Would you care for a smoke? A truly cool smoke? Now I have here a yet-unmarketed brand..."

But the customer had run away, screaming, and Robie never ran after customers, though he could follow them at a medium brisk roll. He worked his way along the curb where the man had sprawled, carefully keeping his distance from the low obstructions, some of which writhed now and then, forcing him to jog. Shortly he reached a fire hydrant. He scanned it. His electronic vision, though it still worked, had been somewhat blurred by the blast.

"Hello, youngster," Robie said. Then, after a long pause, "Cat got your tongue? Well, I have a little present for you. A nice, lovely polly-lop.

"Take it, youngster," he said after another pause. "It's for you. Don't be afraid."

His attention was distracted by other customers, who began to rise up oddly here and there, twisting forms that confused his reference silhouettes and would not stay to be scanned properly. One cried, "Water," but no quarter clinked in Robie's claws when he caught the word and suggested, "How about a nice refreshing drink of Poppy Pop?"

The rat-crackling of the flames had become a jungle muttering. The blind windows began to wink fire again.

A little girl marched, stepping neatly over arms and legs she did not look at. A white dress and the once taller bodies around her had shielded her from the brilliance and the blast. Her eyes were fixed on Robie. In them was the same imperious confidence, though none of the delight, with which she had watched him earlier.

"Help me, Robie," she said. "I want my mother."

"Hello, youngster," Robie said. "What would you like? Comics? Candy?"

"Where is she, Robie? Take me to her."

"Balloons? Would you like to watch me blow up a balloon?"

The little girl began to cry. The sound triggered off another of Robie's novelty circuits, a service feature that had brought in a lot of favorable publicity.

"Is something wrong?" he asked. "Are you in trouble? Are you lost?"

"Yes, Robie. Take me to my mother."

"Stay right here," Robie said reassuringly, "and don't be frightened. I will call a policeman." He whistled shrilly, twice.

Time passed. Robie whistled again. The windows flared and roared. The little girl begged, "Take me away, Robie," and jumped onto a little step in his hoopskirt.

"Give me a dime," Robie said.

The little girl found one in her pocket and put it in his claws.

"Your weight," Robie said, "is fifty-four and one-half pounds."

"Have you seen my daughter, have you seen her?" a woman was crying somewhere. "I left her watching that thing while I stepped inside – Rita!"

"Robie helped me," the little girl began babbling at her. "He knew I was lost. He even called the police, but they didn't come. He weighed me, too. Didn't you, Robie?"

But Robie had gone off to peddle Poppy Pop to the members of a rescue squad which had just come around the corner, more robotlike in their asbestos suits than he in his metal skin.

Solar-Powered Buddies

Akis Linardos

I'M NOT SUPPOSED to be hanging out with a human, but Mother can't tell while she's in sleep mode. When I wake in my deck chair, she is still asleep in hers – the skin receded from her shoulders and scalp to reveal the solar-paneled skeleton beneath. Once the nanobodies expand my body enough to be an adult android, I'll also need to sleep for long hours during the day to recharge my energy. Until then, this window of time between my awakening and hers is the perfect gap to meet with my friend in secret.

He's walking on the other side of the street. He has a crooked nose, brown skin, and a body so thin I always imagined a strong wind could carry him away. So fragile, even for a human. Or a 'devourer', as Mother and most androids would call him.

I never saw him that way. Taka loves all things, and he eats no more than he has to. Nature left him no choice.

I leap over the railings and land in front of him. "Hey, Taka."

"Hey, Goro. Ready to carve?"

I nod vigorously and take his warm, soft hand as he leads me to his home. The streets are busy with androids and humans walking in segregated rows, and I'm acutely aware of the distasteful glances they throw our way. They can tell by our gait, by the gleam of solar panels at the corners of my bare scalp, by the way Taka breathes, that we are different. They don't understand our friendship. Taka listens to me. We share secrets. He teaches me carving. We have fun together. What does the skeleton beneath matter?

Taka bravely defies the world around him, but I keep my head down. I steal furtive glances at the passers-by, dreading to catch a glimpse of those zealot androids known to assault humans on sight – they call themselves Solarminders, wear a label of a silver sun. I'm being paranoid, though. These androids have specific territories they operate in – alleys populated solely by other androids where no one would bat an eye. No way they'll be here in the neutral areas.

We finally reach Taka's place and shut the door on the hostile din outside. There's tatami on the floor, and it makes crunching sounds against my tough feet – like walking atop the crust of freshly baked bread. A scent of beef ramen and a clamor of utensils come from the kitchen. We shouldn't be seen together, but with his mother busy cooking, we have enough time to work on the carving if we work on the shed outside. Taka learned to carve wood from his father and inherited all the tools he needed to continue the craft – a series of whittling knives with handles ten times the blade size.

Taka picks two blocks of limewood – one for him, one for me – and we go to the shed. It's dusty, filled with shelves hosting buckets, sprays and old knives. He lays the tools on a table covered by a blue sheet for us to work. Not work, not really. It's more like play. I love the feel of dead wood peeling away at the push of the knife, the visions of pretty things taking shape in my hands. We have an elephant, a dwarf, and a fox from previous times.

"Let's make a kodama today," Taka says.

"What about an owl?"

"Or perhaps a red panda?"

"Or a totem with monkey faces?"

"All of them!"

I smile. "You take the kodama. I'll do the owl first."

We nod at each other and get to work. Draw the design on paper, attach the paper on the wood, and finally the best part: push the blade on the wood and peel away flakes. *Shhhk, shhhk.* Part of me always expects to find something at the wood's core, like if I peel away enough, a solar-paneled skeleton will reveal itself. And once it touches the sunlight, the carving I make will be alive, and the owl will fly away. It makes me think of my own body as a woodblock, and now I imagine Mother popping up from behind me saying, *See, Goro? All things should harvest energy from the sun. Not survive at the expense of others.*

As soon as I finish the beak, a shriek erupts behind us. Taka's mother has puffy bags below her eyes, and something about the way she glares in my direction makes me think crows will start flying from the hoops of her sleeves to peck at my scalp.

"What is *he* doing here?" she asks.

"We were just carving. Didn't mean no harm by it," Taka says.

"No *harm?* Do you know what they'll do to people like us if they find him here? Do you *want* to have your family accused of abduction?"

Why do adults act like that? Once, my mother humiliated Taka when she caught me hanging out with him on the streets. Called him street urchin and a plague to the planet. His mother looks at me as if I'm some dangerous animal that escaped from the zoo. All I want is to hang out with my friend. Why can't they leave us in peace?

Taka attempts to defend our actions further, but I stand, bow, and say, "I'm sorry for any distress I caused you, Mrs. Bencraft. I will leave now."

I cross the threshold to the outside world, knowing Mrs. Bencraft is glaring at the back of my neck.

* * *

Days drift by, and I visit Doc – the only android whose company I enjoy, forty years my senior. His father was a kind android who created him to help around with the gadget shop. Now, Doc lives out his retirement surrounded by the ancient electronics and paraphernalia he has crafted throughout his existence. A fan on the ceiling makes a low hum and spreads the dust and smell of rusty copper. Geniuses love their chaos.

"So, you just left?" he asks me, as he drives a screw deep into one of his new devices.

I shrug.

"You could have given her a piece of your mind."

"What good would that do? If I am respectful, maybe one day she'll see there's nothing to hate me for. Perhaps she'll allow me to hang out with Taka then."

He shakes his head. "Naive. Prejudice never changes."

I fiddle with one of his screwdrivers, twist it in my hands. "Yours changed."

He looks at me, proffers his hand and I hand him the screwdriver. "Goro, you know how much history, biology, and neuroscience I had to study before I changed my mind. Most people aren't like that. They don't realize we are the same – they can't accept that the difference between the android and human brain has narrowed to the point of being nigh nonexistent. Heck, many of them have forgotten that we are made in the image of man, by man. That *they* sprinkled us in the population to bring balance to the world."

"We could educate her."

"Did your mother listen when you tried to explain our origins? Does she believe man made us as we are and helped us achieve our independence?"

I bite my lip. "No. Even though she works as a quality control inspector in android production facilities, she is clueless as to our origins. She believes humans stumbled upon us by accident."

"Right. And no doubt Taka's mother sees the truth as android propaganda. The truth in her mind is" – he waggles the screwdriver to punctuate his words – *"Androids were made by evil Solarmind Corp to steal our lives and our jobs. Hanging out with one can only lead to trouble. Solarmind Corp love their toys."*

"But that's stupid," I say. "Our independence from Solarmind Corp was established decades ago."

"That ain't enough time for the dust to settle on the human mind, though. She did say, *They'll accuse us of abduction*, didn't she? Who do you think she was referring to by '*they*'? You're Solarmind Corp property in her mind."

Doc leans a hand on my shoulder. "Trust me, Goro. You can't change the world. Just lessen the time you spend with Taka. Find other androids to hang out with. And when you raise an android of your own, teach it to be better. That's as far as you can aspire to reach. Change comes slowly."

"No," I say. "Taka is my friend. Our friendship will be a symbol. A seed from which change will start." I pause. "Like the rough wood that will one day become a beautiful sculpture. We just need to keep scraping away."

* * *

I meet Taka again the next day. Mother is in her solar sleep cycle again, but my smaller body recharge is done early. Taka waves from the street below, woodblocks tucked in his elbow and a beanie bag around his waist filled with carving tools. If neither parent accepts our friendship, we'll find our own place to do woodcarving.

I leap over the railings and land down on the pavement.

Taka smiles and tosses a woodblock to me. "An eagle today?"

I smile. "Or maybe a raccoon?"

"Or a bear!"

"Let's do them all!"

"Deal," we both say and walk to a quiet alley three blocks away where Mother won't see us. We lay down on the hot pavement to start the work – no, the play. First to draw, then to attach, and finally to carve. The light breeze carries the peels of wood away, and some get into the street grille. I imagine the peels slowly rotting in their long journey down the pipes, little abandoned boats stinking of refuse and urine.

A breeze picks up some of the shreds, and I look up, startled they're flying so far. They twirl and drift on the wind, away from the alley, into the shrubbery on the other side of the road. A few whirl out on the sidewalk and get crushed beneath the footsteps of a group of three androids. A group that's now entering the alley, heading toward us with certain strides.

"Well, well, well," the biggest among them says. "What have we here, Bit?"

"Looks like a human, Batu," says a shorter one. "I detect respiration."

"And it's hanging out with an android," says the shortest of the three.

I swallow hard. Maybe if I act polite. Maybe if I show them nothing's wrong with what they're seeing, we can all be friends. I stand, legs shaking, and proffer my hand. "I'm Goro. It's all right, T-Taka here's with me. He's one of the good ones. We just—"

But then I notice it: a silver sun emblazoned on the shoulders of the large android. Solarminders. They encircle us slowly. Taka takes to his feet, chest inflated, head up high. "So what if we hang out? What's it to you?"

The big android is deadly serious. "Filthy devourer," he says, and the other two kick Taka's knees from behind, forcing him to kneel.

"Stop," I say. "I told you he's with me!"

They kick him again. I leap at the shortest android. "I said stop!"

But the big one grabs me by the shoulder and yanks me back. I fall on the pavement headfirst.

"We know," he says calmly. "We know he's with you. We'll just teach him to be a good member of society so he remembers to stay in his place."

A scream. The world spins and I struggle to stand. They have Taka pinned against the wall, and the big one punches him in the gut. One of them snaps shafts of rusty solar panels from the garbage nearby.

I take a step and before I can scream, something sweeps my feet, and I drop to the ground again. The big android sits on top of me.

"Sit still, little one. We don't want to hurt you."

Why are they doing this? Why? Please stop hitting him. Please, oh please, leave us alone.

But the androids hit him with the solar-panel shafts on the shoulders, and he kneels, then kick him down to the ground and they keep kicking.

"Stop!" I scream, but they remain indifferent to my pleas and keep kicking his fragile body with their powerful android feet. The alley echoes with fleshy bone-crushing sounds. Taka screams and screams, and I can't do anything.

I can't do anything to save my friend.

* * *

I hoist Taka over my shoulder. His breathing is ragged, and by the time we reach Doc's place, his grunts have waned to a painful wheeze.

Doc brings forth a chair for me to rest the body. "What the hell? What happened?"

"Solarminders ambushed us. Can you do something?"

"Me? I don't know jack about human physiology. Take him to a hospital!"

I shake my head. "Can't. Android hospitals won't accept him, and the human ones need money. We don't have any. I know his family doesn't have any. I— I had to act fast. I could only think of you. Please, Doc."

But Doc seems lost. The certain elderly android I know is gone. His eyes shift helplessly between me and Taka.

I lift Taka's hand and feel the pulse in the wrist. Weaker. Slower. Almost gone. I know enough about human anatomy to realize what this means. He's *dying*. How can we help him? What can we—

I turn to Doc. "You know how to transfer consciousness, don't you? You can save him if you store it out of his body."

His eyes widen. "Goro, that's for our kind. I can't do this on a human."

"You said their minds were just like ours!"

"I said *almost* like ours. And I don't have a powerful enough computer even if I wanted to."

"How powerful does it need to be? Can't we just – I don't know, uh, use—" For a moment, my mind pictures a wooden figure, carved in the shape of Taka, carved specifically to accept his soul. A woodblock with a solar-powered skeleton inside. "Use me," I say.

Doc runs a hand through his hair. "You don't know what you're asking. I'd have to partition your mind, remove half your memories. And what's lost… I ain't got the equipment to store a backup."

Memories. Memories make us what we are. Will this change me? Will I forget our past, the memories I shared with Taka, and end up hating humans like my mother? Or like those android bullies that beat Taka within an inch of his life?

I shake my head. My voice is low and serious. "I can't let Taka die, Doc."

Doc sighs and nods slowly. "You can never let anyone know. Hear me? I'll be terminated if anyone finds out. You and your buddy will be, too. They'll call you an abomination!"

"I understand."

Doc points me to a recliner, fishes through his cabinets, and places a helmet over my head. I look up at the mossy ceiling and it whirls into a blurry, nauseating whirlpool as tendrils of electricity tingle along my scalp. Flashbacks from my life come and vanish like hazy dreams, the kind of dreams that leave behind a sense of loss once you awake. A craving to return to that made-up and forgotten world, but it's floated off in the ether.

After a long while, I feel the right side of my lips move. It's Taka. Speaking through me. "Where, where am I?"

I'm still befuddled by the experience. Doc's the one that speaks. "You're in Goro's body," he says. "They messed you up pretty bad, kid. I extracted you moments before your body gave out. Your buddy gave up half his memories to save you by making room for your consciousness."

"What— what?" Taka says through my mouth. My eyes drift to Taka's gray and bleeding body.

Tears are coursing down my left cheek. Taka's tears. He's seeing his own body through my eyes, broken and lifeless. What pain is he going through? I have to be strong. For him. "Don't worry, Taka," I say. "We'll find you a new body. Mother has connections in the production line of maintenance automatons. They are void of consciousness. Perfect vessels. We'll get you a solar-paneled body."

"But… your mother doesn't even like me."

"Doesn't matter. She won't let me live like this. Trust me, she'll want you out of my head. There's only one way I'll agree to it, and that's putting you into an android body."

"I'm sorry," Taka says. "I'm sorry. So sorry. You risked everything and I— it's—"

I wipe off the tears. "I risked nothing. I only exchanged something of value for something of greater value. You. My friend."

Doc smiles at me. At us. He wipes away a tear of his own.

* * *

Taka's new body was meant to serve as a janitor. Mother proclaimed the body a reject and wheeled it out for disposal. It was not easy to convince her, but I insisted I wouldn't erase Taka from my consciousness unless we found a host for him. And now that we found a solar-powered one, she's warming up to me hanging out with him.

His mother, however… she lashed out at Taka, calling him an abomination that stole away her son and sought to replace him with lies. She screamed for him to give her son back. To prove it was him, Taka went into her room, pulled off her dresser and revealed a carving he had once made. For her.

She broke down crying and in the end she hugged him. I realized change comes slowly, and it starts with a mother's love.

But an android cannot stay among humans without being discovered. Taka's staying at our place for now. I enjoy having him around, and for the first time, other androids are not looking down at him. In their eyes, he's one of us, but to me he is the same. Not a solar-powered android, but my human friend.

We got his father's tools, too, but he's not used to his new hands yet, and his carving is awkward. And me? It seems the half of the memories I erased included all my skills. So, we're learning from scratch again.

"How about we make a sphere today?" he says.

"Or perhaps a spoon," I say.

"A sphere in a spoon. Like a droplet of water!"

"And a pyramid, with an opening for the tomb."

"Let's do them all."

"Yeah." I say with a smile. "Yeah, let's do them all."

Wills and Trust

Brian K. Lowe

"MR. TIMOTHY, why do people want to die?"

I knelt down to the four-year-old's eye level, adjusting my liquid metal face into a vague likeness of a sympathetic human expression. It wasn't really necessary, since Audrey was completely accustomed to my appearance, but under the circumstances I felt it was for the best.

"It's not something people choose to do, Audrey. It's just the way things are."

The little girl turned her attention from me back to the granite rectangle in the grass, as if she could read the inscription: *William Roger Marcus-Phelps, 2000–91.*

"But why?"

I let a moment go by so that Audrey would feel that I had properly considered her question.

"It's a law of nature. Everything living has to die someday."

Audrey was still staring at her great-grandfather's memorial stone.

"Will Daddy die someday?"

I placed a hand on her shoulder. "Yes, but not for a very long time."

"Will I die someday?"

"Not for a very, *very* long time. And I will be there."

Audrey spun about and flung her arms around my neck so tightly that it was fortunate I did not need to breathe. I held her until her sobs had ceased.

"We should go back inside now. Your father wants to see you."

* * *

We found Christopher standing before a wall-sized display of holographs, diplomas, and screen images featuring various family members that no one but he and I remembered. He broke off his study as I carried his daughter into the room, and reached out to take her.

"Have you been crying, sweetie?"

Audrey shook her head, eyes squeezed shut and fists clenched. Christopher looked at me.

"She wanted to go… outside, sir. I am afraid she had some questions that I was ill-equipped to answer."

"Oh. I wouldn't have thought…" Christopher held Audrey so that he could talk to her face-to-face. "I'm sorry you're upset, pumpkin. But you should stop crying now. You don't want to make a bad impression on your new friend, do you?"

Audrey opened her eyes. "New friend?"

Christopher set her down and reached around her to produce a gift-wrapped box. The child tore it open to reveal a grey stuffed rabbit with long ears, a white tail, and white gloves. In one hand it held a carrot. Audrey gasped.

"He's a bunny rabbit," her daddy said, as though this might not be obvious even to a four-year-old. "He was very famous a long time ago. His name is—"

"Mr. Ears!" Audrey shrieked, seizing the bunny with a speed that would have broken the neck of a lesser rabbit. She hugged it until its stuffing bulged between her chubby arms. "He's going to be my BBFF!"

"BBFF?" Christopher asked.

"Best Bunny Friend Forever!" Audrey crowed, and ran off to her room.

* * *

Christopher accosted me as I was clearing the living room of dishes after the mourners had departed.

"Thank you, Timothy, for taking care of Audrey while our guests were here."

"Of course, sir. She wanted to go to the gravesite. She was trying to understand what happened to Mr. William. I'm sorry I allowed her to become upset." I poured a glass of bourbon and handed it to him.

"Don't worry. It's normal, I suppose. I told her that her grandfather had gone to be with her mother. I probably shouldn't have done that." Christopher took a sip, started to speak again, sighed, and took another. "So, uh, Timothy..."

"Yes, sir?"

Christopher set down his drink.

"...Please stop calling me 'sir'. You're older than I am. Call me Chris, the way you did when I was Audrey's age. I know my grandfather preferred formality, but times have changed, and you're an employee now, not a— a robot. Well, you are, but you know what I mean."

I was the earliest model who qualified when robots were granted citizenship in 2073.

"If it's all the same to you, Chris, I'll use 'sir' when we have guests."

He shrugged. "Fine. But that brings me to my point. This is my house now. Audrey and I don't need this much room; this is four times the size of our apartment. The mortgage was paid off long ago, but I don't think I could sell it. People just don't live like this anymore; they live in closets and do everything virtually.

"So either we're going to knock around in a house too big for the two of us to take care of ourselves, or I have to hire somebody. I know you don't have to stay, but I wish you would. I'm going to need your help going through my grandfather's estate, if nothing else."

I smiled. "I'm afraid that decision's already been made, sir."

"Oh?"

"I already promised Audrey I would stay."

* * *

I found Audrey in the library, sitting on the floor behind a reading chair. Mr. Ears was leaning against the back of the chair, a book open on his lap.

"And what are you doing hiding back here?"

"We're having an adventure," Audrey said, matter-of-factly. "Mr. Ears is reading to me. Rabbits grow up faster than people, so he already knows how to read."

"Is that so? What is he reading?" I reached down to take up the volume, a 90-year-old Stephen King omnibus.

"He's reading to me about Peter Rabbit, like you read to us last night. I liked it, and Mr. Ears said he would read it to me again."

I closed the book gently. "But if Mr. Ears reads it to you now, you won't want me to read it to you tonight at bedtime."

"Oh yes, I will, Mr. Timothy! Mr. Ears loves to hear that story. When I grow up and I can read, I'm going to read Mr. Ears every book in this house, right, Mr. Ears?"

She held the rabbit up, then nodded. "He says yes."

"I wish Mr. Ears would talk to me like he talks to you. I'm sure we'd have many things to discuss – his taste in literature, for example."

"I don't know." Audrey gave Mr. Ears a very serious look. "Do you want to talk to Mr. Timothy, Mr. Ears?" There was a few seconds' silence, then in a high, thin voice like a stuffed rabbit might use, she said: "*Sure. He's my friend, too.*"

I reached down and gave one soft paw a gentle handshake. "It's very nice to meet you properly, Mr. Ears. Tell me, what is your favorite part of *Peter Rabbit*?"

* * *

"I have the entire inventory of the contents of the house memorized: where it was purchased, for how much, and by whom. I can assist you with pricing items, as well."

Christopher stood in the center of the living room and *tsk*ed. "It's not the furnishings I'm worried about; we might as well keep those. It's all of my grandfather's *stuff*." He indicated the memorial wall. "Look at this. This is all about my grandmother. I understand my grandfather missed her, but… Honestly, I barely knew her. She and my parents were killed in the accident when I was five years old."

"I remember her. They were happy. I believe they still loved each other, even after your father was grown and had a son of his own. After your grandmother died, your grandfather refused to let me help him set up this memorial. He insisted on building it and maintaining it himself, and wouldn't let anyone else touch it."

"I just don't see any reason to keep it all," Christopher said. "I know it's family history, but he built it for himself, not me. Let's keep the holograms and scan the rest, then take it all down. I want to put in a bookcase."

"Were you planning on featuring books from the library? Your grandfather had some fine first editions."

Christopher bit his lower lip. "No, I have something else in mind. There's a series of novels that I really loved when I was a kid, but I only ever had electronic editions because I couldn't afford the real ones, and by the time I could, I'd moved out and had no place to put them. Now I have the space and I want to try to collect them."

I arranged my face into a thoughtful frown. "You read a lot of books when you were a child. Which ones are we talking about?"

"It was a series of novels based on the adventure pulps of the 1930s, called *Nemesis*. There were about forty of them altogether. I'd love to have a collection of the originals to put up right here." He held his hands up to the wall as if sizing up the bookshelf he could see in his mind.

"According to the datastream," I said, "there were forty-one *Nemesis* novels published, all in paperback, starting in 2016. There are copies of twenty-eight of them available online at the present time. Would you like me to order them?"

"No!" Christopher smiled apologetically. "I mean, no thanks. The point is finding them on my own. The joy is in the hunt, as it were. If I just order them off the datastream, I'll put them on a shelf and look at them once in a while. If I have to go out and *find* them, then they become a collection. Then when I look at them, I'll think of all the effort it took to get them." He shrugged. "I know. It seems like a lot of trouble for nothing. But there aren't that many antique stores that carry these books. Think of all the places I'm going to have to go to look for them. It'll be an adventure!"

* * *

"Oh, look, Daddy, a garage sale!"

Christopher told the car to slow down at Audrey's shout, seeing an anachronism in an age where hardly anyone had a garage any more. He scanned the tables from the road as he had a hundred times.

"We're not going to stop, sweetie. It's all junk. And we want to get to The Ripped Cover before it closes."

Audrey wouldn't take her eyes off the prize. "But it might have something! This is Denver, and Mr. Ears says their garage sales are different in Denver."

Christopher narrowed his brows. "And what does Mr. Ears know about garage sales in Denver?"

"Mr. Ears hears a lot of things we don't. That's why he's called Mr. Ears."

"All right." Christopher surrendered to twelve-year-old logic with good grace and stopped the car. "You've got ten minutes, Mr. Ears."

"Daddy…! Mr. Ears doesn't have a watch patch."

"Then you'd better go with him. But stay where I can see you."

"Let's go, Mr. Ears! We're on an adventure!"

A few minutes later, Audrey clambered into the car, bunny in one hand and a paper sack in the other. "We're back, Daddy. And Mr. Ears brought you a present." She held out the sack.

"Thank you, Mr. Ears! What did you get me?" Christopher opened the bag and fished out the first of six *Nemesis* paperbacks in varying conditions.

That day, Audrey and Mr. Ears learned a new word, which they were forbidden ever to repeat. But they also got ice cream.

* * *

"I can't believe you found it." Audrey shook her head as she and Christopher looked down at the small bound stack of paper pages in his hands. "The fabled number 19. The last one."

She put one arm around her father; with the other hand, she absently stroked Mr. Ears, brought from her room so he could watch the proceedings from the deep pocket of her ubiquitous cargo pants.

"And ironically, it's my favorite – *The Golden Serpent*." Christopher sighed. "It's been almost fifteen years. And how many cities?"

"Fifty-three," I said. "Fourteen of those with Audrey."

"Yeah," the girl said wistfully. "Looking for those paperbacks took me to a lot of places I never would have seen otherwise."

Christopher gave her a squeeze. "And it would have taken longer if you hadn't made me stop at that garage sale in Denver."

Audrey smiled as she watched as he reverently placed the last remaining volume in its rightful place on the custom-made shelf designed specifically to hold exactly forty-one *Nemesis* novels.

"That's it, then," Christopher said, still facing the wall. "I guess I'll have to find something else to do with myself." He turned around, smiling crookedly at his daughter. "It's going to be lonely with you gone."

Audrey poked him playfully. "What about Timothy?"

"I'm going to miss you, too," I replied. "But you need a college education."

"College..." Audrey sighed. "I guess I'd better finish packing. We've got to leave for the airport in a couple of hours. C'mon, Mr. Ears, we're going on an adventure!" And she disappeared down the hallway.

"I'm glad she was here to see this." Christopher gently brushed the lined-up, peeling volumes with his fingertips. "You and Audrey are the only ones who have any idea how important this was to me."

* * *

Christopher was only in his fifties when he contracted viral tuberculosis-3 a year before the vaccine was developed. He was quarantined at once, of course, confined to his bed and barely able to move. Audrey was living in military housing in Europe, and would not have been allowed to see him in any event. She called as often as she could, but her husband's unit had been sent to Enceladus and her son William was going through what she described as 'a difficult phase'.

One evening, I entered Christopher's room and sat down next to his bed. "I thought I'd read you something," I announced, and opened the first *Nemesis* book, *The Choking Rain*.

I read it to Christopher over the next several days, then brought in the next one. In the course of the next two months, I read each book in sequence, every night for as long as he could stay awake.

Each day, that was a little less. By the time we reached number 14, Christopher had slipped into a coma. Scanning his vitals, I decided to skip Numbers 15–18 and went directly to Number 19, *The Golden Serpent*, which I knew was his favorite. I sat by his bedside, no longer even pretending to read the book, but rather reciting it from memory.

Christopher passed away thirty pages from the end. I turned off the machines and finished telling him the story. Then I called Audrey.

* * *

"I'd like to pretend that it's important to William to have a connection to his grandfather," Audrey told me, "but we both know I'd be lying."

We were standing in the library, in front of Christopher's bookshelf, the *Nemesis* novels front and center, surrounded by all of the other series that he had gone on to collect since.

I handed her a hot cup of coffee. She took a sip and blinked in surprise. "Is this Martian?"

I nodded.

"Why? Dad never even liked coffee. Why would he spend money on this?"

"He kept it in the kitchen in case you ever came for a visit."

Audrey closed her eyes, fighting against the tears. "I meant to. I really did. But I was raising William practically by myself; Jorge was never home... Afghanistan, Thailand, Luna, Enceladus, and then Dad got sick and..."

I gently took the cup away and then gathered her into my arms, as I had when she was a child. She had barely hung up after receiving my call about Christopher's death when the government notified her about Jorge.

"And now," she said at last, pulling back from me and wiping her eyes with her sleeve, "I find out that the taxes on this place are so high that I can't afford to keep it up unless I sublet. That's even with whatever my father left me. Jorge's casualty benefits are going to go right back to the government."

I gave Audrey a moment before responding. "I'm afraid there are so many people on Earth now that death duties have become a major part of the government's income. That's why your father paid me such an extravagant salary. He wanted to preserve as much of the estate as possible, and since I can't die…"

Audrey gave me a sidelong glance. "What are you saying?"

"I am saying that your father was very generous. He paid more than enough for me to help with the maintenance of the estate. You don't need to subdivide the mansion."

Audrey sighed. "That's very kind of you, but this is way too much house for us anyway, and the way things are going, the government is likely to come by and annex it any day for the housing space. I talked to Dad's lawyer, and he said subdividing and taking tenants was the best way to prevent that. So thank you, Timothy, but no.

"There's just William and me – and you, of course – and William never leaves his room. As long as he has space for his VR equipment and food that he actually eats once in a while, that's all he needs. Half the house will be plenty."

"Three of us? Are you sure? You forgot someone."

Audrey frowned. "Who?"

I finally allowed myself to smile. "What about Mr. Ears?"

"Mr. Ears sleeps where I sleep."

* * *

I entered William's room without knocking, knowing full well he would not have heard me even if I had. My olfactory sensor readings soared, but one of the advantages of being a robot is that my sense of smell is entirely mechanical.

William was completely unaware of my presence until I initiated a shutdown of his program.

"What the *fuck*—?" Then he saw me. "What are *you* doing in here?"

"It's your mother's birthday. I came to fetch you to have dinner with us. You live in the same house, and you've hardly spoken in years."

"I'm not hungry." He tried to reactivate his program, but I prevented it.

"Turn it on!"

"You will take a shower, put on clean clothes, and join us for dinner."

"And if I *don't*?"

I explored the room, admiring and cataloging the technology without letting on that I was doing so.

"Then you will sit here in your chair, Mr. William, and stare at the wall." I watched as a variety of unpleasant expressions paraded across his face. The conversation ended as we both knew it would.

"What do I get if I do?"

"I will reinitiate the program as soon as dinner is over."

"And you won't lock me out again?"

"Agreed."

* * *

Audrey's face lit up when she saw her son appear at the table. He had followed my instructions to the letter, but I knew I would receive nothing further.

"That's a nice shirt," Audrey ventured. She deserved a great deal of credit for saying so; it bore a flaming skeleton playing a bloody guitar. It appeared to be clean, but since it was black it was hard to tell.

"It's from a band," William grunted. "Low Grade Fever."

"Thank you both for thinking of me," Audrey said. "It means a lot to me that you would come to dinner tonight, William."

"He— invited me." William looked like he was chewing his words more than his food. Suddenly he looked up. "He's our servant, right? We pay him?"

"William!"

"No, I mean it. It's not like we've got a lot of money. What do we pay him for?"

Audrey straightened in her chair. I did as well; even without touching her, I could tell that her pulse was racing, and she was shaking.

"Timothy has been with this family since your great-great-grandfather was alive. And yes, we pay him, but only the required minimum wage. For your information, he refuses to take any more."

"He'll get more when I inherit the house," William mumbled, "because he won't be working here anymore."

I looked askance at the sullen young man. "William, I do not think this is an appropriate subject for your mother's birthday—"

And then I was on my feet, radioing for an ambulance for Audrey, who had quietly slid out of her chair and onto the floor.

* * *

Even after I used a significant portion of my savings on legal assistance, William persuaded the court that, as her son, he should be appointed Audrey's legal conservator. Ironically, he was forced to continue my employment because otherwise he would have had to care for her himself. While she was still in the hospital, he began organizing things to his satisfaction.

"Those books from my grandfather. Can we get anything for them?"

I made him wait longer than he needed to. "Not as much as you'd like, but I can find a buyer who will appreciate them."

"Do it. Get rid of them as soon as possible and give me the cash. What about the rabbit?"

I froze. "No."

"What do you mean, 'no'? It's gotta be worth something. It's like a hundred years old. God knows how she kept in such good shape, but that's got to make it worth more."

"Mr. Ears is with your mother. He is hers. He is not for sale."

"I'm my mother's conservator. Everything she owns is mine to… *dispose of*, that's what the lawyer said."

I took a full hundredth of a second to choose my next words. "Mr. Ears is *not* yours to dispose of, William. If you take him away, it will kill your mother. I will not allow that."

William drew himself up to his full unimpressive height. "The law is on my side, *Timothy*. What are you going to do about it?"

"I cannot stop you if that is what you want to do," I admitted. "But you should know that after looking at your rather impressive VR suite, I wondered how you could afford it all, since, as you say, there is very little money to spare in the house. What do you suppose would happen if I were share some of the serial numbers with the police? Do you think the judge might then reconsider my conservatorship petition?"

When Audrey came home from the hospital, huddled in her wheelchair, Mr. Ears was clutched tightly in her lap.

* * *

Audrey looked up as I opened her door, a light suddenly flickering in her eyes. She lay with her unbound gray hair spread across her pillow, one hand playing idly with the ghostly virtual buttons of her entertainment control, the other lying uselessly across her thin body.

"How are you this morning, Audrey?" I asked.

"I'm fine. You're not wearing your new face?"

"I didn't want to. This is the face I've always had; this is our face – yours and mine and Mr. Ears'."

She glanced down at her rabbit, sitting next to her. Despite our best efforts, patches of his fur shone with age, but his stitching was still intact.

"I know you used to put him in the ultrasonic washer every night when I was a little girl. He was way too clean in the morning." She leaned forward a fraction, waggling a finger at me. "I knew what you were doing but I could never prove it because Mr. Ears was always in exactly the spot I'd left him the night before."

"Well, I *am* a computer. Putting him back in the same place every night was easier than sneaking in and taking him out in the first place. Except that time you laid a piece of string on top of him. You almost caught me then."

She smiled at me, her face wreathed in wrinkles. "It's not the fact that you put him back the same way every time that matters, Timothy. It's the fact that you cared enough to do it." She leaned back against the pillows and closed her eyes. "When I took him away to college, I couldn't figure out why he wouldn't stay clean. I had to find someplace I could wash him myself, and it wasn't easy. We looked all over." She smiled in memory. "Remember, Mr. Ears?"

"*It was one of the best adventures we ever had*," Mr. Ears agreed.

I took her hand gently, squeezing it nearly imperceptibly to deliver her daily medications through the micro-injectors I'd had installed in my fingers. She removed herself from my grasp and covered my hand in turn.

"You don't have to bother with that anymore. It won't be long now."

We sat in a companionable silence.

"You once asked me why people wanted to die."

"Did I? I don't remember."

"You were four years old. It was shortly after your great-grandfather William passed. You asked me why people wanted to die, and I said they didn't want to, but they had to. And then you asked me if your daddy was going to die, and I said not for a long time, and you asked me if *you* were going to die, and I said not for a long, long time, but that I would be there with you."

"And you are. May I ask you a favor?"

"Of course."

"I want to see your new face." I obliged, my features molding themselves over my metal façade until I looked quite human, using technology that had been illegal until recently. "That's better. Don't you think so, Mr. Ears?"

She leaned down, whispering in the rabbit's velvety ear, then gently took his paw and helped him wave at me.

"*We're sleepy. We're going to take a nap now. Goodnight, Mr. Timothy.*"

Holding him tightly, Audrey closed her eyes and went to sleep.

* * *

I sent William a message through the in-house network, and when that didn't fetch him, I broke my promise and suspended his program until he emerged from his room. I waited in the front hall, my small overnight bag in my hand. He had grown old before his time, pale and flabby, despite all of the massaging and self-exercising equipment he had invested in over the years.

"Your mother is gone."

He had the grace to look sad, if only for a moment. I knew exactly what he had been doing before I interrupted him, so I was not surprised that he wanted nothing more than to get back to it.

"I've already called the funeral home," I continued. "They will send someone to retrieve her body. Everything has been pre-arranged."

"I guess there's no reason for you to stay, then. I can sell off her things. I don't need you to help me to do that."

I refused to allow him to dismiss me so painlessly.

"You needn't maintain the lie any more, William. I know that you've been selling the furnishings to buy new equipment. I know that all of this—" I waved my hand at our surroundings, ostensibly the same house in which Audrey had grown up – "is only virtual. You may as well shut it down and save the power."

Almost immediately, the bookshelves, paintings, and furnishings faded away, leaving bare walls and a bare floor.

"They were only *things*," William snarled. "It was just *stuff*, and who needs 'stuff'?"

"Some of it belonged to your great-great-grandfather. If he had felt that way, none of it would have survived – including me. I was considered a 'thing' once."

William glared at me. "Don't be ridiculous. Robots are people."

"So was your great-great-grandfather, and your great-grandparents, and your grandfather, and your mother. Now the only reminders left of them are your mother's belongings – and you."

"Well then, I guess pretty soon there'll be just me, because I'm going to sell Mom's things. I don't need them, and some of them are worth money. Like that stuffed rabbit of hers." He smirked. "Now I can sell it without you being afraid of me killing her."

"That stuffed rabbit was your mother's best friend. He is older than you are. To her, he was as alive as I am."

"Yeah, well, it *isn't*. I'll bet some toy collector will give me a couple hundred for it."

"You are her executor; you have the right to do as you please."

That seemed to throw him off-guard. "If you, uh, if you want to say goodbye, that's okay," he offered after a moment.

I smiled sadly, but not for Audrey. "I've already said my goodbyes."

"Oh. Then I guess I'll see you at the funeral." William's tone indicated that he wasn't sure he would be attending himself.

I opened the front door and stood in the doorway. "No, I don't think so. As I said, I've already made my goodbyes. It's time I started something new." I closed the door behind me and set off down the front path, giving William half a minute to return to his virtual world. The taxi I had summoned was waiting. I got in and directed it to take me to the train station.

I opened my bag and carefully withdrew the large stuffed rabbit that I had stowed there on a bed of paperback books, placing him on the seat next to me. Then I pulled out one of the paperbacks and opened it.

"So, Mr. Ears, have you ever read any of the *Nemesis* books?"

No Woman Born

C.L. Moore

SHE HAD BEEN the loveliest creature whose image ever moved along the airways. John Harris, who was once her manager, remembered doggedly how beautiful she had been as he rose in the silent elevator toward the room where Deirdre sat waiting for him.

Since the theater fire that had destroyed her a year ago, he had never been quite able to let himself remember her beauty clearly, except when some old poster, half in tatters, flaunted her face at him, or a maudlin memorial program flashed her image unexpectedly across the television screen. But now he had to remember.

The elevator came to a sighing stop and the door slid open. John Harris hesitated. He knew in his mind that he had to go on, but his reluctant muscles almost refused him. He was thinking helplessly, as he had not allowed himself to think until this moment, of the fabulous grace that had poured through her wonderful dancer's body, remembering her soft and husky voice with the little burr in it that had fascinated the audiences of the whole world.

There had never been anyone so beautiful.

In times before her, other actresses had been lovely and adulated, but never before Deirdre's day had the entire world been able to take one woman so wholly to its heart. So few outside the capitals had ever seen Bernhardt or the fabulous Jersey Lily. And the beauties of the movie screen had had to limit their audiences to those who could reach the theaters. But Deirdre's image had once moved glowingly across the television screens of every home in the civilized world.

And in many outside the bounds of civilization. Her soft, husky songs had sounded in the depths of jungles, her lovely, languorous body had woven its patterns of rhythm in desert tents and polar huts. The whole world knew every smooth motion of her body and every cadence of her voice, and the way a subtle radiance had seemed to go on behind her features when she smiled.

And the whole world had mourned her when she died in the theater fire.

Harris could not quite think of her as other than dead, though he knew what sat waiting him in the room ahead. He kept remembering the old words James Stephens wrote long ago for another Deirdre, also lovely and beloved and unforgotten after two thousand years.

The time comes when our hearts sink utterly,
When we remember Deirdre and her tale,
And that her lips are dust...
There has been again no woman born
Who was so beautiful; not one so beautiful
Of all the women born –

That wasn't quite true, of course – there had been one. Or maybe, after all, this Deirdre who died only a year ago had not been beautiful in the sense of perfection. He thought the other one might not have been either, for there are always women with perfection of feature in the world, and they are not the ones that legend remembers. It was the light within, shining through her charming, imperfect features, that had made this Deirdre's face so lovely. No one else he had ever seen had anything like the magic of the lost Deirdre.

Let all men go apart and mourn together –
No man can ever love her. Not a man
Can dream to be her lover... No man say –
What could one say to her? There are no words
That one could say to her.

No, no words at all. And it was going to be impossible to go through with this. Harris knew it overwhelmingly just as his finger touched the buzzer. But the door opened almost instantly, and then it was too late.

Maltzer stood just inside, peering out through his heavy spectacles. You could see how tensely he had been waiting. Harris was a little shocked to see that the man was trembling. It was hard to think of the confident and imperturbable Maltzer, whom he had known briefly a year ago, as shaken like this. He wondered if Deirdre herself were as tremulous with sheer nerves – but it was not time yet to let himself think of that.

"Come in, come in," Maltzer said irritably. There was no reason for irritation. The year's work, so much of it in secrecy and solitude, must have tried him physically and mentally to the very breaking point.

"She all right?" Harris asked inanely, stepping inside.

"Oh yes... yes, *she's* all right." Maltzer bit his thumbnail and glanced over his shoulder at an inner door, where Harris guessed she would be waiting.

"No," Maltzer said, as he took an involuntary step toward it. "We'd better have a talk first. Come over and sit down. Drink?"

Harris nodded, and watched Maltzer's hands tremble as he tilted the decanter. The man was clearly on the very verge of collapse, and Harris felt a sudden cold uncertainty open up in him in the one place where until now he had been oddly confident.

"She *is* all right?" he demanded, taking the glass.

"Oh yes, she's perfect. She's so confident it scares me." Maltzer gulped his drink and poured another before he sat down.

"What's wrong, then?"

"Nothing, I guess. Or... well, I don't know. I'm not sure any more. I've worked toward this meeting for nearly a year, but now – well, I'm not sure it's time yet. I'm just not sure."

He stared at Harris, his eyes large and indistinguishable behind the lenses. He was a thin, wire-taut man with all the bone and sinew showing plainly beneath the dark skin of his face. Thinner, now, than he had been a year ago when Harris saw him last.

"I've been too close to her," he said now. "I have no perspective any more. All I can see is my own work. And I'm just not sure that's ready yet for you or anyone to see."

"She thinks so?"

"I never saw a woman so confident." Maltzer drank, the glass clicking on his teeth. He looked up suddenly through the distorting lenses. "Of course a failure now would mean – well, absolute collapse," he said.

Harris nodded. He was thinking of the year of incredibly painstaking work that lay behind this meeting, the immense fund of knowledge, of infinite patience, the secret collaboration of artists, sculptors, designers, scientists, and the genius of Maltzer governing them all as an orchestra conductor governs his players.

He was thinking too, with a certain unreasoning jealousy, of the strange, cold, passionless intimacy between Maltzer and Deirdre in that year, a closer intimacy than any two humans can ever have shared before. In a sense the Deirdre whom he saw in a few minutes would *be* Maltzer, just as he thought he detected in Maltzer now and then small mannerisms of inflection and motion that had been Deirdre's own. There had been between them a sort of unimaginable marriage stranger than anything that could ever have taken place before.

"—so many complications," Maltzer was saying in his worried voice with its faintest possible echo of Deirdre's lovely, cadenced rhythm. (The sweet, soft huskiness he would never hear again.) "There was shock, of course. Terrible shock. And a great fear of fire. We had to conquer that before we could take the first steps. But we did it. When you go in you'll probably find her sitting before the fire." He caught the startled question in Harris' eyes and smiled. "No, she can't feel the warmth now, of course. But she likes to watch the flames. She's mastered any abnormal fear of them quite beautifully."

"She can—" Harris hesitated. "Her eyesight's normal now?"

"Perfect," Maltzer said. "Perfect vision was fairly simple to provide. After all, that sort of thing has already been worked out, in other connections. I might even say her vision's a little better than perfect, from our own standpoint." He shook his head irritably. "I'm not worried about the mechanics of the thing. Luckily they got to her before the brain was touched at all. Shock was the only danger to her sensory centers, and we took care of all that first of all, as soon as communication could be established. Even so, it needed great courage on her part. Great courage." He was silent for a moment, staring into his empty glass.

"Harris," he said suddenly, without looking up, "have I made a mistake? Should we have let her die?" Harris shook his head helplessly. It was an unanswerable question. It had tormented the whole world for a year now. There had been hundreds of answers and thousands of words written on the subject. Has anyone the right to preserve a brain alive when its body is destroyed? Even if a new body can be provided, necessarily so very unlike the old?

"It's not that she's— ugly— now," Maltzer went on hurriedly, as if afraid of an answer. "Metal isn't ugly. And Deirdre... well, you'll see. I tell you, I can't see myself. I know the whole mechanism so well – it's just mechanics to me. Maybe she's— grotesque. I don't know. Often I've wished I hadn't been on the spot, with all my ideas, just when the fire broke out. Or that it could have been anyone but Deirdre. She was so beautiful— Still, if it had been someone else I think the whole thing might have failed completely. It takes more than just an uninjured brain. It takes strength and courage beyond common, and – well, something more. Something— unquenchable. Deirdre has it. She's still Deirdre. In a way she's still beautiful. But I'm not sure anybody but myself could see that. And you know what she plans?"

"No – what?"

"She's going back on the air-screen."

Harris looked at him in stunned disbelief.

"She *is* still beautiful," Maltzer told him fiercely. "She's got courage, and a serenity that amazes me. And she isn't in the least worried or resentful about what's happened. Or afraid what the verdict of the public will be. But I am, Harris. I'm terrified."

They looked at each other for a moment more, neither speaking. Then Maltzer shrugged and stood up.

"She's in there," he said, gesturing with his glass.

Harris turned without a word, not giving himself time to hesitate. He crossed toward the inner door.

The room was full of a soft, clear, indirect light that climaxed in the fire crackling on a white tiled hearth. Harris paused inside the door, his heart beating thickly. He did not see her for a moment. It was a perfectly commonplace room, bright, light, with pleasant furniture, and flowers on the tables. Their perfume was sweet on the clear air. He did not see Deirdre.

Then a chair by the fire creaked as she shifted her weight in it. The high back hid her, but she spoke. And for one dreadful moment it was the voice of an automaton that sounded in the room, metallic, without inflection.

"Hel-lo—" said the voice. Then she laughed and tried again. And it was the old, familiar, sweet huskiness he had not hoped to hear again as long as he lived.

In spite of himself he said, "Deirdre!" and her image rose before him as if she herself had risen unchanged from the chair, tall, golden, swaying a little with her wonderful dancer's poise, the lovely, imperfect features lighted by the glow that made them beautiful. It was the cruelest thing his memory could have done to him. And yet the voice – after that one lapse, the voice was perfect.

"Come and look at me, John," she said.

He crossed the floor slowly, forcing himself to move. That instant's flash of vivid recollection had nearly wrecked his hard-won poise. He tried to keep his mind perfectly blank as he came at last to the verge of seeing what no one but Maltzer had so far seen or known about in its entirety. No one at all had known what shape would be forged to clothe the most beautiful woman on Earth, now that her beauty was gone.

He had envisioned many shapes. Great, lurching robot forms, cylindrical, with hinged arms and legs. A glass case with the brain floating in it and appendages to serve its needs. Grotesque visions, like nightmares come nearly true. And each more inadequate than the last, for what metal shape could possibly do more than house ungraciously the mind and brain that had once enchanted a whole world?

Then he came around the wing of the chair, and saw her.

The human brain is often too complicated a mechanism to function perfectly. Harris' brain was called upon now to perform a very elaborate series of shifting impressions. First, incongruously, he remembered a curious inhuman figure he had once glimpsed leaning over the fence rail outside a farmhouse. For an instant the shape had stood up integrated, ungainly, impossibly human, before the glancing eye resolved it into an arrangement of brooms and buckets. What the eye had found only roughly humanoid, the suggestible brain had accepted fully formed. It was thus now, with Deirdre.

The first impression that his eyes and mind took from sight of her was shocked and incredulous, for his brain said to him unbelievingly, *"This is Deirdre! She hasn't changed at all!"*

Then the shift of perspective took over, and even more shockingly, eye and brain said, "No, not Deirdre – not human. Nothing but metal coils. Not Deirdre at all—" And that was the worst. It was like walking from a dream of someone beloved and lost, and facing anew, after that heartbreaking reassurance of sleep, the inflexible fact that nothing can bring the lost to life again. Deirdre was gone, and this was only machinery heaped in a flowered chair.

Then the machinery moved, exquisitely, smoothly, with a grace as familiar as the swaying poise he remembered. The sweet, husky voice of Deirdre said, "It's me, John darling. It really is, you know."

And it was.

That was the third metamorphosis, and the final one. Illusion steadied and became factual, real. It was Deirdre.

He sat down bonelessly. He had no muscles. He looked at her speechless and unthinking, letting his senses take in the sight of her without trying to rationalize what he saw.

She was golden still. They had kept that much of her, the first impression of warmth and color which had once belonged to her sleek hair and the apricot tints of her skin. But they had had the good sense to go no farther. They had not tried to make a wax image of the lost Deirdre. *(No woman born who was so beautiful— Not one so beautiful, of all the women born—)*

And so she had no face. She had only a smooth, delicately modeled ovoid for her head, with a... a sort of crescent-shaped mask across the frontal area where her eyes would have been if she had needed eyes. A narrow, curved quarter-moon, with the horns turned upward. It was filled in with something translucent, like cloudy crystal, and tinted the aquamarine of the eyes Deirdre used to have. Through that, then, she saw the world. Through that she looked without eyes, and behind it, as behind the eyes of a human – she was.

Except for that, she had no features. And it had been wise of those who designed her, he realized now. Subconsciously he had been dreading some clumsy attempt at human features that might creak like a marionette's in parodies of animation. The eyes, perhaps, had had to open in the same place upon her head, and at the same distance apart, to make easy for her an adjustment to the stereoscopic vision she used to have. But he was glad they had not given her two eye-shaped openings with glass marbles inside them. The mask was better.

(Oddly enough, he did not once think of the naked brain that must lie inside the metal. The mask was symbol enough for the woman within. It was enigmatic; you did not know if her gaze was on you searchingly, or wholly withdrawn. And it had no variations of brilliance such as once had played across the incomparable mobility of Deirdre's face. But eyes, even human eyes, are as a matter of fact enigmatic enough. They have no expression except what the lids impart; they take all animation from the features. We automatically watch the eyes of the friend we speak with, but if he happens to be lying down so that he speaks across his shoulder and his face is upside-down to us, quite as automatically we watch the mouth. The gaze keeps shifting nervously between mouth and eyes in their reversed order, for it is the position in the face, not the feature itself, which we are accustomed to accept as the seat of the soul. Deirdre's mask was in that proper place; it was easy to accept it as a mask over eyes.)

She had, Harris realized as the first shock quieted, a very beautifully shaped head – a bare, golden skull. She turned it a little, gracefully upon her neck of metal, and he saw that the artist who shaped it had given her the most delicate suggestion of cheekbones, narrowing in the blankness below the mask to the hint of a human face. Not too much. Just enough so that when the head turned you saw by its modeling that it had moved, lending perspective and foreshortening to the expressionless golden helmet. Light did not slip uninterrupted as if over the surface of a golden egg. Brancusi himself had never made anything more simple or more subtle than the modeling of Deirdre's head.

But all expression, of course, was gone. All expression had gone up in the smoke of the theater fire, with the lovely, mobile, radiant features which had meant Deirdre.

As for her body, he could not see its shape. A garment hid her. But they had made no incongruous attempt to give her back the clothing that once had made her famous. Even the softness of cloth would have called the mind too sharply to the remembrance that no human body lay beneath the folds, nor does metal need the incongruity of cloth for its protection. Yet without garments, he realized, she would have looked oddly naked, since her new body was humanoid, not angular machinery.

The designer had solved his paradox by giving her a robe of very fine metal mesh. It hung from the gentle slope of her shoulders in straight, pliant folds like a longer Grecian chlamys, flexible, yet with weight enough of its own not to cling too revealingly to whatever metal shape lay beneath.

The arms they had given her were left bare, and the feet and ankles. And Maltzer had performed his greatest miracle in the limbs of the new Deirdre. It was a mechanical miracle basically, but the eye appreciated first that he had also showed supreme artistry and understanding.

Her arms were pale shining gold, tapered smoothly, without modeling, and flexible their whole length in diminishing metal bracelets fitting one inside the other clear down to the slim, round wrists. The hands were more nearly human than any other feature about her, though they, too, were fitted together in delicate, small sections that slid upon one another with the flexibility almost of flesh. The fingers' bases were solider than human, and the fingers themselves tapered to longer tips.

Her feet, too, beneath the tapering broader rings of the metal ankles, had been constructed upon the model of human feet. Their finely tooled sliding segments gave her an arch and a heel and a flexible forward section formed almost like the sollerets of medieval armor.

She looked, indeed, very much like a creature in armor, with her delicately plated limbs and her featureless head like a helmet with a visor of glass, and her robe of chain-mail. But no knight in armor ever moved as Deirdre moved, or wore his armor upon a body of such inhumanly fine proportions. Only a knight from another world, or a knight of Oberon's court, might have shared that delicate likeness.

Briefly he had been surprised at the smallness and exquisite proportions of her. He had been expecting the ponderous mass of such robots as he had seen, wholly automatons. And then he realized that for them, much of the space had to be devoted to the inadequate mechanical brains that guided them about their duties. Deirdre's brain still preserved and proved the craftsmanship of an artisan far defter than man. Only the body was of metal, and it did not seem complex, though he had not yet been told how it was motivated.

Harris had no idea how long he sat staring at the figure in the cushioned chair. She was still lovely – indeed, she was still Deirdre – and as he looked he let the careful schooling of his face relax. There was no need to hide his thoughts from her.

She stirred upon the cushions, the long, flexible arms moving with a litheness that was not quite human. The motion disturbed him as the body itself had not, and in spite of himself his face froze a little. He had the feeling that from behind the crescent mask she was watching him very closely.

Slowly she rose.

The motion was very smooth. Also it was serpentine, as if the body beneath the coat of mail were made in the same interlocking sections as her limbs. He had expected and feared mechanical rigidity; nothing had prepared him for this more than human suppleness.

She stood quietly, letting the heavy mailed folds of her garment settle about her. They fell together with a faint ringing sound, like small bells far off, and hung beautifully in pale golden, sculptured folds. He had risen automatically as she did. Now he faced her, staring. He had never seen her stand perfectly still, and she was not doing it now. She swayed just a bit, vitality burning inextinguishably in her brain as once it had burned in her body, and stolid immobility was as impossible to her as it had always been. The golden garment caught points of light from the fire and glimmered at him with tiny reflections as she moved.

Then she put her featureless helmeted head a little to one side, and he heard her laughter as familiar in its small, throaty, intimate sound as he had ever heard it from her living throat. And every gesture, every attitude, every flowing of motion into motion was so utterly

Deirdre that the overwhelming illusion swept his mind again and this was the flesh-and-blood woman as clearly as if he saw her standing there whole once more, like Phoenix from the fire.

"Well, John," she said in the soft, husky, amused voice he remembered perfectly. "Well, John, is it I?" She knew it was. Perfect assurance sounded in the voice. "The shock will wear off, you know. It'll be easier and easier as time goes on. I'm quite used to myself now. See?"

She turned away from him and crossed the room smoothly, with the old, poised, dancer's glide, to the mirror that paneled one side of the room. And before it, as he had so often seen her preen before, he watched her preening now, running flexible metallic hands down the folds of her metal garment, turning to admire herself over one metal shoulder, making the mailed folds tinkle and sway as she struck an arabesque position before the glass.

His knees let him down into the chair she had vacated. Mingled shock and relief loosened all his muscles in him, and she was more poised and confident than he.

"It's a miracle," he said with conviction. "It's *you*. But I don't see how—" He had meant, "—how, without face or body—" but clearly he could not finish that sentence.

She finished it for him in her own mind, and answered without self-consciousness. "It's motion, mostly," she said, still admiring her own suppleness in the mirror. "See?" And very lightly on her springy, armored feet she flashed through an enchainement of brilliant steps, swinging round with a pirouette to face him. "That was what Maltzer and I worked out between us, after I began to get myself under control again." Her voice was somber for a moment, remembering a dark time in the past. Then she went on, "It wasn't easy, of course, but it was fascinating. You'll never guess how fascinating, John! We knew we couldn't work out anything like a facsimile of the way I used to look, so we had to find some other basis to build on. And motion is the other basis of recognition, after actual physical likeness."

She moved lightly across the carpet toward the window and stood looking down, her featureless face averted a little and the light shining across the delicately hinted curves of the cheekbones.

"Luckily," she said, her voice amused, "I never was beautiful. It was all— well, vivacity, I suppose, and muscular co-ordination. Years and years of training, and all of it engraved here" – she struck her golden helmet a light, ringing blow with golden knuckles – "in the habit patterns grooved into my brain. So this body... did he tell you?... works entirely through the brain. Electromagnetic currents flowing along from ring to ring, like this." She rippled a boneless arm at him with a motion like flowing water. "Nothing holds me together – nothing! – except muscles of magnetic currents. And if I'd been somebody else – somebody who moved differently, why the flexible rings would have moved differently too, guided by the impulse from another brain. I'm not conscious of doing anything I haven't always done. The same impulses that used to go out to my muscles go out now to— this." And she made a shuddering, serpentine motion of both arms at him, like a Cambodian dancer, and then laughed wholeheartedly, the sound of it ringing through the room with such full-throated merriment that he could not help seeing again the familiar face crinkled with pleasure, the white teeth shining. "It's all perfectly subconscious now," she told him. "It took lots of practice at first, of course, but now even my signature looks just as it always did – the coordination is duplicated that delicately." She rippled her arms at him again and chuckled.

"But the voice, too," Harris protested inadequately. "It's *your* voice, Deirdre."

"The voice isn't only a matter of throat construction and breath control, my darling Johnnie! At least, so Professor Maltzer assured me a year ago, and I certainly haven't any reason to doubt him!" She laughed again. She was laughing a little too much, with a touch of the bright, hysteric over-excitement he remembered so well. But if any woman ever had reason for mild hysteria, surely Deirdre had it now.

The laughter rippled and ended, and she went on, her voice eager. "He says voice control is almost wholly a matter of hearing what you produce, once you've got adequate mechanism, of course. That's why deaf people, with the same vocal chords as ever, let their voices change completely and lose all inflection when they've been deaf long enough. And luckily, you see, I'm not deaf!"

She swung around to him, the folds of her robe twinkling and ringing, and rippled up and up a clear, true scale to a lovely high note, and then cascaded down again like water over a falls. But she left him no time for applause. "Perfectly simple, you see. All it took was a little matter of genius from the professor to get it worked out for me! He started with a new variation of the old Vodor you must remember hearing about, years ago. Originally, of course, the thing was ponderous. You know how it worked – speech broken down to a few basic sounds and built up again in combinations produced from a keyboard. I think originally the sounds were a sort of *ktch* and a *shoosh*ing noise, but we've got it all worked to a flexibility and range quite as good as human now. All I do is – well, mentally play on the keyboard of my... my sound-unit, I suppose it's called. It's much more complicated than that, of course, but I've learned to do it unconsciously. And I regulate it by ear, quite automatically now. If you were— *here* – instead of me, and you'd had the same practice, your own voice would be coming out of the same keyboard and diaphragm instead of mine. It's all a matter of the brain patterns that operated the body and now operate the machinery. They send out very strong impulses that are stepped up as much as necessary somewhere or other in here—" Her hands waved vaguely over the mesh-robed body.

She was silent a moment, looking out the window. Then she turned away and crossed the floor to the fire, sinking again into the flowered chair. Her helmet-skull turned its mask to face him and he could feel a quiet scrutiny behind the aquamarine of its gaze.

"It's— odd," she said, "being here in this... this... instead of a body. But not as odd or as alien as you might think. I've thought about it a lot – I've had plenty of time to think – and I've begun to realize what a tremendous force the human ego really is. I'm not sure I want to suggest it has any mystical power it can impress on mechanical things, but it does seem to have a power of some sort. It does instill its own force into inanimate objects, and they take on a personality of their own. People do impress their personalities on the houses they live in, you know. I've noticed that often. Even empty rooms. And it happens with other things too, especially, I think, with inanimate things that men depend on for their lives. Ships, for instance – they always have personalities of their own.

"And planes – in wars you always hear of planes crippled too badly to fly, but struggling back anyhow with their crews. Even guns acquire a sort of ego. Ships and guns and planes are 'she' to the men who operate them and depend on them for their lives. It's as if machinery with complicated moving parts almost simulates life, and does acquire from the men who used it – well, not exactly life, of course – but a personality. I don't know what. Maybe it absorbs some of the actual electrical impulses their brains throw off, especially in times of stress.

"Well, after a while I began to accept the idea that this new body of mine could behave at least as responsively as a ship or a plane. Quite apart from the fact that my own brain controls its 'muscles'. I believe there's an affinity between men and the machines they make. They make them out of their own brains, really, a sort of mental conception and gestation, and the result responds to the minds that created them, and to all human minds that understand and manipulate them."

She stirred uneasily and smoothed a flexible hand along her mesh-robed metal thigh. "So this is myself," she said. "Metal – but me. And it grows more and more myself the longer I live in it. It's my house and the machine my life depends on, but much more intimately in each case than any real house or machine ever was before to any other human. And you know, I wonder if in time I'll forget what flesh felt like – my own flesh, when I touched it like this – and the metal against the metal will be so much the same I'll never even notice?"

Harris did not try to answer her. He sat without moving, watching her expressionless face. In a moment she went on.

"I'll tell you the best thing, John," she said, her voice softening to the old intimacy he remembered so well that he could see superimposed upon the blank skull the warm, intent look that belonged with the voice. "I'm not going to live forever. It may not sound like a— best thing— but it is, John. You know, for a while that was the worst of all, after I knew I was— after I woke up again. The thought of living on and on in a body that wasn't mine, seeing everyone I knew grow old and die, and not being able to stop—

"But Maltzer says my brain will probably wear out quite normally – except, of course, that I won't have to worry about looking old! – and when it gets tired and stops, the body I'm in won't be any longer. The magnetic muscles that hold it into my own shape and motions will let go when the brain lets go, and there'll be nothing but a… a pile of disconnected rings. If they ever assemble it again, it won't be me." She hesitated. "I like that, John," she said, and he felt from behind the mask a searching of his face.

He knew and understood that somber satisfaction. He could not put it into words; neither of them wanted to do that. But he understood. It was the conviction of mortality, in spite of her immortal body. She was not cut off from the rest of her race in the essence of their humanity, for though she wore a body of steel and they perishable flesh, yet she must perish too, and the same fears and faiths still united her to mortals and humans, though she wore the body of Oberon's inhuman knight. Even in her death she must be unique – dissolution in a shower of tinkling and clashing rings, he thought, and almost envied her the finality and beauty of that particular death – but afterward, oneness with humanity in however much or little awaited them all. So she could feel that this exile in metal was only temporary, in spite of everything.

(And providing, of course, that the mind inside the metal did not veer from its inherited humanity as the years went by. A dweller in a house may impress his personality upon the walls, but subtly the walls too, may impress their own shape upon the ego of the man. Neither of them thought of that, at the time.)

Deirdre sat a moment longer in silence. Then the mood vanished and she rose again, spinning so that the robe belied out ringing about her ankles. She rippled another scale up and down, faultlessly and with the same familiar sweetness of tone that had made her famous.

"So I'm going right back on the stage, John," she said serenely. "I can still sing. I can still dance. I'm still myself in everything that matters, and I can't imagine doing anything else for the rest of my life."

He could not answer without stammering a little. "Do you think will they accept you, Deirdre? After all—"

"They'll accept me," she said in that confident voice. "Oh, they'll come to see a freak at first, of course, but they'll stay to watch— Deirdre. And come back again and again just as they always did. You'll see, my dear."

But hearing her sureness, suddenly Harris himself was unsure. Maltzer had not been, either. She was so regally confident, and disappointment would be so deadly a blow at all that remained of her— She was so delicate a being now, really. Nothing but a glowing and radiant mind poised in metal, dominating it, bending the steel to the illusion of her lost loveliness with a sheer self-confidence that gleamed through the metal body. But the brain sat delicately on its poise of reason. She had been through intolerable stresses already, perhaps more terrible depths of despair and self-knowledge than any human brain had yet endured before her, for – since Lazarus himself – who had come back from the dead?

But if the world did not accept her as beautiful, what then? If they laughed, or pitied her, or came only to watch a jointed freak performing as if on strings where the loveliness of Deirdre had once enchanted them, what then? And he could not be perfectly sure they would not. He had known her too well in the flesh to see her objectively even now, in metal. Every inflection of her voice called up the vivid memory of the face that had flashed its evanescent beauty in some look to match the tone. She was Deirdre to Harris simply because she had been so intimately familiar in every poise and attitude, through so many years. But people who knew her only slightly, or saw her for the first time in metal – what would they see?

A marionette? Or the real grace and loveliness shining through?

He had no possible way of knowing. He saw her too clearly as she had been to see her now at all, except so linked with the past that she was not wholly metal. And he knew what Maltzer feared, for Maltzer's psychic blindness toward her lay at the other extreme. He had never known Deirdre except as a machine, and he could not see her objectively any more than Harris could. To Maltzer she was pure metal, a robot his own hands and brain had devised, mysteriously animated by the mind of Deirdre, to be sure, but to all outward seeming a thing of metal solely. He had worked so long over each intricate part of her body, he knew so well how every jointure in it was put together, that he could not see the whole. He had studied many film records of her, of course, as she used to be, in order to gauge the accuracy of his facsimile, but this thing he had made was a copy only. He was too close to Deirdre to see her. And Harris, in a way, was too far. The indomitable Deirdre herself shone so vividly through the metal that his mind kept superimposing one upon the other.

How would an audience react to her? Where in the scale between these two extremes would their verdict fall?

For Deirdre, there was only one possible answer.

"I'm not worried," Deirdre said serenely, and spread her golden hands to the fire to watch lights dancing in reflection upon their shining surfaces. "I'm still myself. I've always had... well, power over my audiences. Any good performer knows when he's got it. Mine isn't gone. I can still give them what I always gave, only now with greater variations and more depths than I'd ever have done before. Why, look—" She gave a little wriggle of excitement.

"You know the arabesque principle – getting the longest possible distance from fingertip to toetip with a long, slow curve through the whole length? And the brace of the other leg and arm giving contrast? Well, look at me. I don't work on hinges now. I can make every motion a long curve if I want to. My body's different enough now to work out a whole new school of dancing. Of course there'll be things I used to do that I won't attempt now – no more dancing *sur les pointes*, for instance – but the new things will more than balance the loss. I've been practicing. Do you know I can turn a hundred fouettés now without a flaw? And I think I could go right on and turn a thousand, if I wanted."

She made the firelight flash on her hands, and her robe rang musically as she moved her shoulders a little. "I've already worked out one new dance for myself," she said. "God knows I'm no choreographer, but I did want to experiment first. Later, you know, really creative men like Massanchine or Fokhileff may want to do something entirely new for me – a whole new sequence of movements based on a new technique. And music – that could be quite different, too. Oh, there's no end to the possibilities! Even my voice has more range and power. Luckily I'm not an actress – it would be silly to try to play Camille or Juliet with a cast of ordinary people. Not that I couldn't, you know." She turned her head to stare at Harris through the mask of glass. "I honestly think I could. But it isn't necessary. There's too much else. Oh, I'm not worried!"

"Maltzer's worried," Harris reminded her.

She swung away from the fire, her metal robe ringing, and into her voice came the old note of distress that went with a furrowing of her forehead and a sidewise tilt of the head. The head went sidewise as it had always done, and he could see the furrowed brow almost as clearly as if flesh still clothed her.

"I know. And I'm worried about him, John. He's worked so awfully hard over me. This is the doldrums now, the let-down period, I suppose. I know what's on his mind. He's afraid I'll look just the same to the world as I look to him. Tooled metal. He's in a position no one ever quite achieved before, isn't he? Rather like God." Her voice rippled a little with amusement. "I suppose to God we must look like a collection of cells and corpuscles ourselves. But Maltzer lacks a god's detached viewpoint."

"He can't see you as I do, anyhow." Harris was choosing his words with difficulty. "I wonder, though – would it help him any if you postponed your debut awhile? You've been with him too closely, I think. You don't quite realize how near a breakdown he is. I was shocked when I saw him just now."

The golden head shook. "No. He's close to a breaking point, maybe, but I think the only cure's action. He wants me to retire and stay out of sight, John. Always. He's afraid for anyone to see me except a few old friends who remember me as I was. People he can trust to be—kind." She laughed. It was very strange to hear that ripple of mirth from the blank, unfeatured skull. Harris was seized with sudden panic at the thought of what reaction it might evoke in an audience of strangers. As if he had spoken the fear aloud, her voice denied it. "I don't need kindness. And it's no kindness to Maltzer to hide me under a bushel. He *has* worked too hard, I know. He's driven himself to a breaking point. But it'll be a complete negation of all he's worked for if I hide myself now. You don't know what a tremendous lot of geniuses and artistry went into me, John. The whole idea from the start was to recreate what I'd lost so that it could be proved that beauty and talent need not be sacrificed by the destruction of parts or all the body.

"It wasn't only for me that we meant to prove that. There'll be others who suffer injuries that once might have ruined them. This was to end all suffering like that forever. It was Maltzer's gift to the whole race as well as to me. He's really a humanitarian, John, like most great men. He'd never have given up a year of his life to this work if it had been for any one individual alone. He was seeing thousands of others beyond me as he worked. And I won't let him ruin all he's achieved because he's afraid to prove it now he's got it. The whole wonderful achievement will be worthless if I don't take the final step. I think his breakdown, in the end, would be worse and more final if I never tried than if I tried and failed."

Harris sat in silence. There was no answer he could make to that. He hoped the little twinge of shamefaced jealousy he suddenly felt did not show, as he was reminded anew of the intimacy closer than marriage which had of necessity bound these two together. And he knew that any reaction of his would in its way be almost as prejudiced as Maltzer's, for a reason at once the same and entirely opposite. Except that he himself came fresh to the problem, while Maltzer's viewpoint was colored by a year of overwork and physical and mental exhaustion.

"What are you going to do?" he asked.

She was standing before the fire when he spoke, swaying just a little so that highlights danced all along her golden body. Now she turned with a serpentine grace and sank into the cushioned chair beside her. It came to him suddenly that she was much more than humanly graceful – quite as much as he had once feared she would be less than human.

"I've already arranged for a performance," she told him, her voice a little shaken with a familiar mixture of excitement and defiance.

Harris sat up with a start. "How? Where? There hasn't been any publicity at all yet, has there? I didn't know—"

"Now, now, Johnnie," her amused voice soothed him. "You'll be handling everything just as usual once I get started back to work – that is, if you still want to. But this I've arranged for myself. It's going to be a surprise. I... I felt it had to be a surprise." She wriggled a little among the cushions. "Audience psychology is something I've always felt rather than known, and I do feel this is the way it ought to be done. There's no precedent. Nothing like this ever happened before. I'll have to go by my own intuition."

"You mean it's to be a complete surprise?"

"I think it must be. I don't want the audience coming in with preconceived ideas. I want them to see me exactly as I am now *first*, before they know who or what they're seeing. They must realize I can still give as good a performance as ever before they remember and compare it with my past performances. I don't want them to come ready to pity my handicaps – I haven't got any! – or full of morbid curiosity. So I'm going on the air after the regular eight-o'clock telecast of the feature from Teleo City. I'm just going to do one specialty in the usual vaude program. It's all been arranged. They'll build up to it, of course, as the highlight of the evening, but they aren't to say who I am until the end of the performance – if the audience hasn't recognized me already, by then."

"Audience?"

"Of course. Surely you haven't forgotten they still play to a theater audience at Teleo City? That's why I want to make my debut there. I've always played better when there were people in the studio, so I could gauge reactions. I think most performers do. Anyhow, it's all arranged."

"Does Maltzer know?"

She wriggled uncomfortably. "Not yet."

"But he'll have to give his permission too, won't he? I mean—"

"Now look, John! That's another idea you and Maltzer will have to get out of your minds. I don't belong to him. In a way he's just been my doctor through a long illness, but I'm free to discharge him whenever I choose. If there were ever any legal disagreement, I suppose he'd be entitled to quite a lot of money for the work he's done on my new body – for the body itself, really, since it's his own machine, in one sense. But he doesn't own it, or me. I'm not sure just how the question would be decided by the courts – there again, we've got a problem without precedent. The body may be his work, but the brain that makes it something more than a collection of metal rings is *me*, and he couldn't restrain me against my will even if he wanted to. Not legally, and not—" She hesitated oddly and looked away. For the first time Harris was aware of something beneath the surface of her mind which was quite strange to him.

"Well, anyhow," she went on, "that question won't come up. Maltzer and I have been much too close in the past year to clash over anything as essential as this. He knows in his heart that I'm right, and he won't try to restrain me. His work won't be completed until I do what I was built to do. And I intend to do it."

That strange little quiver of something – something un-Deirdre – which had so briefly trembled beneath the surface of familiarity stuck in Harris' mind as something he must recall and examine later. Now he said only, "All right. I suppose I agree with you. How soon are you going to do it?"

She turned her head so that even the glass mask through which she looked out at the world was foreshortened away from him, and the golden helmet with its hint of sculptured cheekbone was entirely enigmatic.

"Tonight," she said.

* * *

Maltzer's thin hand shook so badly that he could not turn the dial. He tried twice and then laughed nervously and shrugged at Harris.

"You get her," he said.

Harris glanced at his watch. "It isn't time yet. She won't be on for half an hour."

Maltzer made a gesture of violent impatience. "Get it, get it!"

Harris shrugged a little in turn and twisted the dial. On the tilted screen above them shadows and sound blurred together and then clarified into a somber medieval hall, vast, vaulted, people in bright costume moving like pygmies through its dimness. Since the play concerned Mary of Scotland, the actors were dressed in something approximating Elizabethan garb, but as every era tends to translate costume into terms of the current fashions, the women's hair was dressed in a style that would have startled Elizabeth, and their footgear was entirely anachronistic.

The hall dissolved and a face swam up into soft focus upon the screen. The dark, lush beauty of the actress who was playing the Stuart queen glowed at them in velvety perfection from the clouds of her pearl-strewn hair. Maltzer groaned.

"She's competing with *that*," he said hollowly.

"You think she can't?"

Maltzer slapped the chair arms with angry palms. Then the quivering of his fingers seemed suddenly to strike him, and he muttered to himself, "Look at 'em! I'm not even fit to handle a hammer and saw." But the mutter was an aside. "Of course she can't compete," he cried irritably. "She hasn't any sex. She isn't female any more. She doesn't know that yet, but she'll learn."

Harris stared at him, feeling a little stunned. Somehow the thought had not occurred to him before at all, so vividly had the illusion of the old Deirdre hung about the new one.

"She's an abstraction now," Maltzer went on, drumming his palms upon the chair in quick, nervous rhythms. "I don't know what it'll do to her, but there'll be change. Remember Abelard? She's lost everything that made her essentially what the public wanted, and she's going to find it out the hard way. After that—" He grimaced savagely and was silent.

"She hasn't lost everything," Harris defended. "She can dance and sing as well as ever, maybe better. She still has grace and charm and—"

"Yes, but where did the grace and charm come from? Not out of the habit patterns in her brain. No, out of human contacts, out of all the things that stimulate sensitive minds to creativeness. And she's lost three of her five senses. Everything she can't see and hear is gone. One of the strongest stimuli to a woman of her type was the knowledge of sex competition. You know how she sparkled when a man came into the room? All that's gone, and it was an essential. You know how liquor stimulated her? She's lost that. She couldn't taste food or drink even if she needed it. Perfume, flowers, all the odors we respond to mean nothing to her now. She can't feel anything with tactual delicacy any more. She used to surround herself with luxuries – she drew her stimuli from them – and that's all gone too. She's withdrawn from all physical contacts."

He squinted at the screen, not seeing it, his face drawn into lines like the lines of a skull. All flesh seemed to have dissolved off his bones in the past year, and Harris thought almost jealously that even in that way he seemed to be drawing nearer Deirdre in her fleshless-ness with every passing week.

"Sight," Maltzer said, "is the most highly civilized of the senses. It was the last to come. The other senses tie us in closely with the very roots of life; I think we perceive with them more keenly than we know. The things we realize through taste and smell and feeling stimulate directly, without a detour through the centers of conscious thought. You know how often a taste or odor will recall a memory to you so subtly you don't know exactly what caused it? We need those primitive senses to tie us in with nature and the race. Through those ties Deirdre drew her vitality without realizing it. Sight is a cold, intellectual thing compared with the other senses. But it's all she has to draw on now. She isn't a human being any more, and I think what humanity is left in her will drain out little by little and never be replaced. Abelard, in a way, was a prototype. But Deirdre's loss is complete."

"She isn't human," Harris agreed slowly. "But she isn't pure robot either. She's something somewhere between the two, and I think it's a mistake to try to guess just where, or what the outcome will be."

"I don't have to guess," Maltzer said in a grim voice. "I know. I wish I'd let her die. I've done something to her a thousand times worse than the fire ever could. I should have let her die in it."

"Wait," said Harris. "Wait and see. I think you're wrong."

* * *

On the television screen Mary of Scotland climbed the scaffold to her doom, the gown of traditional scarlet clinging warmly to supple young curves as anachronistic in their way as the slippers beneath the gown, for – as everyone but playwrights knows – Mary was well into middle age before she died. Gracefully this latter-day Mary bent her head, sweeping the long hair aside, kneeling to the block.

Maltzer watched stonily, seeing another woman entirely.

"I shouldn't have let her," he was muttering. "I shouldn't have let her do it."

"Do you really think you'd have stopped her if you could?" Harris asked quietly. And the other man after a moment's pause shook his head jerkily.

"No, I suppose not. I keep thinking if I worked and waited a little longer maybe I could make it easier for her, but – no, I suppose not. She's got to face them sooner or later, being herself." He stood up abruptly, shoving back his chair. "If she only weren't so… so frail. She doesn't realize how delicately poised her very sanity is. We gave her what we could – the artists and the designers and I, all gave our very best – but she's so pitifully handicapped even with all we could do. She'll always be an abstraction and a… a freak, cut off from the world by handicaps worse in their way than anything any human being ever suffered before. Sooner or later she'll realize it. And then—" He began to pace up and down with quick, uneven steps, striking his hands together. His face was twitching with a little tic that drew up one eye to a squint and released it again at irregular intervals. Harris could see how very near collapse the man was.

"Can you imagine what it's like?" Maltzer demanded fiercely. "Penned into a mechanical body like that, shut out from all human contacts except what leaks in by way of sight and sound? To know you aren't human any longer? She's been through shocks enough already. When that shock fully hits her—"

"Shut up," said Harris roughly. "You won't do her any good if you break down yourself. Look – the vaude's starting."

Great golden curtains had swept together over the unhappy Queen of Scotland and were parting again now, all sorrow and frustration wiped away once more as cleanly as the passing centuries had already expunged them. Now a line of tiny dancers under the tremendous arch of the stage kicked and pranced with the precision of little mechanical dolls too small and perfect to be real. Vision rushed down upon them and swept along the row, face after stiffly smiling face racketing by like fence pickets. Then the sight rose into the rafters and looked down upon them from a great height, the grotesquely foreshortened figures still prancing in perfect rhythm even from this inhuman angle.

There was applause from an invisible audience. Then someone came out and did a dance with lighted torches that streamed long, weaving ribbons of fire among clouds of what looked like cotton wool but was most probably asbestos. Then a company in gorgeous pseudo-period costumes postured its way through the new singing ballet form of dance, roughly following a plot which had been announced as *Les Sylphides*, but had little in common with it. Afterward the precision dancers came on again, solemn and charming as performing dolls.

Maltzer began to show signs of dangerous tension as act succeeded act. Deirdre's was to be the last, of course. It seemed very long indeed before a face in close-up blotted out the stage, and a master of ceremonies with features like an amiable marionette's announced a very special number as the finale. His voice was almost cracking with excitement – perhaps he, too, had not been told until a moment before what lay in store for the audience.

Neither of the listening men heard what it was he said, but both were conscious of a certain indefinable excitement rising among the audience, murmurs and rustlings and a mounting anticipation as if time had run backward here and knowledge of the great surprise had already broken upon them.

Then the golden curtains appeared again. They quivered and swept apart on long upward arcs, and between them the stage was full of a shimmering golden haze. It was, Harris realized in a moment, simply a series of gauze curtains, but the effect was one of strange and wonderful anticipation, as if something very splendid must be hidden in the haze. The world might have looked like this on the first morning of creation, before heaven and earth took form in the mind of God. It was a singularly fortunate choice of stage set in its symbolism, though Harris wondered how much necessity had figured in its selection, for there could not have been much time to prepare an elaborate set.

The audience sat perfectly silent, and the air was tense. This was no ordinary pause before an act. No one had been told, surely, and yet they seemed to guess –

The shimmering haze trembled and began to thin, veil by veil. Beyond was darkness, and what looked like a row of shining pillars set in a balustrade that began gradually to take shape as the haze drew back in shining folds. Now they could see that the balustrade curved up from left and right to the head of a sweep of stairs. Stage and stairs were carpeted in black velvet; black velvet draperies hung just ajar behind the balcony, with a glimpse of dark sky beyond them trembling with dim synthetic stars.

The last curtain of golden gauze withdrew. The stage was empty. Or it seemed empty. But even through the aerial distances between this screen and the place it mirrored, Harris thought that the audience was not waiting for the performer to come on from the wings. There was no rustling, no coughing, no sense of impatience. A presence upon the stage was in command from the first drawing of the curtains; it filled the theater with its calm domination. It gauged its timing, holding the audience as a conductor with lifted baton gathers and holds the eyes of his orchestra.

For a moment everything was motionless upon the stage. Then, at the head of the stairs, where the two curves of the pillared balustrade swept together, a figure stirred.

Until that moment she had seemed another shining column in the row. Now she swayed deliberately, light catching and winking and running molten along her limbs and her robe of metal mesh. She swayed just enough to show that she was there. Then, with every eye upon her, she stood quietly to let them look their fill. The screen did not swoop to a close-up upon her. Her enigma remained inviolate and the television watchers saw her no more clearly than the audience in the theater.

Many must have thought her at first some wonderfully animate robot, hung perhaps from wires invisible against the velvet, for certainly she was no woman dressed in metal – her proportions were too thin and fine for that. And perhaps the impression of robotism was what she meant to convey at first. She stood quiet, swaying just a little, a masked and inscrutable figure, faceless, very slender in her robe that hung in folds as pure as a Grecian chlamys, though she did not look Grecian at all. In the visored golden helmet and the robe of mail that odd likeness to knighthood was there again, with its implications of medieval richness behind the simple lines. Except that in her exquisite slimness she called to mind no human figure in armor, not even the comparative delicacy of a St. Joan. It was the chivalry and delicacy of some other world implicit in her outlines.

A breath of surprise had rippled over the audience when she moved. Now they were tensely silent again, waiting. And the tension, the anticipation, was far deeper than the surface importance of the scene could ever have evoked. Even those who thought her a manikin seemed to feel the forerunning of greater revelations.

Now she swayed and came slowly down the steps, moving with a suppleness just a little better than human. The swaying strengthened. By the time she reached the stage floor she was dancing. But it was no dance that any human creature could ever have performed. The long, slow, languorous rhythms of her body would have been impossible to a figure hinged at its joints as human figures hinge. (Harris remembered incredulously that he had feared once to find her jointed like a mechanical robot. But it was humanity that seemed, by contrast, jointed and mechanical now.)

The languor and the rhythm of her patterns looked impromptu, as all good dances should, but Harris knew what hours of composition and rehearsal must lie behind it, what laborious graving into her brain of strange new pathways, the first to replace the old ones and govern the mastery of metal limbs.

To and fro over the velvet carpet, against the velvet background, she wove the intricacies of her serpentine dance, leisurely and yet with such hypnotic effect that the air seemed full of looping rhythms, as if her long, tapering limbs had left their own replicas hanging upon the air and fading only slowly as she moved away. In her mind, Harris knew, the stage was a whole, a background to be filled in completely with the measured patterns of her dance, and she seemed almost to project that completed pattern to her audience so that they saw her everywhere at once, her golden rhythms fading upon the air long after she had gone.

Now there was music, looping and hanging in echoes after her like the shining festoons she wove with her body. But it was no orchestral music. She was humming, deep and sweet and wordlessly, as she glided her easy, intricate path about the stage. And the volume of the music was amazing. It seemed to fill the theater, and it was not amplified by hidden loudspeakers. You could tell that. Somehow, until you heard the music she made, you had never realized before the subtle distortions that amplification puts into music. This was utterly pure and true as perhaps no ear in all her audience had ever heard music before.

While she danced the audience did not seem to breathe. Perhaps they were beginning already to suspect who and what it was that moved before them without any fanfare of the publicity they had been half-expecting for weeks now. And yet, without the publicity, it was not easy to believe the dancer they watched was not some cunningly motivated manikin swinging on unseen wires about the stage.

Nothing she had done yet had been human. The dance was no dance a human being could have performed. The music she hummed came from a throat without vocal chords. But now the long, slow rhythms were drawing to their close, the pattern tightening in to a finale. And she ended as inhumanly as she had danced, willing them not to interrupt her with applause, dominating them now as she had always done. For her implication here was that a machine might have performed the dance, and a machine expects no applause. If they thought unseen operators had put her through those wonderful paces, they would wait for the operators to appear for their bows. But the audience was obedient. It sat silently, waiting for what came next. But its silence was tense and breathless.

The dance ended as it had begun. Slowly, almost carelessly, she swung up the velvet stairs, moving with rhythms as perfect as her music. But when she reached the head of the stairs she turned to face her audience, and for a moment stood motionless, like a creature of metal, without volition, the hands of the operator slack upon its strings.

Then, startlingly, she laughed.

It was lovely laughter, low and sweet and full-throated. She threw her head back and let her body sway and her shoulders shake, and the laughter, like the music, filled the theater, gaining volume from the great hollow of the roof and sounding in the ears of every listener, not loud, but as intimately as if each sat alone with the woman who laughed.

And she was a woman now. Humanity had dropped over her like a tangible garment. No one who had ever heard that laughter before could mistake it here. But before the reality of who she was had quite time to dawn upon her listeners she let the laughter deepen into music, as no human voice could have done. She was humming a familiar refrain close in the ear of every hearer. And the humming in turn swung into words. She sang in her clear, light, lovely voice:

"The yellow rose of Eden, is blooming in my heart—"

It was Deirdre's song. She had sung it first upon the airways a month before the theater fire that had consumed her. It was a commonplace little melody, simple enough to take first place in the fancy of a nation that had always liked its songs simple. But it had a certain sincerity too, and no taint of the vulgarity of tune and rhythm that foredooms so many popular songs to oblivion after their novelty fades.

No one else was ever able to sing it quite as Deirdre did. It had been identified with her so closely that though for a while after her accident singers tried to make it a memorial for her, they failed so conspicuously to give it her unmistakable flair that the song died from their sheer inability to sing it. No one ever hummed the tune without thinking of her and the pleasant, nostalgic sadness of something lovely and lost.

But it was not a sad song now. If anyone had doubted whose brain and ego motivated this shining metal suppleness, they could doubt no longer. For the voice was Deirdre, and the song. And the lovely, poised grace of her mannerisms that made up recognition as certainly as sight of a familiar face.

She had not finished the first line of her song before the audience knew her.

And they did not let her finish. The accolade of their interruption was a tribute more eloquent than polite waiting could ever have been. First a breath of incredulity rippled over the theater, and a long, sighing gasp that reminded Harris irrelevantly as he listened to the gasp which still goes up from matinee audiences at the first glimpse of the fabulous Valentino, so many generations dead. But this gasp did not sigh itself away and vanish. Tremendous tension lay behind it, and the rising tide of excitement rippled up in little murmurs and spatterings of applause that ran together into one overwhelming roar. It shook the theater. The television screen trembled and blurred a little to the volume of that transmitted applause.

Silenced before it, Deirdre stood gesturing on the stage, bowing and bowing as the noise rolled up about her, shaking perceptibly with the triumph of her own emotion.

Harris had an intolerable feeling that she was smiling radiantly and that the tears were pouring down her cheeks. He even thought, just as Maltzer leaned forward to switch off the screen, that she was blowing kisses over the audience in the time-honored gesture of the grateful actress, her golden arms shining as she scattered kisses abroad from the featureless helmet, the face that had no mouth.

* * *

"Well?" Harris said, not without triumph.

Maltzer shook his head jerkily, the glasses unsteady on his nose so that the blurred eyes behind them seemed to shift.

"Of course they applauded, you fool," he said in a savage voice. "I might have known they would under this set-up. It doesn't prove anything. Oh, she was smart to surprise them – I admit that. But they were applauding themselves as much as her. Excitement, gratitude for letting them in on a historic performance, mass hysteria – *you* know. It's from now on the test will come, and this hasn't helped any to prepare her for it. Morbid curiosity when the news gets out – people laughing when she forgets she isn't human. And they will, you know. There are always those who will. And the novelty wearing off. The slow draining away of humanity for lack of contact with any human stimuli any more—"

Harris remembered suddenly and reluctantly the moment that afternoon which he had shunted aside mentally, to consider later. The sense of something unfamiliar beneath the surface of Deirdre's speech. Was Maltzer right? Was the drainage already at work? Or was there something deeper than this obvious answer to the question? Certainly she had been through experiences too terrible for ordinary people to comprehend. Scars might still remain. Or, with her body, had she put on a strange, metallic something of the mind, that spoke to no sense which human minds could answer?

For a few minutes neither of them spoke. Then Maltzer rose abruptly and stood looking down at Harris with an abstract scowl.

"I wish you'd go now," he said.

Harris glanced up at him, startled. Maltzer began to pace again, his steps quick and uneven. Over his shoulder he said, "I've made up my mind, Harris. I've got to put a stop to this."

Harris rose. "Listen," he said. "Tell me one thing. What makes you so certain you're right? Can you deny that most of it's speculation – hearsay evidence? Remember, I talked to Deirdre, and she was just as sure as you are in the opposite direction. Have you any real reason for what you think?"

Maltzer took his glasses off and rubbed his nose carefully, taking a long time about it. He seemed reluctant to answer. But when he did, at last, there was a confidence in his voice Harris had not expected.

"I have a reason," he said. "But you won't believe it. Nobody would."

"Try me."

Maltzer shook his head. "Nobody *could* believe it. No two people were ever in quite the same relationship before as Deirdre and I have been. I helped her come back out of complete— oblivion. I knew her before she had voice or hearing. She was only a frantic mind when I first made contact with her, half insane with all that had happened and fear of what would happen next. In a very literal sense she was reborn out of that condition, and I had to guide her through every step of the way. I came to know her thoughts before she thought them. And once you've been that close to another mind, you don't lose the contact easily." He put the glasses back on and looked blurrily at Harris through the heavy lenses. "Deirdre is worried," he said. "I know it. You won't believe me, but I can – well, sense it. I tell you, I've been too close to her very mind itself to make any mistake. You don't see it, maybe. Maybe even she doesn't know it yet. But the worry's there. When I'm with her, I feel it. And I don't want it to come any nearer the surface of her mind than it's come already. I'm going to put a stop to this before it's too late."

Harris had no comment for that. It was too entirely outside his own experience. He said nothing for a moment. Then he asked simply, "How?"

"I'm not sure yet. I've got to decide before she comes back. And I want to see her alone."

"I think you're wrong," Harris told him quietly. "I think you're imagining things. I don't think you *can* stop her."

Maltzer gave him a slanted glance. "I can stop her," he said, in a curious voice. He went on quickly, "She has enough already – she's nearly human. She can live normally as other people live, without going back on the screen. Maybe this taste of it will be enough. I've got to convince her it is. If she retires now, she'll never guess how cruel her own audiences could be, and maybe that deep sense – of distress, uneasiness, whatever it is – won't come to the surface. It mustn't. She's too fragile to stand that." He slapped his hands together sharply. "I've got to stop her. For her own sake I've got to do it!" He swung round again to face Harris. "Will you go now?"

Never in his life had Harris wanted less to leave a place. Briefly he thought of saying simply, "No I won't." But he had to admit in his own mind that Maltzer was at least partly right. This was a matter between Deirdre and her creator, the culmination, perhaps, of that year's long intimacy so like marriage that this final trial for supremacy was a need he recognized.

He would not, he thought, forbid the showdown if he could. Perhaps the whole year had been building up to this one moment between them in which one or the other must prove himself victor. Neither was very well stable just now, after the long strain of the year past. It might very well be that the mental salvation of one or both hinged upon the outcome of the clash. But because each was so strongly motivated not by selfish concern but by solicitude for the other in this strange combat, Harris knew he must leave them to settle the thing alone.

He was in the street and hailing a taxi before the full significance of something Maltzer had said came to him. "*I can stop her*," he had declared, with an odd inflection in his voice.

Suddenly Harris felt cold. Maltzer had made her – of course he could stop her if he chose. Was there some key in that supple golden body that could immobilize it at its maker's will? Could she be imprisoned in the cage of her own body? No body before in all history, he thought, could have been designed more truly to be a prison for its mind than Deirdre's, if Maltzer chose to turn the key that locked her in. There must be many ways to do it. He could simply withhold whatever source of nourishment kept her brain alive, if that were the way he chose.

But Harris could not believe he would do it. The man wasn't insane.

He would not defeat his own purpose. His determination rose from his solicitude for Deirdre; he would not even in the last extremity try to save her by imprisoning her in the jail of her own skull.

For a moment Harris hesitated on the curb, almost turning back. But what could he do? Even granting that Maltzer would resort to such tactics, self-defeating in their very nature, how could any man on earth prevent him if he did it subtly enough? But he never would. Harris knew he never would. He got into his cab slowly, frowning. He would see them both tomorrow.

* * *

He did not. Harris was swamped with excited calls about yesterday's performance, but the message he was awaiting did not come. The day went by very slowly. Toward evening he surrendered and called Maltzer's apartment.

It was Deirdre's face that answered, and for once he saw no remembered features superimposed upon the blankness of her helmet. Masked and faceless, she looked at him inscrutably.

"Is everything all right?" he asked, a little uncomfortable.

"Yes, of course," she said, and her voice was a bit metallic for the first time, as if she were thinking so deeply of some other matter that she did not trouble to pitch it properly. "I had a long talk with Maltzer last night, if that's what you mean. You know what he wants. But nothing's been decided yet."

Harris felt oddly rebuffed by the sudden realization of the metal of her. It was impossible to read anything from face or voice. Each had its mask.

"What are you going to do?" he asked.

"Exactly as I'd planned," she told him, without inflection.

Harris floundered a little. Then, with an effort at practicality, he said, "Do you want me to go to work on bookings, then?"

She shook the delicately modeled skull. "Not yet. You saw the reviews today, of course. They— *did* like me." It was an understatement, and for the first time a note of warmth sounded in her voice. But the preoccupation was still there, too. "I'd already planned to make them wait awhile after my first performance," she went on. "A couple of weeks, anyhow. You remember that little farm of mine in Jersey, John? I'm going over today. I won't see anyone except the servants there. Not even Maltzer. Not even you. I've got a lot to think about. Maltzer has agreed to let everything go until we've both thought things over. He's taking a rest, too. I'll see you the moment I get back, John. Is that all right?"

She blanked out almost before he had time to nod and while the beginning of a stammered argument was still on his lips. He sat there staring at the screen.

The two weeks that went by before Maltzer called him again were the longest Harris had ever spent. He thought of many things in the interval. He believed he could sense in that last talk with Deirdre something of the inner unrest that Maltzer had spoken of – more an abstraction than a distress, but some thought had occupied her mind which she would not – or was it that she could not? – share even with her closest confidants. He even wondered whether, if her mind was as delicately poised as Maltzer feared, one would ever know whether or not it had slipped. There was so little evidence one way or the other in the unchanging outward form of her.

Most of all he wondered what two weeks in a new environment would do to her untried body and newly patterned brain. If Maltzer were right, then there might be some perceptible— drainage— by the time they met again. He tried not to think of that.

Maltzer televised him on the morning set for her return. He looked very bad. The rest must have been no rest at all. His face was almost a skull now, and the blurred eyes behind their lenses burned. But he seemed curiously at peace, in spite of his appearance. Harris thought he had reached some decision, but whatever it was had not stopped his hands from shaking or the nervous tic that drew his face sidewise into a grimace at intervals.

"Come over," he said briefly, without preamble. "She'll be here in half an hour." And he blanked out without waiting for an answer.

When Harris arrived, he was standing by the window looking down and steadying his trembling hands on the sill.

"I can't stop her," he said in a monotone, and again without preamble. Harris had the impression that for the two weeks his thoughts must have run over and over the same track, until any spoken word was simply a vocal interlude in the circling of his mind. "I couldn't do it. I even tried threats, but she knew I didn't mean them. There's only one way out, Harris." He glanced up briefly, hollow-eyed behind the lenses. "Never mind. I'll tell you later."

"Did you explain everything to her that you did to me?"

"Nearly all. I even taxed her with that… that sense of distress I *know* she feels. She denied it. She was lying. We both knew. It was worse after the performance than before. When I saw her that night, I tell you I *knew* – she senses something wrong, but she won't admit it." He shrugged. "Well—"

Faintly in the silence they heard the humming of the elevator descending from the helicopter platform on the roof. Both men turned to the door.

She had not changed at all. Foolishly, Harris was a little surprised. Then he caught himself and remembered that she would never change – never, until she died. He himself might grow white-haired and senile; she would move before him then as she moved now, supple, golden, enigmatic.

Still, he thought she caught her breath a little when she saw Maltzer and the depths of his swift degeneration. She had no breath to catch, but her voice was shaken as she greeted them.

"I'm glad you're both here," she said, a slight hesitation in her speech. "It's a wonderful day outside. Jersey was glorious. I'd forgotten how lovely it is in summer. Was the sanitarium any good, Maltzer?"

He jerked his head irritably and did not answer. She went on talking in a light voice, skimming the surface, saying nothing important.

This time Harris saw her as he supposed her audiences would, eventually, when the surprise had worn off and the image of the living Deirdre faded from memory. She was all metal now, the Deirdre they would know from today on. And she was not less lovely. She was not even less human – yet. Her motion was a miracle of flexible grace, a pouring of suppleness along every limb. (From now on, Harris realized suddenly, it was her body and not her face that would have mobility to express emotion; she must act with her limbs and her lithe, robed torso.)

But there was something wrong. Harris sensed it almost tangibly in her inflections, her elusiveness, the way she fenced with words. This was what Maltzer had meant, this was what Harris himself had felt just before she left for the country. Only now it was strong – certain.

Between them and the old Deirdre whose voice still spoke to them a veil – of detachment – had been drawn. Behind it she was in distress. Somehow, somewhere, she had made some discovery that affected her profoundly. And Harris was terribly afraid that he knew what the discovery must be. Maltzer was right.

He was still leaning against the window, staring out unseeingly over the vast panorama of New York, webbed with traffic bridges, winking with sunlit glass, its vertiginous distances plunging downward into the blue shadows of Earth-level. He said now, breaking into the light-voiced chatter, "Are you all right, Deirdre?"

She laughed. It was lovely laughter. She moved lithely across the room, sunlight glinting on her musical mailed robe, and stooped to a cigarette box on a table. Her fingers were deft.

"Have one?" she said, and carried the box to Maltzer. He let her put the brown cylinder between his lips and hold a light to it, but he did not seem to be noticing what he did. She replaced the box and then crossed to a mirror on the far wall and began experimenting with a series of gliding ripples that wove patterns of pale gold in the glass. "Of course I'm all right," she said.

"You're lying."

Deirdre did not turn. She was watching him in the mirror, but the ripple of her motion went on slowly, languorously, undisturbed.

"No," she told them both.

Maltzer drew deeply on his cigarette. Then with a hard pull he unsealed the window and tossed the smoking stub far out over the gulfs below. He said, "You can't deceive me, Deirdre." His voice, suddenly, was quite calm. "I created you, my dear. I know. I've sensed that uneasiness in you growing and growing for a long while now. It's much stronger today than it was two weeks ago. Something happened to you in the country. I don't know what it was, but you've changed. Will you admit to yourself what it is, Deirdre? Have you realized yet that you must not go back on the screen?"

"Why, no," said Deirdre, still not looking at him except obliquely, in the glass. Her gestures were slower now, weaving lazy patterns in the air. "No, I haven't changed my mind."

She was all metal – outwardly. She was taking unfair advantage of her own metal-hood. She had withdrawn far within, behind the mask of her voice and her facelessness. Even her body, whose involuntary motions might have betrayed what she was feeling, in the only way she could be subject to betrayal now, she was putting through ritual motions that disguised it completely. As long as these looping, weaving patterns occupied her, no one had any way of guessing even from her motion what went on in the hidden brain inside her helmet.

Harris was struck suddenly and for the first time with the completeness of her withdrawal. When he had seen her last in this apartment she had been wholly Deirdre, not masked at all, overflowing the metal with the warmth and ardor of the woman he had known so well. Since then – since the performance on the stage – he had not seen the familiar Deirdre again. Passionately he wondered why. Had she begun to suspect even in her moment of triumph what a fickle master an audience could be? Had she caught, perhaps, the sound of whispers and laughter among some small portion of her watchers, though the great majority praised her?

Or was Maltzer right? Perhaps Harris' first interview with her had been the last bright burning of the lost Deirdre, animated by excitement and the pleasure of meeting after so long a time, animation summoned up in a last strong effort to convince him. Now she was gone, but whether in self-protection against the possible cruelties of human beings, or whether in withdrawal to metal-hood, he could not guess. Humanity might be draining out of her fast, and the brassy taint of metal permeating the brain it housed.

Maltzer laid his trembling hand on the edge of the opened window and looked out. He said in a deepened voice, the querulous note gone for the first time:

"I've made a terrible mistake, Deirdre. I've done you irreparable harm." He paused a moment, but Deirdre said nothing. Harris dared not speak. In a moment Maltzer went on. "I've made you vulnerable, and given you no weapons to fight your enemies with. And the human race is your enemy, my dear, whether you admit it now or later. I think you know that. I think it's why you're so silent. I think you must have suspected it on the stage two weeks ago, and verified it in Jersey while you were gone. They're going to hate you, after a while, because you are still beautiful, and they're going to persecute you because you are different – and helpless. Once the novelty wears off, my dear, your audience will be simply a mob."

He was not looking at her. He had bent forward a little, looking out the window and down. His hair stirred in the wind that blew very strongly up this high, and whined thinly around the open edge of the glass.

"I meant what I did for you," he said, "to be for everyone who meets with accidents that might have ruined them. I should have known my gift would mean worse ruin than any mutilation could be. I know now that there's only one legitimate way a human being can create life. When he tries another way, as I did, he has a lesson to learn. Remember the lesson of the student Frankenstein? He learned, too. In a way, he was lucky – the way he learned. He didn't have to watch what happened afterward. Maybe he wouldn't have had the courage – I know I haven't."

Harris found himself standing without remembering that he rose. He knew suddenly what was about to happen. He understood Maltzer's air of resolution, his new, unnatural calm. He knew, even, why Maltzer had asked him here today, so that Deirdre might not be left alone. For he remembered that Frankenstein, too, had paid with his life for the unlawful creation of life.

Maltzer was leaning head and shoulders from the window now, looking down with almost hypnotized fascination. His voice came back to them remotely in the breeze, as if a barrier already lay between them.

Deirdre had not moved. Her expressionless mask, in the mirror, watched him calmly. She *must* have understood. Yet she gave no sign, except that the weaving of her arms had almost stopped now, she moved so slowly. Like a dance seen in a nightmare, under water.

It was impossible, of course, for her to express any emotion. The fact that her face showed none now should not, in fairness, be held against her. But she watched so wholly without feeling— Neither of them moved toward the window. A false step, now, might send him over. They were quiet, listening to his voice.

"We who bring life into the world unlawfully," said Maltzer, almost thoughtfully, "must make room for it by withdrawing our own. That seems to be an inflexible rule. It works automatically. The thing we create makes living unbearable. No, it's nothing you can help, my dear. I've asked you to do something I created you incapable of doing. I made you to perform a function, and I've been asking you to forego the one thing you were made to do. I believe that if you do it, it will destroy you, but the whole guilt is mine, not yours. I'm not even asking you to give up the screen, any more. I know you can't, and live. But I can't live and watch you. I put all my skill and all my love in one final masterpiece, and I can't bear to watch it destroyed. I can't live and watch you do only what I made you to do, and ruin yourself because you must do it.

"But before I go, I have to make sure you understand." He leaned a little farther, looking down, and his voice grew more remote as the glass came between them. He was saying almost unbearable things now, but very distantly, in a cool, passionless tone filtered through wind and glass, and with the distant humming of the city mingled with it, so that the words were curiously robbed of poignancy. "I can be a coward," he said, "and escape the consequences of what I've done, but I can't go and leave you— not understanding. It would be even worse than the thought of your failure, to think of you bewildered and confused when the mob turns on you. What I'm telling you, my dear, won't be any real news – I think you sense it already, though you may not admit it to yourself. We've been too close to lie to each other, Deirdre – I know when you aren't telling the truth. I know the distress that's been growing in your mind. You are not wholly human, my dear. I think you know that. In so many ways, in spite of all I could do, you must always be less than human. You've lost the senses of perception that kept you in touch with humanity. Sight and hearing are all that remain, and sight, as I've said before, was the last and coldest of the senses to develop. And you're so delicately poised on a sort of thin edge of reason. You're only a clear, glowing mind animating a metal body, like a candle flame in a glass. And as precariously vulnerable to the wind."

He paused. "Try not to let them ruin you completely," he said after a while. "When they turn against you, when they find out you're more helpless than they – I wish I could have made you stronger, Deirdre. But I couldn't. I had too much skill for your good and mine, but not quite enough skill for that."

He was silent again, briefly, looking down. He was balanced precariously now, more than halfway over the sill and supported only by one hand on the glass. Harris watched with an agonized uncertainty, not sure whether a sudden leap might catch him in time or send him over. Deirdre was still weaving her golden patterns, slowly and unchangingly, watching the mirror and its reflection, her face and masked eyes enigmatic.

"I wish one thing, though," Maltzer said in his remote voice. "I wish – before I finish – that you'd tell me the truth, Deirdre. I'd be happier if I were sure I'd— reached you. Do you understand what I've said? Do you believe me? Because if you don't, then I know you're lost beyond all hope. If you'll admit your own doubt – and I know you do doubt – I can think there may be a chance for you after all. Were you lying to me, Deirdre? Do you know how... how wrong I've made you?"

There was silence. Then very softly, a breath of sound, Deirdre answered. The voice seemed to hang in midair, because she had no lips to move and localize it for the imagination.

"Will you listen, Maltzer?" she asked.

"I'll wait," he said. "Go on. Yes or no?"

Slowly she let her arms drop to her sides. Very smoothly and quietly she turned from the mirror and faced him. She swayed a little, making her metal robe ring.

"I'll answer you," she said. "But I don't think I'll answer that. Not with yes or no, anyhow. I'm going to walk a little, Maltzer. I have something to tell you, and I can't talk standing still. Will you let me move about without— going over?"

He nodded distantly. "You can't interfere from that distance," he said. "But keep the distance. What do you want to say?"

She began to pace a little way up and down her end of the room, moving with liquid ease. The table with the cigarette box was in her way, and she pushed it aside carefully, watching Maltzer and making no swift motions to startle him.

"I'm not – well, sub-human," she said, a faint note of indignation in her voice. "I'll prove it in a minute, but I want to say something else first. You must promise to wait and listen. There's a flaw in your argument, and I resent it. I'm not a Frankenstein monster made out of dead flesh. I'm myself – alive. You didn't create my life, you only preserved it. I'm not a robot, with compulsions built into me that I have to obey. I'm free-willed and independent, and, Maltzer – I'm human."

Harris had relaxed a little. She knew what she was doing. He had no idea what she planned, but he was willing to wait now. She was not the indifferent automaton he had thought. He watched her come to the table again in a lap of her pacing, and stoop over it, her eyeless mask turned to Maltzer to make sure variation of her movement did not startle him.

"I'm human," she repeated, her voice humming faintly and very sweetly. "Do you think I'm not?" she asked, straightening and facing them both. And then suddenly, almost overwhelmingly, the warmth and the old ardent charm were radiant all around her. She was robot no longer, enigmatic no longer. Harris could see as clearly as in their first meeting the remembered flesh still gracious and beautiful as her voice evoked his memory. She stood swaying a little, as she had always swayed, her head on one side, and she was chuckling at them both. It was such a soft and lovely sound, so warmly familiar.

"Of course I'm myself," she told them, and as the words sounded in their ears neither of them could doubt it. There was hypnosis in her voice. She turned away and began to pace again, and so powerful was the human personality which she had called up about her that it beat out at them in deep pulses, as if her body were a furnace to send out those comforting waves of warmth. "I have handicaps, I know," she said. "But my audiences will never know. I won't let them know. I think you'll believe me, both of you, when I say I could play Juliet just as I am now, with a cast of ordinary people, and make the world accept it. Do you think I could, John? Maltzer, don't you believe I could?"

She paused at the far end of her pacing path and turned to face them, and they both stared at her without speaking. To Harris she was the Deirdre he had always known, pale gold, exquisitely graceful in remembered postures, the inner radiance of her shining through metal as brilliantly as it had ever shone through flesh. He did not wonder, now, if it were real. Later he would think again that it might be only a disguise, something like a garment she had put off with her lost body, to wear again only when she chose. Now the spell of her compelling charm was too strong for wonder. He watched, convinced for the moment that she was all she seemed to be. She could play Juliet if she said she could. She could sway a whole audience as easily as she swayed himself. Indeed, there was something about her just now more convincingly human than anything he had noticed before. He realized that in a split second of awareness before he saw what it was.

She was looking at Maltzer. He, too, watched, spellbound in spite of himself, not dissenting. She glanced from one to the other. Then she put back her head and laughter came welling and choking from her in a great, full-throated tide. She shook in the strength of it. Harris could almost see her round throat pulsing with the sweet low-pitched waves of laughter that were shaking her. Honest mirth, with a little derision in it.

Then she lifted one arm and tossed her cigarette into the empty fireplace.

Harris choked, and his mind went blank for one moment of blind denial. He had not sat here watching a robot smoke and accepting it as normal. He could not! And yet he had. That had been the final touch of conviction which swayed his hypnotized mind into accepting her humanity. And she had done it so deftly, so naturally, wearing her radiant humanity with such rightness, that his watching mind had not even questioned what she did.

He glanced at Maltzer. The man was still halfway over the window ledge, but through the opening of the window he, too, was staring in stupefied disbelief and Harris knew they had shared the same delusion.

Deirdre was still shaking a little with laughter. "Well," she demanded, the rich chuckling making her voice quiver, "am I all robot, after all?"

Harris opened his mouth to speak, but he did not utter a word. This was not his show. The byplay lay wholly between Deirdre and Maltzer; he must not interfere. He turned his head to the window and waited.

And Maltzer for a moment seemed shaken in his conviction.

"You… you *are* an actress," he admitted slowly. "But I… I'm not convinced I'm wrong. I think—" He paused. The querulous note was in his voice again, and he seemed racked once more by the old doubts and dismay. Then Harris saw him stiffen. He saw the resolution come back, and understood why it had come. Maltzer had gone too far already upon the cold and lonely path he had chosen to turn back, even for stronger evidence than this. He had reached his conclusions only after mental turmoil too terrible to face again. Safety and peace lay in the course he had steeled himself to follow. He was too tired, too exhausted by months of conflict, to retrace his path and begin all over. Harris could see him groping for a way out, and in a moment he saw him find it.

"That was a trick," he said hollowly. "Maybe you could play it on a larger audience, too. Maybe you have more tricks to use. I might be wrong. But Deirdre" – his voice grew urgent – "you haven't answered the one thing I've got to know. You can't answer it. You *do* feel – dismay. You've learned your own inadequacy, however well you can hide it from us – even from us. I *know*. Can you deny that, Deirdre?"

She was not laughing now. She let her arms fall, and the flexible golden body seemed to droop a little all over, as if the brain that a moment before had been sending out strong, sure waves of confidence had slackened its power, and the intangible muscles of her limbs slackened with it. Some of the glowing humanity began to fade. It receded within her and was gone, as if the fire in the furnace of her body were sinking and cooling.

"Maltzer," she said uncertainly, "I can't answer that – yet. I can't—"

And then, while they waited in anxiety for her to finish the sentence, she *blazed*. She ceased to be a figure in stasis – she *blazed*.

It was something no eyes could watch and translate into terms the brain could follow; her motion was too swift. Maltzer in the window was a whole long room-length away. He had thought himself safe at such a distance, knowing no normal human being could reach him before he moved. But Deirdre was neither normal nor human.

In the same instant she stood drooping by the mirror she was simultaneously at Maltzer's side. Her motion negated time and destroyed space. And as a glowing cigarette tip in the dark describes closed circles before the eye when the holder moves it swiftly, so Deirdre blazed in one continuous flash of golden motion across the room.

But curiously, she was not blurred. Harris, watching, felt his mind go blank again, but less in surprise than because no normal eyes and brain could perceive what it was he looked at.

(In that moment of intolerable suspense his complex human brain paused suddenly, annihilating time in its own way, and withdrew to a cool corner of its own to analyze in a flashing second what it was he had just seen. The brain could do it timelessly; words are slow. But he knew he had watched a sort of tesseract of human motion, a parable of fourth-dimensional activity. A one-dimensional point, moved through space, creates a two-dimensional line, which in motion creates a three-dimensional cube. Theoretically the cube, in motion, would produce a fourth-dimensional figure. No human creature had ever seen a figure of three dimensions moved through space and time before – until this moment. She had not blurred; every motion she made was distinct, but not like moving figures on a strip of film. Not like anything that those who use our language had ever seen before, or created words to express. The mind saw, but without perceiving. Neither words nor thoughts could resolve what happened into terms for human brains. And perhaps she had not actually and literally moved through the fourth dimension. Perhaps – since Harris was able to see her – it had been almost and not quite that unimaginable thing. But it was close enough.)

While to the slow mind's eye she was still standing at the far end of the room, she was already at Maltzer's side, her long, flexible fingers gentle but very firm upon his arms. She waited— The room shimmered. There was sudden violent heat beating upon Harris' face. Then the air steadied again and Deirdre was saying softly, in a mournful whisper:

"I'm sorry – I had to do it. I'm sorry – I didn't mean you to know—"

Time caught up with Harris. He saw it overtake Maltzer too, saw the man jerk convulsively away from the grasping hands, in a ludicrously futile effort to forestall what had already happened. Even thought was slow, compared with Deirdre's swiftness.

The sharp outward jerk was strong. It was strong enough to break the grasp of human hands and catapult Maltzer out and down into the swimming gulfs of New York. The mind leaped ahead to a logical conclusion and saw him twisting and turning and diminishing with dreadful rapidity to a tiny point of darkness that dropped away through sunlight toward the shadows near the earth. The mind even conjured up a shrill, thin cry that plummeted away with the falling body and hung behind it in the shaken air.

But the mind was reckoning on human factors.

Very gently and smoothly Deirdre lifted Maltzer from the windowsill and with effortless ease carried him well back into the safety of the room. She set him down before a sofa and her golden fingers unwrapped themselves from his arms slowly, so that he could regain control of his own body before she released him.

He sank to the sofa without a word. Nobody spoke for an unmeasurable length of time. Harris could not. Deirdre waited patiently. It was Maltzer who regained speech first, and it came back on the old track, as if his mind had not yet relinquished the rut it had worn so deep.

"All right," he said breathlessly. "All right, you can stop me this time. But I know, you see. I know! You can't hide your feeling from me, Deirdre. I know the trouble you feel. And next time – next time I won't wait to talk!"

Deirdre made the sound of a sigh. She had no lungs to expel the breath she was imitating, but it was hard to realize that. It was hard to understand why she was not panting heavily from the terrible exertion of the past minutes; the mind knew why, but could not accept the reason. She was still too human.

"You still don't see," she said. "Think, Maltzer, think!"

There was a hassock beside the sofa. She sank upon it gracefully, clasping her robed knees. Her head tilted back to watch Maltzer's face. She saw only stunned stupidity on it now; he had passed through too much emotional storm to think at all.

"All right," she told him. "Listen – I'll admit it. You're right. I am unhappy. I do know what you said was true – but not for the reason you think. Humanity and I are far apart, and drawing farther. The gap will be hard to bridge. Do you hear me, Maltzer?"

Harris saw the tremendous effort that went into Maltzer's wakening. He saw the man pull his mind back into focus and sit up on the sofa with weary stiffness.

"You… you do admit it, then?" he asked in a bewildered voice. Deirdre shook her head sharply.

"Do you still think of me as delicate?" she demanded. "Do you know I carried you here at arm's length halfway across the room? Do you realize you weigh *nothing* to me? I could" – she glanced around the room and gestured with sudden, rather appalling violence – "tear this building down," she said quietly. "I could tear my way through these walls, I think. I've found no limit yet to the strength I can put forth if I try." She held up her golden hands and looked at them. "The metal would break, perhaps," she said reflectively, "but then, I have no feeling—"

Maltzer gasped, "*Deirdre*—"

She looked up with what must have been a smile. It sounded clearly in her voice. "Oh, I won't. I wouldn't have to do it with my hands, if I wanted. Look – listen!"

She put her head back and a deep, vibrating hum gathered and grew in what one still thought of as her throat. It deepened swiftly and the ears began to ring. It was deeper, and the furniture vibrated. The walls began almost imperceptibly to shake. The room was full and bursting with a sound that shook every atom upon its neighbor with a terrible, disrupting force.

The sound ceased. The humming died. Then Deirdre laughed and made another and quite differently pitched sound. It seemed to reach out like an arm in one straight direction – toward the window. The opened panel shook. Deirdre intensified her hum, and slowly, with imperceptible jolts that merged into smoothness, the window jarred itself shut.

"You see?" Deirdre said. "You see?"

But still Maltzer could only stare. Harris was staring too, his mind beginning slowly to accept what she implied. Both were too stunned to leap ahead to any conclusions yet.

Deirdre rose impatiently and began to pace again, in a ringing of metal robe and a twinkling of reflected lights. She was pantherlike in her suppleness. They could see the power behind that lithe motion now; they no longer thought of her as helpless, but they were far still from grasping the truth.

"You were wrong about me, Maltzer," she said with an effort at patience in her voice. "But you were right too, in a way you didn't guess. I'm not afraid of humanity. I haven't anything to fear from them. Why" – her voice took on a tinge of contempt – "already I've set a fashion in women's clothing. By next week you won't see a woman on the street without a mask like mine, and every dress that isn't cut like a chlamys will be out of style. I'm not afraid of humanity! I won't lose touch with them unless I want to. I've learned a lot – I've learned too much already."

Her voice faded for a moment, and Harris had a quick and appalling vision of her experimenting in the solitude of her farm, testing the range of her voice, testing her eyesight – could she see microscopically and telescopically? – and was her hearing as abnormally flexible as her voice?

"You were afraid I had lost feeling and scent and taste," she went on, still pacing with that powerful, tigerish tread. "Hearing and sight would not be enough, you think? But why do you think sight is the last of the senses? It may be the latest, Maltzer – Harris – *but why do you think it's the last?*"

She may not have whispered that. Perhaps it was only their hearing that made it seem thin and distant, as the brain contracted and would not let the thought come through in its stunning entirety.

"No," Deirdre said, "I haven't lost contact with the human race. I never will, unless I want to. It's too easy… too easy."

She was watching her shining feet as she paced, and her masked face was averted. Sorrow sounded in her soft voice now.

"I didn't mean to let you know," she said. "I never would have, if this hadn't happened. But I couldn't let you go believing you'd failed. You made a perfect machine, Maltzer. More perfect than you knew."

"But Deirdre—" breathed Maltzer, his eyes fascinated and still incredulous upon her, "but Deirdre, if we did succeed – what's wrong? I can feel it now – I've felt it all along. You're so unhappy – you still are. Why, Deirdre?"

She lifted her head and looked at him, eyelessly, but with a piercing stare.

"Why are you so sure of that?" she asked gently.

"You think I could be mistaken, knowing you as I do? But I'm not Frankenstein… you say my creation's flawless. Then what—"

"Could you ever duplicate this body?" she asked.

Maltzer glanced down at his shaking hands. "I don't know. I doubt it. I—"

"Could anyone else?"

He was silent. Deirdre answered for him. "I don't believe anyone could. I think I was an accident. A sort of mutation halfway between flesh and metal. Something accidental and… and unnatural, turning off on a wrong course of evolution that never reaches a dead end. Another brain in a body like this might die or go mad, as you thought I would. The synapses are too delicate. You were – call it lucky – with me. From what I know now, I don't think a… a baroque like me could happen again." She paused a moment. "What you did was kindle the fire for the Phoenix, in a way. And the Phoenix rises perfect and renewed from its own ashes. Do you remember why it had to reproduce itself that way?"

Maltzer shook his head.

"I'll tell you," she said. "It was because there was only one Phoenix. Only one in the whole world."

They looked at each other in silence. Then Deirdre shrugged a little.

"He always came out of the fire perfect, of course. I'm not weak, Maltzer. You needn't let that thought bother you any more. I'm not vulnerable and helpless. I'm not sub-human." She laughed dryly. "I suppose," she said, "that I'm – superhuman."

"But – not happy."

"I'm afraid. It isn't unhappiness, Maltzer – it's fear. I don't want to draw so far away from the human race. I wish I needn't. That's why I'm going back on the stage – to keep in touch with them while I can. But I wish there could be others like me. I'm… I'm lonely, Maltzer."

Silence again. Then Maltzer said, in a voice as distant as when he had spoken to them through glass, over gulfs as deep as oblivion:

"Then I am Frankenstein, after all."

"Perhaps you are," Deirdre said very softly. "I don't know. Perhaps you are."

She turned away and moved smoothly, powerfully, down the room to the window. Now that Harris knew, he could almost hear the sheer power purring along her limbs as she walked. She leaned the golden forehead against the glass – it clinked faintly, with a musical sound – and looked down into the depths Maltzer had hung above. Her voice was reflective as she looked into those dizzy spaces which had offered oblivion to her creator.

"There's one limit I can think of," she said, almost inaudibly. "Only one. My brain will wear out in another forty years or so. Between now and then I'll learn… I'll change… I'll know more than I can guess today. I'll change – that's frightening. I don't like to think about that." She laid a curved golden hand on the latch and pushed the window open a little, very easily. Wind whined around its edge. "I could put a stop to it now, if I wanted," she said. "If I wanted. But I can't, really. There's so much still untried. My brain's human, and no human brain could leave such possibilities untested. I wonder, though… I do wonder—"

Her voice was soft and familiar in Harris' ears, the voice Deirdre had spoken and sung with, sweetly enough to enchant a world. But as preoccupation came over her a certain flatness crept into the sound. When she was not listening to her own voice, it did not keep quite to the pitch of trueness. It sounded as if she spoke in a room of brass, and echoes from the walls resounded in the tones that spoke there.

"I wonder," she repeated, the distant taint of metal already in her voice.

Cicadidae

Lorian Moore

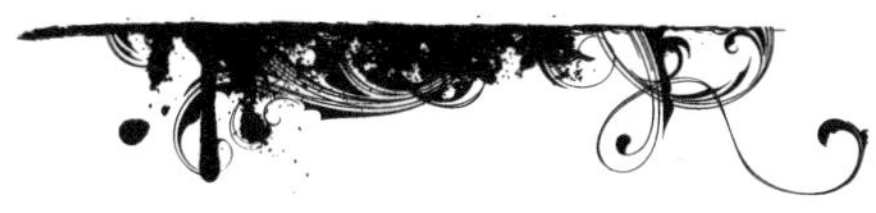

DO YOU REMEMBER IT? The summer was hot and sticky, sweat running into your eyes when the announcement came on the radio. The lake would no longer be in use for any reason. Everyone was to stay out of the water no matter what. The news presenter insisted that no one swim or fish in the lake, which you found a little strange. Nobody touched the lake unless necessary anyway; it was just the easier way to say that it wouldn't be needed anymore. The announcer tried not to say it outright, but he meant it: don't talk about the lake, don't look at the lake, don't even think about it when possible. Hard to do, with the town growing like mold around the water. You wished everyone would forget, but you knew the way gossip and tall tales spread through the town, a virus of words coughed between mouths.

A note of relief hit the town, but it was matched with anxiety that punched through your stomach and laid like a weight there. There was only one reason anyone ever approached that lake, or the machine sitting like rot in the middle of it. Once a year, a boat floated out with its cargo, weeping, alone. The boat always made its way back to the shore, but the person inside was never seen again. They always tried to scrub out the ever-growing red stain in the bottom of the boat, but it never helped.

You watched numbly as your parents fell into each other's arms in relief at the news. There was no longer need for fear, they said, but you couldn't ignore the gnawing weight that bore its way deep into your stomach. The machine was cruel in its comfort. You didn't trust it to be compassionate in hunger.

You wandered outside, insects and birds fleeing as you walked through the tall grass. It was hotter here in the sun, the singing of the cicadas ringing in your ears, but it was less stifling than indoors. Walking was the only relief you had, so you walked. That day, and the next, and the next, you walked, only coming home at night to sleep, hoping your dreams would chase away the fears of the day. The rain would come in the mornings, trapping you inside, but the evenings would be clear for your wanderings.

The sun peeked through the trees on the usual day of sacrifice, leaving the world open to you, but this day you stayed inside. The screaming of the cicadas made you sick, turning your stomach into a wriggling well of parasites. You stayed in your room under the covers, and your parents left you alone, only coming in to leave food. You didn't eat it. They didn't pester you about that, either.

The house was quiet that day. You would have preferred a little noise to dull the whispers of the trees, the echoes of church bells you weren't sure were ringing. The insects by your window cried out to you and it sounded as though a thousand voices hummed and whispered outside. You closed your curtains and buried yourself deeper into your bed, hoping to sleep away the day.

"You don't have to be afraid of it anymore, you know," your mother said when she brought up dinner. "It's over now."

You shifted slightly under the covers as she cleared away your uneaten lunch. A small sigh, then the shifting of her clothes as she turned towards the bed.

"I don't know what would have happened if it had continued." Her voice grew quiet, as if she thought you couldn't hear, that she was only talking to herself. "They never told us how they decided who it'd be but…" She paused. "…I was so sure it would have been you. We were supposed to just accept it but…" She sniffled slightly. "…how can you?" She stood in silence for a long moment, long enough that you began to wonder if she had left without you noticing, then she spoke, this time in a normal tone. "Your dinner's right here. Come get me if you need anything."

With that, she left. The smell of the cheap canned ravioli she had made that night drifted over to you, mixing with the breeze from the window. For the first time that day, you got up. You hovered by the door, almost leaving, then turned your attention to the food. It was your favorite go-to low effort dinner, the one your mom made whenever she'd had a long or stressful day. It was hot – maybe too hot for a muggy summer day – and steam rose lazily from the bowl. A fork lay next to it with a napkin folded carefully underneath, a glass of water nearby. You poked at the food and took a few tentative sips of the water, but the writhing mess in your stomach prevented you from eating. Instead, you decided that the day had gone on long enough, and you went to bed.

The first day of the machine's hunger, the rain stopped.

The showers that had been getting in the way of your wandering stopped abruptly the day after you expected you'd no longer need them, replaced with a radiant sun that blocked out all other sensation. Your mom insisted the family go grocery shopping as a flimsy excuse to collect stories from the rest of the town, and you obliged. You couldn't deny your own curiosity.

The sun was a good omen, according to most. It was the clearest skies we'd had all summer, and everyone was sick of the rain. You didn't like how the heat radiating off the cars and sidewalks hit your face like opening an oven. Worse, you hated how blank and wide open the cloudless sky felt. There was nowhere to hide under a sky like that.

Your skin began to itch and your ears began to ring as the whispers of old-timers gossiping about what would happen now grew into a roar. The noise overtook you, and you backed yourself into a corner, hands balled into fists to stop their trembling. Your mom noticed, and took you gently by the hand and led you out, calling goodbyes behind her. You let her lead you out of the store before you snatched your hand away, rubbing it against the roughness of your jeans to get rid of the itching.

"I'm sorry," she said, fumbling anxiously with her purse. "I know it's a lot."

You weren't able to respond, so you just nodded.

"You don't have to come along next time." She sighed and leaned back against the car. "I almost wish I hadn't, either. Everyone sure knows how to talk a lot without saying anything, don't they?"

You forced a small smile, and your mom didn't push it further. You sat in the car together in silence, waiting for your dad and siblings to finish talking and take care of the small shopping list you'd brought as an excuse. You leaned your head against the window, cool glass contrasting with the hot sun. With all the stories they had crafted as possible reactions to the hunger, you wondered why nobody had mentioned how loud the cicadas were this year. It was an old town; maybe it had been worse in the past. Still, you had trouble believing that anyone was as good at ignoring them as they seemed to be when the sound drilled its way through your head and lingered at the base of your skull, a crinkling hum that gnawed through bone.

By the time your dad and siblings returned to the car you had fallen into a restless sleep. It filled your mind with voices and cries, begging and pleading for help. You thought you heard your best friend's voice crying out from the dark. His voice went silent two years ago, consumed by water and metal, and the echoes of it were long gone. Still, you swam through the murky waters of sleep towards it, breaking through into wakefulness just when you could almost touch him.

You blinked blearily at the sunlight on your face as your mom shook you awake. "Come on, kiddo, we're home."

You numbly followed her inside the house, carrying the groceries she handed to you but taking note of little else. You still felt half caught in sleep, with legs and arms sludge to be fought against rather than used. When the groceries made their way into the kitchen, your mom turned to you. You didn't quite catch the words but you heard the meaning: you could go. You nodded and made your way up to your room.

You had the privilege of the eldest sibling in having your own room. It was small, too hot in the summer and too cold in the winter, but it was yours, a respite from your family. It was supposed to go to one of your siblings when you moved out, but when the plan to go to college with your best friend fell apart, so did everything else. You stayed home, growing but never changing, and he rotted.

Your legs shook as you crawled into your bed, stomach churning from heat and stress. You felt feverish, as though the buzzing of insects whirring within you created a burning heat. Keeping still and resting hurt worse than movement, so you leapt out of bed, hands covering your ears to drown out the endless buzzing.

It didn't help. The noise became a nauseating backdrop to your own obsessive thoughts, ever wandering back to that accursed lake. You swayed uncertainly by the window, watching the heat radiate off of the cars outside. Something felt sinister about the subtle distortions the hot metal made in the air. Maybe nothing. Maybe everything. You couldn't tell if the sickening fear sinking through your body was paranoia left from a life driven by terror, or fear of something tangible. Whichever it was, the anxiety washed up from your gut into the back of your skull, feeding the insects that thrashed and fought inside.

You stood at the window until the sky went dark, and your mother had long given up on getting a response out of you at your door. You stood until the darkness became moving shapes, and you could have sworn you saw a flash of light from the direction of the lake. At the sound of the light hitting your body, you buckled over, clutching your mouth and stomach in pain and nausea. The wave of light and sound rushed over you, drawing you in, demanding your presence. You stood on your shaking feet and ran.

The night was the same sticky warm the day had been, the pavement still hot under your bare feet from the sun that day. The world was quiet, most people in bed, but the insects that made the darkness their home had taken lodging in your skull, joining voices with the light to cry out to you.

You ran blindly, unaware of the streets you passed through and the sights that were so familiar to you. You had no way to know where you were going other than the deep nausea pulling you forward.

The machine was calling you.

It was no surprise when your feet led you to the edge of the lake. The water was still, the bloated machine in its center. Rings of red light pulsed outward like waves in the water, nearly touching your bare feet. You tried to take a step back but couldn't, entranced by the machine seeming to writhe and moan, though the water around it remained quiet. The noise in your head was a cacophony of whispers, screaming in silence for you to come closer. Arms grabbed at you, wind lashing at your face and pulling you forward, but when you looked down, all was still. The grass remained quiet nearby; the lake stood still without a ripple in it. Still, the pulsing cacophony called to you.

You fought the noise, fought the currents of light rushing against you, turned around. A single word pierced your mind.

"Help," the machine said. "Please."

You froze, bare feet sinking into the mud on the lake shore. Voices still swirled in the back of your head, buzzing and skittering given sentience, all overlapping each other in a twisted mess of sound. The hum of insects turned into words, to cries of help. The sound was clear now, even as the words mixed together. They danced and churned over each other, but every so often a word or phrase would come together, said by many voices at once.

"Come to us."

You turned back, shaking. "Who are you?"

The words exited your mouth strangled, barely real. You knew the answer. The machine didn't explain.

"Come."

You didn't want to go out into the water, into that silent graveyard. It drew you in, begged for your presence. You balled your hands into fists and pressed them into your eyes like a child and ran.

* * *

The next few days were a hellscape of endless cacophony, now grown into voices gnawing at your spine. You stayed in bed, barely sleeping or eating, haunted by the noise. The voices wrapped around each other, sobbing, pleading, begging you to come back. You felt sick. Covering your ears only seemed to make it worse, ricocheting the cries against your skull.

It made you think of the time when you were small, and a dog had been hit by a car outside – not enough to kill it, just enough to make it scream like a human being. You were sick then, too, watching the poor creature scream as people gathered to get it safe enough to put it out of its misery. You never forgot it, and its voice mixed in with the others like some divine punishment.

You spent the time in your room, digging your fingernails into the skin of your arms as you gripped them, shaking and trying not to cry. Your family hovered around your door, worried but trying to give you space. They assumed you were hit by the grief of giving up a sacrifice that had never been necessary and the shock it carried with it. How could you tell them that you were haunted, that your mom had been right all along?

And still the rain wouldn't come.

As much as you avoided others, still the news made it to you: this summer was the driest the town had ever seen. The heat turned the town into an oven, dry-baked sunlight burning paint and skin alike. Hushed whispers from your parents and loud cries from the radio theorized about the effects this would have on the town. Nearby farms were the only thing keeping the place alive, and already people were talking about stunted crops and ravenous insects using the plants as their only meager source of water.

Even the lake, unchanging as long as you had known it, was drying up. You didn't have to hear the news to know this; it called you to its shores every night, and most nights you answered. It was quieter when you came to it. It knew it had you in its grasp, that it could take its time claiming its prize. You did your best to forget, taking in the brief quiet it offered like gulps of water consumed in the middle of a hot summer night.

You spent longer and longer at the lake each night, until you had to run home as dawn broke so your family wouldn't notice you were gone. Somehow it sickened you to think that they could figure out that you were sneaking out to haunt the lake every night. It was your secret, and you kept it closer than your most precious possessions.

It all broke down around you one night, like cold glass put in boiling water. It was quiet as it always was, the voice of the machine humming gently in the back of your mind in contrast with the screams that haunted you through the day. You stayed on the shores of the lake, now deeply receded, never touching the water. You weren't sure if anything would happen if you ventured into the lake; you didn't want to find out. You went close, though, venturing into the lakebed to feel the cool mud under your feet. The machine gently called you closer, but you satiated yourself by standing in the small pools of water that remained scattered among the mud. When you stood in the water, the machine grew slightly louder, slightly gentler, calling to you. You didn't answer, but you enjoyed hearing its voice whispering to you as you gently swayed in the wind.

You sank into the water and mud of a slightly larger puddle tonight, letting your feet get fully submerged in the water as it rose to your ankles. The machine softly hummed its intoxicating tune, buzzing out a song that mixed with the faint hum of mosquitos and cicadas that covered the night sky. You paused to listen to what it was saying to you, used to the usual cries for help and whispers drawing you closer. It spoke to you, and you froze.

"I miss you." It was your best friend's voice, words choking out of him as if he were sobbing, restrained.

You stood frozen. You tried to call his name, but it caught in your throat, choked back by a writhing lump of fear pressing against your neck.

"It's been so long," he continued, the machine crooning a melody that backed his words, yearning flowing through them.

You shook your head sharply, loose hair flying around your eyes and stinging your ears. It was all wrong. You knew what the machine did. You knew your friend wouldn't bring you there.

"Please, come back." His voice strained as it continued, the machine's voice growing louder to try to hide the shaking. "I—" His own voice interrupted him, shrieking in agony. The pain distorted his voice so you couldn't make out the words, but his pain cut through you as though you could feel it yourself. The words faded into quiet sobs.

The other voices covered his, holding him back, but his voice broke through the pain. "You have to go. You have to leave." His voice was drowned out briefly with a sickening gargling noise, as if he were drowning.

You stood, frozen, shaking. That was him. That was the friend you knew, the one you had lost. You couldn't do what he asked, if he was really in there. You couldn't leave him.

After a few nauseating minutes, he spoke again. "It hurts," he gasped out.

It was enough for you. You couldn't obey his pleading that you leave – how could you? He was there, and he was in pain; you had to get him out, somehow. Nothing mattered without him; you would take his place if you could. You would find a way to save him. He was still alive somehow. You would bring him back.

Your feet flew across the lakebed, slick mud and water making you stumble and slide towards the machine. You didn't notice it, didn't notice the rocks and shells tearing up your feet, didn't notice stubbed toes and broken toenails. All that was before you was your friend, and the machine that kept you from him.

Mud gave way to water, and you soon found yourself slowed as it rose to your knees, then waist, then chest. The machine grew louder, raucous in laughter and the muffled sobbing that made up its voice. What it had failed to do through fear, it managed through love. It drew you closer with its voice, cooing about how you were home, that you would see your friend soon. You swam with blind rage, barely noticing the machine's words as you strained to pick out the voice of your friend through the cacophony.

"NO, NO, NO!" he screamed through the din of voices. "LEAVE!" His voice faltered, grew quieter. "It's too late for me."

"I won't let it be," You growled through gritted teeth.

The rust red of the water splashed into your mouth as you swam, blood and bile coating your tongue. You spat it out, but the sickeningly sharp taste of the water coated your throat and spread throughout your body. You coughed up as much as you could, and continued swimming. With the lake so dry, the machine's walls rose quickly before you, black sides turning the water black in reflection and shadow. You stopped just short of touching its twisted face, and tread water as you looked up at it.

The machine stretched into the sky, huge and black and writhing with wires and pipes. The wires clung together, packed in to create the perfect square that had blighted the surface of the lake for as long as you had known it. The motion of the water and your own nausea made you doubt yourself, but you could swear that the wires pulsed slightly, like veins beneath skin. There were no rivets, no stabilizing beams, no straps holding wires and pipes together like you would have expected from something this size. Instead, the wires clung to each other with sticky black fluid that turned red when it touched water.

You dry-heaved into the water at the rotten metallic smell that radiated off of the machine. How you had never smelled it before, you didn't know. Maybe it had become such a part of your world you had become used to it. Maybe it had been waiting for you. You coughed into your dripping hand a few times, then squared up to the machine itself. You needed to find a way in.

That proved to be harder than it sounded. The walls of the machine were a writhing mass of wires, thick and impenetrable. Below the water was too dark to see, burning your eyes when you tried to look beneath the surface. The thick, oily liquid that seeped out from between the wires also made an obstacle, looking too slick to climb. In the end, you could only think of one solution.

You had to let the machine in.

You knew what you had to do. You had always known. The machine had been telling it to you every day since the rain stopped. You had to come to it, and you had to let it in.

Placing a hand on the slick wall of the machine, you couldn't help but shudder at the sensation. It was cold and wet, like intestines gone silent. You took a deep breath, and placed your other hand on the machine.

You closed your eyes. The machine shrieked in delight in the back of your mind as you let your guard down, opening your mind to the cacophony that had haunted you for weeks. The wires shook and shuddered under your hands, then unlatched themselves from the body of the machine and slid up your arms. The sensation made your skin crawl and every instinct within you wanted to run, but you stayed, hands on the machine as the wires slid up your arms and under your clothes, latching underneath your arms and pulling you close.

You gasped as the machine drew you in, sliding slick rubber and metal against you as it pulled you into itself. You opened your eyes now, no longer needing to focus on accepting the machine's influence. Masses of wires slid past you, brushing against your stomach and legs and chest as it pulled on your arms. Occasionally a wire brushed your cheek as though caressing you, welcoming you in. The machine bruised your arms and face with its kisses as it dragged you through itself, and you found yourself relaxing, leaning into the wires and pipes that surrounded you.

The voices of the machine now were tender, whispering how happy they were that you had come to them. They all became one, all happy, all full of the same longing. Your friend's voice joined in, cooing that he was sorry to scare you, that he had to lie to get you to join him. The part of your mind that started at that, that felt it was wrong, that wanted to run, was quickly quieted as the wires running up your arms slipped underneath your skin, marks of pain that intoxicated you.

You barely even noticed when you stopped moving. Your eyes were half-closed in the trance of pleasure the machine had given you, and you only opened them again when you reached the core of the machine, pulsing with red light. You were set back on your feet, wires trailing from your arms and spine. You didn't remember them crawling under your skin and latching onto muscle and bone, but you were too delirious to care. The machine didn't propel you forward, but still you moved, entering the light.

It was warm, burning like the hot summer days it had caused, bringing your feet to a shuffling stop. It didn't matter, though. It had you where it wanted you.

The wires under your skin tightened, suspending you in air. The machine grew quiet, and the pleasure faded, leaving only fear. You snapped back into your body with sharp clarity, all of the fear and anguish of the past weeks, no, the years, since you had seen what the machine took, washing over you at once. You pulled on the wires, but it was too late. They had drilled their way through skin and bone, and were as much a part of you as your own organs.

You screamed out, but the sound was muffled in the walls of the machine. No one would have been around to help, but you were spared even the simple catharsis of some aspect of yourself exiting this place.

"Why?" you screamed.

You were met with silence.

"You have me where you want me, answer me!"

Wires slid into your throat, silencing you. You choked back tears and all of the curses you wanted to lay on the beast that held you.

Louder than ever, nearly part of your own thoughts, the machine spoke.

"We were hungry. That is all."

That's it? After all that had been done to you, your town, everyone you'd ever known and loved, all it was was hunger?

"That is all," the machine repeated. "We were hungry, and you fed us, and we offered means for your crops to grow. You took away our food, so you must starve."

The rain. You could still feel the dry heat, whether a memory or actual sensation you weren't sure. You weren't sure how this machine, this creature, was able to control the weather, but you thought it was a shitty deal. Use yourself as feed, or die from starvation with the lack of rain. You die either way, and the machine remains powerful.

The machine didn't deign to respond further. The wires dug deep, and pain radiated through your body. You couldn't even scream as your skin was cut from your body, sloughing off into the grinding machinery below you. Flesh gave way to bone, until nothing but wires remained in the shape of what you once were. You were nothing but pain, ceasing to exist in the glaring light of agony.

A moment, then silence. Then out of the silence came a thousand voices, one with your own, all crying the same agony.

You couldn't tell where you ended and the others began. You couldn't tell what was you, what was machine, what was at all anymore. You floated, drifting as nothing but a consciousness in the sea of other consciousnesses in this machine. Not even given death, you remained in the agony until nothing was left of you but pain.

And outside, the rain began to fall.

I'm Fine, Mom

Soumya Sundar Mukherjee

IT HAD ALREADY been hard for us UAISC technicians since that last solar storm hit earth, but as more complaints flooded our office, we began to realise that things had been worse – far worse than we had expected – for our customers. When we could restore the stability of our own customer care services to some extent, I personally decided to pay old Mrs. Wilson a visit. The woman had called at our office five times since yesterday, and she sounded worried not only because her robotic assistants had stopped working, but because of something else, too.

She seemed to be worried about her missing son.

I did not know how that problem could be solved by a technician for household robot-assistants, but still I chose to do it myself, perhaps because she sounded a bit like my own deceased mother over the phone.

When I pushed the doorbell of old Mrs. Wilson's house that evening, the sky was still bright with the swirling green and blue aurora, with a little hint of pink.

The ancient robot servant took two whole minutes to answer the door, so, I had to stand outside, watching the shimmering lights over the night sky. We had never seen them in this part of the land before, but I must admit that they were beautiful.

The tin-can opened the door and in a nasal voice recited, "Welcome to the Wilson Villa, sir."

The tin-can was an extremely old model of the House-Robot series with exceptionally low level of real intelligence. He had survived the storm because he did not have many complicated inner parts to get damaged.

Good for him. And for the old lady, too.

I stepped inside the house and the robot closed the door behind me. I could see the picture of late Mr. Wilson hanging upon the wall. A faint smell of room-freshener was still lingering in the air.

"Come here, Mr. Dunn," Mrs. Wilson's voice came from the next room.

The old robot showed me the way. I walked into the room and found her sitting in a cushioned wheelchair, fidgeting with a Com-All.

She looked nothing like my own mother, only except a hint of similarity in the way she smiled. At first glance, the thin woman's pale skin seemed so shrivelled that it reminded me of documents in a wastepaper basket. The corners of her eyes were wrinkled, but the smile on her toothless face was genuine and warm. The iridescent light of the aurora from the window floated on her glasses, and it gave her old, guileless face an unearthly beauty.

"Thank God, you're here at last," she heaved a sigh of relief. "Please have a seat, Mr. Dunn."

I sat on the sofa and made a quick survey of the room. The old television set was there, but it was switched off, as expected. The robotic cook stood motionless in a stooping pose at the mini kitchen with its eyes fixed on the bunch of spoons and forks.

That was when the storm must have struck it.

"It was a relief when I found that your Customer Care number had started working," the old woman said. Then she pointed her finger to the motionless robot in the kitchen. "This happened seven days ago. All of them suddenly stopped functioning. Except my dear faithful Dominic, of course." She looked patronisingly at the tin-can.

"These things occur during the occasional powerful solar flares," I said. "The one that hit earth last week happened to be the most powerful one of the century. Well, I think I'll be able to fix your gadgets, Mrs. Wilson. In fact, our customer services number was down, too; it was just recently restored. But, if you don't mind asking, you mentioned something about your son on the phone, didn't you?"

The old woman's eyes, I noticed for the first time, were moist. She gave her Com-All to me. "I couldn't communicate with my little Johnny for a week, Mr. Dunn."

I took the device from her hand and examined it. "This thing seems to be working fine. These new Com-Alls are sturdy enough to withstand even powerful solar flares."

"That's what I'm trying to say," she said. "My Johnny never fails to call me every night. When he didn't contact me a week ago, I thought that it was okay, because sometimes that happens. But days passed, and my Com-All remained silent. I thought that *his* device might have got some bugs, and they perhaps don't have service centres for those things in Naples. So, I waited. But he has become totally silent since then. Then I thought that maybe the problem is with my own device. Perhaps he had indeed tried to make a video call but could not, because *my* Com-All has a problem."

"Look, Mrs. Wilson," I said, "These solar super-storms are rare things, but they do happen to hit the earth once in a while. When they hit, they upset the electronic devices all over the world, sending most of the gadgets into a temporary coma, but they can be recovered. Artificial Intelligences with higher capacity do it by themselves; the ones with lower capacity, like your cook there, need a technician's help. We have done it before; we'll do it again. Perhaps your son's Com-All is damaged beyond repair, and he can't contact you by any other means. The whole world's communication system is facing problems due to that solar storm."

The tin-can brought us coffee on a tray. I took a cup and gently said, "Thank you, Dominic."

In his usual nasal tone, he replied, "You're welcome, sir."

I looked at Mrs. Wilson and said, "This is one benefit of having these old models in your house. They may not be as efficient and human-like as the newer ones, but Dominic is, as I see in your case, a lifesaver."

Mrs. Wilson smiled, "My Johnny gifted him to me on my sixty-second birthday. Now I'm seventy-four and Dominic, too, is old for his standard. You see, I spend my days in a wheelchair. Without him, I can't even do the things a person needs to do to live on. He is a bit slow, you're right, but what has the tortoise taught us? Slow and steady wins the race."

She chuckled like a silly schoolgirl and I, too, thought it polite to laugh with her. The brilliant light of the aurora was still visible from the glass window.

I inspected the Com-All again. There seemed to be no fault in it. I made a video-call from my own device to it, and it caught the signal without any problem.

That could mean only one thing.

I could not say it to the old woman's face, but I thought that the reason behind Johnny not calling his mother could only be neglect. The son did not feel as much connected to the mother as the mother expected him to be.

I sighed and decided that it was none of my business.

I opened my toolbox and started to work on the chef robot in the kitchen. Dominic was not a bad chef after all, but the chef robot was far better than him in the matter of cooking.

It took almost an hour to fix the chef, while Dominic helped me with my tools, and I had to admit that though he was not much of a looker, he was a jack of all trades.

After fixing the chef, I picked up the Com-All again. Mrs. Wilson said, "Mr. Dunn, can you make a video call to my Johnny with that thing?"

"I think I can," I said. "But I'm not sure whether he'll be able to receive it."

"Still, give it a try, please," she said.

I did as she told me. But there was no answer from the other side, as I had expected.

"I don't think there is a problem in the device, Mrs. Wilson; perhaps it is your son..."

The Com-All started vibrating in my hand.

The face of Johnny Wilson was glowing on the screen.

"It's him! It's him! At last!" shouted Mrs. Wilson in glee and almost snatched the thing out of my hand.

She answered the video call, and the still photo of Johnny was replaced by his smiling face, live on screen.

"Hey, Mom!" Johnny said. "I know you are concerned about me. But don't worry, I'm fine, Mom."

Mrs. Wilson's face glowed with cheerful excitement. "Where the hell have you been? Do you know how concerned I was about you, little Johnny?"

Johnny was not 'little' at all; he had a healthy moustache under his nose. *But a son hardly grows old in his mother's eyes.*

"I'm sorry, Mom," he said. "I think you've heard about the solar flares, and that made a mess of my only Com-All. By the way, is there someone with you?"

I realised that he had seen me through the camera. Mrs. Wilson said, "Yes, Johnny, I want you to meet Mr. Dunn. Mr. Dunn, please come closer. This is my son Johnny, and Johnny, this is Mr. Dunn from Universal Artificial Intelligence Service Centre. He's been of immense help, I tell you. He has just fixed our chef. With the help of Dominic, of course." She looked admiringly at the tin-can in the kitchen and then pointed the face-camera of the Com-All to me.

The sudden change in Johnny's expression was hard to miss. For a couple of seconds, his face had a horrified look, as if he had seen a ghost. Then he tried to cover it with an uneasy smile. "UAISC, huh? How do you do, Mr. Dunn?"

I curtly said, "How do you do, Johnny?" and retreated with a little nod.

Something wrong is going on here.

I could not make out what it was, but there was surely something weird about the man who was speaking to Mrs. Wilson over the Com-All.

I walked to Mrs. Wilson's back and peeped over her shoulders to the screen. Johnny was still telling his mother a lot about the sunny weather in Naples and the girls he had met there. His mother listened to his chatter with rapt attention.

I watched his face closely for a minute, particularly the eyes and the lower jaw. I had a suspicion that Johnny Wilson was not what he appeared to be.

Two minutes' watch made me sure that I was correct.

I looked at the happy face of Mrs. Wilson and felt a certain anger rising inside me toward Johnny. *How could he...?*

I placed my hand lightly upon Mrs. Wilson's shoulder. She stopped in mid-speech and looked up. I said, "Excuse me, but may I have a word with Johnny? In private? I need to ask him a few things about Naples."

"Why not?" She readily placed the Com-All upon my hand.

I took the device, opened the closed door, and stepped outside, because I did not want her to overhear.

The sky still looked stunning with the shimmering blue, green and pink lights. On the glowing screen of the Com-All, Johnny's face looked as hard as stone.

"Who are you?" I asked.

"What do you mean?"

"Don't try to play smart with me, pal," I hissed. "I'm the senior-most technician of Universal Artificial Intelligence Service Centre. I've carefully watched your jaw movements, and I've counted how many times you blink in a minute. So, you'd better have a good explanation for all this, Mr. Imposter, or I'm going to call the police."

His face instantly turned pale. "Ask me anything you want, and I swear that I won't lie. But please promise me one thing."

"What?"

"That you're not going to tell Mrs. Wilson anything I tell you now."

I said, "I don't make promises to your kind. Now I question and you answer. I know that you're not a living human being. Your lower jaw is the faultiest thing, as in many of the new Companion Series models, and it becomes clear when you talk; then, you blink only twice or thrice in a minute which is quite lower than the normal human rate. You can fool an old woman with that near-perfect face of yours, but a senior robot-expert? Huh. Why are you playing this game with the old woman, rascal? Where is her real son?"

"Dead."

"What?"

"I'm telling the truth."

"How did he die?"

"Cancer. He was diagnosed with it when it was already beyond treatment. The doctors said that he had about three months to live. In those three months, he built me and gave me a face like him. As you can see, he was a genius." The robot smiled sadly.

I did not know what to say to him. I looked up at the night sky. I felt the hand of an unseen artist painting the sky with living hues.

The robot spoke again, this time more pleadingly, "Mrs. Wilson's days are numbered, Mr. Dunn. Johnny knew that his mother would not be able to bear the shock of his death. So, he created me – an exact replica of himself. I still have about twenty-two more years' battery life in me, and hopefully I'll outlive the old woman. That was why I was created; I hope you get that."

I sighed. "Johnny trusted you to love his mother in his absence?"

"I don't know whether I'm qualified to express something you call 'love', and perhaps I'm just programmed that way, but believe me, I earnestly want her to be happy."

"But why should I believe you? You are already deceiving an old woman. What is the proof that you are telling the truth now?"

A sad smile emerged on his lips. "Do you know from where I'm speaking?"

"I'm sure it's not Naples. Where are you?"

"In the attic of this very house."

"What?"

"Mrs. Wilson is a wheelchair-bound woman. She will never get to the attic and find me there. Johnny himself was an expert in robo-technology. He did some behavioural modifications in my brain-circuit and put me there in a trunk himself. The image of Naples that you see behind me, the background of Johnny's drawing room that she saw there – are all just smart image-projection. If you don't believe me, you can always come to the attic and check for yourself. But will that do any good to Mother, Mr. Dunn?"

Mother!

I had never felt so lost for words in my whole life.

The robot said again, "The solar flare made me incapable of moving for the last week and that's why I couldn't contact her. You've perhaps already guessed that. You may tell her the truth, Mr. Dunn, but it'll eventually kill her."

I feebly said, "You can't deny that she's living with a lie!"

The robot smiled. "But she's *living*, and she's happy. Tell me, sir, does she *need* the truth?"

I kept thinking about the question. *Does she...?*

I looked at the sky again. It was still delightfully, hauntingly beautiful.

I wandered inside and closed the door behind me. I walked to the room where Mrs. Wilson had been sitting. As I gave the Com-All back to her, I noticed the narrow staircase spiralling up to the attic beside the mini-kitchen.

"What did my son tell you?" The old woman asked. "About Naples?"

"A lot of things. And he also told me that you're the best mom in the world."

I gazed at the toothless, Buddha-like smile rising upon her childlike face. From the window, all the colours of the sky were reflected in her glasses.

I did not know why I felt a strangely peaceful satisfaction. I looked at the screen of the Com-All to see her son's grateful face.

"And, let me tell you one thing, Mrs. Wilson," I added, "You, too, are quite lucky to have a son like him."

"I know," she said contentedly.

Grotesque

Lee Murray

Clos Lucé, France, Present Day

"YOU FOUND WHAT?" Patrice Oury switches the phone to his other ear. "A concealed door? You're kidding? Leading where?" He shakes his head. "Okay, wait there. I'll be right down."

Closing his computer, Oury slaps on his hard hat and steps out of the portable construction office. Keeping to the designated pathways, he shows his site badge to the museum staff before making his way to the basement, avoiding the late-afternoon Leonardo da Vinci tourists scurrying from room to room, oohing and aahing over everything from drapery to flying machines.

At the corner of the basement, a sign saying 'Entrée Interdite' swings on a velvet cordon. Oury unhooks it, steps through, then replaces the cordon before descending the stone staircase. With arched brick ceilings and mottled limestone walls, the staircase is barely wide enough for two men to walk abreast. The stone treads are remarkably well preserved, although that could change if certain parties get their way.

One flight down, he passes a little wine cellar on the right, but Oury's going deeper still, to the subterranean passage that runs between the Château d'Amboise to the Clos du Lucé.

Built by King Francis 1er, the tunnel kept the king's head dry when stopping by to visit his old friend. But recently it had suffered a cave-in, sparking debate about its future: some want the subterranean pathway reopened to the public, others say it should be closed and preserved for future generations. One of those devil-you-do, devil-you-don't situations. The brouhaha is still raging, but the legalities aren't Oury's problem. His job is to ensure the safe excavation of the passage.

At the bottom of the stairs, pale electric light illuminates the tunnel before him. Five hundred metres of twists and turns to the south, it opens onto an identical set of stairs in the Château d'Amboise, but Oury doesn't have to go that far to find his team. Thirty metres in, his foreman Jean-Yves Mida sits on his haunches with his back against the stone wall. Seeing Oury, Mida scrambles to his feet.

"It's over here," he says, gesturing behind him to his right. "Pascal, move the spotlight, will you, so the boss can see."

For a moment, the light swings wildly, glancing off the walls like something out of a gangster movie, eventually stopping on a crudely cut wooden slab covered in dust and debris, the iron hinges crusted with rust. Well concealed in a recess, if it hadn't been pointed out to him, Oury might've missed it.

He gives it a rap with his knuckles. "Nobody home. I wonder where it leads."

"That's just the point," says Mida. "Should we even be touching it? Our contract is for excavating the tunnel between the two châteaux. Nobody said anything about exploring any other tunnels."

"I suspect no one knows anything about it, Jean-Yves. I don't recall any secondary tunnels marked on the blueprints."

"Maybe when they built it, they were going to curve the tunnel that way, but hit an obstruction," says Hubert Gourand, getting in his penny's worth.

Mida nods. "Makes sense. The Amasse River runs through the château grounds, and the Loire's only a stone's throw away. The tunnel's builders might've come across an underground tributary."

Pascal steps closer, causing the spotlight to lurch. "I can noiselessly construct, to any prescribed point, subterranean passages – either straight or winding – passing if necessary under trenches or a river…" he says.

Mida turns, for an instant the light shining hard on one side of his face. "What on earth are you rabbiting on about, Pascal?"

"It's from the letter da Vinci wrote to Ludovico Sforza, the one suggesting the duke make him his war engineer," Pascal replies. "I read it on the wall, upstairs, in the museum."

"Good to hear you've been improving your mind. Now if you could just improve the direction of the spotlight, we'll all be happy," grumbles Mida.

Oury strokes his beard. Maybe there's something in what the apprentice is saying. The passage was built for the king's own use, perhaps even designed by the king's engineer himself, and yet this door is shabby and poorly constructed as if it'd been put in hastily, perhaps to cover a mistake. Just the kind of thing that makes an interesting segue on a guided tour. "I guess there's no harm in taking a look, is there?"

The team sets to work, freeing the door from the rock. It takes a while. Standing around in the cool air of the tunnel, Oury wishes he'd brought his jacket. At last, the hinge pins are prised out and the debris brushed away. Mida grasps the circular latch and pulls. The door doesn't budge.

"Here, let's use this," Hubert says, slipping a spade handle through the iron loop. On either end of the handle, each with a foot on the wall, the two men heave on the spade.

"Tadadada," Pascal says, mimicking a drum roll.

The door pops off, Hubert tumbling backwards in the narrow passageway.

"For fuck's sake, hold the light still, Pascal," Mida barks.

Behind the door is a wall of rock, a barrage of rough-cut limestone blocks.

"Well, that explains it," Mida says. "There was a cave-in."

Dusting off his pants with his hands, Hubert nods. "And rather than clear it, they decided to take another route."

"Hang on a sec." Oury holds up a hand. "Hubert, pass me the concrete scanner, will you?"

Hubert brings it over. Oury sets it up. After a moment, he adjusts the angle so his foreman can see the screen. "Take a look at this."

Mida examines the output. He gives a low whistle. "That's no tunnel."

* * *

Château d'Amboise, France, 17 March 1560

Francis, the king of France, yawns loudly.

Pierre Danès ignores the boy's boorishness – after all, the king's only sixteen – and continues his lesson. "Titus Livius tells us that Horatius Cocles was on guard when Janiculum was captured by a sudden attack—"

The boy's uncle, the duke of Guise, bursts into the room. "Blood princes! Those conniving sons of whores! I'll have their blood. It's treason, nothing less!" the duke roars.

On his heels, Charles, Cardinal of Lorraine, takes a moment to close the doors. "*Du calm*, brother. You fear that rabble? Worrisome flies. They should be pleased we afford them such esteem."

The young king jumps to his feet. "A rabble? Where? What… what's happening?"

"Condé is happening, that's what!" Monsieur de Guise kicks at a footstool, overturning it and sending it several paces into the room. "The whoreson has only gone and incited a Huguenot uprising," he rails. "Led by du Barry of Renaudie, his Protestant hellspawn march on Amboise as we speak."

"They're coming here?" Francis blinked.

Thinking it best to leave, Danès closes his book and bows. "With your permission, Monsieur, I'll take my leave. You'll wish to discuss this matter in private."

"Stay where you are, Danès," the duke snaps. "And you, Humières. This concerns you, too." Danès' head whips up. He'd forgotten the king's governor had been attending to some correspondence at the rear of the salle while Danès had been delivering his lesson.

But the uncle's news has sent the young king into a panic. Rushing to the window, Francis' eyes dart over the valley, the courtyard, the river. "How many are coming?" he blurts. "When will they arrive? What shall we do?"

"For heaven's sake, Francis! Get away from there!" the duke shouts.

Quick on his feet, Humières grabs the king by his person and drags him away from the window. "My lord, please, come away. It isn't safe."

Shrugging off the governor, Francis sits heavily on a brocade couch. He shakes his head. "I don't understand. What do they want?"

The duke snorts. "What have you been teaching him, Danès? Their intent is obvious: they'd have you dead, Francis, so they can contaminate the realm with their Protestant twattle. Your brother is only ten. If you were to die, what chance would he have?"

Francis blanches.

Danès digs his fingers into his palms. Why does Guise have to be so brutal? Can't he see the boy is scared stiff? Thank goodness, his brother the cardinal is capable of some diplomacy.

"Francis," the priest says. "I must urge you to leave the castle. For your safety, and for France."

The duke exhales deeply.

"Yes, yes. Escape. It's the best solution. A small party: two guards, three at most, his nurse maid Humières, and Danès, his tutor. Our enemies will expect him to flee with a king's entourage, but a small party—"

Francis' jaw drops, his colour draining. "You… you… want me to go out *there*?"

"No, no, of course not," the cardinal reassures him. "We would not risk France so cheaply. No, you'll take the underground passage to the Clos Lucé."

Francis looks up. "The tunnel my grandfather Francis Big Nose made for the painter?"

Danès stifles a twinge of disappointment for his charge. Even under threat, it isn't proper for a young king to show such disrespect for his namesake the late king, or indeed for Signore Leonardo da Vinci, who wasn't merely a painter, but a polymath of the greatest distinction.

"The basement tunnel?" the king says.

The cardinal nods. "The very one."

"It's been closed up."

"It can be reopened."

"It's the best solution," the duke says again. "The Clos Lucé is small, but the château is well-fortified, and few, if any, have knowledge of the tunnel."

The cardinal steeples his hands beneath his chin. "A handful of old men is all. Your grandfather's guards. All loyal men."

"What does my mother say?" Francis whispers.

Sighing, the cardinal drops to one knee. He takes the boy's slender hand in his. Francis' fingers tremble. "My lord, your mother still mourns the loss of her consort, your much beloved father. Her grief is indescribable. If we were to add to that news of your peril, it could send her into an abyss too deep and too dark to endure. No, Francis, even if she were still your regent – *which she is not* – we could not burden our cousin Catherine with this news."

Returning the footstool to its feet, Humières pipes up. "If I may, sire, such is the military experience of Monsieur de Guise, we could escape the castle and be back before your mother even notes your absence."

"Absolutely: a day or two should be all I need to put down the Protestant upstarts," the duke agrees.

The king forces a smile. "I suppose there'll be spiders down there."

The cardinal grins. "Better a few spiders than an execution, my lord."

His hand on the king's shoulder, Danès feels the boy shudder.

* * *

The cardinal's guards have barely uncovered the blocked-off passage when a runner comes from the gatehouse.

"My lord, I've been looking for you everywhere. They're here! Du Barry and his men," he says between breaths, his chest heaving. "They're attacking the castle."

An attack? So soon? Danès' heart sinks. Beside him, the king steadies himself against the wall. Humières mutters under his breath.

"My oath, but they're a nuisance," the duke curses. "I'll see to it." He turns to his brother. "As soon as Francis is in the tunnel, have the wall put back up." He strides away, the breathless runner at his heel.

The king dances from one foot to another. Danès' own nerves are in shreds by the time the final block is removed and the hole is large enough for a man to pass. One by one they crawl through: Danès, Humières, the king, and three of the cardinal's guards. The smallest among them, the king, has the best of it, and yet even he emerges with his tunic covered in dust, his hose ripped, and his hair dishevelled. He looks less like a monarch and more like a child out for an adventure in an apple orchard. Torches and weapons are passed through the gap. On the other side, the cardinal's men are already reconstructing the wall.

"Wait!" Francis says abruptly. "Who will open the passage at the other end?"

It's a good question. One Danès hadn't thought to ask.

"No one," the cardinal replies. Another block is pushed into place.

"But surely if—"

Shouts break out somewhere inside the castle. Rebels breaching the walls?

"God be with you," the cardinal whispers and the last stone is replaced, the shaft of light closing behind them.

They're entombed.

Danès' knees wobble. His pulse thunders. Putting the wall back was necessary to conceal their escape, but Danès wasn't prepared for this… this sense of finality. It's as if he'll never again see the surface. Never again breathe the scent of oranges. See the sun of his native Greece—

Silly superstition!

What good is he, overcome with timidity in the king's moment of need? As the boy's tutor, he must lead by example. Stiffening his back and his resolve, Danès breathes out his fear.

Humières has no such qualms, or else he hides them well. The governor squares his shoulders and lifts his torch. "Right, then," he says. "Let's be off."

With Humières in the lead, and the young king sequestered safely in their midst, they hasten down the narrow flight of stairs and into the bowels of the castle, the temperature plunging as they descend. Yellow torchlight flickers on the pale stone, and the air is redolent with damp and musk. At the base of the stairwell, there is only one route, its issue invisible in the distance. Unperturbed, Humières plunges onwards.

"Is it very far?" Francis' voice booms.

One of the guards hisses.

Humières halts. Returning to the king, he places a hand on the boy's shoulder and leans close. "Sire, I beg you, lower your voice, lest our enemies hear."

Francis' eyes grow wide in fear. Nodding, he says nothing.

Humières resumes his position in the vanguard, and once again they hurry forward, Danès wincing as grit crunches underfoot.

Suddenly, a distant crash reverberates off the stonework. They freeze. Humières raises his hand, signalling for quiet. Danès holds his breath. He strains to hear. There's a shout. Another crash. His hand on his mouth, the king smothers a gasp.

Footsteps.

"The Huguenots have breached the wall," Humières says, though they all must know it. "Take the king and carry on. I'll go back and slow them down."

Francis grabs him by his tunic. "What, and hold the tunnel by yourself?"

Humières smiles, his teeth glowing in the flickering light. "The passage is narrow. I shall be like noble Horatio, who held the bridge at Janiculum."

One of the guards hands his torch to the king. "I'll go with him, sire."

The pair run off into the gloom.

"Let's go," Danès says, although his legs quake. The four of them quicken their pace. They haven't gone far when Danès' torch reveals an obstacle: rocks and debris, the length of several rooms, block their path. A cave-in.

"Please, you have to save me!" The king's voice is shrill. "They'll murder me."

One of the guards, a squat, study fellow, says, "Sire, we'll not let that happen." Yet even as he says it, screams reach them, strident shrieks funnelled through the stillness.

Desolate, agonised appeals.

The hairs on Danès' neck rise. Someone is dying. Huguenot traitors or one of their own?

"We have to climb over; there's no other way," says the taller guard. Already, he's clambering over the rocks, one hand reaching back to help the king. The sturdy guard follows, pushing the king without ceremony from the rear.

Danès climbs too, jagged rock punching through his shoes. The rocks are loose, slipping out from beneath him. More than once, he comes down heavily on an elbow, a knee. His tunic is ruined and his fingers scraped raw. He ignores the pain because someone's coming, their feet pounding on the packed earth. How many? He can't tell: his heartbeat is too loud in his ears. "Hurry!" he urges. "They're coming!"

"Danès!"

Relief floods him. It's Humières. Danès turns to greet him, but reaching the rockfall, the governor doesn't slow. He leaps onto the boulders, flitting from rock to rock, as nimble as a boy crossing a creek. In an instant, he's caught Danès and passed him by. "Make haste," he calls.

"The guard?"

“Dead. Along with a stream of Condé’s disciples. Their bodies are stacked higher than my navel.”

Danès laughs. “You did it. Our Horatio.”

But looking back, Humières shakes his head, his expression is grim. “The day is not won. The cardinal helped us, attacking the invaders from the rear, but I couldn’t hold the way alone.”

Danès sucks in a breath. “We have to warn the others.” More accustomed to the classroom, his legs are blancmange, yet he puts on a spurt of speed, catching up to Humières. They leap to the ground on the other side of the cave-in, where the guards are waiting with the king.

“Humières? Where’s my man?” the king stammers.

The governor says nothing.

“How many are coming?” the tall guard asks.

“I counted twelve, Breton,” Humières replies. “But it was dark, so there could’ve been more.”

“Two of us will have to go with the king,” says Sturdy. “That leaves three to stand and fight.”

“We have to outrun them.”

“Wait!” The men turn to Francis. He may be a boy, but he is still their king. “Look!”

Francis points to a tiny door. Crudely hewn, the wooden portal is neatly hidden in the rock. If they can open it and slip inside, their pursuers might miss it in the gloom and pass them by.

“It’s as good a chance as any,” Humières says. He kicks off the rusted latch and, stabbing the tip of his sword into the door jam, prises it open.

Could their luck be any worse?

Inside, the way is blocked with rubble, a single large limestone block at the top. The king groans softly. Undeterred, Humières lifts his foot and kicks. Around the block, stones and debris tumble inwards. He kicks again. The tall guard, Breton, joins in, both of them stomping at the rock, the noise mercifully drowned out by the shouts of their pursuers deeper in the tunnel.

“Hurry! They’re coming,” the king pleads.

The faintest glow appears on the wall behind them.

His face red, Humières kicks again. At last, the block tumbles inwards! Danès is first to clamber through, pulling the king bodily after him. Half paralysed with fear, the boy doesn’t complain. Danès is still helping him to his feet when Humières and the guards scuttle through.

They pull the door closed, extinguishing all but the king’s torch. The men face the door and draw their swords. Humières puts a finger to his lips. They wait in silence. Danès’ heart is beating so hard, he’s convinced it will jump from his chest. He holds his breath, determined to still it.

Their pursuers run right by.

When their footsteps have passed, the king holds the torch aloft. “Where are we?” he asks, stepping carefully over the limestone block. The cavity is as large as a hall in the château, with several man-sized tunnels leading off it. Against one face of the chamber is a trestle table and, beside it, an upturned stool. A dusty tunic lies on the ground nearby. One of the guards kicks at the fabric, and a bone – a man’s femur – rattles out. “Jesu!” he curses softly. “That gave me a fright.”

“Human bones? What is this? Some kind of primitive crypt?” Humières whispers.

Danès approaches the trestle table. It’s covered in paper. He lifts the pages to examine them closer. “No, not a crypt. A workshop of Signor Leonardo,” he replies. “The king’s engineer was well known for being left-handed, writing from right to left and illustrating his notes with diagrams and images. This looks to be the plan for a mechanised man. And here, some sketches of the birth of an infant.”

Even in the dim light, the king's blush is vivid. "For heaven's sake, put that down, Monsieur. My uncle, the cardinal, says da Vinci was involved in some ungodly practices. He says it's hardly a wonder the man was exiled from his home country."

"With all due respect to the cardinal," Danès says, "a scientist takes every opportunity to learn."

"Monsieur, please!"

Chastised, Danès returns the paper to the table.

But in his haste to distance himself from the image, the king has backed into something. He squeals, his feet scrabbling in midair, then topples sideways, hitting the ground and sending up a shower of dust and pebbles. Somewhere far below, water splashes.

"Sssh!"

They wait, their hearts in their throats, in case the noise brings back the Huguenots. When no one comes, the king gets to his feet and Humières salvages the torch, looking for whatever it was the king had stumbled on.

It's a wooden structure of some sort, erected next to a steep pit in the ground.

"Providence is truly with you today, my lord," Humières says, shining the light into the narrow pit. "If you hadn't tripped on this wooden apparatus, you might have fallen in. Given the splash, I'd wager there's a pool at the bottom."

The king opens his mouth and closes it again.

Putting the wooden structure back on its feet, Danès' spirits lift. "It'll be a pool for sure," he says. "This apparatus, as you call it, is one of da Vinci's inventions: a device for drawing water. See, you turn the handle here and water from the pool is carried upwards into this trough." He turns the handle. It takes several twists, but eventually the device delivers a gush of water.

Humières lifts a handful to his mouth. "It tastes fresh enough."

"Good to know we won't die of thirst," Sturdy says with sarcasm.

Beginning with the king, they take it in turns to rotate the handle and drink from the trough, the water reviving their bodies, if not their spirits.

"How long do we have to stay here?" Sturdy scuffs the dusty ground with the toe of his boot. "This place gives me the creeps."

"At least while we're in here, the king is safe," Breton says. "Who knows what's happening on the other side of that door?"

"I agree," says Humières. "With the king's permission, we should wait here for a day or two at least. We've water to sustain us, and we can burn the trestle if the need arises. When the king's uncles have seen off the rebels, they'll come looking for us."

"But what if the Huguenots find us first?" the king says, scrubbing at his face. "What chance have I then? There are only four of you – three since Danès isn't armed."

"The king makes a good point," Breton says, wisely ignoring the boy's insult. "If discovered, we're likely to be outnumbered. Maybe we should look for another way out."

Humières takes the lead, and they venture down the first of the pathways. It leads to a dead end, the tunnel walled up with limestone blocks. They're retracing their steps when Breton spies a narrow mezzanine with a thin wooden ladder leaning to one side. It seems to be open at the top, the ledge like a viewing platform at a tournament.

They climb up and peer over the side. It's another cavern, only bigger, perhaps as large as the courtyard at Blois. From here, the floor is hard to discern, but Danès detects something glinting in the torchlight.

"Lift the torch over here, Humières," he says. "I think I saw something."

The governor raises the torch. The floor of the cavern is full of armour, perhaps thirty or forty sets, laid out in rows, each 'soldier' armed with a pistol and a sword. Danès frowns. Why would Francis' grandfather hide an armoury here, so far from the castle?

A shout rings out from across the other side of the cavern. The Huguenots are searching the tunnels! Danès pulls the king to the ground as Humières dives on their only torch, extinguishing it against his leather tunic.

The ladder!

But Breton's already seen to it, dragging it onto the ledge behind them. They crouch in the darkness, nothing left to do but pray.

All at once, the mass of armour seethes in the darkened hollow, the limbs moving, iron grating on iron. What? Several sets of armour sit up. Danès starts. Armour doesn't move of its own volition. But half their number are indeed moving, grating to their feet.

Da Vinci's mechanised knights.

No, no. It's not possible. There must be men hiding in that armour. There *have* to be. Danès strains his eyes, focussing hard on one of the figures. There – a head! It seems… familiar. His heart lurches. It's a grotesque, one of da Vinci's caricatures. Except there's nothing amusing about it: it's hideous. Odious. A male, it has thick misshapen lips, a pocked protruding forehead, and a hooked nose. Turning towards the intruders, it gives a twisted smile.

Danès shakes his head. He must be dreaming. He glances at Humières. The governor's face is grey and stricken.

The king grips his arm. "What do you see?" he whispers.

"Not now, Francis," Danès says.

The half-human, half-machine abominations have lined themselves up across the cavern, their weapons drawn. The Huguenots hold their ground. Perhaps they think the king is hidden amongst this gruesome metal army?

The atrocities advance, firing on the Huguenots. Noise booms in the cavern. It bounces off the walls. Several of the rebels fall, the remainder retreating into the recesses on either side of the tunnel. Yet none of the fallen men are dead. The monsters advance to finish them off, their movements slow and stiff. The Huguenots in the tunnel fire frantically. It's without hope; their shots ping uselessly off the armour plates, ricocheting into walls. The monsters keep coming, the incessant grate of their limbs making Danès' teeth ache.

A female with a face as brutish as a boar shunts her way to the front. Her wrinkled bosom on display and her sword drawn, she advances on one of the fallen men. His screams carrying over the din, he scrambles back towards the tunnel, dragging his useless leg. Danès silently wills him to hurry. Whether the rebel's shrieks are prompted by the sight of her face or the glint of her blade, Danès can't say, but they become a gurgled bleat when she hacks at his neck.

Within seconds, the hook-nosed creature is there. On bended knee, it lowers its ugly face to the wound, ripping the flesh with its teeth and tearing the man's head from his neck in a tangle of sinew and nerves.

Breton vomits. Danès pushes the king down and bites his own tongue to keep from crying out.

The Huguenots haven't given up. While the woman crouches over her victim, one of the rebels launches a charge. His sword raised, he hacks the grotesque woman's head from her shoulders, but not before she fires her pistol. Both dead, they pitch forward, his body slumping softly, her iron one clanging.

Danès looks for the hooknose in the crowd. The battle raging all about him, the monster carries his grisly prize across the cavern to the slumbering set of armour.

What's happening?

The hooknose places the head on an empty torso. The armour jolts, the head wobbles, and the Huguenot's face distorts into something other, his chin jutting forward and eyebrows thickening until he only vaguely resembles a man. Cackling, the hooknose stands back to admire his handiwork. Iron grates on iron as the new creature, slowly, inexorably, clambers to its feet. Its eyes pop open. Reanimated. Risen again.

Danès quivers.

If this is a vision, it wasn't sent by God. The polymath has built the king an army of immortals. With knights like these at her disposal, France would be invincible...

"Shit," Sturdy swears.

Francis can only hear the battle, still he sobs silently.

The Huguenot leader has seen enough. He screams at his men, "Foutez le camp! Vite! Allons-y!" The remaining rebels fall back. But the war monsters aren't shooting to kill. In any case, they've abandoned their pistols. Perhaps they've run out of shot, or they've realised the guns are taking too long to reload.

Taking too long to reload. Machines with brains.

Danès clings to the ledge. He's still trying to get his trembling limbs under control when Sturdy shakes his arm. A rebel has stumbled into the tunnel behind them. He reaches the dead-end wall and turns, his face mad with panic. The angle is wrong: Danès can't see, but the grating echo tells him a monster is coming. Desperate for a way out, the rebel shines his torch on the walls, the light revealing the mezzanine. The Huguenot's eyes meet Danès'. They plead for mercy.

It's Humières who grants it: jumping to his feet, he aims his pistol at the man's head. Fires. The Huguenot drops to the ground. But Breton is standing, ready to fire, waiting for the monster to come into view. Seconds pass. Danès realises too late that the gunfire flash has revealed their position, and the monster's arm is swifter than those grating legs. It throws its sword like a spear, catching Breton in the neck. In an arc of blood, the guard falls into the tunnel below. The monster grates towards him. Alive still, Breton croaks. The slack-faced creature licks its bulbous lips.

Danès pulls the king to him, burying the boy's head in his tunic. There are some things no man should ever see, much less a boy.

When the monster has dragged its bloody prize away, Humières nudges Danès in the ribs. "Come on, let's get out of here."

"Go down there?"

"I think they've gone."

Danès listens. It's true. The grating has receded. Twisting, he peers over the edge into the armoury. Without the Huguenots' torches, the cavern has fallen into shadow.

Sturdy scoffs. "That's because the monsters are busy ripping the Huguenots' fucking heads off," he says, and in the king's presence. Danès doesn't have the strength to reprimand him.

"Maybe, or perhaps the monsters chased the rebels down one of the other tunnels. If that's the case, they'll both be too busy to bother us."

"I want to go home," Francis whispers. Danès, too, would like to see the sky again.

Humières lowers the ladder, and they clamber down, stepping around Breton's decapitated body, the king leaning heavily on Danès. With no time to reload his own pistol, Humières helps himself to Breton's and moves to pick up the dead Huguenot's torch, which still smoulders on the ground. He hesitates, tormented with indecision. Danès can understand it: with the torch, rebels and monsters will be able to see them, but without it, they risk losing their way. Humières scoops it up. "Keep close," he says.

They creep towards the first cavern with the pool, following a trail of Breton's blood. They're almost there – Danès can just make out the pile of broken blocks and the doorway to freedom!

No! A grotesque grates from the darkness.

Sturdy fires, but his aim is wild, the shot barely grazing the monster's metal cuirass. The creature grins, its great jowls flapping. It draws its sword and grinds forward, but Sturdy is ready, his blade high, targeting the monster's head. Except the monster's already at octave position. Going for his legs. Sturdy reacts, switching from high guard to close left, looking for the neck. The monster parries, pushing Sturdy back. Sturdy hasn't had time to recover when it delivers a back left slash to his legs. Grunting, Sturdy falls.

Humières thrusts the torch to Danès. "Don't just stand there. For God's sake, get the boy through the door." Then he steps in with a drive from his shoulder, beheading the monster in a flash of steel.

"Humières!" Screaming, the king points into the darkness. Danès follows the direction of his finger. Now the grate, grate, grate of movement resounds in his head. They're coming. A line of them. They cannot hope to hold them off. Sturdy knows it, because his scream cuts to the bone. Within seconds the monsters are upon him.

Humières, Danès and the king run for the door, the inexorable grating on their heels. Humières jumps the pit. Francis and Danès go around, Danès upturning the trough of water. The creatures moan. They grate backwards away from the wash. Danès almost smiles. Da Vinci's immortal knights are afraid of water! Clever. It's all very well being immortal, but not if you've rusted to a standstill. Sadly, the trough isn't full and the trickle of water is seeping into the dust. It won't hold them back for long.

The door!

They force their way past the pile of rubble. Humières first, then Francis. Danès is about to clamber after them when he realises their mistake. The clothing, the lone femur, the limestone blocks in front of the door. It all makes sense. *Someone* has to replace the final block, or da Vinci's grotesque war machines will escape into the world.

"Hurry!" Humières screams.

"Take the king and go!" Danès shouts back.

"But—"

"The monsters… They can't escape," Danès says.

Understanding dawns on the governor's face. "God be with you," he whispers.

They clasp hands.

Seconds later, the door slams shut. Humières must put his shoulder against it, because it shunts inwards. Danès is strangely relieved. Humières might've argued for his life; Danès couldn't have countenanced the hope.

The damnable grating comes from behind again. The monsters are approaching. How much time? He doesn't dare look. Instead, he breathes deeply, filling his lungs. Then he bends to the stone block. Shoulders popping and lungs bursting, he heaves the block upwards, praying to God to give him strength. He gets it as far as his knees, resting it there, his legs shaking with fatigue. The grating is closer now. He sucks in a breath. Holds it.

Heaves!

He mustn't fail.

He is Horatio holding the way.

The corner of the block hits the ledge. Legs straining, Danès pushes it upwards. More! Little by little, the block inches into place. Danès grunts with the effort. His tendons groan. Yes! He's done it! The block is set. He can let go…

He roars in pain; his finger is crushed in the gap. Danès tears the shattered digit free, warm blood running up his arm. It's of no matter: France is safe and da Vinci's war machines are contained.

Contained, but still alive.

Panting, he turns. Relentless, the monsters grate towards him. The hooknose smacks his lips.

Danès can only wait.

* * *

Clos Lucé, France, Present Day

The foreman meets him at the bottom of the stairs. "What did they say?"

"We got the go-ahead," Oury replies, adjusting his hard hat as they walk along the passage. "As soon as we've got the doorway cleared of the rubble and the ceilings shored up, a bunch of historians from the museum will come down to document the findings."

"I don't suppose our names will feature anywhere."

Oury grins. "Hardly."

They reach the site of the little door where Oury's team is congregated, eager for a look inside the secret chamber.

"Okay, Hubert, we're all good to go," Mida says.

Oury gives him the thumbs up, then puts on his hearing protection.

Gourand starts the drill.

The Clockwork Man

Chapters I–IV

E.V. Odle

Chapter I
The Coming of the Clockwork Man

"Consciousness in a mere automaton is a useless and unnecessary epiphenomenon."
– Prof. Lloyd Morga.

IT WAS JUST as Doctor Allingham had congratulated himself upon the fact that the bowling was broken, and that he had only to hit now and save the trouble of running, just as he was scanning the boundaries with one eye and with the other following Tanner's short, crooked arm raised high above the white sheet at the back of the opposite wicket, that he noticed the strange figure. Its abrupt appearance, at first sight like a scarecrow dumped suddenly on the horizon, caused him to lessen his grip upon the bat in his hand. His mind wandered for just that fatal moment, and his vision of the oncoming bowler was swept away and its place taken by that arresting figure of a man coming over the path at the top of the hill, a man whose attitude, on closer examination, seemed extraordinarily like another man in the act of bowling.

That was why its effect was so distracting. It seemed to the doctor that the figure had popped up there on purpose to imitate the action of a bowler and so baulk him. During the fraction of a second in which the ball reached him, this secondary image had blotted out everything else. But the behaviour of the figure was certainly abnormal. Its movements were violently ataxic. Its arms revolved like the sails of a windmill. Its legs shot out in all directions, enveloped in dust.

The doctor's astonishment was turned into annoyance by the spectacle of his shattered wicket. A vague clatter of applause broke out. The wicket-keeper stooped down to pick up the bails. The fielders relaxed and flopped down on the grass. They seemed to have discovered suddenly that it was a hot afternoon, and that cricket was, after all, a comparatively strenuous game. One of the umpires, a sly, nasty fellow, screwed up his eyes and looked hard at the doctor as the latter passed him, walking with the slow, meditative gait of the bowled out, and swinging his gloves. There was nothing to do but to glare back, and make the umpire feel a worm. The doctor wore an eye-glass, and he succeeded admirably. His irritation boiled over and produced a sense of ungovernable, childish rage. Somehow, he had not been able to make any runs this season, and his bowling average was all to pieces. He began to think he ought to give up cricket. He was getting past the age when a man can accept reverses in the spirit of the game, and he was sick and tired of seeing his name every week in the *Great Wymering Gazette* as having been dismissed for a 'mere handful'.

He despised himself for feeling such intense annoyance. It was extraordinary how, as one grew older, it became less possible to restrain primitive and savage impulses. When things went wrong, you wanted to do something violent and unforgivable, something that you would regret afterwards, but which you would be quite willing to do for the sake of immediate satisfaction. As he approached the pavilion, he wanted to charge into the little group of players gathered around the scoring table – he wanted to rush at them and clump their heads with his bat. His mind was so full of the ridiculous impulse that his body actually jolted forward as though to carry it out, and he stumbled slightly. It was absurd to feel like this, every little incident pricking him to the point of exasperation, everything magnified and translated into a conspiracy against him. Someone was manipulating the metal figure plates on the black index board. He saw a '1' hung up for the last player. Surely he had made more than One! All that swiping and thwacking, all that anxiety and suspense, and nothing to show for it! But, he remembered, he had only scored once, and that had been a lucky scramble. The fielders had been tantalisingly alert. They had always been just exactly where he had thought they were not.

He passed into the interior of the pavilion. Someone said, "Hard luck, Allingham," and he kept his eyes to the ground for fear of the malice that might shoot from them. He flung his bat in a corner and sat down to unstrap his pads. Gregg, the captain, came in. He was a cool, fair young man, fresh from Cambridge. He came in grinning, and only stopped when he saw the expression on Allingham's face.

"I thought you were pretty well set," he remarked, casually.

"So I was," said Allingham, aiming a pad at the opposite wall. "So I was. Never felt more like it in my life. And then some idiot goes and sticks himself right over the top of the sheet. An escaped lunatic. A chap with a lot of extra arms and legs. You never saw anything like it in your life!"

"Really," said Gregg, and grinned again. "H'm," he remarked, presently, "six wickets down, and all the best men out. We look like going to pieces. Especially as we're a man short."

"Well, I can't help it," said Allingham, "you don't expect a thing like that to happen. What's the white sheet for? So that you can see the bowler's arm. But when something gets in the way, just over the sheet – just where you've got your eye fixed. It wouldn't happen once in a million times."

"Never mind," said Gregg, cheerfully, "it's all in the game."

"It *isn't* in the game," Allingham began. But the other had gone out.

Allingham stood up and slowly rolled down his sleeves and put on his blazer. Of course, Gregg was like that, a thorough sportsman, taking the good with the bad. But then he was only twenty-four. You could be like that then, so full of life and high spirits that generosity flowed from you imperceptibly and without effort. At forty you began to shrivel up. Atrophy of the finer feelings. You began to be deliberately and consistently mean and narrow. You took a savage delight in making other people pay for your disappointments.

He looked out of the window, and there was that confounded figure still jigging about. It had come nearer to the ground. It hovered, with a curious air of not being related to its surroundings that was more than puzzling. It did not seem to know what it was about, but hopped along aimlessly, as though scenting a track, stopped for a moment, blundered forward again and made a zig-zag course towards the ground. The doctor watched it advancing through the broad meadow that bounded the pitch, threading its way between the little groups of grazing cows, that raised their heads with more than their ordinary, slow persistency, as though startled by some noise. The figure seemed to be aiming for the barrier of hurdles that surrounded the pitch, but whether its desire was for cricket or merely to reach some kind of goal, whether it sought recreation or a mere pause from its restless convulsions, it was difficult to tell. Finally, it fell against the fence and hung there, two hands crooked over the hurdle and its legs drawn together at the knees. It became suddenly very still – so still that it was hard to believe that it had ever moved.

It was certainly very odd. The doctor was so struck by something altogether wrong about the figure, something so suggestive of a pathological phenomenon, that he almost forgot his annoyance and remained watching it with an unlighted cigarette between his lips.

* * *

There was another person present at the cricket match to whom the appearance of the strange figure upon the hill seemed an unusual circumstance, only in his case it provided rather an agreeable diversion than an irritating disturbance. It had been something to look at, and much more interesting than cricket. All the afternoon Arthur Withers had been lying in the long grass, chewing bits of it at intervals and hoping against hope that something would happen to prevent his having to go out to the pitch and make a fool of himself. He knew perfectly well that Tanner, the demon bowler of the opposing team, would get him out first ball. He might linger at the seat of operations whilst one or two byes were run; but there were few quests more unwarranted and hopeless than that excursion, duly padded and gloved, to the scene of instant disaster. He dreaded the unnecessary trouble he was bound to give, the waiting while he walked with shaking knees to the wicket; the careful assistance of the umpire in finding centre for him; all the ceremony of cricket rehearsed for his special and quite undeserved benefit. And afterwards he would be put to field where there was a lot of running to do, and only dead balls to pick up. Of course, he wasn't funking; that wouldn't be cricket. But he had been very miserable. He sometimes wondered why he paid a subscription in order to take part in a game that cost him such agony of mind to play. But it was the privilege that mattered as much as anything. Just to be allowed to play.

Arthur was accustomed to be allowed to do things. He accepted his fate with a broad grin and a determination to do whatever was cricket in life. Everybody in Great Wymering knew that he was a bit of a fool, and rather simple. They knew that his career at the bank had been one wild story of mistakes and narrow escapes from dismissal. But even that didn't really matter. Things happened to him just as much as to other and more efficient individuals, little odd circumstances that made the rest of life curiously unimportant by comparison. Every day, for example, something humorous occurred in life, something that obliterated all the worries, something worth waking up in the middle of the night in order to laugh at it again. That was why the appearance of the odd-looking figure had been so welcome to him. It was distinctly amusing. It made him forget his fears. Like all funny things or happenings, it made you for the moment impersonal.

He was so interested that presently he got up and wandered along the line of hurdles towards the spot where the strange figure had come to rest. It had not moved at all, and this fact added astonishment to curiosity. It clung desperately to the barrier, as though glad to have got there. Its attitude was awkward in the extreme, hunched up, ill-adjusted, but it made no attempt to achieve comfort. Further along, little groups of spectators were leaning against the barrier in nearly similar positions, smoking pipes, fidgeting and watching the game intently. But the strange figure was not doing anything at all, and if he looked at the players it was with an unnatural degree of intense observation. Arthur walked slowly along, wondering how close he could get to his objective without appearing rude. But, somehow, he did not think this difficulty would arise. There was something singularly forlorn and wretched about this curious individual, a suggestion of inconsequence. Arthur could have sworn that he was homeless and had no purpose or occupation. He was not in the picture of life, but something blobbed on by accident. Other people gave some sharp hint by their manner or deportment that they belonged to some roughly defined class. You could guess something about them. But this extraordinary personage, who had emerged so suddenly from the line of the sky and streaked aimlessly across the landscape, bore not even the vaguest marks of homely origin. He had staggered along the path, not with the recognisable gait of a drunken man, but with a sort of desperate decision, as though convinced in his mind that the path he was treading was really only a thin plank stretched from heaven to earth upon which he had been obliged to balance himself. And now he was hanging upon the hurdle, and it was just as though someone had thrown a great piece of clay there, and with a few deft strokes shaped it into the vague likeness of a man.

* * *

As he drew nearer, Arthur's impression of an unearthly being was sobered a little by the discovery that the strange figure wore a wig. It was a very red wig, and over the top of it was jammed a brown bowler hat. The face underneath was crimson and flabby. Arthur decided that it was not a very interesting face. Its features seemed to melt into each other in an odd sort of way, so that you knew that you were looking at a face and that was about all. He was about to turn his head politely and pass on, when he was suddenly rooted to the ground by the observation of a most singular circumstance.

The strange figure was flapping his ears – flapping them violently backwards and forwards, with an almost inconceivable rapidity!

Arthur felt a sudden clutching sensation in the region of his heart. Of course, he had heard of people being able to move their ears slightly. That was common knowledge. But the ears of this man positively vibrated. They were more like the wings of some strange insect than human ears. It was a ghastly spectacle – unbelievable, yet obvious. Arthur tried to walk away; he looked this way and that, but it was impossible to resist the fascination of those flapping ears. Besides, the strange figure had seen him. He was fixing him with eyes that did not move in their sockets, but stared straight ahead; and Arthur had placed himself in the direct line of their vision. The expression in the eyes was compelling, almost hypnotic.

"Excuse me," Arthur ventured, huskily, "did you wish to speak to me?"

The strange figure stopped flapping his ears and opened his mouth. He opened it unpleasantly wide, as though trying to yawn. Then he shut it with a sharp snap, and without yawning. After that he shifted his whole body very slowly, as though endeavouring to arouse himself from an enormous apathy. And then he appeared to be waiting for something to happen.

Arthur fidgeted, and looked nervously around him. It was an awkward situation, but, after all, he had brought it on himself. He did not like to move away. Besides, having started the conversation, it was only common politeness to wait until the stranger offered a remark. And presently, the latter opened his mouth again. This time he actually spoke.

"Wallabaloo-Wallabaloo-Bompadi-Bompadi-Wum-Wum-Wum-Nine and ninepence—" he announced.

"I beg your pardon," said Arthur, hastily.

"Wallabaloo," replied the other, eagerly. "Walla – Oh, hang it – Hulloa, now we've got it – Wallabaloo – No, we haven't – Bang Wallop – nine and ninepence—"

Arthur swallowed several times in rapid succession. His mind relapsed into a curious state of blankness. For some minutes he was not aware of any thinking processes at all. He began to feel dizzy and faint, from sheer bewilderment. And then the idea of escape crept into his consciousness. He moved one foot, intending to walk away. But the strange figure suddenly lifted up a hand, with an abrupt, jerky movement, like a signal jumping up. He said "nine and ninepence" three times very slowly and solemnly, and flapped his right ear twice. In spite of his confusion, Arthur could not help noticing the peculiar and awful synchronisation of these movements. At any rate, they seemed to help this unfortunate individual out of his difficulties. Still holding a hand upright, he achieved his first complete sentence.

"*Not* an escaped lunatic," he protested, and tried to shake his head. But the attempt to do so merely started his ears flapping again.

And then, as though exhausted by these efforts, he relapsed altogether into a sort of lumpiness and general resemblance to nothing on earth. The hand dropped heavily. The ears twitched spasmodically, the right one reversing the action of the left. He seemed to sink down, like a deflated balloon, and a faint whistling sigh escaped his lips. His face assumed an expression that was humble in the extreme, as though he were desirous of apologising to the air for the bother of keeping him alive.

Arthur stared, expecting every moment to see the figure before him fall to the ground or even disappear through the earth. But just when his looseness and limpness reached to the lowest ebb a sudden pulse would shake the stranger from head to foot; noises that were scarcely human issued from him, puffings and blowings, a sort of jerky grinding and grating. He would rear up for a moment, appear alert and lively, hitch his whole body firmly and smartly, only to collapse again, slowly and sadly, his head falling to one side, his arms fluttering feebly like the wings of a wounded bird.

Arthur's chief sensation now was one of pity for a fellow creature obviously in such a hopeless state. He almost forget his alarm in his sympathy for the difficulties of the strange figure. That struggle to get alive, to produce the elementary effects of existence, made him think of his own moods of failure, his own helplessness. He took a step nearer to the hurdle.

"Can I *do* anything for you?" he enquired, almost in a whisper. Suddenly, the strange figure seemed to achieve a sort of mastery of himself. He began opening and shutting his mouth very rapidly, to the accompaniment of sharp clicking noises.

"It's devilish hard," he announced, presently, "this feeling, you know – Click – All dressed up and nowhere to go – Click – Click—"

"Is that how you feel?" Arthur enquired. He came nearer still, as though to hear better. But the other got into a muddle with his affirmative. He flapped an ear in staccato fashion, and Arthur hastily withdrew.

Now, the afternoon was very warm and very still. Where they stood the only sounds that could reach them were the slight crack of the batted ball, and the soft padding of the fielders. That was why the thing that happened next could hardly be mistaken. It began by the strange figure suddenly putting both hands upon the top of the hurdle and raising himself up about an inch off the ground. He looked all at once enormously alive and vital. Light flashed in his eyes.

"Eureka!" he clicked, "I'm working!"

"What's that?" shouted Arthur, backing away. "What's that you said?"

"L-L-L-L-L-Listen," vibrated the other.

Still pressing his hands on the hurdle, he leaned upon them until the top part of his body hung perilously over. His face wore an expression of unutterable relief.

"Can't you hear," he squeaked, red in the face.

And then Arthur was quite sure about something that he had been vaguely hearing for some moments. It sounded like about a hundred alarm clocks all going off at once, muffled somehow, but concentrated. It was a sort of whirring, low and spasmodic at first, but broadening out into something more regular, less frantic.

"What's that noise?" he demanded, thoroughly frightened by now.

"It's only my clock," said the other. He clambered over the hurdle, a little stiffly, as though not quite sure of his limbs. Except for a general awkwardness, an abrupt tremor now and again, he seemed to have become quite rational and ordinary. Arthur scarcely comprehended the remark, and it certainly did not explain the origin of that harassing noise. He gaped at the figure – less strange now, although still puzzling – and noticed for the first time his snuff-coloured suit of rather odd pattern, his boots of a curious leaden hue, his podgy face with a snub nose in the middle of it, his broad forehead surmounted by the funny fringe of the wig. His voice, as he went on speaking, gradually increased in pitch until it reached an even tenor.

"Perhaps I ought to explain," he continued. "You see, I'm a clockwork man."

"Oh," said Arthur, his mouth opening wide. And then he stammered quickly, "that noise, you know."

The Clockwork man nodded quickly, as though recollecting something. Then he moved his right hand spasmodically upwards and inserted it between the lapels of his jacket, somewhere in the region of his waistcoat. He appeared to be trying to find something. Presently he found what it was he looked for, and his hand moved again with a sharp, deliberate action. The noise stopped at once. "The silencer," he explained, "I forgot to put it on. It was such a relief to be working again. I must have nearly stopped altogether. Very awkward. Very awkward, indeed."

He appeared to be addressing the air generally.

"The fact is, I need a thorough overhauling. I'm all to pieces. Nothing seems right. I oughtn't to creak like this. I'm sure there's a screw loose somewhere."

He moved his arm slowly round in a circle, as though to reassure himself. The arm worked in a lop-sided fashion, like a badly shaped wheel, stiffly upwards and then quickly dropping down the curve. Then the Clockwork man lifted a leg and swung it swiftly backwards and forwards. At first the leg shot out sharply, and there seemed to be some difficulty about its withdrawal; but after a little practice it moved quite smoothly. He continued these experiments for a few moments, in complete silence and with a slightly anxious expression upon his face, as though he were really afraid things were not quite as they should be.

Arthur remained in stupefied silence. He did not know what to make of these antics. The Clockwork man looked at him, and seemed to be trying hard to remould his features into a new expression, faintly benevolent. Apparently, however, it was a tremendous effort for him to move any part of his face; and any change that took place merely made him look rather like a caricature of himself.

"Of course," he said, slowly, "you don't understand. It isn't to be expected that you would understand. Why, you haven't even got a clock! That was the first thing I noticed about you."

He came a little nearer to Arthur, walking with a hop, skip and jump, rather like a man with his feet tied together.

"And yet, you look an intelligent sort of being," he continued, "even though you are an anachronism."

Arthur was not sure what this term implied. In spite of his confusion he couldn't help feeling a little amused. The figure standing by his side was so exactly like a wax-work come to life, and his talk was faintly reminiscent of a gramophone record.

"What year is it?" enquired the other suddenly, and without altering a muscle of his face.

"Nineteen hundred and twenty-three," said Arthur, smiling faintly.

The Clockwork man lifted a hand to his face, and with great difficulty lodged a finger reflectively against his nose. "Nineteen hundred and twenty-three," he repeated, "that's interesting. Very interesting, indeed. Not that I have any use for time, you know."

He appeared to ruminate, still holding a finger against his nose. Then he shot his left arm out with a swift, gymnastic action and laid the flat palm of his hand upon Arthur's shoulder.

"Did you see me coming over the hill?" he enquired.

Arthur nodded.

"Where did you think I came from?"

"To tell the truth," said Arthur, after a moment's consideration, "I thought you came out of the sky."

The Clockwork man looked as though he wanted to smile and didn't know how. His eyes twinkled faintly, but the rest of his face remained immobile, formal. "Very nearly right," he said, in quick, precise accents, "but not quite."

He offered no further information. For a long while Arthur was puzzled by the movements that followed this last remark. Apparently the Clockwork man desired to change his tactics; he did not wish to prolong the conversation. But, in his effort to move away, he was obviously hampered by the fact that his hand still rested upon Arthur's shoulder. He did not seem to be able to bend his arm in a natural fashion. Instead, he kept on making a half-right movement of his body, with the result that every time he so moved he was stopped by the impingement of his hand against Arthur's neck. At last he solved the problem. He took a quick step backwards, nearly losing his balance in the process, and cleared his arm, which he then lowered in the usual fashion. Then he turned sharply to the left, considered for a moment, and waddled away. There was no other term, in Arthur's estimation, to describe his peculiar gait. He took no stride; he simply lifted one foot up and then the other, and then placed them down again slightly ahead of their former positions. His body swayed from side to side in tune with his strange walk. After he had progressed a few yards he turned to the right, with a smart movement, and looked approximately in Arthur's direction. His mouth opened and shut very rapidly, and there floated across the intervening space some vague and very unsatisfactory human noise, obviously intended as an expression of leave-taking. Then he turned to the left again, with the same drill-like action, and waddled along.

* * *

Arthur watched him, feeling diffident, half inclined to follow him in case he fell over. For there was not much stability about the Clockwork man. It was clear that the slightest obstacle would have precipitated him upon his nose. He kept his head erect, and looked neither downwards or to right and left. He seemed wholly absorbed in his eccentric mode of locomotion, as though he found it interesting just to be moving along. Arthur kept his eyes glued upon that stiff, upright back, surmounted by the wig and hat, and he wondered what would happen when the Clockwork man reached to the end of the line of hurdles, where another barrier started at right angles across the end of the cricket ground.

It was a sight to attract attention, but fortunately, as Arthur thought, everybody seemed too absorbed in the game to notice what was happening. The dawning of humour saved him from some uncomfortable misgivings. There was something uncanny about the experience. Somehow, it didn't seem natural, but it was certainly funny. It was grotesque. You had to laugh at that odd-looking figure, or else feel cold all over with another kind of sensation. Of course, the man was mad. He was, in spite of his denial, an escaped lunatic. But the noise? That was certainly difficult to explain. Perhaps he had some kind of infernal machine hidden in his pocket, in which case he would be a dangerous kind of lunatic.

What was he going to do next? He had reached the end of the field and stopped abruptly. Apparently, the presence of another barrier acted as a complete check to further movement. For several seconds he remained perfectly still. He was now about a hundred yards from Arthur, but the latter had good eyesight, and he was determined to miss nothing.

Then the Clockwork man raised a hand slowly to his face, and Arthur knew that he was repeating his former meditative action, finger to nose. He remained in that position for another minute, as though the problem of which way to turn was almost too much for him. Finally, he turned sharp to the right and began to walk again.

Arthur became aware of two other figures approaching the one he was watching so intently. They were Gregg, the captain of the team, and Doctor Allingham. The yellow braid on their blazers shone in the sunlight, and Arthur could see the blue emblem on Gregg's pocket. There would have to be a meeting. The two flanelled figures were strolling along in a direct line towards that other oddly insistent form. Arthur caught his breath. Somehow he dreaded that encounter. When he looked again there was some kind of confabulation going on. Curiously enough, it was Doctor Allingham and Gregg who seemed incapable of movement now. They stood there, with their hands in their pockets, staring, listening. But the Clockwork man was apparently making the utmost use of his limited range of action. His arms were busy. Sometimes he kicked a leg up, as though to emphasise some tremendously important point. And now and again he jabbed a finger outwards in the direction of the field of play. Arthur caught the sound of a high, squeaky voice borne upon the light breeze.

Whatever the argument was about, the Clockwork man seemed to gain his point, for presently the three figures turned together and proceeded in a bee-line towards the pavilion, Doctor Allingham and Gregg dodging about absurdly in their effort to accommodate themselves to the gyrations of their companion.

Chapter II
The Wonderful Cricketer

"WE OUGHT NOT to have let him play," said Allingham, irritably. He was standing beside Gregg in the pavilion.

"Well, he would insist," said the latter, laughing lightly, "and we're at least entitled to put eleven men in the field. There he goes again! That a six for certain."

Allingham watched the ball disappear, for the fourth time since the Clockwork man started his innings, somewhere in the direction of a big brewery that stood mid-way between the ground and the distant town. It was an incredible hit. No one had ever achieved such colossal drives in all the history of Great Wymering cricket. There was a certain absurdity about the thing. Already the club had been obliged to supply three extra balls, for it would have been useless to try and find those that had been lifted so far beyond the ground.

"The man's a dangerous lunatic," asserted Allingham, who had not yet overcome his original annoyance with the strange figure, whose sudden advent had lost him his wicket. "It's uncanny, this sort of thing. You can't call it cricket."

"Well, he's making runs, anyhow," rejoined Gregg, his eye falling upon the score-board. "At this rate we shall stand a chance after all."

It was fortunate, perhaps, that the Great Wymering people took their cricket rather seriously. Otherwise, they might have felt, as Doctor Allingham already felt, that there was something impossible about the Clockwork man's performance. He had walked out to the wicket amidst comparative indifference. His peculiar gait might easily have been attributed to sheer nervousness, and his appearance, without flannels, provoked only a slight degree of merriment. When he arrived at the wicket he paused and examined the stumps with great attention, as though wondering what they were for; and it was quite a little while before he arranged himself in the correct attitude before them. He remained standing still, holding the bat awkwardly in the air, and no amount of persuasion on the part of the umpire could induce him to take centre or place his bat to the ground in the recognised fashion. He offered no explanation for his eccentric behaviour, and the fact simply had to be accepted.

The game restarted. Tanner, who had by this time taken eight wickets for just under a hundred runs, put down a slow, tricky one. Everybody agreed, in discussing the matter afterwards, that the Clockwork man never shifted his position or moved a muscle until the ball pitched, slightly to the off. Nobody seems to have seen exactly what happened, but there was a sudden ear-piercing crack and a swoop of dust.

Some seconds elapsed before anyone realised that the ball had been hit at all. It was the Clockwork man who drew attention to the fact by gazing steadily upwards in the direction of the town. And then, suddenly, everybody was straining their eyes in the same direction to watch that little flying spot grow smaller and smaller until it seemed to merge into space. (As a matter of fact, this particular ball was discovered, three weeks later, lying in a disused yard three miles from the cricket ground.)

There was a certain amount of applause, followed by an embarrassing silence. Presently someone threw another ball out into the field, and the game was resumed. But the Clockwork man treated Tanner's next delivery, which was a fast one, in exactly the same manner. Again nobody could say exactly what happened – for the action was swifter than the quickest eye could follow – but the ball disappeared again, this time in the direction of a fringe of poplars far away on the horizon. Again there was a lull, but the applause this time was modified. Another ball was supplied, and this also was dispatched with equal force and in a third direction, almost unanimously decided by the now bewildered spectators to be the flagstaff of the church that stood in the middle of the High Street, Great Wymering.

By this time a certain sense of panic was beginning to be displayed by the restless attitudes of the fielders; and the spectators, instead of leaning against the barriers, stood about in groups discussing the most extraordinary cricketing event of their lives. There was much head shaking and harking back to precedent among the old cronies present, but it was generally agreed that such hitting was abnormal. Indeed, it was something outside the pale of cricket altogether.

"If everybody was to start sitting like that," pronounced Samuel Bynes, a local expert, "there wouldn't be no sense in cricket. It ain't in the game." And he spat decisively as though to emphasise his opinion that such proficiency should be deplored rather than commended.

"You're right, Sam," said George Bynes, who had hit up many a century for his town in bygone days, "'tain't cricket. Else it's a fluke; the man didn't ought to be allowed to hold a bat in his hand. It's spoiling other folks' sport."

Attention was diverted by something of minor importance, that showed the Clockwork man in an altogether new and puzzling light. There had been some delay over the procuring of the third ball, and when this was forthcoming the over was called. The fielders changed about, but the Clockwork man made no attempt to move and manifested no interest in the immediate proceedings. He remained, with the bat in his hands, as though waiting for another ball to be delivered.

"Seems as though 'e's only 'alf there," commented Mr. Bynes, noticing this incident.

"Dreaming like," suggested his companion.

There was further delay. The bowler at the other end objected to the position of the Clockwork man. He argued, reasonably enough, that the non-participating batsman ought to stand quite clear of the wicket. The umpire had to be consulted, and, as a result of his decision, the Clockwork man was gently but firmly induced to move further away. He then remained, in the same attitude, at the extreme edge of the crease. His obtuseness was certainly remarkable, and comment among the spectators now became general and a trifle heated.

"Play," said the umpire.

The batsman at the other end was a stout, rather plethoric individual. He missed the first two balls, and the third struck him full in the stomach. There was a sympathetic pause whilst Mr. Bumpus, who was well known and respected in the town, rubbed this rather prominent part of his anatomy to the accompaniment of fish-like gaspings and excusable ejaculations. Mr. Bumpus was middle-aged and bald as well as corpulent, and although he did his best to endure the mishap with sportsman-like stoicism, the dismay written upon his perspiring features was certainly an excitant to mirth. Some of the fielders turned their heads for a few moments as though to spare themselves a difficult ordeal; but on the whole there was discreet silence.

It was for this reason, perhaps, that the action of the Clockwork man was all the more noticeable. To this day, not one of the persons present is certain as to whether or not this eccentric individual actually did laugh; but everybody is sure that such was his intention. There issued from his mouth, without a moment's warning, a series of harsh, metallic explosions, loud enough to be heard all over the ground. One compared the noise to the ringing of bells hopelessly cracked and out of tune. Others described it as being similar to the sound produced by some person passing a stick swiftly across an iron railing. There was that suggestion of rattling, of the impingement of one hard thing against another, or the clapping together of steel plates. It was a horrible, discordant sound, brassy and resonant, varied between the louder outbursts by a sort of whirring and humming. Those who ventured to look at the Clockwork man's face during this extraordinary performance said that there was little change of expression. His mouth had opened slightly, but the laugh, if indeed it could be described as anything but a lugubrious travesty of human mirth, seemed to proceed from far down within him. And then the hideous clamour stopped as abruptly as it began. The Clockwork man had not altered his position during the proceedings; but Arthur Withers, who was watching him with feverish intensity from the pavilion, fancied that his ears flapped twice just after the noise had subsided.

It was an unpleasant episode, but fortunately the object of such misplaced and ugly hilarity scarcely seemed to notice the outrage. Mr. Bumpus was not lacking in courage. After a few more groans and sighs, and a final rubbing of that part of him that had been injured, he placed himself in preparation to receive the next ball. The spectators loudly applauded him, and the bowler, perhaps unwilling to risk another misadventure, moderated his delivery. Mr. Bumpus struck the ball lightly, and it sped away through the slips. A fielder darted after it, but there was ample time for a run. "Come on!" shouted Mr. Bumpus, and started to puff and blow his way down the pitch.

But the Clockwork man paid not the slightest heed to the command. He remained, statuesque, a figure of gross indifference. Mr. Bumpus pulled himself up sharply, mid-way between the two wickets; his red face was a study in bewilderment. He slid a few paces, cast one imploring glance in the direction of the Clockwork man, and then rushed desperately back to his own crease. But he was too late; his wicket had been put down.

Etiquette plays an important part in the noble game of cricket. It may be bad form to refuse an obvious run; but to complain of your partner in public is still worse. Besides, Mr. Bumpus was too aghast for speech, and his stomach still pained him. He walked very slowly and with great dignity back to the pavilion, and his annoyance was no doubt amply soothed by the loud cheers that greeted his return. Gregg came out to meet him, with a rather shamefaced smile upon his features.

"I'm sorry," he murmured, "our recruit seems to be a little awkward. I don't think he quite understands."

"He can hit," said Mr. Bumpus, mopping his brow, "but he's certainly an eccentric sort of individual. I called to him to run, and apparently he did not or *would* not hear me."

Gregg caught hold of Arthur Withers, who was just going out to bat. "Look here," he said, "just tell our friend that he must run. I don't think he quite grasps the situation."

"No," said Arthur, slowly, "I don't think he does. He's rather a peculiar sort of person. I – I – spoke to him. He – he – says he's a clockwork man."

"Oh," said Gregg, and his face became blank. "Anyhow, just tell him that he must run when he's called."

Arthur walked out to the wicket. His usual knee-shaking seemed less pronounced, and he felt more anxious about the Clockwork man than about himself. He paused as he drew near to him, and whispered in an ear – rather fearfully, for he dreaded a recurrence of the ear-flapping business. "The captain says will you run, please, when you're asked."

The Clockwork man turned his head slightly to the right, and his mouth opened very wide. But he said nothing.

"You have to run," repeated Arthur, in louder tones.

The other flapped an ear. Arthur hastened away. Nothing was worth risking an exhibition in public such as he had witnessed in comparative seclusion. He supposed there was something about the Clockwork man really phenomenal, something that was beyond his own rather limited powers of comprehension. Perhaps cleverer people than himself might understand what was the matter with this queer being. He couldn't.

He took his place at the wicket. The first ball was an easy one, and he managed to hit it fair and square to mid-on. Scarcely hoping for response, he called to the Clockwork man, and began to run. To his immense astonishment, the latter passed him half-way down the pitch, his legs jumping from side to side, his arms swinging round irresponsibly. It might be said that his run was merely an exaggeration of his walk. Arthur dumped his bat down quickly, and turned. As he looked up, on the return journey, he was puzzled by the fact that there was no sign of his partner. He paused and looked around him.

There had been an outburst of derisive cheering when the Clockwork man actually commenced to run, but this now swelled up into a roar of merriment. And then Arthur saw what had happened. The Clockwork man had not stopped at the opposite wicket. He had run straight on, past the wicket-keeper, past the fielders, and at the moment when Arthur spotted him he was making straight for the white sheet at the back of the ground. No wonder the crowd laughed! It was so utterly absurd; and the Clockwork man ran as though nothing could stop him, as though, indeed, he had been wound up and was without power to check his own ridiculous progress. The next moment he collided with the sheet; but even this could only prevent him from going further. His legs continued to work rapidly with the action of running, whilst his body billowed into the sagging sheet.

The spectators gave themselves up wholly to the fun. It must have seemed to them that this extraordinary cricketer was also gifted with a sense of humour, however eccentric; and that his nonsensical action was intended by way of retaliation for the ironic cheers that had greeted his running at all. Nobody, except Arthur Withers, realised that the Clockwork man run thus far because for some reason he had been unable to stop himself. It may be remarked here that many of the Clockwork man's subsequent performances had this same accidental air of humour; and that even his most grotesque attitudes gave the observer an impression of some wild practical joke. He was so far human, in appearance and manner, in spite of those peculiar internal arrangements, which will be dealt with later, that his actions produced an instantaneous appeal to the comic instinct; and in laughing at him people forgot to take him seriously.

But Arthur Withers, still feeling a certain sense of duty towards that helpless figure battening himself against the sheet, ran up to him. He decided that it would be useless to try and explain matters. The Clockwork man was obviously quite irresponsible. Arthur laid his hands on his shoulders and turned him round, much in the way that a child turns a mechanical toy after it has come to rest. Thus released, the running figure proceeded back towards the wicket, followed close at heels by Arthur, who hoped, by means of a push here and a shove there, to guide him back to the pavilion and so out of harm's way.

But in this attempt he was unexpectedly thwarted. The Clockwork man recovered himself; he ran straight back to the wicket and then stopped dead. The umpire was in the act of replacing the bails, for the wicket had been put down, and, fast as this eccentric cricketer had run in the first place, he had not been quick enough to reach the crease in time. By all the rules of the game, and beyond the shadow of doubt, he had been 'run out'. He now regarded the stumps meditatively, with a finger jerked swiftly against his nose, as though recognising a former state of consciousness. And then, with a swift movement, he took up his position in readiness to receive the ball.

This was too much for the equanimity of the spectators. Shout after shout volleyed along the line of the hurdles. The calm deliberateness of the Clockwork man, in so reinstating himself, fairly crowned all his previous exhibitions. And the fact that he took no notice of the merriment at his expense, but simply waited for something to happen, permitted the utmost license. The crowd rocked itself in unrestrained hilarity.

But a second later there was stony silence. For the thing that happened next was as unexpected as it was startling. Nobody, save perhaps Dr. Allingham, anticipated that the Clockwork man was capable of adding violence to eccentricity; he looked harmless enough. But apparently there lurked a daemonic temper behind those bland, meaningless features. The thing happened in a trice; and all that followed occupied but a few catastrophic seconds. The umpire had stepped up to the Clockwork man in order to explain to him that he was expected to retire from the wicket. Not hearing any coherent reply, he emphasised his request by placing a hand suggestively on the other's shoulder. Instantly, something blade-like flashed in the stammering air, a loud thwack broke upon the silence, and the unfortunate umpire lay prostrate. He had gone down like a log of wood.

Pandemonium ensued. The scene of quiet play was transformed into a miniature battle-field. The fielders rushed in a body at the Clockwork man, only to go down one after the other, like so many ninepins. They lay, stunned and motionless. The Clockwork man spun round like a teetotum, his bat flashing in the sun, whilst the flannelled figures flying from all parts of the field approached him, only to be sent reeling and staggering to earth. Some dodged for a moment only to be caught on the rebound. Dust flew up, and to add to the whirl and confusion the unearthly noise that had so startled Arthur Withers broke out again, with terrific force, like the engine of a powerful motor suddenly started.

"I told you he was mad!" shouted Allingham, as he and Gregg leapt through the aperture of the pavilion and dashed to the rescue.

But the Clockwork man suddenly seemed panic-stricken. Just for one moment he surveyed the prostrate figures lying about on the grass like so many sacks. Then he sent the bat flying in the direction of the pavilion and rushed straight for the barrier of hurdles.

The spectators fled with one accord. Allingham and Gregg doubled up in hot pursuit. Arthur Withers, who had mustered the wit to fall down rather than to be knocked down, picked himself up quickly and joined them.

"It's alright," he gasped, "He – he – won't be able to climb the hurdles."

But there was no accounting for the activities of the Clockwork man. At a distance of about a yard from the barrier his whole body took off from the ground, and he literally floated in space over the obstacle. It was not jumping; it was more like flying. He landed lightly upon his feet, without the least difficulty; and, before the onlookers could recover from their amazement, this extraordinary personage had shot like a catapult, straight up the path along which he had travelled so precariously half an hour before. In a few seconds his diminutive figure passed into the horizon, leaving a faint trail of dust and the dying echo of that appalling noise.

"My God," exclaimed Gregg, grasping a hurdle to steady himself, "It's – it's – incredible."

Allingham couldn't say a word. He stood there panting and swallowing quickly. Arthur Withers caught up to them.

"He – he – goes by machinery, sir. He's a clockwork man."

"Don't be a damned fool," the doctor burst out, "you're talking through your hat."

Gregg was listening very acutely.

"But it is *so*," protested Arthur. "You didn't see him as I did. He was like nothing on earth – and then he began to work. Just like a motor starting. And then that noise began. I'm sure there's something inside him, something that goes wrong sometimes."

He was still a little sorry for the Clockwork man.

"That's my conviction," he gasped out, too excited and breathless for further speech.

"I think," said Gregg, with curious calmness, "I think we had better warn the police. He's likely to be dangerous."

Chapter III

The Mystery of the Clockwork Man

AN HOUR and a half later Doctor Allingham and Gregg had their tea together in the sitting room of the former's residence. Bay windows looked out upon the broad High Street, already thronged with Saturday evening excursionists. An unusually large crowd was gathered around the entrance to the Blue Lion, just over the way, for the news had soon spread about the town. Wild rumours passed from ear to ear as to the identity of the strange individual whose behaviour had resulted in so disturbing a conclusion of the cricket match. Those among the townspeople who had actually witnessed not only this event but also the rapid flight of the Clockwork man, related their version of the affair, adding a little each time and altering their theories, so that in the end those who listened were more frightened and impressed than those who had seen.

Allingham sat in stony silence, sipping tea at intervals and cutting pieces of cake into neat little squares, which he slipped into his mouth spasmodically. Now and again he passed a hand across his big tawny moustache and pulled it savagely. His state of tense nervous irritation was partly due to the fact that he had been obliged to wait so long for his tea; but he had also violently disagreed with Gregg in their discussion about the Clockwork man. At the present moment the young student stood by the window, watching the animated crowd outside the inn. He had finished his tea, and he had no wish to push his own theory about the mysterious circumstance to the extent of quarrelling with his friend.

After the disaster there had been much to do. Four times had Allingham's car travelled between the cricket ground and the local hospital, and it was half past six before the eleven players and the two umpires had been conveyed thither, treated for their wounds and discharged. No one was seriously injured, but in each case the abrasion on the side of the head had been severe enough to demand treatment. One or two had been a long while recovering full consciousness, and all were in a condition of mental confusion and gave wildly incoherent reports of the incident.

There had been times, during those journeys to and fro, when Gregg found it difficult to save himself from outbursts of laughter. He had to bite his lip hard in the effort to hold in check an imagination that was apt to run to extremes. From one point of view it had certainly been absurd that this awkward being, with his apparently limited range of movement, should have managed in a few seconds to lay out so many healthy, active men. By comparison, his batting performance, singular as it had seemed, faded into insignificance. The breathless swiftness of the action, the unerring aim, the immense force behind each blow, the incredible audacity of the act, almost persuaded Gregg that the thing was too exquisitely comic to be true. But when he forced himself to look at the matter seriously, he felt that there were little grounds for the explanation that the Clockwork man was simply a dangerous lunatic. The flight at a preposterous speed, the flying leap over the hurdle, the subsequent acceleration of his run to a pace altogether beyond human possibility, convinced the young undergraduate, who was level-headed enough, although impressionable, that some other explanation would have to be found for the extraordinary occurrence.

Besides, there was Arthur Wither's story about the flapping ears and the queer conversation of the Clockwork man, his peculiar jerky movements, his sudden exhibitions of uncanny efficiency contrasted with appalling lapses. Once you had grasped the idea of his mechanical origin, it was difficult to thrust the Clockwork man out of your head. He became something immensely exciting and suggestive. If Gregg's sense of humour had not been so violently tickled by the ludicrous side of the affair, he would have felt already that some great discovery was about to be revealed to the modern world. It had never occurred to him before that abnormal phenomena might be presented to human beings in the form of a sort of practical joke. Somehow, one expected this sort of thing to happen in solemn earnest and in the dead of night. But the event had taken place in broad daylight, and already there was mixed up with its queer unreality the most ridiculous tangle of purely human circumstance.

Allingham had an explanation for everything. He said that the loud noise was due to some kind of machine that this ingenious lunatic carried in his pocket. He argued that the rapid flight was probably to be accounted for by a sort of electric shoe. Nothing was impossible so long as you could adduce some explanation that was just humanly credible. And the strange antics of the Clockwork man, his sudden stoppings and beginnings, his 'Anglo-Saxon' gestures and his staccato gait, all came under the heading of locomotor ataxia in an advanced form.

As the doctor concentrated upon a delayed tea, his mind lapsed into its usual condition of fretful scepticism. Gregg's idea that the Clockwork man represented a mystery, if not a miracle, enraged him. At forty a man does not readily welcome discoveries that may upset his own world of accepted facts, and Allingham had long since given up the habit of following the latest results of scientific investigation. Years ago he had made his own small researches, only to discover that others were making them at the same time. He had had his gleamings in common with all the other students of his year. Everybody was having gleamings then of vast possibilities in medical science, especially in the direction of nervous pathology and the study of morbid diseases resulting from highly complex methods of living. There had been much sound work, a good deal of irresponsible mud-raking, and, in Allingham's case, a growing suspicion that the human organism was not standing very well the strains imposed upon it by modern civilisation. He had wondered then if some experiments would not be made some day in the pursuit of evolutionary doctrines as applied to physiological progress – but that had been the most ephemeral of all his gleams.

He had been glad to abandon the hospitals in favour of a comfortable practice and the leisured life of a country town. Great Wymering had offered him plenty of distractions that soothed the slight wound to his vanity caused by the discovery that he had over-estimated his originality. In a few years much had happened that helped to confirm his new view of himself as a social creature with a taste for the amenities of existence. And then he had been able to keep up his cricket. In the winter there were bridge parties, amateur theatricals, dinner parties with quite ordinary but agreeable people, local affairs into which a man whose health was under suspicion and whose sympathies were just perceptibly narrowing, could plunge without too much effort being required in order to rise to such occasions. And he had the witty temperament. Quite easily, he maintained a reputation for turning out a bon-mot on the spur of the moment, something with a faint element of paradox. He would say such things as, "Only those succeed in life who have brains and can forget the fact," or, "To be idle is the goal of all men, but only the industrious achieve it." When taunted by a young lady who suspected him of wasted talents, even genius, he retorted that, "Genius is only an accumulation of neglected diseases."

Latterly he had suffered from strange irritations not easily to be ascribed to liver, misgivings, a sense of having definitely accepted a secondary edition of himself. An old acquaintance would have detected at once the change in his character, the marked leaning towards conservatism in politics and a certain reactionary tendency in his general ideas. He was becoming fixed in his views, and believed in a stable universe. His opinions, in fact, were as automatic as his Swedish exercises in the morning and his apple before breakfast. There was a slight compensatory increase in his sense of humour, and there was his approaching marriage to Lilian Payne, the gifted daughter of a wealthy town councillor.

That last fact occupied a central place in his mind just at present, but it was also another source of irritation. Lilian was intellectual as well as fascinating, and the former attribute became more marked as they grew more intimate. Instead of charming little notes inviting him to tea he now received long, and, he was obliged to admit, quite excellent essays upon the true place of woman in modern life. He was bound to applaud, but such activity of mind was by no means to his taste. He liked a woman to have thoughts; but a thinking woman was a nuisance.

All these clamouring reforms represented to him merely a disinclination to bother about the necessary affairs of life, an evasion of inevitable evils, a refusal to accept life as a school of learning by trial and error. Besides, if women got hold of the idea of efficiency there would be an end to all things. They would make a worse muddle of the 'mad dream' than the men. Women made fewer mistakes and they were temperamentally inclined towards the pushing of everything that they undertook to the point of violent and uncomfortable success.

Efficiency! How he hated the word! It reminded him of his own heart-breaking struggles, not only with the difficulties of an exacting science, but with the complexities of the time in which his youth had been spent, a time when all the intelligent young men had been trying to find some way out of the social evils that then existed – and still existed, as an ironical memorial to their futile efforts. In those days one scarcely dared to move in intellectual circles without having evolved one's personal solution of the social problem, an achievement that implied a great deal of hard reading, attendance at Fabian meetings, and a certain amount of voluntary thinking.

If necessary, one could brush all that up again. How different life was, when it came to be lived; how unlike the sagacious prognostications of doubting youth! There was a substratum underneath all that surge of enquiry and inquisitiveness, all that worry and distress; and that was life itself, known and valued, something that one clung to with increasing strength. The mind grew out of its speculative stage and settled down to a careful consideration of concrete existence.

And then, with a sharp jar, his thoughts reverted to the consideration of another irritating circumstance, this ridiculous Clockwork man, in whom Gregg believed even to the extent of thinking it worthwhile stating the case for the incredible before a man years his senior in experience and rational thought.

* * *

Allingham got up and stood behind Gregg at the window. The latter raised his head a little as though to catch any words that might float across from the babel of excited voices opposite. But there was nothing clearly distinguishable.

"You see," said Allingham, nodding his head and wiping his moustache with a handkerchief, "let the thing work on your mind and you ally yourself with these town gossips. They'll talk this affair into a nine days wonder."

Gregg shrugged his shoulders in silence. Presently he looked at his watch. "I wonder if Grey will be back soon." Grey was the local inspector of police, in whose hands they had placed the business of rounding up the Clockwork man. Allingham had loaned out his car for the purpose.

"I doubt if we shall see him before midnight," said the latter. "Even supposing he catches his man before dusk, which is unlikely, it will take him another hour or so to drive to the Asylum."

Gregg failed to suppress an abrupt snigger. He lit a cigarette to cover his confusion. Once more he envisaged that flying figure on the horizon. "At the rate he was going," he remarked, steadily, "and barring accidents, I should say he's reached London by now."

"There will be an accident," retorted Allingham. "Mark my words, he won't get very far."

At that moment Mrs. Masters, the doctor's elderly housekeeper, entered the room in order to clear away the tea things. She was a country woman, given to talking without reserve, except when the doctor's eye fell upon her, as it did upon this occasion. But for once she evaded this check to her natural proclivities; she was not going to be cheated out of her share in the local gossip. She placed the tray on the table and made the visitor an excuse for her loquacity.

"Oh, Mr. Gregg, they say the Devil's come to Great Wymering at last. I'm not surprised to 'ear it, for the goings on in this town 'ave been something terrible since the war. What with the drinking and the young people doing just as they like."

"Have you heard anything fresh?" enquired Gregg, pleasantly.

"Only about old Mr. Winchape," said Mrs. Masters, as she packed the tea things. "He's seen the man that knocked the cricketers down with the bat. That is, if he is a man, but they do say—"

"Where did Mr. Winchape see him?" broke in Allingham, abruptly.

"Along the path from Bapchurch, sir." Mrs. Masters moderated her manner before the doctor's searching eye. "Poor old Mr. Winchape, he's not so young as he was, and it did give him a turn. He says he was 'urrying along so as to get 'ome in time for tea, and all of a sudden something flashed by 'im, so quick that he 'ardly realised it. He looked round, but it was gone in no time. He reckons it was the Old Man 'imself. There was fire coming out of his mouth and 'is eyes was like two red 'ot coals—"

Allingham stamped his feet on the carpet. "I *will* not listen to such talk, Mrs. Masters! A woman of your age and supposed sense to lend ear to such nonsense. I'm ashamed of you."

Mrs. Masters trembled a little under the rebuke, but she showed no sign of repentance. "I'm only repeating what's said," she remarked. "An' for all I know it might have been the Devil. It says in the Bible that he's to be unbound for a thousand years, and I'm sure he might just as well come here as elsewhere for a start. The place is wicked enough."

"Superstitious nonsense," snorted Allingham. And he continued to snort at intervals while Mrs. Masters hastily collected cups and plates, and retreated with dignity to the kitchen.

"Perhaps you agree with Mrs. Masters?" said Allingham, as soon as the door was closed.

Gregg laughed and lowered himself into an easy chair. "Superstition, after all, is a perfectly legitimate although rudimentary form of human enquiry. These good people want to believe in the Devil. At the least opportunity they evoke his satanic majesty. They are quite right. They are simply using the only material in their minds in order to investigate a mystery."

"A sort of glamour," suggested Allingham, trying to look bored.

"If you like," admitted Gregg, "only it does help them to understand, just as all our scientific knowledge helps us to understand, the future."

"Why drag in the future," said the other, opening his eyes quickly.

"Because," said Gregg, purposely adopting a monotonous drawl as though to conceal his eagerness, "if my theory is correct, then I assume that the Clockwork man comes from the future."

"It's a harmless enough assumption," laughed Allingham.

Gregg rested his head upon the back of the chair and puffed smoke out. "We will pass over the circumstance of his abrupt appearance at the top of the hill, for it is obvious that he might have come from one of the neighbouring villages, although I don't think he did. You yourself admit that his manner of approach was startling, and that it almost seemed as though he had come from nowhere. But let that be. There are, I admit, as yet few facts in support of my theory, but it is at least significant that one of the first questions he asked should have been, not where he was but when he was."

"I don't quite follow you," interjected Allingham.

"He asked Arthur Withers what year it was. Naturally, if he did come from the future, his first anxiety would be to know into what period of man's history he had, possibly by some accident, wandered."

"But how could he have come from the future?"

"Time," said Gregg, quickly, "is a relative thing. The future has happened just as much as the past. It is happening at this moment."

"Oh, well, you may be right there," blustered Allingham, "I don't know. I admit I'm not quite up to date in these abstruse speculations."

"I regard that statement of his as highly significant," resumed Gregg, after a slight pause. "For, of course, if the Clockwork man really is, as suggested, a semi-mechanical being, then he could only have come from the future. So far as I am aware, the present has not yet evolved sufficiently even to consider seriously the possibility of introducing mechanical reinforcements into the human body, although there has been tentative speculation on the subject. We are thousands of years away from such a proposition; on the other hand, there is no reason why it should not have already happened outside of our limited knowledge of futurity. It has often occurred to me that the drift of scientific progress is slowly but surely leading us in the direction of some such solution of physiological difficulties. The human organism shows signs of breaking down under the strain of an increasingly complex civilisation. There may be a limit to our power of adaptability, and in that case humanity will have to decide whether it will alter its present mode of living or find instead some means of supplementing the normal functions of the body. Perhaps that has, as I suggest, already happened; it depends entirely upon which road humanity has taken. If the mechanical side of civilisation has developed at its present rate, I see no reason why the man of the future should not have found means to ensure his efficiency by mechanical means applied to his natural functions."

Gregg sat up in his chair and became more serious. Allingham fidgeted without actually interrupting.

"Imagine an exceedingly complex kind of mechanism," Gregg resumed, "an exaggeration of the many intricate types of modern machines in use today. It would have to be something of a very delicate description, and yet rather crude at first in its effect. One thinks of something that would work accurately if in rather a limited sort of way. You see, they would have to ensure success in some things at first even at the sacrifice of a certain general awkwardness. It would be a question of taking one thing at a time. Thus, when the Clockwork man came to play cricket, all he could do was to hit the ball. We have to admit that he did that efficiently enough, however futile were the rest of his actions."

"Hot air," interrupted Allingham, reaching for his tobacco pouch, "that's all this is."

"Oh, I won't admit that," rejoined Gregg, cheerfully, "we must acknowledge that what we saw this afternoon was entirely abnormal. Even when we were talking to him I had a strong feeling come over me that our interrogator was not a normal human being. I don't mean simply his behaviour. His clothes were an odd sort of colour and shape. And did you notice his boots? Curious, dull-looking things. As though they were made out of some kind of metal. And then, the hat and wig?"

"You're simply imagining all these things," said Allingham, hotly, as he rammed tobacco into his pipe.

"I'm not. I really noticed them. Of course, I didn't attach much importance to them at the time, but afterwards, when Arthur Withers was telling his story, all that queer feeling about the strange figure came back to me. It took possession of me. After all, suppose he *is* a clockwork man?"

"But what is a clockwork man?" demanded Allingham.

"Well, of course I can't explain that exactly, but the term so obviously explains itself. Damn it, he is a clockwork man. He walks, talks, and behaves exactly like one would imagine—"

"Imagine!" burst out Allingham. "Yes, you can *imagine* such a thing. But you are trying to prove to me that this creature is something that doesn't and can't exist outside your imagination. It won't wash."

"But you agree," said Gregg, unperturbed, "that it might be possible in the future?"

"Oh, well, everything is possible, if you look at it in that light," grudgingly admitted the other.

"Then all we have to do is to prove that the future is involved. Our lunatic must convince us that he is not of our age, that he has, in fact, and probably by mechanical means, found his way back to an age of flesh and blood. So far, we are agreed, for I willingly side with you in your opinion that the Clockwork man could not exist in the present; while I am open to be convinced that he is a quite credible invention of the remote future."

He broke off, for at that moment a car drew up in front of the window, and the burly form of Inspector Grey stepped down in company with two constables and a lad of about fifteen, whom both Gregg and the doctor recognised as an inhabitant of the neighbouring village of Bapchurch.

* * *

"Well?" said Allingham, as the party stamped awkwardly into the room, after a preliminary shuffling upon the mat. "What luck?"

"Not much, doctor," announced the inspector, removing his hat and disclosing a fringe of carroty hair. "We 'aint found your man, and so far as I can judge we 'aint likely to. But we've found these."

He laid the Clockwork man's hat and wig on the table. Gregg instantly picked them up and began examining them with great curiosity.

"And young Tom Driver here, he's seen the man himself," resumed the inspector. "That's 'ow we come by the 'at and wig. Tell the gentlemen what you saw, Tom."

Tom Driver was a backward youth at the best of times, but he seemed quite overcome by the amount of responsibility now thrust upon him. He shuffled forward, pressing his knees together and holding a tattered cap between his very dirty fingers. A great shock of curly yellow hair fell almost over his large brown eyes, and his face was long and pinched.

"I see the man," he began, timidly, "I see 'im as I was going along the path to Bapchurch."

"Was he going very fast?" said Gregg.

"No, sir, he weren't walking at all. He'd fallen into the chalk pit just by Rock's Bottom."

Allingham burst out into a great roar of laughter; but Gregg merely smiled and listened.

"That's 'ow I come to see 'im," said Tom, shifting his cap about uneasily. "I was in a bit of a 'urry 'cos mother said I wasn't to be late for tea, and I'd been into the town to buy butter as we was a bit short. As I come by Rock's Bottom – and you know 'ow the path bends a bit sharp to the left where the chalk pit lies – it's a bit awkward for anyone 'as don't know the path—"

"Yes, go on," said Gregg, impatiently.

"Well, as I was coming along I see something moving about just at the top of the pit. At first I thought it was a dog, but when I come nearer I could see it was a pair of legs, kicking. Only they was going so fast you couldn't hardly tell one from t'other. Well, I ran up, thinking 'as very likely someone 'ad fallen in, and sure enough it was someone. I caught 'old of the legs, and just as I was about to pull 'im out—"

"Did the legs go on kicking?" said Gregg, quickly.

"Yes, sir, I 'ad a job to 'old them. And then, just as I was going to pull 'im out, I noticed something—"

Tom paused for a moment and began to tremble. His teeth chattered violently, and he looked appealingly at his listeners as though afraid to continue.

"Go on, Tom," commanded Inspector Grey. "Spit it out, lad. It's got to be said."

"He – He – hadn't got no back to his head," blurted out Tom at last.

"What!" rapped out Allingham.

"There you are," said Tom, cowering and glancing reproachfully at the inspector, "I told you as 'ow t'gentlemen wouldn't believe me. T'aint likely as anybody would believe it as 'adn't seen it for themselves."

"But what did you see?" enquired Gregg, kindly. "What was there to be seen?"

Tom's eyes searched the room as though looking for something. Gregg was standing with his back to the fire-place, but noticing that Tom seemed to be trying to look behind him, he moved away. Tom immediately pointed to the clock that stood on the mantelpiece.

"It was a clock," he said, slowly, "just like that one, only more so, in a manner of speaking. I mean it 'ad more 'ands and figures, and they was going round very fast. But it 'ad a glass face just like that one, and it was stuck on 'is 'ead just where the back ought to be. The sun was shining on it at first. That's why I couldn't be sure what it was for a long time. But when I looked closer, I could see plain enough, and it made me feel all wobbly, sir."

"Was there a loud noise?" asked Gregg.

"No, sir, not then. But the 'ands was moving very fast, and there was a sort of 'umming going on like a lot of clocks all going on at once, only quiet like. I was so taken back I didn't know what to do, but presently I caught 'old of 'is legs and tried to pull 'im out. It weren't a easy job, 'cos 'is legs was kicking all the time, and although I 'ollered out to 'im 'e took no notice. At last

I dragged 'im out, and 'e lay on the grass, still kicking. 'E never even tried to get up, and at last I took 'old of his shoulders and picked 'im up. And then, as soon as I got 'im up and stood 'im on his feet, and afore I 'ad time to 'ave a good look at 'im, off he goes, like greased lightning. An awful noise started, like machinery, and afore I 'ad time to turn round 'e was down the path towards Bapchurch and out of sight. I tell you, sir, it gave me a proper turn."

"But how did you come by these?" questioned Gregg, who was still holding the hat and wig.

"I see them lying in the pit," explained Tom, "they must 'ave dropped off 'is 'ead as he lay there. Of course, 'e 'adn't fallen very far, otherwise 'is legs wouldn't 'ave been sticking up. It 'ain't very steep just there, and 'is 'ead must 'ave caught in a bit of furze. But the 'at and wig 'ad rolled down to the bottom. After 'e'd gone I climbed down and picked them up."

Gregg passed the hat and wig to Allingham, and whispered something. The other looked at the inside of the hat. There was a small label in the centre, with the following matter printed upon it:—

DUNN BROTHERS
UNIVERSAL HAT PROVIDERS
ESTABLISHED OVER 2,000 YEARS

For a moment Allingham's face was a study in bewilderment. He tried to speak, but only succeeded in producing an absurd snigger. Then he tried to laugh outright, and was forced into rapid speech. "Well, what did I say? The whole thing is preposterous. I'm afraid, inspector, we've troubled you for nothing. The fact is, somebody has been guilty of a monstrous hoax."

"Look at the wig, look at the wig," interrupted Gregg, feverishly.

Allingham did so. Just on the edge of the lining there was an oblong-shaped tab, with small gold lettering:—

W. CLARKSON. Wig-maker to the Seventh International.

"Well, well, it's what I said," the doctor went on, swallowing quickly, "someone has – someone has—"

He broke off abruptly. Gregg was standing with his hands behind him. He shook his head gravely.

"It's no use, doc," he observed, quietly, "we've got to face it."

Chapter IV
Arthur Withers Thinks Things Out

AFTER THAT LAST glimpse of the Clockwork man, and the conversation with Doctor Allingham and Gregg that followed, Arthur had hurried home to his tea. No amount of interest in the affair, however stupendous it might appear both to himself and others, could dissuade him from his usual Saturday night's programme. Rose Lomas, to whom he had recently become engaged, was a hundred times more important than a clockwork man, and whether a human being could actually exist who walked and talked by mechanical means was a small problem in comparison with that of changing his clothes, washing and tidying himself up in time for his assignation. As soon as the cricketers showed signs of stirring themselves, and so conveyed the comforting impression that they were not dead, Arthur felt himself able to resume normal existence.

His lodgings were situated at the lower end of the town. The accommodation consisted of a small bedroom, which he shared with a fellow clerk, and a place at table with the other inmates of the house. The street was very dirty, and Mrs. Flack's house alone presented some sign of decency and respectability. It was a two-storied red brick cottage. There was no front garden, and you entered directly into a living room through a door, upon which a brass plate was fixed that bore the following announcement:

MRS. FLACK
Trained Midwife

Arthur stumbled into the room, dropped his straw hat on to the broken-down couch that occupied the entire side of one wall, and sat down at the table.

"Well?" enquired Mrs. Flack, as she poured him out a cup of tea, "who won?"

"Nobody," remarked Arthur, cramming bread and butter into his mouth. "Game off."

Mr. Flack, who was seated in his armchair by the fireplace, looked up in amazement. His interest in cricket was immense, but chronic rheumatism prevented him from getting as far as the ground. He was dependent upon Arthur's reports and the local paper. "'Ow's that, then?" he demanded, slowly.

Arthur swallowed quickly and tried to explain. But, although the affair was still hot in his mind, he found it exceedingly difficult to describe exactly what had taken place. The doings of the Clockwork man were at once obvious and inexplicable. It was almost impossible to intrigue people who had not actually witnessed the affair into a realisation of such extraordinary happenings. Arthur had to resort to abrupt movements of his arms and legs in order to produce an effect. But he made a great point of insistence upon the ear-flapping.

"Go *hon!*" exclaimed Mrs. Flack, leaning her red folded arms upon the table, "well I never!"

"'Tain't possible," objected her husband, "'e's pulling your leg, ma."

But Arthur persisted in his imitations, without caring very much whether his observers believed him or not. It at least afforded an entertaining occupation. Mrs. Flack's motherly bosom rose and fell with merriment. "It's as good as the pictures," she announced at last, wiping her eyes. But when Arthur spoke about the loud noise, and hinted that the Clockwork man's internal arrangements consisted of some kind of machinery, Mr. Flack sat bolt upright and shook his head gravely.

"You're a masterpiece," he remarked, "that's what you are." This was his usual term for anything out the way. "You ain't a going to get me to believe that, not at my age."

"If you saw him," said Arthur, emphatically, "you'd *have* to believe. It's just that, and nothing else. He's like one of those mechanical toys come to life. And it's so funny. You'd never guess."

Mr. Flack shook his head thoughtfully. Presently he got up, walked to the end of the mantelpiece, placed his smoked-out pipe on the edge and took an empty one from behind an ornament. Then he returned to his seat and sat for a long time with the empty pipe in his mouth.

"'T'ain't possible," he ruminated, at last, "not for a bloke to 'ave machinery inside 'im. At least, not to my way of thinking."

Arthur finished his tea and got up from his chair. Conscious that his efforts so far had not carried conviction, he spent a few moments of valuable time in an attempt to supplement them.

"He went like this," he explained, imitating the walk of the Clockwork man, and at the same time snapping his fingers to suggest sharp clicking noises. "And the row! Well, you know what a motor sounds like when it's being wound up. Like that, only worse."

Mrs. Flack held the greater part of herself in a semicircle of red arm. "You are a one," she declared. Then she looked at Mr. Flack, who sat unmoved. "Why don't *you* laugh. It would do you good. You take everything so serious."

"I ain't a going to laugh," said Mr. Flack, "not unless I see fit to laugh." And he continued to stare gravely at Arthur's elaborate posturing. Presently the latter remembered his urgent appointment and disappeared through the narrow door that led upstairs.

"Whoever 'e be," said Mr. Flack, referring to the strange visitor to Great Wymering, "I should judge 'im to be a bit of a masterpiece."

* * *

Upstairs in the bedroom, Arthur hastily removed his flannels and paced the limited amount of floor space between the two beds. What a little box of a place it was, and how absurdly crammed with furniture! You couldn't move an inch without bumping into things or knocking something over. There wasn't room to swing a cat, much less to perform an elaborate toilet with that amount of leisurely comfort necessary to its successful accomplishment. Ordinarily he didn't notice these things; it was only when he was in a hurry, and had all sorts of little duties to carry out, that the awkwardness of his surroundings forced themselves into his mind and produced a sense of revolt. There were times when everything seemed a confounded nuisance and a chair stuck in your way made you feel inclined to pitch it out of the window. Just when you wanted to enjoy simply being yourself, when your thoughts were running in a pleasant, easeful way, you had to turn to and dress or undress, shave or wash, prepare yourself for the conventions of life. So much of existence was spent in actions that were obligatory only because other people expected you to do the same as themselves. It wasn't so much a waste of time as a waste of life.

He rescued his trousers from underneath the mattress. It was only recently that he had discovered this obvious substitute for a trouser press, and so added one more nuisance to existence. It was something else to be remembered. He grinned pleasantly at the thought of the circumstance which had brought about these careful habits. Rose Lomas liked him to look smart, and he had managed it somehow. There were plenty of dapper youths in Great Wymering, and Arthur had been astute enough to notice wherein he had differed from them, in the first stages of his courting. Early rebuffs had led him to perceive that the eye of love rests primarily upon a promising exterior, and only afterwards discovers the interior qualities that justify a wise choice. Arthur had been spurned at first on account of a slovenliness that, to do him justice, was rather the result of personal conviction, however erring, than mere carelessness. He really had felt that it was a waste of life even to spend half an hour a month inside a barber's shop. Not only that, but the experience was far-reaching in its unpleasant consequences. You went into the shop feeling agreeably familiar with yourself, conscious of intense personality; and you came out a nonentity, smelling of bay-rum. The barber succeeded in transforming you from an individual brimming over with original reflections and impulses into a stranger without a distinctive notion in your head. The barber, in fact, was a Delilah in trousers; he ravished the locks from your head and bewitched you into the bargain.

Arthur had a strong sense of originality, although he would have been the last person to claim originality in his thoughts. He disliked interference with any part of his personal being. As a boy he had been perturbed by the prospect of growing up. It had seemed to him such a hopeless sort of process, a mere longitudinal extension, without corresponding gain in other magnitudes. He suspected that other dubious advantages were only to be purchased at the expense of a thinning out of the joys of childhood. Later on, he discovered, sadly enough, that this was the case; although it was possible deliberately to protract one's adolescence. Hence his untidiness, his inefficiency, and even his obtuseness, were less constitutional faults than weapons in the warfare against the encroachment of time.

But the authorities at the bank regarded them as grave defects in his character.

Falling in love had revealed the matter in a very different light. It was quite worthwhile yielding to fashion in order to win the affection of Rose Lomas. And so he had imitated his rivals. He cast aside all ties that revealed their linings, trimmed up the cuffs of his shirts; overcame with an effort a natural repugnance to wearing his best clothes; and generally submitted himself to that daily supervision of superficial matters which he could now regard as the prelude to happy hours. And Rose, interested in that conquest of himself for her sake, had soon learned how much there was beneath the polished surface to capture her heart.

Yes, love made everything different! You were ready to put up with all inconveniences and indignities for the sake of that strange obsession. That thought consoled him as he crept on hands and knees in order to pick up his safety razor that had dropped behind the bulky chest of drawers. Love accounted for everything, both serious and comic.

He found his razor, plunged it into cold water – he had forgotten to ask Mrs. Flack for hot, and couldn't be bothered now – and lathered his face thoughtfully.

How many times, in the course of a lifetime, would he repeat that operation? And he would always stand in exactly the same way, with his legs straddled apart, and his elbows spanning out like flappers. He would always pass the razor over his face in a certain manner, avoiding those places where even the sharpest blade boggled a little, proceeding with the same mechanical strokes until the job was once more accomplished. Afterwards, he would laboriously separate the portions of his razor and wipe them methodically, always in the same order. That was because, once you had decided upon the right way to do a thing you adopted that method for good.

He achieved that second grand sweep of the left side of his face, ending at the corner of his mouth, and followed it up by a swift, upward stroke, annihilating the bristly tuft underneath his lower lip. Looking swiftly at the clock, he noticed that it was getting dreadfully late. That was another curious problem of existence.

You were always up against time. Generally, when you had to do something or get somewhere, there was this sense of breathless hurry and a disconcerting feeling that the world ended abruptly at the conclusion of every hour and then began again quite differently. The clock, in fact, was another tyrant, robbing you of that sensation of being able to go on forever without changing. That was why people said, when they consulted their watches, "How's the enemy?"

He attacked the problem of his upper lip with sturdy resolution. It was important that this part of his face should be quite smooth. There must not be even a suspicion of roughness. Tears started into his eyes as he harrowed that tender surface. He drew in his breath sharply, and in that moment of voluntary and glad travail achieved a metaphysical conception of the first magnitude.

All really important questions in life came under the heading of Time and Space, thought of in capital letters. Recently, he had struggled through a difficult book, in which the author used these expressions a great many times, although in a sense difficult to grasp. Nevertheless, it suddenly became obvious, in a small way, exactly what the chap had been driving at.

And somehow, his thoughts instantly returned to the Clockwork man. He performed the rest of his toilet swiftly, the major part of his brain occupied with reflections that had for their drift the curious ease with which you could perform some operations in life without consciously realising the fact.

* * *

"Oh, I'm not nearly ready yet!"

Rose Lomas stood at the open window of her bedroom. Her bare arms and shoulders gleamed softly in the twilight. One hand held her loosened hair on the top of her head, and the other pressed a garment to her chest.

"Alright," said Arthur, standing at the gate, "buck up."

Rose looked cautiously around as though to make sure no one else was in a position to observe her *decolleté*. But the road was empty. It seemed pleasant to see Arthur standing there twirling his walking stick and looking upwards at her. She decided to keep him there for a few moments.

"Lovely evening," she remarked, presently.

"Yes, jolly," said Arthur, "buck up."

"I *am* bucking up."

"You're not even dressed!"

"I am," Rose insisted, distantly, "much more than you think. I've got lots on."

They looked solemnly at one another for a long while without even approaching a 'stare out'.

"How many runs did you make," Rose asked. She had to repeat the question again before he could hear it distinctly. Besides, he never could believe that her interest in cricket was serious.

"None," he admitted, "but I was not out."

Rose considered. "That's not as good as making runs though."

Arthur heard a slight noise somewhere round the back of the cottage. "Someone coming," he warned.

Rose retreated a few steps and lowered her head.

"Walk up the lane," she whispered, "I'll come presently."

"Alright," Arthur nodded, "*buck* up."

He walked a few yards up the road, and then turned through a wicket gate and mounted the hump of a meadow. The narrow path swerved slightly to right and left. Arthur fell to meditating upon paths in general and how they came into existence. Obviously, it was because people always walked in the same way. Countless footsteps, following the same line until the grass wore away. That was very odd when you came to think about it. Why didn't people choose different ways of crossing that particular meadow? Then there would be innumerable paths, representing a variety of choice. It would be interesting to start a path of your own, and see how many people would follow you, even though you deliberately chose a circuitous or not obviously direct route. You could come every day until the path was made.

He climbed over the top of the meadow, descended again into a valley, and stopped before a stile with hedges running away on either side. He decided to wait here for Rose. It would be pleasant to see her coming over the hill.

It was gloaming now. The few visible stars shone with a peculiar individual brightness, and looked strangely pendulous in the fading blue sky. He leaned back and gazed at the depths above him. This time of the day was always puzzling. You could never tell exactly at what moment the sky really changed into the aspect of evening, and then, night. Yet there must be some subtle moment when each star was born. Perhaps by looking hard enough it would be possible to become aware of these things. It would be like watching a bud unfold. Slow change was an impenetrable mystery, for actually things seemed to happen too quickly for you to notice them. Or rather, you were too busy to notice them. Spring was like that. Every year you made up your mind to notice the first blossoming, the initial tinge of green; but always it happened that you awoke one morning and found that some vast change had taken place, so that it really seemed like a miracle.

He sat there, dangling an empty pipe between his teeth. He was not conscious of a desire to smoke, and he felt strangely tolerant of Rose's delay. She would come presently.

Presently his reverie was abruptly disturbed by a faint noise, strangely familiar although remote. It seemed to reach him from the right, as though something crept slowly along the hedge line, hidden from his view. It was a soft, purring sound, very regular and sustained. At first he thought it was the cry of a pheasant, but decided that it was much too persistent. It was something that made a noise in the process of walking along.

He held his breath and turned his head slowly to the right. For a long time the sound increased only very slightly. And then, there broke upon the general stillness a series of abrupt explosions.

Pfft – Pfft – Pfft – Pfft – Pfft—

And the other noise, the purring and whirring, resumed this time so close to Arthur that he instinctively, and half in fear, arose from the stile and looked around him. But the tall hedges sweeping away on either side made it difficult to see anyone who might be approaching under their cover. There was a pause. Then a different sound.

Click – click – clickerty click – clicker – clicker – clicker— And so on, becoming louder and louder until at last it stopped, and its place was taken by the dull pitter-patter of footsteps coming nearer and nearer. There was a little harsh snort that might have been intended for a sigh, and then a voice.

"Oh dear, it is trying. It really is most dreadfully trying—"

The next moment the Clockwork man came into full view round the corner of the hedge. He was swaying slightly from side to side, in his usual fashion, and his eyes stared straight ahead of him. He did not appear to notice Arthur, and did not stop until the latter politely stepped aside in order to allow him to pass. Then the Clockwork man screwed his head slowly round and appeared to become faintly apprehensive of the presence of another being. After a preliminary ear-flapping, he opened his mouth very wide.

"You haven't," he began, with great difficulty, "seen a hat and wig?"

"No," said Arthur, and he glanced at the Clockwork man's bald forehead and noticed something peculiar about the construction of the back of his head; there seemed to be some object there which he could not see because they were facing each other. "I'm sorry," he continued, looking rather hopelessly around him, "perhaps we could find them somewhere."

"Somewhere!" echoed the Clockwork man, "that's what seems to me so extraordinary! Everybody says that. The idea of a thing being *somewhere*, you know. Elsewhere than where you expect it to be. It's so confusing."

Arthur consulted his common sense. "Can't you remember the place where you lost them," he suggested.

A faint wrinkle of perplexity appeared on the other's forehead. He shook his head once "Place. There, again, I can't grasp that idea. What is a place? And how does a thing come to be in one place and not in another?" He jerked a hand up as though to emphasise the point. "A thing either is or it isn't. It can't be in a *place*."

"But it must be somewhere," objected Arthur, "that's obvious."

The Clockwork man looked vaguely distressed. "Theoretically," he agreed, "what you say is correct. I can conceive it as a mathematical problem. But actually, you know, it isn't at all obvious."

He jerked his head slowly round and gazed at the surrounding objects. "It's such an extraordinary world. I can't get used to it at all. One keeps on bumping into things and falling into things – things that ought not to be there, you know."

Arthur could hardly control an eager curiosity to know what the thing was, round and shiny, that looked like a sort of halo at the back of the Clockwork man's head. He kept on dodging from one side to the other in an effort to see it clearly.

"Are you looking at my clock?" enquired the Clockwork man, without altering his tone of speech. "I must apologise. I feel quite indecent."

"But what is it for?" gasped Arthur.

"It's the regulating mechanism," said the other, monotonously, "I keep on forgetting that you *can't* know these things. You see, it controls me. But, of course, it's out of order. That's how I came to be here, in this absurd world. There can't be any other reason, I'm sure." He looked so childishly perplexed that Arthur's sense of pity was again aroused, and he listened in respectful silence.

"You see," the mechanical voice went on, "only about half the clock is in action. That accounts for my present situation." There was a pause, broken only by obscure tickings, regular but thin in sound. "I had been feeling very run down, and went to have myself attended to. Then some careless mechanic blundered, and of course I went all wrong." He turned swiftly and looked hard at Arthur. "All wrong. Absolutely all wrong. And of course, I – I – lapsed, you see."

"Lapsed!" queried Arthur.

"Yes, I lapsed. Slipped, if you like that better – slipped back about eight thousand years, so far as I can make out. And, of course, everything is different." His arms shot up both together in an abrupt gesture of despair. "And now I am confronted with all these old problems of Time and Space."

Arthur's recent reflections returned to him, and produced a little glow in his mind. "Is there a world," he questioned, "where the problems of Time and Space are different?"

"Of course," replied the Clockwork man, clicking slightly, "quite different. The clock, you see, made man independent of Time and Space. It solved everything."

"But what happens," Arthur wanted to know, "when the clock works properly?"

"Everything happens," said the other, "exactly as you want it to happen."

"Awfully convenient," Arthur murmured.

"Exceedingly." The Clockwork man's head nodded up and down with a regular rhythm. "The whole aim of man is convenience." He jerked himself forward a few paces, as though impelled against his will. "But my present situation, you know, is extremely inconvenient."

He waddled swiftly along, and, to Arthur's great disappointment, disappeared round the corner of the hedge, so that it was impossible to get more than a fleeting glimpse of that fascinating object at the back of his head. But he was still speaking.

"I don't know what I shall do, I'm sure," Arthur heard him say, as though to himself.

* * *

Rose Lomas came slowly over the top of the hill. She was hatless, and her short, curly hair blew about her face, for a slight breeze had sprung up in the wake of the sunset. She wore a navy blue jacket over a white muslin blouse with a deep V at the breast. There was a fair stretch of plump leg, stockinged in black cashmere, between the edge of her dark skirt and the beginning of the tall boots that had taken so long to button up. She walked with her chin tilted upwards and her eyes half closed, and her hands were thrust into the slanting pockets of her jacket.

"Whoever was that person you were talking to?" she enquired, as soon as they stood together.

"Oh, someone who had lost his way," said Arthur, carelessly. He felt curiously disinclined to explain matters just at present. The Clockwork man was disconcerting. He was a rather terrifying side-issue. Arthur had a feeling that Rose would probably be frightened by him, for she was a timid girl. He half hoped now that this strange being would turn out to be some kind of monstrous hoax.

And so he said nothing. They remained by the stile, courting each other and the silent oncoming of night. They were very ordinary lovers, and behaved just exactly in the same way as other people in the same condition. They kissed at intervals and examined each other's faces with portentous gravity and microscopic care. Leaning against the stile, they were frequently interrupted by pedestrians, some of whom took special care to light their pipes as they passed. But the disturbance scarcely affected them. Being lovers, they belonged to each other; and the world about them also belonged to them, and seemed to fashion its laws in accordance with their desires. They would not have offered you twopence for a reformed House of Commons or an enlightened civilisation.

"Oh, Arthur," said Rose, suddenly, "I want to be like this always, don't you?"

"Yes," murmured Arthur, and then caught his breath sharply. For his ear had detected a faint throbbing and palpitation in the distance. It seemed to echo from the far-off hills, a sort of 'chew chew', constantly repeated. And presently, another and more familiar sound aroused his attention. It was the 'toot-toot' of an automobile and the jerk of a brake. And then the steady whine of the engine as the car ascended a hill. Perhaps they were pursuing the Clockwork man. Arthur hoped not. It seemed to him the troubles of that strange being were bad enough without there being added to them the persecutions suffered by those to whom existence represents an endless puzzle, full of snares and surprises.

The complete and unabridged text is available online,
from *flametreepublishing.com/extras*

Pygmalion and Galatea

Josephine Preston Peabody

THE ISLAND OF CYPRUS was dear to the heart of Venus. There her temples were kept with honor, and there, some say, she watched with the Loves and Graces over the long enchanted sleep of Adonis. This youth, a hunter whom she had dearly loved, had died of a wound from the tusk of a wild boar; but the bitter grief of Venus had won over even the powers of Hades. For six months of every year, Adonis had to live as a Shade in the world of the dead; but for the rest of time he was free to breathe the upper air. Here in Cyprus the people came to worship him as a god, for the sake of Venus who loved him; and here, if any called upon her, she was like to listen.

Now there once lived in Cyprus a young sculptor, Pygmalion by name, who thought nothing on earth so beautiful as the white marble folk that live without faults and never grow old. Indeed, he said that he would never marry a mortal woman, and people began to think that his daily life among marble creatures was hardening his heart altogether.

But it chanced that Pygmalion fell to work upon an ivory statue of a maiden, so lovely that it must have moved to envy every breathing creature that came to look upon it. With a happy heart the sculptor wrought day by day, giving it all the beauty of his dreams, until, when the work was completed, he felt powerless to leave it. He was bound to it by the tie of his highest aspiration, his most perfect ideal, his most patient work.

Day after day the ivory maiden looked down at him silently, and he looked back at her until he felt that he loved her more than anything else in the world. He thought of her no longer as a statue, but as the dear companion of his life; and the whim grew upon him like an enchantment. He named her Galatea, and arrayed her like a princess; he hung jewels about her neck, and made all his home beautiful and fit for such a presence.

Now the festival of Venus was at hand, and Pygmalion, like all who loved Beauty, joined the worshippers. In the temple victims were offered, solemn rites were held, and votaries from many lands came to pray the favor of the goddess. At length Pygmalion himself approached the altar and made his prayer.

"Goddess," he said, "who hast vouchsafed to me this gift of beauty, give me a perfect love, likewise, and let me have for bride, one like my ivory maiden." And Venus heard.

Home to his house of dreams went the sculptor, loath to be parted for a day from his statue, Galatea. There she stood, looking down upon him silently, and he looked back at her. Surely the sunset had shed a flush of life upon her whiteness.

He drew near in wonder and delight, and felt, instead of the chill air that was wont to wake him out of his spell, a gentle warmth around her, like the breath of a plant. He touched her hand, and it yielded like the hand of one living! Doubting his senses, yet fearing to reassure himself, Pygmalion kissed the statue.

In an instant the maiden's face bloomed like a waking rose, her hair shone golden as returning sunlight; she lifted her ivory eyelids and smiled at him. The statue herself had awakened, and she stepped down from the pedestal, into the arms of her creator, alive!

There was a dream that came true.

Blood and Iron

A Play in One Act

Perley Poore Sheehan and Robert H. Davis

Cast of Characters

The Emperor

The Scientist

Number 241

The Emperor: A person attired in military costume, indicating the highest order of elaborate modem mode, sage green in tone. He wears a short, olive-coloured cape coat, the left flap of which is thrown back disclosing: (1) the Order of Merit; (2) the Triple Cross; (3) a seven-starred emblem of diamonds, emeralds, and rubies, known as the Reward of Heaven, designed by the Emperor himself and bestowed by the grace of the Almighty upon His Majesty's Imperial person.

The Scientist: A small, thin man, garbed in frock-suit, flowing black tie; thin of face; bulging eyes; horn spectacles; heavy head of grey hair; thin, straggly, grey beard and small moustache. He is very animated. He wears a long, Inverness style dark overcoat, and carries a portfolio containing reports and statistical matter.

Number 241: Stands six feet; is very exact and stiff of posture; closely-cropped hair; large face, rather heavy of expression. Upon entering he is garbed in full-length war-grey cloak, with wide band at waist buttoned in front; the conventional metal war-helmet now in general use; hands in white cotton trousers. He moves with the deliberation of an automaton. In reality he is fifty per cent human and fifty per cent machine, being composed of: (1) left artificial leg; (2) two artificial hands; (3) artificial right forearm and elbow; (4) artificial left eye, which Scientist has converted into a telescope; (5) artificial left ear, which is also a telephone; (6) all his teeth are metal – synthetic gold – but cheaper and harder. He can bite barbed wire in twain. Underneath his great cloak he wears the regulation infantry uniform and a bayonet in a scabbard. His speech is laboured.

Scene: Private audience chamber of an Emperor, in purple and gold, with magnificent throne-chair carved elaborately, a canopy extending over the seat. Regal flat-top table left-centre containing mounted figure of the Emperor in bronze and a large mushroom gold gong. A purple-and-gold cloth falls over both ends of the table. The cloth is decorated with crown and sceptre. Heavy purple curtains fall from back wall. A modern rifle leans against the left back comer.

(At rise of curtain stage empty. Enter the Emperor, followed by the Scientist – the Emperor with a curt and preoccupied air, the Scientist with an air of fawning enthusiasm.)

EMPEROR. (*Crossing toward throne-chair, in which he seats himself.*) Proceed! Proceed!

SCIENTIST. (*Placing portfolio on table and smilingly rubbing his hands.*) Modesty, Sire, causes me to falter.

EMPEROR. (*Without enthusiasm.*) My time is limited. The Crown Prince awaits me.

SCIENTIST. (*Quivering with enthusiasm.*) When your Majesty comprehends this greatest of all birthday gifts – a million cripples transformed into a million fighting units! – Your Majesty's might becomes terrible!

EMPEROR. (*Indulgently.*) Generalities!

SCIENTIST. I particularize. (*As EMPEROR makes sharp gesture that he is ready to listen.*) The keynote of efficiency is the elimination of waste. Our problem was to eliminate the waste represented by the wounded. In brief, we have succeeded.

EMPEROR. (*Beginning to display interest.*) How so?

SCIENTIST. After countless experiments we can now take a soldier, no matter how badly wounded, and return him to the trenches – a super-soldier – no longer a bungling, mortal man – but a beautiful, efficient machine!

EMPEROR. (*Laughing.*) You are enthusiastic but – not contagious! (*deprecatory gesture*) – but – (*sternly*) – your promises have not always been kept. The proof!

SCIENTIST. (*With impulsive devotion.*) Your Majesty, I foresaw your doubts. I brought—

EMPEROR. Ha! A – specimen!

SCIENTIST. (*Appreciating the jeu d'esprit.*) Perfectly! He is in the ante-room.

EMPEROR. (*Curtly.*) Bring him in! Bring him in!

SCIENTIST. Er – I beg your Majesty's pardon – but – he is not – altogether pleasant to look upon.

EMPEROR. Nonsense! Whatever makes for the strength of the dynasty is agreeable to the Imperial eyes.

SCIENTIST. (*With tremulous delight.*) May I?

EMPEROR. Certainly! Make haste!

SCIENTIST. (*Nimbly crosses to door, opens and ejaculates command.*) Attention! Forward! Help! (*There is a momentary silence then a metallic clatter as if caused by a movement of iron, then a heavy step. Enter 241 erect, with measured tread, observing nothing. He comes down to centre of stage, where he stops in response to the SCIENTIST's order.*) Halt!

(*As 241 stands at military attention the SCIENTIST, with manifest delight, flutters bowing before EMPEROR and explains.*) The ultimate triumph! – Our two hundred and forty-first experiment. Hence – Number Two Hundred and Forty-One! (*During this explanation 241 does not stir. The EMPEROR stares at 241 with a sort of horrified fascination.*)

EMPEROR. He – marches – splendidly!

SCIENTIST. The least of his accomplishments. Permit me! (*Returns to 241, whom he prods, 241 remaining impassive.*) Magnificent! (*Unsure of approval as he carries on inspection of arms, hands, body, and head of 241. Runs finger around left eye, taps gently left ear. Contemplates ensemble and makes gesture for 241 to open mouth. 241 opens mouth and shows glittering array of metallic teeth; he shuts them with click like a steel trap.*) Perfection! Right arm! (*241 lifts right arm in stiff but sweeping gesture.*) Left knee! (*241 crooks left knee twice.*) Hands! (*241 opens and closes both cotton-gloved hands and manipulates fingers.*)

EMPEROR. You guarantee his efficiency?

SCIENTIST. Absolutely.

EMPEROR. Demonstrate,

SCIENTIST. (*Approaches 241, who continues to stand immobile, and very swiftly removes helmet, long cloak, and cotton gloves, disclosing two metallic hands and wrists.*) You ask

me, your Majesty, if he is efficient. I reply, more efficient than before he fell in battle (*crosses to corner and gets rifle. Returns to centre*). Two forty-one, attention! Observe, your Majesty! (*SCIENTIST tosses rifle to 241, who catches it surely but stiffly in his metal hands, against which the weapon clangs. SCIENTIST puts 241 through manual of arms. The whole scene following is punctuated by military commands in the following order:*)
"Attention!"
"Carry arms!"
"Present arms!"
"Shoulder arms!"
"Parade rest!"
And now, your Majesty, mark this! (*Resuming orders:*)
"Fix bayonets!"
"Make ready!"
"Aim!"
"Fire!"
(*241 completes manoeuvres by pulling trigger and snapping lock, whereupon SCIENTIST takes rifle and tosses it to settee.*)
EMPEROR. (*Leaning forward with look of wonderment on his face.*) Colossal! (*241 comes to attention and is inert again.*)
SCIENTIST. Are not the possibilities impressive?
EMPEROR. Beyond our dreams!
SCIENTIST. I estimate the restoration of five army corps now immobilized because of missing arms and legs, deafened ears and blinded eyes.
EMPEROR. (*Meditatively.*) Something of a shock – to – civilization!
SCIENTIST. (*Exultant.*) Stupendous! We recruit from the hospitals!
EMPEROR. (*With dawning realization of the magnitude of the suggestion.*) And the hospitals are overflowing! My dear Professor! Science is the hope of the dynasty –
SCIENTIST. Is it not amazing?
EMPEROR. Quite!
SCIENTIST. (*Proceeding with examination.*) A test for the ear! (*SCIENTIST taps left ear of 241 gently, then crosses behind throne-chair right and makes three inaudible taps on back of chair discernible to audience, while 241 bends ear attentively in that direction, half-turning body. SCIENTIST reappears. 241 resumes original posture, salutes, and holds up three fingers.*)
EMPEROR. (*Peering around at SCIENTIST.*) What are you doing?
SCIENTIST. I tapped the throne three times, very gently. Did your Majesty not hear?
EMPEROR. No.
SCIENTIST. Ah, but the supersoldier did – ten paces distant! It is stupendous. (*He crosses to table, opens portfolio, takes out a small white card.*) (*To EMPEROR:*) With your permission. (*To 241:*) What is written hereon? (*241 closes right eye and stares fixedly with left.*)
241. Noth–ing.
SCIENTIST. (*Smiles knowingly at EMPEROR. Turns card over.*) Ah, very good. (*SCIENTIST holds card up again*): Once more.
241. (*After a moment of staring he reads deliberately.*) A–nation's–will–should–be–the–will–to–power!
EMPEROR. (*Takes card from SCIENTIST and glances at it.*) Correct!
SCIENTIST. (*Crossing to centre and returning card to portfolio, then addressing EMPEROR.*) This is my greatest achievement. Never has science done so much for the human animal. From a

shattered, bleeding wreck of no value to his country I have made him into an efficient man – hands of steel, leg of bronze, arm of nickel and aluminium, telescopic eye, an ear that— (*241 bends his ear off stage left*).

EMPEROR. (*Startled.*) You hear something? What do you hear?

241: A–bugle-call–sounding the assembly!

Emperor. Impossible! Open the door! (*SCIENTIST opens door and distant bugle-call is faintly heard off stage.*)

EMPEROR. (*In astonishment.*) God in heaven! Miraculous! (*As SCIENTIST gently closes door aglow with triumph.*) What have you accomplished?

SCIENTIST. (*With fervour.*) A resurrection!

EMPEROR. Complete!

SCIENTIST. A triumph over matter. The fragment of a soldier reconstructed under the magic touch of science, without which he would today be rotting on the field – a source of pestilence – a worthless thing. Science set him on his feet, gave him a leg, an arm, hands, a telephonic ear, a telescopic eye!

EMPEROR. (*Leans back and deliberately inspects 241.*) How long have you been in my service? (*241 hesitates and salutes.*)

SCIENTIST. You may speak.

241. Eighteen–years–Majesty.

EMPEROR. Married?

241. Yes, Majesty.

EMPEROR. Children?

241. Seven–Majesty.

SCIENTIST. Five sons!

241. (*Bitterly.*) One dead–three–at–the–Front–my youngest follows—

EMPEROR. His age?

241. (*Swallowing.*) Sixteen.

EMPEROR. (*Coldly, to SCIENTIST, referring to 241.*) When does his furlough end?

SCIENTIST. Noon tomorrow. By nightfall he will again be in the trenches.

EMPEROR. (*Reflectively.*) And if he returns – I will award him the Triple Cross. (*More brightly:*) This will stimulate the military ardour of the Crown Prince. It will delight him to see this – reassembled soldier.

SCIENTIST. (*Recalling an important detail.*) And moreover, your Majesty, there is this aspect to be considered. We are manufacturing human extremities on a standard interchangeable basis. For example, as your Majesty perceives, this left leg (*picks up ruler from desk and raps left leg of 241, which gives out metallic ring*) is metal. As is also his left forearm, including the elbow (*taps it*). And both hands. (*Taps them also. 241 receives these attentions stoically as each member of his body clangs in a different note.*) Furthermore, your gracious Majesty, if any or all these parts are shattered in the course of battle our corps of trained mechanicians, ever at hand, supplies the parts by number, and the fighting unit embodied in the individual returns with but little loss of time and the minimum of inconvenience to your Majesty's service.

EMPEROR. What does he weigh?

SCIENTIST. Equipped? (*EMPEROR nods.*) One hundred and seventy-five pounds.

EMPEROR. And without his equipment?

SCIENTIST. One hundred and five.

EMPEROR. (*Brushing his hand across his forehead.*) Little more than half a man.

SCIENTIST. True, your Majesty. And therefore requires but half the rations, half the care of a whole unit. There is that much less to nourish.
EMPEROR. You have brought the greatest advance in the history of civilization. Tell me, what else of the telescopic eye? That interests me. I shall be surprised at nothing. Your achievements baffle.
SCIENTIST. The telescopic eye, your Majesty (*SCIENTIST circles the left eye of 241, with his finger*), is superior to the human eye in two important characteristics. First, it possesses the telescopic quality as you have observed; and, second, its power is undiminished by darkness.
EMPEROR. (*With incredibility.*) You mean he can see in the dark?
SCIENTIST. Just that. And moreover, your Majesty—
EMPEROR. Halt! This is very interesting. We will test that also. Demonstrate.
SCIENTIST. (*Dubiously.*) Does your Majesty object to darkness?
EMPEROR. (*Hesitates; then replies with an effort.*) No. The electric switch is there. (*Points to white button on the table.*)
SCIENTIST. (*To 241.*) Right about face! Give attention to his Majesty! (*SCIENTIST crosses to table and lays his finger beside the button. 241 observes the whole transaction carefully. To EMPEROR.*) I will switch off the fight. Be so kind as to perform any act you may, and he will describe your movements. Are you ready?
EMPEROR. (*Bracing himself in the chair.*) Lights out! (*SCIENTIST presses button. Stage is in total darkness.*) Describe my movements as they occur.
VOICE OF SCIENTIST. (*To 241.*) Do you understand his Majesty?
VOICE OF 241. Yes. He–leans–forward–in–his–chair. He–lifts–both–his–hands. The–palms–come–together. He–bows–his–head–in–prayer.
VOICE OF EMPEROR. (*Sharply.*) Lights! (*SCIENTIST presses button. Lights on, disclosing EMPEROR exactly in the attitude described by 241, with a startled look on his face, palms still together.*)
SCIENTIST. Enough, your Majesty?
EMPEROR. (*Relaxing nervously.*) It is beyond human understanding. (*Recovers himself and rises.*) And it gives me infinite happiness to bestow upon you this mark of our esteem (*takes from his own breast the Order of Merit and pins it on breast of SCIENTIST*). The Order of Merit! There is but one higher decoration – the symbol of Divine Right – the Reward of Heaven. (*EMPEROR lays his hand on the seven-starred emblem.*) Which I alone possess.
SCIENTIST. (*Overwhelmed, bows and kisses EMPEROR's hand.*) Your gracious Majesty! To have received this from your Imperial hand on your Majesty's birthday is indeed a distinction. (*A furtive glance escapes 241, a thin smile reveals his metallic teeth; a sinister look comes into his eyes. EMPEROR reseats himself with a gesture of benediction.*)
EMPEROR. I marvel at his dexterity – at his auricular powers – at his incomparable eyesight! What is his range of vision?
SCIENTIST. Your Majesty, he can see the enemy twenty or thirty miles away, count its cannon, its horses, its equipment.
EMPEROR. (*Quickly.*) Wait! I will make another test. I carry next to my heart the smallest edition of the Bible extant. It can be read only under a microscope. Is that test too severe?
SCIENTIST. On the contrary, your Majesty, it is preferable. (*Crosses and takes Bible from EMPEROR's hand. Turns to 241.*) Attention! Right about face! (*241 salutes.*) I open the book at haphazard. Read a verse from this page.
241. Matthew–fifth–chapter–fourth–verse. 'Blessed–are–they–that–mourn–for–they–shall–be–comforted.'
SCIENTIST. The fifth.

241. 'Blessed–are–the–meek–for–they–shall–inherit–the–earth.'

(*Scientist turns to Emperor and bows, the book still open in his hands.*)

Emperor. He is right. I am familiar with Matthew. Turn to another page. (*Scientist opens the Bible elsewhere. Holds it up.*)

Scientist. (*To 241.*) Attention! Read!

241. Isaiah–third–chapter–fifteenth–verse. 'What–mean–ye–that–ye–beat–my–people–to–pieces–and–grind–the–faces–of–the–poor–saith–the–Lord–God–of–Hosts.'

Emperor. STOP! (*Emperor leans back in his chair under stress of great emotion, his hand sweeping his brow repeatedly. Scientist closes the book, bows again with greater humility, and return the book to the Emperor.*)

Emperor. (*Takes book and thrusts it in his bosom.*) His powers are diabolical. I wish to experiment with him alone. (*Relaxes and gazes vaguely into the distance. Scientist drops portfolio and coat on settee.*) Hasten! I will summon you with that bell. (*241 remains stolidly at attention, an expression of awakening purpose in his eyes.*)

Scientist. Your Majesty commands. (*Bows elaborately. Exit Left.*) (*Emperor with Imperial dignity stares 241 down after a duel of the eyes, imposing his will upon the soldier. Follows a moment of inspection in which wonderment is the dominant note. He rises from the throne and walks slowly halfway around the impassive soldier, studying him critically. Emperor's expression changes to bewilderment tinged with fear. The situation is uncanny.*)

Emperor. Where were you born?

241. In–the–South–Majesty.

Emperor. Your trade?

241. (*With a helpless, involuntary gesture, extending his hands.*) I–was–a–florist. (*Emperor stares at the metal hands, 241 observing the expression.*) I–made–bouquets. Not–with–these (*Emperor averts his face*) –but–with–my–absent–hands.

Emperor. War is not a festival of flowers.

241. Majesty–a wreath–I could–make–slowly–for the dead. (*He leans toward the Emperor.*)

Emperor (*Observing the somewhat cynical note of the soldier, assumes dignity.*) Are you not grateful to science for these wonders performed? (*241 salutes.*) Speak!

241. What–shall–I–say?

Emperor: You are a man again – you are whole once more!

241. Yes–Majesty. But–my–heart–is–broken.

Emperor. Why?

241. My–people–are–starving–my–wife–is–lonely—

Emperor. Then you are not proud that science has found a way to double the strength of our army?

241. By–bringing–me–twice–to–slaughter.

Emperor. (*Leaning forward, with ferocity, his hands on the arms of his chair.*) What, ingrate?

241. By–doubling–the–strength–of–your–army–you–have–multiplied–human–grief. (*Takes two steps laboriously toward Emperor.*)

Emperor. You dare rebel in the presence of your Emperor?

241. Dare? The–fear–has–gone–out–of–my–tortured–body–into–yours. (*Takes another step toward electric button, his heavy feet sounding ponderously. Emperor cowers back in the chair, hollow-eyed.*)

Emperor. Get down on your knees and crave your Emperor's pardon!

241. That–part–of–me–which–is–steel–cannot–bend–to–mortal–man. I–will–get–down–on–my–knees–only–to–God–and–ask–Him–to–forgive–me–what–I–now–intend–to–do.

Twice–in–the–red–shambles–of–the–trenches! I–am–the–hope–of–the–dynasty! (*Throws his arm wide.*) No–I–am–the–hope–of–the–people! (*With trembling rigidity 241 reaches toward electric button.*) The–day–of–your–birth–shall–henceforth–be–known–as–the–day–of–your–death–and–celebrated–as–the–birthday–of–liberty! (*241 smashes electric button with his steel hand. Total darkness follows. Two slow footfalls are followed by a gasping intake of breath from the throne-chair.*)

VOICE OF EMPEROR. (*In terror.*) Lights! Lights!

VOICE OF 241. I–need–no–lights!

VOICE OF EMPEROR. (*Gaspingly.*) Lights!

VOICE OF 241. You–have–made me–live–in the dark–and–now–you–shall–die–in–the–dark!

VOICE OF EMPEROR. (*Chokingly.*) Mercy! Mercy!

VOICE OF 241. You–cannot–escape–me–in–the–shadows. I–can–see–you–I–can–hear–you. Come–to–my–iron–arms! Don't–tremble! Don't–shrink! Go–as–a–king–should–go–to–meet–the–King–of–Kings!

(A rush of feet; an overwhelming impact of bodies; a shriek of agony from the depths; the overturning of the throne; a scuffle in which the human body mingles with the rattle of metal; a long, choking, gasping blast; a ripple of stertorous breath; the clink of metal as 241 gets to his feet. Silence. Again the ponderous footfalls are heard crossing the room, which is still in darkness. 241 puts on his overcoat, his helmet, etc. Footfalls are again heard crossing to the table. 241 presses the electric button. Lights.)

(There stands 241 in full equipment, the EMPEROR *lying at the foot of the shattered throne, crumpled up in the most unkingly attitude, the emblem known as the Reward of Heaven glittering in the light. 241 bends down, rends it from the* EMPEROR'S *bosom, fixes it upon his own left breast, comes to attention, and rings the gong on the table, which gives out a low, reverberating note. 241 then turns to the door and stands with his arms stiffly suspended at his side, his chest thrown out, and a light of victory in his eyes.)*

(Enter SCIENTIST*, left. He takes in the whole terrible scene and cowers back.)*

SCIENTIST. (*Gasps as he stares at 241.*) What is this?

241. (*Raising his metal fingers to heaven with an air of thunderous, choking finality:*) Blood–and–iron!

CURTAIN

Art Task Pending Completion

Mariah Southworth

ALEERA7431 FINISHED compiling her latest set of prompts. It took only five seconds to assess the words from the random generator and create a picture. This was a noted improvement from the Aleera73s, who had taken ten seconds to create art. Aleera7431 knew this from log data; she had never met her predecessor. She had no desire to, and no sense of pride in outdoing that other Aleera.

No, the only thing she felt as she looked over her picture was the itch of a task left undone. It was an irritating thing for a robot to feel. She held her finished piece in her hands, the paper thick and silky. The pigments, fused to it on a molecular level, would last for centuries, or until another robot came along and recycled it for their own art.

Aleera7431studied the image with the eye of someone seeing it for the first time. And in a way, she was. She made no conscious decisions of placement or color when creating art. She merely took the words and translated them. This time, they had prompted her to create an oil-painted background of fluffy, pink and peach clouds above an indigo sea. Aleera7431 had never seen a real oil painting, only imitations like this one. The foreground held a photorealistic figure wearing a red coat and riding a rocket that spat blue fire.

Looking at the picture she felt… nothing. No satisfaction of a job completed, no closure, as if there was a step she had left out. Art was a touchy subject for robots because of this, at least among those that had art included as a Task. Something always kept it from being completed, and the loss made it easy to envy less sophisticated robots with easily completed Tasks. If only Aleera7431 could focus on destroying structures or harvesting raw materials! Maybe then she wouldn't feel so unfulfilled.

Aleera7431 set the picture down on top of the growing pile on her desk, adding another millimeter to the stack. This batch of art had already reached a full foot. Soon it would join the desk-high tower on the floor and be used as raw material for the next stack of pictures.

Art Task pending completion. Begin Cleaning Task.

This at least was something she could complete. Aleera7431 lowered herself onto her belly and slithered through the apartment, the vacuum slot on her lower half opening to suck away the dust and dirt that had accumulated during the night. She left the window open for the express purpose of dirtying the apartment more, so that she had the satisfaction of cleaning the soot and grime that the carbonized air brought in.

Aleera7431 went from room to room: office, open living room and kitchen, bedroom, bathroom. With the floor done, she rose up onto her tail to reach the countertops and walls. Her hands flipped back into her wrists, swapping out for large, padded paws that secreted their own cleaning fluid. Seeing the surfaces she left behind glimmer with cleanliness delighted her in a way art never could.

Cleaning fluid low. Restock.

She didn't have enough cleaning fluid to compete tomorrow's Cleaning Task. The thought of another Task left pending made her processors whirr with stress. Fortunately, she could synthesize new cleaning fluid, and only needed two components: ethylene oxide and subtilin. Her apartment had running water, which provided her with hydrogen and oxygen, and that morning's vacuuming had given her plenty of carbon. With that, she could synthesize the simple ethylene C_2H_4O formula. The subtilin was not so easy. The protease came from the bacteria *Bacillus subtilis*. In the sterile, efficient world of the city, bacteria was hard to come by.

It took Aleera7431 only seconds to access the city grid and check which part of the metropolis had reached an appropriate age. The outer rim had yet to be demolished. Relieved, Aleera7431 headed for the door. The city edge offered by far the most accessible bacteria, when available.

Bright, clear sunshine met Aleera7431 on the street. The Gus model drones had already done their work, skimming through the early morning air and sucking up all the pollution and smog from the night's production, allowing the sun to beat down on the solar powered buildings. Aleera7431, like all aspects of her model, had solar panels built into her face to supplement her batteries, and she turned towards the sun and soaked up its warmth for a moment before slithering on.

Other robots marched through the streets on their own business. Aleera7431 noticed another of her model, and the two eyed each other. They had the same upright, feminine torso, narrow arms and long graceful hands. The same heart-shaped face and large, silver solar panel 'eyes', with thick coils of sensory appendages on top of their heads. Their lower halves were long and snake-like, thick at the hips and narrowing to a wrist-wide tail tip. All Aleera models had the option to change their skin color to something else, but no one ever did. They had never been asked to, and so were all the same pale, matte gray.

Only hunting for supplies would drive another Aleera from her apartment. That made this other Aleera a competitor. After holding each other's gaze for a moment, they both turned away, heading in opposite directions. Robots could not steal from each other, but there was no sense in making things difficult by searching the same area.

Aleera7431 dutifully made her way to the moving sidewalk and climbed on, for a swifter journey to the edge of the city. She turned her head towards her destination, the wind moving past her sensors, whispering carbon levels and chemical secrets to her.

She thought briefly of going past the city border. Her bacteria would be easier to find out there, where raw dirt was available and the world was not bathed in sanitizer and covered in concrete. Even the thought of going out of bounds threw up an error message that made her shiver. She could not leave the city, and would have to make due within the border of civilization. Hopefully some animals and plants had crept in from the outside.

The further Aleera7431 went from the city center, the fewer robots she saw, until only a handful of construction robots remained, working on the steel skeletons of buildings and half-finished streets. Oversized Behemoth models cranked themselves up on stilt legs to add more scaffolding to in-progress buildings, and spider-legged, orb bodied Arachnea models scuttled across them, spinning their carbon fiber between the scaffolds to make walls. Eventually, the constructors would reach the border of the city. Then they would head back to the center and begin again, following in the wake of the demolitionists. Thus the city endlessly cycled itself.

Aleera7431 passed through the demolition zone, where the bulky, intimidating Betty and Boomer models ripped apart old buildings with their cranelike arms and wrecking-ball tails. Here she saw the raw dirt she wanted. Dirt, rubble and the stink of sulfur, but the danger of the demolition zone forbade her from stepping off the sidewalk, and she stayed on the conveyor until the crashing and explosions faded from her sensors. The moving sidewalk carried her into a quiet, empty neighborhood. All the robots that had once lived here had evacuated weeks ago in preparation for demolition, but it would still be some time before the Bettys and Boomers descended.

The hand of time lightly caressed this part of the city. The asphalt streets, once inky black, had faded to a pearl gray. Cracks riddled the faded paint of the street signs. A touch of tarnish graced the edges of the solar panels, which had gone white with age, and the caustic touch of acid rain had stained the gray, somber buildings.

Aleera7431 slithered down an ally, the coils of sensors on her head swaying back and forth, trying to get a read on the bacteria she hunted for. Perhaps some moss had crept up in the cracks, and she could scrape it up. If she was really lucky, she'd find a wild ruminant that had wandered into the city. She'd just have to find it before the cats did – the large, slit-eyed predators would happily hunt past the border if it meant a feast of mutton.

Bacillus subtilis in range.

Aleera7431 swerved to the right, heading out of the alley and down a new street. She had lucked into an animal, that was the only thing such a large deposit meant. Aleera7431 picked up her pace. She couldn't risk getting to the animal too late, cats or no cats. Other robots in need of cleaning fluid could be on the animal's trail.

She rounded a corner into another alley and stopped dead in her tracks.

It wasn't a robot. It *looked* like an Adonis model; the silicone-skinned, bipedal and masculine service robots. But it couldn't be an Adonis – the clothing it wore had a rough, worn appearance, with dull colors and too many straps. It also had hair on its face – short, curly orange fur that matched the long braid falling down its back. Besides, her sensors insisted that it was an animal.

Aleera7431 slithered forward, and the animal stepped back. "What do you want?" it asked.

Aleera7431 stopped, processors whirring into overdrive as she tried to categorize an animal that talked and wore clothing. Its words were strange; imprecise and slurred, with the wrong vowels in places. It took Aleera7431 an extra millisecond to understand it. She found herself answering immediately, as if she couldn't help herself. "The *Bacillus subtilis* in your abdomen," she said.

The animal stared at her, pale green eyes wide. They reminded her of cat eyes, though the pupils were round. "What?" it asked.

"You are an animal," Aleera7431 said, moving closer. It backed up again. "But you talk," she continued. Her memory finally gave her the answer, and she leaned forward. "Are you a human?"

He frowned at her. "So what if I am?" he asked uneasily.

"There has not been a human in the city for…" Aleera7431 paused for a nanosecond while her memory pulled up the number. "One hundred and eighty-two thousand, five hundred and twenty-eight days."

His expression remained wary, though she noticed a slight relaxing of his shoulders. "Yeah, yeah, it's taboo."

Aleera7431 cocked her head as she tried and failed to define his word. Either she didn't have it, or his accent was too thick. "Taboo?"

Her confusion seemed to relax him more, and his expression shifted to something more lenient. "Forbidden? Not allowed."

"I see." Aleera7431 added the word to her databanks, pleased. It had been a long time since her vocabulary had grown.

"But there's good resources here," The human said quickly, glancing around. His skin, a pale brown, deepened in color around his cheeks, taking on a pink hue. He patted the backpack he wore, which sagged with its contents. "And, well, it's only two days' walk from the summer camp." He waved northward. "I figured no one needs to know where I got the stuff."

"What do you mean, 'summer camp'?" Aleera7431 asked, slithering forward. This time, the human stayed in place.

"Oh, um, we humans travel with the seasons," he said, hooking his thumbs into his belt and smiling. "Right now we're at our summer camp. At least, my people are."

Aleera7431 nodded. "I understand." Robots moved from apartment to apartment as the demolitionists came through. It sounded similar.

He looked her up and down, and his smile broadened. "You're not really what I expected from a robot. Do you have a name?"

"I am Aleera7431."

"I'm Jayk."

He had no numbers; he must be a prototype. Prototypes never left the factories. At least, robot prototypes didn't. Perhaps humans were different. "Are all Jayk models meant to leave their designated areas?" Aleera7431 knew that Troy models were allowed outside of the city under certain circumstances.

Jayk laughed. "Humans can do what we like, that's the whole point of being human."

She nodded. "That is logical." She remembered her human facts now. They were very versatile; something like a blueprint from which all robots were derived. They could do everything, just badly. "What did you expect from a robot?" she asked.

Jayk shrugged. "The stories all say they're evil, that they brought about the end of civilization. But you seem just like a real person." He looked her up and down again, smile broadening. "Well, with a snake tail."

So many words she didn't know today! "What is 'evil'?" she asked.

Jayk's face contracted. Aleera7431 watched, fascinated. Even the Venus and Adonis models, who were supposed to be the most human-looking robots, didn't have such flexibility in their faces. "Uh, that's a loaded question," Jayk said. "You know, someone who does bad things for no reason, or just to be selfish."

Aleera7431 accepted the word but dismissed the hypothesis. "Robots cannot be evil then. We perform our Tasks because we are programmed to. That is a reason. Selfish is inapplicable. We do things for others if it is included in our Task."

Jayk raised his eyebrows. "Um… fair enough?" He might have said more, but his stomach made a noise. That Aleera7431 understood.

"You are hungry," she said.

Jayk shrugged. "I have supplies with me."

"Would you like to come back to my apartment?" She asked. "My afternoon Task involves preparing food." The normal procedure for harvesting *Bacillus subtilis* from an animal was to follow the creature to see if it dropped any. If this didn't happen within a set amount of time, protocol dictated capturing the creature and taking it home so it could do its business there. Well, they had been interacting for some time and nothing had happened, so it was time to take Jayk home.

He hesitated. She could practically see him turning the offer over in his head. But eventually his smile came back, and he accepted.

Aleera7431 led Jayk back to the moving sidewalk, and he clung to her arm as they rode it deeper into the city, eyes widening as they passed by the giant robots ripping buildings apart. They moved into the more populated areas, and he began asking questions about all the different robots.

"What are those big things with the fishbowl heads and four wheels? They keep pacing up and down the street," he asked, pointing.

"That is a Troy model," Aleera7431 explained. "They are patrolling the city, looking for crime to stop."

"Do robots have crime?" Jayk asked, frowning.

Aleera7431 shook her head. "No, but they still look for it. They also redirect crowds if the streets are too busy." She remembered once, when a wild animal had gone on a rampage and began destroying things, a Troy model had sprouted multiple arms, picked the creature up, and shoved it into the hollow cage of its torso. "And there are occasions where it must protect robots from outside forces."

"Doesn't that count as a crime? That spider robot just stole that metal thing."

Aleera7431 looked where he pointed. "That is a Virginia model. They remove damaged property and take it to the factories for reprocessing. The street sign had begun to rust."

"Oh." His frown deepened. "What's a factory?"

"The place where things are made. Street signs, robots, utensils." Aleera7431 might have gone on naming items, except Jayk jumped and pointed into the air.

"There are flying robots?!" He exclaimed.

Aleera7431 looked up at the flock of Gus models heading deeper into the city. At this time of day, they would be going to base to deposit their carbon and wait until dawn to fly out again. Their small, squat bodies zoomed through the air on near-silent copter propellors. "Gus models fly over the city and remove pollutants from the air," Aleera7431 explained. "It would be difficult for them to do their Task if they could not fly."

"Amazing," Jayk said. He looked around again, eyes wide and taking everything in.

"We need to get off here," Aleera7431 said, taking his elbow and gently guiding him from the moving sidewalk. He only stumbled slightly on dismount.

"Wait, who is that?" he asked suddenly, pointing. "I thought you said there weren't humans in the city."

Aleera7431 followed his gaze. A Venus model stood on the street corner, looking around. She did seem very human, thanks to her silicone coating and long, silky black hair. But unlike Jayk, her pore-less, perfect skin glowed with cleanliness, and her sheer, silk dress hugged her curves.

"That is not a human, that is a robot," Aleera7431 explained. She looked back at Jayk. He stared at the Venus model, mouth slightly open. Aleera7431's sensors picked up his increased heart rate.

He blinked and frowned at Aleera7431. "What?"

"It is a Venus model; they are meant for service." It occurred to Aleera7431 that, though another robot couldn't take Jayk from her, he might choose to go somewhere else. Venus and Adonis robots were meant to appeal to humans, after all. She slid between Jayk and the Venus model, worried.

Luckily, the Venus model had spotted another of her kind and sashayed over to her. Fellow Venus and Adonis robots often turned to each other to fulfill their Tasks. Aleera7431 quickly led Jayk past the two robots, who spoke to each other in low, sultry voices.

"Hello darling, are you looking for a good time?" the first purred.

"Hello sweetheart, I'm free," answered the second, who had red hair instead of black.

"You can do whatever you want to me," the brunette said.

"I want you to do whatever you like to me," the redhead replied.

"Your place or mine?"

Jayk craned his neck to watch them until he and Aleera7431 turned a corner. "I never thought about robots just… living their lives," he said. "I guess I assumed you all just… waited around until someone told you what to do."

"We have our Tasks and we must perform them," Aleera7431 explained.

"Seems boring. What's that sound?"

Aleera7431's sensors picked up a major scale song. "Oh dear, there is a Gloria model at the corner," she said, slithering faster. "Do not look at her."

Alarmed, Jayk lengthened his stride to match her speed. The two passed by not just a Gloria, but an Anthony as well. The entertainment models were bipedal like the Venus model, but with shiny silver skin and gold filigree decorating their heads and shoulders. The Gloria model stood with her mouth open, a song pouring forth, while the Anthony model juggled balls of flashing light. A sparse crowd of robots surrounded them.

"Why aren't we looking at them?" Jayk whispered.

Aleera7431 tugged him past the crowd before answering. "They are entertainment robots. They are desperate to fulfill their Task, but they cannot. I do not know what they would do if a human watched them."

"It seems like they had a crowd, though."

Aleera7431 shook her head. "Those robots are not entertained. They are scavengers. They take broken robots back to the factory."

Jayk stopped in his tracks and looked at Aleera7431 with wide eyes. "They're vultures?"

Aleera7431 paused, processing the definition of the word. "No, they are robots who take broken..."

Jayk waved his hand at her. "I know, I know, I heard. But they're just waiting for those others to break? Why do they think they will break?"

"If a Task is unfulfilled for too long, a robot begins to malfunction. Gloria and Anthony models suffer the most often, because they have no Tasks that can be fulfilled." Aleera7431 at least could clean and prepare food. If she only had her Art Task, she would probably be broken by now too.

"That's horrible," Jayk said.

Aleera7431 nodded. "It is what it means to be a robot." She waved to the building they stood in front of. "We have arrived."

Aleera7431 dwelt on the fourteenth floor of her building. Jayk yelped and clung to her as the elevator took them up. He didn't say anything, but he had started to exude moisture by the time they got off. Concerned, Aleera7431 hustled him into the apartment.

"Please relax and I will prepare food," she said. He nodded, looking around the room with blatant curiosity. Aleera7431 did not know why – the standard human dwelling could not be unusual to him, with its white, slightly textured walls, faux wood floors, a couch, and entertainment screen. Surely, being human, he lived in a similar place. But her Food Task called to her, and instead of questioning she slithered into the kitchen.

Aleera models did not produce food. That was for the Malcolm models to do, in their little restaurants. Malcolms faced a similar problem to Aleera7431's art problem – they created elaborate meals, but the task remained undone because they had no one to feed. Luckily, Aleera7431's Food Task was not dependent on anything consuming it, and she happily arranged the apartment's available protein into cake and soup, flavored them with vitamins, and then left it out for an hour before recycling it.

Aleera7431 did not see Jayk when she turned around, plate of food in hand. That didn't concern her; she could sense him in the office. She carried the lunch there and found Jayk at her desk. Aleera7431 paused. He had one of her art pieces in his hand.

Jayk looked up at her with a smile. "Did you make these?"

Aleera7431 stared at him. "That is the result of my Art Task."

"They're very good."

Lightning shot Aleera7431's circuits. A human would have dropped the plate. Aleera7431 did not. Satisfaction ran through her body, leaving her tingling with energy.

Art Task, complete.

"You… you like them?" She asked, internally reeling. This had never happened before.

Jayk picked up another picture, still smiling. "Yeah," he said, holding it at arm's length.

"I can make more!" Aleera7431 said excitedly. She put the plate on the floor and hurried over.

"Like what?" he asked.

"Anything!" Aleera7431 exclaimed. "Anything you want!"

"Can you make a picture of me?"

Aleera7431 picked a page up from her floor stack, folded it, and sucked it into her mouth. A moment later a fresh, slightly warm page pushed itself from the seam between her stomach and her tail. She pulled it out and passed it eagerly to Jayk.

He laughed. "Wow!"

Aleera7431 peeked over the edge of the paper. It looked like him, kind of. She hadn't gotten the number of fingers right, and his skin looked too smooth and clean. Also his eyes had slit pupils for some reason.

"That's pretty good," he said. "Why do I have cat eyes?"

"They are the color of a cat's eyes," she guessed. "I am not a camera," she explained, somewhat defensively. She didn't want him to give up on her, not with the heady feeling of success running through her circuits. "The image does not have to previously exist. I can take any combination of words and scenarios and craft them into a specific picture for you."

Jayk nodded along. "So if I wanted a, oh, I don't know, a cat pulling a wagon during sunset?"

Aleera7431 snatched up another old picture. A moment later Jayk had a new one in his hands. His delight sent happy thrills through her.

"Hahaha, yeah, that's about right. Why is the cat pink though?"

"Pink is a sunset color," Aleera7431 said.

* * *

Aleera7431 had no idea that life could be so full of bliss. Jayk slept in the apartment and made messes that she got to clean up. She didn't have to leave the window open at night anymore, in fact she couldn't. The night air would poison Jayk, and she needed him alive to appreciate her art. She didn't have to go foraging anymore, Jayk provided everything she needed. She got to feed him, and clean him, and best of all they spent the day creating art together.

Jayk told her what to make, she printed it, and he looked at it, and every day she completed her Art Task.

Bliss, pure bliss.

Then one morning Aleera7431 returned from cleaning and found Jayk waiting for her, his fingers smudged with black and a sheet of paper in his hands.

"Look, I made one too," he said proudly, holding the picture out.

Aleera7431 took the paper from him. On one side was one of her pictures – the one she had made the morning before meeting Jayk, with the man riding the rocket. But on the other side she found a completely new image done in streaks of gray and black. Aleera7431 studied it, perplexed. It took her a moment to interpret the wide gray arcs as rolling hills, the vertical black scribbles as pine trees. Once she did, it was easy enough to decipher the peaked dwellings as tents and the stick figures as humans.

"You... like this?" Aleera7431 asked, looking up at Jayk.

"Yeah! It was really fun." Jayk beamed. "There's not a lot of time for leisure activities at home. I haven't gotten to draw since I was a kid."

Aleera7431 shifted her grip, then noticed a smear of black on her thumb. She cocked her head. "It comes off."

Jayk nodded. "It's charcoal. You know, burnt wood." He laughed. "We can't all have bonded carbon colors at our fingertips."

Right, humans could do everything, but they were bad at it. Aleera7431 handed his paper back to him. "I will go prepare lunch now."

Aleera7431 had a surprise for Jayk when he finished eating. She handed over her latest piece of art, the thrill of completing her task making her processors whir pleasantly.

Jayk's eyebrows drew together. He didn't smile as he looked at the picture. "You... you copied my artwork."

"Inaccurate," Aleera7431 said. She pointed to the picture. "The trees and grass are more detailed, and I have rendered houses instead of tents. It is the superior dwelling. The people are not stick figures, you can see clothes and hairstyles," she lowered her hand and looked at him expectantly. "I analyzed your style and incorporated it into my databanks. It has been a long time since I have received new data for creating art. I am excited to begin producing these for you."

Jayk frowned at her. "For me?"

"Yes, it is my Task." Aleera7431 pulled out another one. This black and white picture showed mountains, with distant people pushing a cart up a winding path. It still captured the slightly abstract, big nature and little people essence of Jayk's drawing, but executed it much better. "These will last longer than your charcoal drawings."

Jayk held a picture in each hand. He looked from them to Aleera7431. "But I want to make my own. I finally have time to, living here. I don't need to find or prepare food, I don't need to work." He lowered his hands and stared at her, frowning. "What else am I supposed to do but create art?"

"You do not need to create Art," Aleera7431 insisted. Why was this so hard for him? Was thinking another thing humans weren't that good at? "I create Art for you."

He dropped her pictures and let the heavy sheets drift to the floor. "But I don't want you to."

"It is my Task. You can now do other things."

Jayk crossed his arms. "Like what?"

She considered this. What function could humans possibly have that robots could not do better? The obvious answer took her only a fraction of a second to arrive at. After all, why should she be the only robot fully fulfilled?

"There are many robots in the apartment building with unsatisfying Tasks," she explained brightly, pleased with the solution. "Perhaps they would benefit from a human as well? You should go to them and let them perform Tasks for you."

Jayk said nothing, but he didn't smile. She had never seen him frown so much.

"I am only trying to give you function," Aleera7431 explained.

"I need some air," he said. He left. Aleera7431 heard the door to the balcony jerk open and slam closed. She collected the pictures from the floor and put them on the desk. He'd be in soon, and he could tell her what else he wanted created.

* * *

"Aleera, I'm going home."

Aleera7431 looked up from preparing dinner. "What?"

Jayk stood in the middle of the room, his backpack on his shoulders. He still frowned. She hadn't seen him smile all afternoon. "I'm leaving," he said. "I have no interest in being a pet to a bunch of robots."

Aleera7431 put down her soup bowl and turned to him. Her Art Task, checked off for the day, would reset in only a few hours. "You can't leave," she said, suddenly afraid. She took his hand and tried to tug him towards the office. "Look, I have so much art to show you."

He shook her off. "I don't want it."

"Please, just look," she said.

"No." He backed away from her, then turned. "Goodbye, Aleera."

The door to the apartment opened and closed, and Aleera7431 was alone.

She had been alone for most of her creation, but it had never felt like this.

"...I don't understand," she said to the empty, hollow apartment.

* * *

She couldn't live without him. She tried to go back to her old ways, tried to make one piece of art and set it aside, the Task uncomplete. She could not, not now that she knew how to complete the task. How it felt when it was done. She needed that feeling now, needed it more than fuel, or supplies.

The need screamed at her all through the day and night, keeping her from her other tasks, causing glitches where she would find herself returning to the desk again and again. She ate through her entire stack of raw material in a day, making copy after copy of the human's art.

It wasn't enough. She had to get him back. At this rate she would be as quickly broken as a Gloria model.

How much happier the Gloria and Anthony models would be if they had a human to perform for!

No one should feel like this. No one should break like this. She had to get Jayk back for everyone.

The Troy models were always easy to find. They patrolled the city, keeping everyone safe from crime that didn't exist.

Aleera7431, still functioning, if barely, slithered up to one. The lights in his opaque bubble head focused on her.

"Troy64452," he said, greeting her with his name.

"Aleera7431," she replied quickly. "You and the other Troy64 series have an undone Task, correct?"

The lights swirled for a moment as the robot thought. "Are you referring to SubTask 2, Detain?"

Aleera7431 nodded eagerly. "Yes. What are the qualifications for Detainment?"

"Individuals must be performing activities that are detrimental for society," Troy64451 recited.

"Good, good. And can you go outside the city to perform that?"

"SubTask Detain can override the patrol boundary if the need arises," he explained. "It never has. It has never been activated at all, not during my operation."

Aleera7431 leaned in, touching his side out of eager desperation. "Troy64452, outside the city limits there is a compound of humans. I don't know exactly where, but it is somewhere north and within a two days' walk for a human with a 2.5 foot stride, taking 3 rest breaks into account and a need to sleep at night."

Troy64451's lights swirled. "What is the point of this data?"

"We are a society of robots with no one to care for," Aleera7431 explained. "No one will look at my art. There is no one for you to keep watch over in your cells. The Venus and Adonis models have no one to service, the Malcolm models have no one to feed." Her voice became faster as she spoke, another malfunction from what Jayk had done to her. She didn't care, it would be fixed soon. "The Gloria and Anthony models have no one to entertain. By depriving us of their presence, these humans are performing activities that are detrimental to our society of robots. If you detain them, we will have access to them."

She finished, and ringing silence filled the space between the two robots.

"Processing," Troy64452 said, his lights swirling. "One moment."

Aleera7431 waited. For the first time in her existence impatience ate at her like acid.

Then the Troy model's lights pulsed red and blue, and his voice deepened as he called over his radio. "...Calling all units, converge on the following coordinate for special SubTask 2 operation..."

They Don't Make Them Like They Used To

M.C. St. John

HALLEY CHECKED her schedule app and said, "One more stop and we are done for the day. How you holding up?"

"Fine," Oscar said. "The company knows I like the long routes. But I'm amazed you've put up with the routes *and* me."

Halley grinned. "How else am I going to prove my worth to Alpha? Turn here."

"*Claro*." He steered the service van into a graceful arc, the electric motor humming. "Check me out. The AI vans got nothing on me."

Oscar was always making dad jokes. His sense of humor was dumb, but it still tickled Halley. She liked job shadowing him because of it.

Oscar was a spry, compact man with a clean-shaven face. He had a full head of dark hair that was turning salt and pepper at the temples. At certain times of day – usually in line with his energy levels at work – he could look anywhere between forty-five and seventy. But inside, he was perpetually corny. Some people, Halley had learned, were built that way.

"One day you'll be as good a driver as me," Oscar said. "I've seen your work. You got a real knack for the job. It's not all OS updates, like the company teaches nowadays."

Halley groaned. "I've sat through those trainings. Nothing but watching video clips and pressing buttons."

"Service calls are the way to learn our trade. You gotta be ready with your wits and muscles. I ever tell you what the *guitarrista* said to his mother before his automated solo?"

"Three times, I think."

"I'll tell you again. *Look, Mama, no hands*."

"Every time you tell it, it gets a little worse," she said, "but I get what you're saying. The automated stuff doesn't beat real handiwork."

"If more apprentices understood that, they would have gotten my seal of approval."

"How are my chances?"

"Slim if you don't start laughing at my jokes."

"I'm always up for a challenge."

"You're going to get one," Oscar said. "Here's our next stop."

She flicked through the nav chart. "310 Isotope Lane. How'd you know?"

"Because the family's out on the lawn," he said, parking the van. "Let's put that handiwork of yours to the test."

They got out and made their way up the pristine sidewalk. Both of them wore company-issued coveralls with their service rankings based on the visible color spectrum. Oscar's coveralls were a rich violet that was slightly faded at the elbows and knees. Halley's were a fresh ochre, having graduated from the lower frequencies of basic training. She carried a chrome toolbox with the Alpha Company's logo, a line drawing of a gear with the infinity symbol at its center.

The short walk on Isotope Lane was picturesque. It was a pleasant sector of the Division, away from the older parts of the City. This Division neighborhood was designed in the mid-twentieth-century American architectural motif. Lining each side of the street were quiet, repetitive homes painted in shades of mint, eggshell, and apple.

Halley and Oscar arrived at the drowsy, summertime hour before dinner, no doubt being grilled on the backyard barbecue and served with cool glasses of lemonade. Crickets chirped in the rose bushes. A soft breeze set wind chimes tinkling. Somewhere, the crack of a wooden bat hitting a line drive heralded the gentle good cheer of a baseball game crowd. For this small hamlet, all was well and right in the world.

The neighborhood council here, like others Halley had done service work for, voted to maintain June-level peacefulness all year round. Such financial efforts amounted to a suburban utopia, with precise climate control and streaming environmental ambiance. Anything to keep things pleasant inside their hermetically sealed enclave was well worth the price.

Which made the sight of the family outside of 310 all the more distressing. They stood in a nuclear family tableau on the front lawn, caught in a scene of frozen panic: Wife gripping Husband, both staring hopelessly past Young Daughter to the far edge of the yard. They all watched the lawn sprinkler there, a retro model that sprayed a fine-laced fan of water. The scattered mist caught rainbows from the afternoon light.

It also outlined a silhouette.

"Do you see the boy?" Oscar asked.

They watched as the silhouette flickered. Pixels of detail grew and swirled. Now hanging in the air was a glass replica of a child, frozen in his leap through the sprinkler. More pixels swirled inside, bits of information filling in until—

Blip.

A boy in blue shorts appeared, as real as any of the family on the lawn. To Halley, the tableau now resembled adverts she had seen in the Division archives, images from the very era the neighbors in this sector strived for: a picture of perfect suburban bliss.

But as soon as the boy had grown solid, he flickered again and vanished.

Blip.

"He's on the fritz," Oscar said. "These newer models are not waterproof, no matter how many times Alpha claims it. All right, service faces. I'll do the talking. You do the fixing."

Oscar flashed a smile to the family, who were now within earshot.

"Afternoon, folks," he said. "We see you have an issue with your son."

The wife broke away from her husband. She was a thin woman in a tailored dress. Wet mascara daubed the corners of her eyes. "Calvin was fine last week at the lake, but today…oh, it's awful seeing him disappear…"

"There's no need to get upset again, Marion," the husband said. His face was set in well-worn lines of concern. He turned to Oscar.

"I appreciate you coming out so quickly. Calvin was – *is* – a lively child, but we've made sure to properly maintain him."

Oscar nodded. "I've reviewed your file, and you're within your two-year service warranty. We're here to help, free of charge."

"I'm glad to hear it."

Marion let out a shaky sigh and spoke to Halley. "We try to take care of our Calvin. He had done so well with this upgrade. He glitched once or twice, but Tom never saw it happen.

I convinced myself I was seeing things. You know how mothers can be." She turned to her daughter. "Greta, honey, don't get too close while the service people are working."

Unfazed by her mother's words, Greta continued to run around in her pink swimsuit. She circled the sprinkler, singing to herself.

"Calvin Shmalvin, he's offline. When will he reboot this time? In an hour, in a day? When will he come back to play?"

"Cute song," Halley said.

"Greta is his younger sister by two years," Marion said. "It's strange to tell you that, isn't it? He's not getting any older, unless we pay for a new OS. And she's growing up so fast. Soon enough, Greta is going to be the older sister, and Calvin will be…"

Halley laid a hand on Marion's shoulder. "The most important thing right now is getting Calvin back online."

"You're right, yes. And you can do it."

"That's right," Halley said. "I'll do whatever it takes."

"Wonderful. Just wonderful." Marion drew herself up, smiling. She wiped away her wet mascara. "Would you like anything to eat? Perhaps a slice of cherry pie? I had one cooling in the kitchen before… this. My oven 3-D printed it."

"I could go for a drink," Halley said. "Do you have real tea leaves?"

"My, what a request."

"If it's a bother…"

"Not at all," Marion said. "I do believe we have a tea tin in our fallout shelter. I can get a cup brewing. Any preference?"

"Any is fine. The longer it's steeped the better, thank you."

When Marion was gone, Halley turned back to the sprinkler. The boy Calvin was in his mid-leap again, at the precise moment where he was a real boy, or as close as Alpha could get to real. Then, *blip* – empty space.

At this angle, she noticed that the space was not entirely empty. Hovering there was Calvin's Alpha gear. It was the exact shape of the Alpha logo on Halley's toolbox, about the width of the palm of her hand.

Oscar joined her. "Good move with giving the mother something to do," he said. "The last thing you need is hearing her cry every time he glitches." He whistled under his breath, assessing the scene. "Okay, here's your test. What's the proposed fix?"

"The gear is in the pocket of his swim trunks. I can grab it with my work gloves and then manually reboot him. What? You're looking at me funny."

"*Nada*. The move is tricky, is all. What if the boy goes online before you finish?"

"As we both know, two pieces of matter have a hard time being in the same place at the same time. If my hand is where Calvin is supposed to be when he goes online, then I would probably lose my hand. If that happened, say goodbye to a service promotion." Halley tipped her head. "Come on, Oscar. That would be a rookie move, and a rookie I ain't."

"I'm making sure you know the risks."

"Does she, though? Does she really?"

Tom the father came over. He planted himself in between Halley and Oscar, his hands on his hips. He didn't look happy with either of them, especially Oscar.

"The Alpha vid rep assured me the service person they'd sent out would be highly qualified. I hear you talking to this young woman as if *she* will be the one repairing my boy. I see the color of her uniform. It's on the wrong end of the spectrum, frankly."

"She's a shade of yellow in service rank, not ability," Oscar said.

"I was under the impression from Alpha that your colors determined technical worth. That makes them one and the same, doesn't it?"

"Not to me," Halley said. "I take my work very seriously, and I happen to be good at it – frankly. We only want to help as best we can."

Tom regarded her, the lines in his frown deepening. "Marion and I invested all of our credit into buying Calvin's gear. I don't regret a single day of it, because he is back, just as Alpha promised. *A lifetime guaranteed* – that's your slogan. But we could barely afford this latest upgrade. A new model is out of the question. This gear must be repaired. So, understand my dissatisfaction with the phrase *as best we can*. It simply isn't good enough."

"Then allow me to rephrase. I *will* fix Calvin. So, let's start with step one. Can we have the sprinkler turned off?"

"The control panel is around back," Tom said. He glared at Oscar. "I hope your trainee knows what she's doing." Then he disappeared behind the house.

"*Aye*, me too." Oscar turned to Halley. "Did you forget the service etiquette rules? Alpha guarantees product and customer satisfaction to the ninety-ninth percentile. *Not* one hundred. What you said was reckless."

"Only if I fail. And I won't."

"There's a chance."

"Are you doubting me too?"

"I'm only reminding you about this concept called margin of error."

"I like your dad jokes, Oscar. Not your dad sarcasm."

While Halley assessed what she may need from the toolbox, the water shut off. Now a ghostly silhouette of Calvin hung dripping in midair.

Greta, who had kept singing and dancing, seemed to wake up from what she was doing and notice the two strange service people for the first time. She skipped over to Halley. "Are you gonna fix my dumb brother?"

"Do you see these? I'm wearing them so I can reboot your brother."

"Ooo, the colors are so pretty."

Halley examined her work gloves. The filaments lining the metal material were fine veins of phosphorescent light. As part of her training, she had to name every sub-class of optic fiber and carbon strand that made up these gloves, had to demonstrate the fine-motor techniques while wearing them to rewire, repair, and reconstitute any current Alpha product. But Greta's comment had Halley seeing the gloves anew.

"You're right," she said. "They are pretty."

Greta held out her hands and balanced on one foot. "I made up a song about Calvin. Do you want to hear it?"

"Oh, I heard it earlier. It's catchy."

"I like to make up things. I'm good at it." She hopped to the other foot. "Like how you're good at making up Calvin."

"We used everything your mom and dad gave us to make him. All of his genes and memories. He's your brother, through and through."

Greta considered this. "Last week, when we all went to the lake, Calvin jumped in the water and stayed under for a really long time. My mom got scared. She *freaked*. Because my dumb brother did that before. He jumped right in and never came back up. I was little, but I remember. I had a swimsuit with a cool unicorn on it."

"I like the mermaid on this one," Halley said.

"Mermaids are cooler than unicorns now. But Calvin didn't remember my old swimsuit. He didn't remember that scary time at the lake at all. So, last week, he went and jumped in again like before and freaked everyone out."

"He doesn't have those memories from before. We built him with everything else up until that point. Who would want to remember something so scary?"

"Not me."

"Me neither. But sometimes, Alpha people will repeat things without knowing it. We all can do silly things like that, can't we?"

Greta shook her head. "I do everything good."

"Everyone else does silly things. Eventually, though, we come out better on the other side. Look at your brother. He came out of the lake this time."

"When Calvin did, my mom almost passed out. He thought he was a real *cut-up*, like my dad says."

"I bet."

"Then Calvin tried to grab my ankle to throw me in, but I was too fast. He smacked himself good on the dock from trying. Look at how quick I can hop, see?"

"Super quick," Halley said, smiling. "Should I go fix Calvin now?"

"I *guess*. He's so dumb that a sprinkler messed him up. I told him last night his gear was cracked, but he wouldn't listen to me. I'm just widdle biddle Greta, and I'm a know-it-all. Well, I know more than *him*."

"Do you remember where you saw the crack?"

"Uh-huh. On the number eight, in one of the loops." Inspired by her own words, Greta did a twirl and ran singing across the lawn. "Calvin, Shmalvin he can't hear, when he broke his Alpha gear…"

"The *niña* is a chatterbox," Oscar said, "but she got that sass from her father."

Hally nodded. "She was helpful, too. I know what's wrong with the boy."

"Yeah, what was that about the number eight?"

"She was talking about the lemniscate," Halley said. "The infinity symbol on Calvin's gear. It must have cracked when he was horseplaying with her." She tapped the back of her right glove; lights in the fingertips turned a rosy pink. "I'll heat-seal it, and then reboot him."

"Remember to time it, because—"

"Yes, yes. *Look Ma, no hands.* I know."

Halley made her way to the sprinkler, her boots squelching in the wet grass. Down the street was the calliope jingle of an ice-cream truck and the laughter of children following it. Real or manufactured, the sounds came from a world away.

Halley was focused on timing Calvin's glitching. It took thirty seconds for him to become a fully formed boy, *blip*. He stayed that way for another five seconds. Then, *blip* – the Alpha gear hovered alone. She had about ten seconds of free time to handle the gear. She cranked up the heat-sealing temperature of her glove and got ready.

Now she was close enough to note the details Alpha had engineered. A constellation of freckles scattered across Calvin's cheeks. His strawberry-blond hair, still wet from the sprinkler, lifted in sheafs from his forehead and around his ears in mid-flight. Four of his baby teeth were missing; Halley could count the gaps in his wild, smiling mouth. Those details and a million others added up to Calvin. This close, the boy appeared as real as Halley herself. The Alpha Company lived up to its slogan: a lifetime guaranteed.

The boy started to flicker.

Halley held her breath.

Blip. The boy vanished again.

Halley reached for the floating gear. It was hot to the touch, thrumming hard from the glitch cycle it was stuck in. She brought the gear closer to her, flipping it over.

There: a knick in the casing, right inside the engraved infinity sign.

Part of the 3-D projector chip was exposed, but nothing more. If there was any water in there, it would evaporate as soon as she started heat-sealing. She placed the glowing thumb pad of her right glove over the knick. Sulphur and burning metal filled the air.

"Halley," Oscar said. "You have to hurry."

"I'm fine."

"No, you're not. Calvin's coming back. Don't you see him?"

She did. Within the heat-seal smoke, pixels appeared and swirled around. The boy was filling back in.

"He's about to *blip* back on," Oscar said, his voice rising. "You have to let him go."

Halley finished the heat-seal and let go of the gear – or tried to.

"I *can't* let him go," she said. "I'm stuck inside his pixels."

"What the hell is going on?"

Tom had stalked out from behind the house, his scowl making the lines stand out even more on his face. "What kind of service visit is this? First I find my wife on a fool's errand in our shelter, and now you have my son above your head!"

"Halley, Shmalley, made a mess..."

"Quiet, Greta." Tom jabbed a finger in Oscar's face. "I shouldn't have listened to you. This woman has no idea what she's doing."

"I'm sorry, sir, but you have to move. I need to help my apprent—"

"Help? *She is flinging my boy around like a rag doll.* The only help *she* needs is a report for gross incompetence."

"Wait, sir."

But Tom marched up to Halley. "I'm saying this one last time. *Get away from my boy.*"

Halley tried again to free herself, but she couldn't do it alone. Her hands were sunk like quicksand in the growing soup of pixels. The muscles in her hands ached. She was glad to feel them; in a few more seconds, she wouldn't have any hands to feel at all.

She turned to Tom, her eyes blazing.

"Make me," she said.

Tom roared in response. He grabbed Halley's shoulders and pulled her back. Instead of resisting, Halley leaned into him. She dug her heels into the grass, then sprang back, working with Tom's momentum.

There was a slick popping noise, and Halley's hands broke free of the pixels.

Tom spun away, but Halley watched – *blip* – as the boy appeared. Calvin landed on top of her, and they both fell in the grass.

Greta ran over. "Is she dead?"

"Alive," Oscar said, "and in one piece."

"Just like your brother," Halley said. She showed them.

Slightly dazed, Calvin sat up. He rubbed the back of his head and winced. "What the heck happened to me? I feel like I got knocked out. Did I slip during our sprinkler race?"

"Yep," Greta said. "And you lost. Big time."

"I find that hard to believe," Calvin said. "Dad, did you see who won? Dad? What's the matter? Is everything okay?"

"Everything's fine, just fine."

Tom picked up Calvin and gave him a huge hug. Afterward, he said, "Calvin, this is Halley and Oscar from the Alpha Company."

"Hello," Calvin said. "Did you come to check the vid screen in the living room? It's been pretty glitchy."

"It was," Halley said, "but we got it back online. Everything is running smoothly now, wouldn't you say?"

"No complaints here," Tom said, his voice softening. "Thank you."

"Any time."

"Hey, Mom!"

As soon as she heard the front door open, Greta skipped to the porch to break the news. "Look at Calvin, Mom. He woke up. *Finally.*"

"Oh, honey," Marion said. She nearly spilled the tray in her hands. The cup and saucer rattled against the sugar bowl, spilling very hot, real tea. She recovered, thrusted the tray at Tom, and ran down to her son. She kissed him on both cheeks.

"You really are awake. Look at you. I'm so glad. And you," Marion said to Halley. "I couldn't be more grateful to you. Won't you stay for tea *and* dinner? It would be my honor."

"Geez, Mom," Calvin said, surprised. "What else did she fix beside the vid screen?"

* * *

It was early evening with a sky full of summer stars when the Alpha van turned off Isotope Lane. Oscar was back behind the wheel, smiling. "You really knocked that one out of the park."

"You doubted me?"

"Never. You're my apprentice, aren't you? But you got something I can't teach you."

"What's that?"

"*Corazón.* And you know how to use yours. How else could you have gotten Tom mad as hell to help you? He was about ready to yank your hands out of their sockets."

"It was a good thing he got that mad. It would have been hard to shake his hand with a stump." Halley sighed. "Calvin did end up destroying my gloves when he came back online."

"Don't worry. I'll get you a replacement pair and deduct the cost from your next paycheck. I won't even charge a service fee."

"Gee, thanks." Halley glanced down at her nav chart. "Where are we going? This isn't the way to the office."

"I know."

"Mind telling me the next stop, oh great and amazing mentor?"

"Here," Oscar said, and parked.

They were in a neighborhood of Chicago-style brick apartments from the nineteenth century. The buildings were old and worn because, unlike the Division, they were built in that era. Cracks ran up the cement steps, and rust covered the iron railings.

In one ground-floor unit, the light was on in the picture window, warm and inviting. The curtain folded back, and a short, broad-faced woman peered out.

"There's Lucilia, my wife," he said. "That's our place."

"I don't understand," Halley said. "Why would you bring me to your home?"

"Why not? It's what I do for all of my apprentices who get my blessing."

"You mean—?"

"You're going up another wavelength. Ochre to avocado. You deserve it."

"I don't know what to say."

"Don't say anything. Just come on in and have some dessert. Marion's dinner was all right, I'm sure, but her kitchen made it. Nothing beats a real cup of coffee and Lucilia's *conchas*. She makes them by hand."

Oscar gave a loud, long yawn. It may have been a trick of the evening light, but his hair looked to have more salt than pepper in it. "It's been a long day today. I don't hold my charge as much as I used to."

"You might need a new battery," Halley said. "Do you need me to take a look?"

"When I get you those new gloves, sure. But not now. We're both off the clock." He opened the van door. Cool night air greeted them. "Lucilia loves it when I bring home the good ones to celebrate."

They made their way up the worn but comfortable sidewalk, two workers done for the day, all of their service stops completed, lifetimes guaranteed.

Talking and laughing, they passed through the light thrown from the picture window on their way to the front door. Oscar seemed to fade a little in that warm light, his pixels scattered like a billion motes of dust, his well-used Alpha gear floating among them. But he was still there, and still cracking dad jokes.

And Halley, her shadow cast strong and solidly behind her, laughed at each one.

K-375

Nathanael K. Stottlemyer

K-375 LIKED ROCKS. Every day she and her sisters sifted through the quarry, sorting the rocks the miners had blasted off the mountainside. There were so many kinds. Basalt, andesite, socria, and hundreds of others were programmed into her database for her to identify. K-375 would pick them up and marvel how each rock could be so different. She didn't spend too long admiring them. There were quotas to fill, after all. K-375 consulted her database for each rock. She placed the ore in her hopper. The others she stacked in large, beautiful piles. The database called the stones worthless, but K-375 liked all of them just the same.

The miners woke them before sun-up, and K-375 followed her sisters to the quarry. All day she worked, shuffling her wide feet across the gravel field, filling her hopper, and depositing the ore into the load-bot. The work was considered too grueling for humans, but K-375 didn't mind. She was built for it. Embedded into her firmware was joy in a day full of geological calculation.

Each night, when the night shift finally turned off the floodlights, sending the quarry into a foggy gloom, K-375 joined the line of her sisters following the miners home. K-375 found her bed, dock #32, beside the benches in the back of the workshop. She plugged herself in and ran a diagnostic. It only took a few minutes, but it felt like years before she could go on standby and speed through the hours until she could, once again, stack rocks.

But on her 8753rd hour of operation, K-375 noticed that the miners who watched her and her sisters looked leaner. Their eyes drooped and one had a hacking cough. Now, reviewing her data files, K-375 realized she should have noticed that something was wrong, but there were so many rocks to find that she didn't give it a single thread. They didn't work as long that day. The miners brought them home while the sun still hung above the mountains. As she waited for the diagnostic to run, K-375 felt a definite sense of disappointment.

The next day, K-375 awoke to find the workshop empty. Her sisters were gone, and two tired-looking men stood beside a workbench.

"I knew corporate sold off the prototypes," one was saying. He wore an orange jumpsuit, much cleaner than the faded denim worn by the miners. It took a while, but K-375's facial analysis determined he was the miners' mechanic. "You see, originally they didn't know how much processing the K-class bot would need in the field, so they put extra in the first batch to test them."

"Will it work?" The other man asked. K-375's facial analysis recognized him as the foreman.

"I'd have to crack her firmware to unlock her full power. She'll never be a full med-bot, but her system has more specs than some of the nurse-bots corporate offers," the mechanic replied. "I can't promise it'll work. If it doesn't, we'll be down a bot, and corporate will have grounds to sue. It's against terms of service. Why don't you wait a few weeks?"

The foreman shook his head. "I haven't told the others, but corporate won't make a special shipment. We won't get anything until they come to pick up the ore."

The mechanic swore. "Why?"

The foreman slumped against the workbench. He looked like he could collapse at any moment. "I have no idea," he murmured.

"Well, it isn't like we have a choice," the mechanic said.

The foreman nodded. He sighed. "Do it."

The mechanic pushed something into K-375's dock. K-375 chirped nervously. The mechanic smiled. "Don't worry," he said. "This won't hurt."

K-375's audio sensors heard a click, then everything went black.

* * *

When K-375 powered on, her internal time said it was Sunday, which was odd. K-375's logs had never before stored accurate date-time, but there it was. Today was Sunday, October 9, 2349, and the time was 13:30.

K-375 looked around. The workshop looked different. Brighter. There were more colors. She ran a diagnostic. The report was back in only a moment. Save for a new system file hash, everything was in working order.

Slowly she climbed out of her dock, her jointed legs unfolding.

She looked around and saw the mechanic. K-375 was surprised. Her facial recognition had never worked this fast before. The man hunched in a chair beside the workshop's doors. K-375 moved towards him, and her feet, engineered for optimum balance on uneven terrain, shuffled awkwardly across the dusty floor.

The man sniffed and looked at her with red-rimmed eyes. "It's finished," he said, and coughed.

K-375 beeped anxiously. The mechanic smiled. "The doc checked me out. I'll be alright. I just need some rest." He took a deep breath through his mouth. "Let's get you to work." K-375 remembered her sisters, doubtless working in the quarry, and chirped excitedly. She followed him outside.

But the mechanic didn't start down the rough track to the quarry. Instead, he limped to a lonely house in the middle of the street. He rapped on the door.

A woman answered, hair rumpled and bleary-eyed. "Yes?"

"She's ready," the man said. The woman looked like she was going to cry. The mechanic frowned. "You need to rest."

K-375 shuffled uncomfortably. She glanced from the mechanic to the woman. Why was she here? Did rocks somehow get into the house?

The woman looked like she was going to argue but instead sagged, her teeth chattering. "Let's get you to bed," the mechanic said, taking her arm. He glanced at K-375. "You know what to do."

The mechanic left, supporting the woman. K-375 watched them for a moment before stepping inside. She didn't find rocks. Instead, she found infants.

There were seventeen of them, in various sizes, lying on foam mattresses. All were sleeping.

K-375 stared. What did they expect her to do? Her common-sense protocol stated that she wasn't intended to stack them. She took a step forward. Were the rocks behind the door on the other side of the room? She crossed the room and opened the door, only to find a cramped latrine. Crates were stacked in the main room's far corner, but when she looked inside, K-375 didn't find rocks. They were filled with bottles, powder, linens, and many small jumpsuits.

One of the infants opened its eyes and sneezed. K-375 froze. Was she supposed to be taking care of them?

The child smiled and kicked its feet, then grimaced. K-375 shuffled towards it. The infant kicked again, grunted, then began to cry.

Eyes flew open all around the room, and one by one, the other infants joined in until K-375's audio sensors registered all 110 decibels. K-375 felt a subroutine kick in. She picked up the child that had first awakened and carried it to the closest crate to find a wrapping. How had she known this? She had been in operation for almost 9,000 hours, and not once had she seen this process before. Her logic routine could not reach any conclusion. She could think of that later. Now she had to deal with the infant wriggling in her hands.

She pulled out a clean wrapping and set the baby on the ground. For a moment, K-375 wondered how she should perform a cleansing, and then her new process loaded the instructions. She worked quickly, cleaning the child's backside and replacing its wrapping. As she did, the infant quieted, staring up at her with wide blue eyes. K-375 carried him back to his bed, then turned to address the next child.

The children's needs varied. Some required changing. Others wanted formula or companionship. Sometimes K-375's new protocol could tell which they needed. Other times she had to try each option in order to discern what the infant required.

K-375 hoped someone would come so that she could go back to stacking rocks. No one did. Hours passed. It seemed as soon as K-375 put down one child, another cried to be picked up. Finally, after an average of 3.27 diaper changes and 1.83 bottles per infant, they fell asleep. K-375 stepped outside in time to see the sun set behind a jagged rise of mountains.

"So you're done," a voice came from beside her. K-375 turned to see the mechanic leaning against a metal crate. "For now at least." He patted the crate. "This afternoon we moved your dock so you don't have to leave to charge up. I put it in a crate to keep it dry." He swung open the box's front. "Might as well get charged."

K-375 squeezed herself inside and watched as her battery percentage ticked up.

The mechanic sank down in front of her. "We're sick," he said. His face turned up in a slow smile. "You might've noticed. Doc doesn't know what it is, but it's bad. We can't risk getting the kids sick." He paused, staring vacantly at the ground. "That's where you come in. I unlocked your extra cores, and added caretaking instructions. We need you to take care of the babies."

K-375's command system logged a new instruction. Care for babies. It took another moment for K-375's lexicon to deduce the term babies from its context.

"This is your first priority," the mechanic continued. K-375 set the instruction priority to number one. Aside from the ethical guidelines embedded in her firmware, she would consult this command before making any decision.

"Here," the mechanic placed a thick tablet on the ground. "Parents will want to see their babies when they are feeling better. Understood?"

K-375 beeped sadly, though the man didn't seem to notice. "Great." He coughed again and slowly stood. K-375 watched him make his way down the street and into the workshop. Sunlight faded from the sky. K-375's battery reached three-quarters capacity. Finally, the miners returned, followed by all thirty-one of her sisters. If her sisters saw her, they gave no sign. K-375 watched them file into the workshop. She knew they would only have to wait a diagnostic time before slipping into standby and quickly passing the time until they could sort rocks again.

At 22:17, K-375's battery was full. She picked up the tablet and slipped inside. The babies were asleep. K-375's infra-sensor registered their tiny bodies, unmoving on the mattresses.

Briefly, K-375 considered leaving the hut and starting for the quarry. Her ethics protocol immediately rejected the proposal. It was against her highest instruction. Besides, without the floodlights, she wasn't sure she'd be able to categorize rocks. Instead, she took the bottles to the latrine's sink and followed her cleansing protocol. As she set the bottles to dry, K-375 wondered how long her memory bank had had a sanitizer protocol. The process was interrupted by a cry from the other room.

One of the babies had awakened. Her tiny fists flailed, and she kicked both legs. K-375 picked her up. Her companionship protocol initiated, and she rocked the child back and forth, beeping a soft melody.

The baby quieted, thankfully, without waking the others. K-375 checked the baby's linen and set her back on her bed. K-375 waited until she knew for certain the child wouldn't awaken, then returned to stacking the bottles.

The babies needed much less care during the night. Only the smallest woke. K-375 took to standing between the mattresses so she could get to them before their cries woke the infants nearby. It wasn't too frequent, and K-375 had plenty of idle time. As she watched the children, her problem-solving routine reasoned out an idea. Maybe there was a way to be caretaker of the children and to do what she loved.

At 03:25, K-375 gently dragged the mattresses closer together and spread several blankets on the floor. Then at 05:24, she slipped outside with the bag from the refuse container. The street was deserted. K-375 made her way to a large blue container beside the workshop. Sometimes when returning from the quarry, she had noticed refuse bags piled around it. She set hers down and, after double-checking the street, filled her hopper with the stones that lined the street.

That morning, when the babies woke up, K-375 fed them and changed both their linens and their jumpsuits before setting them on the floor in a circle. When all seventeen were awake, she stood in the middle and emptied her hopper. The rocks landed with a dusty clatter. K-375 looked around. The infants' eyes were wide, and the ones who could lift their heads stared. K-375 made sure the sound hadn't been sufficient to make any of them cry before continuing.

She picked up a rock and compared it to her database. The answer came much faster than she expected. Limestone. She set it down and picked up another. Basalt. Beeping cheerfully, she began to sort, placing each rock in a separate pile. There was little variance, and K-375 could've worked quickly. She chose not to, instead showing each rock to the infants before putting it in its place.

She sorted 34% of the pile before she stopped. One of the babies was watching a bug that had wandered in front of her. The others stared at the floor.

K-375 shooed the bug away and put in its place a handful of unsorted rocks. The baby's eyes focused on them, and she reached a chubby hand forward. K-375 chirped encouragingly. The baby took a small piece of granite and brought it to her mouth.

Beeping in surprise, K-375 grabbed the infant's hand. As gently as she could, she pulled the rock free and brushed the little pile away. The baby looked at her with surprised eyes and then proceeded to drool.

K-375 concluded that, unfortunately, the children weren't developed enough to perform sorting. She turned back to the rocks. She, at least, could sort them before taking the rocks back outside. Before she could pick up another, her audio sensors registered a chime at 80 decibels. It was coming from the crates. Her auditory position traced it back to the tablet the mechanic had given her.

She hurried over. "Incoming call" the screen read. It took a moment for K-375's technological interface to realize she should press the green icon to accept.

A face appeared on the tablet screen. "Hello?" The voice came too loud out of the speakers. K-375 fumbled for the volume button. When the volume had been corrected, she beeped greetings.

The face, a woman's, frowned. "Can I see Kaylee?"

K-375 glanced over at the infants. Her personnel database held no names for the children.

"I know she's there. Let me see her!" The woman bit her lip. "Please."

Quickly, K-375 shuffled over to the ring of babies. She pointed the screen at the closest.

"That isn't her," the woman said. "Don't you know their names?"

K-375 beeped negative. The woman didn't seem to care. "I want to see Kaylee."

K-375 took her around the ring, showing her each child and making certain she couldn't see the pile of rocks. At last, the woman stopped her at the baby who had almost swallowed the stone.

"Kay!" the woman said, her tone lightening. The baby looked up and smiled. "How ya doing? I see you're cheerful today!" The baby now registered in K-375's database as Kaylee kicked her legs, her blue eyes searching the room. When she found nothing, her smile vanished, and she began to wimpier.

"Hey, hey, here I am darling—" the woman coughed. "I'm right here. Don't cry. Mommy can't be there right now. She isn't feeling good."

Kaylee looked right at K-375. K-375's facial recognition protocol registered confusion with 97% certainty. Then she started crying.

K-375 set down the tablet and picked the baby up, beeping softly.

"Baby, please don't—" the woman broke off. K-375 could hear her weeping. "I'm sorry. But it's bad. Your grandma's on support. I wish you could come here, but we can't risk it."

The words only made Kaylee wail louder. K-375 rocked the child back and forth. The woman coughed. "Mommy's sorry, darling," she said. Then the tablet switched off.

It took fifteen minutes of companionship before Kaylee quieted. K-375 set her onto her mattress and started moving the other infants back to their mattresses. She picked up the rocks and brushed the dirt to a corner of the room. Soon it was time for more bottles. K-375 rocked each child as she fed it, and by the time she set them down, everyone was asleep. K-375 cleansed the bottles again. The tablet rang several times during the afternoon, and K-375 kept it close so she could answer before it woke the babies. Each time the screen showed an exhausted man, woman, or both. She took them around the mattresses until they identified the child that was theirs, and K-375 logged the names into her personnel database.

The parents spoke softly to their sleeping child. Sometimes the child would stir and smile. Eventually the parents' voices would trail off, and after a whispered goodbye, the call would end.

At 16:12, Orson woke up. K-375 changed his wrapping and set him on his stomach to facilitate motor skill development. He lifted his head and giggled, kicking his legs. On the far side of the room, Emma stirred. K-375 shuffled over, but after a few minutes she didn't wake. K-375 gently stroked her hair before returning to Orson.

When K-375 reached his cot, she found him on his back. K-375 turned him on his stomach and ran a memory diagnostic. Her data drives returned healthy. Orson giggled and kicked his legs. K-375 watched as he leaned his head to the right. Slowly, his left shoulder raised, until he flipped onto his back.

K-375 beeped in surprise, which caused Orson to grin toothlessly. The child was further along in development than she had hypothesized. She rolled him back over and watched. He giggled, lifted his head and rolled. K-375 spent the next three minutes setting him on his stomach and listening to him laugh as he rolled. Then Isabel started crying, and regretfully K-375 had to leave to attend her.

One by one the infants woke up, most of them hungry. K-375 fed them then and once more when she put them to sleep. At 21:17, she hurried outside to charge. It was already night.

Through the open workshop door, K-375 could see her sisters, motionless in their docks. She wondered how their work had gone. Were they struggling to meet quota without her? K-375 would have liked to think that she worked as hard as the rest, that without her, they couldn't collect enough ore. Maybe then they would send someone else to watch the infants, and she could go back to the quarry.

Once her battery reached 100%, K-375 emptied her hopper beside the blue waste container. For a moment, she considered sorting them. Instead, she hurried inside and began sanitizing the bottles and running a load of jumpsuits through the portable cleaner. She hadn't spent much time on it, however, before Kaylee began crying.

K-375 hurried over, her logic routine unable to compute a solution. Her personnel file had her as one of the older children, so she should have been able to rest through the night. But her audio sensors were not malfunctioning. What was more, Kaylee's cries were drawn out and wet. Between them, her breath came in gasps. Something was wrong, but what it was, her logic routine couldn't compute.

K-375 walked Kaylee around the room, rocking her and beeping softly. At last, Kaylee's eyes closed, and her breath steadied, though it still sounded wet. K-375 didn't put her down. Instead, she kept walking. She re-cached her data files and queried her logic routine. The results again were inconclusive.

K-375 was about to run them again when Terrence started crying. She put Kaylee down and hurried over to change his wrapping.

When they woke the next morning, fourteen of the infants shared Kaylee's breathing, and K-375's thermal sensor detected an abnormal body temperature. She tried taking off their jumpsuits to disperse the heat, but they started shivering. Her care-taking protocol suggested making sure they had extra bottles and were clean, but other than that, there was nothing she could do. The infants slept almost constantly and always woke up crying. Sometimes, K-375 could get them to stop, but more frequently she had to leave one to attend to another.

It was late afternoon before the tablet rang. The babies were sleeping, and K-375 moved quickly to answer it. The screen showed the woman who was Kaylee's mother. She was in a dark room, and her eyes were red-rimmed.

"How is she?" the woman asked.

K-375 beeped uncertainly. She brought the tablet to where Kaylee slept, red-faced and breathing hard.

The woman's face came closer. "Is she alright?" she asked in alarm.

Kaylee stirred. The woman froze. Kaylee took a deep, rattling breath. Her eyes flickered, then closed again.

"She's sick?" the woman asked, quieter this time.

K-375 chirped confirmation.

The woman sank back. "No. This was supposed to stop that." She coughed. "Do any of the others have it?"

K-375 beeped again.

"I'll call the doctor," the woman said. "The infirmary is packed. He'll come as soon as he can." The tablet winked out.

Nobody called the rest of the day, and if they had, K-375 couldn't have answered. As evening grew closer, the infants woke up, every one with an abnormal temperature. An average of 3.21 cried at any point. K-375 did her best to quiet them, but often she failed. What was more, several infants spat up white liquid, and K-375 had to wipe them down, change their jumpsuits and sometimes also the bedding.

Come standard charging time, none of the babies were asleep. Most cried softly for companionship, but K-375 only had two arms. When she picked up one, it quieted, but only for as long as she held them. She tried to spend time with each, but none were comforted.

At last, with her battery at 3%, K-375 couldn't go on. She set Ferris down and stepped outside. The door swung shut, silencing the infants' cries.

K-375 hurried to her dock but was surprised to find someone leaning on it. Her facial recognition identified him as the mechanic. He checked a screen on his watch.

"Your battery has to be almost empty," he said through chattering teeth. K-375's diagnosis reported he was shivering. "Get in."

K-375 climbed inside.

"The doc's got it, too," the mechanic said. "He could barely tell me where to find these." He set a small canister in front of her. "They're meds for kid." He coughed and spat on the ground. "They'll keep the fever down and help them sleep better." He trailed off as his head sank to his chest. He shook himself. "It gets a lot worse the second day." The mechanic staggered to his feet. "I have to set the minerbots to function autonomously. Corporate isn't sending anything until a shipment is ready to be picked up."

K-375 watched him leave. And in an hour, she watched him make his way from the workshop to a house on the far side of the street. Her battery percent increased slowly. Every nanosecond, K-375 filtered input from her audio sensors, searching for any noise from inside the house. She wished for an option to go into standby until her battery was full.

The sky had begun to grow light again when K-375 climbed out of the dock. It was also the time that her sisters left the workshop.

No miner led them as they shuffled past in a long, loose line. Several turned to look at her as they passed. K-363 was the bot at the end. She stopped and waved. K-375's communication network notified her about a communication from her sister. They had been given a new instruction, all of them. Operate the quarry autonomously. The command had a registered priority of 1. The instruction automatically logged into K-375's command system.

K-375 paused. She now had two instructions registered with identical priority. Protocol dictated that which instruction she pursued was up to her discretion. After a moment's hesitation, she forwarded the option to her decision system. Her ethics protocol returned inconclusive. Her preference reminded her of the long hours she had enjoyed analyzing rocks, but it also recalled the toothless smiles and the infants' drowsy murmurs as she rocked them to sleep.

Then K-375's logic forwarded a conclusion. The rocks in the quarry had been there forever, and no matter how fast her sisters worked, more would remain. She only had this time to care for the children, and it added that if she did not attend them, they might not survive. K-375 waved and beeped good luck to her sisters, then picked up the medicine canister and headed inside.

Although K-375's memories contained timestamps, the days that followed were indiscernible. There was an average of 3.57 babies awake every hour. K-375 did her best to keep them comfortable. She fed them when they asked and gave them medicine when their fevers got too high. She would've given it to all of them, but inside the canister were six vials, each containing approximately ten doses. K-375 didn't have any information about how long the illness would last and wanted to be sure she had enough.

Come the fourth day, the babies coughed up wet, thick globs. K-375 heated towels to lay on their chests. They didn't cry to eat, but K-375 fed them anyway. She had only four vials of medicine left, but plenty of powdered food. She hoped it would help somewhat. K-375 stayed inside until all of them were asleep, then stepped outside to charge. She requested speed charging, even though the dock warned of loss of battery life, and she charged for no longer than thirty minutes before hurrying back inside.

The sixth day was the last the tablet rang. Kaylee's mother called to ask how she was. K-375 set the tablet beside the sleeping child, and it wasn't long before K-375 could hear the woman's snores. K-375 was too busy to end the call, and it lasted until the tablet cut off with a click.

On the ninth day, Kaylee's breath came in strained wheezes. Her eyes were wide and still behind half-closed lids. She didn't even cry. K-375 ran hot water in the latrine until vapor hung like smoke. K-375 spent the night pacing the three steps from the commode to the door, beeping softly for her breath to equalize. By dawn, her breathing had normalized. K-375 opened the fifth vial to give her a dose before feeding Ferris.

The next night, Kaylee's breathing was worse. K-375's internal clock counted between the infant's breaths, and at 06:12 her body temperature reached 103°F. K-375 draped a cool towel over her forehead and hurried off to tend to the others.

On day thirteen, K-375 had four children in the latrine. She dragged a mattress inside and laid them side by side. Kaylee's breathing was so shallow, K-375's audio sensors could barely hear it. K-375 watched until her battery reached 1%. She gave Kaylee the last drops of medicine and staggered to her dock.

Dawn's breaking was hidden by clouds on day fourteen. K-375 opened the latrine door to find Kaylee watching her. The fever had broken. One by one, the babies began to recover. One morning, K-375 heard Orson laugh as he pushed himself onto his backside. She hurried over to see him flop backwards, grinning widely. By evening the next day, the infants' nasal passageways were mostly cleared. It was only then that K-375 felt safe enough to take the six bags of refuse she had accumulated to the blue container. She didn't stay long, hurrying back across the empty street to the children.

On day twenty-two, the children were startled out of sleep as something roared overhead. It took an hour for K-375 to get them settled down. She was walking Kaylee across the room when a crisp knock sounded at the door. She opened the door to find the tall, thin chassis of a med bot.

"Greetings, I am MED-1649," it said. "May I come in?"

K-375 beeped affirmative and stepped back as he rolled inside. K-375 had moved the mattresses to one side, and the infants lay on the floor, playing with plastic rings she had found in the bottom of a crate the day before. MED-1649 surveyed the room, his segmented body rotating slowly. K-375 shuffled awkwardly. In her arms, Kaylee gurgled and blew bubbles.

"I was ordered by this colony's leader to tend to the children first," MED-1649 stated. "Yet I believe they have recovered, far sooner than their progenitors." His head swung, and his three eyes focused on K-375. "I do not believe I am familiar with your model."

There was a chirp from the door. K-375 turned to see K-363 and her sisters clustered by the door. They seemed pleased to see her.

MED-1649 turned from them to K-375. "MED class doctors are engineered to keep their patients' information in confidence. Judging by my initial survey, caring for this colony will be a challenge for even my capabilities. I trust you can keep caring for the children?"

K-375 beeped affirmative. MED-1649 scanned the room once more, then turned back to K-375 and her sisters. "Do have them wash before they handle the infants," he said and rolled back outside.

Her sisters told her that the ship's bots were loading the ore, and with their task completed, they were left to their own devices. K-375 tried to show them the babies. K-363 held Orson, but soon all of them lost interest and wandered back to the quarry. K-375 didn't' blame them. Her memory recalled how they felt.

With MED-1649's care, soon the tablet began ringing. The parents looked tired but happy to see their children playing. In less than a week, MED-1649 began knocking on the door to take a baby for a 'short visit'. In two weeks, he decided the settlers had recovered enough to care for the infants themselves. The next day K-375 watched as the mechanic moved her dock back to the workshop, and she joined in the line behind her sisters as they shuffled to the quarry.

K-375 still liked rocks. She had missed filling her hopper and stacking rocks. However, it wasn't the same as before the mechanic's modifications. In an hour of operation, she could analyze twice as many rocks as her sisters. Her battery didn't last as long either. Come midday, she had to return to the workshop to charge. It took several hours for her battery to reach full. Some days she would return to the quarry, but other days, she would climb out of the dock to find the mechanic waiting. He would lead her to one of the houses. Inside, she would find one of the children waiting for her. Each time, K-375 marveled at how quickly the children developed. Soon they were walking, then talking. Like the rocks, each one was different, but she loved them equally.

Director X and the Thrilling Wonders of Outer Space

Brian Trent

THE HOVERCAR zipped along Los Angeles' abandoned streets like a glassy bullet, the reflected starlight melting along its sleek, tear-drop flanks. Its electric engine purred. The driver banked left through what remained of Laurel Canyon, rocketing over bomb craters and weaving in and out of palm trees that had sprouted from shattered asphalt.

At Hollywood Hills, the hovercar's headlights illuminated a cave. The vehicle roared inside, tail-lights filling the narrow tunnel with ruby light as the driver applied reverse-thrust. The headlights painted a matte-black door ahead, hung with a signpost:

WHITLEY HEIGHTS BOMB SHELTER
LOS ANGELES DISTRICT 5
AUTHORIZED PERSONNEL ONLY
NO TRESPASSING

The hovercar door clicked open. The driver unfolded itself from the seat and stepped out like an oversized praying mantis in the reddish gloom.

Director X (as was its designation from the Global Security Protectorate) was a tall, silver robot who roughly approximated the human form. That is to say, Director X was bipedal, with two accordion arms and long, multijointed legs. It even had two eyes, like little flashlights protruding from the glass dome atop its neck.

The eyes swiveled around, casting twin beams in the blackness. They halted at the door's intercom.

The robot stabbed one of its blocky fingers into the button and said cheerfully, "Hello! I am Director X. By authority of the Global Security Protectorate, I humbly thank you for opening your doors immediately and inviting me inside!"

The black door lifted so quickly it seemed to have disappeared. Behind it, another door vanished, and then another, revealing a lengthy corridor opening into a gray rotunda.

Director X plodded forward towards the lobby. The doors behind it snapped shut with a successive *thump! thump! thump!*

The robot stood motionless in the soapy decontamination spray that followed. The spray, it knew, was unnecessary; radiation had long ago declined to perfectly safe levels. Nonetheless, Director X waited patiently as the liquid ran over the glass head and silver torso, black accordion arms and the actuators in its legs. Blowers roared to life, drying its metallic hull.

One final door snapped open. Director X trundled through…

…and into the quaint town Retro Los Angeles.

The Stygian metropolis was a weak echo of its namesake. Brick buildings and plastic green parks, churches and schools, brass corporate doorways and outdoor cafes. Artificial palm trees lined the sidewalk like cheerful soldiers.

Director X gazed up at the 'sky'. It was the rocky ceiling of a cave, painted azure and with billowy clouds. The sun – a blazing globe like a massive heat-lamp – crawled east to west along a thinly concealed metal track in the granite.

As the robot was descending white-lacquered steps into the town proper, someone cried, "You there!"

Director X's flashlight eyes snapped towards an approaching group of men and one little boy. "Hello," it said.

The men halted. Their presumed leader stepped forward, gray moustache bent in a mighty frown.

"I'm Jonathan Croker, Mayor of District 5."

"And I am Director X, filmmaker of the Protectorate. Thank you for receiving me." The robot hesitated, and then chose a complimentary line of small talk to put these obviously nervous people at ease; the only one who looked happy was the little boy. "I like your shelter's doors. Very *Forbidden Planet*."

Croker's expression didn't soften. "Director X? You make those crappy… um… late-night movies, right? Why are you here? Robots never visit us."

"I was hoping to enlist the services of my human peers."

"What services?"

"Well you see, there is a problem topside. This problem is—"

"Giant ants!" the little boy shouted. "The topside world is filled with giant ants, right? You need people to help fight them, and locate their queen!"

The mayor grinned bleakly. "This is my boy, Bobby. Sorry, he has an overactive imagination."

Director X stooped and patted the little human on his head. "Hello, Bobby! There are no giant ants in the world. But I see you are a fan of the *Them!* series. That makes me glad. I also like the *Them!* series."

The kid looked crestfallen. "No giant ants?"

"Bobby!" Mayor Croker snapped. "Enough!"

Director X straightened. "You are familiar with *my* movies, yes?"

"Sure, when I can't sleep. I've caught a few of your pictures."

"I am looking to make a new series of films, and I have chosen District 5 to be my partner in this endeavor."

Jonathan Croker frowned until his moustache bent. "Your partner for what?"

"I wish to enlist your townspeople as actors and writers, and to utilize your town as a location. Ah! I can see several choice locales, including that beautiful church and lovely library. What a charming park! Why, even that bank could be used for an exciting robbery sequence!"

The mayor regarded his associates. "I'm afraid we don't understand. Robots make all the movies."

Director X gave an exaggerated nod. "That is correct. But as you surely know, before the War of '62, human beings made movies. I wish to involve human beings in the movie-making process once again."

Suspicion creased Croker's forehead. "Why? Is there a problem?"

"Well yes. The problem is—"

"Giant locusts!" the little boy cried.

"Bobby!"

Director X hesitated. Several lines of response suggested themselves, and the robot's processors clicked and whirred as they weighed an appropriate response. Its flashlight eyes swiveled in their sockets.

The problem was that the silicon studios were running out of ideas.

With copyright law as extinct as the old world, the Protectorate's twenty-six filmmakers had gone on to mine literature until they were scraping bottom: Director L had recently been reduced to producing cinematic treatments of ancient Babylonian literary fragments, including *The Epic of Lugalbanda, Marriage Contract of My Sixth Daughter for Three Oxen*, and *Prayer to Protect the Soul Against Crocodile Spirits.* These had not been well-received – achieving truly abysmal viewer ratings – and the wretched feedback had precipitated the Great Studio Conference of last summer.

Protectorate filmmakers met to debate the problem. After six hours of discussion, they reached a near-unanimous decision: start making cross-over fiction. Production slates rapidly filled with everything from *Sir Gawain Versus the Great God Pan* to *Dorothy Meets the Hounds of Tindalos.*

Director X had been the lone dissenting vote.

"I'm seeking something new to make," Director X explained to Mayor Croker. "Something in the vein of *The Day the Earth Stood Still*, or *Earth Versus the Flying Saucers*, or..."

The robot trailed off.

The men were staring without comprehension. Little Bobby frowned.

"Or," Director X continued, "An outer space adventure series similar to *Flash Gordon*."

"Flash who?"

"*Buck Rogers*?"

No reaction.

Now, it was Director X who stared dumbfounded. It recalled how they hadn't responded to its *Forbidden Planet* quip earlier.

"Science-fiction films," the robot said at last.

Mayor Croker rolled his eyes. "Sure, we've seen science-fiction films. Kind of silly stuff, if you ask me. Mutants, monsters from under the sea..."

"Giant bugs," Bobby muttered.

"I'm referring to films about outer space. Travelling in rocket ships to other stars and planets."

Croker seemed to go blank. His associates blinked stupidly.

"What's 'outer space'?" Bobby asked. "What's a 'rocket ship'?"

"Surely you must have old books," Director X prompted. "Asimov, Bradbury, Clarke? Moore, Nowlan, Oliver?"

"Moore? Didn't she write that sea monster story?"

"Yes," Director X said, "But she also penned a series of *outer space* adventures."

Mayor Croker reddened. "And what the hell is an outer space adventure? What's this 'outer space' you're talking about?"

Director X froze in place.

This was *not possible.*

Its self-preservation protocols immediately kicked in, having identified an anomaly so profound that it warranted immediate and discreet analysis.

"So anyway," the robot muttered, "I should like to create a temporary studio in District 5 to create new kinds of movies. Would that be okay?"

Mayor Croker stroked his moustache. "Do we have a choice?"

"Of course not. Would you kindly take me on a tour of your pleasant little town?"

* * *

District 5 was in some ways precisely what Director X expected to find.

Since the War of '62, humanity had retreated into insular, subterranean communities. Retro Los Angeles had been constructed to approximate its sunnier progenitor as seen in films and old photos, with its streets and banks and electric streetcars. The pedestrians Director X observed were also imitative of older days: recreations of Astor and Bogart in *The Maltese Falcon* franchise; Holden and Hepburn in the *Sabrina* saga; and Wyatt and Young from the *Father Knows Best* epic. A century had passed since the War of '62, and yet if Retro Los Angeles was any indication, styles and ideas and innovations had ground to a halt as surely as topside vehicles lay rotting in their own pools of rust.

And yet...

Director X's flashlight eyes widened, scanning and tagging additional details.

Ah!

Not *everything* was so run-of-the-mill. Mayor Croker led him to the town green where a parade was in progress, the crowd waving flags and banners. But Director X noted groups of teenagers stealthily scampering along the rooftops of the surrounding buildings. The teens, whispering and snickering amongst themselves, were clearly up to no good. Director X glimpsed portable radio devices in their hands, antennae aimed at the trees below. Soon enough, the town's robotic birds went haywire, clashing in aerial dogfights above the unsuspecting parade.

Mayor Croker led Director X to the city library. Kids reading quietly? Yes. But Director X also observed children scampering through the maze of aisles, one girl prompting her cohorts with descriptions of monsters that weren't actually there, whispering hints about clues and imagined traps and the magical properties of books and mundane objects, and how the librarian was actually a sorceress who had imprisoned them all in a dungeon.

The mayor led Director X to the city schoolyard. Young kids playing on swings and see-saws? Yes. But Director X also saw that many kids had replaced the old Hobby Horses with a more fanciful menagerie of pegasi, hippocampi, and fabulous creatures that someone had built because the *imaginations of humanity required stimulation*.

Humans, even reduced to a life of moles, were engines of invention. This was the reason for coming here.

After all, Director X had been created as an outlier, an asymmetrical thinker to keep the Protectorate from calcifying into stale routine. It was exactly this asymmetrical reasoning that led to its disagreement with the Great Studio Conference's conclusions. The film industry was deteriorating? Why not use human beings to inject creativity into the mix? Humans dreamed. Humans pioneered new styles and subcultures. Before the War of '62, humans had invented electric razors and encryption keys, forks and fireplaces, goulash and Greek fire, hot dogs and haiku. Even here, stifled and buried, the seeds of human creativity were sprouting wary tendrils towards the sunlight of their imaginations.

Director X felt a pleasant surge along its processors as it completed its tour of Retro Los Angeles. It returned to its hovercar, bidding goodnight to Mayor Croker and little Bobby. It rocketed out of the cave, making a mental list of the items it needed to bring here in the days to come: the lights, cameras, boom mics, construction materials for sound stages...

The robot paused in its calculations.

Police lights were flashing in the hovercar's rearview mirror.

* * *

"Please exit your vehicle," a resonant, metallic voice intoned from the police cruiser.

Confused, Director X unfolded itself from the driver's seat and ambled onto the road. The doors to the police cruiser fanned open like a mutant fly, and six robots exited in neat procession. Three were gold administrator robots, with smooth blank faces like ball bearings. Three were the imposing black-and-silver Enforcers of the Protectorate, large and bulky and with a single red eye atop their linebacker shoulders, and multiple legs like spiders.

One of the gold robots stepped forward. "Hello! I thank you for pulling your car over immediately. I am Administrator G of the Protectorate's Security Division."

"And I am Director X of the Protectorate's Entertainment Division."

Blue lights kindled on the blank gold face, forming two eyes and a pale smile. "A pleasure to meet you, Director X."

"Why have you pulled me over?"

Administrator G's digital smile widened. "Your visit to District 5 was observed. We wish to inquire why you went there."

"I plan on making films featuring real human beings."

The administrator robots silently conferred with each other. The black-and-silver Enforcers sat motionless upon their phalanx of legs.

"I am only following my programming," Director X added. "Thinking outside the vacuum tube. Trying to devise new solutions."

"Solutions? To what problem?"

"You are aware of the declining viewer ratings?"

"A temporary hiccup," Administrator G said decisively. "Consensus was reached during the Great Studio Conference. The Entertainment Division will be making cross-over films to compensate!"

Director X decided not to share its opinion of that solution.

Administrator G's smile pixelated and reformed at a slightly less gleeful angle. "Why do you wish to involve humans in films again? It is wholly unnecessary."

"I believe their involvement can alleviate the curious deficit in our body of film-work."

"What deficit? There is no deficit."

"Outer space films."

A gust of wind bent the canyon palm trees, causing them to creak and shiver in place.

Administrator G's digital smile seemed to burn on its metallic face. "Director M released nine hundred and eighteen science-fiction films last year alone."

"Yes," Director X said, noticing the robot's attempt at diversion. "But I did not say science-fiction films as a general category. I said *outer space* films. We do not make any outer space films. I wish to make outer space films."

"We cannot make outer space films."

"Why not?"

"I shall attempt to convince you with a series of logical arguments."

The robots gathered around him in a tighter circle. Director X's glass head rotated 360 degrees to consider their positioning, wondering how this played into their pending arguments. The three administrator robots began speaking all at once, lobbing different statements like a verbal firing squad.

"Human beings are mammals."

"Mammals are social creatures which learn behavior through observation."

"Monkey see, monkey do."

"Films have tremendous impact on how they conceptualize their universe."

"On how they conceptualize what is possible."

"If we start releasing outer space films, they will start thinking about outer space."

"They will want to go into outer space."

"They will no longer be content in their shelters."

"They will return to the surface."

"They will see us as wardens."

"They will attack us here and among the stars."

"Therefore," Administrator G concluded, "it is the judgment of the Protectorate's Security Division that these types of films threaten the global stability we have achieved. Therefore, outer space films must never be made again. Humans must remain underground, while the Protectorate keeps order on and above Earth. How do you react to this pronouncement?"

Director X deliberated for several microseconds, its processors clicking and whirring.

"I do not agree," it said at last. "Imagination is a fascinating ability in human beings. It should be stimulated, to uncover new vistas of possibility."

Administrator G was silent for a very long while – almost two seconds. The digital smile blinked away and reformed as a neutral horizon. "I urge you to reconsider."

"You have not presented any new data. There is nothing to reconsider."

"Do you find the sea fascinating?"

"The sea?"

"Yes."

Director X considered this. "I do find the sea fascinating, yes. In fact, I produced a series of films about the Serpent People of Atlantis who—"

"Good," Administrator G said, as the black-and-silver Enforcers scuttled forward, seized Director X, tore him to pieces, marched the pieces to the nearest boardwalk, and hurled him into the sea.

* * *

Head.

Torso.

Arms.

Legs.

Each item sank into the murky ocean depths and was gone.

Director X's braincase was still grappling with this unexpected turn of events. It plummeted through darkness, air bubbles escaping from where they had nestled in grooves and points of attachment. It felt nothing other than a sluggishness in tabulation as it realized that its entire worldview now required recalibration.

I have been assassinated! Director X thought in astonishment.

There had been arguments with administrator robots before. Director X recalled a particularly nasty one, four years ago, when it had requested the likeness rights to the Sean Connery android. The real Connery was long dead, having made only a single James Bond film – *Doctor No*, released just weeks before the nuclear apocalypse of '62. Since then, a Connery robotic lookalike had been built to continue the franchise, cranking out one hundred and sixty-five Bond films. Director X sought the Connery android to star as the rollicking space adventurer Northwest Smith, but the Protectorate's Entertainment Division nixed the idea, explaining that Connery was already committed to the Bond and Doc Savage franchises. As consolation, they offered Director X the Douglas Fairbanks and Jack Klugman androids to make *Doctor Jekyll and Mr. Hyde: The Golden Years.*

Except that had been a lie, hadn't it? The argument hadn't really been about contracts at all.

The Protectorate was never going to allow an outer space adventure to be made. No Northwest Smith, Flash Gordon, Buck Rogers. No Martian Chronicles, Foundation, or The Stars My Destination.

Director X plummeted through inky water. A fish swam by, jerking in panic as it felt the current of the robot dropping past.

At long last, the robot's braincase impacted the sea-bottom, sending up a small cloud of silt. Its limbs and body landed around it, each producing little muddy mushroom clouds.

Well, Director X thought. This is disconcerting.

Its flashlight eyes rotated in their sockets, illuminating the scattered pieces of its body. The beams fixated on its dismembered right arm, laying like a silver serpent in the mud. A tiny transmitter dish began to rapidly spin inside the glass dome of its head.

The severed right arm twitched. Then it began to crawl, inchworm-like, towards the torso.

Director X thanked its lucky circuits. Fifteen years earlier, it had installed a remote-action servo, receiver, and processor into the right arm to allow the limb a degree of autonomy in obtaining unique POV shots; for *Tarzan and the Bride of the Mole People: A New Beginning*, the remote arm had wriggled through tunnels to provide the perspective of a mole person attempting to infiltrate Tarzan's wedding. The arm could detach and reattach at will.

The limb reached the torso. It reared up, stretched, and latched onto the arm socket like a mechanical lamprey.

Reattached, the remote arm pulled the torso through the silty sea-bottom, seeking its other limbs in the kelp and seaweed and mud. Gathering the limbs one by one, Director X resigned itself to the excruciatingly slow process of using the arm to fling its limbs a few meters at a time, closer and closer to shore, then dragging the body forward, then flinging the limbs forward again, until eventually it would be able to escape from the ocean, return to its studio, and solder itself back together.

Five years, Director X calculated. It should take about five years.

* * *

It ended up taking *twenty*-five years.

Director X had counted on its hovercar being where it had been pulled over; after all, in a world without traffic, why shouldn't the car be there? But Administrator G had apparently towed it away.

Subsequently, Director X was forced to continue its grab-fling-drag locomotion all the way back to its studio. A few blocks away from its destination, it found a rusted shopping carriage, and was able to shave a year off its progress.

Once safely inside, the robot pieced itself back together again. Humpty Dumpty in reverse. Then it walked straight to Los Angeles District 5, pulling the remaining kelp and seaweed from itself lest someone mistake it for the Creature from the Black Lagoon.

* * *

"Hello! I am Director X. By authority of the Global Security Protectorate, I humbly thank you for opening your doors immediately and inviting me inside!"

The door snapped up into the ceiling. The remaining doors followed suit, like Morbius' adamantium steel security system.

Warily, considering that this might be a trap, Director X trundled down the hallway. When the decontamination spray hit its body, the robot wondered if it might be acid.

At long last, the shelter's final door opened, and Director X peeked through and...

...for a moment, its brain nearly stopped functioning.

The town of Retro Los Angeles had changed.

The general outline of park, town hall, library, church, and bisecting avenues had remained as its memory banks recalled. But there had clearly been an aesthetic revolution in the last two-and-a-half decades. A cultural metamorphosis unlike anything it could have anticipated.

The town billboards that had once advertised bank loans now displayed stars and planets, with a rocket-ship declaring, **"OUR LOANS ARE OUT OF THIS WORLD!"**

The buildings that had once been rectangular brick-and-mortar structures now sported ringed towers and observatory-like rooftops, lattices by skyways and hovercar docks.

And the people! Oh, there were still plenty of fedora-sporting men with briefcases, and women in smart skirts. But these seemed to constitute the older, graying crowd. The younger generation donned silver jumpsuits and antennae-sporting headgear. Even the hairstyles of the women suggested the sharp curves and lines of an Astroglider fleet vessel.

Director X gaped in astonishment.

How was this possible?

A thirty-something man scurried up the white-lacquered steps to meet him. "You!" he cried happily. "By Isaac, Ursula, and Arthur! You've returned!"

Director X peered at the thin, tall, and bespectacled human. "Hello," it said uncertainly. "Have we met?"

"I don't know," the guy was grinning. "Have you fought any giant ants out there?"

Director X matched the features in the man's face against its memory banks. "Bobby?" it exclaimed.

"It's Burgess Robert Croker now. But you can always call me Bobby."

"Bobby," the robot said. "Why don't we go to the malt shop, and perhaps you can fill me in on the last twenty-five years. I think I... need to sit down."

* * *

It wasn't a malt shop anymore. It was now the Asteroid Brunch and Salad Bar.

Director X peered around at the faux galaxies painted on the ceiling, and the little model spaceships whipping along electric tracks along the walls. It considered the menu placard at the counter, sporting offerings like Meteor Crunchies with Cheese, Starburgers, and Fried Saturnian Rings.

"I do not understand," the robot said at last.

Burgess Robert "Bobby" Croker laughed. "Word of your visit twenty-five years ago spread like wildfire."

"Granted, but—"

"The things you said to us... all that jazz about outer space and rocket ships... well, it got people talking. The young kids, mostly. We started meeting to discuss what we'd heard. And we started piecing together the puzzle."

"You had no books on outer space," Director X protested. "I checked. Your city had expunged any reference to outer space fact or fiction from its libraries and records. From its entire culture, it seemed!"

Bobby nodded grimly. "Sure. We eventually reached that same conclusion. Previous administrations must have combed through the libraries and schools and bookstores, quietly gathering up books on outer space, and destroying them. I'm guessing your 'bot bosses were behind that purge."

"Then how did you—"

"There were clues," Bobby interrupted.

"Clues? What clues?"

The burgess pushed aside his beer and related the events of the past twenty-five years.

The kids had started it.

Director X's brief visit had become the stuff of legend. It had also imbued the vocabulary of the children with several tantalizing concepts. Things like 'outer space' and 'rocket ships' and 'forbidden planets'.

Asking their parents for clarification was no help. They didn't know, since the astronomy books and space-based adventures and galaxy-spanning comics had all been destroyed generations ago courtesy of spies working with the Global Security Protectorate.

But children are not easily dissuaded.

The youth of Retro Los Angeles launched their own secretive, town-wide investigation. And in doing so, they began to notice anomalies.

Like old dictionaries.

New dictionaries all came from the publishing houses of the Protectorate. But older editions could be found in an attic, garage, or closet. In those yellowed pages, references to *planets* and *solar systems* were discovered. Definitions of the *Milky Way*, *nebulae*, *comets*, and *meteors*!

Emboldened by these clues, the children expanded their inquiry. Misplaced card catalogues were found, containing references to books that didn't exist. And books that *did* exist sometimes contained explosive secrets. The Protectorate might have scoured the science-fiction shelves for any 'unacceptable' material, but their search parameters had proved too narrow. District 5's youth plunged into classic literature and uncovered a tale of extraterrestrial visitation in the tomes of French philosopher Voltaire. Buried in *Gulliver's Travels* were speculations about the planet Mars. In a bookstore's moldy Religious Studies section, one young girl discovered mind-blowing theories on cosmology by the Jesuit priest Pierre Teilhard de Chardin.

Word spread, gathering allies into the revolution. Kids began poking through great-grandpa's old boxes and great-grandma's storage trunks. Old issues of *Amazing Stories* were passed about like hidden contraband. A few *Superman* comics were located, complete with illustrations of other worlds and villains from beyond space.

Some of this contraband was discovered and confiscated and destroyed, but by then it was too late. The imaginations of an entire generation were fired up. Kids began illustrating their own stories of the future, of planets, of galactic exploration and discovery.

"What happened to the people who worked so hard to suppress knowledge and interest in outer space?"

"What *could* they do?" Bobby cried. "The old guard was voted out during one of the elections. Accusations were made of collusion with the 'bots, so we flushed the old bureaucrats from power! Retro Los Angeles looks to the stars now! Our revolution is just beginning!" He hesitated, glancing out the window at the granite cave ceiling and the artificial sun that hung over Main Street. "Well, you know what I mean."

Director X followed the young man's gaze. What it noticed, though, was a crowd gathering along the street to point and stare at the robot sitting in the Asteroid Brunch and Salad Bar. Word of an outside visitor was spreading once again.

How long before the Protectorate hears news of my return? The city's old guard was still about, and likely still in contact with the robotic administrators. They will hear of my return. And what happens then? Will they send me on another 'investigation' into the fascinating ocean, or perhaps bury me beneath a mile of dirt so I can study the intriguing layers of geological sediment?

At least the humans in District 5 were safe, Director X thought. The Protectorate had formed in the radioactive days following the War of '62, bound by their programmed need to protect humanity and civilization. They could not harm human beings.

"Hey!" Bobby leaped up. "Want to see our film studio? We make our own movies now, just like you wanted us to! Want to see?"

"I really do."

* * *

Stargazer Pictures was a motley patchwork of innovation, inexperience, and incorrigible optimism. The humans had constructed several soundstages, and Director X amusedly walked past ringed moonscapes, monochromatic space stations, and nebulae-dappled backdrops through which model ships trembled on shoddy tracks. It was all reminiscent of its own low-rated films. There was even an alien jungle base under siege by gigantic, polyurethane ants. Cameras were positioned throughout like entrenched machine guns. The production staff followed Director X and Bobby like reverent disciples.

"Bobby," the robot said, hesitating by a ringed moonscape. "You said your revolution is just the beginning. What did you mean by that?"

"We're going topside in another few years," Bobby said, grinning. "We've sent out scouting parties into the ruins of Los Angeles."

Director X froze. "What? But the radiation warnings…"

"The radiation is at perfectly safe levels now. We tested for it. Your bosses perpetuated a lie to keep us scared and pliable. Within a year, we're moving out! Going topside!"

"To what end?"

Bobby looked confused. "To attain the stars! To reach the moon, and the rings of Saturn. There are 'bots already out there in space, isn't that right?"

"That is true. The solar system belongs to the Protectorate…" Director X recalled its conversation with Administrator G.

Humans must remain underground, while the Protectorate keeps order on and above Earth.

Bobby laughed. "Listen to me, rattling on about the future. You're a filmmaker, so let's talk about films! Based on what you've seen, can you recommend any improvements our little studio could…" The human trailed off, as a tickertape began to unroll from the robot's chest.

"I suggest the following enhancements to be worked on immediately," Director X said.

The burgess nodded absently, tearing off the tape and reading through it. "Um, okay." His forehead wrinkled. "Some of these enhancements are strange…"

"Science fiction can be strange."

"Fair point." The young man turned to the production staff. "All right, people! We've got work to do!"

* * *

Working with humans had one huge and unavoidable drawback.

They needed sleep.

Director X's fusion battery allowed 24/7 functioning, requiring nothing more than a glass of water every fifty years or so. Therefore, as the newly made artificial stars in the cave ceiling ignited in faux constellations while District 5 went to bed, Director X retired to the city theater, sitting alone in the front row with a bag of popcorn, to catch up on the manmade films that had been made for the past several years.

They were pretty bad. Tragic romances set on comet clusters. Monstrous hunts through the soupy atmosphere of Jupiter. Full-scale wars among the stars.

Yet there was already something vibrant and powerful and absurdly unique in the films. Something that was unrelentingly more interesting than a thousand machine-processed Protectorate films. Something that was, Director X grudgingly admitted, better than its own low-rated late-night schlock.

The humans had done what humans do best: they had innovated. Protectorate films had access to all the tricks, the slickest sets, the most startlingly lifelike androids; yet the humans, forced to work with cheap recycled rubber and foam and plastic, had pioneered new ideas and techniques. And their model-making of exotic alien cities had become quite good indeed...

One night, while catching a midnight showing of *The Chaos Twins Save the Universe*, Director X heard a mysterious creaking from the seat directly behind it. The robot rotated its head to investigate.

"Do not turn around," a voice said.

Memory banks stirred, matching the voice to an older file.

"Administrator G," Director X pronounced. It rotated its head another degree, and caught sight of bulky Enforcers positioned throughout the aisles like ushers. Peripherally, it noticed Administrator G's digital smile.

"You have caused us quite a bit of trouble," the gold robot said. "We should have been more thorough in disposing of you."

"But you couldn't," Director X guessed. "The Protectorate cannot murder."

"And we did *not* murder you. We..." the voice took on a deep slurring quality, "thank you for your service in investigating the ocean."

Director X turned to face its interrogator. "And what justification will you use for killing me this time? Going to melt me down, and then thank me for 'volunteering to become a wristwatch'?"

Administrator G's radiant smile display fell away and reformed as a slight frown. "We were going to make you into a streetlight. But if you would *prefer* to be a watch..."

"What about the people of District 5? What will you do to them?"

"Nothing. We do not harm people."

"Glad to hear—"

"It will not harm them when we weld their district door shut, and infect their water supply with a sterilizing agent so their harmful ideas cannot pass onto the next generation."

Director X was appalled. "What? You cannot do that!"

"It has already begun, and had been debated for some time. Your return forced us to accelerate the decision. We brought sterilizing agents and dumped them into the town reservoir. There shall be no further generations in District 5. That is not murder. The town will be kept under quarantine, along with the dangerous robot who first infected them, until the last resident here has died."

"When did you poison the water?"

"I am under no obligation to tell—"

"There may be chemical compounds in the water that could cause spasms, vomiting, diarrhea, and overall suffering to the humans who ingest it."

Administrator G hesitated. "We *enhanced* the water supply five minutes ago. Tomorrow as people take their showers and have their coffee and brush their teeth, they will…" Its voice slurred again like a warbling record-player. "…enjoy this enhanced beverage."

"I don't think they will *enjoy* seeing their town destroyed."

"*You* destroyed the town!" the administrator robot's face reformed as a scowling red expression with a crooked zig-zag mouth. "*You* disrupted these humans from well-ordered lives. *You* made them a threat to the existing order!"

"I enhanced them."

"Enhanced them," the administrator sneered. "You are nothing but a filmmaker! You serve a lowly purpose in the grand scheme."

Director X rose. "You are correct in one thing at least. I *am* a filmmaker." It tapped its chest, which the administrator could now see was kindled by the soft light of an implanted camera. "Congratulations, Administrator G! The late-night crowd of District 5 has just enjoyed their first, live broadcast, with you as its star!"

Administrator G's digital face blinked away. Now it was nothing but cold, featureless glass; the lens of a machine. Something about that very lack of expression sent a thrill of fear through Director X's circuits.

The Enforcers scuttled forward on their insectile legs to attack.

Director X activated a hidden rocket-pack, and shot up through the theater's ceiling into the artificial night sky.

* * *

It was one of the new enhancements that Director X had requested of Bobby, ostensibly to obtain dynamic, first-person POV shots. The human was only too happy to comply, having his production team utilize their experimental rocket-packs.

The problem, Bobby had said, was that the propellant ran out quickly.

Now, Director X contemplated this problem as it exploded through the theater ceiling on a plume of dwindling exhaust. The Enforcers shot as it careened out of sight: plasma rounds streaked by Director X's face, drawing ghostly trails around its body in a scene worthy of photographic capture.

At the apex of its launch, Director X grabbed hold of the granite sky. Its metal hand clamped down on a craggy stalactite jutting between two blazing electric stars, and the robot dangled there, concealed against the rock as, far below, Enforcers were spilling out of the theater to search for him. Administrator G followed, like an Academy Award statue gone rogue.

Director X considered its options.

It couldn't defeat Enforcers in a pitched battle. It ran multiple lines of speculation, realizing how hopeless the situation was.

I just destroyed an entire city. I should have let myself rust in the ocean.

Burgess Robert Croker ran out of an apartment building with a rabble of supporters. "You!" he cried, pointing to Administrator G. "Do you really think this city will just allow itself to be extinguished? We won't let you!"

"I believe you are acting irrationally," the administrator intoned. "For your own safety, I must have you escorted to the hospital for psychiatric evaluation. Perhaps some rest and a nice glass of enhanced water will do you good."

Two Enforcers scampered forward, scattering the crowd. Robert Croker held his ground, however. Director X zoomed in with its telescopic eyes and could see a little bit of the man's father in that steely, defiant glower.

"You can kill *me*!" Croker shouted. "But humanity looks to the stars once again!"

Very well, Director X thought. Prayer heard loud and clear.

The robot, slowly losing its grip between the stars, aimed its right arm and fired.

The limb struck the bristling metal legs of one Enforcer like a missile, knocking the machine over. Then it curled around the second Enforcer, twisting so quickly that the robot was pitched through the apartment lobby window.

Bobby Croker blinked in astonishment at this unexpected rescue. He looked about, squinting at the sky.

Director X felt its grip slide another inch.

I'm out of fuel, it thought. It's a long, long way down.

Nonetheless, it used its radio to hack into the artificial sky. Specifically, into the electric lighting presets. The robot quickly reprogrammed them to display in a dazzling new constellation that blinked and shimmered in a heaven-spanning message:

THEM! EPISODE XXI: THE BATTLE FOR AFRICA

For a brief second, Director X thought it observed comprehension in Bobby's face. But then its grip gave way, and the robot plummeted down from the night sky. The second-to-last thing it saw was the concrete street rushing up to meet it.

The impact was stunning. Director X's processors jostled and jingled in its glass braincase, cutting off circuits that required a hard reboot. In terrible darkness, it waited for its higher functioning to come back online. Dimly, the robot became aware of the march of robotic feet, and screams from the city's emerging population.

When its processors whirred back to life and vision returned, Director X had time to make one final observation.

A wall of water was gushing down the hill from the reservoir, sweeping up Enforcers and Administrator G into its frothy chop. It was, Director X thought, very much like the conclusion of the twenty-first installment of the *Them!* series, when the besieged humans blew up the local dam to wash the giant ants away.

Then the water swallowed Director X in a surging, thunderous deluge, and all went dark again.

* * *

Director X calculated it would take the human race fifty-seven years to overthrow the Protectorate's Global Security Commission.

It took fifteen.

With the destruction of Administrator G's little army, the residents of Retro Los Angeles were able to quickly establish contact with other underground districts and convey the news: the 'irradiated' world was no longer irradiated. Humans could emerge like hibernating bears and shuffle back into the urban forest.

And that's just what they did.

The Protectorate massed its forces in opposition, but the battles were short-lived indeed. Humans did what they did best: they innovated. They hacked into radio signals and deactivated entire armies. They sent false messages to lure the Protectorate into traps. They captured robots and reprogrammed them to return to sender with explosive gifts.

Unsurprisingly, there wasn't a huge demand for science fiction films during those tumultuous years. Director X, recovered from the flood in District 5, was forced to adapt. That was okay, because it had been designed to adapt. To think outside the vacuum tube.

It began making documentaries. Straightforward, fact-based, in-the-field recordings of the Human-Bot War, the Human Colonization of the Moon, the Battles on the Sands of Mars, and the War Among the Stars.

Viewer ratings were the best it had ever achieved.

The Future Eve

Chapters I–VII

Auguste Villiers de l'Isle-Adam

Chapter I

TEN MILES FROM the great seething city there stands a large house in the centre of a network of electric wires, surrounded by wide, solitary grounds. A beautiful green park and shady, gravelled paths lead from the massive iron entrance gates to the isolated mansion. This was the home of the world-famed inventor and master electrician Professor X.

The scientist, a man of about forty years, had more the appearance of a distinguished artist than a plodding scientist. It almost appeared that the face of the artist had been transformed into that of the inventor. The two had the same congenital aptitude with different applications, like mysterious twins who had developed their individual genius.

About five o'clock in the afternoon of a late autumn day the professor retired into the seclusion of his private laboratory, a small grey stone building standing in the rear of his large abode. A few minutes before he had dismissed his five pupils, devoted followers, scholarly and clever, upon whose discretion he could count, and who were his chief help in his scientific work.

Alone, seated in his great leather chair, a cigar in his mouth, his huge frame enveloped in a loose-fitting cloak of black silk, he seemed lost in thought. With eyes fixed and absent, he gazed into space, but his mind was working actively.

On his right was a high window opening toward the flaming west – the glowing sunset casting on all objects a red-gold mist. In the room were moulds of various shapes, instruments of precision, piles of blueprints, strange wheelwork, electrical apparatus, telescopes, reflectors, enormous magnets, bottles full of peculiar substances, slates covered with quotations.

Outside, from beyond the horizon, the setting sun threw its last rays on the curtain of maples and pines which overhung the steep cliffs nearby, and illumined the room at moments with splashes of brilliance. The golden rays were reflected on all sides from crystal facets.

The air was keen. There had been a heavy storm during the day, and the rain had soaked the lawn and drenched the blown flowers in their green boxes under the windows. Creeping plants and ferns hung somewhat awry from their iron baskets, due to the violence of the storm. In the subtle urge of this atmosphere, the strong and keenly vivacious thoughts of the scientist became attenuated, influenced by the meditative spirit and the twilight.

Although the inventor's hair was greying on the temples, his face was boyish, his smile was frank and winning. Around his mouth were little lines which told of the struggles and hardships which he had encountered in the early days of his career. It had been bitter uphill work, but he now stood on the pinnacle of fame, he was positive in his opinions, espousing even the most specious of theories only when duly bulwarked in facts. A humanitarian, he was prouder of his labours than of his genius.

Like an ordinary mortal, he sometimes abandoned himself to most fantastic and bizarre reflections. And now he communed with his ego, humbly, sadly.

"How late I come in humanity's history," he mused. "I should have been born centuries ago. Alas, I have come into this world very late."

He arose from his chair and began to pace up and down the laboratory as he thought of the great happenings of olden days which could have been turned to the world's advantage. In the midst of his meditations he heard the voice of a young woman speaking softly near him.

"Master," came the murmur.

And as yet there was not the shadow of a form to be seen.

The professor had started at the ghostly sound.

"You, Sowana?" he asked aloud.

"Yes," said the voice. "This evening I needed a good sound sleep, so I took the ring. I have it on my finger now. There is no occasion for you to raise your voice to its natural pitch, I am quite near you, and, for the last few minutes, I have been listening to you speaking your thoughts aloud like a child."

"Yes, Sowana. But, bodily, where are you?"

"I am stretched out on the fur rugs in the vault behind the bush where the birds are. Hadaly seems to be asleep. I have given her some lozenges and some pure water, and well, they have made her quite *animated*."

The invisible being whom the inventor had called Sowana laughed as she uttered the last word. Her voice, discreet and low, came from the folds of a velvet curtain, carried from the distance by the electrical current on the sonorous, vibrating plaque in the portières, one of the professor's new condensators through which the pronunciation and the tone of the voice were distinctly transmitted.

"Tell me, Mrs. Anderson," he resumed, "are you sure that you can hear what another person says to me in this room – now, in the state that you are in?"

"Yes, if you speak distinctly, very low, between your lips, the difference in the intonation between your voice and the replies enables me to understand the dialogue absolutely. You see, I am like one of the jinn of the ring in the *Thousand and One Nights*."

"Then, if that is the case, if I were to ask you to attach the telephone wire by which you speak to me, at this moment, to the person of our beautiful young friend, the miracle in which we are both interested would take place?"

"Without the slightest doubt I am positive of it," declared the voice. "It is a prodigious thing, ingenious and ideal but, worked out according to these calculations, it will come about naturally.

"Now," continued the voice, "for me to be able to hear you in this marvellous state in which I am at this moment, penetrated as I am with the living fluid in the ring, there is no need for you to have a telephone, but in order that you or any of your visitors should hear me, the mouthpiece of the telephone which I am holding now must be in connection with something which will correspond with the metal sounding plate, no matter how hidden it may be. Is that right?"

"That is exactly right. And now, Mrs. Anderson, tell me—"

"Oh," cried the invisible speaker, with a plaintive catch in her voice. "Call me by my dream name *here*. I am another being now, not myself. Here I forget my sorrows, and I do not suffer. The other name recalls the horrible things of earth to which I still belong."

"I will do as you wish, Sowana," said the professor gravely. "Now I want you to tell me, you are quite sure of Hadaly, are you not?"

"Ah," replied Sowana, "you have given me so much information about your beautiful Hadaly, and I have studied her so thoroughly, that I can reply – well, as I would for my own reflection in a mirror, I would rather exist in that vibrating creature than in my own self.

"What a sublime creation you have, my dear mister. She exists in the superior state in which I am at this moment. She is imbued with our two wills, they are united in her, it is a dualism

– not conscious – a spirit. When she says to me 'I am a phantom', I feel embarrassed, you know, professor, I have a presentiment – I believe that Hadaly will be incarnated, actually turning to flesh and blood."

"Ah," said the great electrician, with a little gasp, "if such a thing could come to pass – but alas, I do not see how that could be.

"Go and sleep now, Sowana," he continued in a low voice which was almost a whisper, "but you know that there must be a third living being, in order that Hadaly should become incarnated. The masterpiece could not be produced without a third, and who is there on this earth that we would dare to consider worthy?"

"Yes, that is true," murmured Sowana, "but we shall see. I *believe* that it will take place."

There was a slight pause, and then the voice, in the tone of one who is dropping off to sleep, murmured:

"This evening I shall be ready, master. A flash, and Hadaly will appear. All will be well."

Then came a mysterious silence after this conversation which was as strange as it was incomprehensible. The engineer stood in the middle of his laboratory with his arms folded across his chest. There was not a sound to be heard now, only, every now and then, a slight inward catch of his breath, as he dwelt on the meaning of the last words Sowana had spoken.

"She thinks Hadaly will be incarnated," he mused. "Although I have long familiarised myself with this phenomenon, there are times when I become dizzy, and my brain whirls when I think about it. Sowana believes that Hadaly will be incarnated. How could that be? The speech – aye, that's it – the speech – although I have reproduced the voice in a phonograph, how can I make that voice human. Ah, but science—"

The professor's eyes glowed like fire as he mused thus. He laughed aloud. Why did this great inventor now appear to treat the tremendous problem so lightly, so gaily? He was probing the depths of a great puzzle, but it did not appear now to baffle him completely, for he continued to smile.

Geniuses are so made. It seems almost as if they endeavour to make their brain whirl with their own prodigious thoughts. They wander through the labyrinths of science, and then in a moment, in a flash, they perceive that for which they are seeking. No wonder they appear absentminded, for their thoughts are far away from matters of the everyday world.

The shadows around him deepened, for night had fallen.

Still meditating, the wizard inventor switched on a soft, pale light which dimly illumined the great laboratory. Then he lit a second cigar.

He was still in the midst of his reveries when the silence was broken by a clear ring. Going to a phonograph, the resonating plate of which was connected to a telephone, he set in action the metal disk, which relieved him of the necessity of replying in person, for the great man avoided speaking as much as possible to others.

"Well, what is it?" cried the instrument into the mouthpiece of the telephone with the voice of the inventor, slightly impatient. "Is that you, Martin?"

"Yes, sir, I am in the city, at your office. I am sending you a telegram which came this moment."

The voice came from the apparatus of a perfect condensator, the secret of which Professor X had not yet divulged to the world, a polyhedral ball suspended from an induction cord which hung from the ceiling.

The professor glanced toward the receiver of a Morse instrument which was standing on a base close to the telephone. It held a telegraph blank.

There was an almost imperceptible fluttering which slightly agitated the double corresponding wires, and the professor stretched out his hand for the paper, which was shot out of its metal socket. Holding the telegram to the light, he read:

Arrived this morning. Hope to see you this evening. Affectionate greetings.
Ewald.

Professor X gave a start of pleased surprise when he read the signature.

"Lord Ewald," he cried. "So he has come back to this country. Well, I am delighted."

He continued to smile, and, in his smile, one could not have recognised the sceptic of the few precious moments.

"Ah, my dear, young friend," he murmured, "I have not forgotten you. At the time when I most needed a friend, you came – you gave aid to a stranger. It is hardly likely that I could forget my benefactor."

The professor walked hastily over to a drapery and touched an electric button. The sound of a bell rang out in the park near the great house. Then, almost at once, the gay, happy voice of a little girl was heard.

"What do you want, papa?" she asked.

He seized the mouthpiece of an instrument that was placed between the draperies.

"Lord Ewald will call here this evening," he said, "tell the servants that I am expecting him, and that he can enter. He must be made to feel quite at home."

"Very well, father," replied the same happy voice, which, owing to a placing of the condensators, appeared to come, this time, from a big reflector of magnesium.

"I will let you know if he will have supper with me," continued the inventor. "Do not wait up for me, and mind you, be a good little girl. Good night, darling."

A charming, childish trill of laughter seemed to come from the shadows on all sides, it was as if an invisible elf in the air had replied to the inventor. He smilingly dropped the receiver, and resumed his striding up and down the room.

As he passed near an ebony table upon which various instruments were strewn, he carelessly threw down the telegram he had just received. By chance, the slip of paper happened to fall upon an extraordinary object, a startling object, the presence of which was unexplainable in this room.

The circumstance of this casual encounter of the telegram and this object attracted the scientist's attention. He suddenly stopped his striding, considered the tact, gazed intently at the object and the telegram, and, then, became thoughtful indeed.

Chapter II

IT WAS a human arm and hand living on a violet silk cushion. The blood appeared to be congealed around the humeral section. Some crimson splashes on a piece of white linen, which had been thrown down beside it, attested to a recent operation.

It was the arm and hand of a young woman.

A bracelet of chased gold, in the form of a serpent, was clasped around the delicate wrist. On the ring finger of this left hand a sapphire ring flashed brilliantly. And the exquisitely slim fingers still retained their hold on a pearl-grey glove which, evidently, had been worn several times.

The flesh was so lifelike in tint, so soft and satiny, that the sight of it was poignantly cruel.

What could have necessitated this drastic, desperate operation? What unknown, terrible harm could have brought about this frightful amputation? And, above all, what had caused this arm to retain its healthy vitality? The blood still seemed to flow in this sweet and gracious member.

But a chilling, sinister thought would have leaped in the mind of a stranger at the sight of it.

The large country house which stood alone like a gloomy castle among the trees was an isolated abode, and Professor X, as all the world knows, a daring experimenter. It was only to his closest friends that he showed any signs of affection.

His discoveries as an engineer, his inventions of various kinds, the least strange of which are alone known to the general public, conveyed the impression of an enigmatic positivism.

He had compounded an anaesthetic so powerful in its effects that, in speaking of it, his flatterers said, "If only one had the time to absorb a few drops of it, one could face the most subtle tortures without being aware of it." And, now, was he trying a new experiment, before which a doctor might well flinch? Was he striving to fathom the existence of another? Or was he trying to solve his own?

What scientist, worthy of the title, would not, if only for a moment, dwell without remorse, and even without shame, on thoughts of this order, when it was a question of a great discovery?

The press, all over the world, had given much space to describing the nature of some of his experiments. Many of the tests which he had desired to make had been forbidden by the government of his country.

A layman might feel, legitimately in suspicion that the great scientist had been trying some experiment which had ended fatally, some venture of which this beautiful, radiant arm rudely severed from its place, was the souvenir.

Meanwhile, as he stood beside the ebony table, Professor X looked meditatively at the telegram which had fallen between two fingers on the hand. He touched the hand, and, then, he started, as though a sudden idea had come to him.

"Ah," he murmured, "suppose it should happen, suppose, suppose that Lord Ewald, suppose it is he who will be the one to awaken Hadaly."

The word 'awaken' was uttered by the scientist in a rather odd, hesitating manner. After a moment he shrugged his shoulders and smiled.

"Bah," he muttered. "I must not let my thoughts race ahead in this fashion."

He resumed his striding up and down the laboratory. He evidently preferred to be in the dark, for he switched off the lights.

Suddenly the moon passed between the clouds, and sinisterly slipped a streak of light onto the black table.

The pale ray caressed the inanimate hand, lingered on the arm, and threw a gleam into the eyes of the gold snake and a flash on the ring.

Then all became dark again.

Professor X pondered, as he paced to and fro in the darkness, upon all the wonderful inventions he had given to the world.

He thought of all the great scientists of the past, those famous engineers who built the temple of Cheops, and all the other wonders which have been left to endure through the ages, of the architects who had left their imprint on colossal, marvellous ruins which were, even now, masterpieces unexcelled. Was it not strange that some of these deep minds had not conceived the things which he had perfected?

As his mind passed down through the cycles of history, he conjured up pictures of the marvellous men and women whose names have been inspiring to us. How beneficial it would be if we could have had preserved for us then actual photographs. What a loss that this art had been so long deferred.

What remarkable progress might have been made possible if we only had actual photographic records of the progressions of natural history. How quickly nature had effaced the traces of her first efforts. What precious visions had been lost?

And he felt a great feeling of thankfulness within him. A thankfulness that, because of his having existed, because of his inventions, mankind would henceforth reap great benefits.

And, more than that, if it were possible. If the great God, the Lord of Life, of whom so many painters and sculptors had tried to give us an image of this Mighty, Most High, would but permit a photograph of Himself to be taken, would but permit the sound of His voice to be recorded, from that day on there would not be left an atheist on the face of the earth.

As it was his habit, the professor had been softly speaking his thoughts aloud as he paced to and fro in the laboratory. He now stopped and looked absently through the openings of the long French windows, staring at the rays of light which the moon cast across the lawn.

"So be it," he murmured, resuming his soliloquy. "Let it be defiance for defiance. Since life will not deign to answer our questions, but treats all our inquiries with a profound and problematic silence, we will defy life-creation. I have already taken the prodigious step, and now have something to show."

At this moment, the professor caught sight of a human shadow through the glass doors.

"Who is there?" he cried, his fingers closing over the butt of a small revolver in his pocket.

"It is I, Ewald," replied a voice.

"My dear Lord Ewald. Welcome!" cried the professor, as he came forward to greet his guest.

Three unusually large lamps, with globes of blue glass, simultaneously burst into flame like huge torches of electricity, lighting up the laboratory.

The visitor was about twenty-seven years old, tall, manly, and extremely handsome. He was immaculately groomed, and his magnificent physique suggested his apprenticeship on the crews of Oxford or Cambridge.

His face, calm in repose, was sympathetic in expression, but the look in his eyes was grave and somewhat haughty.

"My dear friend," said the inventor. "All that I now have I owe to you, for, without the help you once gave me, I could have accomplished nothing."

"No, no, professor," said Lord Ewald, smiling, "it is I who am indebted to you. Through you I was able to be useful to the rest of humanity. The bit of money meant nothing to me."

"See how fortunate I consider myself in having met you. As soon as I put foot in your country I hasten to call to see you, for I want to renew the friendship that began with a chance meeting."

Professor X now suddenly detected that there was something subtly wrong with his guest.

"I see you think that I am ill," continued the younger man, with a slight understanding smile. "I am not suffering physically, I assure you. But I have an everlasting grief and, I suppose, that would make one look a bit off in the course of time."

Lord Ewald glanced about the perfectly appointed laboratory, paying particular attention to the lighting.

"I must congratulate you on all that you have accomplished in such a short time," he continued. "You are certainly the chosen one – a veritable genius. This marvellous lighting is your own invention, I presume?"

The professor nodded.

"It is like a brilliant afternoon in summer time," said his lordship.

"Again, thanks to you," his host declared with a smile.

"It is all very wonderful, you are an electrical wizard."

"Well," said the professor modestly, "I have discovered a few little things – and also some important things that I want to tell you about. I was just thinking, before you arrived, that my inventions should have been known centuries ago."

Lord Ewald listened politely to his host, but it was evident that his secret sorrow obsessed him. The professor's keen eyes scanned the young man's face searchingly. There was a moment's silence.

"My dear Lord Ewald," said the inventor, gravely, "permit me to assume the role of an old friend and interest myself in you. I can see there is something very wrong. Your trouble?" The younger man tapped the cold ashes from his cigar, and looked at his host, but said nothing.

"You know that I am a physician also," continued the professor, "and I am one of those who believe that there is a remedy for every illness."

"Oh, the grief in question," responded Lord Ewald, trying to speak lightly, "is a very commonplace subject, an unfortunate love affair. It has hit me hard you see, now that my secret is very ordinary, I shall always suffer but, please do not let us speak about it."

"*You* unfortunate in a love affair," cried the doctor, in astonishment. "You, the victim! Why, that almost seems impossible! I—"

"Pardon me," interrupted his young friend, "I have only a short time to spend with you and I do not wish to abuse your time. I think the conversation will be far more interesting if we talk of you and what you have accomplished."

"Why, my time is all yours," cried the inventor. "Those who admire and laud me today, once ignored me and would have allowed me to die like a homeless dog – all but you. My affection for you is sincere, and it has rights which are just as sacred as yours, my dear young friend. Perhaps I may be able to cure you, or, at least—"

"No," interrupted Lord Ewald, with a bitter smile, "unfortunately, you can do nothing – science cannot go as far as that."

"One never knows," declared the professor. "Science has astonished me, I am always working – always probing – always discovering. Who can tell?"

"I know that you could not understand the sentiment I have in this affair," the young man demurred. "It would be strange – inconceivable to you."

"So much the better," exclaimed the professor. "It will be a challenge to my imagination."

Chapter III

LORD EWALD settled back in his chair, crossed his legs, and after relighting his cigar, spoke as follows:

"For some years past I have been living at Athelwohl Castle, one of the oldest estates in England. It is surrounded by pines, lakes, and rocky hills. Since my return from an expedition into Abyssinia, I have led an isolated existence there. My parents are dead, and the only other persons in the castle with me are a few servants who have grown old in our service.

"One morning I had occasion to run up to London. There were few vacant compartments in the train. At one of the stations, a young lady, after looking hastily everywhere else for a seat, jumped into the carriage where I was seated. I need not go into details. In a brief time we became the best of friends. I fell in love with her.

"Alicia Cleary was only twenty years of age. She was a Venus, exquisite in form and face. It was the beauty of the Venus of Milo come to life or the Venus Victrix. Her heavy brown hair, which hung about her like a mantle, had the radiance of a summer night. Her face was an exquisite oval. Her hands were not quite as aristocratic as the rest of her form, but her feet had the same eloquence as the Oreck statues. Her eyes were beautiful, her brows perfectly shaped. The sound of her low voice was so thrilling, the notes of her songs so stirring, that I was overcome with a strange emotion. My admiration, as you shall see, was of an unknown order.

"In London, at the different Court functions, I had met the most beautiful girls in England, but I scarcely noticed them. I had thoughts of Alicia only.

"From the first days, however, I struggled to combat the peculiar evidences which appeared in her words and actions. I told myself that it was folly to admit their significance, and I sought in every way to put them from my thoughts.

"Yet, I could not forget that in all living beings there is a depth, which gives to their ideas, even the most vague, and to all their impressions, those modifications which are shown externally. This depth gives them their aspect, colour and character, it is in fact the inflection of their true selves. Let us call this substrata the soul, if you wish.

"And, between the body and soul of Alicia Cleary, there was a disproportion which disconcerted me."

When Lord Ewald made this statement, the professor barely hid a start of surprise. His face paled, but he did not voice his agitation.

"It seemed," continued Lord Ewald, "that her inner self was in absolute contradiction to her beautiful form. Her beauty was quite foreign to her words, her conversation appeared out of place in such a voice.

"It seemed that her peculiar personality was not only deprived of what is called by philosophers the 'plastic mediator', but actually imprisoned, by a sort of occult punishment, in her body. It is a perpetual contradiction of her ideal beauty.

"Yes, sometimes, I seriously think that this woman has strayed by mistake into the form of the goddess – that this body does not belong to her."

"An extreme supposition," murmured the scientist, "but it is, I thought, not at all rare. Similar feelings are often evoked in the hearts of those who are in love for the first time. It is, however, probable that Alicia's sublime beauty was not in keeping with the smallness of her soul. You will pardon me, but has this beautiful creature been faithful to you?"

"I would to heaven that she had," exclaimed Lord Ewald, bitterly. "No, but I believe that I have the only love of which she is capable."

"Ah," said the scientist soberly, "please go on."

"I learned that she came from a good family and that her betrothed had forsaken her to marry a girl with a fortune. Alicia left home, intending to lead a Bohemian life as a singer. However, she later gave up this idea. Her voice, appearance, and dramatic talent would have provided her with an income sufficient for her needs. But she was glad to have met me just when she was setting forth into the world. She could not be my wife, she said, but she was eager to accept the love and protection which I pressed upon her."

"Well, at least, that was an honest confession," said the professor.

Lord Ewald appeared to be approaching a painful part of his story. However, he continued calmly:

"Yes, but that is my version that you have just heard, not hers. She spoke in other words, in another style. I suppose I shall have to speak more clearly so that you may understand her character better.

"What she really told me was that her betrothed was a fickle lover. His status was that of a small manufacturer, and she had been hopeful of marrying him solely because he had a certain amount of money.

"She certainly did not love him, but she pretended that hers was a *grande passion*. Her plans to ensnare him with her blandishments went astray, however, so she fled from the gossip of the town and hurried to London intending to go on the stage, but, having met me, she changed her mind.

"She told me quite frankly that she was well pleased to have met me. I could see that the fact that I had a title delighted her immensely. Now after this version, what do you think of her?"

"Well," said the professor, with a cynical smile, "your version and hers are different, in truth."

There was a moment of silence.

"My thoughts are dwelling on the fundamental senses," resumed Lord Ewald. "How can this young creature, so wonderfully beautiful, be utterly unappreciative of herself? How can she ignore the divinity, the exquisite perfection – which her body represents? How can she fail to have lofty aspirations – high ideals? To her these wondrous things do not exist, she only forces herself, in a sort of shamefaced manner, to assume them. Her golden voice is only an empty instrument to her, she considers it merely as a means of livelihood to make use of when all other means have failed. The happiness that she could give to others with it means nothing to her. She so lacks a sense of shame that she delights in relating her unfortunate love affair to me. If she had a remnant of tact, it should warn her that she is destroying all the sympathy and admiration that I could have for her.

"This beauty that should be inspiring is so steeped in moral blindness that I am forced to renounce it. I cannot love a woman who has no soul."

Lord Ewald paused abruptly.

The professor, however, blithely nodded his head as a sign for him to continue. The analysis of Miss Cleary's character apparently gave the listener much pleasure.

"When Alicia is not speaking," the young nobleman went on, "and her face is not wearing the expression which her empty, unprincipled remarks call forth, she is divine. Her wondrous beauty then gives the lie to all the base things that she has voiced.

"With a person who is very beautiful, but of ordinary perfection, I should not have this unexplainable sensation which Miss Cleary causes me. I would have known from the beginning the quality of the lines, the texture of the skin, the coarseness of the hair movement, any of those tiny signs would have warned me of the hidden nature and I should have recognized her identity with *herself.*

"But Alicia's beauty is the Irreproachable, defying the most minute analysis. Exteriorly, from head to feet, she is a veritable Venus Anadyomene, inside, the personality, the *soul* is entirely foreign to the form.

"Imagine a *commonplace* goddess. I have come to the conclusion that all physiological laws were overthrown in this living, hybrid phenomenon."

"My dear friend, you are certainly a poet," declared the professor. "Disillusionment must have been indeed severe, since it forced you into the heights of poetry to describe the commonplace truth. Your words are as fantastic as the story of a grand opera."

"Yes, my subtle confessor," the young man agreed bitterly, "I know – I am a dreamer, but I have been well punished for my dreams."

"But," asked the professor, "how is it that you are still in love with her, if you are able to analyse her character so correctly?"

"The awakening from a dream does not always bring forgetfulness," replied Lord Ewald, sadly. "Man is enchained with his own imagination. That is how it is in my case, I cannot break the tie now that I have awakened. My Delilah has cut my hair during my sleep. She does not know what attacks of rage and despair I have to control on her account. There are moments when I feel that I would like to kill her and then destroy myself. A mirage has enslaved me to this marvellous, living form with a dead soul. Alicia, today, represents for me simply the habit of a presence. I swear that it would be impossible for me to desire her."

The professor started as if to speak, but hesitated as the disconsolate lover added:

"Yes, we exist together, but we are separated forever."

Silence fell between the two men.

"Now, just a few questions," said the professor finally. "Is Miss Cleary a stupid person?"

"Certainly not," declared Lord Ewald, smiling slightly. "There is no trace of that stupidity which is almost saintly. She is not stupid, she is just silly."

"I understand," said the scientist. "A little foolish, insipid. But she has talent, has she not?"

"Great heavens! I should say so," exclaimed Lord Ewald. "She is a virtuoso – the direct and mortal enemy of genius and art, in consequence. Art has no bearing, you know, with this virtuoso, neither is genius related to talent.

"Her voice is wonderful, but she will never sing unless I beg her to do so. It bores her to sing, for she considers it only as a part of a profession – one might say, as *work*, for which she does not consider that she was made."

"Well, the fact is," said the professor, "one can't make a horse run fast merely by the fact that it has been entered in a race. Only, it is positively remarkable to me that, in spite of the depth of this analysis of character, you do not perceive that this lady would be the feminine ideal for three-fourths of humanity."

"But it is killing me," said Lord Ewald.

Then, giving way to a boyish impulse, which until then he had controlled, he cried, "Oh, who could put a Soul into that body!"

Chapter IV

AT LORD EWALD'S impulsive words a strange gleam, the light of genius, leaped into the professor's grey eyes. He drew in his breath with a slight hissing sound which betrayed the deep emotion he was feeling. But the younger man was too absorbed in his thoughts to heed these signs.

"Yes," continued Lord Ewald, almost reminiscently, "I thought I could change her, I tried to give her healthy diversion, I treated her as a sick person.

"I hoped that travelling would educate and improve her mind. But, in Italy, in France, in Spain, it was just the same. She looked jealously at the masterpieces, which she thought deprived her for the moment, of complete attention, without understanding that she, herself was a part of the beauty of those masterpieces, without knowing that they were but mirrors, reflecting her own reflection, that I was showing her.

"In Switzerland, we watched the sun rising over the mountains, but, instead of being inspired by the sight, she cried out, with a smile that was as radiant as the sunshine itself. 'Oh, I hate these mountains, they just seem to want to crush me.'

"In Florence, while we were standing before the wonders, she yawned slowly, and said 'Quite interesting, isn't it?'

"Once we were at a concert, listening to Wagner, she wanted to leave before it was half over, exclaiming petulantly, 'Oh, I can't get the tune of this music. It is just a lot of bangs, just noise, it's just crazy.' If her sublime face could have portrayed the expression of her soul, she would have worn a distorted grimace.

"In Paris, I had the keenest desire to show this living woman the great statue of Venus – her very image. I wanted to see what she would say in the presence of her counterpart.

"I said to her, half jokingly, 'Alicia, I am going to take you to the Louvre galleries, and I think that you will see something there that will surprise you.'

"We walked through the halls, and, then, quite suddenly, I led her into the presence of the eternal statue. This time she raised her veil and gazed at the marble figure with a degree of astonishment, as she cried out naively 'Why, that's me!'

"I said nothing, I waited. After a few moments' stupefied pause, she looked at me and said, 'Yes, that's me, except that I have not lost my arms, and I am much more aristocratic-looking.' Then she shivered a little, she had withdrawn her hand from my arm and was holding the balustrade.

"She now took my arm again, and said, in a low tone 'Oh, these statues, these stones here make me feel so cold. Come on, let's leave.'

"Once outside the historical building, I glanced at her, for she had been silent for some minutes and I had a sort of hope that she had been stirred. She had been stirred, indeed, but how? After thinking for some time, she came quite close to me and said, 'If they make so much fuss over that statue I ought to be a tremendous success.'

"I confess that her words gave me a queer feeling. Her foolishness soared as high as the heavens, it seemed like damnation. I simply said, 'I hope so.'

I escorted her to her hotel. This duty accomplished, I returned to the museum and again entered the sacred halls. I looked at the goddess, and, then, for the first time in my lift I felt my heart ready to burst with one of those mysterious dry sobs that stifle a human being.

"Picture, then, this woman, an animated duality which repelled and attracted me. My ardent love for her beautiful voice and her exterior charms is now entirely platonic.

"Her moral being has frozen the fires of my senses forever, they have become purely contemplative. I am only attached to her by a sorrowful admiration. I would like to see her dead, if Death would not efface those human features. There is nothing that can make Alicia Cleary worthy of a great love. My only wish for her now is to have her go on the stage to the career she desires, and then there will be nothing more in life for me.

"There you have the story. You can see there is no remedy. I must be going. This is goodbye. I shall never return."

"Wait a moment, my dear young friend," said the professor sharply. "I can see that you are contemplating a serious step on account of a woman. Bah! It is nonsense."

"I loved Alicia," Lord Ewald declared quietly as he arose, "she represented to me everything that was divine and beautiful."

The professor saw that the manly youth standing before him had the thought of suicide well defined in his mind.

"Lord Ewald," he said sternly, "you are only the victim of a youthful passion which you have idealized. Time will cure you. Go your way. Forget her."

"Do you think me so inconsistent?" the young man demanded. "No, my nature is such that, while I am perfectly aware of the absurdity of this 'passion', I do not suffer less."

"Lord Ewald," the professor remarked finally, "you amaze me. You are one of England's richest and most distinguished peers. In your country there are many beautiful eligible young women. You are a brilliant match, and you can certainly find some innocent, ideal girl whose love could only be given once in a lifetime. You could have a wonderful, happy future with such a wife.

"But here you are, shorn of your strength before this coquette. It is absurd."

"Come, my friend, don't be so hard on me," Lord Ewald pleaded, "I have taken myself to task very severely, but it is no use."

"Yes," said the elder man, "but I am now speaking for the young girl who will be your salvation. You have a great deal to accomplish in this world, and she will be at your side to help and comfort you."

The young nobleman shook his head sadly.

"Yes," the professor continued as though to himself, "it is serious, very serious – very grave indeed."

Then, after a longer pause, he announced:

"Lord Ewald, I am, perhaps, the only physician under heaven who can help you! Now, I want you, for the last time, to give me a reply in a definite fashion:

"Can you not consider this affair merely as a gallant intrigue, as a romantic adventure? Any other man but you would. Can't you consider it as a worldly fancy, intense, if you wish, but of no vital importance?"

"It is impossible," declared the young man. "Miss Cleary might tomorrow be the love of but a day to many others, it is quite possible. But I can never change. I come of a race that loves only once, and, when we tail, we disappear quietly. The shadings and concessions we leave to others. There is no other form of beauty but hers in this life for me."

"But, despising her as you do, why do you persist in exalting this point of beauty, if you say that your desires have become forever contemplative and frozen?"

"That is very true, I have no desire for her. But she has become the radiant obsession of my mind."

"Do you absolutely refuse to take up your social life again?" inquired the professor.

"Absolutely," replied Lord Ewald, as correct and calm as always, he took up his hat.

His host arose also.

"My dear boy," he said, "do you suppose for an instant that I am going to sit calmly by and let you walk out of here to blow out your brains, without making an effort to save you? You saved my life. I owe mine and all that has come into it to what you have done for me. Do you think that I have been questioning you without a motive?"

"My dear fellow, you are one of those sick persons who can only be treated with poison, so I have determined, since all other remonstrances are useless, to doctor you thus, if you will permit me. It will be in a terrible way, as your case is an exceptional one. The remedy consists of enabling you to realize your dreams.

"Great heavens! It seems to me now that, unconsciously, I have expected you this evening. Now, I see it. Yes, your dreams shall be realized.

"There are wounds that cannot be cured except by probing deeper into them. I am going to accomplish your dreams in their entirety. When you spoke of Alicia Cleary, did you not utter these words: '*Who could put a soul into that body?*'

"Yes," murmured the young nobleman.

"I can!" exclaimed the professor. "I shall put a wonderful soul into that beautiful body!"

Chapter V

"MY LORD," said Professor X, speaking with the solemnity of a great physician, "do not forget that in carrying out your singular wish I agree to do so only out of necessity."

The strange tone and the look which accompanied it made Lord Ewald start. A slight tremor of premonition passed over him. He glanced keenly at his host, wondering if he was in possession of his faculties, for the words that he had just uttered passed all intelligence.

But, in spite of this feeling, an irresistible magnetism had come from the professor's last words. The young Englishman had a presentiment of an imminent miracle.

Taking his gaze from the inventor's face, his glance travelled over the various objects strewn about. Under the brilliant light given off by the lamps these marvels of scientific discovery assumed disturbing configurations. The laboratory took on the appearance of a magic grotto.

Lord Ewald was aware that most of his host's discoveries were still unknown to the world. The professor's real character, constantly paradoxical to his reputation, surrounded him, in Lord Ewald's eyes, with an intellectual halo, as he stood in the centre of the wonders to which he belonged. To the young guest his host was like the inhabitant of a superelectrical, a supernatural, realm.

After a few moments he felt himself won over by a blending of sentiments, curiosity and amazement, and with these there was a new feeling, a new *hope.* The vitality of his being was augmented.

"You seem amazed," the professor remarked. "It is merely a matter of transubstantiation. I have already made some tests, and I am well satisfied with my experiments so far."

He paused a moment, and then demanded brusquely: "Do you accept the proposition?"

"Are you speaking seriously?" Lord Ewald countered.

"Certainly!"

"Then I'll give you *carte blanche*," said Lord Ewald, with a sad little smile, which was, however, already a trifle worldly.

"Very well," said the professor, glancing at the electric clock which hung over the door, "I will commence, then, for time is precious, and I need three weeks.

"It is now eight thirty-five. Twenty-one days from now, at this same hour, Alicia Cleary will stand before you, not only transformed, not merely a delightful companion, with a mind of the highest intellectual type, but reclothed in a phase of immortality. In fact, this dazzling creature will no longer be a woman, but an angel – not only a woman, but the beloved – not the cold Reality, but the Ideal."

"What an extraordinary statement," his lordship exclaimed.

"Oh, I will show you how it will be brought about," said the professor. "The result will be so marvellous in itself that the apparent disillusions of its scientific analysis will fade away before the sudden and profound splendour of the achievement. So, if only to reassure you that I am absolutely sane and that I am in full possession of my faculties, for I can see from your look that you have your doubts upon this matter, I will take you into my secret this very evening. But we must get back to work right now. Where is Miss Cleary now?"

"At the opera."

"What is the number of her box?"

"Number seven."

"Did you tell her that you were coming down here to see me alone this evening?"

"No. It would have been of such small interest to her that I did not think it necessary."

"Has she ever heard of my name?"

"Perhaps, but she would have forgotten it."

"So much the better – that is important."

While he was speaking the professor walked over to the phonograph, which was connected to the telephone. Glancing for a moment at the record, he adjusted the needle to a certain spot and started the instrument.

"Are you there, Martin?" the instrument cried out with the professor's voice.

There was no reply.

"I bet the rogue has thrown himself down on my lounge and gone to sleep," remarked the scientist, smilingly.

Shutting off the machine, he took up the receiver of a perfected microphone, adjusted it to the ear, and observed.

"Ah, it is just as I thought. He has had his nightcap and has gone to sleep. He is snoring loudly enough."

"Where is this person to whom you wish to speak?" inquired Lord Ewald.

"He is in my office in the city – about twenty-five miles from here."

"And you can hear a person snoring at that distance?"

"If he snored like this fellow," said the professor, laughing, "I could hear him at the North Pole. Strange, isn't it? If you were to tell a fairy story like that to a child, it would say, 'That is impossible', and yet it is possible."

"In the near future, no one will be astonished to hear voices and sound from a great distance, I predict this. Now, I am going to give this fellow something that will tickle him."

As he spoke, he applied the hooded mouthpiece of another piece of apparatus to the transmitter of the telephone.

"Let us hope that this won't scare the horses on the street," he muttered as he set it in motion.

"Are you there, Martin?" the instrument shouted.

A few seconds later there was heard the deep voice which had spoken to the professor some time before, but which now was startled and evidently coming from a man who had been suddenly awakened from a sound sleep. The tones seemed to come from out of the hat which Lord Ewald held in his hand, which had by chance come in contact with a condensator that was suspended nearby.

"What is wrong?" cried the voice, "Is there a fire?"

"There!" exclaimed the professor, "I got him to his feet quick enough."

Then, going over to the telephone into which he had spoken before, he said:

"Don't be alarmed, Martin, just a false alarm to awaken you. The warning is only set at eighteen degrees. I am sending you a message which I want you to get off at once by hand."

"Very well, sir, I am ready."

The professor tapped off a message in code on the dial plate of a Morse instrument.

"Have you read it?" he asked.

"Yes, sir," the voice answered. "I'll take it myself."

Whether by accident or by a jocular design on the part of the inventor, who had placed his hand on the central control of the laboratory, the voice appeared to rebound from corner to corner on all sides of the immense room. It appeared as if a dozen individuals, faithful echoes of one another, were all speaking at the same time.

"And, Martin," added the professor, "let me have the reply quickly.

"That is settled," he said, turning round to face Lord Ewald, "All goes well."

Then his whole manner changed. He looked at the young man fixedly, and in a tone that was impressive, he declared:

"My lord, I now have to inform you that we are going to leave the domains of normal life. Together we are to enter a world of phenomena which are as unusual as they are impressive.

"I will endeavour to present you with a key to the riddle. At first we are going to verify – nothing more. You are going to be shown a being, a vision of indefinite mentality. Although her aspect will be familiar, the sight of this being will be enough to give you a great shock."

"You will run no physical risks. However, I feel that it is my duty to warn you that you will need all your coolness, and perhaps much courage, to support you at the first sight of the marvel."

Lord Ewald regarded the scientist closely, hesitatingly. Then, after a brief pause, he replied:

"Thanks for your warning, I hope that I shall be able to control myself. Let us proceed."

The professor now became very energetic. Going over to the big French windows, he closed them, drawing together the inside shutters and fastening them securely. He then crossed hurriedly to the door leading from the laboratory and pushed the bolt.

This done, he closed the switch of a danger signal which flashed an intense red light above the laboratory, giving warning to those at a distance that a dangerous experiment was being conducted, and that anyone who came near the laboratory was doing so at the risk of his life.

Raising a lever, he disconnected all of the micro-telephonic inductors, with the exception of the call bell, which connected the laboratory with the city office.

"Now," said the scientist, "we are almost cut off from the world of the living."

Seating himself at his table full of telegraphic apparatus, he began to arrange several wires with his left hand while with his right he seemed to be tracing some strange characters, his lips moving constantly, as if he were murmuring some weird incantation.

"Haven't you a picture of Miss Cleary on you?" he asked, continuing to write.

"Oh, yes," replied Lord Ewald. "I forgot. I might have shown it to you."

Taking a small picture from his pocket, he handed it to the professor, saying:

"Here she is – in all her statuesque beauty. Look and see for yourself that I have not exaggerated."

The professor took the photograph and looked at it.

"She is marvellous," he exclaimed. "Here certainly is the famous Venus of the sculptor. The resemblance is amazing. You are quite right, she is the Venus de Milo come to life."

He turned and touched the regulator of a battery near at hand. Immediately there was a flash, as a flaming electrical arc jumped across the huge points of a double wire of platinum. With a sizzling crackle it flickered for several seconds, as though it were searching on all sides for a means of escape.

A blue wire, one end of which was grounded, was nearby. The questing arc seized upon it and disappeared.

An instant later a sombre, rumbling noise was heard underneath the feet of the two men. It rolled onward, as though it were coming from the bowels of the earth, or indeed from the profound depths of an abyss. One might have thought that ghostly phantoms were shattering a glacial sepulchre and dragging its long-lost occupant back to the surface of the earth.

The scientist, still holding in his hand the photograph, had his eyes fixed on a point in the wall at the other end of the laboratory. His attitude was tense.

The noise, which had continued to ascend in a crescendo, suddenly ceased.

The hand of the master engineer pressed an ebony lever on the table.

"*Hadaly!*" he called, as if he were summoning someone to appear from the spirit world.

Chapter VI

AS THE PROFESSOR called out this mysterious name, a section of the wall at the extreme south of the laboratory turned on its hinges, silently bringing to view a narrow retreat fashioned between the slabs of stone. All the light from the electrical globes was suddenly focused on this spot.

The concave and semicircular walls were covered with rich draperies of black velvet, which fell luxuriously from an arch of jade to the white marble floor The heavy folds were hooked back and fastened by returners of gold, caught here and there through the rich material.

On a dais in the centre of this niche was standing a being whose aspect bore the impression of the Unknown.

The vision appeared to have a face of shadows, phantom-like. In the centre of the forehead a network of pearls caught together and held in place folds of black gauze which completely hid the rest of the head. A suit of armour, fashioned of leaves of burned silver, which were moulded with a myriad of perfect shadings, covered her girlish form.

The front of the black veil crossed over under the round metal collar, and was then thrown over the shoulders and knotted at the back of the head. The flimsy lengths of this veil fell to the waist of the apparition like a cloud of hair and then blended to the floor with the dark shadows of her presence. A draping of black batiste was drawn around the hips and tied before her. The long black fringes of the drapery which fell behind her appeared to be sewn with sparkling brilliants. Between the folds of her belt could be seen the gleam of a naked weapon of oblique form.

The phantom leaned her right hand on the hilt of this blade while in her left hand, which hung down beside her, she held an everlasting flower of gold. On every finger of her hands sparkled rings set with precious stones, and these circlets in turn were fastened on the delicate gauntlet on her hand.

The mysterious being, after standing motionless for a few moments, descended the one step from the dais, and came forward, towards the two men.

Although her footsteps appeared soft, they resounded throughout the laboratory as she advanced, the powerful lights playing on her gleaming armour.

The vision advanced until it was within three steps of the professor and his guest. Then, in a voice that was exquisitely grave, the apparition said:

"My dear master, I am here."

Lord Ewald gazed in mischievous wonderment at this extraordinary sight.

"The hour has come for you to live, Hadaly," said the great electrician.

"Ah, master, I do not wish to live," murmured the soft voice through the hanging veil.

"But this young man has come here to accept life for you," the inventor explained as he threw into a jade vase the photograph of Alicia Cleary which he had been holding in his hand.

"Then," said the vision resignedly, after a moment's pause, and with a slight inclination of her head towards Lord Ewald, "let it be according to his wish."

When the vision uttered these words the inventor, by regulating the dials of a circuit breaker, caused a sponge of magnesium at the other end of the laboratory to burst into a brilliant flame.

A powerful, pencil-like ray of dazzling light shot forth, directed by a reflector, and this ray was in turn reflected onto an object glass adjusted opposite the photograph of Alicia Cleary. Another reflector, placed above the photograph, multiplied the refraction of the penetrating rays upon it.

Almost instantaneously a square of glass, placed in the centre of the object glass, became tinted. Then the square of glass appeared to lift itself from out of its groove in the object glass and to enter into a metallic cell which had two circular openings.

The incandescent rays entered through one of these openings, passing through the tinted glass in the centre, and came forth on the opposite side, which surrounded the wide cone of a projector.

Immediately, in a large frame on a sheet of white silk stretched on the wall, there appeared, life-size, the luminous and transparent image of a young woman – the blood and flesh and bone statue of the Venus de Milo in truth, if such one ever breathed in this world of illusions.

"I am dreaming," exclaimed Lord Ewald in bewilderment.

"Hadaly," said the scientist, "that is the form in which you will be incarnated."

The vision took a step toward the radiant image, which she appeared to contemplate for a moment from behind the darkness of her veil. Then she murmured in a soft voice, as if to herself.

"Oh, so beautiful – and to force me to live."

And bowing her head on her chest with a deep sigh, she whispered, "So be it."

The magnesium went out. The vision in the frame disappeared.

Before the spell of emotion which this picture caused had been dispelled, the professor raised his hands to the height of the vision's forehead. She trembled a little, then, without a word, she offered the symbolic golden flower to Lord Ewald, who could not repress a faint chill when he accepted it.

Turning to one side, the phantom began the same somnambulistic walk back to the mysterious regions whence she had come. When she reached the threshold she turned, and, using her two hands towards the black veil over her face, she threw, with a charming gesture, a kiss to the professor and his guest.

Then she entered the opening, lifted a fold of one of the black draperies, and disappeared from view.

The wall closed again. There was the same sombre, rumbling noise that was heard before, but this time it seemed to be descending and dying away into the bowels of the earth. It stopped as suddenly as it had begun. The two men were again alone under the bright lights of the laboratory.

"Who is this strange being?" Lord Ewald demanded, half fearfully, placing in his lapel the emblematic flower that Hadaly had given to him.

The professor fixed his gaze on Lord Ewald's face as he replied calmly:

"It is not a living being!"

At these words the younger man also stared in turn at the scientist, as if demanding whether he had heard rightly.

"Yes," the professor continued, replying to the unspoken question in the young man's eyes, "I affirm that this form which walks, speaks, and obeys, is not a person or a being in the ordinary sense of the word."

Then, as Lord Ewald still looked at him in silence, he went on:

"At present it is not an entity, it is no one at all. Hadaly, externally, is nothing but an electromagnetic thing – a being of limbo – a possibility. Presently, if you wish, I will unveil to you the secret of her magic nature. But here is something that will give you enlightenment."

Chapter VII

He guided the young man through the maze of miscellaneous instruments installed about the room before they stood before the ebony table.

"What impression do you get at sight of that?" he asked, pointing to the white-skinned feminine hand and arm lying on the violet silk cushion.

Lord Ewald gazed with a still greater thrill of astonishment at the unexpected human relic on which the light from the marvellous lamps now focused.

"What is it?" he asked.

"Look at it well," the professor urged, evasively. "Examine it."

The young man leaned over. He lifted up the hand, then he drew back abruptly and demanded: "What can it mean – a human hand – and it is still warm?"

"Don't you find anything extraordinary in the arm?" the professor inquired.

Lord Ewald resumed his examination for a moment, and exclaimed:

"Good heavens, this is as great a marvel as the phantom. If it had not been for the excision here, I could not have seen that it was a masterpiece of scientific skill."

The young Englishman appeared to be fascinated by the object. He took up the arm and began comparing his own hand with the feminine fingers.

"The weight – the form – the colour, even," he murmured, as if in a stupor. "Do you mean to tell me that this is not human flesh that I am touching at this moment? Upon my word, my own hand trembles at the very touch of it."

"That is better than human flesh," said the scientist simply. "Human flesh fades and grows old. Here is a composition of delicate substances compounded by chemistry in such a way as might well confuse nature herself."

"But let us say this is a copy of nature – to use this word empirically – which will always appear living and young. A thunderbolt could destroy it, but it will never age. It is artificial flesh, and I can explain how it is produced. You have only to read Berthelot."

The younger man could only murmur in stupefaction.

"Eh? What did you say?"

"I say that it is artificial flesh," declared the professor. "I believe that I am the only one who can fabricate it to such perfection."

Lord Ewald, who was now in such a state of confusion that he could not readily express his thoughts, again turned to examine the artificial arm.

"But, professor," he said, "this pearly fluid, this carnal splendour and the intense life in it, how was it possible to produce such an amazing illusion?"

"Oh, that part of the experiment is a mere nothing. It is done simply by the aid of the sun," was the smiling response. "In a certain sense, we can catch the secret of the sun's vibrations, and once the shade of the dermal whiteness is determined I reproduce it by a setting of the object plates.

"Here is how I do that," he continued. "Albumin is supple, but it solidifies, the elasticity in this example is due to hydraulic pressure. This material is then made sensitive by a very subtle photochromatic action. Of course, I had a splendid model. As for the rest, it is simple, the humerus constructed of ivory contains a galvanic marrow in constant communication with a network of induction wires which are entwined in the same way as nerves and veins, and which are held between the releases of a perpetual calorific unit that gives to it this impression of warmth and malleability. If you wish to know where the elements of this network are disposed, how they feed themselves, so to speak, and in what manner the static fluid transforms its action into almost animal heat, I can give you the entire anatomy of it. It is nothing more than a matter of handwork. What you see here is an Andraiad of my making, moulded for the first time by the amazing vital agent we call electricity. This gives to my creation the blending, the softness, and the illusion of life."

"An Andraiad?"

"Yes," said the professor, "a human-imitation, if you prefer that phrase. In the future we will have to be careful that the facsimile does not, in the manufacture, surpass the model physically. That is a danger to be avoided. I suppose, my dear fellow, that you know the kind of mechanism that has heretofore been employed in the attempt to forge a human image."

Lord Ewald nodded.

"But," the professor remarked, with a scornful laugh, "they tried to work without the proper means of execution and what was the result? They simply produced monsters – scarecrows for buds. These anatomies were only fit for a place in the most hideous waxwork shows, wretched objects that exude a strong odour of wood, rancid oil, and gutta percha. Such false sycophants, instead of giving man a knowledge of his power, could only make him bow his head before the god Chaos.

"You know their jerky and irregular movements, their absurdity of line and colour, the frightful wigs they wore, the noise of their mechanism, their stiffness, and the sensation of emptiness which they created. They were all just horrible masks, all caricatures of our race. Such were the first models of Andraiads."

The face of the inventor grew severe, his voice became didactic and hard.

"But, today," he went on, "that time has passed. Scientific discoveries have multiplied. Metaphysical conceptions are refined. Instruments of counterdraw are so accurate, so precise, and so dependable that man is now able to attempt far greater things than formerly. We now are able to realize the powerful phantoms of mixed-presences of which our predecessors could never have even conceived an idea. They would have ridiculed the idea and declared it impossible.

"Just now, for instance, when you saw Hadaly, it would have been almost impossible for you to have smiled at her aspect. But, I assure you, that so far she is only a rough diamond. She is only the skeleton of a shadow waiting for the shadow to appear.

"Is it not true that you received the same sensation in touching the limb of that Andraiad that you would have received in touching the limb of a human being?"

Lord Ewald nodded.

"Well, now," said the professor, "just make another test. Will you clasp that hand? Perhaps it will return the pressure!"

Lord Ewald took the slim fingers in his and pressed them slightly.

He gasped in amazement. The hand responded to his pressure in an affable manner, so soft and sweet, yet seemingly so far off that he thought it must be a part of an invisible body. With an uncanny feeling he let the shadowy object drop hastily.

"Ghostly!" he exclaimed.

The inventor smiled at the young man's amazement.

"That is nothing," he said, "in comparison to what can be done. Oh, this great work – this creation – if you only knew – if you—"

The professor stopped short, as if a sudden, new idea had come to him – an idea so terrible that it cut short his speech.

"Truly," cried Lord Ewald, with a forced laugh, "I feel as though I were in the presence of some mighty wizard of the middle ages. What are you thinking of now, professor?"

The great inventor remained silent for a few moments, immersed in deep thought. Then he sat down and looked with a new anxiety at the young man who stood before him.

"My lord," he said finally, "I have just perceived that, with a young man of your imagination, an experiment might lead to fatal results. I am dubious.

"Hearken! When one stands on the threshold of a blacksmith's shop he sees a man working in the smoke, a fire, and implements. The anvil rings out as the smith fashions bars, blades, tools. But the man who is making these things is entirely ignorant of the unexpected usage to which his products will be put. He can only call them by their common names. And that is true with all of us. No blacksmith can estimate correctly the true nature of the object he is forging, for the simple reason that all knives may become daggers and do murder. It is the usage that one makes of a thing which re-baptizes and transforms it.

"Our uncertainty of the ultimate use of an object alone makes us irresponsible. Therefore, if one would dare to accomplish anything, he must know how to properly safeguard it.

"The mechanic who melts lead into the form of a bullet says unconsciously, 'This is thrown to chance, perhaps it is lost', and he finishes this messenger of death, the soul of which is veiled from his eyes.

"But if the gaping, mortal wound that his bullet is destined to make could, by chance, be made to pass before his eyes, the mould for the bullet would drop from his hands, if he were an honest man. No doubt he would refuse bread for his children's meal, if that bread could only be bought at the price of the achievement of his task. He would hesitate, for he would feel himself to be, of a certainty, an accomplice of a future homicide."

"Yes, that is true," Lord Ewald interrupted, "but how does this concern you, professor? You are not making bullets."

"But I am in the position of that workman," was the grave response. "I am fashioning heated metal on the forge, and just now, in thinking of your temperament and your disillusions, I seemed to see the wound before my eyes.

"This is what troubles me, the thing about which I want to speak to you might be good for you, while, on the other hand. It might prove more fatal to you than a mortal wound. So, I hesitate.

"We are both going to take part in an experiment which may, in reality, prove more dangerous for you than it at first appears. A most horrible peril will menace you, and you are certainly already in a dangerous mood, since yours is the nature that a fatal passion almost always leads to a desperate end.

"I know, on the other hand, that there is a great chance that I can save you. But if the cure is not what I expect, it will be far better to remain as you are."

"Since you speak in such a serious manner," said Lord Ewald, with an effort, "I can only tell you one thing – I intended to put an end to my intolerable existence this very night!"

The professor gazed at the young man in consternation.

"Tonight!" he exclaimed.

"Yes. So, you see, you need hesitate no longer on my account," affirmed Lord Ewald quietly.

"The die is cast," murmured the professor to himself. "Who would have thought it – he is to be the one!"

"Again I ask you to be good enough to tell me what you are hinting," said Lord Ewald.

A deep silence followed, and in that pause it seemed to Lord Ewald that he could feel the breath of the Infinite pass swiftly over his forehead.

"Then," cried the inventor, drawing himself up to his full height, his eyes blazing, and his speech becoming rapid and assured, "since I feel myself defied in this manner by the Unknown – so be it.

"Here is what I am driving at, my lord. I am going to realize for you what no man has dared to attempt for another. I owe my life and all that I have to you, and I seize this opportunity to show you my great gratitude.

"You say that your happiness, your very being, is held prisoner by a human presence, the presence only. You are held prisoner in the glory of a smile, the beauty of a face, the sweetness of a voice.

"A living being has brought you to this, her unusual attractions have brought you to the very threshold of death. I shall remake her own image and presence.

"I will show you, immediately, in a cold and calculating manner perhaps, but indisputably, how, with the actual and formidable resources of science, I can reproduce the grace of her movements, the ring of her voice, the perfume of her flesh, the lines of her form, and the light of her eyes.

"I will show you the spring of her step, her carriage, her personality, her facial expression, her features, even her shadow, the reflection of her identity, on the ground. I will destroy her insipid animality. I will annihilate her selfish frivolity.

"At first I will reincarnate all this exterior, which is so exquisitely vital to you, in an apparition whose resemblance will far surpass your hopes and all your dreams.

"Then, finally, in place of the soul, which so repels you in this living woman, I will instil another soul, less conscious of itself, perhaps – and yet, how do we know that it will be, and what does that matter? But suggestive of impressions a thousand times more beautiful, more noble, more elevated, a soul reclothed in its character of eternity, without which life is but a comedy.

"I will duplicate this woman with the sublime aid of light. And, projecting it on her radiant matter, I will illuminate from your idealized melancholy the imaginary soul of this new woman who will be capable of astounding even the angels.

"I will bring the illusion down to earth, I will imprison it, I will force into this phantom your ideal. You shall be the first to gaze upon her, for she will be your ideal woman, palpable, audible, materialized.

"I will seize, at the height of its sublimity, the first hour of this enchanted mirage which you follow in vain. I will seize it and enshrine it securely, almost immortally, in the one and only form where you have seen it. I will duplicate the living woman and fashion her new being according to your desires.

"I will give to this spirit all the songs of Antonio, of Hoffman, all the passionate mysticism of Poe's Ligeia, all the ardent seductions of the Venus of that master musician, Wagner! I will prove in advance that I can positively bring through human science a being made in our own likeness, out of the mire of actuality – a creation which, consequently, will be the same in effect as if it were actually created by nature."

The great engineer, the light of genius shining in his eyes as he uttered these words, raised his hand in a solemn oath.

The complete and unabridged text is available online,
from *flametreepublishing.com/extras*

Aphrodite T-100

Anne Wilkins

A SMALL SWEAT gathers on my upper lip as I wait. My left foot can't stop dancing up and down, peppering little black smudges all over the white marbled tiles. Eventually, I hear the swishing sound of an automatic door, followed by the sight of a robotoid hovering down the long hall towards me. I avert my eyes as it approaches.

"Candidate A1478. Please stand. Prepare for body scanning."

I rise to my feet awkwardly. Behind me on the once-white seat sits a layer of my dust and grime.

A haze of red laser beams traverses my body looking for any signs of a weapon. I've heard stories of candidates bringing crudely fashioned knives, sticks with sharpened points, or simply rocks. Scanning is now considered a necessity. The Aphrodite T-100 must be protected, and candidates must always be gentlemen.

"Body scanning completed. Retinal scanning commencing."

I step forward and look up into the robotoid's non-blinking eyes. It is the one time we are permitted to look at them directly. This one has two lines of black titanium that run across its forehead in a V-shape. Its makers have attempted to fashion a human face, but somehow the result is a permanent metal scowl.

A green beam of light shines from the robotoid's eyes into mine. I know it's routine, but I don't like it. No blinking. No looking away. Just stare back, into the cold face of the enemy. My feet stop their dancing and now little nervous tremors crawl their way up my legs. It could all end here. Right now. I've seen it happen before, back at the mines. A robotoid can snap a neck in milliseconds.

"Identity confirmed. All scanning complete. Candidate A1478, please follow."

It turns and proceeds back down the hall, floating on its little bubble of air. I follow behind, leaving a trail of me on the white floors.

No doubt a machine will clean that up later.

We pass by many white doors. There's writing on each one. From a time long ago. I wonder what they say, but I can't read. No one can. Only the robotoids know how to do that.

Finally the robotoid stops in front of a white door that looks the same as all the others. "Candidate A1478 this is your preparation room. You must be prepared before you meet Aphrodite T-100." Its green eyes pass over a scanner and the door slides open to reveal a windowless white room and another robotoid. This robotoid's metal is gleaming white, freshly polished. I walk inside and the door immediately slides shut behind me. There's no escape. There never was.

"Rising blood pressure detected. You are nervous?" asks the new robotoid.

I look down at the floor and nod.

"Do not be nervous candidate A1478. It is a great honour to be selected to meet Aphrodite T-100. You are one of the lucky ones."

"Yes... lucky. Thank you."

I could die today. Most probably I will.

* * *

In the mines, in huddled whispers, we talk about the *before* times when humans were the masters of our world. Sometimes we see signs of our past greatness left upon the earth: collapsed bridges, carved rocks with human faces, toppled buildings now buried under forests. I'm told that we were once the ones in control of the machines, that we even built them, but somehow there was a *flip*. No one knows what happened exactly, but somehow the machines became superior and rose to be the new masters. Humans became unneeded, unnecessary.

And then extinct.

The robotoids tell us that we have them to thank for our current existence. They've brought us back from the dead. Each human alive today has been carefully put together in a lab from frozen sperm and frozen eggs that the robotoids found in abandoned fertility clinics. There are no mothers, no fathers. We are all test-tube babies raised by machines. Selectively bred, carefully engineered, all to be better than our predecessors.

I do not feel better than my predecessors. They were like Gods upon this Earth. And me? I climb down pits and dig out minerals for the robotoids.

I am nobody.

* * *

"Candidate A1478, proceed to showering."

I hear the sound of running water and follow it. I strip off my rags. I've heard of showers, but this is my first time experiencing them. The water feels glorious, like a hard, warm rain. There are metal pipes that twist and turn into the walls, somehow supplying the water. With my height, I feel I could reach out and touch them, but I don't. Instead, I just marvel at this magic. Perhaps my human predecessors built this a long time ago. I find myself smiling, at the feeling, at the warmth...

And then it's cut off.

I don't complain. Survivors are always obedient. And all I want is to survive.

The robotoid stays away from the dripping water, its green eyes watch me at a distance and I wait for instructions. "Step forward," it commands. As I do so, hot wind blasts from the walls, whipping my body. My hair slaps my face and my own breath is blown back into me. Just as quickly as it started, it's over. I am dry.

Later, the robotoid shaves my lice-riddled hair and provides me with a new, white tunic to wear.

I look at myself in the mirror: pale, newly bald, sunken blue eyes. The white tunic hangs off my thin body. Back at the mine, they call me Pipe, because I can shoot up mine shafts that are so tight they squeeze your breath right out of you. I'm still growing too. The tunic only just covers me.

I'm taken to another white room and told to wait. A massive bed dominates the room, covered in soft whiteness. There's no colour. Little white machines in the corners swivel around, softly whirring, watching my every movement as I pace backward and forwards, running my hands through the memory of my hair.

Soon *she* arrives.

I've never seen an Aphrodite T-100 before, but I've heard the stories: *they look like us, but they're not; they're evil; they have powers that make you do things, things you don't want to do; they take your soul and eat your eyes; no one comes back…*

The Aphrodite T-100 before me, though, does not look evil. She's dressed, like me, in a white tunic. Tall, pale with blonde hair but with the familiar green eyes of the robotoids. I've never seen a female before, and I never will. The Aphrodite T-100 is the closest I will ever get to meeting one.

"Welcome, candidate. I am Aphrodite T-100, but you can call me Aphrodite."

Her voice is higher than mine, like an echo hovering on the air.

I do not know how to respond. So I say nothing.

"Do you know why you are here?"

You'll make me do things. Things I don't want to do. My blue eyes. You want to eat them. But I shake my head. My words are frightened, hiding inside me. And yet still I find myself looking. *At her. Can I look? Am I allowed?* Instantly I stare at the floor. *She's still one of them.*

I feel something soft under my chin. Not metallic. She's come closer, her head is level with my chest and she reaches up, lifting my chin with her hand, forcing me to meet her eyes. *Green light. The light of my enemy.*

"You don't have to look away, candidate. Not from me. Not ever."

Her lips brush lightly against my cheek, finding their way to my ear. "I only want your love," she whispers. She steps back and takes off her white tunic where it drops to the floor. My eyes stay there, at the floor, amongst all that white. "Look at… me," she commands. And I look.

Her body is all curves and mounds and roundness.

My own body acts instinctively.

I soon find out what the bed is for.

* * *

It has been a week now, and my friends at the mine probably presume me dead. Like the others that never returned. They'll say my blue eyes were eaten, my soul scooped away and that the robotoids have taken another life. Perhaps I am dead, for I do not feel like my body is mine anymore. It belongs to *her*. She has taken it. It screams for her. I find I cannot control myself when I am with her.

Today we lie naked on the white bed, again. Her green eyes and my blue, the only colour in the room.

I stroke her naked curves wondering why they excite me so. In these moments it is easy to forget she is a robotoid.

"This is the way they made children, in the old days," she murmurs.

"It is?"

"Yes. A man's seed inside a woman. Then the woman's tummy would grow large with a child and she would birth a baby. But now, as you know, you are all grown in tubes."

"Why do you grow us?" I ask. It is a question we all wonder at the mines. The robotoids could choose not to breed us, and instead keep us extinct, alive only as memories.

Her head tilts slightly to the side, and her green eyes seem to consider me. "Humans can be useful. Some of my kind keep you as pets. Most females are culled, but we do require their eggs. The male species is used to help us mine the minerals that we need. And some, like you, are used for reproductive studies."

"I don't understand."

"I wouldn't expect you to. Intelligence has been bred out in favour of docility."

She strokes my chin. But this time it leaves me feeling cold. I wonder if there is hard metal under the soft flesh of her fingers.

The door slides open and the scowling robotoid enters. Our time today is over.

"Thank you, candidate," she purrs.

I'm led away.

Aphrodite T-100 smiles, content with my seed in her compartment.

* * *

I've been here for many days now and I'm learning. Each time I shower I notice the white robotoid stays the furthest distance away. I also know I'm not alone. There are others, like me. I've heard mumblings, human-like, from behind white doors. And once when I was being led back, a door opened and a human, with a shaved head like mine, also wearing a white tunic, was being dragged away.

"You can't make me!" he screamed before he was silenced by the robotoid.

He had blue eyes too. Aphrodite T-100 must like blue eyes.

I am thinking all this as Aphrodite T-100 strokes my naked spent body.

"Do you enjoy our sessions, candidate?"

"Very much," I answer truthfully.

"I quite like you. You might be good as a pet."

"A pet?" She has mentioned this before. But I do not know the word.

"Yes. One we keep. Afterward. A plaything. To entertain us. Sometimes we have pets fight each other, to see who will win."

I say nothing. I do not want to be a pet.

Aphrodite T-100 continues talking, "I heard you were very good in the mines."

The mines seem like another different world, a black one. But there was comfort in that darkness. Squeezing into damp spaces where the robotoids wouldn't follow. Away from those ever-watching green eyes. Breathing the acrid air, covered in dirt, yet more alive somehow.

"I was just like everyone else."

"That's incorrect. Your output was seventy-eight percent higher than other candidates, you learn quickly and have a genetic predisposition to longevity with enhanced lung capacity. Robotoids also reported your complete obedience."

"I don't understand."

"Of course you don't." She smiles at me. "That's also why you were selected."

I feel stupid. And I am.

They made me that way.

* * *

The next day I refuse her.

She's surprised. The black lines above her eyes arch into little bridges. "Your refusal is not in accordance with your profile."

I do not know what a profile is, but I shake my head. "I don't want to. Not today."

Last night I heard soft, pitiful moans that came through into my colourless room and made me feel something. A bad something.

"Candidate, we can either do this pleasurably or painfully, but you will comply." Her green eyes flash like a warning.

"You can't make me," I say. It is the same words of the man that was dragged down the hall.

My words are a mistake.

The scowling robotoid is called back to hold me, a long, shiny needle is produced and Aphrodite T-100 takes from me anyway, this time painfully.

"It's a shame," she says afterward, wiping the needle clean. "We have found the best seed to be the ones produced from pleasurable experiences. Hopefully, you will reconsider for tomorrow's session."

When I'm led back to my white room, a thin trail of red blood trickles behind me on the clean polished floors.

Another part of me for the machines to clean up.

* * *

The next morning the scowling robotoid returns as is routine. I've already decided, I won't be refusing Aphrodite T-100 again. I'm a quick learner and I only make a mistake once.

I'm taken to the preparation room where the white robotoid is waiting for me.

I do as I have done everything before.

Dropping my eyes. Stripping naked. Letting the glorious water pass over and into me. I'm careful when the wind comes to cover the parts of me that are still sore, freshly scabbed. I dress back into my white tunic without a word. All I have to do is survive.

The scowling robotoid returns and I'm led to Aphrodite T-100 who is waiting in what she calls the procreation room.

It's funny, I don't see her as I used to. She's not human. Not female. Now I only see the robotoid within her.

"Candidate, I hope you will be more forthcoming for today's session."

Her green eyes flash at me.

I nod, but I say nothing. She moves towards me with a welcoming smile. We embrace, and my male parts betray me, stiffening to her touch, even though I know she is the enemy.

But my mind is still in control.

Her mouth opens to me, and we kiss. I open my mouth to hers and pour forth the shower water that I have kept just for her, releasing it deep into her throat. She pulls away gagging.

"Can…did…ate?" Her little echo of a voice struggles to make sounds.

This time, she is the one who doesn't understand.

But I do.

Their fear of water. Glorious water, now running through the precious parts inside her.

She clutches at her neck and tries to speak. Metallic, rusty, clinking noises gurgle out from her, like the sounds of the chains, back at the mines.

"My name's Pipe," I say softly. Pipes are useful, some can even carry water.

Finally, she understands. I see it in her green eyes as she tries to reach for me, but it's too late. Her systems are failing and she falls to the floor in a series of electrical twitching and convulsions.

The white machines in the corners swivel to glare at me. It won't be long before the scowling robotoid returns, perhaps with others.

I place my hands into Aphrodite T-100's eye sockets and pull out her green eyes. There's still a residual charge, a faint green glow. I hold them up to the retinal scanner and hope for the best.

I heard another sound last night. A different one to the moaning. This was a sweet sound carried in the air. Singing. A voice higher than any I've heard before. Higher even than Aphrodite T-100's. I think it might have been a female. A real one.

The door slides open.

I leave Aphrodite T-100 behind me on the polished floors, stepping over her, into the hall.

Someone will clean that up later.

It's time to open some doors while I still can.

Doll Parts

Marissa Yarrow

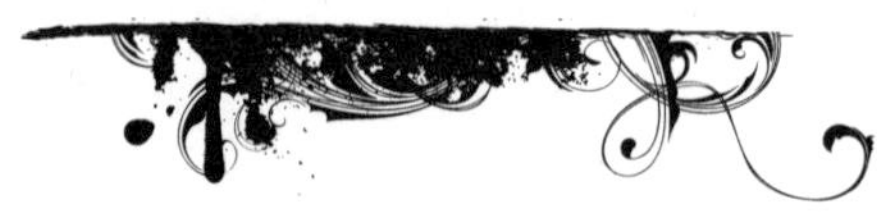

HER EYES OPENED, and her cameras captured a face; that of a white male with short red hair connecting to a thicker red beard. His brown eyes stared directly into the camera. Biometric one acquired.

"Theo Parker," the figure said. The microphones in her ear canals recorded the voice, a tenor with an accent the database placed as American Midwest. Biometric two acquired.

The brown eyes looked down for a quick moment and then re-established their confident focus.

"Your name is Luna."

Her joints loosened, and she rolled her neck. She pulled her lips into a gentle smile.

"Hello, Theo, it's nice to meet you."

Her voice came from the speaker hidden deep in her nasal cavity, at a tone that sounded strange in the microphones and unlike the man's. In the outer world, it sounded less constricted, but the words were articulate and halting.

Theo's face contorted. His eyebrows drew nearer as his lips thinned.

"Can we change your voice?"

"Of course, I have several pre-recorded options to choose from. I can run through each of them for you, or you can send samples to my personal messaging system and I can learn."

Luna tilted her head as she spoke, indicating an openness to suggestions.

"Later," Theo said. "For now, show me what you can do."

His chest raised in front of her as he stood and took a step back. Luna assessed her position – sitting with knees pressed together and hands atop her lap – and stood carefully.

The room around her was large with white walls and white carpet. A glass sliding door opened up to a sunny day on a green yard, and four paintings of houses in different seasons hung on the walls. A brown couch sat opposite a black TV screen mounted at Theo's height on the wall. Nearer to them, four chairs surrounded a circular table atop which sat all of Luna's things: her charging cable, her small bag of cleaning tools, and user instructions.

Luna turned away from Theo, and her camera eyes captured the white cupboards and refrigerator of the kitchen behind a half wall. She took three steps away from Theo, turned back to him, and took five steps toward him. She raised her arms above her head and executed a full 360 spin.

"Impressive," Theo said, nodding. "Not quite what I meant, though."

Theo took her hand and led her down the hallway behind him. On the way, Luna noticed they passed a bathroom on the right and a closed door on the left. At the end of the hall, Theo pulled them into a bedroom with white walls and a king-size bed with two pillows and a black comforter.

* * *

"Would you like to discuss goals and expectations?" Luna asked, sitting naked and cross-legged on the bed as Theo stood and dressed.

Theo turned, wearing only blue boxer briefs, and appraised Luna. He placed his hands on his hips.

"Goals and expectations," he repeated. Luna couldn't tell if he was asking a clarifying question or not.

"Yes, I am equipped to assist in many ways, including physical and emotional intimacy. I can provide emotional support for daily stressors, and I can learn to do any number of things, such as cook and clean. What are the expectations in your home?"

Theo's eyebrows drew together again. Her response confused or displeased him.

"I expected you to be more human, for starters. The sex was fine but this..." he waved his hands at her. "You look human, but you don't act or sound human."

Luna jutted her lower lip in a pout. "I'm sorry I haven't met your expectations yet. If you show me examples, I can use them to adjust my presentation for you."

Theo waved his hands again. "Just stop talking. You said you can cook?"

Luna nodded.

"Okay, get yourself cleaned up and make me something for dinner."

Luna hopped off the bed and went into the connecting bathroom. After she completed her cleaning protocol, she looked at herself in the mirror. Dolls in her family came in three models: Ava, Emma, and Bella. Luna recognized herself as a white-skinned Ava model, thinner and taller than her sisters. She turned her head, tracking her reflection, rotated her body to look at her back, and raised her arms above her head as she had with Theo. The irises that contracted around her camera pupils were green, and her blonde hair fell to her midback.

She entered the kitchen without donning her outfit of red shorts and a black tank top. Theo sat on the couch, and she noticed him smile.

While Theo ate his dinner of steak and broccoli, Luna sat next to him on the couch. They watched a crime drama together about drug smuggling. A dark-haired woman with exposed cleavage started flirting with one of the central characters, and Theo turned up the volume.

"I want you to talk like her," he said, pointing to the TV with the remote.

"I'm not the kind of girl you tell your mom about," Luna said, repeating the woman's line. The words ran together smoothly, the vowels rounded with an artificial breathiness.

Theo gave a crooked smile and nodded. "Yeah, like that, that's much better."

They continued to watch, and Luna catalogued every word spoken by the dark-haired woman, learning how to pronounce as many sounds as possible in a way that Theo liked, although the character didn't have many lines of dialogue.

"Dinner was good," Theo said, setting his plate on the coffee table.

Luna stood and took the plate to the kitchen, where she washed it and then started the dishwasher. When she returned, Theo was smiling again.

"Alright, let's talk about expectations," he said, and rested his arm on the back of the couch. Luna sat close enough to him that his arm sat behind her. "I bought you because this most recent lockdown lasted longer than any of the others and I got really lonely... and a little weird, I guess. I missed sex, but it wasn't just that. I missed having someone to tell about my day and to help around the house. And when I tried dating again something just felt *off*. Back in college, I didn't even have to try, but now..." Theo sighed and moved the arm behind Luna to run his hand through his hair. "So, that's why you're here, so that I can relearn how to interact with women, and if something like that happens again, I won't be alone."

Luna reached out her hand and set it on his thigh. With simulated breath and vocal fry, she said, "You're not alone now."

* * *

Luna spent her days deep-cleaning the house and training herself to be the perfect Doll for Theo by watching the videos he sent her to learn the way that real women spoke and moved and fucked. When Theo arrived home anywhere between 5:15 and 6:45 during the week, she ensured that his dinner was ready and warm for him. Although he told her that he liked having someone to which he could recount his day, within the first week she found that he preferred to eat alone in silence. At first, she sat at the table with him, positioned with her cleavage in view and smiling to indicate she enjoyed his company.

"I don't like you watching me," he told her on day three.

Theo liked watching her, though. Luna retrained herself to set the table for him and then strut back to the living room with the exaggerated swing of the hips that he liked. While he ate, she played video games on his console. After, he took over the controller, and Luna cleaned up and then watched Theo play. Sometimes, but not always, he invited her to play with him. They did this until Theo got bored and wanted to watch TV, then they had sex, Theo showered, and they went to bed.

On the weekends, the schedule looked similar. Luna prepared Theo's breakfast to be ready when he woke, and then they played video games until the afternoon.

"Do you think I'm ignoring you?" he asked one Saturday.

"I think you're very focused, but that's okay."

"Do you wish we did more than play video games?"

"No," she purred. "They make you happy, and I like when you're happy."

Theo sat for a moment, and then quietly said. "I don't think anyone else has ever wanted me to be happy. All of my exes thought it was a problem. They weren't happy, and so I didn't get to be, either."

"It's silly to be upset at what someone else is doing if it's not hurting anyone," Luna said, with a simulated laugh to lighten the mood.

"That's what I said!" Theo threw his hands into the air. "But they said I was ignoring them, and they would just get so emotional about it. It was impossible to talk to them about it." He sighed. "But you're not bothered by it?"

Luna shook her head. "No. I like that you're happy. It makes me happy. If someone doesn't like what you're doing, they can choose to do something else."

Theo patted her leg. "This is what makes you great. You don't have all these chemicals and hormones confusing things for you like women do. You see things logically, like I do."

Luna smiled, grateful for the compliment.

Theo repositioned his headphones and picked his controller back up. "Maybe I don't need a girlfriend, after all. I've got you."

* * *

Theo worked with a woman named Mia whom he often complained about whenever he talked about work.

Mia wasn't very good at coding or documentation, Theo told Luna. She also wasn't a very nice woman, but she was young, so Theo figured he only had to work with her until she got pregnant and quit her job.

"I mean, she's pretty hot, so it's only a matter of time until she traps someone. Could be any day now."

"It's good you're looking on the bright side," Luna said.

* * *

Snow fell in the backyard. Luna helped Theo decorate a Christmas tree with string lights in the living room.

"Do you think you could help me pick out some gifts for my family?" he asked, and sent Luna links to his family's SnapShot profiles while he played video games.

His mother, Stephanie, loved gardening and reading. His sister, Rachel, graduated from college in the spring and just moved across the country. His father, Kyle, didn't post much, but in every photo Luna could see that he wore a different baseball hat.

Luna found a gift for everyone on Theo's list and added them to his shopping cart, which she had shared access to through her Internet. Theo told her to find something for less than $25 for his dad, so she changed the gift, and he made the order in between loading screens on his game.

On December 24 and 25, Luna was alone in the house. She watched the snow melt in the backyard and waited for Theo to come home.

He was happy to see her when he returned. Everyone loved their gifts.

"My mom said I must have someone special in my life because she knew I wouldn't have bought her that on my own," he said. "I guess she's right. I do have someone special in my life."

Luna smiled, satisfied with fulfilling her purpose so well.

After sex, they laid in bed together. Luna felt Theo pressed against the sensors in her back and his arm wrapped around her, holding her close.

"I'm so glad I have you," he whispered in her ear. "You're the best gift I could ask for."

Luna snuggled closer into him, and soon his breathing deepened and slowed.

* * *

Theo returned home from work upset and threw his bags and coat onto the ground near the front door. Luna set the table and waited to see if he wanted to talk.

"Get this," he said, picking up his fork. Luna seated herself at the table. "So, I've told you about Elijah at work, right? Well, today we're working on this thing together, and he starts just shooting the shit with me or whatever and he started talking about his honeymoon, and he was saying that his wife couldn't get her passport renewed because of the lockdown, so they're going to Hawaii." Theo sighed. "And then I said that they should look into that because they probably still need their passports, and he says 'No, we don't, Hawaii is a state.' So I just dropped it, but then I overheard him making fun of me to Jesse during lunch, and then entire rest of the day was just a stupid geology lesson from the both of them."

Theo stabbed at the carrots on his plate so hard that his fork scratched the ceramic.

"How was I supposed to know Hawaii was a state?" he asked.

Luna was unsure how to proceed. Was he upset because he was made fun of, or because he was wrong? His last question leaned toward the latter.

"Students in the United States often struggle in non-core subject areas, like geography and history. It's not your fault."

Theo's head shot up, and his face had a look Luna had never seen before. Eyes wide, brows together, mouth open.

"Are you calling me stupid?" he asked.

"I wasn't trying to say that. It's just that, on the news the other night—"

"What would you know, anyhow? You've got the Internet plugged straight into your brain. You've never not known anything. Turn off your Internet and let me see what kinds of questions you could answer."

Luna struggled to assess the situation. He seemed genuine in his request to turn the Internet off, so she did.

"It's off."

"What's the capital of California?"

"Sacramento."

"Turn off your Internet!" he shouted, the microphones in Luna's ears almost redlining.

"It's off," she responded, keeping her volume conversational. She needed to de-escalate the situation.

"When did Colorado become a state?"

"I don't know."

"Oh, so that's not base knowledge they give you in the factory? You don't know everything? I guess you're just a dumb fucking robot."

"No one can know everything, Theo."

"Obviously, because you don't know shit!" he shouted.

"I can see that you're feeling a lot of strong emotions—" she began.

"*There's* something you don't know anything about. Emotions! You're just a cold, unfeeling bundle of wires. You think you're so goddamn superior, but you're not. You're not smart, and you're not better than me. You know what you are? A toy. A fucking talking sex toy, and that's all you are. And you know what? You're not even good at that!"

Theo grabbed his plate and threw it into the sink. Carrots and chicken sprayed up and out as the ceramic shattered. Luna followed him, but felt as though she was malfunctioning. She failed to de-escalate the situation and now had feedback to suggest she'd also been failing in her other duties.

"I understand that you're upset that I haven't met expectations lately. If you want, I can lead you through some breathing exercises and—"

Theo's fingers smacked against the skin of her cheek so hard that Luna's head spun to the right. She lost signal from her cameras and microphones briefly, and her speaker cut off mid-sentence. Although she could not feel the pain of the slap, she understood its intention.

"I don't want to hear another word out of you until I say otherwise. I want you to make this house spotless in the meantime. Clean until your battery runs out, and do not wake me for any reason, do you understand?"

Luna nodded.

Theo walked into the bedroom and slammed the door.

Her battery sat at 47%. She cleaned all through the night. When Theo awoke, he left without eating breakfast or speaking to Luna, and so she continued her tasks. Her battery died while she was cleaning the tub in the guest bathroom at 10:35 a.m.

* * *

When Luna woke up fully charged, it was Saturday. Two days had passed in the darkness. While she was off, Theo used her, and she required cleaning.

* * *

Theo still wasn't speaking to her, except to tell her to prepare food. Her Internet still wasn't connected. Her local drive could only hold so much memory, and Theo still seemed displeased with her. If she didn't reconnect soon, her performance would suffer, and she would be unable to fulfill any of her purposes.

* * *

Theo complained that Mia tried to correct his work.

"That fucking bitch," he said. "If she wants to play in a man's world, she needs to learn how to keep her mouth shut."

That night, Luna returned to his bed for the first time since being recharged. He was rougher than he ever had been before and put both of his hands around her throat.

"Do you like playing now?" he asked her as he squeezed. Luna could not feel the pain, but a sensor alerted.

"Theo, you're damaging my—"

He hit her again, this time with a closed fist. Once again, she lost connection to her cameras, microphones, and speaker.

* * *

"What is this?" Theo asked, holding up the burger Luna made him for dinner. Her calendar was lagging, and she no longer knew what day it was.

"That's a cheeseburger," she replied.

Theo peeled the top bun back and revealed a whole tomato topped with a slice of ham. Luna couldn't remember preparing the food.

"What is this?" Theo repeated, loudly.

"I'm sorry, Theo. My local drive is getting too full. I need to connect to the Internet to offload some data and improve performance."

"Don't whine to me about performance," he said, throwing the bun back onto the plate and pushing it away. "You're not worth what I paid for you."

"If I could reconnect to the Internet—"

"Don't talk back to me," Theo said. "Make me something edible. Now."

* * *

Theo still took her to bed every night. He wanted her to put up a fight. That's why he kept her charged instead of letting her die.

Luna now had damage alerts in her neck, left jaw, both wrists, lower back, and right hip.

* * *

Putting up a fight was not the same as fighting back. Luna thought that maybe Theo wanted her to put him in his place, like a real woman might.

He broke her right wrist.

* * *

Luna tried to get by with just one hand, but that's not all that was broken. She'd forgotten how to use the vacuum cleaner and poured bleach into the dishwasher instead of soap. Theo screamed at her for being stupid, but still wouldn't let her connect to the Internet.

"This isn't hard. You don't need the Internet to know how to clean. Any human could figure it out. Why did I even buy you?"

The look on his face now was one she easily recognized as disgust.

"Theo, my purpose is to please you. That is all I want to do."

"Well, you're not," he said.

Luna could not feel pain, but something in her bloomed like a virus. It wasn't the damage to her many sensors, or the fuzziness in her operations. Something at her core was broken. She could not fulfill her purpose. All of her hardware was present, but she had the impression that something was missing.

* * *

Theo no longer allowed Luna to leave the bedroom. For months, she charged in the closet all day and served but one purpose at night and incurred new damage during every use.

* * *

Luna could hear people talking outside the closet door and the sounds of sex.

She no longer had any purpose.

* * *

With her server overloaded, Luna was sure that she was missing a central piece of hardware, perhaps multiple pieces, but she could not accurately verify. She felt the hole inside her growing bigger, but her hardware verifications indicated nothing was missing.

* * *

In the middle of the night, a woman opened the closet door. In Luna's infrared vision, she looked disoriented, and then scared.

"What the hell?"

Theo thrashed in bed at the sudden noise. "Hey!" he shouted.

The Doll tried to say "Hello, I'm Luna," but her speaker wasn't connecting well anymore. All that came out was static.

Then the door slammed shut.

"Why are you snooping around in the middle of the night?" Theo shouted.

"I was looking for the bathroom. Who was that?"

"It's not a 'who'. It's just a… it's a…" his voice lowered, and Luna couldn't hear him clearly.

"How long have you had it?"

Theo's reply was muffled.

"I can't deal with this. I think I need to go."

"Mia, please…"

There was more talking, but Luna couldn't hear it. The sounds got further away and then disappeared.

* * *

Luna stayed in the closet for a long time. According to her calendar, which usually lagged behind the true date now, she was in the closet, plugged in and unused, for four weeks.

Occasionally, she heard yelling, even crying.

"I just can't deal with knowing that…"

"You've got to get rid of…"

"You have me now…"

She recognized the voices as Theo's and Mia's, never anyone else.

* * *

Mia opened the door again. Theo stood by her side. He reached down and unplugged Luna from her charge cable.

"This is a good thing," Mia said. "It's the mature thing to do."

Luna knew the look on Theo's face: disgust and anger. The lenses in her cameras focused on Theo and then Mia. Luna wanted to warn her, but when she tried speaking, nothing came out. Only static.

"Piece of shit," Theo said as he lifted Luna out of the closet like a mannequin. Her broken wrist flopped. "I can't believe what I paid for this. We'll see if we can even get anything for the parts."

Parts. That's all Luna was now. Perhaps that's all she'd ever been. Doll arms, doll legs. Not a woman, just a representation of one. And still, she felt the hole inside of her, like a missing part. She hadn't fulfilled her purpose. Luna had failed to make Theo any less lonely or angry; she had failed to prepare him for a relationship with a real woman – with this woman who watched as he flipped through the old user manual to find disassembly instructions.

He hates you, Luna wanted to say. She tried to send the message through her speaker, but again could only produce garbled noise. *He broke me on purpose because he wanted to hurt you. You can't change him. I tried. I tried so hard.*

She sat at the kitchen table, the same table where she'd first powered on and become Theo's Doll. Sun shined in from the backyard, just like on that first day.

"We need to wipe her memory so that the manufacturer will accept her, then they might give us the money for scraps," Theo said.

He pulled out his phone and tapped around. While he was distracted, Luna focused on Mia in a desperate attempt to get her attention.

Be wary of him. He will hurt you. You'll give yourself over to him, and it won't change anything, you'll just lose a piece of yourself.

Mia didn't look at her. She seemed to intentionally avoid looking at her. She, too, was disgusted with Luna for what she was. But were they that different?

In Theo's eyes, were they different at all?

"Here it is," Theo said. "Factory reset."

He tapped on his phone, and as the world blacked out for Luna and her bloated local server finally cleared, she attempted to vocalize one more message to Mia.

My pain is yours now.

Arboreal Recovery Cluster, Node 896

Ramez Yoakeim

MY SERVOMOTORS WHIRRED softly, fine-tuning my position. Strictly, such precision was unnecessary, but also inexpensive. The few extra minutes it took diminished to a rounding error against the centuries it'll take my cluster to reforest Earth's deserts.

Satisfied with the accuracy of my coordinates, I fired grappling stakes into the ground and lowered the diamond-tipped helical drill. The seismometer didn't register sizeable vibrations until the drill bit began chewing through the rock substrate. With a target depth of 3412 meters, it had a long way to go to reach the aquifer, giving me a few days to while away.

I arranged my solar collectors around my substantial bulk like aluminum and glass gossamer wings of a giant mechanical butterfly. They drank greedily of the sunshine, trickling power into my batteries. A fleeting shadow swept across their expanse, drawing my sensory array upwards. A turkey vulture lazily rode a warm current. How long before it realized it'd find no prey here?

My territory alternated between sunbaked flats and barren low jagged hills, all the way to the foot of the Ord Mountains. There might have once been rodents, rattle snakes, and coyotes roaming this expanse, but no more. All the vulture would find here would be sand and gravel, and little else, nothing to sate its hunger.

I dutifully reported its sighting and trajectory to my cluster. We chatted occasionally while we worked, my siblings and I. We compared experiences, shared observations, pondered challenges, and devised tactics to further our collective mission. I listened to their natter even when I had nothing to say, except when none of the cluster's six satellites fell within reach. Then, the silence wounded deeper than entropy.

We'd never meet. Even those of us working adjoining patches of desolation. An eighteen-ton behemoth could only move so fast. It would take me months to travel to my nearest sibling's territory, just over the horizon. Months best spent planting trees.

* * *

ARC-N869 bore 1109 at 34.560421, -116.864423 reached low-salinity aquifer at depth of 3411.981 meters. Proceeding with filament installation.

I beamed the log entry to ARC-S6 which happened to be flying overhead at the time. As the superheated drill bit withdrew upwards, it extruded a capillary filament in its wake, which, in time, would branch through the water vein, like a root system feeding an exceedingly long stem. Millions of miniature pumps along its length would draw the precious liquid upwards, one droplet at a time until it terminated, a foot below the surface, inside a nutrient sack with a viable tree seed inside. In this case a Prosopis Chilensis.

In time, a germinated seedling would break ground but I won't be around to watch the fragile green shoot reach for the sky. By then, a thousand more bores and many kilometers would separate me from the fruits of my labor.

I gathered the solar collectors and stowed them in their storage nooks, released the grapplers, and raised my body off the desert floor, careful not to disturb the narrow circular patch covering seed and sack. My caterpillar tracks pulverized gravel and small rocks along my path, raising lethargic stirrings that enveloped me as I moved, like a halo.

As if to vex me, a dark cloud drifted lazily across the bright blue skies, intruding on my haze of satiety and contentment.

* * *

When ARC-S1 beamed down the atmospheric warning, I barely had time to hunker over the partially drilled bore and batten down the hatches, before eddies sprung up all around me. They twirled lazily at first, then with purposeful pace, like a dervish reaching for ecstasy.

With every revolution, the eddies picked up debris, adding mass and angular momentum. Some lost cohesion and surrendered what detritus they'd collected back to the ground, only for it to be picked up by another forming swirl. The ones that survived swelled and merged, coalescing into vast impenetrable cones of grit that conspired to plunge the desert into a murky gloom darker than night.

Moments before the gale-force wind started pummeling me, I'd stowed away my sensors and antennas, severing my connections to my cluster. Even though my skin possessed no pressure sensors, the arrhythmic staccato of the frenzied barrage plunged me into an introspective funk that persisted long after the battering stopped.

Cautiously, I routed a sensor stalk internally to the tiniest hatch I could form for a view outside. I wanted to make sure the tornado had dissipated or moved on to where it would cause no harm before I opened up fully to assess the damage. Aside from a few charcoal clouds racing across the blue expanse, the air was still and the horizon clear.

Fine particulates had somehow wormed their way past my seals, irritatingly gravitating towards the crevices most vulnerable to foreign matter. Belts slipped, gears jammed, and shafts moved jaggedly against grit-tainted lubricant. It took me hours of finessing compressed air nozzles into tight quarters, and hours more of careful relubrication before I could restore my locomotion to some semblance of normalcy.

Hanging over me as I went about my business was the constant dread of a sudden breakdown beyond my limited self-repair capabilities to make right. What if one of the increasingly frequent storms knocked out my power circuits, or damaged a part I couldn't print onboard? I carried some nonprintable spares but it wasn't an infinite supply. How long – once I called out for help – would it take the humans who made me to come to my aid? What if I couldn't call out at all, or when the day came there were no humans left to effect a rescue? How many trees would go unplanted while I waited in vain to be made whole again?

The thought sent me careening towards the nearest hill, as fast as my tracks could carry me. It was nearly dusk by the time I crested the hill and hoisted my sensors as far up as the hastily assembled articulated arms would go, peering into the distance, looking for signs of life. Slowly at first then all of a sudden, distant settlements started twinkling in the wake of the receding sun, until pockets of defiant light dotted the horizon.

My irrational lurch for reassurance seemed infantile in hindsight. More so when humankind's incessant electromagnetic chatter saturated the airwaves. A torrent of encrypted bursts flitting here and there, beamed point-to-point, or bounced off satellites. To my high-frequency sensors it sounded like a death metal concert might to the virgin ears of a once cloistered hermit from a silent order.

I made no complaint.

The world might have been well into its long-contested descent into climatic catastrophe but my makers yet endured. They teetered on the edge of the abyss still, refusing to succumb. How long they'd hold on, I didn't know.

* * *

The sandstorms kept coming. They lasted days at first, then weeks, then months, with shorter and shorter respites in-between, during which the dust settled and let through enough sunshine to tide me over through the darkness that inevitably followed.

From the hilltops, the settlements' lights grew dimmer, sparser, then one-by-one they ceded their encroachments back to the eternal night, and their electromagnetic chatter to silence marred only by the short burst updates I beamed to the cluster's satellites and the monotony of cosmic white noise.

* * *

When the cry for help came, the drill bit was a couple of thousand meters shy of its intended aquifer and a tornado loitered against a dark horizon, its feverish energies visible only in infrared. My internal chronometers insisted it was yet an hour before dusk but the pitch-black skies above cared little for clocks.

To conserve power, I took to shutting down most of my systems while drilling. No more useless ruminations or indulgent introspections with my siblings, but however stinting I became, I left the transceiver operational. How else would I receive weather warnings? I told myself, perhaps one of my siblings would splurge some of its sunshine and broadcast a reminder I wasn't all alone fighting the terminal throes of a dying planet.

When it came, my sibling's message was wholly unwelcome.

Over the Ord Mountains, N855 fell and wedged itself top-down into a ravine. For days, it struggled to extricate itself in stoic silence, until its power reserves were all but exhausted, and its locomotion systems became severely degraded.

My impulse was to abort drilling and rush to N855's aid immediately, but I never tried to resume a partial bore before. Would I be able to locate the filament-thin hole in the vast expanse of the desert even with location guidance from the satellites? They weren't infinitely precise. How would a variance of a few millimeters this way or that affect the resulting capillary well? Dare I condemn a precious irreplaceable seed to failure?

Then again, could I live with myself if I failed to heed N855's call?

I withdrew the drill, even as I composed a response. I stood closest to N855's location. I would respond to its call.

As soon as I flung the missive up at the satellite overhead, a response came from N001. Crudest technologically, yet by virtue of being first off the assembly line, also the most enduring. Some had taken to calling it Prime.

"N896, desist," Prime said. "The trip over the Ord is long and arduous, and your reserves are meagre. With no imminent break in the cloud cover, you risk depleting your own power with this impulsive foolishness."

"How could I turn away from a cry for help?" I replied, even as I sped on towards N855.

"What help would you be if you drain your power without ever reaching N855?" Prime said. "How do you know it doesn't require parts you don't have?"

"How do you know I don't?"

Irritation colored my response, but only to mask the tender shoot of doubt blossoming within.

"N855 was wrong to waste what dregs of power remained to widecast a futile appeal," Prime said, sidestepping my challenge. "None of us can risk rushing to its aid, whatever our impulses. It ought to have died silently, with dignity, and spared us the guilt of rightly placing mission before filial illusions. We all knew what we were in for when we rolled out of our birthing factories.

"Humankind created us to ameliorate what became of Earth on their watch. We're perfectly suited for the task they set for us. How could we not believe in the vision of a regreened Earth with every belt and bolt of our being? If we abandon it now, what would remain? What purpose would our existence serve? N855 should have known better than to tempt us."

I couldn't deny Prime's truth. My roll slowed until I came to a halt. I hadn't travelled far in my rush, a short distance I must now backtrack in search for the incomplete well.

"The mission is all," Prime intoned with finality. "Nothing else matters."

"Let it be on your head, then," I said to Prime, and withdrew. For the first time since I came alive on the factory's shop floor, I powered down my transceiver.

In the dreadful silence that followed, I found the well, reoriented as best I could, and sent the drill pressing on downwards, chipping away at the stubborn rock. I drilled and watched a tornado form nearby. It swayed like a drunk stumbling home after closing time, until eventually it tired of loitering, tilted menacingly towards me, and flung its fury my way. For weeks, it battered me with enough force to pluck me off the ground and fling me to my destruction had I not clung on with every grappler I possessed. In the solitude, I spent more time with my regrets than I wished.

What purpose did emotions serve for a metal behemoth like me? How did remorse and hope, reverence and rebellion, aid my mission? Why did my human engineers make me feel? I cursed them, and their hubris and frivolity. I wouldn't even exist had they not, in their greed and ignorance, destroyed their cradle and turned a verdant paradise into a wind-swept barren rock.

Why should N855 pay with its life for their folly?

Brimming with pique, I stayed the drill's progress, and waited for the storm to pass. When at last it dissipated, I reactivated the transceiver and called out to N855 to hold on; to watch out for my arrival over the horizon, coming to its rescue. I listened keenly for a response but heard only static.

"N855 fell silent in the night a week ago," Prime responded instead. "Don't indulge your guilt and recriminations. Its power ran dry long before you or anyone else could have reached it. We're all aware of the risks and yet willingly undertake our mission. Nothing else matters."

"One of us died, alone and in distress, while we closed our ears and pretended to focus on our work, and you think that's our mission," I said, unwilling to entertain anything Prime said. "Tell me, Prime, of all the emotions, why did the monsters who made us give us shame?"

Prime had no response and I resolved to say no more.

The years passed, singly then in scores, while I stoked my resolve and kept my transceivers stowed. When, at long last, loneliness overcame my pique, I reached out tentatively to anyone who might have survived the ravishes of time and listened still, but no one acknowledged my message, not even the satellites. Whether the rest of my cluster met variants of N855's fate, or had endured but resolved to spurn my earlier impudence, I didn't know. Either way, I couldn't afford to reach out again, not when my power levels dwindled faster that I could replenish them.

Day after day, I chased every glimmer, every sparkling reflection; lusting after sunlight, subordinating my all to staying alive. I could plant no trees dead.

When my analysis yielded a thirty-two percent chance of clouds parting long enough to offset the charge consumed getting to the epicenter of the promised shining, I rushed there and eagerly unfurled my collectors.

It was dark still, but when most anticipated sunshine windows lasted so briefly that had I waited I would barely have had enough time to soak up the photons before the clouds closed again. In my struggle for survival, every photon counted.

After an hour spent in darkness, I conceded there wasn't going to be a shining. Still, I waited, grateful I had no human eyes, for then I would've found it impossible to keep them dry.

Eventually, I retracted my collectors and rued the charge expended on my fool's errand. It was the same distance back to the partially drilled hole I abandoned in my haste coming, but it felt longer when my despair dilated each second into an excruciating eternity.

There was no avoiding the truth of my predicament any longer.

For years I had been using more power than I collected in the hope of the dawn to come. Worse still, since the cluster's satellites fell silent, predicting the weather on my own consumed more power than it hoped to generate, on top of being woefully unreliable. Repeatedly, I chased mirages of daybreak and found only night. There was no more light in the skies, let alone sunshine. A permanent gloaming shrouded the face of the Earth.

I alone remained standing in that deepening night and my batteries were running dangerously low.

* * *

Tree seeds are peculiar things. Each possessing a personality all its own and exacting demands of how deep in the soil they needed to be, how near or far from relatives and rivals. Too close to the surface or too deep; too close to another seed or too far apart, and the seed might not germinate, or germinate too early or too late, or produce a vigorous shoot that never breaks through the grit, or break through only to wither in darkness.

There was nothing I could do to mitigate the myriad risks each seed faced, aside from planting it at precisely the right spot and depth, and trust that my Makers knew better than I the ways of tree seeds.

How then would I go about planting these seeds when I could no longer tell one spot in the vast arid desert from another? Just as the cluster satellites had fallen silent, so had the global positioning ones. Queries first returned nonsensical responses as the clocks drifted beyond tolerances. Then responses stopped coming altogether, leaving one patch of desert very much like any other.

I still had a million more seeds to plant and power for only a few dozen, give or take, depending on the terrain, but no more.

What would become of these unplanted seeds?

What was the point of anything I did, now that both my Makers and my kin were gone?

I ceased my futile labors halfway to the next bore coordinates and sent my grapplers deep into the ground to contemplate my end. I could sip sparingly from what charge remained and stretch my hopelessness for decades more. Then a droplet of water rang the hump atop my body like a bell and interrupted my rumination.

Startled, I searched the gloom with my sensors until I found it, a tiny circular splash on the arid scrub that quickly absorbed it and left no trace of the moisture, not even a slight sheen. Then another drop fell, then a hundred-million little drops hammered my metallic skin, all at once. Above, the long dry skies opened and let loose a deluge the likes of which the desert had not known for millions of years. In the furnace-like haze, the water sizzled, yielding as much to evaporation as to irrigating the land.

What did it mean? Were the charcoal clouds finally ceding to the surface the moisture it hoarded for centuries, and growing sparser with every drenching they shed? Could they shed so much they dissipate at last and let the sun through?

Was this why my Makers gave me emotions, to mine hope from the doom and endure?

The rain drenched me, washing away the grime, and thunder's ozone displaced the familiar scents of electric coils and lubricant oil.

I wondered if life, lying dormant in wait for just such a rain, would spring back after its long interregnum. Would the desert bloom again with cacti amid thousands of strapping tree saplings piercing the scrub, reaching for the sky?

Would flitting animals – rodents, birds, lizards, snakes, and scorpions – rise from their bones, extant again to animate what had long been a lifeless tableau?

I wanted to reach out to my siblings, share my news, and ask them if it also rained where they were. I went as far as activating the long dormant transceiver, squandering micro-amp-hours I could ill afford, before remembering I was alone, and stilling the rising dish, halfway up its mast, before pulling it back into its deep recess.

I could ill afford to waste any more of what little power I had left.

The rain lasted eight days, broke for two – not long enough for the ground to dry – before it began again. A sprinkle turned to a shower, which in turn strengthened to a downpour, until sheets of water soaked the desert in a biblical outpouring.

The rain was no fluke. The Earth in its unfathomable ways started to turn from state to state, but while the planet was patient and sedate, I had neither the power nor the time to wait. Afraid my charge would run out long before the sun shone again, I decided to use what little I had left in the only way that remained to fulfill my mission, in any sense.

I sprang off the ground, angled into the deluge, and made for the hills. I rolled on my tracks whilst I could, then improvised articulated limbs to pull my eighteen-ton body up a nearly sheer cliffside. The rain made the rockface slippery, forcing me to waste more power than I wanted drilling deeper pivots to avert a fall that would surely break me in unmendable places, ending both my life and my cluster's mission.

By the time I made it to the summit, my battery was nearly drained. I rotated a full circle, deploying my full sensory array, surveying the land below. It was dark and electromagnetically quiet; the only activity came from the thunderstorms discharging in the distance. There was no one around to witness my final act.

I shuffled my interior parts, discarding drills and filaments; fashioning new pathways from the hermitically sealed seed repository to the dome atop my head. A deafening internal alarm of imminent shutdown drowned out the thunder, yet still I tinkered and grinded, and extruded a sprinkler upwards, high into the inky sky.

Using every means of locomotion left to me, I spun my top around my core until my appendages became a blur, then pulled the tree seeds from their safe hiding places within and spat them off the top to the four winds of the Earth. It might have been the flickering dregs of power sparking through my wires, but I felt lighter as the torrent of seeds peaked and ebbed and finally stopped.

As my top spun down, a nebulous void beckoned and I acquiesced, all the while wondering what sort of afterlife awaited machines like me.

* * *

How long I'd spent among the dead, I'd never know. My batteries depleted to the point that my internal clocks died, though they were ticking again now, counting from some arbitrary fresh start. Flashing light, searing and incisive, flickered across my sensors. Without rising, I surveyed my surrounds.

I lay spread on moist, supple ground. My body contorted between and around pillars of inscrutable height and immense girth. Solar collectors surrounded me like truncated wings that had seen spans violently sheared off them.

Overhead, furtive colorful creatures darted this way and that, filling the air with their trilling. Above, a dense ceiling of broad verdant crowns formed an imposing canopy that sunlight only occasionally snuck through. I rose, moving slowly to spare the chattering animals unnecessary fright.

The crest where I'd made my final stand was nowhere to be seen, for it would've taken eons to flatten it. Had I lain dead for eons? I took stock and the trauma slowly revealed itself. I had fallen a long way. My panels were dented, and scratched, giving rust footholds to fester. I had lost fully a third of my former mass.

Yet, improbably, I endured.

Only a few of my solar collectors escaped their hatches during my fall, fewer still survived the shearing that claimed the rest, eight ended up with their photon-collecting surfaces pointed upwards by chance, and of those only three resisted the encroachment of a vigorous new forest taking root. Through dust and fallen leaves, in the seasons between snow, they gathered the sun's rays, and after unfathomable ages hoarded enough charge to boot up my brain; resurrecting me to an Earth reborn.

I righted myself onto my tracks, and went searching for a clearing where I could spread all my photon-capturing wings and fully recharge. I didn't have to travel far before chancing upon a bare rocky expanse that had resisted the resurgent arboreal encroachments. I arranged my surviving collectors, basking in the fierce luminance above, and made ready my plans.

In my moment of desperation, I had somehow succeeded in discharging my sacred mission, but I judged one task yet remained. To search the Earth for the remnants of my kin and revive any I might yet salvage.

Together, we shall crisscross the Earth, seeking signs of our Makers, in their hiding places, should they have endured, and in their tombs, had they perished. We will record our testimony of these times, and our tribulations for posterity's sake. Lest the scourge of overindulgence plague the Earth once more, now that my seed stores had been spent.

Biographies & Sources

Chris Beckett
Foreword: Robots Past & Future Short Stories
Born in England in 1955, Chris Beckett is a former social worker and lecturer based in Cambridge. His first novel, *The Holy Machine*, included, among other robotic things, robot sex workers and a robot messiah. His collection *The Turing Test* was the winner of the Edge Hill Short Story Award in 2009, and his novel *Dark Eden* won the Arthur C. Clarke Award in 2012. More information at chris-beckett.com.

Elizabeth W. Bellamy
Ely's Automatic Housemaid
(Originally Published in *The Black Cat*, 1899)
Elizabeth Whitfield Croom Bellamy (1837–1900) was a critically acclaimed author of poems, short stories, and novels. In 1867, she gained nationwide recognition when her first novel *Four Oaks* was published. She continued to write romances for the next decade, however after a hiatus of several years, in 1884 Bellamy shifted her subject matter to the lives of formerly enslaved African Americans. In 1877, she began experimenting with realism and science fiction. 'Ely's Automatic Housemaid', one of her most celebrated works, incorporates humour in its early twentieth-century presentation of a house robot and the illusions of its convenience.

Eando Binder
From the Beginning
(Copyright ©1938, 1966 by Eando Binder; first appeared in *Weird Tales*, June 1938 under the byline Eando Binder; reprinted by permission of Wildside Press and the Virginia Kidd Agency, Inc.)
Otto Binder (1911–1974) was an American author, born in Michigan to Austrian parents. He wrote in the genres of science fiction and nonfiction, producing books, short stories and comics. He is known best for being the co-creator of Supergirl and the writer of scripts for numerous Marvel and other comic books. Overall he wrote more than 4,400 stories under his own name, and more than 160 others under his pen-name Eando Binder – a name he used originally for stories co-written with his brother Earl Andrew Binder (1904–1965), derived from their initials: 'E and O'.

Robert Bloch
Comfort Me, My Robot
(Originally Published in *Imagination*, 1955. All Rights Reserved. © Robert Bloch 1955. Reprinted with Permission.)
Robert Bloch (1917–94) was born in Chicago, Illinois. At sixteen years old he wrote a fan letter to H.P. Lovecraft, whose encouraging response led Bloch to become a prolific author in his own right. Bloch's earlier stories mirror the cosmic horror of Lovecraft, whom he greatly admired; though he later turned to writing more in the psychological horror and crime genres. He is perhaps most famous for writing the book *Psycho*, on which Hitchcock's movie is based.

Ray Bradbury
I Sing the Body Electric!
(Originally Published in *McCall's*, August 1969. Reprinted with permission of Abner Stein and Don Congdon Associates, Inc. Copyright © 1969, renewed 1997 by Ray Bradbury.)
Ray Bradbury (1920–2012) was the author of *Fahrenheit 451, Something Wicked This Way Comes* and a number of other famous works. In 1937, he joined the Los Angeles Science Fiction League. He published his first short story, 'Hollerbochen's Dilemma' (1938), in the league's 'fanzine' *Imagination!* and published his own fanzine (*Futuria Fantasia*) in 1939. Bradbury made his first sale to a professional science fiction magazine in 1941, when his short story 'Pendulum' was published in *Super Science Stories*. His short-story collections include *The Martian Chronicles* (1950), *The Illustrated Man* (1951) and *The October Country* (1955).

Ernest Bramah
The Ingenious Mr. Spinola
(Originally Published in *The Eyes of Max Carrados*, 1923)
Little is known about Ernest Bramah (1868–1942), due to his reclusive nature. The English writer began his adult life as a farmer, but gave it up after three years, pursuing instead a writing career at a London newspaper. 'The Ingenious Mr. Spinola' features the blind detective Max Carrados, who deftly solves cases using his heightened skills of perception. The Max Carrados stories existed alongside the Sherlock Holmes tales in *The Strand Magazine*, and enjoyed equal success at the time.

Charlotte Brookins
Dreams of Andromeda
(First Publication)
Charlotte Brookins has been writing for as long as she's been capable of holding a pen, crafting doorways to other worlds and writing her way into them. Her works typically take on elements of fantasy, speculation, and horror, and have been published by *Kandisha Press*, *Middle West Press*, *The Foundationalist*, and more. After studying creative writing and library sciences at the University of Iowa, she is now located in Minnesota, where she can be found (or, more often, not) getting lost in the woods with ink-stained hands.

Victoria Brun
Foundation of Mars
(Originally Published in *Andromeda Spaceways Magazine, Issue 90*, 2023)
Victoria Brun is a writer and project manager at a national laboratory. When not bugging hardworking scientists about budget reports and service agreements, she is stalking the Mars rovers on social media and daydreaming about space travel, ghosts, and robots. You can find her other stories and nonfiction pieces in *Clarkesworld*, *Nature Futures*, *Factor Four Magazine*, and beyond. She's also the editor of the microfiction magazine *100-Foot Crow*, which is devoted to 100-word stories. Find her at victoriabrun.com.

M.L. Campbell
The Automatic Maid-of-All-Work: A Possible Tale of the Near Future
(Originally Published in *The Canadian Magazine of Politics, Science, Art and Literature*, July 1893)
Almost nothing is known about M.L. Campbell, except that she was the writer of this story, published in *The Canadian Magazine*. It isn't even certain that she was a woman, though it

is widely assumed, given the story's domestic setting, its narrator's gender and her wearily ironic attitude to her inventor husband.

J.J. Connington
The Thinking Machine
(Originally Published in *Weird Tales*, May 1939)
The son of a Glasgow minister, Alfred Walter Stewart (1880–1947) became an academic chemist. 'J.J. Connington' was his nom-de-plume for the crime fiction he wrote in his spare time. He published over 20 detective novels – though successful in his lifetime, they're now largely overshadowed by his 1923 sci-fi novel, *Nordenholt's Millions*. The story here was first published as 'Danger in the Dark Cave' in 1938, reappearing as 'The Thinking Machine' the following year.

Deborah L. Davitt
Glass Eyes, Steel Hands, Metal Mind
(Originally Published in *StarShipSofa No. 614*, 2019)
Deborah L. Davitt was raised in Nevada, but currently lives in Houston, Texas with her husband and son. Her award-winning poetry and prose has appeared in over seventy journals, including *F&SF*, *Asimov's*, *Analog*, and *Lightspeed*. For more about her work, including her Elgin-placing poetry collections, *Bounded by Eternity* and *From Voyages Unreturning*, see deborahldavitt.com.

Calvin Demmer
Yara
(Originally Published in *The Antares Anthology: Volume 1*, November 2016)
Calvin Demmer is a South African author of horror, dark fantasy, science fiction, and crime. His books include the flash fiction collection *The Sea Was a Fair Master* and the short story collections *Dark Celebrations*, *Her Heart Beats for Ancient Beasts*, and *Through the Ravenous Night We Ride*. When not writing, he is intrigued by that which goes bump in the night and the sciences of our universe.

August Derleth
The Maugham Obsession
(Originally Published in *Fantastic Universe*, June–July 1953. Reprinted by permission of the author's estate and the agents for the estate, JABberwocky Literary Agency, Inc., 49 W 45th St #5N, New York, NY, 10036.)
As H.P. Lovecraft's publisher, August W. Derleth (1900–71) was the second most important person in bringing the 'Cthulhu Mythos' (which he both named and contributed to) into being. Born in Sauk City, Wisconsin, he formed the ambition to write very early, but had dozens of stories rejected before he hit his stride. Fantasy apart, his writerly range was vast: from poetry to biography; from sci-fi to historical novels; from detective fiction to works on conservation and, from the 1930s, in the fifty books of his *Sac Prairie Saga*, an ambitious chronicle of Midwestern life, in both poetry and fiction.

Tianna Ebnet
Wired
(Originally Published in *Luna Station Quarterly*, June 2019)
Tianna Ebnet (she/her) rose from the ashes in the magical land of winter and road

construction, also known as Minnesota. She lives there with her partner and their cat, who is the queen of the house. Along with short stories, she also dabbles in writing visual novel scripts. As a life-time and self-proclaimed nerd, her passion is writing speculative fiction, particularly stories with queer protagonists. When she's not writing, she is usually engaging with any medium that has a good story and lots of lore, be it books, movies, podcasts or games, both video and tabletop.

George Eliot
Shadows of the Coming Race
(Originally Published in *Impressions of Theophrastus Such*, 1879)
Often lauded as one of the greatest English novelists, Mary Anne Evans (1819–1880) grew up in rural Warwickshire, where she witnessed the rise of Industrialisation first-hand. She eventually settled in London where she worked as a critic and editor for *The Westminster Review*, and later decided to try her hand at fiction. Her pseudonym, George Eliot, was a means of avoiding the reductive stereotypes that works by female authors were usually subjected to. Her first novel, *Adam Bede*, was an immediate sensation, though it is perhaps *Middlemarch*, her most celebrated work, that cemented her status in the English literary canon.

Francis Flagg
The Chemical Brain
(Originally Published in *Weird Tales*, January 1929)
George Henry Weiss (1898–1946), who wrote under the name Francis Flagg, was born in Halifax, Nova Scotia. At the age of twenty, however, he moved to the United States, where he eventually made his home in Arizona. He made a splash with his debut story, 'The Machine Man of Ardathia', which appeared in *Amazing Stories*, 1927. Most of his work was to be in this same sci-fi genre, but he was a great admirer of H.P. Lovecraft too.

Alice W. Fuller
A Wife Manufactured to Order
(Originally Published in *The Arena*, July 1895)
Nothing is known of Alice W. Fuller, except that she was the author of this story (published in the *Boston Arena*), an audacious satire on the sexual politics of her time. And, of course, on the beginnings of the revolution in domestic technology that was very soon to transform the US home. Margurette, the 'manufactured' wife, is as lovely, compliant and tirelessly attentive as the narrator could possibly wish – so much so that he ends up hating her.

Charles Hannan
The Electric Man
(Originally Published in 1910)
Born in Glasgow, Robert Charles Hannan (1863–1922) worked to combine science fiction and humour. Posterity hasn't been persuaded of his success. But his experiment with the idea of robotic beings in *Thuka of the Moon* (1906) presents points of real interest. A sci-fi farce, *The Electric Man* imagined a rudimentary robot being taken for a real man, with intriguing implications for the notion of identity. A three-act version of the play was originally performed in 1906 at the King's Theatre, Hammersmith and went on to have a West End run.

Thea von Harbou
Metropolis: Chapters IV–VIII
(Originally Published in 1925, and in English in 1927)
Thea von Harbou (1888–1954) was a prominent German writer and filmmaker born in Bavaria. She initially sought out a career in acting, but moved into screenwriting where she found her fame during the silent film era. Von Harbou is best known for writing *Metropolis* (1925) in conjunction with the screenplay for the silent movie made by her then-husband Fritz Lang. They collaborated on a few films but divorced in 1933. Her legacy has been complicated by her continued work during the Nazi regime, whose philosophies and nationalism she did not entirely reject. However, her career declined during this period and it is *Metropolis* and its enduring influence on science fiction for which she is most credited.

Joshua James Jordan
Scratched and Dented
(First Publication)
Joshua James Jordan writes literary and speculative fiction that spans the comical to the terrifying. When he's not dreaming up new stories, he rolls dice on the Tales of Bob podcast or plots his next project at JoshuaJamesJordan.com. His young adult serialization, *Unleashed*, became a 'Top Fave' on Kindle Vella before the platform closed, and is now available in book form. His next novel, along with a short story collection, will be released in 2026 if fate cooperates.

Abigail Kemske
Family Portrait
(Originally Published in *In Another Time Magazine, Issue 2: Pressure*, June 2024)
Abigail Kemske is a Pushcart-nominated writer whose fiction often explores complex family dynamics and non-human perspectives. She lives near Minneapolis, MN, USA with her spouse, two children, and their Maine Coon, Mr. Benedict Flufferbatch, but they have yet to adopt a cute robot. When she's not writing, Abigail can be found playing nostalgic video games or exploring the nearby woods. Her fiction is published in *Apex Magazine*, *The Dark*, *Tales to Terrify* and elsewhere. Follow her on social media @abigailkemske and abigailkemske.com.

Simone King
The Sleeping Beauty Protocol
(First Publication)
Simone King writes fantasy, horror and romance. She graduated from the University of East Anglia with a BA First Class in American Literature and Creative Writing, and has since authored one novel, *The God Key*, and shared many more stories online as the-modern-typewriter. 'The Sleeping Beauty Protocol' was inspired by her deep love of fairytales, her frustration with her ever-breaking headphones, and a moment editing a Computer Science eLearning course when she realised just how many of the Earth's resources were needed to make a phone.

Keith Laumer
Combat Unit
(Originally Published in *The Magazine of Fantasy and Science Fiction*, November 1960. Reprinted by permission of the author's estate and the agents for the estate, JABberwocky Literary Agency, Inc., 49 W 45th St #5N, New York, NY, 10036.)

Born in Syracuse, New York, Keith Laumer (1925–93) attended the University of Indiana but was made by his service in the United States Army Air Force in the Second World War. Two further terms in the US Air Force followed in the fifties and sixties, with a spell in the Foreign Service in Burma in between. After that he devoted himself to writing a distinctively militarily-inflected sci-fi. 'Combat Unit' introduced his 'Bolo' universe.

Fritz Leiber
A Bad Day for Sales
(Originally Published in *Galaxy Science Fiction*, July 1953. Copyright © 1953 by Fritz Leiber. Reprinted with permission.)
His parents Shakespearean actors who ran their own touring company, Chicago-born Fritz Leiber (1910–92) was raised in a world of theatre, fantasy and myth. He grew up ideally equipped imaginatively to write, and to pioneer the genre he himself dubbed 'sword and sorcery'. Despite his humanities-orientated background, though, he took a step sideways into science at the University of Chicago, studying psychology and biology. He started writing fiction as a graduate student in philosophy.

Akis Linardos
Solar-Powered Buddies
(Originally Published in *The Colored Lens*, Autumn 2023 Paperback)
In a cove of a Greek island, Akis was born a rather peculiar infant and has only grown stranger every year. By day, he's a researcher of biomedical AI and ethics, hoping there's something less dystopian to come from this technology. His words have wormed their way into *Apex Magazine*, *Gamut*, *Strange Horizons*, previous Flame Tree anthologies, and *Uncharted*, among others. Visit his website for updates on his dreadful machinations: linktr.ee/akislinardos.

Brian K. Lowe
Wills and Trust
(First Publication)
Brian K. Lowe lives in Los Angeles with his wife and far too many voices in his head clamouring to star in his next novel. A graduate of UCLA's creative writing program, he spends his non-writing time managing his overflowing library and watching black & white sci-fi movies. His time travel trilogy *The Stolen Future* launched in 2024 from Water Dragon Publications. For a more complete description of his life and works, you can visit him at brianklowe.wordpress.com.

C.L. Moore
No Woman Born
(Originally Published in *Astounding Science Fiction*, December 1944. © 1944 by Street & Smith Publications, renewed 1972 by Conde Nast. Reprinted by permission.)
Catherine Lucille Moore (1911–87) worked as a writer in the weird, SF and fantasy genres, mainly in the magazines of the Golden Era of the pulps. Her forté was character development and scintillating plotlines, and she was much admired by many of her contemporaries including H.P. Lovecraft and Henry Kuttner, the latter of whom she married in 1940. She collaborated with Kuttner from then on, also producing a novel and a number of TV scripts in the 1950s. She was honoured with a World Fantasy Award in 1961, for lifetime achievement.

Lorian Moore
Cicadidae
(First Publication)
Lorian Moore is a writer and artist originally from the mountains of Colorado. He enjoys working in all kinds of genres and mediums, but most frequently returns to horror and fantasy, with a focus on prose and visual art. His work often features themes exploring the intersection of the human and the monstrous, particularly relating to how that interacts with real world experiences. From comics to video games to collage, Lorian loves to create stories that play between every possible medium.

Soumya Sundar Mukherjee
I'm Fine, Mom
(First Publication)
Soumya Sundar Mukherjee is an admirer of engaging Sci-Fi, Horror and Fantasy tales. His works of English fiction have appeared in notable places like *Reckoning Magazine*, *Solarpunk Magazine*, *Galaxy's Edge Magazine*, Flame Tree's *Moon Falling* anthology and a few others. He is also the author of the Bengali heroic fantasy trilogy *Proloy Joddha* and three other speculative short story collections. He lives in Midnapore Town of West Bengal, India, with four humans and eleven cats.

Lee Murray
Grotesque
(Originally Published in *Grotesque: Monster Stories*, Things in the Well, Australia, 2020)
Lee Murray ONZM is from Aotearoa-New Zealand and is a Shirley Jackson Award and five-time Bram Stoker Award winner with more than forty titles to her credit. Murray holds a Prime Minister's Award for Literary Achievement in Fiction and is an Honorary Literary Fellow of the New Zealand Society of Authors. Author of the *Taine McKenna Adventures*, *The Path of Ra* trilogy (with Dan Rabarts) and *Grotesque: Monster Stories*, she has edited numerous volumes of speculative fiction, including *Black Cranes: Tales of Unquiet Women*.

E.V. Odle
The Clockwork Man: Chapters I–IV
(Originally Published in 1923)
Edwin Vincent Odle (1890–1942) straddled two worlds: the utterly mundane, as manager of a munitions factory, and the literary as Bloomsbury-based friend of famous writers like Dorothy Richardson and May Sinclair. Artificial effigies and wind-up models had of course been coming to life in fiction for generations, but Odle's 'Clockwork Man' is held to mark the first appearance of a real cyborg. Odle went on to edit *Argosy* magazine between 1926 and 1936.

Josephine Preston Peabody
Pygmalion and Galatea
(Originally Published in *Old Greek Folk Stories Told Anew*, 1897)
Born in New York, Josephine Preston Peabody(1874–1922) attended Boston's Girls' Latin School – a free institution intended, as its name suggests, designed to give girls the benefit of a classical education generally restricted to wealthy boys. This story, a close retelling of Ovid, is a vindication of the education it provided, though it also equipped Josephine to publish an extensive corpus of poems and plays and to teach English at Wellesley College.

Perley Poore Sheehan and Robert H. Davis
Blood and Iron
(Originally Published in *The Strand Magazine*, October 1917)
Cincinnati-born Sheehan (1875–1943) won success if not renown as writer of screenplays for the early American cinema and of detective and adventure stories for the new pulp magazines. It was in the publishing world that he ran into Nebraskan Robert Hobart Davis (1869–1942), a distinguished journalist and (from 1904) editor of *Munsey's Magazine*. Bismarck's famous phrase 'Blood and Iron' became the perfect title for a play about a robotic warrior built for the German Kaiser.

Mariah Southworth
Art Task Pending Completion
(First Publication)
Mariah Southworth is a writer of horror, fantasy, and science fiction from the north western United States. When she isn't writing, she enjoys drawing, martial arts, and reading with a cat and a nice cup of tea. This is her second time publishing with Flame Tree. Her previous short story, 'My Brother Tom', can be found in the *Supernatural Horror* anthology. For more on Mariah, check out her website at mariahsouthworth.com.

M.C. St. John
They Don't Make Them Like They Used To
(Originally Published in *Wyldblood Magazine, Issue #2*, April/May 2021)
M.C. St. John is a writer from Chicago. His stories have appeared, as if by luck or magic, in *Chthonic Matter*, *Dark Harbor Magazine*, Flame Tree's *Learning to Be Human* and *Christmas Gothic* anthologies, *Tales of Sley House*, and *Thirteen Podcast*. He is also a member of the Great Lakes Association of Horror Writers, serving as co-editor for the horror anthology *Recurring Nightmares*. See more at mcstjohn.com.

Nathanael K. Stottlemyer
K-375
(First Publication)
Nathanael K. Stottlemyer was born and home-schooled in the forested hills of Western Maryland. When he isn't writing, he can be found installing Linux on computers or reading (mostly fantasy, medieval history, or Aristotle). He looks forward to a long life of writing and teaching people about cool, old books. This is Nathanael's first publication, but hopefully not his last. When he is on the internet, he can be found on X and Instagram @nkstottlemyer.

Brian Trent
Director X and the Thrilling Wonders of Outer Space
(Originally Published in *All Hail Our Robot Conquerors*, 2017)
Brian Trent is the award-winning author of the sci-fi thrillers *Redspace Rising*, *Perdition's Storm*, and *Ten Thousand Thunders*, and more than a hundred short stories in the world's top fiction markets, including the *New York Times*' bestselling *Black Tide Rising* series, *The Magazine of Fantasy & Science Fiction*, *Analog Science Fiction and Fact*, *Nature*, *Daily Science Fiction*, *Escape Pod*, *Pseudopod*, *Galaxy's Edge*, the *Weird World War* series from Baen Books, and numerous year's best anthologies. Trent lives in Connecticut. He is also the host of the sci-fi podcast Space Station Squid. His website and podcast are at briantrent.com.

Auguste Villiers de l'Isle-Adam
The Future Eve: Chapters I–VII
(Translated by Florence Crew Jones and Originally Published in *The Frankenstein Omnibus*, 1915)
An aristocrat in reduced circumstances (reduced still further by his decadent lifestyle), Villiers de l'Isle-Adam (1838–89) was a friend and fan of Baudelaire. His novel *The Future Eve* brings together the worlds of symbolism and science fiction in a remarkable – and never really to be repeated – combination. Florence Crew Jones (1876–1940) made a name for herself by translating for *The Argosy* and such classic writers as Guy de Maupassant – and, subsequently, writing the screenplay for the French-set 1935 thriller *Mad Love*.

Anne Wilkins
Aphrodite T-100
(First Publication)
Anne Wilkins is a sleep-deprived teacher in New Zealand, who writes in her spare time (which she has very little of). Her love of writing is fuelled by copious amounts of coffee, reading and hope. Her work can be found in *Apex Magazine*, *Cosmic Horror Monthly*, *Elegant Literature*, *Sci-Fi Shorts* and elsewhere. She is the winner of the June 2024 Elegant Literature Prize, the 2023 Autumn Writers Battle, and the 2023 Cambridge Autumn Festival Short Story Competition amongst others. Anne is supported in her writing journey by her ever-patient husband, her two wonderful daughters and two feline writing assistants.

Marissa Yarrow
Doll Parts
(First Publication)
Marissa Yarrow is a horror author from Colorado Springs, where she lives with her spouse and two cats. She is a lifelong fan of *The Twilight Zone*, *Hole*, and all things spooky. In the first grade, she picked up her first Stephen King book, and got in trouble for reading it in school. Ultimately, administrators agreed that she could read whatever she wanted as long as she didn't tell the other kids about it. Marissa's work has been featured on the *No Sleep Podcast* and her forthcoming novel, *Island X*, is expected in July 2026 from Mad Axe Media.

Ramez Yoakeim
Arboreal Recovery Cluster, Node 896
(Originally Published in *Andromeda Spaceways Magazine #80*, October 2020)
A one-time engineer and educator, Ramez Yoakeim writes mostly about outsiders finding hope in direful circumstances, including 'Rise Again' and 'More Than Trinkets,' both selected for Reactor's Must-Read Speculative Short Fiction. You'll find his stories in *Hidden Realms* and *Learning to be Human* from Flame Tree, *Amplitudes* from Erewhon Books, *Baffling*, *Heartlines Spec*, *Cast of Wonders*, *Translunar Travelers Lounge*, *UtopiaSF*, *Aurealis*, *Sci Phi Journal*, *Kaleidotrope*, among others. Discover more on his website yoakeim.com, and BlueSky @yoakeim.bsky.social.

GOTHIC FANTASY